A MATTER OF HONOR

The lorry driver had helped them to gather the dead. And to bury them.

They said it was anthrax that killed so many. A whole village. Every animal. Every bird. All of them now in that pit they made us dig.

But he knew that you don't die from anthrax in the middle of eating a sandwich. A mother doesn't die while she's giving her little girl a bath. A young man doesn't die with his hand still under his girfriend's sweater. This night, he had seen all these things.

The lorry driver and his helpers were dead men as well. He knew that. No question, the men with guns would never let them leave.

He revved up his engine.

They would die here or on the road to Vigirsk. If not there, then later.

But he would make the bastards work for it.

Other books by John R. Maxim

Novels
PLATFORMS
ABEL BAKER CHARLIE
TIME OUT OF MIND
THE BANNERMAN SOLUTION
THE BANNERMAN EFFECT
BANNERMAN'S LAW

Non-Fiction
DARK STAR

A MATTER OF HONOR

John R. Maxim

BANTAM BOOKS

NEW YORK · TORONTO · LONDON · SYDNEY · AUCKLAND

For Tamara, Tatiana, and Pyotr
For Aleks and his Moscow cops
And, always, for Christine

A MATTER OF HONOR

A Bantam Book / August 1993

ISBN 0-553-29920-4

Published simultaneously in the United States and Canada

Bantam Books are published by Bantam Books, a division of Bantam Doubleday Dell
Publishing Group, Inc. Its trademark, consisting of the words "Bantam Books" and
the portrayal of a rooster, is Registered in U.S. Patent and Trademark Office and in
other countries. Marca Registrada. Bantam Books, 1540 Broadway, New York, New
York 10036.

PRINTED IN THE UNITED STATES OF AMERICA

OPM 0 9 8 7 6 5 4 3 2 1

The burial pit took a full day to dig.

It was sixty meters in length.

The place they chose was a beet field, hidden by pines, outside the village of Vigirsk. A single bulldozer, brought in by flatbed, worked in a drenching rain. The rain was good. It muted the sound of the heavy equipment and made it all but invisible from the nearest paved road, nearly two kilometers distant.

But the rain was also bad because water poured into the pit, seeped in from the sides, almost as quickly as the black earth could be moved. There were frequent mud slides. Twice, the flatbed's winch was needed to pull the bulldozer free.

The operator of the bulldozer was exhausted. They brought him hot tea and encouraged him with promises of great rewards. But they could not let him rest because they had no one else with his skills.

When night fell, the rain became mixed with snow and the mud began to harden. The flatbed and a canvas-covered lorry drove off. It was time to begin gathering the dead.

The trucks made many trips.

There was a driver and two helpers in each truck. These men, conscripted at a roadblock near Vigirsk, were to find and collect the corpses. To see that they did, two other men with guns rode with them.

The men with guns told them that they had nothing to fear. Finish this before sunrise, their leader said, and you can go home to your families.

Guns or no, he seemed a decent sort. They wanted to believe him. He had promised that they would not become ill, that the time of contagion had passed. The best proof, he said, is that we are here as well.

This much they believed. For the rest, they could only hope. They, like the man on the bulldozer, had been promised a reward. You'll see, he told them. You are doing a great service for your country. You won't just get a medal for it. You'll get something much better.

A reward.

More likely, the driver of the flatbed feared, they would end up being the last into the pit. With all the talk of democracy, the new Russia, they still snatch you off the street any time they like. It was that way in the time of the czars. It was that way in Stalin's time. It is foolish to think that this will ever change.

But the lorry driver disagreed. These are not the old days, he argued. All they want is to prevent a panic. If we play along, we might do all right. Besides, if this crowd shot everyone who ever helped them bury their dead, there would be no one who knew how to drive a truck.

They worked almost through the night. They went house-to-house, to every vehicle, every outbuilding, gathering the dead of Vigirsk. That done, they began gathering the animals. They finished before sunrise.

The man who had promised a reward told them to rest now. Climb into the lorry, get under the canvas. It stinks a little but it's dry. We're going to bring you some food and some vodka. All you can eat. All you can drink. Even American cigarettes. A whole carton for each man.

This was more than they could believe. But the man did seem sincere. He seemed very nice indeed. This reassured some, but it unsettled others. If a man can see this much death and still have a cheerful way about him, they said, it means that he has seen death so often that it no longer touches him.

They had not asked, of course, who these men were. Internal Security, probably, but better not to know. They were certainly well disciplined, which at least meant they weren't gangsters. Not one of them took rings off the fingers of dead women or went looking for valuables or took the icons that hung in the little church.

The nice one, judging by his accent, had grown up in the Urals, probably right around here. He had made conversation with them, asking about their hometowns, what they did for a living, and if they liked to go fishing. He told them about his favorite streams for catching the fattest trout. To some, this was more proof that he meant them no harm. To others, it meant only that he was clever. He was keeping their minds off trying to make a run for it.

The snow had changed back to sleet again. The six of them sat shivering, caked with mud, listening to the freezing rain which slapped at the canvas. It is best, they decided, to plan for the worst. They loosened the ties of the canvas so that they could dive out through the sides if it came to that. Each one was assigned an exit so that there would be no confusion. They would scatter six ways, every man for himself. You can't outrun a bullet, but a small chance, they agreed, is better than no chance at all.

Soon they heard the noise of the bulldozer starting up again. It was very near. They fell silent, listening, half expecting that it would come and shove them into the pit, truck and all.

But the sound, much clanking and grinding, came no closer. The lorry driver peeked under the canvas. He saw that the bulldozer had begun filling the burial pit at the near end. The operator was having a hard time of it. His treads were slipping in the mud and the motor was coughing badly. Very old machine. His task was made all the more inefficient by his fear of getting too near the edge and having it give way beneath him. Or perhaps he simply did not want to see what he was burying.

The driver of the flatbed had been a tank commander in Afghanistan. There, he told the others, he had seen many pits for the dead. But never one like this. Not one with whole families from babies to grandmothers on the bottom and hundreds of animals on the top. Goats, cows, pigs, even horses. This was why they needed a flatbed with a winch. Try to lift a dead cow without one.

One of the men who rode with him said that the hardest part was the babies. But after that, he said, the hardest part was wasting all that good meat. It's more than a year, he said, since he got his teeth around a decent piece of beef or even horse.

"That meat is full of anthrax," said the flatbed driver. "One bite and you're dead the next day."

"Shit," muttered his other helper.

The flatbed driver raised an eyebrow. "Shit means what? You think the meat is good? I didn't see you stuffing chickens into your coat."

The helper snorted. "Even after Afghanistan," he said to the others, "this one still believes everything they tell him."

The flatbed driver bristled. "And you know better, I suppose. You, who have hardly been a hundred kilometers from the farm where you were born."

"That farm is why I know better. You think I have never seen anthrax?"

The veteran of Afghanistan frowned. "Have you?" he asked. "Or are you only good for talk?"

The helper looked away. "Forget I said anything. When a man with a gun says it's anthrax, it's anthrax."

The lorry driver leaned forward. "Tell me how you know it isn't."

A long sigh. "With anthrax," he said quietly, "you don't just keel over. You get sick first. Everything comes out both ends, you get carbuncles all over your body, and you cough up blood. You don't die in the middle of eating a sandwich. A mother doesn't die while she's giving her little girl a bath. A young man doesn't die with his hand reaching under his girlfriend's sweater. Tonight, I have seen all these things."

The lorry driver touched a finger to his lips.

"They are coming back," he said.

Outside, car doors opened and closed. Quiet voices, then silence. Now footsteps sucked at the mud. They grew closer and stopped. The rear flap tore open. All six men froze, fearing that the men with guns had come to finish them. But it was only the nice one and another who had never spoken. They carried not guns but cardboard boxes. Right away, the six could see bottles in one of them. Big bottles. Whole liters.

"You see?" the one from around here said. "I keep my word."

The two left their boxes and walked back to their car. One

opened the trunk. They returned, this time, with a kerosene heater which the nice one lit for them. The silent one carried two large thermos jugs, some towels, and a cake of brown soap.

"Now you can be warm," said the one who was in charge. "And there is hot water in the jugs. You'll feel better when you get some of the mud off you."

They wet two of the towels and passed them around. Steam rose from them. It did feel good to get the death off their hands.

Meanwhile, the one who had never spoken or smiled is suddenly behaving like Father Winter. From one box he took small loaves of bread which he handed to each man. Next there is real butter in a wooden tub and a big jar of blackberry jam. Underneath are perhaps ten kilos of sausage and a knife for slicing it. In the box with the vodka there is more of the same plus the cartons of cigarettes. They were Marlboros. Best kind. If these men meant to shoot us, they said with their eyes, they would not waste all this. They would surely not give us a knife.

The one from around here took out a vodka bottle and unscrewed the top. He handed it to the lorry driver. "Take a good swallow and pass it," he said.

The vodka was Stolichnaya, the driver noted. The good stuff. Meant only for export. The label was even in English.

"Get a little drunk," he said. "Eat all you want. You don't have to save some for later because this is only the beginning."

All six men blinked.

"Before you go home," he told them, "I will give you an address in Yekaterinburg. From now on, at the beginning of every month, you will all come and visit me. You will come on the same day. If each of you can say that he has kept his promise, that he has not spoken of this—even to his wife or his priest—you will each get a food parcel as good as these. I don't have to tell you what they are worth."

They knew. The richest of them could work a full year and not have enough for even one. They smiled, one after the other.

"How long will this continue? That is up to you. If one of you gets a case of loose lips, it ends for all of you."

He paused to let this sink in. He watched as they glanced at each other, noting their expressions and where the glances lingered. Their faces told them what he wanted to know. They were clearly in agreement that this was too good to pass up. Some glances lingered longest on one of the flatbed helpers. This told the man that this one probably had the most to say already. But the helper answered them with a shrug that said, *Hey. No problem with me.*

A distant car horn sounded. Their benefactor looked toward its source, then nodded to the other.

"We'll be back in a few minutes," he told them. "Meantime, enjoy yourselves. Try to save us a swallow and enough for a sandwich."

The lorry driver waited for one of those minutes, then lifted the canvas a little. Through the sleet and the morning mist, he could make out a limousine picking its way across a field. A big black Zil. Someone important. The limousine came to a stop near the far end of the pit. The chauffeur climbed out first. He had a powerful-looking flashlight in one hand and an umbrella in the other. Unfurling the umbrella, he stepped around the Zil and opened the rear door.

His passenger, an older man, was still pulling on galoshes. He was dressed like a big shot, black suit, black coat, except that on his head he wore one of those Scottish caps, red plaid, and it had a little pom-pom on the top. What sort of man, the lorry driver wondered, rides in a Zil and wears a hat like that? The man climbed out under the umbrella.

This was a good development, thought the lorry driver. Someone in authority had arrived. It was no longer just men with guns who, so far, had no names.

The man in the tam-o'-shanter stood on the edge of the pit, looking into it. He was shaking his head, wearily. The others joined him there.

He nodded toward his chauffeur, who turned the flashlight on and shined it where he pointed. The man from the Zil could see better now. Before, they had been only shapeless mounds, glistening under a glaze of sleet. He seemed confused.

"Only animals?" he asked. "Where are the villagers?"

"Underneath," said the one who had been in charge. "This way, if anyone should ever start digging . . ."

"Good idea." The older man nodded. "Well done."

"This is a sugar beet field," said the younger man, "but the soil of this whole collective has been exhausted. It is not scheduled to be worked again for at least two years. Even so, we'll plow it up and plant alfalfa to hide all the tracks."

Another nod. "How many dead?"

"Not as bad as we thought. Ninety-two."

"You're sure that you have all of them?"

"We've combed this whole valley. Every building, every vehicle, even the privies."

"Some will have relatives elsewhere. How will you deal with inquiries?"

"An outbreak of anthrax," the younger man answered. "The dead, we'll say, have been cremated to destroy the bacillus. Their clothing and personal effects with them, for obvious reasons. Their livestock burned in pits. We'll quarantine their homes as well and restrict all access. Anyone who knows anthrax will understand the need for these measures."

"Anthrax kills like this? No survivors?"

"It can. Not as quickly, perhaps, but in a day or so. Without treatment, the pulmonary form is always fatal."

The man in the plaid hat seemed doubtful. He put that question aside. "What have you learned about the accident? How it happened, I mean."

The younger man blinked. "Accident? Who told you it was an accident?"

"General Borovik told me. You say it wasn't?"

"Borovik!" He spat the name. "A worse accident was Borovik being born. A catastrophe was trusting this shipment to him and those morons he uses."

"Colonel . . ." A weary sigh. "Just tell me what happened, if you please."

The younger man took a breath. Count to ten, he told himself. Don't go too far.

"Two of Borovik's . . . people . . . picked up the shipment in Yekaterinburg and drove it out under a truck-load of pigs."

"Pigs." The older man frowned. "That means Borovik used the Kerenskys for this?"

"Young ones. Nephews. Same blood." Which guarantees subhuman, he thought but did not say. "They had barely started back to Moscow when they decided to take a little off the top for themselves."

"They didn't know they were carrying nerve gas?"

"Of course they knew," he said sharply. "I told them myself. For one hour, I drilled into them how to handle those canisters."

"And yet they opened one of them?"

"Smashed it open. With a hammer. The hammer was still in his hand."

"But why would they . . . ?"

"Why?" The younger man threw up his hands. "Because all Kerenskys are criminals. Because they are low-lifes. For two years now, I have protested the use of such people. For two years I have warned you about General Borovik. The man is . . ."

Again, he caught himself. He apologized. It has been a long two days, he said. We are all very tired. No insubordination was intended.

"What happened was this," he said, his words now measured. "When I told them it was gas, I saw them wink. I said to them, No, no. Don't wink, you idiots. I do not say it's gas because it is really emeralds or gold from the mines of Yekaterinburg. I do not say it's gas because it is really wads of American dollars. *I say it's gas because it is gas.* I tell you not to open the canisters because you will die in ten seconds if you do."

The older man said nothing.

"There are babies down there," said the man who had once been a colonel. "There is a pretty little girl in a ballet costume and an old man who lost both his legs fighting Hitler."

The older man chewed his lip. His eyes found those of the silent one. The silent one shrugged, barely perceptibly. The visitor looked away. For a few moments, he watched the work of the bulldozer. The pit was nearly half filled in.

"That driver. Is he reliable?"

"He'll keep his mouth shut. So will the others."

"What others?"

"In the lorry. We had to round up some drivers and some strong backs. I think I . . . we"—he included the silent one—"have reached an understanding with them."

The old man looked at the silent one. He looked into his mind. He saw the doubting flick of an eyebrow.

"You can't let them go," he said. "Any of them."

The former colonel took a breath. "I'll be responsible," he said. "Leave them to me."

"Are they from this place?"

"From Kemensk. Five towns away."

"Miners or farmers?"

"One farmer. The rest work for the mines."

"You don't suppose a farmer would know anthrax when he sees it?"

The younger man hesitated. "If he's seen it, perhaps. It's not so common in the Urals."

The older man rubbed his chin. "Coming here," he said, "I saw dead birds on the road. Does anthrax make birds fall from the sky?"

No answer.

"Does it kill chickens? I see chickens in the pit."

"General . . ."

"If those men talk, you'll be up before a firing squad. You realize that, don't you?"

He started to speak. The older man raised a hand.

"That means you, Captain Sostkov here, and all of your men. You would take such a risk?"

"General . . ." He gritted his teeth. "I will not execute those—"

"And where will it end? How many more will follow you to the wall?"

He stiffened. "If you're suggesting that I would betray you . . ."

"Nothing of the sort. You would die first. You would die for your country and perhaps even for me. But would you die for General Borovik?"

The former colonel knew what he was being asked. Would he give up his life knowing that Borovik still had breath in him? Or would he first give up Borovik?

There could be little doubt where that would end. Borovik

would switch sides in two seconds. Still, to go back on his
word, to sacrifice those six men before he's had a chance to
make them understand . . . the future . . . how wonderful it will be . . . don't let this one tragedy ruin it . . . he
could not bear the thought of it.

He straightened. "General," he said again, firmly, "I
will not execute those men."

The older man studied him. He sighed, then moved to
embrace him. "I understand you," he said with a sigh.
"Babies and war heroes. Enough harm has been done
already."

His voice had softened but his eyes had not.

They had locked upon those of the young former captain.
The man who did not speak. The man whose eyes had
flashed with pride when his hero, General Arkadi Kulik,
remembered and spoke his name.

The lorry driver watched them through the flap.

He could hear little of what they were saying. Only a
word here and there from the man who had just come. He
had one of those voices that carried.

But all would be well, he told himself, because the man
in the Scottish cap looked so very sad. Now he was hugging
the one from around here. Giving him a squeeze.

The lorry driver turned to the kerosene heater, lighting
one of his Marlboros off the mantle.

When he looked back, the two men were heading toward
the truck again. The one in the cap stood with his chauffeur,
watching them go.

Suddenly, the silent one halted. He was looking toward
the pit as if something there had caught his attention. Now
he was walking toward it. He stopped at the edge, scanning
it. Now he called out to the nice one.

"He has a tongue after all," remarked the lorry driver.
The others, busy eating sandwiches, were not so interested.

The one who called out ran back toward the chauffeur. He
reached out a hand, came away with the flashlight. Now he
called again to the other.

"It's a woman," the lorry driver heard him say over the
growl of the bulldozer. "She's still alive."

Impossible, thought the lorry driver. Did she climb up

through dead livestock? But the other man rushed over to look.

"Where?" he seemed to be saying. "Shine the light on her."

The first one did so. The nice one leaned closer. Suddenly, a dull pop. The nice one went rigid. He staggered for a step or two, then turned to the other, disbelief on his face. Another pop, sharper this time. The lorry driver saw the pistol. He saw the nice one fold up and sink to the ground, his whole body twitching.

The one who shot him swung his beam toward the bulldozer. At the same time, he aimed his pistol. He held both of these on the driver, but the driver, it seemed clear, had neither seen nor heard. He kept working. Now, with the beam still blinding the driver to him, he pressed his pistol against the fallen one's neck. Another pop. Almost silent. He holstered his pistol. He stood erect. With his boot, he pushed the nice one over the side.

At first, the lorry driver felt frozen in place. For a moment, he could not think. A part of him was not even surprised. That's what trying to be decent gets you, it told him.

"We're dead men," he said at last.

The others scrambled to the flap. They lifted it too much. The man with the Scottish hat saw the light from the heater. He called to the other and pointed. In the truck there was confusion. What did you see? Why do you say that? Only the Afghan veteran took him at his word. In an instant, he was out of the truck, running for the flatbed. One helper followed. The other yammered stupidly.

No time to discuss this. The lorry driver leaped from the back and ran to his cab. He pressed the starter. Nothing. He tried again. This time God was good. He threw it into gear. His own helper, his face white, clawed his way in from the other side. He collapsed at once, dead or dying, into the footwell. Something slapped at the door of his cab. Bullets. The window exploded, cutting his face. It's only glass, he told himself. Go. From the back came another scream of pain.

The flatbed roared past him, drawing fire. Even the chauffeur was shooting. The flatbed steered directly at him.

The chauffeur hesitated, then ran, dragging his boss with him. The flatbed smashed into the Zil, knocking it aside.

But it did not accelerate. It was slowing. Drifting into the thickest mud. The Afghan veteran must have taken a bullet. The lorry driver wanted to stop. Help him. But he knew that all of them were finished if he did. Even the driver of the bulldozer had finally caught on to what's happening. He was on foot. Running for his life. The lorry driver stepped on the gas.

No question. They would get him.

If not here, then on the road to Kemensk.

If not now, then later.

But he would make the bastards work for it.

1

From the air, thought Lesko, Russia could have been Nebraska.

The Finnair jet from Zurich had begun its long descent, bouncing through scattered clouds. He peered out toward the south, looking for some sign of the Moscow skyline. He saw nothing but farmland. Spring crops coming up.

It was all very flat. Not that many roads. Not many trees either except for an occasional stand of pine or birch. But at least it was green, mostly. Somehow, he had always thought of Russia in black and white.

He felt Elena's hand on his arm, squeezing it. The squeeze was her promise that this would be fun. He grumbled inwardly. For her sake he would try to enjoy it but this was still dumb.

No one goes to Russia on a honeymoon.

Nebraska . . . Illinois . . . Kansas.

This could have been any of them, not that he'd ever been to the Midwest either. Like now, he'd only seen those places from the air. Couple of times.

Once, ten years ago, he and his partner flew to Los Angeles to pick up a young female fugitive. She had hired two kids to snuff her husband because he was cheap and boring. It was in all the papers. She made bail, climbed into her car, then drove out to California because she always wanted to be an actress. Six months later, she actually got a job. She's in this mouthwash commercial, the dumb shit, like it never occurred to her that about half of Queens would recognize her the first day it ran.

Anyway, that was the first time in an airplane for either

of them. Katz, then his partner, was like a kid. Even kept the vomit bag for a souvenir.

The second time was last year when Carla Benedict's kid sister got killed. He and Elena flew out for the funeral, partly to pay their respects, but mostly because his daughter was already out there with Bannerman and he wanted to make sure Susan was far out of harm's way in case Carla, who is not known for her stability, started leaving bodies all over the streets.

But Lesko didn't want to think about Carla. Or bad times. Sad times. He blinked the picture away and replaced it with one of Elena. The way she looked, the ceremony. Looking up at him. Saying "I do." And then mouthing the words, *"Oh, I do, Lesko. I surely do."* Susan in the front row, crying. She even got him doing it. Half the church, in fact, was holding hankies and the other half were shaking their heads like they still can't believe this is happening. He didn't blame them.

Those two flights to California . . .

Sometimes, like now, he could not help but be amazed at the way his life had turned between them.

Five years ago, he was still a New York cop. His total travel experience had been a cut-rate cruise to Bermuda with his wife before she divorced him and that one plane ride with David Katz. It was then, come to think of it, when Katz first developed the expensive tastes that ended up getting most of his face blown off.

They had two extra days due to some screwup with the paperwork. Katz couldn't believe all the good-looking women. And he couldn't get enough of Rodeo Drive. A month later he's wearing Italian shoes and these baggy California clothes that make you look like you just lost forty pounds. One day, a few months later, he runs into Katz out at Giants Stadium and Katz is wearing a gold Rolex. He swore that he hit a trifecta up at Milford Jai Alai in Connecticut. Said he had witnesses. Said don't worry, he won't wear it on the job. He knows how it could look.

What Katz was really hitting was couriers. Not for the drugs. For the money. It still bothered Lesko that he should have known. He should have broken Katz's face while he still had one. But if he had, he wondered, where would he be right now? It was Katz getting killed that changed his life.

His own biggest ambition had been to put in his twenty-five, buy into this sports bar in Queens that had three big-screen televisions, and spend a little more time with his daughter before she meets the right guy and gets too wrapped up with a family of her own. Take her to some Knicks and Giants games. Have some good talks. Check out, like any good father, the guys she's seeing.

He sure as hell blew that one.

Anyway, now all of a sudden he's a globe-trotter.

Raymond Lesko, a third-generation Polish Catholic cop, has gone from a one-bedroom walk-up off Queens Boulevard to a villa in Zurich filled with about a zillion dollars' worth of art and antiques. It's Elena's house, of course. And there's also a summer place in Antibes and an apartment in London, both of which Elena tried to have her lawyers put in his name until he found out and stopped it. She said it was a wedding present. She said it was nothing compared to what he'd given her. But no way.

Lesko looked at his watch. In two hours, they'll have been married one week. It seemed to be lasting.

As for what he'd given her . . . A month ago Elena had taken him out to a crowded restaurant and, while he had a slab of roast pork in his mouth, broken the news that she was already four months pregnant. He almost needed a Heimlich.

She sits there, tears rolling down her face, asking him not to be angry with her. She would have told him sooner, she says, but the mood was never right and he had so much on his mind already—she was babbling now—and she was frightened that he would feel entrapped now that she was actually pregnant. That he would leave her. But please don't, she says. In no way, she says, does this require that he marry her unless, of course, marriage is a thing that he might consider. This is the way Elena talks.

"Elena . . . that's wonderful," was how he answered.

"What . . . what do you mean? What is wonderful?"

"The roast pork, Elena. What do you *think* I mean?"

Then she began bawling. Out loud. Hardly stopping for air.

The whole idea of taking him out to dinner was so that he wouldn't yell and scream, and here she is acting like he'd just told her that the dinner was really her pet Pekingese. He had to walk around the table, kneel down at her side, hold her, and say all the things she needed to hear, whether he was sure that he meant them yet or not.

The Finnair jet was dropping quickly. Now he noticed that most of the roads seemed to be unpaved. A lone truck was kicking up dirt on one of them. He saw very little traffic otherwise.

No towns either. This was more like the Russia he'd imagined.

One large cluster of buildings caught his eye. It was well away from any main artery. The buildings, shaped like barracks, were painted a dirty white and their roofs were of rusting corrugated steel. Leo Belkin, leaning from the seat behind him, said it was a collective farm. Lesko thought it looked more like a prison farm, but Elena dug her nails into his hand before he could say so.

Be polite, Lesko.

This is Leo's homeland. We are his guests. Relax and enjoy.

Guests, my ass, Lesko said in his mind.

It was not that he didn't trust Leo Belkin. They were not going to be shipped off to some gulag as soon as they landed. This was the new democratic Russia. Maybe, just maybe, the trip really was a wedding present and Leo did not have some kind of a hustle going.

It was just that lately he seemed to catch Belkin staring at him an awful lot. And then looking away. It's like when you do have a scam going and you keep looking at the intended patsy to see if he's started to catch on yet.

Well . . . benefit of the doubt. By any standard, Leo has been a good friend. He'd certainly helped them clean up Zurich. Felony drug arrests down almost forty percent. Most of the known dealers either out of the business, out of town, or dead. A few Swiss bankers in jail and several more under

indictment. The Platzspitz was a park again instead of an
open-air drug market. There was still some small shit on the
street, of course, but most of the heavy users have followed
the dealers.

And in California, when Carla went crazy, Leo was right
there. Carla came back to Switzerland with Leo's young
assistant, Yuri, who got shot up, and Leo's been helping
Carla make a life over here. And then, two years ago, he
also helped Bannerman track down that bunch who ambushed Elena's car and put a couple of holes in her. Her left
arm still isn't right. She says it's fine, but it isn't. There's
nerve damage.

Looking at Leo, you'd never guess. He's a rumpled little
guy, looks like a college professor, bald, always sucking on
a pipe he never lights or sipping at a glass of wine he never
really drinks. Accent sounds more continental than Russian.
Good guy, gets invited to a lot of parties, can play any song
Cole Porter ever wrote. Everyone likes him. Even Bannerman likes him. But even Bannerman said be careful.

What you'd never guess is that Leo is a KGB general.

Or was. Or still is.

It's hard to keep track, these days, of what he is and what
they call themselves. The Russian leaders keep coming up
with new names for the KGB, trying them on for size,
looking for something that sounds a little more benign, but
nobody else pays much attention.

For a while, the KGB had become the MSB. Stands for
"Inter-Republican Council for Security." But when the republics went their own way, there were suddenly twelve new
names for the KGB. Russia's, last he heard, was the Agency
for Federal Security.

Bannerman says don't get a headache over it. Regardless
of what anyone else calls them, he says, KGB is still what
they call themselves. They're still entrenched and they still
have teeth.

Anyway, back to Leo . . .

Leo used to work for Department 4 of the First Chief
Directorate, which was and still is Foreign Intelligence.
Department 4 takes in all of Switzerland, Germany, and
Austria. Bannerman says it still does. He says Leo is still top
dog, their senior *Rezident,* for all three countries. His base is

at the Soviet embassy in Bern, but he hangs out mostly in Zurich because that's where the money and the power is. He stays close to Elena's family, the Bruggs, because that's where the biggest money is. And the most power.

Elena brought his hand to her lips. She kissed the spot where she'd dug her nails into it. Then she held it against her cheek.

Elena.

Even now, Lesko could scarcely believe that this was happening. That he was here with her. That she could love him.

Beauty and the Beast.

Lesko could not count the times he read those words on the lips of people who saw them together. Or else they would assume he was her bodyguard.

"You imagine this, Lesko," she would say. "It is not true."

"It doesn't bother me. But yeah, it's true."

"Nonsense. You are an extraordinarily attractive man."

"Elena, face it. I look like a bouncer. When I was a cop it was at least useful, but now it's, well . . ."

"It's what?"

"Nothing. Forget it."

There was hardly a morning when he wouldn't stand in front of a mirror and wonder if this is the day when she'll take a good look at him. It wasn't that he was ugly. His features were okay, he supposed. But, like Katz used to say, there was something about his eyes and his mouth, even when he was feeling good, that made him look like he was about to eat someone. Even more so when he smiled.

Plus which, he was an ox. Especially when he stood next to Elena. She had just turned forty-nine, only six years younger than he was, but she was very small and trim and elegant, and in the right light she could have been half his age. If that was a gap, the difference in their upbringings was an ocean.

Elena was born in Zurich but she was raised in Bolivia. Her mother had been sent to Switzerland to be educated but got trapped there by the war. Meanwhile, she fell in love with one of the Bruggs, got knocked up, got married. The war ended and Elena's mother went home for a visit, but her family wouldn't let her come back because the husband wasn't a Catholic. Elena grew up in La Paz with English nannies, Swiss tutors, and more servants than your average hotel.

By the time she was twenty, Elena could speak five languages. It was no surprise, therefore, that all the big coca growers used her first as an interpreter and then as a negotiator. One thing led to another.

The cocaine wars of the seventies wiped out most of her family. Elena rose up, partly by attrition but mostly because she was smart and tough. And in her own way, she was straight. Anyway, before long, every DEA chart showing the cocaine hierarchy of Bolivia would have this little box, right at the top, with her name in it, but the box would always have dotted lines and a question mark, because no one had ever taken her picture and they weren't really sure whether Elena was a code name or more than one person or what.

Lesko shook off this train of thought. That was then. This is now.

One thing about those five languages. She hardly ever used anything but English in his presence. This was mostly good manners. The only other language he knew was some street Spanish, and not much of it was very polite. But he was learning German on the sly and one day soon he was going to surprise her with it.

"Such a rough man, Lesko. But such a good and brave heart."

She would say things like that. Often. Out of the blue.

He'd catch her staring at him from across the room. She would say how lucky she feels. He would get tongue-tied.

His bathroom mirror aside, he had come to accept that Elena loved him. It was no less difficult to accept that he loved her. What she was before, the things she did before they met, had faded so completely in his mind that they were not even distant memories. It was only in a rare half-awake dream that he saw her standing in the back room of a Brooklyn barbershop with three dead men at her feet.

She was scared to death. Trembling. But she wouldn't

beg and she wouldn't lie. She stood there, back straight, chin high, waiting for him to finish her as well.

Now here he is, five years later, fifty-five years old with a daughter who's twenty-six, about to have a kid with the woman who ordered the death of his partner.

Belkin was at his ear again, pointing out a monument and cemetery that marked how close the Nazi tanks got to Moscow before the Russian winter turned motor oil into glue. Says he had two uncles in that battle. One died later at Kursk. The other still lives in Moscow. Somewhere. His voice trailed off. It was Lesko's impression that they didn't stay in touch.

He had asked Belkin about his father. A normal question, right? But Belkin gave him this funny why-are-you-asking look. Just for a second. Then he looked away, muttered, "He's dead . . . many years," and began glancing around the way you do when you're eager to change the subject. Lesko didn't push.

The subject he changed to was Leningrad, where he still has family, on his mother's side, still living in the same big house her family had owned before the Revolution. The way things are going, he said, they might own it again soon. For now, however, it's still shared with several other families.

Belkin especially wanted to show them Leningrad— which he had trouble calling St. Petersburg. Lesko didn't read anything into that. He himself had still called New York's airport Idlewild for years after they changed its name to JFK, and to this day you can't find a New Yorker who calls Sixth Avenue the Avenue of the Americas. Anyway . . . Leo wanted to take them to this museum outside Leningrad where the Russian art treasures he'd brought back from California were back on display after being missing for nearly fifty years. That's what really got Leo his star . . . or whatever it is they give Russian generals. And it was Bannerman who told him where to look by way of payback for his help.

Still, he owes Bannerman and he knows it. He also needs him because being wired into Bannerman's network, to say nothing of the Bruggs, is what gives him his clout in the KGB.

Elena knows all this. She says that's why he shouldn't let himself get paranoid about Leo's invitation. Don't look for a hidden motive, she says. You've been a policeman too long.

He'd tried telling her that his real reason for not wanting to go involved her pregnancy. Elena wasn't a kid anymore. Even if she stayed flat on her back for nine months, there were no guarantees that she'd carry the baby full-term.

But she didn't want to know that. Nothing could go wrong, because she had it in her mind that this kid was a miracle, an act of God, a reward for the way she'd redeemed herself and, not least, a gift to her new husband of the son he'd probably always wanted.

This, of course, was horseshit.

What it really was, was dragging him off to their bedroom three nights in a row last Christmas when she saw that her temperature was up. This was after several months of appointments with this new doctor she was seeing, probably getting pumped full of hormones and getting him, Lesko, to have his sperm tested. If you can picture that.

Even Susan was in on this somehow. All those calls back and forth between them. A sudden visit by Susan last December. In fact, all four of the future bridesmaids were around back then. Lots of whispering, sudden silences, smug expressions. Funny, he had forgotten about that until now.

Anyway, the bottom line was that Elena wanted a kid. She'd adopt one if she had to, she said. But first she wanted to try. She wanted a kid from her own belly. She wanted *his* kid whether he chose to stay with her or not.

In a way it was flattering, but in most ways it was crazy. To hear Elena tell it, he was—almost literally—the first man she'd ever loved. She was experiencing, for the first time, many of those romantic notions that most women outgrow by the time they're twenty. Like, that having a child is the fullest expression of love. That the offspring of a love so fine and pure must necessarily be perfect. Lesko, however, knew that having kids was a total crap-shoot. The kid was just as likely to be a creep.

He had lucked out with his daughter. From day one, Susan was all he could have asked for. She was bright, nice, good at sports, and she grew up drop-dead gorgeous. Katz used to say that Susan was the one who lucked out. That Lesko's genes had somehow skipped a generation. Katz said it was actually more than luck. It was a trick God pulled to keep the species going. Otherwise, he said, no wife would ever take a chance on having another you.

Yeah, well . . . fuck you, David.

Anyway, if Susan has a kid with anyone, it will probably be with Bannerman. Two years now, they've been living together. If they have one, and Bannerman runs screaming from the hospital when the nurse brings it to the window, he can't say he wasn't warned.

Susan could have done worse, he supposed. She also could have done better. Like a nice boring dentist—or even a lawyer, if she could find one with his hands in his own pockets.

It was not that he didn't like Bannerman. In most ways, Bannerman was every parent's dream of what their daughter might bring home. Well traveled, good manners, enough money, basically a straight arrow.

But Bannerman is a killer. You can dress it up any way you like, but that was what it comes down to.

In his head, Lesko heard a snort from David Katz. He tried to ignore it.

Fucking Katz.

He listens in to private thoughts, adds his two cents, and, most times, totally misses the point.

Lesko knew what he'd say. *"Give Bannerman a break, Lesko. It's not like you never killed anyone."*

Maybe. But not for money.

"The city paid us, Lesko. And the Bruggs are paying you now. What do you call that?"

It's not the same. There's still a difference.

"Hey, Lesko?"

"Leave me alone."

"I didn't say anything about Bannerman. That was you. A lot of times you think it's me when it's you."

Lesko grunted. He knew that this was probably true.

"But while I got your attention, you thought about what you're going to name the kid?"

Lesko blinked. *"David . . . I'm going to be fifty-six*

*years old when that kid comes. You think all I got on my
mind is what to call it?"*

Katz laughed. *"How about Moose?"*

Lesko didn't need this. His free hand curled into a useless
fist.

"That's if it's a girl." Katz was enjoying himself. *"If it's
a boy, you could—"*

"You're an asshole, David."

A sigh. *"Come on, Lesko. Lighten up."*

"David. Go away."

"What's wrong with thinking about a name?"

*"First things first is why, you putz. What's first is that it
gets born without me losing Elena. The second thing is that
it's . . . healthy."*

He'd almost said *normal*.

Lesko had read some statistics about the risks of having
a kid at her age. He wished he hadn't.

And even if everything worked out okay, what was he
going to do with a kid? He knows a little bit about
daughters, but what if it's this son Elena is so sure about?
They don't even have Little League in Europe. Or Pop
Warner football. The kid will probably want to play soccer
all summer and go skiing all winter, and he'll have an old
man who cares diddly about either sport.

"Look on the bright side," Katz told him. *"Having a kid
in Europe, you probably won't have to sit through Ice
Capades again."*

Lesko dismissed this with a flick of his free hand. This
time, Elena reached for it, caressed it. He glanced at her,
knowing that he'd been caught. She looked away, pretending otherwise, but she couldn't hide the dimple that shows
up even when she's trying not to smile.

It was another thing he liked about her. She didn't mind
about Katz.

Except for one night, maybe.

It was the second or third time they made love. She had
asked him to undress her because her arms were still in
slings from being shot. Then she stopped him. He thought it
was because he was hurting her, but he saw that she was
looking around the room. She asked, in this very small
voice, "Are we alone, Lesko?"

But except for that one time, Katz didn't bother her. She understood that Katz was strictly in his head. A habit. Ten years of being partners. Ten years of being so close you know what the other guy is going to say before he says it. Not that he didn't wonder, in the beginning, whether he was going nuts. Or being haunted. Or whether he was just holding on to Katz because he was so lonely back then.

Whatever.

The engines of the Finnair jet changed their pitch. Lesko checked Elena's seat belt to see that it was fastened but not too tight. He groped for a pillow and tried to slide it under the buckle. Elena gave an exasperated sigh. She slapped his hand with the book she was reading. *Doctor Zhivago*. But she used the pillow.

2

The man in the grinding vat had been caught stealing.

He knew that he was going to die. And he knew how. That knowledge had brought madness to his eyes.

That this little hair-ball was stealing came as no surprise to Kerensky. He was, after all, an Armenian. Nearest thing to a gypsy.

But this particular Armenian was more stupid than most. He had stolen from a consignment of ham and sausage that was intended for General Borovik's mother. Her name and address were written on it, plain for all to see. To Borovik's way of thinking, this could only be a deliberate insult. He had insisted that an example be made.

The question of insult aside, Borovik is extremely sentimental about his mother. For that reason alone, this man is about to become a sausage.

• • •

The Armenian lived in a basement room which he shared with several cousins. There, in addition to the missing meats, Kerensky had found nearly five kilos of caviar, sixty cartons of Kent and Marlboro cigarettes, a whole box of panty hose in many different patterns—even one with yule trees on it—and several pornographic videotapes from Germany. Also more than five hundred American dollars and a like amount in assorted other Western currencies. Also a stack of Yugoslav notes, but those were for cheating American tourists who did not know a dinar from a ruble.

If the Armenian had stolen from some other consignment, Kerensky might only have had him beaten, his trade goods and hard currency confiscated, and perhaps left swaying from a hook in the smoke room for a day or two.

That would cure him.

This last remark was made by Sasha, Kerensky's older brother.

It was several hours later, on the metro going home, when Kerensky got the joke. People thought he was crazy, he was laughing so hard.

Also it was good to hear Sasha making jokes again. It's three months since he lost both his sons. Nice boys, if you overlook a few things. Very sad. This was good tonic for Sasha.

The Armenian was naked. His arms and legs were bound with lengths of intestine. He glistened, head to toe, with pork fat. Kerensky wished that he had thought to run a skinner over the little man's head and torso to scrape off some of that body hair. Armenians all look like monkeys.

Twice now, Kerensky had touched the button that activated the grinders, watching this man thrash atop the mixture as its level sank by thirty centimeters each time. The Armenian, now exhausted, had somehow managed to hook his jaw and one shoulder over the rim of the vat. He was making cat noises. They came through his nose because a fistful of tripe had been stuffed into his mouth. He had tried to draw his body into a ball, but much of his lower half remained immersed in the pork snouts, organs, eyeballs, and animal genitalia that would soon be ground into a mustard-colored paste and then pumped into the entrails of sheep to make sausages as big as a fat woman's arm.

There is a saying which Kerensky supposed is known to every butcher in the world. And probably to every politician. It goes, "If you love sausage or the law, you must never watch either being made."

Only three, not counting the general, would be watching this particular batch. The others were Kerensky's brothers, Sasha and Feodor, who had prepared the Armenian and hoisted him into the vat. Their stained and torn smocks gave evidence of the struggle. Sasha and Feodor would serve as witnesses. They would let all the others know what was done here. Tomorrow, they would bring a sample to the Armenian's cousins and make all of them eat a mouthful.

This was Feodor's idea.

A nice touch. Borovik will like it.

Besides, Borovik needs to be shown that the Kerensky brothers are capable of disciplining their own gang members. He has still not forgotten that business with the shipment from Yekaterinburg.

Kerensky didn't know what happened, exactly. All Borovik would say was that Sasha's boys opened one of the crates which they were warned not to touch and set off a booby trap meant for possible hijackers. It ruined the whole shipment. Even killed thirty pigs.

Funny thing, though. They brought back the pigs, but not Sasha's boys. The pigs came back gutted and dressed and were sealed in a freezer. You'd think they could have cleaned the boys up while they were at it and brought them home for a proper burial.

But it was not a time to complain.

There were no other workers in the sausage section.

This was not because Kerensky had dismissed them, but because it was a Monday and only half of the usual number had bothered to appear for their shift. Those who had, had put in their customary three-hour day and then slipped off to a bathhouse where they would spend the afternoon drinking beer and eating salt fish as a cure for their hangovers.

The hangovers were a consequence of all the home-brewed concoctions they had consumed since Friday. A favorite was beer mixed with equal parts hair spray, foot deodorant, and white-lilac eau de cologne. Another was bread saturated with shoe polish and heated on a radiator until dry.

It was Sasha who told him about these recipes. At first, Kerensky thought that this was another of Sasha's jokes, but it turned out to be the truth. Also a very bad practice. Already, this year, Kerensky had lost three workers dead from alcohol poisoning, two to blindness, and six more in jail for repeated public drunkenness. Those who remained, of course, had not worked on Friday afternoon either, because that was when they stood in line for their weekly half-liter of legal vodka. But real vodka was mostly for bartering, not drinking.

Workers.

They are ten times more trouble than they are worth. Kerensky and his brothers would have been out of there two years ago, enjoying their money, eating lunch every day at good restaurants, had General Borovik not insisted that they stay on the job to keep everything looking legitimate.

Where else, asked Borovik, can you control a fleet of trucks? Where else would you have freezer vaults which are better than bank vaults for our purposes? Where else can you have ten, fifty, a hundred ex-convicts ready at the snap of your fingers?

Perhaps, thought Kerensky. But it still isn't fair. You would think that the leader of the most powerful brigade in Moscow, bigger than any two other mafias combined, should at least have a regular table at the Metropole.

As for having all those men, it's one thing to snap your fingers and quite another to hope that they're not drunk out of their minds when they show up.

Today, as it happened, quite a few of them had been brought back to work, although not to the sausage rooms. Two truckloads of pigs, nothing special about them, had arrived unexpectedly. Kerensky had to pay the police to go and scour the local *banyas*—bathhouses—rounding up those who were still sober enough to slaughter and scald the pigs, preferably in that order and hopefully not each other. By the sounds of the shouts and squeals now coming from the killing room, some confusion remained.

It was just as well. The noise would drown out the Armenian, who had now managed to spit out the tripe and was screaming up at the ceiling in the apparent hope that God, whom he had rediscovered in the past five minutes, would cause a power failure. A rasping buzzer sounded, as if to dash that hope.

Kerensky turned toward the sound and glanced at his watch, then nodded to Feodor, who stood nearest the barred double doors. Feodor spoke through it, listened, then shrugged in Kerensky's direction before lifting the bar and admitting a tall, slender man wearing a dark Italian suit and carrying a briefcase. Kerensky tried not to reveal his disappointment. General Borovik, it seemed, had sent Viktor Podolsk in his place.

The Armenian, however, showed no such reserve. He loosed a babbling stream of pleadings, prayers, and even flattery toward the person of Major Podolsk. His hope of redemption, it seemed, had shifted from the God of his grandparents to the mercies of the KGB.

Better to believe in God.

Kerensky smiled and nodded in the direction of the major, but he was looking past him, still hopeful that Borovik himself might be coming. That hope quickly faded when Podolsk flicked a finger toward the door, directing that it be locked behind him.

Kerensky did not care for this one. He was from Leningrad and it showed. Effete. Excessively Westernized. Features more Nordic than Russian. His sense of humor and his grasp of irony were also Nordic, which is to say nonexistent.

The KGB talks of its new breed. This one was a good example. University-educated, technologically inclined, eats and drinks in moderation, goes to fitness clubs. This one, it is said, sits on an exercise bike reading Agatha Christie. He travels to Italy and goes sailing on yachts. He wears Italian shoes, soft like a baby's ass and with little tassels on them. How, Kerensky wondered, does such a man call himself a Socialist?

The Armenian was mewing again. The major, for the first time, noticed him. Kerensky watched as Podolsk, eyes blinking, slowly approached the mixing vat. This would be good, thought Kerensky. He signaled Feodor. Feodor had to cover his mouth to keep from laughing. The effort made him fart.

Major Podolsk stiffened. The tan from Italy faded by several shades, but he seemed unable to turn away. This always amused Kerensky. It's the pig eyes that do it. No one is ever quite prepared to see his sausage ingredients looking back at him.

The major stood for a long moment, composing himself, before he turned to face Kerensky. His mouth was a straight line. Blue eyes, smooth skin, blond hair. His grandma must have spread her legs for the Nazis.

The major gestured toward the vat. "You can't be serious," he said quietly.

Kerensky blinked to show his innocence.

"In what regard, Comrade Major?"

"This man." Podolsk tossed his head, frowning. "You don't actually intend to grind him up."

"Ah!" Kerensky showed that he now understood. "The general said that this one and his cousins should be taught a lesson. This way, I think, leaves the strongest impression."

Podolsk seemed slow to grasp the poetry of Kerensky's solution. The frown deepened. He seemed at a loss for words.

"And . . . what then?" he asked finally. "What becomes of the, ah . . . result?"

Kerensky scratched his head. He pulled a greasy clipboard from a nail. "Ah, yes," he said, suddenly amused. "This consignment goes to a refugee camp for Azerbaijanis."

Podolsk stared blankly. Kerensky was disappointed. To him, it was abundantly clear that an Azerbaijani might be perfectly happy to eat an Armenian, all things considered.

The KGB major, however, failed to grasp this nuance as well. He was still immersed in fundamentals.

"You . . . intend to grind him up *alive*? All of him?"

The Armenian tried to speak. But his eyes rolled back in his head. He fainted.

In truth, Kerensky did have some misgivings. He was certain that the extruder would filter out those bone fragments and teeth that could not be ground to powder. An extra few kilos of meal should absorb the blood and the bowel contents, and he expected that hungry refugees would be philosophical about the odd clump of long black hair. His more immediate concern involved the grinding machinery. The gears worked sluggishly at best. They might jam. The three of them could be there well into the next shift pulling the machine apart. He could tell his brothers to climb in with their electric saws, but if what's left of the Armenian is still thrashing around, they might argue whose idea this was in the first place.

"Kerensky . . ." The major shook his head slowly. "You are an even greater piece of shit than I imagined."

The heavier man reddened. He glanced toward his two brothers, grateful that they did not seem to have heard.

Podolsk turned away, hefting his briefcase, looking for a clean surface on which to lay it. He chose the top of a cereal drum and opened the snaps. He cocked his head toward the mixing vat.

"Let that one go," he said curtly.

Up your ass, thought Kerensky.

"You will have no time for him. The general will be satisfied that his point has been made."

He beckoned Kerensky to the drum where he opened his briefcase and produced a file folder. He laid out three passport photographs, enlarged, several copies of each.

"These three"—he waved a hand over the photographs—"will arrive in Moscow this afternoon. They will stay five nights at the Savoy hotel before going on to St. Petersburg."

Next, he produced a single sheet of paper which detailed a tourist itinerary and another which contained brief biographical sketches.

"Read these," he said. "I will wait."

Kerensky read, one eyebrow slowly rising. The woman was Swiss, not much said about her except that she was a woman of some influence. Her husband was an American, a former policeman. He looked more like a gangster. The second man, who did not in the least look Russian, was a Soviet diplomat, now based in Switzerland. Kerensky suspected that he was also KGB, but Podolsk's paper did not volunteer that detail. He did not like this.

"What do you want of me?" he asked quietly.

"Watch where they go every minute of the day and make note of who they see. If you can, listen to what they talk about."

The eyebrow reached its apogee. "For this, the KGB needs Kerensky?"

"It is not a need. It is a preference."

The heavier man grunted. "But if they suspect that they are being watched, will this man"—he touched Belkin's photograph—"not assume that my people are KGB all the same?"

Podolsk closed his eyes. He smiled, briefly, as if savoring some private joke. "More likely," he said, "they will think that you are petty criminals. If they notice you, therefore, try to sell them things."

"What may I sell them?"

"Anything. Just let me know what they ask for. If they seek information, offer to get it for a price. Then come and tell me what they wish to know."

Kerensky, his lips pursed, read the itinerary and biography pages once again, hoping to find some clue to the KGB's interest in these three. All that was clear was that the general wished to distance himself from this. And if Borovik did not wish to use his own men—they were so much better at this—perhaps his interest was more personal than official.

"How will I report?" he asked.

"I, too, will be staying at the Savoy. Room sixteen. Call me every two hours except when they are in their rooms."

Kerensky's eyebrow twitched but he kept it under control. The Savoy, he thought, is a walk of less than a minute from KGB headquarters and yet Podolsk stays at the Savoy. This is definitely not official.

"Intending no offense, Comrade Major, but I would like to speak with General Borovik on this matter."

Podolsk glared at him. "I am most assuredly not your comrade, Kerensky. And you have your instructions."

He took the papers from the sausage-maker's hand and slid them into his briefcase, leaving the photographs. He walked toward the metal door. Feodor Kerensky hurried to open it. Podolsk hesitated. He turned.

"This once," he said. "You may call and speak with General Borovik."

Kerensky groaned inwardly. This was what he wanted. It was also what he was afraid of. Podolsk was as much as telling him that he didn't like this business either.

Podolsk lifted his chin. "But never again, Kerensky. Never question an order from me again."

Kerensky spread his hands as if in supplication. He stood that way until Podolsk was gone.

Nearly an hour passed before the general returned his call. The Armenian had lapsed into an exhausted stupor. As the telephone rang, Kerensky told his brothers to revive the man, slap his face, blow pepper up his nose.

The voice on the telephone gave no name or greeting, but there was no mistaking it. It was very soft, somewhat high-pitched, almost fatherly in tone. Stalin's voice was like this. Kerensky knew well that the resemblance was both practiced and deliberate.

He repeated the instructions given by Major Podolsk, first assuring the general that he did not doubt that they were authorized. It was only that they seemed lacking in specifics. If the general could give him some better idea of what he was looking for . . .

"Where they go," Borovik interrupted him, "who they see, what they talk about. The specifics are implicit, Kerensky."

"Yes. Of course, they are."

"What else, then?"

"Comrade General . . . It is only that . . . in the course of watching them, I will surely learn more about them. Would it not be better if I knew more at the outset?"

"Such as?"

"Well . . . Belkin. The diplomat. It has entered my mind that he might be KGB. If that is so . . ."

"I am all the KGB which need concern you, Kerensky."

His heart sank. He liked the feel of this even less.

"Is there anything else?"

"No. Only . . . that I had hoped to see you."

"It was not necessary."

"I mean, for the thief. The Armenian who stole from

your mother. But . . . I will release him now, as Major
Podolsk ordered.''

A hollow silence. "You still have him? In that vat?''

"Yes.''

"De . . . describe him. Tell me what you see.''

The stammer. The faint tremor in the voice. It was what
Kerensky was hoping to hear. He began relating how they
lured the man to the sausage room, overpowered him, bound
him in entrails, gagged him with the snout of a pig. This last
was not accurate, but a pig snout is easier to envision than
tripe. He added details that Major Podolsk would not have
known, such as the plan to feed part of this man to his
cousins and such as watching the Armenian try to flop on
the surface like a fish whenever they approached the red
button.

"Press it again," said the general. His voice was now a
croak. "Tell me what he does.''

Kerensky signaled his brother, Feodor. Feodor pressed
the button. The Armenian squealed and thrashed. Kerensky
described what he saw. The level was dropping quickly. The
Armenian had no hope now of gripping the rim. Kerensky
had to stand on a chair to see. The man's feet seemed
dangerously close to the grinding gears. Kerensky said this
to Borovik.

"Shall I stop it?" he asked.

The reply, amid heavy breathing, was an impatient grunt.
Kerensky understood. He was to keep talking. He turned the
phone from his mouth so that it could capture the Armenian's shrieks. Suddenly, the man began to vibrate, shaking
violently as if electrocuted. The shrieks became gasps. The
eyes popped wide and the mouth opened into what seemed
a frozen grin. There, in a blink, the mind was gone. Both
legs to the hips as well.

Borovik's breath came more rapidly. Kerensky wondered
if he was masturbating.

"Comrade General?''

Kerensky had given him time to gather himself.

"Yes . . . Yes.'' The voice sounded tired but content.
A man lost in reverie.

"What will I tell Major Podolsk? He ordered me to release that man."

A small sigh. "You did. He went into hiding. Left Moscow. That's the end of it."

"This other thing you have asked of me . . . Is it . . . a sensitive matter?"

"What? Oh. You mean the tourists."

"Is it dangerous, general?"

"No."

"Could I ask why a KGB officer is traveling with an American policeman?"

A pause. "This is what I wish to know, Kerensky."

Kerensky grunted. No evasion this time. Leonid Belkin was definitely KGB. But Borovik's tone had become impatient. Kerensky had hoped that the lifting of his spirits would make him more communicative.

"Comrade General, I ask these questions only so that I might choose the proper people. Might it come to pass that I would be asked . . . to take strong measures?"

"One must always remain flexible, comrade."

"I see."

"Choose well, Kerensky. Not like last time."

"No. No. This time, no boys."

"And get busy on this. Their flight has already landed."

"Immediately. Yes."

"Do this for me, Kerensky, and the next service I ask of you will take you to America."

The sausage-maker blinked. Borovik knew well that this had been his dream.

"To New York, Kerensky. And to Miami."

Drugs, he realized. It must involve drugs. But he thought about meat as well. In America, he had heard, meat like most Russians eat was reserved for dogs. And not just pork from old pigs. In America, the dogs get beef. Even liver. Whole sections of supermarkets have food only for dogs, and this much space is given also for cats. One may even buy toys for them so that they are not left unamused while their owners work.

"Kerensky?"

America has meat-packing plants, they say, where dogs are brought in and allowed to choose what recipes they like best. This, then, is what goes to the supermarkets. Kerensky found this very hard to believe, but everyone who has been to America says it's true. They claim that dogs and cats are even put on television and shown expressing their preferences. This, it seemed to him, was a demand economy gone mad.

"Kerensky!"

"Yes . . . Yes, Comrade General."

"When you bring the sausage to the cousins, you will watch them eat it?"

"My brothers will."

"No. You. And do it where there is a telephone."

Kerensky understood. He rolled his eyes.

General Borovik broke the connection. The grinding machine groaned and shook. Feodor kicked it. The machine shuddered to a stop. Kerensky's brother cursed.

Well, Kerensky decided, Feodor will have to dismantle it himself. He must get to the Savoy. Take Sasha because he is the more clever of the two while Feodor is better with machines. Also their cousin, Yakov. Yakov used to drive a taxi and he knows the city inside out. Kerensky gathered the photographs.

Miami.

The very thought of it made him smile.

Miami is nothing but rich old Jews. Tell them that you are from Russia, and also a Jew, they give you everything. Kerensky had heard this.

Not so far from Miami is also Disney World.

3

"**Moscow is what? Eight** hours ahead of us?"

Susan Lesko's voice rose over the crackle of bacon. Bannerman, still in his white terry robe, sat on the deck of his Westport home, sorting through snapshots of the wedding. There were two prints of each.

"Seven, this time of year. They should be on the ground by now."

While he was showering, Susan had set two places for breakfast on the umbrella table outside. Too pretty a morning to waste, she said. At his place, she had left a fresh mug of coffee, a glass of grapefruit juice which he had just poured into the shrubbery, and a second juice glass containing an assortment of vitamin pills. He had given up trying to persuade her that the coffee at his elbow was all the breakfast he wanted.

She had also left the snapshots and a pencil, asking that he go through them, matching names to some of the less familiar faces. She would then arrange them into two albums, one to keep and the other for Elena.

"Paul? Have you ever been there?"

"Not to Moscow, no."

"But you've been to Russia."

Bannerman hesitated. "Only to St. Petersburg once. Just in and out."

He heard a long silence broken only by the rattle of utensils. He knew that she was deciding whether or not to probe further.

"Could you ever go back?" she asked. "As a tourist, I mean?"

"I suppose so. Sure."

Well . . . maybe.

The Russians, he imagined, might grit their teeth and grant him a visa. And Susan would love that city. She could happily spend three days in the Hermitage alone. On the other hand, he knew what Leo's advice would be. Let more time pass. The . . . insult . . . runs deep. Wait five years. Maybe ten. The Hermitage will still be there. For right now, it would not be worth the trouble.

Leo would be right.

Being watched, every second of every day, would be the least of it. He would have to make some sort of insurance arrangement and be sure the Russians knew about it. That the price would be high. Even then, there was always the chance that some loose cannon might decide to act out a revenge fantasy. And, the KGB aside, a dozen other intelligence services would be wondering what he was *really* doing there. As they're probably wondering, right now, about Lesko's visit. As they had about the wedding.

In the United States alone, four different agencies had already contacted him, asking him why *else* so many of his people had gathered in Zurich last week.

He was patient with them. He went out of his way to calm them. There was no *else*. The ten who flew over from Westport were those who were closest to Lesko and Elena. More than twice that number had been invited, but Bannerman, as quiet as the past year had been, did not care to risk leaving Westport too thinly defended.

Then, once in Zurich, a new round of assurances became necessary because other contract agents began showing up from all over Europe. Some thirty in all. They had not been invited, but they were not entirely unexpected. Word gets around. They came by to say hello. No, Mama's Boy is not back in business. It was not a hiring hall. Put that out of your heads. It was a wedding celebration, pure and simple.

He could not blame them for wondering, he supposed. After all, each of these men and women had worked for him, at one time or another, when he was Mama's Boy. Many had worked for Mama before him. But that was over. If they'll let it be over.

He sorted through several snapshots of the ushers and bridesmaids. These were taken at the rehearsal by one of Elena's cousins, using Susan's camera while Susan ran around arranging the wedding party into a series of poses. He was in many of these. He remembered seeing Roger Clew from the State Department, standing out of range, shaking his head bemusedly as the camera clicked away.

"You wonder why people get curious?" Clew said to him afterward.

"It's just a wedding, Roger. Like any other."

"No, no. My *parents'* wedding was like any other. My parents didn't have a wedding party consisting of you, two KGB officers, a former GRU colonel, and a deputy chief of operations from the Drug Enforcement Administration."

"I'm sure it was very nice all the same."

"And that's just the men." Clew brought his fingers to his temples as if to contain his disbelief. "We also have

bridesmaids—all very pretty, very virginal, by the way—
who include Carla Benedict, who works with a knife, Molly
Farrell, who makes bombs, and Janet Herzog, who favors a
knitting needle. Not to mention Susan Lesko, who seems to
fit right in now that she's been blooded as well.''

This last had bothered him. The various intelligence
services had probably begun building a file on Susan during
the first month of their acquaintance. Roger's certainly had.
That, he supposed, was to be expected. But, at a more
visceral level, he didn't like hearing her name lumped in
with Carla and the others. She was not like them. Blooded
or not.

''And here they are, people who spent most of their lives
trying not to be photographed, all posing with shit-eating
grins like this was the junior prom.''

Bannerman shrugged. ''Shouldn't that tell you something?''

''I know. You're all retired. It makes me crazy.''

''Roger . . . don't start.''

The man from State raised his hands. A gesture of
surrender.

He cocked his head toward a short, muscular man of
indeterminate age who stood off to one side drinking beer
from a bottle. ''Is that John Waldo, by the way?''

Bannerman smiled. ''Pretty much.''

''Why the new face?''

''There isn't any why. He wanted it done and he did it.''

''Is there anyone else here I'd have trouble recogniz-
ing?''

''Roger . . .''

The hands again.

''Anyway,'' he said, ''thanks for letting me come. I mean
that.''

Bannerman shook his head. ''I had nothing to do with
it.''

Clew was silent for a long moment. ''But you didn't stop
it. Thanks for that.''

Bannerman said nothing.

''If I should ask Susan to dance tomorrow . . . will she
turn and walk away?''

''She understands you, Roger. She doesn't dislike you.''

Clew grunted distantly. The answer fell short of an all-is-forgiven, but he supposed it would have to do. He scanned the room in search of a different subject. He looked at John Waldo again. The job did seem to be purely cosmetic as opposed to a serious attempt at disguise. No facial reconstruction except for straightening his nose. Hair darkened but no change in the cut. Still, except for that bottle of Guinness, Clew might have walked right by him.

Further on, by the buffet table, he saw a tiny woman, short red hair, dressed in a Banana Republic jumpsuit. A nice-looking man, fiftyish, deeply tanned, stood with one hand rubbing her shoulder as he, also, was scanning the room.

"Carla looks good," he said. "She's gained back some weight."

"A couple of pounds. She thinks it's too much."

"How's she doing, generally?"

"Much better. Thank you."

"Do you think she'd dance with me?"

Bannerman had to smile. "That might be pushing your luck, Roger."

In truth, Bannerman had been surprised to learn that Roger Clew was on the invitation list. Elena knew that he and Roger had been close for fifteen years, but she also knew that Roger hatched one manipulative scheme too many aimed at getting Bannerman and his people back to work. Water under the bridge, she'd said. A wedding is a time to mend fences.

That, he supposed, might have been one motive. Gratitude might have been another. It was Roger who had quashed two outstanding indictments against her a couple of years back, without which she could never have returned to the United States. Lesko gave another reason. Better to have him inside the tent pissing out, he said, than outside pissing in.

Bannerman heard the sound of vegetables being chopped. It meant that Susan was making one of her western omelets. He rose from the table and walked to the sliding door, hoping to persuade her that the bacon and an English muffin would be plenty. Her omelets were delicious, but if he ate one he would either have to forgo lunch or take a three-mile run this evening.

Instead, he stood watching her. She was at the counter, her back to him, wearing one of his shirts, open to the fifth button, and not much else.

She owned two robes, including a gorgeous oriental, but she seldom wore them in the morning. This was mostly, he suspected, because she knew perfectly well what wearing that shirt did to him. No designer of lingerie had ever come up with anything remotely as sexy as a man's shirt on a beautiful woman in the morning.

She half turned while he was watching, using one of those long straight legs to kick a cabinet shut. The same motion pulled the shirt tight against one breast and partially exposed the other. She was pretending not to notice that he was standing there. She yawned, or pretended to yawn. The yawn turned into a catlike stretch, an arching of her back which caused her breasts to rise as her head rolled languidly across her shoulders. A toss of her long brown hair revealed more of her face. Now he saw the tiny contented smile tugging, just barely, at one corner of her mouth. He knew the look. He also knew that there was no use in protesting the western omelet. She would only suggest that there was more than one way to work off a big breakfast.

Bannerman turned from the deck door without speaking. No use in rewarding smugness, either. He took his seat at the umbrella table that Susan had purchased the summer before.

She'd chosen the rest of the deck and patio furniture as well, plus the several hanging plants on wrought-iron poles and all of the azaleas and dwarf rhododendrons that bordered the area. His own contribution had been a plum tree which, according to Susan, would not bear fruit for another two seasons.

He could wait. In the meantime, he was quite proud of it. It was the first tree, the first *anything,* he'd ever planted. He'd bought two books that showed him how to care for it, unwilling to trust a single source. Typical, Susan had muttered at the time.

All the same, it seemed to be doing quite well. A few weeks ago, it had exploded into a million pinkish blossoms, and the slender purple leaves had since pushed through. He would check it every morning, pull a weed or two from its base, and then just stand back and look.

The deck had been bare before Susan entered his life. Sometimes, at night, before Susan, he would wander out here with a Scotch and sit against the railing, being careful to stay in deep shadow. All house lights turned off. Even then, he didn't make a habit of it. Habits kill. He would not have dreamed that one day soon he'd think nothing of lolling around out here in his bathrobe, in broad daylight.

His first-ever breakfast on the patio came the day after the umbrella table and chairs were delivered. Susan took his mug and his Sunday *New York Times* from his hands and told him to get out there and enjoy the morning. That time, he'd stalled for about thirty minutes, long enough to get two of his people to come and check out the area, being careful not to let Susan see them. She found out later. Hit the ceiling.

"That's a crummy way to live, Bannerman," she told him.

He had not thought of it in those terms. Over the years, caution had become such a part of his nature that there was barely any thought process to it at all. He likened it to the buckling of a seat belt, but Susan dismissed that analogy.

"You don't strap on a seat belt," she said, "just to warm up the car, and you don't call in a SWAT team every time you feel like getting some air."

He could offer no argument that did not sound paranoid. By the fourth or fifth Sunday, he had even stopped slipping a pistol into the folds of his newspaper.

4

General Vadim Borovik's mood had darkened again.

He stood, hugging himself, at the tall arched window of his fourth-floor office which looked out upon Dzerzhinski Square. The pleasure of Kerensky's Armenian had not lasted.

He was a small man, of Stalin's height. Like Stalin, he wore lifts in his boots. He had even practiced Stalin's manner of speech. Soft voice, quiet menace. But the angrier Stalin got, the quieter he became. Borovik could never quite manage that. These days, he was angry more often than not. Also, when Stalin spoke softly, everyone leaned close to listen. With Borovik, they just pretended not to hear.

For a while he wore a mustache like Stalin's and he smoked the same kind of pipe. But then the changes came. People who once fell silent when he passed began to point and whisper. Some laughed behind his back. One day, a young girl, a tourist, approached him in a restaurant and asked him if he was an actor in a movie. There were other KGB officers in this restaurant. They hid their faces, snickering. Borovik still seethed at the memory.

After that, he had shaved the mustache. Without it, he realized, the resemblance suffered. Stalin was a Georgian whose blood had mostly Greek while Borovik's was mostly Tartar. A warrior's blood. But one day he would grow that mustache again. One day there would be order again. Let them laugh while they can.

Borovik's eyes grew hard. Across the square, peeking at him from behind the Detsky Mir department store, as if taunting him, stood still another insult. The Savoy Hotel. Belkin and his companions would be staying there.

Of all the hotels in Moscow, Leo Belkin had chosen the Savoy. A hotel for foreigners, managed by foreigners. One need not ask why. Belkin had selected the one hotel which stood practically in front of Number 2 Dzerzhinski. Facing this window. The choice could only have been deliberate. A thumbing of the nose.

Their rooms had been readied for them. Every whisper would be recorded. Belkin, of course, would expect nothing less. He would caution the American and his new Swiss wife to guard their words, leave no notebooks, no address books. But the American would probably forget. Americans are children about such things.

A movement, off to Borovik's right, caught his eye. There, below him, on a corner outside Detsky Mir, Borovik spied an old woman who was aiming a camera in his direction. Now he saw the reason for it. A small group stood in the square, waiting for a lull in traffic so that they could pose for a souvenir photograph with Moscow Center in the background. The old mother was clearly ill at ease.

From her gestures, Borovik knew that she was telling the others to arrange themselves quickly so that she could be done with it. The others were trying to calm her, chiding her for her timidity. One of them, a young man, now sought to provoke her by striking a pose that Borovik recognized at once. He was aping the posture of Feliks Dzerzhinski's statue, now gone, melted down for scrap.

Borovik had been at his window that night as well, his office darkened, when they took it away. Thousands out there, cheering and mocking, scrawling slogans on the statue's base. Painting swastikas on Moscow Center itself. And what did the so-called authorities do when they tried to pull the statue down? Did they move to prevent this desecration? No. The mayor of Moscow sent cranes and trucks. He showed them how to commit this sacrilege more efficiently.

They had even erased his name. No more Dzerzhinski Square. Today it was Lubyanka Square. Tomorrow, the wind will change again and they will call it something else. But to Borovik, it would always be Dzerzhinski.

At last, the old woman snapped her picture. She quickly lowered the camera, concealing it against her thigh, and blessed herself. Ten years ago, she would have been arrested for taking a picture of this building. It is good that she remembers.

Ten years ago, Borovik reflected, not many would even have walked along the sidewalk in front. Every Muscovite claimed to know of someone who did so and heard the sounds of torture coming from the barred ground-floor windows. Some said that the shrieking and wailing caused the hair of this man or that woman to turn white in just one day. Others say that this or that pedestrian stopped to listen at one of the windows and was dragged inside, never to be seen again. Not his wife or husband, either. His grandparents soon vanished as well.

None of this was true, of course. Nothing can be heard from the street. The interrogation rooms were soundproofed and they were two floors further down.

Even for two years after the back-stabber Gorbachev started his *glasnost,* if foreign tourists would ride past in their buses and ask, "What was that big yellow building back there?" the Intourist guide would pretend not to hear. Or she would say that it is just an office building. An insurance company. Which it was before Lenin. She would never say that it is KGB headquarters. If she had, she might have seen those rooms firsthand.

Now, he thought disgustedly, we have guided tours. The tourists come right into the building. Not just into the KGB museum. They are taken everywhere. Even to parts of the basement.

In every group there is a bumpkin who says, "Tell me confidentially. Is Wallenberg, the Swede, still down below?" or, "Can I see my father's old cell? Perhaps he wrote a forwarding address on the wall."

Under Gorbachev, suddenly we had a KGB museum where children could touch pieces of the American U-2 and see weapons of assassination taken from agents of the CIA. We gave them KGB comic books and we sold them KGB T-shirts which they wore not with respect but with impudence. To show that they are not afraid. They wear them even to their disco clubs and to rock concerts. Once, at such a concert, with his own eyes he saw a Russian girl pull off her KGB shirt, exposing herself, to trade it for a T-shirt of the Oakland Raiders, an American football team which, even in its own country, is known to be a pack of thugs. So bad, he'd heard on good authority, that even Oakland threw them out.

This is the new Soviet Union . . . what is left of it. This is what has become of Socialist values. Now the KGB has a chairman who denounces all who came before him as criminals. He brings reporters with their cameras into the courtyard where tens of thousands had their last look at the sky before they got a bullet in the head. He shows them the cells of the Lubyanka itself. He appears on their television programs and permits the most impertinent questions to be asked, even taking calls from those who are watching.

It is good that he knows so little.

Borovik could not imagine exposing himself to such nonsense. Not that he was ever asked. The Chairman would not allow it in any case. Television is not for you, Vadim Yakovich. It is only for handsome officers who look European and have good teeth. Perhaps this is not exactly what he said, but it is what he meant. No short, squat officers with Tartar blood. No brutish faces. No Stalin impersonators. Only those who fit the benevolent image of the new KGB. You would embarrass us, Vadim Yakovich. You would scare the children.

So, thought Borovik, we endure the insults. We smile. We wait. Meanwhile, we write down the names. We write down all their names. And his is very near the top.

"General Borovik? Sir?"

Major Podolsk's voice. Borovik had not heard his knock. He raised a hand to show that he was deep in contemplation. Let the young fop cool his heels awhile.

He was a reliable enough officer, Borovik supposed. Another of the new breed but more pragmatic than most. Knows where his bread is buttered. But should he ever forget, Borovik would remind him that his alternative is twenty years in Lefortovo prison.

Drinks daiquiris, however. What Russian drinks daiquiris and reads Agatha Christie? He must be homosexual. For him, Lefortovo might be paradise.

"What do you have for me, Major?" Borovik did not turn from the window.

Nor, he noticed, did Podolsk answer at once. There was

always that little delay. A slow filling of the lungs. The merest hint of insolence.

"There is quite a lot, actually," Podolsk said at last.

Borovik heard the sound of file folders being slapped against his desk.

"Here is a list of the wedding guests." Another slap. "Profiles on about half of them. The computers are working on the rest."

"Any surprises?"

"A great many." Viktor Podolsk added a stack of photographs to the other documents. "The American State Department was represented by the undersecretary for foreign affairs. The Drug Enforcement Administration by its deputy chief of operations. This was no ordinary wedding."

Borovik sniffed. Also Mama's Boy, that butcher, that murdering bastard, with a small army of his criminals. Also the Bruggs with all their millions, and two KGB officers who should long ago have been shot. No ordinary wedding, he says. How very perceptive. "What have you learned from Yasenevo?"

The reference was to the headquarters of the First Chief Directorate—now called the Foreign Intelligence Service—at Yasenevo on Moscow's Outer Ring Road.

"They say . . . that it is none of our affair."

Borovik heard the hesitation. He could imagine the actual language they used. *"Tell that twisted little toady . . ."* His color rose.

"Comrade General," Podolsk said these words through a grimace. "You realize that they are technically correct."

Borovik cleared his throat and spat toward the sidewalk, watching the phlegm tumble until it struck. He was right about this one. The glamor boys insult him and he defends them. Definitely a pansy.

As for Yasenevo being *technically* correct . . . that was true only while those three remained outside these borders. "They are in Moscow now, Podolsk. In Moscow, they are mine."

"General . . ." The major tried again. "Have you looked at their itinerary?"

"What about it?"

"Except for a few special courtesies, it is a very full, very ordinary tourist itinerary. A different restaurant every night, the Bolshoi, the circus, and the Pushkin. There is simply no reason to suspect that they are—"

Borovik turned at last, his expression pained. "If you lived in the West, Podolsk, would you honeymoon in Moscow?"

"Perhaps. If I had never been here. If a friend invited me."

"This friend. Would you want him with you on your wedding trip? Answer as if you were normal, Major."

With effort, Viktor Podolsk ignored this last. "He is . . . more of a host, actually. The trip was his gift to them."

Borovik snorted. "Belkin's pay is less than mine. How does he afford such a gift?"

Perhaps he is a greater thief than you are, thought Podolsk, but he knew this to be unlikely. "Yasenevo has clearly authorized the expense," he answered.

"Obviously. But to what purpose?"

Podolsk spread his hands. This discussion would get nowhere. Point out to this hack that any intelligence organization worth the name would leap at the chance to cultivate the Bruggs and he will call you a fool. How can you not see, Podolsk, what they intend? Right here in Moscow. Right under this window.

Borovik snorted again. He stepped to his desk and began sorting through the enlarged photographs. He took his time, staring thoughtfully at some, pausing to scowl at others. He came to one of Mama's Boy. With the nail of his thumb, he scored a line across Bannerman's throat. And another across his eyes. The nail pushed through the paper.

Podolsk cleared his throat. Borovik turned away, gathering himself.

"How many did we have at this wedding?" he asked. "Two?"

"Only one. Barca."

"Why not the Sicilian?"

"He might have been recognized. There was no need to risk it. Barca was there as an invited guest, right in the thick of everything."

"Ah, yes. Barca." Borovik saw him in one of the photographs, a drink in his hand, working his charm on a group of older ladies. And, in a second photo, there he was with Belkin himself, this time with a champagne glass in his hand. Borovik frowned. He had told him not to drink. "Do we have his report?" he asked.

Podolsk had been dreading this. "He . . . is withholding it. He wishes to discuss a new arrangement with you."

Borovik stiffened. His eyes grew cold. "He *bargains* with me?"

"He . . . acknowledges that terms have been agreed upon. But he asks—and these are his words—'What is it worth to the general to be able to penetrate Mama's Boy's inner circle?' The question, however, is rhetorical. What he wants is a contact to broker all heroin shipments through—"

Borovik's eyes became glazed. "He can do this? Penetrate Bannerman?"

"He claims to have found a way."

Borovik's fingers were at his temples. "Penetrate means what? Earn his trust? Get close to him?"

"Apparently. But what use is it? If Bannerman is retired . . ."

"What did he promise? Quote him exactly."

Podolsk gritted his teeth. "That you can have your own man in this private town of Bannerman's, fully accepted, and eventually trusted. When the time is right, he will kill him for you."

Borovik could only stare.

"Remember, General, this is Barca talking. He is hardly the man one would choose for such a . . ."

The shorter man was not listening. His expression had become strangely distant. The fingers of his left hand drummed against the desk. They began to walk in the direction of another photograph, expensively framed, that of his mother, but he stopped them halfway.

"When does Barca report again?" he asked.

The major checked his watch. "He's overdue, actually."

Borovik sorted through the wedding pictures. He found another shot of Mama's Boy. An enlargement. Bannerman chatting amiably with Roger Clew. He held it up to the light.

Podolsk watched his eyes, hoping to read them, the better to anticipate what this stupid man might do. What Podolsk saw startled him. Borovik's eyes had become moist. They were welling with tears.

"Make the agreement," said Borovik quietly, his voice slightly thickened. "Promise him what you must, but make the agreement."

Podolsk took a breath. "Ah . . . may I ask what this Mama's Boy is to us? By all reports, he is retired and wants nothing more than—"

"Do it, Podolsk."

"But what use is it? Besides, we need Barca where he is."

A low growl began in Borovik's stomach. He raised one hand as if to strike a blow. Podolsk stood his ground. The hand slammed against his desk, then swept the files to the floor.

Podolsk said nothing. He turned to leave.

"This other business," Borovik said to his back. "Does he know why General Belkin has come to this country with an American policeman and a born-again drug trafficker?"

The younger man turned. "Barca tends to agree with my assessment but he expects to know more today. However, regardless of what he thinks . . ."

"Enough, Podolsk."

The major closed his eyes.

"I want voice contact with Barca."

"Voice contact?"

Borovik gestured toward an olive-colored phone, one of five on his desk along with three different pictures of his mother. The other phones were black.

"Signal the Sicilian on his communicator, tell him to have Barca call. When he does, put him through to my green line."

"But voice contact is . . ."

Borovik waved him off. "Decoding, last time, took four hours. My line is secure."

Podolsk wanted to laugh. "General . . ."

"Do it, Podolsk."

"But you might as well—"

"Do it," he rasped.

"—stick your head out your window and shout his name." But Podolsk did not finish his thought. He chewed his lip, then nodded.

Borovik turned once more to his window, this time to conceal his emotions. The pain was leaving him. Excitement was taking its place. He could feel himself swelling. He gestured toward the Savoy with his chin. "Kerensky's people, meantime. They are in place?"

"Yes, General." For what they're worth.

Borovik tossed a hand, dismissing Podolsk. As an afterthought, he snapped his fingers and gestured toward the mess on the floor. He knew that Podolsk saw the gesture, because he heard a hesitation in his step. But Podolsk continued on. The door clicked shut before Borovik could speak.

He resisted the urge to call that pansy back, make him kneel down, pick up those files. Putting Podolsk in his place could wait. Right now, what he needed was to think. Borovik stepped to his desk and took, from the bottom drawer, a bottle of peppered vodka. He drank deeply.

Bannerman.

Oh, to have just three days with him. Just the two of them alone. And a good pair of pliers.

The vodka seemed to ease the pressure at his groin. But soon he would need stronger relief.

There was once a house nearby where whores could be bound and beaten. It was also the place where Beria kept his young girls, sometimes for weeks. He would drive through the streets, they say, pointing out the ones he wanted. He should have stuck with the whores. It was for all those girls, as much as anything, that the prudes in the Politburo lynched him.

But even the whores were gone now. They would no longer work there, and ever since Gorbachev, you couldn't make them stay. More money was to be made at the tourist hotels, where rich foreigners pay ten times as much and do not make them scream.

Perhaps he would go down to the basement. There, if one concentrated, the screams can still be heard.

5

Bannerman had returned to his task of sorting pictures. He was now on those of the wedding reception. He wished that Susan was in more of these. She'd been too busy taking them.

Here she was, however, in a shot with Yuri Rykov, Leo Belkin's aide. They were dancing. Yuri was looking at her feet as she demonstrated a step. In another, she was grinning at the camera, one arm around Irwin Kaplan and the other around Belkin. Belkin was sucking on his pipe, a mischievous glint in his eye. Kaplan's expression was more of a blush. Belkin seemed to be enjoying the DEA man's discomfort at being photographed with a KGB general.

Irwin had known Lesko since his early days in New York when Lesko had just made detective and Irwin was a young assistant district attorney. He and his wife would probably have come to the wedding at their own expense, but it would have stretched their budget. Instead, at Lesko's suggestion, he told his superiors about the invitation and then feigned a reluctance to accept.

"Here's what you do," Lesko had advised him. "You tell your boss you're not going. Too many unsavory characters. Name names, watch his mouth drop. Play this right and he'll send you over on Air Force One."

Irwin's boss very nearly did. The DEA provided first-class tickets to Zurich and four nights in a junior suite at the Dolder Grand Hotel. The trip would not be charged as vacation time. The only price Irwin paid was to endure a day-long briefing by some CIA types and some instruction in the use of a special pinhole camera in the event that ordinary cameras were banned. Irwin dropped it into a trash basket upon clearing customs in Zurich.

A nice, if wasteful gesture, thought Bannerman, who

promised him a set of Susan's pictures. Well . . . give or take a few.

Similarly, Yasenevo was delighted to have two of its own in the wedding party, but Leo would not have missed it for the Order of Lenin or whatever their highest medal is these days. His relationship with the Bruggs went back more than a decade.

Certainly, he had cultivated old Urs Brugg for professional reasons—the patriarch of the Brugg family was the sort of asset on whom careers are built—but for all of that, Leo's affection for that splendid old man was no less genuine. Urs Brugg was gone now. Almost two years. Elena, who had hoped to live a quiet life for a change, having given away most of her money, discovered that her uncle had left her the bulk of his estate, which included an art collection valued in excess of twenty million dollars and a controlling interest in a dozen corporations.

A cordial relationship with Mama's Boy had not hurt Leo Belkin's career either. Bannerman had been friendly with him for those same two years although he had known Leo by reputation long before that. Leo, Bannerman felt sure, would never do anything that might risk either relationship. Not if he had a choice. But Leo did seem to have a lot on his mind during the days leading up to the ceremony. Bannerman had asked him, finally, directly, whether he was having second thoughts about the upcoming wedding trip. Belkin said no, but a bit too emphatically for Bannerman's comfort.

Susan was particularly fond of the other KGB officer, Yuri Rykov, recently promoted to major although he was only twenty-nine. Yuri was a handsome, good-natured young man with an engaging boyishness about him. He had only just returned to limited duty after being shot last year in Los Angeles. His face still needed some work. The jaw was now fully functional, but the right cheekbone would require further reconstruction and some of the scarring would need to be reduced. None of this, however, had stopped him from courting a young Swiss widow and concert cellist named Maria.

On the day of the wedding he had taken Bannerman aside to tell him, shyly, that he and Maria had also talked of

marriage. Having said that, and after a searching look, he let
the subject lie.

Bannerman understood. Marriage to a European would
certainly mean the end of a career in foreign intelligence.
Even the thought of it, if known, would result in his
immediate recall. Policy was still firm in that regard. Leo,
although sympathetic, would not be able to help him.
Through that eye contact, Yuri was asking whether Westport might be an option if it came to that.

A fact not lost upon young Yuri was that Anton Zivic, the
former GRU colonel who was also in the wedding party,
had defected some years earlier and was now living unmo-
lested in Westport. Running a successful art and antiques
business and chairing the council that exercised a measure
of control over about thirty retired but occasionally ram-
bunctious agents. Yuri was also well aware that Zivic had
already been ordered home, under guard, when Mama's
Boy not only spirited him out of Rome but successfully kept
him out of the hands of the American intelligence authorities who might have kept him under lock and key for up to
three years of debriefing. But that, of course, was before the
Gorbachev/Yeltsin era.

Things might be easier now, thought Bannerman, but far
from relaxed. And Yuri was not Anton. Anton had no ties at
home, no family, and might well have been arrested if he'd
returned. Yuri was in no such danger, and his parents and
sisters were still living. Russia's attempts at democratiza-
tion notwithstanding, the defection of a KGB officer was
still the crime of desertion. If he bartered information for
sanctuary, the crime would become treason. The effect on
his family, even now, might be considerable. Bannerman
was not sure that Yuri could deal with that. And Bannerman, in any case, could not take him in without Leo
Belkin's blessing. To do so would be a breach of faith.

"Let me know what you decide," Bannerman had told
the young officer. "But talk to Leo first."

This brief exchange with Yuri had been the extent of
anything resembling a conspiracy during Bannerman's several days in Zurich. Certainly, an informal job mart had
developed. Leads were swapped among the free-lancers
regarding government agencies or businessmen who might

be hiring and for what purpose. A select few were quietly put on retainer by the Bruggs. Bannerman didn't ask why. It was none of his business.

At one point, he had seen Elena walking arm in arm with John Waldo. Telling him, among other things, how much younger he looked. Waldo trying not to grin or blush for fear of causing wrinkles. A while later, Waldo said that he might hang around for a couple of weeks. If Bannerman had no objection. Bannerman had none. Elena had already told him what she had in mind. He told Waldo to take all the time he needed.

Most of the guests, invited or otherwise, were more or less equally discreet. They were sure that at least some of their conversations were being recorded via long-range listening devices and would soon be making busywork for assorted intelligence analysts. With that in mind, a few amused themselves by sharing outlandish gossip and inventing colorful stories for the benefit of the eavesdroppers. Otherwise, the nearest thing to an intrigue that he noticed was a series of obviously conspiratorial conversations between Susan and Elena.

Bannerman had often thought that some sort of virus must be released at wedding ceremonies. Other than Yuri, he had heard at least a half-dozen people make wistful comments about settling down, perhaps starting a family. They regarded Lesko as proof that almost any man could find a woman who'd marry him and Susan as proof that no genetic mutation need result.

They would point to Billy McHugh—called Bannerman's monster, although not to his face—who had stunned the European crowd by showing up with a wife. He had finally married his widowed Westport landlady, the former Mrs. DiBiasi, after a courtship of almost Sicilian propriety. Back when Billy worked Europe, he had never even stroked a cat as far as anyone knew. Some had never heard him speak. Now here he was tending bar at Elena's wedding.

There was no need for him to do so, of course. The affair was elaborately catered. He was simply more comfortable behind a bar. It was behind the bar at Mario's, a Westport restaurant, one of the several CIA-owned businesses that

Bannerman had seized, that he'd gradually learned to be at ease with ordinary people.

Even more dazzling was the sight of the equally dangerous Carla Benedict, who appeared with a gentleman friend—a former movie actor from Genoa—and was actually seen smiling at him and holding his hand. Seeing Calamity Carla in a public display of affection was not unlike seeing Dracula at mass.

Carla had not returned to Westport after her sister's funeral. She stayed with Yuri until he was able to travel and then flew back to Switzerland with him. Once there, she elected to stay until she could get some of her own emotions sorted out. She'd found a little apartment above an old stone boathouse on Lake Zurich where she kept pretty much to herself. Yuri looked in on her regularly, as did Elena, and they did their best to coax some life back into her. Thank God for her Italian. He was probably exactly what she needed. Someone not from her world. Someone who was not at least a little bit afraid of her. Someone who saw only a pretty little woman with sad eyes who took long lonely walks after dark. It was good to see her smiling again.

As for Susan and those chats with Elena, complete with furtive glances in his direction and private little smiles, there could not be much doubt about their content. Neither he nor Susan had ever actually raised the subject of marriage but the undercurrent was certainly there. Her father had expressed a preference, though marginal, of marriage over cohabitation. And Susan had remarked more than once that she'd like to have all her children by the time she turns thirty. Bannerman neither encouraged nor resisted either prospect. If pressed, however, he would ask her to give it more time. Thirty was almost four years off.

His circumspection was rooted not so much in the difference between her world and his. That difference had narrowed considerably. His Westport people had fully accepted her. A few, Molly Farrell and Billy McHugh in particular, had grown especially close to her. Even Carla Benedict had eventually come around. Up to a point.

It helped, of course, that Carla now had an outsider of her own, but it was more than that. Last year, Susan had passed what in Carla's eyes was a critical test. She had shot a man.

She didn't kill him, not directly, and she'd had little choice but to shoot. Still, she was deeply affected by it. She learned that there was a world of difference between shooting at paper targets or dead trees and seeing what a bullet could do to human flesh. Carla, not having returned to Westport, never saw that Susan had become moody, often distant, and was drinking somewhat more than her occasional glass of wine. Carla never saw the night sweats or heard the tears. This went on for many weeks.

Bannerman, during this time, would hold her, take long walks with her, listen to her, love her. He tried to tell her that he fully understood what she was feeling. She thanked him for that. But she doubted that he understood and said so.

It was this doubt that made him wonder if Carla had not been right all along. That Susan, Lesko's daughter or not, could never really adapt to his world any more than he could go back to hers.

Anton Zivic, though fond of Susan, tended to agree.

Bannerman had asked him to lunch at Mario's, the restaurant now managed by Molly Farrell.

"When she denies that you could know what she feels," he told Bannerman, "she intends no insult. She simply realizes that, in her place, you would have felt very little."

"That's not necessarily true, Anton."

"For you, for all of us," Zivic corrected him, "it is both true and necessary."

"And for Susan?"

"For Susan, remorse is necessary. It affirms that her humanity remains intact."

"In her eyes, what does that make me?"

Zivic shrugged and sighed. "She believes that you are a fundamentally decent man. In fact, you are."

Bannerman waited, expecting a qualifier. For a moment, Zivic seemed to be chewing on something other than his veal chop but, whatever it was, he left it unsaid.

"Anton, do you think this can last?"

Another shrug. "Relationships change. You know that."

"Sure, but that's not what you're suggesting. You think I'll have to end it."

Zivic blinked. "I said no such thing."

Bannerman retreated, taking time to regroup as he adjusted his napkin. His friend's discomfort was clear to him. And Bannerman realized that pressing him for advice on such a personal matter stretched the bounds of Zivic's role. But Zivic still seemed to regard Susan as an outsider, and Bannerman had thought that that issue, of Susan being a danger to them, had long since been put to rest. Time and again, Susan had shown what she was made of. All of them, Anton included, no longer watched their words in her presence. There was almost nothing of substance that she didn't know about them. Bannerman so reminded Zivic.

"She knows only stories, Paul. She listens to anecdotes. True, she has been involved in one or two, peripherally, but—"

Bannerman interrupted him. He pointed out that Susan had very nearly been killed on two occasions. This could hardly be described as peripheral. Further, it was her involvement with him that had put her at risk. She understood that. And yet she stayed.

"These . . . occasions you speak of. Has she ever discussed their resolution with you? In specific terms, I mean."

Bannerman made a face. "I don't cut off ears and bring them home to her, if that's what you're asking."

"I know you don't."

"Then would you please tell me what's on your mind?"

Zivic toyed with the vegetable on his plate. "The man Susan knows," he said, "is a rather nice man. Excellent manners, a sense of humor, never unkind or profane, and, having discovered the pleasures of gardening, he becomes more domesticated by the day."

Bannerman waited.

"Yes, Susan has heard the stories. But these stories, I think, are not quite real to her because the man she lives with is nothing at all like this Mama's Boy. She knows only Paul Bannerman."

Bannerman could see, more in Zivic's eyes than in his words, what was coming. "One doesn't rule out the other, Anton."

"No. But Susan has never seen the other. Or she has chosen not to."

Bannerman shook his head. "Susan grew up with New York cops. And she knows that her father has killed. I don't think that changed the way she feels about him."

Again, a shrug.

The gesture, thought Bannerman, implied that Susan might have different standards for her father and the men she sleeps with. Zivic's eyes, at least, were asking how Bannerman thought she might feel about sleeping with him if she had heard other kinds of stories. Not of adventures, told with dark humor, but of executions. Not those of narrow escapes, but of the innocent passersby who had sometimes died to facilitate escapes. Of prisoners never taken. Of witnesses seldom left alive.

"That's over," Bannerman said quietly. "It's in the past."

"So we keep saying." The Russian took a sip of his wine, holding it in his mouth before swallowing. "Not bad for a house wine. Pino Grigio, I think."

Zivic glanced around the restaurant, as if searching for still another subject that involved neither the constancy of Susan Lesko nor the wishful thinking of Paul Bannerman. He felt sure that the two were related. Remove Susan from the equation, thought Zivic, and Paul would certainly know better than to think that he would ever be left in peace.

Molly Farrell caught Zivic's wandering eye. She was standing behind the bar with Billy McHugh. They were in conversation with two female customers who were showing them an assortment of travel brochures. Those of cruise ships. Molly raised her chin, asking Zivic if he needed a waiter. Zivic smiled and shook his head.

He recognized one of the women. She sold real estate, lunched there once or twice a week, was fond of Billy's bacon cheeseburgers. She was smartly dressed, middle forties, formerly a battered wife, now a widow. Her late husband had been a lawyer who had twice put her in the hospital. This came to light during a rare evening visit. Billy noticed fresh bruises and swelling which she had attempted to conceal under makeup, asked about them, and the woman began to weep. Molly took over, brought her to a quiet table, got her talking. The woman was afraid to go home, afraid not to. Molly put her up for the night. By morning, her husband was dead. An accident on his basement stairs. His neck was broken.

This sort of thing was happening rarely enough these days that he had chosen not to burden Paul with this particular episode. Nor did Zivic insist upon knowing which one, Molly or Billy, had visited the lawyer. It was almost certainly Billy. Once again, Zivic found it necessary to define, for Billy's benefit, the limits of customer service and to berate Molly whose task it was to keep Billy's concept of friendship in focus. During his first two years in Westport, and before the rest of them realized it, the big bartender had performed similar services for at least eleven patrons who had told their Uncle Billy of their troubles.

His thoughts returned to Susan Lesko. This was not, of course, the sort of anecdote that they would share with her. Too close to home and, strictly speaking, it would make her an accessory. Not that Susan would have shed a tear for the lawyer, necessarily, but her tennis games with Molly and her banter with Billy might lose some of their easy-going camaraderie. Her relationship with those two, however, was not the question at hand.

''Anton?''

Bannerman had been waiting, his arms folded, while Zivic pretended interest in the vacation plans of those two women. Zivic turned to face him, one eyebrow cocked, a look of innocence.

''Anton, why are you ducking me on this?''

Zivic spread his hands. ''Because you ask questions I can't answer. For this, you should speak to a woman.''

''I have. Molly says go for it. Carla says go slow.''

''Which of them did you thank?''

''Um . . . both of them?''

Zivic snorted.

Bannerman couldn't help but smile. He rubbed his jaw until it faded. ''I wish you'd help me think this out, Anton.'' he said.

''You speak as if there were options. You will not leave Susan, nor will you send her away.''

''No, I won't.''

''But you fear that she will turn from you one day. This could happen in any case.''

"I know that."

"Do I gather that you are contemplating marriage?"

"I'm contemplating how to deal with the subject when it arises." Bannerman grimaced. "Anton, what if we had children?"

"Children." Zivic stared blankly.

Bannerman looked away.

"This is the price of my lunch? I am to advise you about having children?" Bannerman's color rose slightly.

"Here is my advice." Zivic leaned forward. "If you want Susan, keep her. If you want a family, have it. If you also want a golden retriever, buy it. Or are you one of these people who will not have a pet for fear that it will die before you do?"

Bannerman grunted. "Live for today. Is that what you're saying?"

Zivic softened his voice. "It is true, I think, that Susan sees you through a prism. She knows what you are and yet she doesn't. Is it your concern that her vision will one day clear?"

"It's crossed my mind."

"What will she see?"

"I'm not always such a nice person, Anton."

"You are also not Heinrich Himmler. Also you have been more than two years with Susan. Why does this arise only now?"

"I told you. I think she wants to get married. I know she wants a child."

"And this child may one day discover that his tree-planting father is Mama's Boy."

A pained expression. "It's something to think about."

"So is bowel cancer from not enough roughage. If you like, I will help you worry about that as well."

A tickle of hair and a kiss from Susan brought him back to the present. She set his breakfast plate in front of him, then slipped into the chair opposite. The shirt teased him again. Her omelet was a third the size of his.

The lunch with Anton Zivic had not resolved much of anything. Perhaps it had helped to give form and voice to random thoughts, but he had left the table feeling a little stupid.

Still, although his concern about a nonexistent child might have been ludicrous, he thought that his concerns about Susan had substance. Susan had never even heard him shout at another human being, much less do harm to one. A woman can see a man . . . beat up another one, for example . . . and never quite get over it. Regardless of what caused the fight. And especially if he showed no distaste for it afterward. She might even begin to fear him.

"I will tell you the greater danger," Zivic had scolded him that day in the restaurant. "One day, in Susan's presence, an emergency will arise. It will be a time to act but you will hesitate."

Bannerman began to answer, but didn't.

"You see?" Zivic rapped the table. "Even now you hesitate. The best thing for you . . . tonight, take Susan down to the Bronx and do a few drive-by shootings. If you need a motive, shoot one of those annoying young men who extort money for wiping windshields at stoplights. That way you put this behind you before you end up risking your own life and those who depend on you for the sake of Susan's good opinion."

It was not the most helpful advice Anton had ever given, but he'd made his point. If you're not going to end it, stop brooding about this and deal with it. Bannerman knew he was right. He should probably sit Susan down and speak his mind, but he knew perfectly well what she'd say. She'd said it before:

"Bannerman . . . eat your breakfast. I never thought you were Robin Hood."

She had also told him that she's not "some Mafia princess whose husband brings her furs that keep falling off trucks and then says 'Never ask me about my business.'" She would tell him that there's no need to protect her, no need to pretend.

But he liked protecting her. He liked pretending. He liked pretending that he was just another Westport businessman, owner of the travel agency that those women at the bar had just visited. No, not pretending. Being. Having people stop him on the street and chat with him. Having neighbors, like the young doctor next door who occasionally comes over for some one-on-one in his driveway, using the hoop left by a previous owner. Loser buys the beer.

Bannerman even liked raking leaves. He liked grilling steaks. Going to garage sales. Most of all, he liked being loved by Susan Lesko.

From inside, he heard the muted ring of a telephone. The call was on a private line, connected to an answering machine and scrambler which he kept locked in a cabinet. Bannerman chose to ignore it, let the machine take it. It was too nice a morning for the sort of calls that came in on that line.

The ringing stopped. Susan took a piece of bacon with her fingers and brought it to her lips. She paused, listening. Bannerman heard nothing but he knew that Susan probably could. She had ears like a bat.

"That sounds like Carla," she said. "She wants you to pick up."

Bannerman grumbled. He pushed to his feet.

As he neared the locked cabinet after first grabbing his keys, he began to pick up words and phrases. They seemed disjointed. Something about Aldo, the man she was seeing. Her voice was profoundly sad. Now she cited a telephone number, which she said was Yuri Rykov's. Bannerman's first thought, due perhaps to his own state of mind, was that Carla and her Italian had a fight and she had gone to Yuri for solace. Perhaps she was calling to say she wanted to come home. He wished that she had called Anton instead. It would serve him right.

Bannerman had the cabinet open and was reaching for the handset when he heard the words . . . "I had to cut him. I cut him good."

Then came a choking sound. The beginnings of a sob.

Carla broke the connection.

6

"Keep an open mind, Lesko.''

Belkin kept saying that.

''Moscow is not Zurich.''

Lesko shrugged and nodded.

''You land at JFK, first impressions of New York are not so positive either.''

''Leo . . .'' Lesko spread his hands.

''Just keep an open mind.''

The thing was, he hadn't said a word.

True, he was less than overwhelmed so far, but he was trying not to let it show for Leo's sake. No, it wasn't Zurich, but it wasn't Calcutta either. Relax, Leo.

The Finnair jet had landed at Sheremetyevo Airport. It was fairly new, according to Belkin. He said it was built for the 1980 Olympics and designed by the French. With that, thought Lesko, you'd expect it to have just a little glitz.

It didn't. Everything was brown, poorly lit, low ceilinged, only a few little shops and snack counters, half of which were closed. Guards everywhere. No smiles.

But he was trying to keep an open mind because Leo Belkin kept reminding him that he had to. Near the passport control booths, they walked past a tour group from England whose guide was telling them the same thing. It's like a blind date, thought Lesko. When the person fixing you up keeps telling you to keep an open mind, this girl has great qualities, a terrific personality, you know right away she's going to be a bowser.

Belkin got their bags through pretty quickly. No one with a Western passport seemed to have any trouble either, although most of the Russians were getting their luggage picked apart item by item. A customs agent took his time writing down what Elena's diamonds looked like so that they didn't grow bigger by the time she came back out.

One thing was really dumb. Sheremetyevo had these red
and green customs lanes like in every European airport.
Green was for "nothing to declare" and you're supposed to
walk right through. But in Russia you had to declare all
currency, any currency, in excess of fifty dollars' worth.
Nobody, therefore, ever got to use the green lane.

A border guard checked his passport and visa, very
carefully, then looked him up and down, then handed it back
with a look that said *We know all about you. Don't think we
won't be watching you.* Lesko did not take this personally,
because every tourist got the same look. They must teach it
in guard school. Welcome to Russia.

Belkin had arranged for a limousine and driver. The car,
waiting at the curb, was a roomy but ponderous-looking
thing called a Chaika. It reminded him of the old Packard
sedans. The driver, named Valentin something or other, was
a good-natured young guy who reminded him of Yuri. He
seemed genuinely delighted to see them and eager to
practice his English.

"We show you beautiful places, beautiful things," he
said. "Totally awesome," he added. This cracked him up.
Belkin winced.

The ride into Moscow, he said, would take forty-five
minutes. Belkin spent the first twenty of them tempering
Valentin's enthusiasm and finding new ways to say they
should keep an open mind. In one way it was kind of sad.
The guy really wanted them to like his country, but he was
as much as saying that he's ashamed to show it to them. In
another way, it kept raising these little red flags that Lesko
had been sensing for at least the past week. If he thinks his
country is such a toilet, why didn't he buy them a toaster or
a salad bowl and let it go at that.

There was not much to see during the ride in. They passed
one more monument showing how close the Germans got. It
was a group of tank traps in the shape of giant red jacks,
maybe ten miles out. Almost everything else along this road
had been bulldozed before the airport opened. Before that, it
was mostly shacks and shanties. Might have given the
wrong impression.

Lesko knew this because he'd asked John Waldo about
Moscow the day before the wedding. He'd heard that Waldo

had been there. Waldo explained Moscow in terms he could visualize:

"You been to the Motor Vehicle Bureau, right? In New York."

"So?"

"You been there, in this peeling dump, standing in line, waiting for some putz who hates his life, who can't be fired, couldn't give a shit, to try being a little helpful."

Lesko thought he understood. Bureaucracy. But it's probably the same all over. No big deal.

Waldo read his mind. "Now imagine that anything you want to do with your life, any change you want to make, like painting your kitchen, you have to go to maybe five different places just like it for a permit."

Lesko grunted.

"It gets worse. Next imagine an entire country that is not only run like the Motor Vehicle Bureau but also looks like it. Imagine whole cities where one of those shlubs behind the desk also designs all the buildings."

Lesko was still doubtful. From pictures, it didn't look that bad. And he heard the subways were nice. "When were you there, by the way?"

"Last time was '85, I guess." Waldo rubbed his chin. He did this very gingerly. "Couple of times before that."

"They say it's loosened up since then."

"You should live so long."

Waldo was careful about his chin because it was still fairly new. Last year, in Los Angeles, Waldo had gotten it into his head that he was the only person in the whole city who looked his age. Also, some young punk with diamond studs in his ear had called him *Pop*.

This, to make a long story short, makes John Waldo crazy. So he sneaks off to some Beverly Hills knife to get maybe a little tuck here and there and ends up getting sold on $15,000 worth of reconstructive surgery. That, plus the same Clairol color Ronald Reagan uses, takes off a good twenty years. Then Belkin tells him he could have had the same job done for $80 at the Moscow Cosmetological Clinic and Waldo says that's fine if he wanted to spend the rest of his life looking like he'd just been goosed.

Waldo could be very negative.

Lesko never asked him why he went to Russia or how he got in and out, but Waldo could get in and out of anything. Basically, he was Bannerman's cat burglar. The trips were probably for paybacks of some kind. Lesko didn't want to know. But Leo Belkin probably knew, because, of all Bannerman's people, it took him the longest to be comfortable around John Waldo.

The Chaika sedan suddenly veered right, tires squealing, and exited the airport expressway. Valentin grinned an apology. He turned east onto the Moscow Ring Road, massively wide, sixteen lanes, and accelerated.

"Big, big road," he said. "Good that you see it."

The young driver was smiling into the rearview mirror, but Lesko could see that he was also watching the road behind them. Instinctively, he started to turn in his seat.

"Apartments for the people," Valentin said loudly, pointing forward. "All new, very nice."

Lesko took the hint. He settled back.

Ahead, as far as he could see, were row upon row of pink or off-white concrete buildings, all prefabricated, most in various stages of assembly, but quite a few were completed. They were a uniform eight stories high, long rectangles, and some had a row of storefronts across the street level. All the apartments seemed to have terraces. He did not see much in the way of landscaping, but there was no graffiti either. Good-sized playgrounds. A couple of swimming pools. In fairness, they looked a lot better than some of the projects in New York.

Belkin said that the Hitler war had left 25 million people homeless and they were still playing catch-up. Until the sixties, he said, anyone who had a three-room apartment could be forced to take in a family of perfect strangers. By law, even now, the individual space allotment was only seven square meters per person. This, thought Lesko, was roughly the size of one of Elena's guest bathrooms. It would also explain Moscow's divorce rate. Over eighty percent, according to Waldo. Highest in the world.

In a democracy, Belkin went on, this sort of law could not have been imposed. But in a democracy, most of those millions would have had no roof at all over their heads. Marxism. To each according to his needs.

Lesko could have done without the captive lecture. It seemed to him that they could have built a lot of housing for the cost of all those klunky monuments and war memorials he'd seen in the tourist books, but he said nothing. Once again, Valentin lurched onto an exit ramp. Elena lurched into Lesko. Another apology from Valentin. Belkin turned to add his voice to it, but, as he spoke, his eyes washed over the road behind them.

"Prospekt Mira," said Valentin. "More interesting to go this way."

Lesko couldn't see why. More apartment blocks. Except these were much bigger, not so new, and on closer inspection they seemed to be falling apart. Cracks everywhere, tapering streams of rust, no terraces, no visible amenities of any kind, few cars parked outside. Come to think of it, Lesko hadn't seen more than a handful of passenger cars on the road since they left the airport expressway, let alone a possible tail. He wondered what those sixteen lanes were for. From what he could see, Moscow had fewer private cars than Westport.

He remembered something else that Waldo had told him. A lot of these apartment blocks had no numbers on them. They had addresses, said Waldo, but the address of one building might have no sequential relationship at all to that of the building right next to it or even to another section of the same building. Waldo said that this was deliberate. The idea was to make it hard for people to get together, keep them from moving around too much.

Lesko found this hard to believe. Even in Russia, he argued, there had to be a line between repression and chicken shit. Waldo said just wait. Try to find an ordinary street map of Moscow. Also try to find a phone book. You can get a phone if you behave yourself and you wait long enough, but no one can find out your number—because there aren't any phone books. The last batch was printed maybe ten years ago, and only fifty thousand copies for a city of eight million. You can go to these little booths on the street and ask for someone's number, but you have to know the full name—first, middle, and last—and the exact address. This is fine if the number you want is your mother's. Otherwise, don't waste your time.

Valentin was pointing again.

Off to the left there was a sprawling farmers' market where there seemed to be plenty of produce. "All private," said the young Russian. "All capitalist. You see? Market economy."

They continued southward, Valentin describing an enormous sports complex on the left and the massive Kosmos Hotel on the right, both also built for the 1980 Olympics. Ahead, Valentin pointed out the soaring monument to Soviet space exploration, a 300-foot rocket trail, chrome-plated, with a little rocket on top and, further on, a stupendously turgid statue called "Worker and Collective Farm Woman." They seemed to be striding forward as if into the future, determined expressions on their faces, the worker holding a hammer aloft, the woman holding a sickle. Judging by the buildings nearest it, the statues and pedestal must have been fifteen stories tall. For this, people went homeless.

Valentin's description of these monuments was more dutiful than enthused. It did not seem that he counted them among his beautiful things.

Belkin told them that the statue marked the entrance to the Economic Achievements Exhibit, which was easily twice the size of anyone else's World's Fair. He said they were shutting down a lot of it now because it was too expensive to maintain, but mostly because the people had stopped coming to see it. They regarded this exhibit as belonging to another era. It had no relevance to the struggle of their daily lives. They no longer believed in its promise of the future. These days, he said, anything communist was totally and automatically discredited.

This was shortsighted, he said.

The past is fact. One does not reject the past. One learns from it, builds on it, or one repeats it.

Lesko blinked. He nudged Elena with his elbow.

The future, said Leo Belkin, could be beyond their wildest dreams.

With the right sort of leadership. The right sort of help.

This last was followed by a flicker of eye contact between Belkin and the young driver.

Lesko saw it. So did Elena. She placed her hand on Lesko's thigh and patted it. The gesture said, *Be patient.*

7

The number, Bannerman realized, had a Zurich exchange. Yuri Rykov lived in Bern. He punched it out all the same. Yuri answered on the first ring. At hearing Bannerman's voice he asked, ''You are home, sir?''

''Yes.''

''Ten minutes, please.'' The line clicked off.

While Yuri, presumably, hurried to a public phone, Bannerman replayed Carla's message. Susan listened at his side. At the words ''I had to cut him,'' she only frowned. A year ago, thought Bannerman, she would have been horrified.

Some of Carla's words were slurred as if she'd been drinking. That was not like her. Bannerman had never known her to drink anything but wine, two glasses at most, and only with a meal.

Susan found a snapshot of the man Carla brought to the wedding. ''Here,'' she said. ''What was his name again?''

''Corsini. Aldo Corsini.''

''She sounds heartbroken. Do you suppose she caught him with another woman?''

Bannerman shrugged helplessly. He doubted it. In that circumstance, Carla would probably not have bothered calling. Or if she did, having used her knife, her manner would have been defiant. *''I taught the fucker a lesson. Leave me alone.''*

The telephone rang. He snatched the handset and said, ''Yes.''

''Mr. Bannerman, sir?''

''Paul is fine, Yuri. What happened?''

''You have scrambler, yes?''

''Yes.'' He pressed two more buttons. ''Yuri, I'm recording this call and Susan is listening. Do you object?''

"Not to the first. But for Miss Lesko, subject is unpleasant."

Susan folded her arms to show that she was going nowhere.

In for a pound, thought Bannerman. "She can deal with it. Go ahead."

"News is not good. Carla killed this man, Aldo."

Bannerman groaned within himself.

"Best I give background? Is important."

"Go on."

Yuri took a breath. "This morning is a lawn party at Willem Brugg's house. Is for Sunday brunch. Carla is invited. She comes with Aldo Corsini. I am also invited. I go with Maria. Willem tells me that Corsini is asking many questions about General Belkin and about Lesko. I tell this to Carla but she says it is harmless. She says that since the wedding, Aldo has become a . . ." He searched for the word. "It is an Americanism for *aficionado*."

"Groupie?"

"Ah, yes. Groupie. She says for a week now all he talks about are you and your people who he met at the wedding. Such fascinating people, dangerous people, who tell wonderful stories, all true. He is especially . . . enthralled? Enthralled by tales of Carla. So suddenly at the party, he asks her to be his wife."

"Wait." Bannerman shook his head as if to clear it. "He proposed marriage? To Carla?"

A brief silence. Then, quietly, "Carla is not a handsome woman?"

"Of course she is, Yuri. Go on."

The wedding strikes again, thought Bannerman.

"Carla does not say yes or no. At first she thinks that he has sipped too much champagne with orange juice but she is very pleased all the same. In a little while she asks him to take her home because her . . . blood is up?"

"I understand."

"He is reluctant to leave so soon but Carla prevails. He drives her to this boathouse where she lives but he does not wish to enter. Always he goes in but this time he has headache. Carla insists. He says maybe for five minutes. She opens more champagne, gives aspirin. She wants to make love and now she makes overtures. Forgive me. I cannot relate this if I must be delicate."

"It's okay, Yuri. What happened?"

"Carla tries to embrace him. He resists her, saying that he must shower first. But his cleanliness is not foremost in Carla's mind. She throws off her dress. She begins to open his trousers. He tries to get away but she persists. She tears the buttons off his shirt and—"

"Um . . . Yuri. How would you know all this?"

"Carla told me."

"She described, in detail, her attempt to arouse Aldo?"

"It was so I would understand how she . . . I may finish, please?"

"Go on."

"She tears his shirt, he pushes her away. But not before she sees wires."

Bannerman closed his eyes. "A transmitter?"

"Yes. Very short range. I found recording device in his automobile."

"What happened with Corsini?"

"Carla says he tries to explain. That this is his hobby. Is groupie, remember. Carla does not believe, says get out. At last he tells her that he can become rich. He will share everything with her because he loves her. She spits at him. He strikes her."

"Uh-oh."

"She responds with champagne bottle. Broken glass. Very big mess."

"Where is Carla now?"

"Number you called is my Maria's house. Maria is performing in concert. Carla is there but she cannot stay because Maria must not know of this. I will take her to Bern, my flat. Tonight, if you ask it, I will go back to Carla's boathouse, clean up."

Bannerman hesitated.

"There will be no debt." Yuri sighed. "Carla has been my friend."

Bannerman could think of no alternative. No use involving the Bruggs.

"Thank you," he said. "Have you played Corsini's tape?"

The Russian grunted. "When Carla is near, he makes charming conversation. When she is not, he asks about Lesko wedding trip. He asks different people in different ways so that he learns something here, something there. When he is alone, he summarizes, I think. He speaks softly into the microphone he wears."

"Saying what, exactly?"

"I do not know because, to himself, he speaks Italian. But I hear 'Lesko' . . . 'Elena' . . . 'Belkin.' And in his manner, I hear satisfaction, I think."

"I know some Italian. Can you play it for me?"

Now Yuri hesitated. "Here I have conflict. I must report first to General Belkin, then you with his permission."

"Fair enough. Can you also get to your computers tonight? See what you have on Corsini before you call Moscow?"

"Yes. You do the same?"

"Immediately, yes."

"We go to Bern now but, for computers, best I wait until embassy staff is gone home. I call General Belkin at perhaps eight P.M. Moscow time. Then I drive back and clean."

Bern. Ninety minutes away, thought Bannerman. Yuri will be at this all night, leaving Carla alone. "Have Carla call me as soon as you get to your flat. What is her state of mind, Yuri?"

"Sad. Very sad. She thought this man cared for her."

"Tell her that we all care for her. That we'll . . ." He stopped when he saw Susan wince and shake her head. He knew the look. It said, *You know zero about women, Bannerman.*

"Um . . . Yuri?"

"Yes."

"If there's anything I should know about that trip to Russia, tell me now."

"Is . . . nothing. Truly."

"Yuri?"

"Elena and Lesko are not endangered. This much I promise."

Bannerman did not like the sound of that assurance. He was silent for a long moment, then broke the connection without saying good-bye. The breach of manners was deliberate.

8

The Chaika continued on toward central Moscow.

Other than an occasional bust of some poet or other—and several pedestals whose statues had been removed—there were few monuments or points of interest to see after crossing the Inner Ring Road.

The area was residential but the apartment buildings here were older, more gracious, most dating to the czarist era. Elena spent the time watching people although she saw surprisingly few. Just the odd cluster of old men playing chess or dominos and a handful of women pushing strollers.

Valentin told her that every Muscovite tries to get out of the city on a Sunday. "Too much bigness," he said. "In Moscow, everything is bigness because this is what Stalin liked. Must go to country to find your soul. Also to pick a few mushrooms."

Prospekt Mira, meaning Peace, twice changes its name before ending at Lubyanka Square, formerly Dzerzhinski Square, named for the Pole who had founded the Soviet secret police. The television image of his statue coming down was still vivid in Lesko's mind. It did not strike him, all things considered, that the change to Lubyanka was much of an improvement. Berlin, he assumed, did not have an Auschwitz Square.

"We turn here," said Valentin. "On right, comes now famous Lubyanka Prison. Was czarist prison before Communists. Many bad stories."

Lesko twisted in his seat. He rolled the window down.

"Next building, joined to it, is longtime KGB headquarters. No so popular, even with KGB. To have an office here these days is almost punishment. You see it better when we get to Lubyanka Square."

"Ah . . . our hotel is just ahead," said Leo Belkin.

Valentin did not hear the hint. He rolled his own window down and gestured with his thumb. "Gray building on left is also KGB but is new KGB. In English, is now Ministry of Security. On right is old KGB, old Moscow Center."

Lesko turned further in his seat for a better look at the old one. He leaned out through the window, grimacing from the effort of his contortion, one hand holding his hair in place.

"You watch." Valentin's hand made a circular gesture that took in the entire square. "This year . . . next year, Lubyanka Square becomes Sakharov Square, maybe even George Bush Square. Half of all street names in whole Soviet Union would be changed tomorrow except for confusion and expense."

It would not have surprised Lesko if Valentin suddenly began talking about Jesus. For the moment, however, he was more interested in a building that he had always thought of as one big dungeon.

"Comes now hotel," said Valentin. "Was once called Luxury Savoy, then Berlin Hotel, and now is Savoy again, this time run by Finns. Savoy's street name is also changed. Was once named for Stalin's henchman, Zhdanov, but now is . . ."

Elena saw Belkin touch his arm. She assumed it was to settle him down, but Valentin peered ahead and then cut the wheel sharply to his right. The suddenness of the turn slammed Lesko's head against the Chaika's roof. One arm flailed. Elena grabbed him and pulled. She looked back. She saw two men who had been loitering on the sidewalk outside the hotel. They had suddenly become animated. One of them was jabbing a finger toward the departing Chaika.

"Forgive, please," said Valentin. "Too soon for hotel. I show you more *big*."

Elena whispered into Lesko's ear. His expression darkened, but he only nodded.

After two short blocks, Valentin made a second right turn. He was pointing now at a colonnaded building, creamy pink with white detail, that would have seemed more at home in Paris than in Moscow.

"Bolshoi Theater," he said, with pleasure that now seemed forced. "Bolshoi means big. Is also best ballet, best opera, best place to meet nice young girls. I tell you why?"

"Love to hear it," said Lesko bloodlessly.

"Tickets," Valentin explained, "cost only few rubles but are impossible for ordinary Muscovites to get. Easier for tourists but they pay much more. Also still easy for KGB. I buy two and I come early to the Bolshoi. Many people are waiting. They hope that someone has extra ticket to sell. I look for prettiest girl and I offer my ticket as gift. I do not take rubles for it. Better to sit with her, maybe later get gift in return."

Belkin winced. He turned toward the back seat. "It is not as it sounds, Elena. In Russia, a gift is always answered with another gift. This girl, for example, will bring Valentin to a jazz club she knows about or she will bake something for him. She is not expected to . . . ah . . ."

Valentin was mortified. "No, no," he waved a finger. "These are *nice* girls. Very serious about music, very knowledgeable. You must not think . . . "

Belkin put a reassuring hand on his shoulder. "In two nights," he said gently, "our guests will see for themselves. I have arranged tickets. You are invited to join us."

Valentin gasped. "To see Boris Gudenov?"

"Boris Gudenov." Belkin nodded. "Go now. Drive."

"To Red Square," he suggested brightly. "We show you Red Square?"

"I'd like that." Elena smiled.

She sat back, urging Lesko, through a touch, to do the same. Whatever happened back at the hotel, she decided, was clearly less important to young Valentin than the prospect of going to the opera. And of far less moment than having his respect for Russian women called into question.

Relax, Lesko.

It was probably nothing.

9

"They mocked me."

Borovik was still at the window. Still hugging himself. In one hand he held a pair of binoculars.

"Ah . . . who mocked you, General?"

"The driver pointed toward this window. And then the one called Lesko looked up here. He saluted me."

Viktor Podolsk could only guess what this meant. The driver pointed? What KGB driver would not point out Moscow Center to a guest?

As for the rest of it, he knew that the car had not stopped. That a sudden decision had been made to bypass the Savoy. But first, the American must have turned to look at this building. This was natural. Same way Soviet tourists in Washington go to look at the FBI building. He wondered if Hoover ever saw them doing this and said, "They mock me." Very possibly, he thought.

"Podolsk?"

"I am here."

Podolsk had been staring at the general's desk. He saw several photographs of Mama's Boy. All had been mutilated.

"He put his hand up . . . so." Borovik touched his left temple. "And when they sped off, he threw it down . . . so." The general made a chopping gesture.

Podolsk could not be certain, of course, but the first might have been a shielding of the eyes. The second, if the car turned sharply, might be explained by the laws of physics. That either was a calculated insult seemed unlikely. The general's window was only one of perhaps two hundred.

"Come here, Podolsk." He held out the binoculars. "Look down at the Savoy."

The major stepped to his side.

"Do you see Kerensky?"

"Yes. And two others."

"*Should* you see Kerensky and his two others?"

Podolsk sighed. "Sir, they are not professionals." Worse, they were amateurs behaving as they imagined professionals to behave. Nothing could be more conspicuous. "I will . . . go and speak to him."

"What of Barca?"

"Still no word."

"Have you tried his hotel?"

"Sir, that would violate—"

Borovik banged a fist against the window's frame. "I was catching spies and traitors while your mother was still wiping your ass. Don't lecture me about tradecraft."

"Sir . . ." This man, thought Podolsk, would not know tradecraft if it fell from the sky. He tried again. "Sir, he is not so very late. We know he is with the woman. In that circumstance, situations arise which can preclude—"

"You mean he is fucking. I wait while this Italian is fucking."

Podolsk groaned inwardly. How can it be, he wondered, that this man is a major general? Who did he pay? Who is he still paying?

"You are, of course, correct," said Podolsk. His cheek had developed a tic. "I have sent a coded message to the Sicilian asking him to . . . remind Barca of the time."

"By transmitter?" Borovik lifted his chin.

"In code, yes."

"I told you to use the communicator."

"Sir . . . that device is for emergencies."

"That *device* is also always with him. His radio is who-knows-where. It could be hours before he—"

"Sir . . . the communicator only transmits flash codes. Such codes can say 'Report' or 'Break Off' or 'Terminate.' We have no flash code that says 'Go find Barca and when Carla Benedict is not looking tell him to get out of bed and give us a call on a Swiss telephone.'"

Borovik stared at him coldly. That speech would cost Podolsk dearly one day.

"These codes. They can say 'Barca—Report—Voice'?"

The major took a breath. "Yes."

"Send that message, Major. Do it now."

Podolsk backed away.

"And see to Kerensky."

"At once."

Borovik raised a finger. For a long moment he held it upright, then, slowly, pointed it toward the open window.

"That man . . . the American."

"Lesko, General?"

"He mocked me."

"Yes, General." Podolsk eased toward the door.

10

Aldo Corsini.

Bannerman typed the name onto his computer screen, hit the search key, and sat back.

"Everyone in this file," he told Susan, "is a contract agent. I have most of ours and a lot of theirs. Yuri's files would have it the other way around."

"You think that's what he is?"

Bannerman shrugged. "I doubt it. Someone at the wedding would have known him. Besides, he talked about getting rich. Contract agents have a nice payday now and then, but they don't do it to get rich."

"Then he wasn't a reporter, either. Same logic. Or a writer planning to do a story about people like you."

"I hope not," he said.

That possibility had not occurred to him. If that's all Corsini was, an investigative reporter, then his death was murder and he died for nothing. He would not have learned much that he could prove. Anything he'd write would be no more than gossip. Tall stories. Officially denied by any of the governments involved. But Bannerman tended to agree with Susan.

Yuri's manner still nagged at him, however. He had sounded calm enough on the telephone but he wasn't. Under stress, Yuri tends to forget his English which is otherwise quite good. He tends to drop his definite and indefinite articles. There are none in the Russian language.

Whatever had shaken him, Bannerman doubted that it was seeing Aldo's body. Yuri had seen *big messes* before. Tears might have done it. Carla's tears. She was special to Yuri. Or else Yuri might know more than he's saying.

The computer drive made chugging sounds, opening drawers, slamming them shut.

Susan had watched as he took his computer disks from a safe, of sorts, that was one of Molly Farrell's creations. Molly had hollowed out Volumes 1 through 6 of an outdated Encyclopædia Brittannica and inserted a series of metal boxes, each with a simple combination lock of the type used on luggage. To Susan, this had not seemed such a terribly clever arrangement until Bannerman explained why she must never touch these volumes.

The trick was that the lock had to be opened while the volume was upright, an awkward and unnatural thing to do. If it was tilted more than thirty degrees from the vertical, or forced, or if the wrong combination were tried, a battery-powered magnetic device would scramble the disks. Originally, he told her, Molly had built in a small explosive charge, but he had no wish to maim a cleaning woman who decided that his encyclopedia needed dusting. The scrambled disks could always be recopied. Anton Zivic had the master.

"Are you worried about Elena? Tell the truth."

He raised an eyebrow. "Why Elena, especially?"

"I meant . . . my father, too."

He exhaled, then shook his head. "I'd like to know why Corsini was so interested and in whose behalf. And what Yuri was holding back. But no, I can't imagine Leo putting them in danger."

The chugging stopped. The words SEARCH ENDED appeared on the screen. Bannerman slid Volume 2—ANNU TO BALTIC—from his shelf and opened it carefully. He removed a set of silver lead-lined envelopes and began booting another series of disks.

She watched in silence as he scanned, in turn, lists of known drug traffickers, smugglers, arms dealers, and even corporate executives. The latter, he explained, were known to be involved with the former. There seemed to be hundreds of such companies, most of them European, German, and Italian firms.

He lingered longest over the drug-trafficker files. They were by far the most extensive. Much of the data, many of the names, organization charts, international connections, had been provided by Irwin Kaplan to supplement and update what the Bruggs already knew. Leo Belkin contributed more of it from the KGB computers in Bern.

She knew how these files had been used when the Bruggs and her father, with Leo's help, set out to clean up Zurich. Key drug traffickers, dealers, and laboratories were hit at random. It was a terror campaign, basically. The idea was that they would have no idea who was hitting them or why. The effect was chaos, paralysis, interfactional warfare. Drug traffickers blamed covetous rivals or their own ambitious lieutenants. They began killing each other. In the end, all that was left for the Bruggs was a mopping up.

Their interest, and that of her father, was limited strictly to Zurich. Zurich is to them what Westport is to Bannerman's people. It's their home. They protected it.

Leo Belkin's interest, quite aside from his friendship with the Bruggs, was certainly to use Zurich as a test of this strategy. To gain experience with it. To try it out on a larger scale. As Bannerman pored through his drug-trafficker files, she wondered aloud whether that larger scale might be Moscow.

That had crossed his mind as well, he said, but he didn't think so. Russia has a drug problem, he told her, but it's far less serious than their problem with alcoholism. Further, there's no real money in it. Even if the ordinary Russian could afford drugs, the ruble is useless to the international traffickers. Finally, he said, what internal trafficking there is should be none of Leo's business. It's the job of the former Second Chief Directorate, which, as it's now organized, is the equivalent of the FBI and the DEA combined.

The computer made a shuddering sound. SEARCH ENDED. Bannerman had scanned the last of the disks.

"Still nothing?" she asked.

He shook his head, disappointed.

"Why would you think Aldo was a drug dealer?"

"I didn't, especially." He had hoped, he explained, to find something in the drug file if only because traffickers were the most obvious common thread between Belkin, Lesko, and Elena. But there was no Aldo Corsini, not even as a known alias.

"Paul?" Susan was staring into the distance. "Should Carla be alone? Shouldn't somebody be with her?"

He'd been thinking about that, he said. Yuri will be out half the night. Carla, who had apparently gone from a romantic high to slashing her lover to death, all in the course of an hour, will not be thinking dispassionately.

"I'm considering sending Molly," he said, "but she can't get to Bern before tomorrow morning, Swiss time. By then, Yuri could have Carla on a flight to New York."

"I could go. We could fly back together."

Absolutely not, he thought. Even Molly might have trouble handling her. He looked at his watch. Yuri should be halfway to Bern.

"Well . . . let's see how she sounds first. You can talk to her when she calls."

"There had to be more to it. Carla wouldn't have killed him over a slap. Would she?"

"Sweetheart . . . I don't know."

At the moment, he was more interested in Aldo. Interpol might have something, but he had no discreet access to that agency's files. Even if he had, he couldn't very well ask about a man who might be found dead in the morning. He had neglected, he realized, to ask Yuri what he intended doing with the body.

The Bruggs had excellent contacts at Interpol, but Bannerman was reluctant to involve them for the same reason. That left Roger Clew.

He knew that Roger could telex Interpol and have the information, if there was any, within the hour. But Roger would want a favor in return. And Roger, if he found anything, would surely begin snooping on his own. It almost wasn't worth getting him interested.

Except, he realized, Roger had seen Aldo at the wedding

and was probably as startled as anyone to see Carla
Benedict in love. He might have run a check on the man
already. Just out of curiosity. Just because he could.

Bannerman reached for the phone.

11

For several blocks, Valentin had twisted and darted
through traffic, making more sudden turns, slowing and
speeding up for no apparent reason. At last, he parked the
Chaika in what Lesko presumed to be an illegal spot, all
four wheels on the sidewalk in front of a hotel.

"Hotel Rossiya," said Valentin, spreading his arms.
"Biggest in Soviet Union . . . Europe . . . world."

"I know," Lesko muttered, climbing out. "Stalin liked
big."

It was big but dull. Featureless. As if someone had taken
about ten of those concrete apartment blocks and encased
them in glass. The revelation, if true, that it was the world's
biggest came as less of a surprise than the Baskin &
Robbins ice cream store that stood just to the left of the
lobby entrance and the lunch truck featuring Nathan's
Famous Hot Dogs that stood at one end of a tour-bus
parking area.

"Oh, look." Elena seized his hand and pointed. Uphill
from the Rossiya was a postcard view of the Kremlin, its
crenellated red brick battlements and watchtowers extending far in two different directions. Inside, a forest of white
bell towers topped by golden domes. In the foreground, the
familiar milticolored towers of St. Basil's Cathedral.

"Come," said Belkin. "A good time to stretch our legs."

Valentin, Lesko noticed, did not bother to lock the car.
Nor did he remove his windshield wipers to prevent their
theft, a practice that John Waldo said was universal. Unless,
thought Lesko, you happen to be driving a KGB car. He saw
no obvious identification on the windshield. Maybe the

license plate. It read MOC331. Lesko memorized it. It seemed a good idea.

Leo Belkin led them to a long pedestrian tunnel that passed under the traffic to the edge of Red Square. Two young men, early twenties, stood at the tunnel's entrance. They were dressed in three-quarter-length jackets, blue jeans, and they carried gym bags that said *Adidas* on them. One seemed about to approach them, his expression bright and friendly. The other whispered something. The first backed off.

In the underpass itself, they encountered other young men who seemed equally hesitant and several children who, taking their cue from the older boys, affected looks of idle innocence.

They were there, Belkin explained, to trade with foreign tourists. Each carried wads of rubles which they would sell at black-market rates. The gym bags contained caviar, fur hats, and probably lacquered boxes for sale or trade. They would buy virtually anything a Western tourist wore or carried. The children trade lapel pins for one or two cigarettes, although Lenin pins, now collector's items, can be worth a whole pack. Meanwhile they watch and learn the business.

Much of this was still illegal, he warned, certainly the exchange of currency. Although the risk of dealing with them was not great, arrests were occasionally made. Best to steer clear of them. Belkin appeared to consider saying more, but he did not.

Lesko slowed, allowing Elena to gain a few steps. He glanced behind him. Already, he saw, two separate trans-actions were under way with tourists who had entered the underpass after them. Money openly exchanged. Nothing furtive about it.

"They made you, right?" he asked Leo. "They know you're KGB."

Belkin doubted it. The first two, perhaps. They had seen the letters MOC on the license plates. For the others, it was more likely Lesko's face, not his or Valentin's, that had caused them to be circumspect. Stalin would have loved a few hundred Leskos. This one, he would have used as breeding stock.

"They were not frightened," he said. "Only prudent. The time of fear is over."

Lesko curled his lip. "Glad to hear it."

Belkin stared ahead. A sigh. "Very well, Lesko. What's on your mind?"

Lesko shrugged innocently. "I'm relieved, is all. The new Russia, right? No more looking over your shoulder."

"Lesko . . ."

"I mean, if there was a problem here, you would not have involved my pregnant wife, right? You would have told us to stick with the Poconos."

Belkin understood the sense if not the reference. He waited.

"Things are so loose here, if I decide to trade my old Levi's for a few jars of caviar, it's no big deal, right?"

"You brought Levi's?"

"Hypothetical. What if I did?"

"Don't even think of it. It's against the law and the caviar is probably stolen."

Lesko shook his head. This is from a guy whose life's work is stealing other people's secrets.

"I mean, as long as I'm prudent about it. Like Valentin, who never drives in straight lines. Like those kids back there who deal black-market in an underpass that could be sealed off in two seconds."

Another sigh, more weary than the last. "What are you saying, Lesko?"

"I don't know. I just want to score some caviar."

"I'll show you where to buy it. Don't trade for it."

"Leo . . ." He placed a hand on the smaller man's shoulder, stopping him. "Is that because I'm going to be watched all the time I'm here?"

Belkin hesitated.

"Yes or no, Leo."

"Assume yes. Prudence, remember?"

"Were we tailed from the airport?"

"I don't think so. I truly don't."

"Okay. They waited at the hotel instead."

Belkin grunted. "You noticed."

"No, Leo. Elena did. I was too busy banging my head against the roof of your car."

"My apologies for that. The sudden turn was to see if they would react to us."

"They did. Were they KGB?"

Belkin almost smiled. "If they were, I'd be ashamed of them. More likely, they are street informers of the sort you used in New York."

"And like the KGB uses here. Right or wrong, Leo?"

He heard Elena calling him. She was up ahead, in the daylight, pointing at something, grinning like a kid, urging him to come look. Belkin started in her direction. Lesko held him back.

"Why, Leo? Why are they interested?"

Belkin shrugged. A gesture of dismissal. "There are rivalries . . . jealousies in any organization," he said. "Your New York police force was no exception. Break no laws and this will not affect you."

"You're saying their interest is in you. Not me or Elena."

"Curiosity is a better word. But yes."

"This rival you have. Any chance of Elena getting caught in the middle?"

"If I thought there were, I would have you both on an airplane in one hour."

"What's your rival's name?"

"I'm . . . not certain. That's the truth."

"Say I believe you, Leo. But say, with the right kind of bait . . . maybe you could flush him out."

Belkin's eyes flashed. "That was an insult. Did you intend it so?"

"Hey. Fuck you, Leo. This is Russia we're standing in and you're still KGB."

"And you are Raymond Lesko," he answered angrily. "You have married Elena Brugg. You have a close personal association with Paul Bannerman. Your daughter even shares his bed in Westport. Do you imagine, Lesko, that there's a country in the world, including your own, which you could visit without the local authorities wondering what you're doing there?"

Lesko fingered the smaller man's lapels. He started to speak. Belkin brushed the hand away.

"Yes, you will be watched," he said. "Accept that and

behave accordingly. But as a favor to yourself, try not to become tiresome about it just because you're being watched in *my* country."

Elena called again, this time impatiently. Belkin turned and walked toward her.

"Come, Lesko," he said over his shoulder. "I will show you Red Square. You can tell me how ugly it is."

12

When asked where he got that Scottish hat, and why he wore it all the time, Arkadi Kulik would only sigh.

"Ask someone else," he would say.

This, of course, encouraged gossip.

The story most often repeated was that it had belonged to a KGB defector who had gone over to British Intelligence. He was a major who had served under Kulik. The British gave him a new name and a house in the town of Dumbarton near Glasgow. He took up golf. The British gladly paid for his lessons because this defector had so much to tell them. No fool, he doled it out a little at a time.

Kulik, they say, took this defection personally. He tracked this man to Dumbarton. He tied him to a chair and beat him, starting at the knees and elbows, with something called a niblick. Humming an aria, they say, all the while. General Kulik is known for his singing voice.

Fully half the bones in this man's body were broken, but he was still alive and conscious when Kulik burned his house down around him. He kept this man's new Scottish tam as a trophy. Here, in his dacha at Zhukovka, there is also a bent and twisted golf club leaning by the fireplace.

The man who never smiled—his name was Sostkov—believed this story. It was why he did not hesitate that morning near Yekaterinburg when General Kulik's eyes told him that a certain former colonel had let sentiment get

the best of him and there was a need for more aggressive
leadership.

Sostkov had seized the opportunity. He showed what he
was made of. He finished off the flatbed driver who had
wrecked the general's Zil. The lorry driver, however, had
led them on quite a chase before they boxed him in on
the other side of Vigirsk. He was easy to follow because his
truck was on fire from the smashed kerosene heater in the
back. But he was a stubborn one. He turned on them and
rammed one of their cars, head on, his fuel tank exploding,
cooking two of their men but also himself and his helper.

General Kulik was not so pleased at such a mess. All that
fire and smoke. But at least it was still near enough to
Vigirsk where there was no one left alive to see it.

What did impress him, however, was when Sostkov told
him that he could operate a bulldozer. He filled in the rest
of the pit. He pushed the lorry in, still smoking, and the car
it crashed into. The Zil, a total write-off, was the last
addition. It went in right on top of the colonel who had gone
soft.

General Kulik picked that moment to ask if we are sure
we got them all. Did we make a count in the confusion?
Sostkov had not, but the answer from the others was firmly
yes. Six of them, they said, plus three of ours. If you need
proof, they said, you can dig them up yourself.

"Sostkov?"

"Sir." The former captain, far richer now, sprang to
attention. He stepped to the door of the general's library
where the general had been working with his figures and his
charts. As he entered, he glimpsed one big chart that seemed
to show a chain of command. One name at the top, many
names in many boxes beneath it. He knew the name at the
top was not yet that of General Kulik. But it would be one
day. Of that he had no doubt. Kulik covered the chart as he
approached.

"What have you got for me, Sostkov?"

He hesitated. "It might mean nothing. A call from your
man at Ostankino. General Borovik has asked for voice
contact from one of his Italians in Zurich."

Arkadi Kulik peered up over his spectacles. "Any idea
why?"

"None."

"Might it concern Leo Belkin's visit?"

The younger man shrugged. "Not necessarily. If it were not for the timing . . ."

"I take it that Belkin's party has arrived."

"About an hour ago, yes." Sostkov anticipated the general's next question. "Our people in Customs saw no sign that he is under surveillance. He was definitely not followed when he left Sheremetyevo."

Kulik nodded, somewhat satisfied. "And it's been made clear to Borovik that he is to take no action?"

"Very clear."

"No surveillance for Belkin to spot? No microphones for him to find? We stay far away from him?"

"He argued, but he agreed."

The former general grumbled. "Borovik agreeing and Borovik using his head are two different things. You will monitor this voice contact?"

"It's arranged, yes."

Kulik frowned. "Leo Belkin, the Brugg millions, and this Lesko who is practically related to Mama's Boy. With all we have happening, that's one row of dominos we don't need falling in our direction."

Sostkov said nothing.

"Borovik says he's got Bannerman out of his system. Do you believe him?"

Sostkov hesitated, then shook his head. "If it were me, I could not forget."

"You would be so . . . sentimental?"

"Not sentiment. Humiliation. I could not live while Bannerman lived."

Kulik nodded with a sigh. He lifted one corner of the chart he had been working with. His eyes fell on Borovik's box. "More trouble than he's worth," he muttered after a time. He chewed his lip thoughtfully. "What is your opinion of Viktor Podolsk?" he asked.

A shrug. "He hates working for Borovik."

"This makes him normal. But what do you think of him personally?"

"You've never met him?"

"He doesn't know I exist. But that might have to change."

Sostkov pursed his lips thoughtfully. "By all accounts he is . . . intelligent. A realist. A good organizer. And he has a natural head for business."

"In other words, everything that Borovik is not. What got him in trouble?"

"A number of things." Sostkov wrinkled his nose as if to say that they did not amount to much. "First, he was selling fuel to Latvia during the embargo a few years ago. He would trade it for Baltic bricks and textiles which he would sell to the Leningrad cooperatives. There was also a scheme involving lottery tickets."

"You mean printing counterfeits?" Kulik seemed disappointed.

Sostkov shook his head. "He had someone in the lottery office who would give him the names of those who held winning tickets. He would then buy those tickets for more than their face value and sell them to black-market operators who needed a way to account for their income."

Kulik nodded appreciatively. "A clever idea," he said. "How did a dolt like Borovik catch on?"

A shrug. "Someone informed. Say what you want about General Borovik, but at least he recognizes talent when he sees it."

Kulik's expression soured. Sostkov realized his mistake. Borovik had also recruited those clowns, the Kerenskys. And through them, two criminally stupid drivers who managed to wipe out an entire valley.

But Kulik was on another train of thought. "Talent is one thing," he said. "Can Podolsk be as ruthless?"

"Ruthless as Borovik?"

Kulik rocked a hand. "With Borovik, it's more of a sickness. A man needn't be a brute or a bully. Merely decisive."

"I suppose . . . he would have to be tested."

"As you were tested, Sostkov?"

The former captain said nothing.

"Your colonel was a decent man, you know. A humane man."

"Yes . . . I know he was."

"Any regrets?"

He started to shake his head but stopped himself. "From time to time," he answered truthfully.

"Of the act itself? Or the necessity?"

"It had to be done. I didn't have to like it."

The older man smiled, ruefully, then more warmly. He rose to his feet and, one hand on Sostkov's shoulder, walked him toward the door of his library.

"You cannot know," he said, "how good it is to hear you say those words. The world has enough monsters. It doesn't need more."

Sostkov blushed a little. The older man patted his back, and closed the door behind him. The general returned to his desk.

He had his own regrets, he said within himself.

This Sostkov was a good one. Very steady.

But he was also the only man still living who could place Arkadi Kulik at that burial pit.

The others were gone. His chauffeur, Mischa, had seen to four of them. Then Mischa's own turn came. That was hard. Mischa had been with him for six years and he had, after all, saved him from being flattened against the Zil.

Nor was a new Zil so easy to find.

But there was no great hurry, Kulik supposed, as long as Sostkov stayed where he could keep an eye on him. There was time to pick and choose his replacement. Perhaps he did not have so far to look. He liked what he had been hearing about this Podolsk.

Well . . . that could wait.

He looked at his watch.

Another hour or so with these charts and then it's time to think about dressing for dinner. Sostkov seems very pleased that he's been invited. But it's good for him. All work and no play, et cetera.

In the outer room, dialing the number of their man at Ostankino, Oleg Sostkov felt good inside. It was nice to be understood. Nice to be respected. It also wasn't bad to have some money.

His thoughts turned to the BMW which was coming in just ten more days. Silver with black leather seats. Fuel

injection. Getting high-octane petrol that won't clog it will
be a problem but . . . such a car . . . it was worth the
extra effort.

His call was disconnected. He grumbled and tried again.

Someday soon, he would drive his new car all through
Europe. Find a pretty girl to go with him. Or pick up a
French girl along the way. General Kulik says it's easy. He
says that these days, saying that you're KGB—even former
KGB—gets them very excited.

It had bothered him, for a while, that all the others were
sent on missions to the West and he had to stay home. Even
Kulik's driver, big Mischa, got to go. On the other hand,
none of them got a BMW with leather seats.

General Kulik was a good boss so far. The best he ever
had. The only one, certainly, who invited him along when
he went out for dinner.

He was not all puffed up like some. He was a man you
could talk to as long as you didn't go too far. As long as you
kept in mind that bent-up golf club leaning next to his
fireplace.

13

"Where are we?"

Carla's head jerked up at the bleat of a nearby horn. She'd
been dozing.

"Only forty kilometers to Bern," Yuri told her. "Not
long now."

For a moment, as her head cleared, she seemed to panic.
Yuri knew what was happening. Memories were flooding
back. She was trying to believe that they were only dreams.
But then she saw that this was Aldo Corsini's car and it was
Yuri who was driving. Her head sank forward. She hid her
face in her hands.

Yuri Rykov reached for the back of her neck and began

massaging it, gently. She did not respond. She waited until
he took his hand away, then drew up her knees, holding
them tight against her chest.

Yuri groped for the ice bag, which had slid into the well
of her seat. It was watery but still cold.

"Put this back against your cheek," he said. "It is still
very swollen."

She took it. With her other hand, she turned down her sun
visor and looked at her face in the small vanity mirror. She
moaned softly. Her left eye was partially closed. The
swelling extended down one side of her nose and to half of
her upper lip. She brought the ice bag to her face, hiding
once again.

"Are you going to stay with me?" she asked.

"While it is daylight, yes. Then I must go back to Zurich,
also to my embassy in Bern."

"I mean, are you going to *stay* with me."

He eased off the accelerator, moving his lips as if
searching for a reply that would be correct.

"Don't do me any fucking favors, Yuri."

The Russian sagged.

"Never mind." She hugged herself tighter. "I'm not in
the mood anyway."

A part of her hated Yuri for knowing what he knew. For
having seen her like that. For having Maria. She had no one
now. She needed him to hold her, not rub her neck. She
needed to get lost in him.

A bigger part of her hated herself, not least for taking this
out on Yuri. He'd been kind to her. He deserved better.

Still . . .

She was embarrassed by the way he bathed her. As if she
were a child. She did not resist when he eased her out of the
raincoat with which she'd covered herself. Or when he knelt
to peel off her torn and splattered panty hose. He had lifted
her onto her bathroom counter, sat her there, washing the
blood from her arms and chest, sponging it from her hair.
She did not resist. Nor did she help.

It was not so much that she'd been naked. He'd seen her
body before. In California. But then it was a woman's body

and not just a thing to be scrubbed. In California, he thought she was beautiful. She needed to hear that now.

Such perfect skin, he told her then. Like coffee with cream. No freckles, unusual for red hair. No scars, except for the one across her throat that even Yuri mistook for a natural crease. Perfect breasts, he said. Not large, but that is good. Always, he said, they will stay high and proud.

Now she was just one more part of a mess that needed cleaning. Fixing. He stuffed cotton into her cheek to control the bleeding where her teeth had cut into it. He took ice from the kitchen and fashioned a compress. Then he dressed her, choosing a skirt, blouse, and blazer because they required less cooperation than her customary jeans and leathers. He found her wigs in a bedroom closet. They were her working wigs. Disguises. Worn to hide red hair when needed. He chose one for that purpose. Blond, a helmet cut. The look was ten years out of fashion, but it changed the shape of her face. She did not resist when he sat her down on her toilet-seat cover and put the wig on her. She sat there, holding the compress as he stuffed more of her clothing into a bag. He rolled Aldo up in the ruined carpet and hoisted him onto his shoulder. He took Aldo out, stashed him someplace. She wasn't sure where. Yuri was all business. He never even put his arms around her when she shivered. Or when she cried.

She had called him at Maria's house, needing him. She called five times before he finally got home from the garden party. Even then, he could not come, not right away. You must wait, he whispered, until Maria takes her daughter to her parents' house and then leaves for her concert. Carla had understood that. But she needed him right then.

Aldo.

Dear sweet Aldo.

You bastard.

"Yuri?"

"Yes, Carla."

"His eyes changed."

"The Italian's eyes? How so?"

"They just changed. One second he was Aldo, the next he was someone else."

"In his eyes, what did you see?"

She wasn't sure. When you step in dog shit, see it on your shoe—that was how he'd looked at her. An hour before that, for weeks before that, he had looked at her the way Yuri did in California.

The punch came so fast. Too fast, too well aimed, for an amateur. And he used the butt of his palm so that he wouldn't risk a knuckle. That has to be learned.

"He would have killed me," she said quietly.

"You saw . . . rage?"

She shook her head. Not rage. At least not for being spit at. It was more like resignation. Whatever it was that he was after, she had ruined it for him. Now she was shit on a shoe.

"He thought I was nothing. A naked little nothing."

Yuri reached for her knee. Another squeeze. This time she placed her hand on his.

"How did you meet him, Carla?"

"He was feeding the swans."

Yuri saw a mental picture. An irrelevancy. He blinked it away. "I mean, which of you initiated this contact?"

She understood. "Me. Not him."

Or she thought so until now. Perhaps not. Perhaps he was just very patient. Very professional. 'Slow and steady wins the race.' A cardinal rule. Right up there with 'Never risk a knuckle.'

Yuri wanted details.

She was already remembering.

The first time she saw him, she told Yuri, she was having dinner. By herself. It was at the Kronenhalle in Zurich. She ate there once a week on average, usually at the same table but not always on the same day.

She saw Yuri's frown. She understood it. It was not a strict routine but it was a routine nonetheless. Routines kill.

Yuri made no issue of it. But he knew the restaurant. Just off the Quay Bridge where the Limmat River flows into Lake Zurich. Quite good as Swiss-German restaurants go. A very nice art collection on the walls.

She was dining alone, she told him, and so was he. She had barely noticed him. Over coffee, she was sitting back, getting lost in a Matisse which she particularly admired. Their eyes met. He smiled, apologetically, as if to say he had not meant to intrude upon her privacy. He made no further overture. He paid his bill and left the restaurant, first taking the unused bread from his basket and wrapping it in a handkerchief.

She finished a second cup of coffee and, as she often did, chose to walk off the meal along the shore of the river, going up as far as the tramway station, crossing at the Banhofstrasse and coming down the other side. She saw him again on the Quay Bridge. He was breaking small pieces from a dinner roll and giving them to a small boy who was there with his mother. It was the boy, actually, who was feeding the swans. Carla walked past them. The man did not seem to notice her. She stopped and watched. The boy spoke to her, in German, calling her attention to all the birds below. Several families of them.

Only then did the man turn. A hesitation, and then a smile of recognition. He offered her some of his bread. The offer was made in German. She answered in that language but he heard her American accent. They conversed briefly in English. Carla wished him a pleasant evening and walked to her car.

A week later, when she dined at the Kronenhalle again, he wasn't there. If he had been, she supposed, she might have wondered. She fed the swans by herself.

By the time another week had passed, she had forgotten him. But once again, there he was at the Kronenhalle, sitting under the Matisse. She caught his eye. She nodded a greeting. He smiled and stood. He asked if she would care to join him for dessert and coffee. She did so, bringing her own bread to his table. They fed the swans together.

Soon they were seeing each other, trying new restaurants, taking walks, talking. Carla told him about herself, inventing where necessary. She had grown up in California, then moved to Connecticut where she managed certain properties owned by the Brugg family. She created a husband who had died in an auto accident. There were no children. She told him of her sister, a film student, who had been murdered last year in Los Angeles. Carla, after burying her, had come to Europe to escape the pain.

His name, he said, was Aldo Corsini. A widower, also no children, a fact he regretted. His wife had died when their

lake house in Lugano caught fire. He still owned their flat in
Genoa, but he lived on his boat because the flat contained
too many memories.

When he was younger, he acted in films, many westerns,
was killed three different times by Clint Eastwood and twice
by Lee Van Cleef. Most of his other roles were as dissolute
young Romans and then as dissolute aging Romans. Finally,
he said it was time to grow up. He founded, with the
backing of some friends, a small business which he ran from
the boat as well. It was a venture-capital firm. Actors make
good salesmen, he said. What he did was help other
companies find markets for their products, cut bureaucratic
red tape, get financing. For this last, he was often in Zurich.
He enjoyed dancing if it was slow, any sort of sailing but
especially by moonlight, a good meal with the right wines,
and American ladies if they had red hair and green eyes that
seemed sad and lost. He understood, he said, the emptiness
she felt. He, too, was trying to rebuild his life.

They became lovers. He made love in the manner of a
man who likes women. Constantly aware of her, constantly
attentive. Pausing now and then just to look at her, talk to
her, laugh with her. Carla's pain began to recede.

A month of weekends at her boathouse passed before he
asked, or rather hinted, that he would very much like an
introduction to the Brugg family. She answered that she
would prefer, for now, to keep business out of their
relationship. If he didn't mind.

She watched his eyes. She saw no disappointment.

Not long after that, they were dining at La Rotonde, the
restaurant in the Dolder Grand Hotel, when Willem Brugg
entered with a party of six. Willem saw her before she
noticed him. He approached, was introduced, and asked
them to join his table. Aldo tried to decline. Willem insisted.
Throughout the meal, he and Aldo talked a great deal. Carla
saw, however, that this was none of Aldo's doing. He was
trying as best he could to converse with the others, but
Willem and his wife were fascinated by him, intent on
learning what sort of man could bring a glow to the cheeks
of Carla Benedict.

That evening led to other invitations. Several charity
functions. At a reception following one of Maria's recitals,

Carla introduced him to Yuri Rykov and Leo Belkin. She introduced them only as Russian diplomats. He also met and chatted with the several contract agents who were already on retainer to the Bruggs. She did not tell him what they were. She introduced them as friends of the family, accountants, factory managers, or by whatever job function crossed her mind.

Carla realized that it would only be a matter of time before Aldo learned more about her. She decided that she must tell him something of the truth. If he could not deal with it, better to know sooner than later.

She told him, during one of their walks, which parts of her life were real and which were lies. The dead husband was a lie, the sister was not. She told him that she was an intelligence operative, or had been, and that her life had been a violent one. She told him of her years in Europe with the man known as Mama's Boy and of their expropriation of a sanatorium and a goodly amount of other real estate in a small Connecticut town called Westport.

It was far more than he had any right to know. She realized that. It was just that once she began talking she found it hard to stop. Expropriation? You say you helped yourself to an entire American town? How could this be possible?

Well . . . sort of.

She explained to him that the CIA had been running a number of safe houses there for more than forty years. They were originally intended for the debriefing and supervised retirement of agents brought in from the field after years of deep-cover operations. The sanatorium was for those who were too dangerous or too damaged ever to be released. The others, over the years, became a sort of private army for certain people in the government.

Several years ago, she told Aldo, they lured Mama's Boy there from Europe. Why is too long a story. But once they got him inside that sanatorium, he was never going to leave. Mama's Boy—Paul Bannerman—saw it coming. About a dozen of us, she said, slipped into Westport.

We freed him, but now we were all on someone's hit list and there was nowhere to hide. So Bannerman decided that we might as well stay there. We threw the federals out. We moved into their houses, took over their businesses. They

couldn't do much about it because the Westport facility was
illegal to begin with. We let them know that if they tried to
retake it with guns, what they'd get was a bloodbath and a
front-page scandal. It's been a standoff, more or less, ever
since.

Aldo could scarcely believe a word of all this.

But he had heard of this Bannerman, he said. Several
years ago, there was an article in the German magazine
Stern entitled "America's Terrorists." The nom de guerre,
Mama's Boy, struck him as a strange choice for a man who,
one assumes, wished to be feared. Aldo had thought that he
must be dead or in prison by now. As for the rest of it, it was
too much to absorb. He said that he was shocked and—he
would admit it—more than a little afraid of such people. He
would need time to think.

A month went by. Carla heard nothing from him, not
even a letter. Her depression had returned. Then, early one
Saturday, the florists' trucks began arriving. Yellow long-
stemmed roses, a dozen at a time, each with a single red rose
in the center. Then came lilacs, her favorite, in every
imaginable shade. By late morning, her apartment over the
boathouse had no room for more.

Aldo appeared at noon, bearing a picnic basket. A
chartered airplane was waiting, he told her. It was time that
she saw the coast of Italy by moonlight.

He told her, as they sailed, what he had decided. The past
could not be changed, nor would he wish it. This past had
made her the woman whom he had grown to love.

He had many questions, he said. So many that he scarcely
knew where to begin.

"There's a lot I can't tell you, Aldo. Not now or ever."

"Of course. Spies must have their secrets."

"I wasn't a spy, exactly, but . . . close enough."

"And yet, how can I resist asking?"

"Ask whatever you please. But if I tell you that I can't
answer, you have to be able to accept that."

"This is fair. Same rule for me?"

"Absolutely."

"All I will ask is that there be no lies. You may say,
'Aldo, I will not speak of this or that because I have made
a promise,' and I will not ask again."

"Thank you."

"But if you say, 'Aldo, I will not speak of this because you will think the less of me,' that is not so good. That much, you should trust me."

Carla said nothing.

"There is also the matter of your associates."

"What about them?"

"At the end of these past weeks, I thought, 'Aldo, you must get her away from them. They are cruel and hard. They will destroy her.' But then I think, 'No, Aldo, you have no right.' "

She nodded, agreeing with this last. "You don't know them, Aldo. They're good people."

He grunted doubtfully.

"You'd like them. Most of them."

He appeared to consider this. "Perhaps . . ." he said. "Perhaps you have a good idea. I should meet your friends. I must learn to be at ease with them. And they with me."

Glad I thought of it, she said in her mind.

But no warning bell sounded.

Or if it had, she had not been listening for it.

14

Bannerman tried Roger Clew's Georgetown number on the chance of catching him alone. He broke the connection when a machine answered.

On Sunday mornings, weather and global events permitting, Roger usually played tennis. For several years now, his boss, Barton Fuller, had hosted an informal round-robin and brunch at Briarwood, his Virginia home. Roger was a regular. So was Irwin Kaplan.

Bannerman had Fuller's number, but he was reluctant to use it. The call would only invite speculation as to why a simple inquiry regarding Carla Benedict's current boyfriend was worth interrupting their game.

He tapped out the memory code for Roger's direct number at the State Department. A female staffer, young, Texas accent, answered on the fifth ring.

"Mr. Clew's office. Maureen Tobin speaking."

"Hi. I don't suppose he's in."

"No, sir. Not until Monday afternoon." She did not insist that he identify himself. The line he'd called on was enough. "I'll take a message if you'd like."

He gave his name. The line went silent for a moment.

"I'm . . . sure that he'll want to talk to you, Mr. Bannerman. Are you in Westport?"

"It's not urgent, Maureen. It can wait until Monday."

"But he'll be calling in, sir. Any minute, I expect."

More accurately, thought Bannerman, Roger's beeper would be sounding in about thirty seconds.

"If he does, fine. But please don't interrupt his Sunday on my account. This is strictly a personal matter."

"Does he have your number, Mr. Bannerman?"

"He does. I'm at home. Are you as pretty as you sound, Maureen?"

The voice hesitated. It took on a chill. "I suppose . . . if you like freckles."

Bannerman assured her that he did. He thanked her and said good-bye, aware that Susan was looking at him, one eye in a squint.

"That was sexist, Bannerman," she said.

He grunted an acknowledgment.

"And disillusioning. She now thinks that Mama's Boy is a twerp."

He nodded absently. A small price, he thought, if it distracts young Maureen from rushing to her duty officer and getting the place in an uproar. Other than at the wedding, he had not spoken to Roger in a year. He had not called him in two.

The phone rang five minutes later. He affected a yawn as he said hello.

"Paul? It's Roger."

The voice betrayed a measure of surprise and it was

slightly muffled as if a hand was held over the mouthpiece. Bannerman heard birds in the background. He expressed dismay that the young staffer had seen fit to call, repeating that the matter could have waited.

"No problem. We just finished a set."

"Where are you? At Briarwood?"

"Yes. Bart Fuller says hello."

"My apologies to Mr. Fuller as well. As long as I've got you, Roger, did you meet Aldo Corsini at the wedding?"

"Corsini . . . ." Clew pretended to be searching his memory. "Oh, Carla's friend. I didn't meet him, actually. Elena told me who he was."

"Did you run a check on him?"

Another silence. "Why would I do that?"

"Roger . . ."

The voice relaxed a notch. "Okay. Yes. Didn't you?"

"Just through my own files. He's not in them. I wouldn't have bothered except that he's just asked Carla to marry him."

Silence. Then, "What did she say?"

"She's . . . sorting it out."

"And this guy knows what Carla is?"

"*Was,* Roger, but yes. Is there anything I should know about him?"

"He might be straight. A wheeler-dealer, maybe, but nothing that waves a red flag."

"Can I look at his dossier?"

"He doesn't really have one. No criminal record. No file of any kind. Most of his life he's been a salesman for one import-export firm or another when he wasn't making spaghetti westerns. Seems to have made a decent living but never really grabbed the brass ring. A few years ago, he set himself up as a venture capitalist, but he doesn't seem to fund anything himself. He's more of a broker. He puts people together for a fee."

"How would you know all that if there's no file?"

"Well, there's his tax return. The income he reports falls well below his apparent lifestyle, but this is Italy, right? That's not to say he's rich, however. He's in debt as often as not. The Italian police have heard of him but that's as far as it goes. His name pops up at Interpol but only as a "known associate" of Italians for whom they do have active files. Most are businessmen, exporters, some of them fairly shady. If Corsini's taking money under the table from them, my guess is he does their laundry."

"Launders their money? How? By setting up dummy companies?"

"They're not dummies. They're real businesses. He set up several in Eastern Europe, even before the wall came down. Over the past couple of years, however, Corsini seems to be concentrating on the Russian Republic."

Bannerman frowned at the mention of Russia. "What sort of businesses?"

"Food products, mostly. Last year, for example, he brokered a joint venture between the Italy's Bellisima Food Company and a Russian cooperative. They've already opened a string of pizza parlors in Moscow. Bellisima is controlled by the Sicilian Mafia, by the way."

Bannerman made a face. Moscow. And now the Mafia.

"What good is Russia," he asked, "for laundering cash if nothing but rubles comes out the other end."

"No one's in Russia for rubles. It's a barter economy. Pepsi, for example, got distribution rights to Stolichnaya vodka in return for building a few bottling plants."

"What would the Mafia get?"

"A wild guess? Morphine base."

Bannerman sighed inwardly.

"Up to now, these particular Sicilians have been getting it from the Palestinians in return for assault rifles. But Irwin says that source is drying up. He's here. You want to talk to him?"

"Not now. Russian assault rifles?"

"Mostly the old AK-47s, but they're available, cheap, on the open arms market. Don't look for a connection between pizza and guns."

"Drugs, then. You think Corsini is a trafficker."

"I didn't say that."

With effort, Bannerman masked his irritation. "Well, which is it?" he asked. "You say he's straight and in the next breath you say he launders cash. You say he helped set up a Moscow pizza chain and then you mention, with a thud, that the Mafia's involved."

"Paul . . . the guy's a middleman. He makes introductions. If those introductions result in criminal activity, that doesn't necessarily make him dirty."

"Um . . . are you this man's lawyer, by any chance, Roger?"

"Lawyers are a good example. Lawyers put these kinds of deals together all the time. Are they all dirty?"

Bannerman didn't bother to answer. "Whatever he is," Bannerman asked, "are you satisfied that he's in business for himself?"

"As opposed to what? An intelligence agent?"

"No harm in wondering."

"Paul . . . does Lesko's honeymoon have anything to do with this line of questioning?"

He avoided a lie. "You're right. I suppose I'm reaching."

Clew grunted in agreement. "If he's an agent, he's not ours. If you think he's a Russian agent, why don't you ask Leo Belkin?"

"Never mind. There's no need." Again, not quite a lie.

"For that matter, why would the Soviets need to put an agent on you? Half of your new friends these days are KGB."

A petulant remark. Bannerman ignored it.

"Your report on Corsini . . . could you fax it to me?"

"For old times' sake?"

"If that pleases you. For a reasonable quid pro quo if it doesn't. And I'm recording this, by the way."

"Be my guest. As for the report, you'll have it this afternoon but it won't tell you much. The danger is that you'll make too big a deal out of Corsini's Mafia connection. There probably isn't a businessman in Italy without one, or, for that matter, a venture capitalist anywhere in Europe who's not looking for ways to carve out a piece of Russia."

"I suppose. Thanks, Roger."

"Not so long next time, okay? How's Susan?"

"She's right here. Waving hello."

An odd silence.

"Next time you're up this way, drop in. I'll grill some steaks."

Another pause. "Was that an invitation? Or are you being polite?"

Clew had raised his voice a bit. From the sound, he had also turned his head, probably toward Barton Fuller.

"An invitation, Roger. I suppose we're overdue."

15

No warning had sounded, Carla told herself, because there was no reason why one should. He wanted to meet her friends, was all. It was natural. And it was not as if he'd made an issue of it.

"I meet them . . . I don't meet them," he said to her when she hesitated. "It is entirely up to you."

"No big deal," she told him. "Sure. Why not?"

He'd already met several anyway, plus Leo and Yuri. Boozed with them. Told jokes with them.

The wedding, at this point, was only three weeks away. Her invitation read Carla Benedict and Guest. Aldo could meet Paul Bannerman. He'd probably be disappointed. Socially, Paul's a sweet, friendly guy. Very polite. Even a little shy.

As for the rest of the Westport crowd, some are more housebroken than others, but she could pick and choose. And he could meet Lesko and Elena. If Elena liked him, just knowing her was all the business contact he'd ever need.

Another thought was to have Yuri and Maria over for dinner in the meantime. No. Bad idea. They wouldn't be able to say much in front of Maria. And Aldo would learn, too soon, that she couldn't cook worth a shit.

But she could ask Lesko and Elena to join them at the Kronenhalle for lunch. If Lesko didn't scare him off, nothing would.

Lesko didn't. Aldo even invited them to come down to Genoa, sail on his boat. Lesko's response was polite but unenthusiastic. His only experience with boats, he told them, had been the Hudson River Circle Line when his daughter was small and a Sheepshead Bay party boat one July with a bunch of sweaty and besotted cops who hooked their own ears and fingers more than they did bluefish.

During the last few days before the wedding, a score of old friends began drifting into town. Most of them looked her up. She held a sort of open house for them. Each morning, on arising, she and Aldo would find at least two who had crashed in her small living room.

She was pleased to see that Aldo made a genuine effort. He would talk to them for hours on end, especially the women. He would take them fishing on the small runabout that the landlord kept in the boathouse. It took him no time at all to conclude that most were very much like anyone else except for the stories they told. Comfort grew into enthusiasm. He reveled in the stories.

By the time Paul and Susan appeared, he was thrilled at the prospect of meeting them, although some encouragement was needed before he would approach Billy McHugh or John Waldo. At the ball following the wedding, he danced with Molly Farrell—who was always warm and friendly—and with Janet Herzog, from whom he actually coaxed a smile.

"Marry me," he had said this morning.

"Wh-what?"

"I love you. In this, I am helpless. You are the most beautiful woman I have ever known."

She stared at him. The man was positively glowing. It must be the champagne.

"Look . . . Aldo . . . maybe we'd better . . ."

He touched his fingers to her lips.

"All your life," he said earnestly, "you have taken chances for money. Now it is time to take a chance for happiness."

"Hold it. I mean . . . have you thought this out? Where would we live?"

"Where would we . . . This is important to you?"

"I don't know. I guess I'm just trying to picture it."

"Very well," he told her. "For the first year, we live half on my boat and half here in Zurich. You don't like boats? I buy a house."

"No, the boat is . . ."

He brightened. "A better idea. Half on my boat and half in Westport. It is good that you be with your friends again. After one year of this, we decide again."

It was totally unexpected. Carla had no idea what to say, what to think. The last time anyone proposed marriage to her she was a sophomore at UCLA. She had gotten an abortion instead.

She would think about it, she decided. Maybe talk to Elena when she got back from Russia. Talk to Anton Zivic.

But not Paul. Not just yet. He'd want Aldo checked out up, down, and sideways. He'd be right, but he might also ruin this. Aldo had made her feel in a way she hadn't felt in years and she was going to fuck his brains out for it. She dragged him from the garden party.

"Yuri?"
    "Yes, Carla."
    "Who was he?"
    "We will find out."

Those eyes.

Looking into hers. Seeing that they were glazed and hurt. Blood dripping from her mouth.

He backed away, one hand holding his trousers up. His eyes now seemed to turn inward. She saw a certain wistfulness in them. Self-reproach, perhaps. It was the look of a man who knew that, perhaps because of the champagne, he had made an unredeemable error. The eyes flickered again. The self-reproach was gone. In its place, the look of a man who realized that all that was left was to cut his losses.

Slowly, in no hurry at all, he secured the top button of his trousers and picked his necktie from the floor. He wrapped the ends around his fists. He stepped toward her, then hesitated, his expression suddenly wary. He was recalling, perhaps, all those stories. Calamity Carla. But, he seemed to decide, this thing on the floor is not dangerous. Naked except for panty hose, stunned, no weapon within reach. Not even her shoes. She had kicked them off. Not even her feet because one leg was pinned beneath her and the other was splayed to the side. Still, better safe than sorry. He would break the leg. It would make the rest easier. He moved in, half turning, to deliver the kick. He did not see the champagne bottle, which had fallen with her. Not until he saw it again, a greenish blur, whipping in an arc against his upraised knee.

A scream. Shock of pain. The blur came again, this time against the hand that gripped the damaged knee. He tried to spin away. A mistake. The next blow slammed against his kidney. He went rigid, gasping, then crashed to the floor.

Those eyes. Wild now.

He scrambled into an awkward crouch. He was snarling at her, taunting her, trying now to lure her in, ready to seize the bottle if she came at him again.

Carla looked past him, toward the studio kitchen, where the knives were. She knew that he would lunge if she tried for them. She had only the bottle, still whole. She darted sideways, snatching a brass lamp from an end table. She tore it loose and, in measured blows, rapped it against the bottle until the bottle fractured. The thick bottom thumped to the carpet. She tapped one side. More glass fell away, leaving her with the neck and a jagged four-inch shard.

Carla told herself, looking back, that she had not meant to kill him. To an extent, it was true. A part of her brain still tried to believe that this was all a mistake. This man loved her.

He saw the shard. He threw himself to his right, grasping for a chair with which to defend himself. Carla slashed at the reaching hand. He rolled again, the hand spraying blood. He tried to kick at her. The single button of his trousers popped loose. They slid to his thighs.

Something new appeared in his eyes. A different kind of rage. Humiliation. He was crippled, cut, his pants were falling off, and it was a woman who had so emasculated him.

What happened next, she thought, could not have happened. Not the way she saw and heard it in her mind. She remembered stepping between his legs, pinning them with one foot on the crotch of his fallen trousers. She remembered that he reached for the foot, as she hoped he would, so that she could leap upon his chest, straddling his outstretched arms. Her instincts told her that she would have him then. With her left hand she would seize the hair, jerking his head to one side, exposing his throat. She would press the green shard against it near the hinge of his jaw. It would not matter if he freed a hand. He would have to yield or be cut. It would give her time to think.

Carla did all this.

She begged him, as she remembered it, not to make her kill him. And he did seem to yield. To relax. The eyes, which had bored into hers, now softened. He refilled his lungs. The eyes lowered to her chest, lingering there. His upper lip curled.

"No tits," he murmured.

Carla blinked. She could not have heard correctly. But he said it again.

"Like a boy. No tits."

Perhaps he said it, if he actually did, to break her concentration. Perhaps to show her that he was not afraid. Perhaps to hurt her. She didn't know.

She sat back slightly, easing the pressure against his throat. She looked down at her breasts but she was feeling him, waiting for his muscles to tense, waiting for him to buck. He did nothing. Only those eyes.

Carla cut him. She cut deep.

A knee slammed into her spine. He arched his back and heaved. He threw her. She scrambled out of reach, circling him, counting in her head. Five seconds. Ten.

He did not try to rise. He stared, horrified, at the three-foot arcs of blood that were pulsing from his neck. He snatched at his necktie, bunching it, trying to pack it against the wound. But the necktie was silk and it absorbed almost nothing. Blood flowed through his fingers and down his wrist.

Fifteen seconds.

Carla closed in on him. With her bare foot she kicked at him, trying to make him move so that the blood would pump faster. He rolled onto his back, using his good leg to push himself away from her. He was near her front door. He used the knob to raise himself. There was a mirror on the wall. He looked into it, lifting the necktie compress so that he could see the cut. It spurted as before.

"Why? Oh, Carla, why?" he moaned these words.

She backed away. Thirty seconds.

"Carla?" He turned to face her. "What have you done to me?"

He was Aldo again. A part of her wanted to save him. But it was too late. Forty seconds. She felt tears on her cheeks.

She watched as his blood-starved brain lost one function, then another. It no longer controlled his legs. They became dead weights. The damaged knee went into spasm. His balance gone, he flailed his arms like a drowning man and tumbled backward against the wall. It supported him, but briefly. The legs collapsed. He crumpled to the floor, mouth slack, a puppet without strings. She watched as the light drained from his eyes.

"Yuri?" She was still squeezing herself. "Am I crazy?"

He had listened to her account in silence.

The details, most of them, were new to him. The events that he had described to Paul Bannerman went only as far as this man's first blow and her response to it. The rest was left for him to deduce from the dead man's appearance and the way the blood was distributed. One thing had confused him. Aldo's eyes had been closed. His face had been washed. His hair was put neatly in place. Carla, in her account, made no mention of these ablutions.

"You are hurt. Not crazy."

He reached for her, drawing her close.

"Yuri?"

"Yes, Carla?"

"The things I told you. The things he said?"

"Yes?"

"I'm not sure he even said them."

He touched his lips to her forehead. "Try to rest, Carla."

Yuri was not sure that it mattered, but he, too, had wondered. That Aldo would insult her to no purpose made no sense. Even with too much champagne. But he was inclined to believe that the remark about her breasts—an exaggeration, certainly—had indeed been made. To make her blink. The man had simply waited too long to try for his advantage.

As for the other business—"Carla, what have you done to me?"—nothing that a dying man might say or do surprised him. They say that Brezhnev, in his final delirium, called out to the God of Abraham and that the lecher Beria, while being strangled, tried to grope for his spectacles, which had fallen to the floor.

Also, he reflected, Aldo was an actor.

And agents in deep cover are very much like those actors who live their roles even when they are not on the stage. Under stress, or in shock, such an agent might well revert to the part he had been playing. Or perhaps he, not Carla, was the one who was unbalanced.

He tried to tell her this but she was no longer listening. Her melancholy had deepened. He considered being firm with her, reminding her that she was Carla Benedict and that self-pity did not become her. But in his head he heard Maria's voice telling him to say nothing of the kind. His thoughts turned back to Aldo Corsini.

The man had certainly been trained but by whom? Yuri had considered several possibilities and was forced to reject all but one. Aldo could not have been working for the Italians, or the Americans, or for any Western intelligence service, because if any of these wished to know why Lesko and Elena were in Russia they would simply have asked Mama's Boy.

And yet, that Aldo was *svoi*—one of us—was equally hard to believe. The KGB would have asked General Belkin. And, most convincingly, Aldo Corsini had spoken of becoming rich. These days, the KGB had enough trouble just meeting its payroll.

The computer in Bern might have the answer. But if those files showed Aldo to be an agent, what then? Can a KGB officer reveal this to Mama's Boy? Can Major Yuri Rykov now assist in concealing the evidence of his death?

Yuri saw no choice. He had given his word. Unless General Belkin gives an order to the contrary, he must keep it. But even then, he would have to ask Bannerman to release him from his promise.

Oh, Carla, he sighed within himself. You are a great deal of trouble.

16

Susan wished, uselessly, that she could have been a fly on the practice wall at Briarwood. At this moment, Roger would be briefing the secretary of state, Barton Fuller.

Mr. Fuller, assuming that he knew nothing about Aldo Corsini, would tend to take Bannerman's call at face value. So would Irwin Kaplan. Some guy wants to marry Carla. Bannerman wants to know more about him. Period.

But Roger, being Roger, would be reading between the lines, searching for some advantage. Paul, therefore, had given him one. The invitation to come to Westport. Two years had passed since Roger was told never to return. The hope was that he would weigh the potential benefits of a reconciliation against anything he might gain by trying to milk an *apparent* connection between Aldo's *apparently* shadowy business dealings and her father's wedding trip.

She sat cross-legged on the den floor, a pencil in her mouth, a notepad in her hand, as Bannerman played the tape of their conversation a second time. He listened, deep in thought, his fingers steepled against his lips.

Now it was Paul who was trying to read between the lines. Listening for nuances. She hated that he had to.

If anyone wants to know why he built a wall around Westport, she thought, all they'd have to do is see him now. In Westport, he looks out for his friends and they look out for him. Nobody looks for angles. She almost wished he hadn't made that call.

The tape ended.

Paul began pacing. Still that thousand-yard stare. He'd glanced at her just once, at her loose-fitting shirt, and quickly looked away.

"Maybe Roger's being straight this time," she told him.

He cocked his head but didn't turn.

"I mean, what if what you see is all there is? Of course, if you'd rather hear a conspiracy theory . . ."

He shook his head. "We have Roger for that. Finish your thought."

He stood at the sliding-glass door to the deck, peering into the distance. She knew better than to approach him. He would turn away rather than have the sight of her distract him. It was flattering, she supposed, but annoying. She shouldn't have to throw on a chador every time he wanted her to help him think.

"Roger says that Aldo is an entrepreneur, maybe a hustler, but not necessarily a crook. That description fits a lot of middle-aged Europeans. Carla could have met any one of them. It just happened to be Aldo."

He started to shake his head. He checked himself. "Okay. Let's assume that."

"He didn't . . . necessarily . . . need a motive for being interested in Carla. She's an exciting woman. She has interesting friends."

"Including me?"

"To brag that he knew you? Sure."

"What's his interest in your father and Elena?"

"Any European businessman would love to know Elena Brugg. My father comes with the package."

"Why was he wearing a wire?"

"Don't jump on this. But maybe it was a hobby."

A doubtful grunt.

"It could fit," she insisted. "Yuri said he was a spy groupie. Besides, he kept that recorder in his own car. Does a professional work that way? You tell me."

"Probably not," he acknowledged. "Certainly not alone."

"Would a professional walk around at a lawn party, obviously pumping for information about the *real* reason behind the Russia visit?"

"No. But then why would Aldo?"

"A honeymoon in Moscow? Paid for by a KGB general? To a groupie, that's better than *Murder on the Orient Express*."

"Why did he hit Carla?"

Susan made a face. "Because he's a macho Italian? Because she spit in his face?"

"Why did she kill him?"

"Because she's Carla Benedict."

Bannerman nodded slowly.

On the face of it, he thought, Susan's version made decent sense. Aldo, according to Yuri's account, had told Carla that a great deal of money was at stake. He'd been, after all, an invited guest at Elena Brugg's wedding and he'd been seen socializing with the Bruggs otherwise. He might have used that apparent intimacy as leverage in a deal with someone else. Not so unusual.

But then, there's the darker view.

"Try it another way," he said. "Aldo helped to set up a drug deal between these Sicilians and some Russian entrepreneurs under the cover of that pizza chain. Assume that he did so knowingly. Aldo then contrives to meet Carla because Carla just happens to be close to all three architects of a successful antidrug effort in Zurich who now just happen to be traveling to Russia together."

Susan closed one eye but did not interrupt.

"Those computer files you saw were more than a list of names, Susan. They were a killing strategy. You might as well know that."

She knew it. She said nothing.

"Aldo, or whoever pays him," said Bannerman, "knows that Leo Belkin didn't participate in the Zurich cleanup out of the goodness of his heart. He did it to gain experience with, and full access to, that computer program in order to put it to use, down the road, in his own country."

"And this someone wants to know where and when?"

He nodded. "And whether the trip puts this particular deal in jeopardy. Carla is targeted as a possible way in because she's thought to be vulnerable to seduction. She's still mourning her sister, she's lonely, and, after a year, she still can't bring herself to come back to Westport and the only life she knows. Offer her a new one. Ask her to marry you."

Susan twisted her lip. "That's it? That's your conspiracy theory?"

"I know. It has a hole or two."

"Like the fact that Aldo knew Carla long before those three had any thought of a Russian honeymoon?"

He rubbed his chin. "Aldo had been working his way in for several months. Leo's wedding gift took him by surprise. It forced his hand. Made him take chances."

"Okay." Susan made a note. "But on whose orders? The Mafia?"

A slow nod, or rather the start of one. Then a shrug and a shake of the head.

He had trouble believing that the Mafia would have bothered. All that effort and intrigue just to protect one source of morphine base? Or even a new market for the finished product? There were too many others. Too many easier ways to do business.

That left the Russians.

But which Russians? No criminal organization can function in Russia without the help of corrupt officials. Criminals need protection. More basically, they need cars, apartments, and freedom of movement. Weapons and luxury goods can be had on the black market, but these other things need documentation and that means large-scale bribery. For that matter, he had trouble imagining that such an organization could be in business for very long without being infiltrated by the KGB.

This last thought troubled him.

It had been floating in the back of his mind since his talk with Yuri. Had the KGB sent Aldo?

Within Soviet borders, control of drug traffic, all forms of smuggling, all organized criminal activity, is the responsiblity of the . . . what's *left* of the Second Chief Directorate. Technically, it's none of Leo Belkin's business. Until this moment, Bannerman realized, he had assumed that any plans Leo might have had for using the Zurich program must necessarily be a cooperative effort between the First and Second Chief Directorates.

But what if his target is the SCD itself?

Who else would try to penetrate the Brugg/Mama's Boy axis? Certainly not the drug traffickers. They would have neither the subtlety nor the patience. And obviously not the First Chief Directorate, because Leo was already there.

"What are you thinking?" Susan asked.

"I'm . . . not sure. Give me a minute."

What he wasn't sure of was how far he wanted to take this line of reasoning. An actionable conclusion was one thing. A paranoid swamp was another.

The paranoid view was that the late Aldo Corsini took his orders from someone in the Second Chief Directorate who was actively involved in drug trafficking and that Roger Clew knows it.

Why do we think Roger knows it? Because Roger was more than *just curious* about Carla's new friend. Just curious would be running the name through his own computers and, finding nothing, checking with Interpol for good measure. But Roger hadn't stopped there. He had gone back to Interpol a second time, asking for a supplementary run against "known associates." According to Roger, he found nothing incriminating, but, if so, why did he keep digging? He knew that Aldo had no criminal record, even within Italy, which means that he must have checked with the *carabinieri* as well. His information about Aldo's lifestyle means that he contacted the Italian tax authorities.

Why does Roger think . . . or even know . . . that Aldo works for the SCD? Probably through the same logic we've used. He's also had more time to think about it.

He would have wondered, for example, how Aldo managed to do business all over Eastern Europe for several years before the barriers came down. The answer was simple. He had a rabbi there. Someone corrupt. Someone big.

But the time to make real money in Eastern Europe is now, because money is pouring in and state property is being picked up for a song. And yet, Aldo the dealmaker had shifted his focus to the Soviet Union, where the pickings are far more doubtful. The reason? His rabbi must have been transferred home.

Okay. Who was this rabbi? Not some local party leader. Someone with real influence whose authority had once cut across all boundaries in the Eastern Bloc but who no longer had that authority. Not the military either, because the Soviet military is only now pulling out. That left the KGB. Internal Security when the Eastern Bloc was still internal. The Second Chief Directorate.

The rabbi, now back at Moscow Center, has set himself
up in business again. Smuggling of one kind or another. Not
necessarily limited to drugs, but drugs might be the currency. But why would Aldo go along? He doesn't seem to
have gotten rich in their previous dealings.

Bannerman chose to put that question aside. There could
be a dozen reasons. Fear among them.

The paranoid view, taken to its conclusion, is either that
Leo Belkin has gotten wind of what this rabbi is doing or
that the rabbi thinks he has.

Put another way, Leo Belkin is either using Lesko and
Elena as bait, to flush this person out, or this person thinks
they're all on to him, which is why he tried to put a mole
inside.

Round and round she goes, thought Bannerman.

All of this might be true. Or almost none of it. Roger
would have reached the same conclusions. Why didn't he
say so? Because Roger's style is to lay back and watch. Let
it cook. Look for the advantage. What Roger wants most in
the world right now is for Mama's Boy to be in his debt.

More paranoia.

''Bannerman?''

Susan's voice. As if from a distance. He turned his head
slightly.

''Remember me? Susan Lesko.''

''Sorry.'' He tossed a hand. ''I was . . .''

''I know what you were doing. I want you to share it with
me.''

He was staring at the telephone. Willing it to ring. Hoping
that Carla or Yuri might give substance to shadow. Failing
that, he was tempted to call Moscow and get Lesko out of
there. Tell him his father died. Lesko's father had been dead
for nearly thirty years, but Lesko would get the message.
The problem would be trying to explain, afterward, why
he'd ruined Elena's wedding trip.

Substance and shadow.

Aldo's corpse was certainly substance.

And he almost certainly didn't work alone. Someone
would be wondering where he is. And his rabbi, his
whatever, would be waiting for a report on Willem Brugg's
garden party.

"I have to run out," he said, undoing his robe. "If Carla calls, tell her to stay put. In the meantime . . ."

"Out where, Bannerman? To see Anton Zivic?"

"And Molly Farrell. Yes."

"What can you tell them that you can't tell me?"

"Sweetheart . . ." Bannerman answered from the bedroom. "When that phone rings, you 'll know more than I do. As for Anton, I might want some of our own people in Europe. We need to decide who to send."

"Besides me, you mean."

No answer. Just the scrape of coat hangers.

"You're going to send whoever knows Zurich best because that's where the body is and whoever knows Moscow best because that's where my father is. How am I doing so far?"

"Nobody's going to Moscow. There's no need."

"Which means you don't think he's in trouble."

Bannerman emerged from the bedroom shaking his head. "I don't think so. Someone might be keeping an eye on him, but they'd be doing that anyway."

She watched as he took the tape from his machine and dropped it into his pocket. He had answered her distractedly as if to say that her father was the least of his concerns.

"Okay, then Carla's my friend and I want to be useful. Whoever else you're sending, they'd be wasted doing the things I can do."

"Susan . . ."

"Like staying with Carla, setting up a communications center, driving a chase car . . ."

She stopped herself. Bannerman had formed a time-out signal with his hands.

"Susan we're not mounting Desert Storm here," he told her. "The most I'm going to do is a little spin control."

"Are you going to Zurich?"

"Maybe nobody is. It depends on what we hear from Yuri. In the meantime, it couldn't hurt to book some flights."

"The minute you land, won't Roger know?"

She saw in his expression that he'd considered this. Some of his people might slip in unnoticed, but not Mama's Boy himself. Not unless he smuggled himself into Switzerland

and that would take time. He had either accepted that or decided to stay home.

"After that talk you had"—she gestured toward the tape in his pocket—"what could be more natural than you and me popping off to Zurich for a nice get-acquainted chat with Aldo Corsini?"

Bannerman started to say no. But in his eyes, a flicker of interest.

"Picture us," she said, "you and me, cheerfully strolling toward Passport Control, me carrying a big gift-wrapped box as if we're bringing Carla a present. What would Roger—or anyone else—make of that?"

Bannerman chewed his lip thoughtfully.

"Maybe I'm even seen taking Carla shopping. Buying her a yachting outfit, some foul-weather gear. What would that look like?"

"A trousseau," he said, nodding.

"How about it? Do I pack for both of us?"

Bannerman had to agree that it might be smart to bring her. He had already made a point of letting Roger know that she could hear their conversation. That was to further disarm him . . . persuade him that there can't be much going on here if Susan is in on it. The cheerful scenes she's just described might also disarm whoever else might be concerned about Aldo's disappearance. And that might buy him some time.

Time, as before, was the problem. It would be four hours, at least, before they could reasonably catch a flight and then seven hours en route. Too much time. Too much could happen. A whole night will have passed in Zurich. Yuri busy through most of it. The others out of reach in Moscow.

Moscow.

He had not lied when he said no one is going there. Not immediately, at least. But by morning he could have people in Helsinki, with good paper waiting for them, looking for a tour group to join. Two women would attract the least attention. Maybe Molly and Janet.

"Pack as if we're going for a week," he told her. "That gift is a nice touch, by the way."

She nodded an acknowledgment, trying not to smile. "Any special needs?"

He shook his head. "Pack normally. Assume that the bags will be examined. Bring evening wear as if we expect to attend parties."

Special needs.

He knew that she didn't mean weapons. But the last thing he wanted in his bag was Susan's idea of a cat-burglar outfit with blackened tennis shoes and a ski mask.

17

Red Square wasn't ugly.

Behind him, Lesko heard Valentin explaining that in old Russian the word for *red* was the same as the word for *beautiful*.

It wasn't beautiful either.

To be fair, thought Lesko, parts of it were gorgeous. St. Basil's belonged in a fairy tale. And those white bell towers inside the Kremlin walls were like giant candles, especially now. The onion-shaped domes flickered red and gold in the light of the late afternoon sun. And the buildings that formed the perimeter of the square were handsome enough, taken individually.

Still, for some reason, the overall effect was like a cold rain in your face.

He understood why. Partly.

In all of Europe, he thought, you couldn't find a single major square that wouldn't be mobbed with people at this hour, even on a Sunday evening. Saint Mark's in Venice, for example. You'd see sidewalk cafes, all kinds of vendors selling postcards and tourist junk, street artists doing caricatures, lots of pigeons.

Here, there were more guards than people. The guards, apparently soldiers, were strung out every hundred feet or so all around the square. Just watching. But watching what? In an area that must have been half a mile long and a quarter mile wide, he counted no more than twenty tourists wearing cameras and maybe ten pedestrians, cutting across, carrying shopping bags. Including one woman who, for some reason, Elena was now flagging down. Not a single pigeon. Here, a pigeon could starve to death. Or more likely, end up in a pot.

Red Square was definitely not a place to hang out. You're supposed to come, be awed by it, take your pictures, then get lost. No loud talking, no running, no nothing. It struck him that a few tables with Cinzano or Heineken beer umbrellas would go a long way toward brightening this place up.

These were his impressions, but he would keep them to himself. Belkin would only get all out of joint again.

Belkin.

What he said had made sense, Lesko supposed. Even the part about getting used to the idea of being watched every place he goes. But, shit. Call me naive for hoping that a honeymoon would be seen as an exception to the rule. Call me a dreamer for thinking that traveling with a KGB general, for Christ's sake, would be insurance against finding a microphone in your fucking mattress.

Elena was calling him, waving her camera.

She already had Belkin and Valentin lined up with St. Basil's in the background. The woman she'd stopped was going to take the picture with all of them in it. The woman, shy smile, nice face, said hello as he approached.

"An American, yes? Where in America?"

"Um . . . New York, originally."

"Oh." Huge grin. "Is it wonderful? I would love to see New York. Big Apple, yes? Stand here, please."

She was a tall woman, slender, about forty. She wore a flowing purple coat, unbuttoned, a pink sweater underneath, green slacks over vinyl boots. Three pink carnations, tied with a bow, were pinned to her lapel.

She snapped the St. Basil's picture, then suggested one with the Kremlin in the background. She chatted, trying out her English as they reorganized themselves. She took the second picture, plus one more for good measure, and returned the camera to Elena. Her eyes suddenly went wide. She was staring at Elena's hands for some reason. But then she seemed to catch herself.

She straightened, now asking the others where they were from. Only Elena told the truth. Belkin said he was a musician from Leningrad. Valentin was a law student. Lesko understood. When he was a cop, he wouldn't have said so either in a situation like this. It broke the mood. The woman said her name was Katya. She taught math at a Moscow high school where she was also a volleyball coach.

"Best time for visit," she told Elena. "Not so many tourists yet. But many flowers."

Then, shyly but with grin intact, she removed her carnations and pinned them to Elena's coat. Elena began digging into her purse. Katya backed away, hands raised, refusing a gift in return. But she melted when she saw what Elena had been looking for. It was a bottle of nail polish. The color that she was wearing, Lesko realized, was a deep purple. It went nicely with the taller woman's coat. A minute ago, the woman had noticed the color on Elena's nails but then tried to pretend she hadn't for fear of letting on how desperately she wanted it. Lesko liked her for that.

Elena forced the bottle into her hand. The taller woman blushed, but she was thrilled. Elena reached into her purse again and this time produced the paperback novel she had been reading on the plane.

"For your English," Elena said to her. "To practice."

Once again, Katya tried to refuse but she seemed unable to manage the words. Her eyes glazed over as she reached, very slowly, for the volume, brushing her fingertips across the embossed foil of the cover. She took it at last, then kissed it. Near to tears, she hugged Elena, and squeezed each of their arms. Still unable to speak, she hurried off clutching Pasternak's *Doctor Zhivago* to her breast.

"All that?" Elena asked Belkin. "For just a book?"

He shook his head. "Not just a book, dear Elena." He gestured with his chin. "That woman has trouble finding food, she might never travel abroad, or have a car, or more than a few square meters of living space. She can live with all that. She cannot live without food for the mind."

"She couldn't have bought a copy?" Lesko asked.

"For two weeks' pay, perhaps. If she could find it. Which she probably could not."

He turned away in the direction of the Kremlin. With a flick of his eyes, he invited Lesko to walk with him.

"What do you think?" he asked. "Of what you've seen so far, I mean."

"I liked that lady."

"But not this? Our beautiful Red Square?"

Lesko considered being tactful. "No offense, Leo. This place is a morgue. That lady was alive."

Far from being offended, the answer seemed to please him. "That lady was Russia, Lesko. Not all this. Not those men at the Savoy. Not even men like me. That good lady is the soul of Russia."

This last, the warmth behind it, and the hint that Leo felt distanced from the woman, surprised Lesko. He chose to say nothing. The two men walked on in silence. Elena and Valentin followed.

As they passed the Spassky Gate, the main entrance to the Kremlin grounds, Lesko paused to look through the open passageway. An armed sentry waved him off with a snap of the fingers. Lesko was not annoyed, especially. Traffic cops make such gestures all the time, and Valentin had just been saying that this particular gate was kept clear for those on official business. But the sentry's manner seemed to ignite a slow burn in Leo Belkin.

"Wait here," he said. "I will deal with this."

Belkin flashed his ID at the sentry, berated him for rudeness, demanded to see an officer, berated him as well, then escorted his party through the gate. Once inside, Lesko could see that there were dozens of tourists up ahead taking pictures of a giant cannon. But ropes had been strung to keep them away from this area. Belkin, somewhat distractedly, told them the names of the two churches they could see and then asked if anyone needed to use the facilities. No one did except Leo. He disappeared for five minutes inside a big yellow building that Valentin identified as the meeting place for the old Congress of People's Deputies. When Belkin came out, he announced that there was no need to stay because they would be touring the Kremlin the next afternoon.

All in all, it seemed a pointless episode. An excuse to pull rank. Even Valentin seemed a bit embarrassed by it. He had

trouble looking Lesko in the eye. But he did look at Elena.
And Elena, thought Lesko, gave him a little nod in response.

What's going on here? he wondered.

They were outside the wall again, walking in the direction
of Lenin's tomb. Lesko had seen it a thousand times on
television. It seemed less impressive in person, dwarfed by
the expanse of the Kremlin walls. Same wine color. Black
trim, boxy lines. For a shrine, it looked more like a bunker.

The mausoleum was closed for the day. Two guards on
duty, spiffy uniforms. The guards looked about eighteen.

Belkin said that they could come back when it's open but
there wasn't much to see inside. Just Lenin's face and hands
and no close inspection allowed. The guards keep visitors
moving. Even generals.

This, Lesko had heard, was because it wasn't really
Lenin. Just a wax dummy. The real one turned into King Tut
when someone forgot to turn the heat down once. It wasn't
true, but that was the rumor. He could see, however, that
Belkin was waiting for him to make some crack about it.
Waiting to pounce if he did. Belkin was not in a holiday
mood.

"I hear they're going to move the body, close this
down," he said instead.

Belkin grunted. "They are, and then they aren't," he
answered. "My guess . . . they'll leave well enough alone
as long as tourists want to come and see him."

Lesko nodded.

"He never wanted this, you know."

"Wanted what? This tomb?"

"He wanted to be buried in St. Petersburg next to his
mother. This was all Stalin's idea. Stalin wanted to be
enshrined in there with him. He was, for a time."

Elena snapped a picture.

"Thirty thousand a day," said Belkin.

"Beg pardon?"

"Every day," said Belkin, "thirty thousand people
would line up for hours just for one passing glimpse of him.
Now they line up at McDonald's instead."

This was said, thought Lesko, more than a little bit
ruefully. He let it pass.

They walked along the Kremlin wall. Belkin called their

attention to a long row of plaques behind which various
writers and composers, and a couple of cosmonauts, were
buried in the wall itself. Further on, behind the mausoleum,
they came to the graves of all the other Communist leaders
since Lenin. Stalin's was the simplest. Just a black marble
slab lined with low flowering plants. The area smelled
faintly of urine. Since guards were stationed not ten feet
away, day and night, Lesko assumed that one of them must
have offered an opinion of his former boss.

Even Leo showed no particular reverence as he read the
names from the Cyrillic inscriptions. Kosygin, Chernenko,
Brezhnev. He warmed up considerably when he showed
them Andropov's grave. Smartest of them all, he said. Came
up through the KGB. Hated corruption. Sacked hundreds of
thieves and incompetents. A real family man, by the way.
Didn't just talk about it, either. Things might have turned
out differently if he'd lived.

This last, and especially the part about family, Belkin said
wistfully. And with something approaching anger. To
Lesko, it seemed personal.

"You knew him?" he asked.

Belkin nodded. "He did me a favor once."

"What kind? You mind my asking?"

"It was . . . of a personal nature."

Lesko wasn't going to pry. He continued walking.

Belkin's mood swings aside, it was beginning to sink in
on Lesko that he was actually here. The Kremlin. Red
Square. There was a balcony on the roof of Lenin's tomb
from which the Communist leadership would watch the
May Day parade. All his life, he'd seen pictures of them
standing there. A few generals. The rest wearing topcoats
and fedoras. They all looked like truck drivers. Lots of
saluting and waving. Rockets and tanks going by. Giant
banners saying "We Do Not Falter In Our March Toward
World Communism" and "Produce More Than You Are
Asked For The Motherland."

Klutzy shit like that.

Waldo says that the crowds you saw—all those people
smiling and cheering—were there by invitation only. Like
from central casting. They were all party members, all

reliable. An ordinary Russian couldn't get within half a mile of Red Square on May Day.

Now, no more parades. Most of the generals and fedoras are dead or pensioned off. Some of them getting pissed on. In a way, thought Lesko, it really did seem sad. So much wasted energy. People spending their whole lives trying to believe in something, *needing* to believe in it because God knows it was all they had. He had to wonder what would have happened if the Communists had lost. Back then, judging by the buildings he could see, Moscow must have been as interesting as any big city in Europe until Stalin came along and decided everything had to look like a brown wedding cake or a post office.

Valentin was at his side, pointing. The long blue building with the white trim, he said, was the GUM department store. It was still open, shoppers streaming in and out. It seemed twice the size of Macy's on Thirty-fourth Street. The brick building at the far end was the State History Museum. No one going in. Maybe it was closed. Or maybe no one goes there because it breaks their hearts.

But at least no one screwed around with this area too much. They left St. Basil's alone. Lesko would have thought it would be the first thing the truck drivers torched.

Valentin saw him staring at the cathedral. He offered some history—said it wasn't really a cathedral, but basically a collection of chapels. Ivan the Terrible had it built about four hundred years ago. Was said to have been so pleased that he had the architect blinded so that he could never build anything more beautiful.

Belkin didn't like that story. The same one, he said, is told about the Taj Mahal. No matter how often it's refuted as the probable invention of some tourist guide looking for new patter, the legend persists. The only blinding that's happened is to the very considerable accomplishments of that particular czar.

Not worth getting worked up over, thought Lesko, but he had to agree. At least about the legend. If old Ivan ever wanted to build anything else, he couldn't expect bidders to line up around the block if they knew he'd poked the last guy's eyes out.

Valentin, showing signs of discomfort again, had

launched into another story about St. Basil's. Something about those ten chapels being used to stable horses for a while. Lesko had missed the beginning, but since this was said with displeasure, he assumed that Valentin was taking another shot at Stalin and muttered something to that effect.

"Not Stalin," said Belkin, testily. "Napoléon."

Lesko raised an eyebrow.

"As an act of spite, he also ordered it blown up, and those Kremlin churches burned when he began his retreat. Fortunately, the officer to whom he gave that order was too busy saving his own skin."

"Yeah, well . . . thank God, right?"

Belkin glared at him. "What is that? Sarcasm?"

Lesko blinked.

"Your God-fearing West, Lesko, has had more than its share of monsters. Hitler would have turned Moscow into a wheatfield and Russians into fertilizer."

Now what? thought Lesko.

"We did not invent despotism. The curse of this country, however, is that for eight hundred years it has known almost nothing else. That, and invasion by foreigners. Lenin was not the first of our people to say that enough was enough and to lead a revolution. He was merely the first to survive one."

"Leo . . ."

"Our grandparents would have followed the devil himself if he could feed them and give them some measure of pride. But Lenin was not a devil. He was a decent man who made mistakes."

Lesko cleared his throat.

"If you doubt that," Belkin snapped, "I suggest that you read a book."

"Hey." Lesko raised a hand. "All I asked was who put the horses in St. Basil's."

Belkin took a breath. He glanced self-consciously at Valentin, who was studying the cobblestones. "My apologies," he murmured. "That was totally inexcusable."

"No offense." Lesko shrugged. "You're right. I should read a book."

Lesko felt Elena at his arm. He sensed, rather than saw, that her eyes were on Belkin. More vibrations between them. She was telling him to let it go. Lesko was getting a little tired of this. He decided to push.

"You still a Communist, Leo? I mean, can anyone still believe in that crap?"

He felt a hard pinch from Elena but from Belkin only a rueful smile.

"A belief in anything, Lesko, is better than a belief in nothing. Lenin, to us, was our George Washington, our Lincoln, and our Jesus all rolled into one. Now we learn that everything he tried to build has been corrupted and was, in any case, a house of cards. Stalin, the corrupter, built us into a world power nevertheless. He made us proud to be Russians. Now, for all the tanks and rockets, we are fast becoming a second-rate power with a third-world economy. If that happened in your country, my friend, what would be left for you? What would you believe in?"

"Myself, Leo."

"Ah, but you see, there is no *self* here. For seventy-five-years, the self has been nothing. There has only been the state, the dream, and the enemy, all of which united us and gave our lives purpose. If the dream is gone and the state has collapsed of its own weight, if the enemy has demeaned us by offering us charity, all the while picking at our bones, what is left to us?"

Lesko still wasn't sure what had set Belkin off. If Elena knew, he'd get it out of her later. Maybe it was those bozos at the Savoy or maybe it was just being home. Here, he thought, is a basically upbeat guy, life of the party back in Zurich, who's in Moscow one hour and all of a sudden he's the Volga Boatman. The lights of GUM caught Lesko's eye.

"Any place in there to buy a beer?" he asked.

"There are juice bars," said Valentin quietly. "They sell champagne."

"What do you say we lighten up?" He put a hand on Belkin's back, steering him in that direction. Belkin planted his foot.

"My question was not rhetorical, Lesko."

"Leo . . . give me a break."

"I insist. I would very much like to hear some street-cop wisdom from my former enemy."

"Street-cop wisdom? Why didn't you say so?" He started walking, pulling Belkin with him. "This street cop says stop your whining, Leo. Stop your whining and get off your ass."

18

Viktor Podolsk stood at the concierge desk in the lobby of the Savoy, a phone at his ear, waiting for his call to be put through to General Borovik.

The desk amused him. It was still only the service bureau, as in any Intourist hotel, but the Finns who managed the Savoy chose to mount a brass plaque with the word *Concierge* on it.

A harmless enough pretension. And he supposed that a concierge desk was to be expected in any hotel that charged 300 dollars American for a single night's stay, hard currency only. And which had spent 2 million, they say, on gold leaf alone. Statues of nude women everywhere you turn.

There were two such statues flanking the interior entrance. One had a hand cupped to her ear and the other had an arm outstretched, fingers down in a sort of sweeping motion. The first seems to ask, "You say you're a Russian?" The second says, "In that case, go away." To the Finns, this must have seemed more subtle than to hang a sign that said "No Russians or dogs allowed."

The concierge desk, apparently, was a source of additional profit. A fat German salesman, taking him for one of the Finns, had just pressed a five-Deutschmark note into his hand and asked him to keep an eye on the mound of luggage he had stacked near the desk. The German had barged off before he could protest, crossing to the Detsky Mir children's store for some last-minute shopping.

It occurred to Podolsk that there might be no need to stay in his room when the Belkin party arrived. His dark Italian suit, his Nordic features, seemed a perfect disguise in this hotel.

But perhaps not.

The bumbler, Kerensky, was certain to address him as "Comrade Major" at the worst possible moment. He doubted that there was a hundred people in all of Moscow who still used "comrade" as a form of address, or a single one who knew less about Marxism than did Kerensky.

Kerensky sat on a lobby chair nearby, perspiring in a heavy, fleece-lined coat that by the look of it had never been cleaned. His expression, sullen and resentful only moments ago, when he wasn't leering at the statues, now had a certain slyness to it. Perhaps, thought Podolsk, that expression was Kerensky's idea of alertness. More likely he was wondering how much a few strips of that gold leaf might fetch.

Podolsk drummed his fingers impatiently. Come on, Borovik. Pick up.

The Finn at the desk caught his eye and, glaring, motioned toward Kerensky with his head. *Please,* his look was saying. *Get that creature out of here. Any longer and we'll have to halve our rates.*

Podolsk turned his back on Kerensky. He could not stand the sight of him either.

Kerensky welcomed the change in posture.

One eye on the major, the other on the front desk, he eased his chair nearer the fat German's luggage.

Only when the major bent over the telephone did he allow both eyes to caress the unmistakable shape of a laptop computer which that soon-to-be-departing guest had left among his suitcases and sample kits.

Kerensky was looking at a million rubles, at least.

Forget rubles.

Thirty thousand dollars, American, or the equivalent amount in any hard currency. Perhaps twice that much depending on the software packed with it. But worth nothing at all unless he could get rid of Viktor Podolsk for two minutes.

If only General Borovik would snap his fingers and tell him to come running. Podolsk and his snotty advice with

him. His hopes rose when he saw the major straighten and
begin speaking into the telephone.

"Yes," Podolsk said wearily. "I signaled Zurich before I
left the building."

"Yes, the Sicilian has acknowledged. Even now, he is
looking for Barca . . . Yes, Kerensky's people have been
redeployed . . . No, I have seen no sign of General Belkin
or his party."

Borovik snorted into his ear.

"Must I do everything, Podolsk? They are in Red Square.
What is more, they are making sure that I know it."

"Ah . . . what are they doing, General?"

No answer at first. Just Borovik's mumbled voice to
someone else, a question followed by silence. Podolsk
understood. A militiaman or a Kremlin guard was reporting
on another of the general's four telephones. Could Borovik,
he wondered, be so indiscreet that he had spread those
photographs all over the city?

Borovik came back on.

"It is as you said, Podolsk." His voice now dripped of
sarcasm. "Just some innocent sightseeing. They have paid
their respects to our departed leaders and they are now
standing in the middle of Red Square having a nice innocent
chat for all the world to see."

And there you have it, thought Podolsk. He had argued
that they might indeed be in Moscow as tourists. Since they
are now in Red Square, behaving as the most typical of
tourists, only a fool, in General Borovik's view, could fail to
see that they cannot, therefore, be tourists.

Borovik was speaking into the other phone again, his
voice rising slightly. Podolsk waited, certain that more
damning revelations were imminent.

Distractedly, he stretched the cord in order to see the
street outside. Kerensky's thug cousin, Yakov, was sitting
behind the wheel of a taxi whose owner had been encouraged to take the evening off. His brother, Sasha, the
ponderous oaf who had been loitering outside and had
witlessly shouted and pointed when the Chaika appeared,
was now safely deployed in the dim light of the Hermitage
Bar. Kerensky, whom he had just lectured on the subject of

calling attention to oneself, was now doing it again. He was making a show of being hot. Wiping his brow, opening his jacket, and fanning his shirt. Podolsk grimaced as the aroma of sweat and rancid pork reached him. Kerensky shrugged helplessly. He stripped off his fleece jacket and looked about him for a place to drape it, finally choosing the German's stand of luggage.

"Podolsk?"

"I am here, General."

"They seem to have made a contact. There was a second woman. She took their picture, or pretended to, and then engaged them in conversation. The Brugg woman slipped something into her hand."

A *contact*, sighed Podolsk. In the middle of Red Square. Perhaps this woman held up a sign saying, *Here I am. Your co-conspirator*. Perhaps that German boy, Mathias Rust, flew her in with his Cessna again.

"Purple coat, no hat." Borovik was repeating words spoken by the other caller. "Brown hair tied back, coat is to her ankles, green slacks with bell bottoms."

A good inconspicuous choice of garment, thought Podolsk, rolling his eyes. Clearly a professional. "We will . . . watch for her, General."

"The others are now walking toward GUM. Send someone to Red Square. Watch them as well."

"At once, General."

The line made a clattering sound and went dead.

For a useless task, a useless man, thought Podolsk. He hooked a finger in the direction of the bar, summoning the obese, crew-cut Sasha Kerensky, who managed to knock over an ashtray as he entered the lobby.

Speaking as if to a child, Podolsk instructed him to take a taxi—not Yakov's, please—to Red Square, locate the Belkin party, keep an eye on them, break off at once if they seem to notice him and, if they do, do not, repeat *not,* return to this hotel. Go to the Metropole next door. Call from there.

Kerensky intercepted his brother at the inner door of the entrance. He carried his thick fleece jacket bundled against his chest.

"Change with me," Podolsk heard him say. "Mine is warmer, too warm for indoors." Sasha seemed confused, but he did not resist as his brother pulled the lighter jacket from his shoulders and guided him toward the street.

Podolsk watched as he climbed into a taxi without first speaking to the driver. The driver turned to protest. Sasha Kerensky smacked his cap off. Podolsk could watch no longer.

The driver made no move toward his gear shift. He had folded his arms.

"To GUM," commanded the sausage-maker. "The October entrance."

"From you," the angry driver sputtered, "I don't need a sixty-kopek fare. You can walk to GUM in three minutes."

Sasha seized him by the hair. "To GUM," he barked. "This is KGB business." He shoved the head forward, releasing it. The driver, red-faced, put the car in gear.

That matter settled, Sasha Kerensky unfolded the fleece jacket and sat back. A grin split his face. With his fingers he traced the Toshiba brand name and caressed the textured surface of the laptop's case. A Toshiba, no less. And his brother had stolen it right under the nose of that major who thinks he knows everything.

The driver placed a hand over his tender scalp and smoothed his hair. He replaced his cap. Sasha took no notice. He did not see the fury that burned from those eyes in the rearview mirror. If he had, he might have smacked him again for good measure.

But Sasha was thinking. He could not very well wander through GUM carrying a computer worth more than its weight in gold. One of his brother's storage rooms was only ten more minutes in the Shelepikha district. A nice dark little street where people mind their business. Except this driver would never wait for him there. It is a bad part of town. Besides, he is indignant.

Sasha knew what he would do. The driver had a Marlboro box on his dashboard. It was a signal, these days, that in his trunk he had something worth buying. These drivers set up shop behind the hotels when it is dark.

"What do you have to sell?" he asked.

"Nothing."

"You don't have to lie. Tell me."

The driver shrugged. "Maybe some smoked fish. Tangerines. Mostly tea."

"Turkish or Georgian?"

"Turkish. But good."

Sasha sneered. Turkish tea is bird shit.

"I have a friend who will take all you have. Drive out to Kalinin. I will show you where to turn."

The driver hesitated. "No GUM?"

"First the tea, then GUM."

"One American dollar for each ten grams."

"We charge my friend two dollars. I keep one."

"Out of two dollars, I give you half of one dollar," the driver countered, "but I don't charge for the fare."

"Good. I agree."

Disgusting, thought Sasha Kerensky. A man sees a chance to rob his fellow citizen and the rest of his mind goes dead. In five minutes, this man will be in his trunk with his tea. Best way to make sure he waits. Best way to make sure he does not see where the Toshiba goes.

19

Yuri had prepared a bubble bath for her.

It smelled of fresh lemons. Very clean. He did this because in the elevator she began to cry again. He reached for her, holding her, letting her bury her face against his chest. But then she pushed him away.

"Don't," she said. "I'm disgusting."

This was not true. To show it, he scooped her up in his arms and he kissed her. He kissed every part of her head and shoulders that he could reach.

"What part is disgusting?" he asked her. "Is it this? Or this? Or am I on the wrong parts?" With that, he kissed each of her knees. When he did so, she laughed. But the laugh became a sob and she hid her face again. Laughter and tears.

So alike. He did not put her down until they were inside his flat, not even when he dropped his keys, not even as he closed his blinds, not even as he fumbled with the door of his freezer and pulled out a bottle of iced vodka.

Her remark, he felt sure, was not one of self-abasement. It was Aldo Corsini. She still felt him on her skin. At the boathouse he had cleaned her as well as he could, but it was not the same as a good soaking.

She would not drink the vodka. She would only wash her mouth with it, cleaning the cut inside her cheek, spitting blood into his kitchen sink until its color faded to pink. Meanwhile, he prepared her bath. To do so had required some deception.

As she was bent over his sink, Yuri palmed a bottle of dishwashing liquid. It was called Brio. The detergent smelled strongly of lemons, and he remembered that the television commercials for it gave assurance that Brio was gentle to the skin. Also on television, he had noticed that many Western women were fond of taking bubble baths. The total effect seemed both soothing and modest. An additional advantage was that in such a circumstance, it seemed acceptable for him to sit in a chair by the tub and talk to her.

From his bathroom cabinet he took one tablet of Demerol and one of Seconal. A Swiss doctor had prescribed these to help ease his discomfort after the operations that had restored his face and also to help him sleep. They would do the same for Carla. Upon reflection, he realized that she might refuse them as she had refused the vodka. Best to take two more of each pill, he decided, and put them in his pocket. One way or the other, he would get her to take them.

She was in bubbles up to her chin. She looked up at him.

"You're a sweet guy, Yuri. You know that?"

"Thank you. Open, please."

He sat by the tub, spooning tomato soup into her mouth. She had, as he had anticipated, refused the medication. Only two aspirin and a fresh ice pack. The Demerol and Seconal, therefore, were in the soup. The sleeping pill had not had time to take effect, but she seemed drowsy nonetheless. With the kind of day she'd had, and now the hot bath, this was not so surprising.

The tub was of normal length, but like many Swiss tubs, it was several inches deeper than was typical elsewhere. It was deep enough that even Yuri could submerge his whole body except for his knees. For a small woman like Carla, however, this could be a problem, especially if the tub was slick. She had to brace herself to keep from sliding under the water. But she did not seem to mind.

"You even put bath oil in the water, didn't you." She felt the texture between her fingers. A smile of appreciation.

"Um . . . you like it?"

"I like it. It's just a little slippery."

The label of the detergent bottle listed two kinds of "surfactants" among the ingredients. He did not know this word, but the German root suggested some sort of lubricating effect.

Carla blew a hole through a cloud of bubbles. Some of them danced in the air.

"Yuri?" She closed one eye. A look of confusion. "Do you take bubble baths?"

"Me? Well . . . I mean, ah . . ."

"Oh. It's Maria's, right? She left it here."

Yuri shrugged ambiguously, gratefully. His deception had gone undiscovered. He scraped at the soup bowl. "Drink," he said. "One more spoonful."

She obeyed. "Yuri?"

"Yes, beautiful Carla."

She smiled. "Don't start that beautiful Carla stuff. I'll drag you into this tub."

Yuri blushed. "What was your question?"

"What made a guy like you join the KGB?"

He pursed his lips. "Good pay. Travel. To help my country."

"How did you avoid the shit jobs?"

He knew what she meant. Intimidating dissidents. Standing outside churches, taking photographs of those who entered. Arresting citizens for talking to foreigners. All of that seemed so distant now. Like bad dreams. "They did not arise," he told her. "From the beginning I was First Directorate although it was three years before I was trusted to travel."

"Have you done any wet work?"

"Carla . . ."

"Come on. You know all about me."

"The answer is no."

"Bullshit."

"Wet work is assassination. It is very rare and it is seldom useful. Also, it was permitted to refuse. I would have refused."

She reached for his hand. She studied it, tracing her fingers over its surface. "I've heard about these hands. In Los Angeles, you ripped a man's throat out with this."

He tried to pull away. "An exaggeration. He shot me. I groped blindly."

"But he wasn't your first, was he."

Yuri cleared his throat. "Could we not find a more pleasant subject?"

"I just . . . like to know that you can protect me."

"Hmmph."

"What's *Hmmph*?"

"More likely that you would protect me."

It was meant as a compliment, said with respect. She did not seem to appreciate it. The sadness came back in her eyes. He felt her grip tighten around his fingers. She began pulling him closer.

"I . . . should leave you to rest." he said. "I can call Mr. Bannerman for you if you wish. And then I must . . ."

She guided the hand to her lips. Caressing it. Tasting it. Now she lowered it to her chest and held it against her, submerged beneath the foam. She stifled a yawn.

The yawn gave him hope that the pills would work quickly. There was little time for this, much on his mind, much to do. But now she was pulling him again. He yielded. She turned her face toward his. Her lips parted. He dropped to one knee. Her arms twined around his neck.

Her kiss, the things that she did with her tongue, sent shocks through his body. In all his life, he had never been kissed in this way. Her tongue was alive. Almost violent. Probing deeply. It seemed to him, almost, that she was trying to force herself inside him. To hide there. Her small arms held him with a strength, an intensity, that he would not have imagined in her.

In his mind, he saw Maria's face. Her expression, at first,

was one of surprise and then of confusion. In his mind, he explained to her that this had not been his intention but now, perhaps, it cannot be avoided. Maria seemed to understand. She turned away, going about her business as if she had seen nothing at all.

More shocks. One of Carla's hands was now against his chest, the fingers reaching inside his shirt. He slid his own right hand behind her back, the other beneath her knees, ignoring the effect upon his wristwatch and jacket. He lifted her as he had in the elevator. From her waist down, all was foam. She was like a mermaid.

It was true, he thought, that Maria would understand. Carla was in pain. She had need of him. To refuse a woman, when she offers herself, is something that is never forgiven. To refuse a woman such as Carla, in this circumstance especially, might also be unsafe. That he also wanted her, was thrilled by her, was in this case irrelevant. He would never have taken the initiative. Maria would know that. She would understand.

Best, however, not to mention it.

He carried Carla to his bed.

20

"You're an ungrateful prick, Lesko."

He heard Katz in his head while he was urinating.

"You got no appreciation, you know that?"

Lesko was in no mood for this. Elena was already sore at him.

"She should be," Katz scolded. *"Guy invites you to Russia, picks up the whole tab, and all you do so far is noodge."*

He had left them at the large fountain on the main floor of GUM, sipping sweet champagne from paper cups, while he went to find a toilet.

"Guy sees that his whole country is in the shithouse and all you can say is stop your whining, Leo. Get off your ass, Leo."

"David . . . he asked for it. He was pushing for it."

"Would you have said that in the South Bronx? In Harlem? You've been living off the Bruggs too long, Lesko. You got no compassion."

"I earn my keep, David. Fuck you."

Lesko said this aloud. The little man selling folds of toilet paper was suddenly nervous. He began edging toward the door.

"David?" Lesko returned to his mind. *"Something's going on here. What?"*

"It sure as hell isn't sensitivity training."

Lesko showed his teeth. But maybe, he thought, Katz was right.

Katz . . . his own conscience . . . whatever. Even so, he didn't need this.

Sometimes he could will Katz away. He tried it. He waited until Katz opened his mouth again and then he zapped him. Katz exploded into a flash of light. Lesko gathered the light into a ball and sent it to Lenin's tomb where he rematerialized him, unconscious, inside the glass coffin. Let him wake up there in the morning. Lenin was probably a bargain compared to some of the skags Katz woke with over the years. Meanwhile, if it gets too dark and scary in there he can always use Lenin as a candle.

Lesko sighed.

There he went again, getting smart-ass disrespectful. If Belkin wanted to feel bad about Lenin being thrown out with the bathwater, he had a right. Lesko would try to be nice.

He finished at the urinal and went to rinse his hands. Rusty water, cold, no soap, no paper towels. He checked the stalls. No paper there either and the little guy selling it was gone, probably to find a cop. Place stank, he thought, rubbing his hands dry. It hadn't been hosed down in a month.

See that? He was still doing it. Being negative. He was beginning to sound like John Waldo.

Here he was, he told himself, in this incredible department store. They'd been wandering up and down the first-floor gallery for about a half hour and he had yet to say anything positive. But it was really an amazing place. You look at the architecture, the details, and this was every bit as awesome as the Gallerias of Naples or Milan. Here, that first-floor gallery was the length of two football fields, and there were two more levels above it with little bridges running across. Maybe a hundred little shops on each level. The whole thing covered with a greenhouse roof. And Belkin said there were two other galleries, running parallel, just like this one. Probably just as mobbed.

Valentin said that most of the shoppers were from out of town. Some, he said, traveled hundreds of miles because they had nothing like this selection of goods back home. That was the thing. What made it hard to say anything nice was that he'd never seen such crap in his life.

Years ago, back in Queens, there was this old Kresge Five & Dime. A new mall opened just down the street on Queens Boulevard. The Kresge's hung on for about a year and then it went out of business. By the time it finally closed, about half the shelves were empty, but they were still trying to unload whatever dusty, picked-over junk they still had for ten cents on the dollar.

That was what these shops looked like. Cheap clothing with seams already coming loose. Bath towels you could push your thumbnail through. One place sold hand tools, hammers and such, that were dumped in a bin and coated with rust. Raincoats made out of oilcloth which you could smell from three shops away. Sales clerks with expressions that said if you want it, fine, if you don't, go away. Any halfway-decent merchandise was easy to spot because it always had a sign or a little flag saying it was from Hungary, Czechoslovakia, Italy, the implication being that if it was made in Russia it was probably a piece of shit.

Still . . . maybe on the way back he could find some little gift for Elena. Some flowers, anyway. Make up for being such a jerk.

As he started back toward the fountain, he noticed a little costume jewelry stall with a display of amber necklaces. Elena liked amber. It went with her coloring. One necklace was particularly unusual. It was a long strand of unpolished chunks in several shades. The tag said 600 rubles. If he remembered correctly from his guidebook, that was a month's pay for most Russians, but it was only a few bucks American.

He approached the counter. The sales girl did a double take. Her lips parted. Lesko was used to that. He tried a smile. It didn't help. He pointed toward the necklace of mixed amber and peeled a five-dollar bill from his roll. He held it up, questioningly.

She seemed tempted but, ''Only rubles,'' she muttered. Nuts.

Lesko thought of the kids outside. He gestured that he'd be back and walked toward the exit. He realized that this was not the smartest idea he'd ever had. On the other hand, he wasn't planning to walk outside waving American dollars either. If someone approached him, fine. If not, okay. But he wanted that necklace for Elena.

When he passed through the exit, expecting to see St. Basil's all lit up, he realized that he'd been turned around. He was at the opposite end of GUM. He had barely oriented himself when a kid in his early twenties started toward him, then hesitated like the others. Lesko made a peace sign with his fingers. The kid came on.

''Good evening, sir. Are you enjoying your visit?''

''The time of my life.''

It never failed to amaze Lesko. He hadn't opened his mouth. Everything he wore was German or Italian. Haircut was Swiss. And yet everyone in the world seems to know an American on sight. ''I need some rubles,'' he said. ''How many for ten bucks?''

''Such transactions are illegal, sir.''

''Kid . . . give me a break. How much?''

The young man smiled. ''For ten dollars, twelve hundred rubles. For more dollars, the rate is better.''

''The ten's all I need.''

He held the bill in one hand and extended the other, palm up. The kid hesitated for just a beat more and then reached into his pocket. From a thick wad, he separated six little bundles of twenties. Lesko assumed that he was being cheated to some degree. Kid would be crazy not to start off

low. But this made that necklace about a two-dollar purchase, and there was no point being greedier than that.

It looked like Monopoly money. Little colored bills less
than half the size of a dollar. Lesko suddenly realized that
he'd never seen Soviet currency before. They could have
been kopeks for all he knew.

"Listen," he said, "I have a better idea. There's a
necklace I want inside. It's six hundred rubles. Buy it for me
and you can keep the five bucks plus the rest of the rubles."

The young man brightened. "Agreed," he said.

Lesko watched as the kid paid with the same twenties. He
was straight after all. As he turned from the jewelry counter,
Lesko held out a hand for the necklace, but the kid kept
moving toward the exit. Must be safer to do business
outside, Lesko realized. Lesko followed him onto the street
where the young man did a sweep with his eyes and then
passed him the small package. Lesko thanked him and
started back toward the doors.

"Sir? If you want more amber . . ."

Lesko stopped. "This necklace. Is it any good?"

The kid rocked a hand. "Not so bad. Nothing in shops is
the best. You always do better by trading."

"Just out of curiosity, what else do you deal in?"

He shrugged. "I have good unpressed caviar. Better than
in Berioska shops. Fur hats made of muskrat, not rabbit.
Also military hats and belts."

"That's all?"

"Tell me what you want. Probably I can find it."

"Drugs?"

A flicker of contempt. "Not from me."

"Glad to hear it. What kind of stuff do you trade for?"

"Almost anything from America. Cigarettes, magazines,
clothing, anything electronic, cosmetics . . ."

"You can't buy any of that stuff legally?"

He shook his head. "Hard to find. Someday, perhaps."
He cocked his head toward the shops of the gallery. "In
there, someday you will see Waldenbooks, Radio Shack,
even Safeway and Sears Roebuck."

Lesko believed it. GUM was already a mall. Half the
cities in Europe already looked like Cincinnati.

"Won't that put you out of business?"

"By then, perhaps, I will be in America. Do you think I could find work there?"

"How many languages do you speak?"

"English is adequate. German and French are better. I am learning Spanish."

"Offhand, I'd say you can't miss."

A shy smile. "Could I be a policeman? Like you?"

Lesko made a face. He knew that the kid wasn't serious. He was just letting him know that he knew. It was the eyes. You can always spot a cop by his eyes. The way they're always looking around.

"You're sure I'm not CIA?"

The kid almost laughed. "You are not CIA."

Lesko extended his hand. "Nice talking to you. Name's Lesko."

"Mikhail." He shook it. "Your necklace," he said. "The pieces are good but you must have them restrung."

"Thanks. I will."

The young man gestured toward the exit. "If you decide to buy or trade, I am there most evenings."

"Take care of yourself." Lesko slapped his shoulder. He reentered GUM in search of Elena.

The taxi driver's name was Ratmir. He was humiliated. He was furious.

His passenger, that lying pig of a man, was holding fast to his collar to keep him from taking the keys and running.

His clothing, his entire taxi, now smelled of oranges and Turkish tea. His pants were wet and sticky where he had crushed his tangerines. Three packages of tea had been split open. Totally destroyed. Their contents now clung to his knees and elbows. Only the smoked fish and about half of the tea could now fetch a decent price. On the tangerines he would lose money.

That pig.

He never wanted the tea. He had waited until the trunk was open. Then he seized Ratmir by the neck and by the crotch and threw him inside, slamming the lid shut against his head.

"For your own good," came the muffled voice of the pig.

"Very bad area, the Shelepikha. Nothing but ex-convicts and those who live in Moscow illegally. You are safer in the trunk. Also you are here when I return."

Now he promises to pay the fare plus twenty rubles extra if he is driven back to GUM. Ratmir did not believe him. Even if he paid it, the ruined tangerines and the tea were worth many times more.

"Don't stop. Go past," said the pig, twisting his collar. Blood hammered at Ratmir's temples.

He glanced into his mirror. The pig was staring ahead, off to the right. Now, with his free hand, he was reaching inside his coat. Ratmir tensed. But the pig had no weapon, only squares of paper. No . . . they were photographs. He was spreading them with his thumb and now staring again. Two men, talking together, had caught his interest. They were standing by the entrance of GUM. One looked like a foreigner. He was even bigger than this one.

"Go past," he said again, pointing. "Go in front of those trucks."

The pig had released his collar, but Ratmir could feel his breath against his neck and he could smell him even through the tea and the juice of the tangerines. He smelled like rancid fat. Ratmir leaned away from him. With his fingers, he felt for the mallet that he kept under his seat. It was still there. He gripped it and tucked it under his thigh as he shifted gears and eased forward.

The trucks were parked for the evening outside a small loading area between the galleries. Ratmir could expect no help from the drivers. Either they were drunk by now or they were out selling whatever they had stolen from their shipments. At his passenger's order, Ratmir pulled in beyond the second truck. There was an alley there. The pig urged him forward, into it.

Ratmir feared that once again this man would try to put him in the trunk. But as the taxi turned he was looking back up October, back toward the two men. Ratmir surged forward, then hit his brakes hard. The pig bounced off the front seat. His hat went flying. The motor shuddered and stalled. Ratmir scrambled from the taxi. The mallet clattered to the cobblestones. Ratmir groped for it, at the same time throwing his weight against the door that the pig was trying to push open. Once more, Ratmir's fingers found his mallet.

"First you pay me," he shouted. "Not twenty rubles. Two hundred." His voice was high in pitch.

Two pig eyes looked out at him. No fear, not even anger. Only contempt. The eyes also said that he had no time for this.

"Two hundred is fair," he said.

He leaned away from the door as if to reach into his pocket for the money. Instead, his leg came up. He kicked at the door.

But Ratmir had expected this. He pulled the door open as the foot came forward. He swung hard at the ankle. The pig yelped. The leg bucked and flailed. Ratmir hammered at it. To do this, he let the door swing wide. It was a mistake.

The man lunged, his left hand clawing at Ratmir's hair. Ratmir threw his head back, but the hand now gripped his jacket. It jerked him forward, banging his face against the roof of the car, then throwing him backward against the alley wall. For a moment he was dazed. When his eyes could focus again, the man was climbing from the car. Ratmir heard him grunting from the effort but he saw a cruel light in his pig eyes. The man was going to beat him. Break his bones. Already he was finding pleasure in the thought of it. But now the man put weight upon his ankle and he cried out in angry pain. He swung the other leg from the taxi and, both hands gripping the door, pulled himself erect. He prepared to hurl himself at Ratmir.

Ratmir swung the mallet in a chopping motion. It glanced off the side of the bigger man's skull, tearing his ear. The man bellowed. He clapped a hand to it. Ratmir swung again, blindly, this time catching his elbow. The sound was that of an ax striking wet wood. The man's right hand, still clutching the photographs, grabbed at the elbow. His head, the right side of it, was unprotected. Ratmir sidestepped so that the open door was between them. He reached over it and swung the mallet again. It tore at the other ear. The head dipped forward. Now Ratmir pounded at his neck. He did not know how many times he struck him. He did not stop until the pig stopped grunting.

The man was not moving. He sat, hunched over, part in and part out of the taxi. Ratmir was afraid. Had he murdered him, he wondered, or was the man faking? A shadow passed from the sidewalk. Footsteps receded. They were not hurried. Ratmir knew that the next passerby might look in and then run to Red Square for a policeman. He had to get away from there.

Ratmir eased into the driver's seat. He started the engine, praying that there would be no backfire. The prayer was answered. It caught quickly. He engaged the clutch, playing it, letting his taxi creep forward, deeper into the alley, in short jarring spurts. He could hear the big man's shoes clopping along the stones. At last, as he had hoped, the big man tumbled out the still-open back door. His face hit first under all his weight. He rolled until he hit the wall. Ratmir stopped. He reached through his window and pushed the rear door shut, wincing at the noise it made. He put his taxi in reverse and eased back past the fallen man.

Ratmir stopped once more. He had to think. The money crossed his mind, but he swept that thought aside. Not for a thousand rubles would he risk getting within that man's reach again. Unless he first made sure. Unless he finished him. Not for the money, but in case that man woke up remembering his name or the number of his taxi. Even if this man did not go to the police, Ratmir knew that he would be looking for him, for weeks to come, outside the tourist hotels.

It is not fair, Ratmir screamed in his mind.

He had done nothing wrong. If this man lives, he must live in fear. He must stay away from the hotels, but for a taxi driver that was not possible. If this man dies, it's Lefortovo prison and a bullet in the back of the head. Or worse. Unless this man was a liar, that business about KGB, they might take him to Lubyanka. At Lubyanka they would castrate him first. He had heard that they still do that.

Ratmir stiffened. He thought he saw movement. Yes. There it was again. The man's right hand. Even now, it still held those photographs. He was trying to raise the hand. Perhaps to signal. But he had no strength. As Ratmir watched, the hand opened and the crumpled photographs fell from it like leaves. They settled on his chest.

An inner urge told him to go forward again. Cut the wheel to the left. Crush him once and for all. But now he saw that

one foot had begun to twitch violently and he heard a sound
like the chortling of engine valves. The big man's chest
shuddered, coughed once, and was still.

Ratmir touched the gas pedal. Struggling to compose
himself, he eased his taxi back out across the sidewalk.
There were no pedestrians on it. Up at the corner, a few
people were leaving GUM but they were crossing to the
metro station. That big man was gone but the younger one
still lingered. Ratmir backed out further between the trucks.
From there, he looked into the alley. To him, that dark mass
was clearly a body, but he forced himself to realize that to
anyone else it was only a shadow. A bundle of trash. Still,
he knew that it would be discovered soon. In a few hours the
old women will be out with their brooms and they will find
him.

Calm yourself, he said. Drive away. Do not speed. First
thing is to wash the car, get rid of the smell, also get rid of
the mallet. He would go to his uncle Pyotr's garage on
Kurskaya. Uncle Pyotr would help him. He would know
what else to do.

21

Irwin Kaplan's nose was bleeding. His glasses were bent
cockeyed. A net smash by Roger Clew had caught him just
on the hinge.

Add to that a skinned knee from when he tripped on his
shoelace, a sour stomach which would keep him from even
enjoying Barton Fuller's brunch and a tennis game which, if
a passing doctor should see him playing, would immediately be diagnosed as cerebral palsy.

And now, so the morning should be a total loss, Clew gets
a call from Mama's Boy.

Kaplan had urged him to take Bannerman at his word.
Call him back on Monday. Better yet, call him back next

week. That would give Kaplan a chance to put about ten time zones between himself and whatever Bannerman was calling about.

It was not that he disliked Bannerman personally.

Personally, the guy was hard not to like; and Susan, of course, was practically family. At the wedding, Bannerman couldn't have been nicer. Danced with the wife. Asked about the kids. Wanted to see pictures. But he was being Paul Bannerman then. Mama's Boy was a different story. Kaplan hated that there had to be people like Mama's Boy. He hated that his country, a nation of laws, sometimes felt the need to use them.

Clew had returned the call, not waiting to play out the point. And yet he tells Bannerman that they finished a set. Already, this was enough for Kaplan. He didn't want to hear, not even Clew's end of it. He wanted to stick his fingers in his ears except that it would have looked too stupid. Then Clew mentioned his name. Quoting him. Even asking Bannerman if he wanted to talk to him. Bannerman didn't, thank God.

The next bad sign came right after the call. Their fourth for tennis this morning was Kevin Aylward—he's this loopy, right-wing columnist for the *Washington Post*. Roger had asked him to go have some coffee, give the rest of them a few minutes of privacy. But he did it with a wink as in, "Be cool, Kevin. I'll fill you in later."

Kaplan tried to excuse himself as well. But Clew says, "No, no. You might as well hear it. Otherwise, you'll wonder about it and it's not that big a deal."

On his mother's grave, thought Kaplan, he would not have wondered.

Also, when Roger says it's not that big a deal, especially in connection with Bannerman, it usually means that the potential loss of life is only in the single digits. Kaplan knew this.

He *knew* it.

Which is why he should not have been surprised when, as Clew was briefing Barton Fuller, he kept seeing these little flickers of eye contact that said, "I'll fill in the blanks after Irwin goes. You know how he gets. Bannerman makes him nervous."

He tried to tell himself he was imagining it. That it was just a conditioned reflex to Roger's personality. But Fuller was doing it, too. Or at least he was failing to ask obvious questions, or he was frowning at places that did not seem to call for a frown.

Fine.

There was something they didn't want him to know about. Fine with him. If it didn't relate to his job, he didn't want to know anyway.

"Tell you what," he said, rising. "I think three's a crowd here." Kaplan fished for his car keys.

Barton Fuller nodded with a sigh, then raised both hands. "Please stay," he said. "It's not what you think."

"What I think is that you two are playing games with Bannerman again and I don't want any part of it. I particularly resent Roger, here, bringing my name into a conversation that was less than candid."

"Roger did not lie to Paul."

Kaplan twisted his lip doubtfully. "Carla's boyfriend," he asked. "Is he a Russian agent or isn't he?"

Clew started to speak, the beginnings of a denial, but the older man stopped him. "We're not sure," he said. "That's the truth, Irwin."

"Fine. Except that Roger as much as swore that this Corsini guy is just another wheeler-dealer who just might have had a nodding acquaintance with a Maf or two over the years but is otherwise basically clean."

"Irwin . . ." With a gesture, Fuller put this last aside. "What made you ask that question? About Corsini being an agent, I mean."

"Look where he's done business. He had to have had a connection, high up, and, at the very least, he'd do favors to protect that relationship."

"That would make him an asset. Not an agent."

Kaplan turned to Roger. "Is the guy making money?"

"Some."

"But not big bucks, right?"

"Not that I could find."

"So whatever he does, it doesn't seem to be making him rich. To me, it sounds like he gets mostly crumbs. Take away the profit motive and you've got either a lousy businessman or an agent-in-place."

Neither man answered. More eye contact.

Kaplan grimaced, his expression pained. "You know what offends me here? With all due respect? You think I'm stupid."

"I promise you," said Fuller, "that I don't."

"Is Bannerman stupid?"

Fuller's eyes narrowed. "What's your point, Irwin?"

"Do you think it'll take him any longer than it took me to draw the same conclusions about Carla's boyfriend? Why didn't you level with him?"

"About what? All this guesswork? Irwin, what we actually know is very little indeed."

"So instead, you've got him wondering why Roger here was checking this guy out all the way down to his dental charts."

Fuller stared for a long moment, then nodded slowly. It was clear that this line of thought disturbed him.

"Believe it or not," he said finally, "Roger was genuinely trying to be helpful."

Kaplan's cheek twitched. But he said nothing.

"As you know," said Fuller, "we have made mistakes with Paul in the past."

No shit, thought Kaplan.

Especially Roger the Dodger, here. Him and some of his grand schemes aimed at getting Bannerman and his people to end their wasteful, selfish, and unpatriotic retirement and coming back to work—exclusively, no more foreign clients—for State Department Intelligence, which is to say Roger Clew.

"The mistake here, *if there was one,*" said Fuller, "was that we tried to avoid the appearance of attempting to manipulate him again. When Roger came to me with what he learned about Aldo Corsini, I instructed him to say nothing to Paul unless asked and, even then, to let Paul make of it what he will."

"Yeah, well . . ." Kaplan's eyes said that he believed him. "You should have talked to him yourself."

"Meaning that he will be suspicious of anything Roger says?"

Kaplan shrugged. No offense, he thought, but Roger will zigzag if you ask him what he had for lunch.

It's funny, though. There was a time when Roger was the only human in the entire fed who Bannerman trusted. Which is how Bannerman ended up doing jobs for State as opposed to any of the intelligence services. Roger built his career on that. Being Mama's Boy's control. But Roger gets promoted again, back to the U.S. and the next guy, CIA this time, discovers that no contract agent, none of the good ones, will take a job unless Bannerman gave it the green light. The CIA guy saw this as contrary to the national interest and his solution was to make Mama's Boy disappear, probably under the pachysandra outside that dry-out clinic in Westport. In the end, Bannerman made him disappear instead.

Roger, meanwhile, is now a diplomat, but he hates it. Diplomacy is too slow. He yearns for the good old days when he could spell out a problem to Bannerman and Bannerman would say, "Let me think about it." A few days later, Clew would pick up a newspaper and find out that he didn't have a problem anymore.

Clew misses all this. It bugs him that Bannerman doesn't. Bannerman likes the quiet life in Westport too much and, besides, he's involved with this girl who is straight and who doesn't know from Mama's Boy—in the beginning anyway—and who, incidentally, happens to be Ray Lesko's daughter, which is how Irwin Kaplan got involved.

Long story. Forget it.

No . . . better not to forget. In short strokes, Clew hatches this scheme. The idea was to show Bannerman how vulnerable he is, how much he still needs friends in high places, but the scheme is so fucking intricate it naturally goes out of control and a bunch of people get dead. Roger, by rights, should have been one of them. Bannerman gave him a pass for old times' sake.

Kaplan had not answered Barton Fuller's last question. His mind had wandered. He waggled his fingers in apology. Fuller repeated it.

"He'll wonder," Kaplan answered. "Like I'm wondering."

"What Roger is holding back?"

"Among other things."

"What action, if any, will he take?"

Another pained expression. "What are you hoping for, Mr. Secretary?"

"It's Bart here, Irwin."

The grimace deepened. "It's Bart when all we're doing is playing tennis. With all respect, I think we're playing something else now."

Fuller sighed. "Tell him, Roger."

Clew leaned forward, anger in his eyes. "For the record, Irwin, I didn't call Bannerman. He called me."

Kaplan shrugged. He said nothing.

"No one is playing games with Bannerman. On the contrary, we're hoping that he will do nothing at all. If Aldo Corsini is an agent, we want him just where he is."

"I'll ask again. Is he or isn't he?"

"Somewhere near Genoa," Clew answered, "the former Soviet Union has in fact had an agent-in-place. The NSA has been intercepting his signals for years. First to the KGB compound at Karlhorst in East Germany and then, over the past two years, to Moscow Center. Except for a word here and there, his signals haven't been decoded, he's never been triangulated, and he's never been identified. The truth is that nobody cared that much. The only thing that was even interesting about this character was that the Karlhorst Compound was strictly Second Chief Directorate. Normally, an agent-in-place would have reported to the First Chief Directorate."

Kaplan saw what was coming at the mention of Genoa. He started to speak, but Clew waved him off.

"Don't get ahead of me," he said. "Moscow Center, these days, is basically a sort of elephants' burial ground for the old SCD hard-liners. The moderates prefer to use the building across the street. A signal to the First Chief Directorate, in any case, would go to Yasenevo, not Moscow Center. The SCD, whether hard-line or moderate, was tasked with Internal Security. They had no business running agents in Italy any more than our FBI is permitted to run agents abroad. That agent's sign-off, incidentally, is 'Barca.' You know what that means in Italian?"

"Boat?"

"It means *sailboat*, actually."

22

Elena could not stay mad at Lesko.

True, he was behaving boorishly. But she could hardly blame him. She had as much as lied to him.

At the very least, she had excluded him. And that in itself was wrong. This good man was her husband. She was carrying his child. To deceive him was to dishonor him. All that aside, he was entirely too perceptive not to have smelled several rats by now.

"I have to tell him," she said to Leo Belkin.

She said this as they waited at the fountain in GUM, sipping sweet champagne, after Lesko had gone to relieve himself. He was gone a long time. Twenty minutes. He had said that he would be back in five.

She could guess what he was doing with that time. He would have found a quiet place, perhaps a toilet stall, and he would sit there allowing his impressions of the last two hours to settle.

"What the hell is going on here?"

She could hear him asking that question, not of himself but of the dead policeman who was still a part of him.

"David? Why am I getting the feeling that I'm only along for the ride, here? Why do I think that, right now, those three are back at that fountain trying to decide how to handle me? That as soon as I show up, they're going to suddenly be talking about the weather."

Belkin lowered his eyes, nodding slowly, sadly.

"It's my fault," he said.

"No more than mine, Leo."

His lips moved as if searching for words. "When . . . I am in the West, I think with this." He touched his forehead. "I come home, I'm here two hours, and suddenly my soul is Russian again. Everything comes from here . . . and here." He touched his heart and then his gut.

She smiled, a hand on his arm. "If that is what makes a Russian, my friend, then Lesko is as Russian as you are."

A slight nod, more of politeness than of conviction.

Yes, he thought, Lesko is definitely emotional. He is generous, impulsive, utterly loyal to his friends and family. His word, once given, is inviolable. These are certainly Russian qualities.

But there is a difference.

In Lesko's entire life, Belkin felt sure, he had never done a thing of which he was thoroughly ashamed. Not once.

Lesko, himself, would probably argue to the contrary. He might even cite examples of those words and deeds that he regretted most. But they would be only that. Regrets. The occasional stupidities that come with being human. One would never hear, however, that Raymond Lesko stood mute as a friend was unjustly condemned. Or that he followed loathsome orders, without complaint, from men he despised. That he made no protest when good men, better men, were sent to prison on evidence that he knew to be false. That the man who murdered his own father . . .

"Leo . . . don't."

Elena had been watching him, seeing his thoughts on his face. She had heard them before, some of them, those he could bring himself to speak of. She looked up at Valentin. With her eyes and a small movement of her head, she asked that he go and see what was keeping Lesko.

"You are much too hard on yourself," she said when Valentin had gone.

He didn't answer. A quick shake of his head said, *Thank you, but you have no idea.*

"You and I, Leo," she answered as if she had heard him, "we both have had to find our souls."

He drained the champagne from his paper cup and crushed it. "I never should have brought you here," he said.

"I insisted, Leo," she reminded him. "It is only that I should have told Lesko."

He was thoughtful for a moment. "Let me tell him," he said. "I want him to understand how it was."

"He will understand. Simply tell him the truth."

A doubtful grunt. His shoulder was still tender where Lesko had gripped it. But he nodded.

"Leo?" She touched his chest. "I would like to hear the truth as well. The *whole* truth this time."

He looked at her. Then he had to look away. But again he nodded.

"Can I tell you both at dinner?" he asked. "At dinner it will be easier."

She understood, she thought. A restaurant. The more crowded the better. So that Lesko might think twice before reaching across the table for him.

"Dinner will be fine, Leo."

"You'll say nothing until then?"

"I'll try. I'll ask him to wait."

"But say nothing in your room, Elena. Not even with the shower running and the radio turned up loud. Not even—"

"Leo. I know all that."

He took a breath. "At dinner, then."

He would tell them, he thought. He would even show them. At the restaurant, if all goes well, they will see for themselves.

23

Barca.

Sailboat.

Irwin Kaplan said nothing at first.

His mind turned to his youngest daughter. This morning she had asked him to bag tennis just this once and take her out for an Egg McMuffin instead. The kid, he thought, must be psychic.

He knew whose line it was. He was supposed to say, *Aha! Sailboat! Carla's boyfriend must be Barca. He signals Moscow while he's out on his boat, which is why you had trouble triangulating him. His KGB control moved from Karlhorst to Moscow, which explains why Aldo switched his cover operations from Eastern Europe where there's money to Russia where there's colored paper.*

"If Aldo is Barca," he asked Roger instead, "what's it to you?"

"To State, you mean? As opposed to the CIA?"

Kaplan nodded.

"The State Department is the instrument of the President's foreign policy. Don't read too much into this, Irwin, but that is not necessarily true of the Central Intelligence Agency just as the KGB is not necessarily an instrument of Soviet reform."

"Okay, you want this guy for yourself. What's so important about Barca all of a sudden?"

"He might be part of a bigger picture. Something we've been trying to get a handle on. That's all I can tell you for now."

"In the meantime, you're going to let Carla Benedict marry a suspected KGB agent?"

Clew shook his head. "We'll intervene if it comes to that. And we'll explain to Paul why we were circumspect about sharing what is, as you point out, only a suspicion."

Kaplan could hear that conversation already. *Gee, Paul . . . even Irwin-the-straight-arrow-Kaplan said we should make sure before we said anything.* But that would cut very little ice if Carla got hurt because she had her guard down or if . . .

"Assume Aldo is Barca," he said. "What does he want with Carla Benedict?"

"Beyond the obvious?" Fuller tossed a hand. "We simply don't know."

"I guess I'm slow. Aside from sex, what's the obvious?"

"What he's achieved already, I suppose. Potentially exploitable connections with the Brugg family, with Paul Bannerman's network, and with virtually everyone else he met at that wedding."

Kaplan didn't buy this. If Aldo's an agent, his instructions would have been specific. A possibility, if Kaplan had to guess, was that the guy's interest in penetrating that bunch had to do with Elena's war against the Zurich druggies. But Aldo doesn't work for the traffickers. If Clew is right, he works for . . . Oh shit.

"Tell me straight out," Kaplan leaned forward. "Whatever you've got going here, are Lesko and Elena in on it?"

"Not at all."

"Could they find themselves in the middle of it? Being in Moscow, I mean?"

"It's crossed our minds. But we don't think so."

"Are we talking drugs here, or aren't we?"

Fuller hesitated, choosing his words. "If we're right, there are drugs in the equation but they're not central to it. I'll tell you this much. It involves the smuggling of a number of . . . commodities . . . into and out of several of the Russian republics."

Kaplan waited. Then, "That's all you're going to tell me?"

"Need to know, Irwin," Fuller reminded him. "Having said that, we're not even sure how much *we* know."

Kaplan cocked his head toward the terrace where the *Post* columnist, their fourth, was talking to one of Fuller's dogs. "Why would he know more about this than I do?"

Clew affected surprise. "Aylward? Who says he does?"

"Don't fuck with me, Roger."

Fuller cleared his throat. He grimaced, his face registering several different reactions in rapid succession. The first was annoyance, then dismay, and then something akin to admiration, this last directed at Irwin Kaplan.

"Kevin is a source," he said finally. "He heard some whispers. He investigated, picked up a piece here, another there. He came to Roger a few weeks ago, laid out his conclusions, and said that he was going to publish them. That would have been premature."

"So you made a deal." Kaplan nodded. "He sits tight in return for an exclusive."

A wan smile. "That, and getting to come here for tennis."

Irwin Kaplan grunted. He took a breath and blew it out slowly, taking time to think. Other questions were forming in his mind. He was not sure, now, that he wanted to ask them.

Why, to pick the most obvious one, did Barton Fuller give a rat's ass about smuggling in Russia? The answer? It depends. It depends on what they're smuggling.

Next question. Why doesn't Barton Fuller just call in the appropriate ambassador, tell him what he knows, and suggest that the ambassador call it to the attention of the KGB? The answer? The KGB, or someone within it, is probably involved. Who is that someone? It has to be Barca's control. Do we know who that person is? No. Which is why we're now probably going to put a serious surveillance team on Carla's boyfriend—if they haven't had one on him right along—establish that he is in fact Barca—if they don't know damned well already—and, if so, try to identify his KGB control through him.

But surveillance on the boyfriend, assuming that he and Carla are playing house, is also surveillance on Carla. What happens if she spots it? Carla, likely as not, might carve the spook up just on general principles. And how do you surveil Carla without, at the very least as a courtesy, clearing it with Bannerman? And yet, so far, they clearly intend to leave Bannerman in the dark.

"I'm going to make a prediction," he said to Fuller. "No. First I'm going make a judgment."

"Go ahead."

"What I think is going on here, is that the KGB, or a faction within it, is involved in large-scale smuggling. They're supposed to be controlling it, but instead they're grabbing a piece of it. How'm I doing?"

Blank faces. Clew asked, "Why would you think that?"

The DEA man curled his lip. "This takes a rocket scientist? What have we been talking about here?"

He could have gone further. He could have asked, for example, What else is new? Show me a law-enforcement agency in the whole world that doesn't have a problem with sticky fingers. We have cops and DEA agents who pocket confiscated cash and sell confiscated drugs. We have a CIA which, for years has been protecting the traffickers in return for intelligence while skimming drug profits to build up a war chest they don't have to tell Congress about. We have . . .

Kaplan stopped himself. "A KGB war chest?" he asked Fuller. "Is that where your head is?"

The secretary hesitated. "Partly. Perhaps."

"You're going to worry about the KGB building up a

stash? That's your big rumor? Of course they're building up a stash.''

Fuller's expression was thoughtful. Clew's bordered on petulance. He asked, "Does your omniscience suggest a reason why, Irwin?"

"Why? Because they can. Why does a dog lick his ass?" Another hard stare from Clew.

"Okay." Kaplan threw up his hands. "You want a conspiracy? It's a religious thing. The stash is for the second coming of Lenin and to buy new statues for all those empty pedestals. Any money left over, they'll buy retirement dachas in Palm Beach."

Barton Fuller's mouth showed the hint of a smile. It quickly faded. "It might be a bit more serious than that, Irwin."

"So you keep hinting. I don't want to know."

Fuller held his gaze. "Fair enough," he said finally. "You mentioned a prediction. What is it?"

"Predictions are fallible. This is more like a prophecy." Fuller waited.

"Whatever Roger here wants to do, it's going to go wrong." He turned to Clew. "This is no offense, Roger. You're a smart guy and your heart's mostly in the right place. But you want to know what your problem is?"

Clew's eyes were cold. "Some other time, Irwin."

"You're so fucking . . . circuitous. You got a mind like a corkscrew. You hatch these plans that are so goddamned complex, they're like Murphy's Law waiting to happen."

Clew reddened. He started to speak. Kaplan waved him off.

"And I'll tell you something else. You have learned absolutely nothing from the last two times you tried to diddle Bannerman. I'd watch out for that third strike if I were you."

Fuller frowned. "Explain that, Irwin."

Kaplan sat back. "It's all I have to say."

"I, Barton Fuller, am telling you straight that we've gone out of our way not to involve Paul. Why do you think otherwise?"

"I don't know. Past experience."

"We've made mistakes. We've learned from them. What else?"

"You can't not involve Carla Benedict. Your best hope is that Bannerman will decide she's a big girl and that he has better things to do than wonder about this Corsini guy."

Fuller nodded thoughtfully. He reached for his racquet but made no move to rise. He tapped it against his knee.

"Good advice, Irwin," he said. "And with your usual candor."

"Like I said, no offense."

"Well . . . on that score, you might owe Roger an apology. The fact is . . . the subject at hand happens to be fairly straightforward. A particular thing is happening or it isn't."

Kaplan's lips moved. He seemed to be struggling with himself.

"The phrase you're trying to think of," said Clew icily, "is *I'm sorry*."

Kaplan blinked, then shook his head. That was not where his head was. Then, to Fuller, very softly, reluctantly, "Is it nukes?"

"I beg your pardon?"

He hated asking. Repeating was even worse. "Tactical nuclear weapons," he said at last. "Is that the commodity? Is that what you think someone's peddling?"

"In for a penny, Irwin."

"Forget I asked."

But he had asked. And he realized what had put the thought in his head. Kevin Aylward's column. Aylward, maybe three weeks before, had done a series dealing with the redeployment of the Soviet nuclear arsenal after the breakup of the old Soviet Union. He said, basically, that we'd never get a reliable accounting of the Soviet weapons inventory because many were hidden after the START treaty was signed and more disappeared during the chaos that followed the Gorbachev coup.

He also ran a story about a mini-Chernobyl that's supposed to have happened in the past two or three months. Something, he thinks maybe radioactivity, got into the air and wiped out a couple of villages in the Urals. The source was a truck driver who was brought in to help bury the dead and then realized he was worm food if he hung around. The truck driver, bloody, his face all blistered, staggered into the next village where he told someone who told someone else. Then the truck driver stole a bike and took off. But one witness, according to Aylward, claimed to have snuck back to the guy's burned-out truck where he says armed men were winching it onto a flatbed. He says he counted dozens of bullet holes in both trucks.

The Russians hit the ceiling. Said the whole thing was nonsense. If this truck driver exists, produce him. If others claim to have spoken to him, produce them. If the villages you name have become radioactive wastelands, why are they now fully occupied and their citizens busy with spring planting? Come see, they told the American ambassador. We invite you. We invite even this xenophobic, red-bashing drunk of a columnist and ask him finally to put up or shut up.

The ambassador sent a couple of aides, but the trip wasn't necessary. Satellite photographs had already showed normal activity, normal occupancy. The NSA said its sensors picked up no evidence of nuclear contamination. This cut no ice with Aylward, who now claimed a massive cover-up. Everyone's in on it. Even the NSA.

This, however, was typical Kevin Aylward. The voice of doom. Someone pointed out that Aylward has accurately predicted ten of the last three recessions. For twenty years now, the guy's been predicting the imminent collapse of the American economy, mass cancer due to ozone depletion, not to mention nuclear winter. Once, just before he checked into Betty Ford, he was telling anyone who'd listen that Ronald Wilson Reagan, six letters in each name, translated to 666, which is the symbol of the Antichrist.

For all that—and not that Kaplan believed the story—he hoped that truck driver made it. The guy, if he existed, had a lot of heart.

"Irwin?"

"I'm not playing tennis here anymore, either. Not with that wacko."

"That wacko has sources. They've been reliable in the past."

"And he won't reveal them, right? That's because they're probably on Venus."

Kaplan pushed to his feet. He turned away, one hand in his pocket, fingering his car keys again.

"Is it nukes?" he asked again.

Fuller wet his lips. "No."

Kaplan stared out over the tennis court. "Okay. What?"

"A question first. If I should ever ask you, as a personal favor, to sit down with Paul Bannerman on my behalf, would you do it?"

"What for?"

"To keep him out of this. I thought Roger had. Now you've caused me to wonder."

"Why me?"

"You won't lie to him. He knows that."

"Anyway, no."

"With Lesko, then. The two of you could see Bannerman together."

"Maybe. If I can know I'm not lying."

"You won't be. How much do you know about nerve gas, Irwin?"

24

At the Russian embassy in Bern, ten minutes from his flat, Yuri Rykov signed in and made his way to the KGB communications center on the top floor, rear.

He pushed his ID card into a slot and waited. A recording asked him to give his name and rank. He did so, waiting again as a machine verified his voiceprint. After several seconds, the door clicked open electronically.

He would not be alone, as he had hoped. Another officer, a woman, was seated at one of the computer consoles. Her presence made him uncomfortable.

This discomfort, he realized, was in part reactionary. Until the reforms, there had been no female officers in the KGB except for bookkeepers and archivists. Otherwise, all

KGB officers were male, strictly Russian, and were members of the Communist party. Now, he thought, it is like affirmative action in America. Recruitment is from both sexes, and you can come from any republic as long as you are not a Moslem or a Jew. Party membership, of course, is no longer a requirement, but a respect for Socialist ideals remains an unwritten prerequisite. Better, as General Belkin says, to believe in something than to believe in nothing. It is why the CIA recruits so many Mormons and the FBI so many Catholics.

There were two other reasons why he wished that this woman was not there. The first was that they had briefly been lovers. For just one night, and regretted even before breakfast. The second was that she would smell Carla on him. All women have that gift. Even Susan Lesko, from three thousand miles away, heard in his voice that he had done more than put Carla to bed.

"She is better now," he had told her. "Even in her sleep she has a little smile."

"Um . . . good work, Yuri," was what she answered. In Susan's voice as well there was a smile.

Perhaps he imagined it. Perhaps it was simply an expression of relief after he finished relating, in possibly excessive detail, Carla's account of her confrontation with Aldo Corsini.

During that part of the call, all she could say was, "My God." She said it many times. This and "Poor Carla."

Susan explained that they would be coming. She and Bannerman. There would probably be others, but that was not yet decided. They would come as if nothing were amiss. Bringing gifts as if to celebrate Carla's betrothal and as if to become better acquainted with Corsini.

As she told him this, he thought he heard a measure of satisfaction in her voice, a level of enthusiasm that one would normally associate with the author of a plan. She might well have been. It seemed the sort of notion a woman might come up with, but a sensible way to proceed nonetheless. This made it all the more urgent, however, that he clean up Carla's boathouse.

Yuri had also placed a call to General Belkin at the

Savoy. His party had not yet arrived. It was just as well. In a few minutes, Yuri might have more to tell him.

He took a seat at one of the consoles, turned on the power, and tapped into the mainframe. Next, he entered his identifier. A menu appeared. He called up the file on KGB field agents and assets.

Yuri's clearance did not permit him full access to this file, but at least he could see if a file existed. He entered the name CORSINI, ALDO, and hit a key.

The machine chugged and mumbled as if considering his request. The words CORSINI, ALDO—REF. BARCA—ACCESS RESTRICTED—02–4–238–4412 crept across the screen.

Yuri grimaced in annoyance. There was a file. It was something. But it might mean very little. He had no idea what "Ref. Barca" meant, and that series of numbers did not look like any designator code he'd ever seen. He tried typing in BARCA. He hit a key. More chugging. A similar response. BARCA—REF. CORSINI, ALDO—ACCESS RESTRICTED— 02–4–238–4412.

Interesting, he thought. Corsini and Barca must be the same. Or, on second thought, Barca could be almost anything. A cable address for Corsini, the name of a group of which he was part, even a company name. Not very helpful.

The problem was in the design of the filing system. It listed both agents and assets together. A security measure of sorts. A spy or a potential defector would not be able to distinguish between the two unless he could decipher the designator and then ask for still another code through an automatic hookup with either Yasenevo or Moscow Central. Which meant he would need to have a collaborator there. All very complicated.

This listing for Aldo Corsini showed no designator code. For all Yuri knew, he was only an asset, albeit a particularly ambitious one. To be listed as an asset, however, meant very little. Once, in London, Yuri had rented a furnished room from a distracted old woman with terrible breath who had asked no questions and dealt strictly in cash. Even that woman was now on this list. He had put her there. She was an asset of some possible future use, but for all an intruder

would know, that old woman in London could be Mata
Hari.

"Lydia?" He leaned back in his chair, turning toward the
young female officer who had been studiously ignoring
him.

She did not answer. He tried again, a little louder.

She raised her head slightly. "You will address me
correctly." She bit off the words. "I am Lieutenant Voinovitch."

Yuri sighed. Again and again, he had tried to be cordial
with her. The problem was that on the night when he took
her home with him, she had been quite drunk. There had
been a party celebrating General Belkin's promotion. Too
many toasts. Voinovitch, a code and cipher officer whose
behavior was normally very correct, was finally letting her
hair down. Normally it is in a bun, tied tight like the rest of
her.

She became a coquette. But this role was clearly unfamiliar to her and she played it awkwardly. Her intentions,
however, were clear. From his point of view, she was not so
bad looking, and also he was a little drunk himself. He and
Maria had not yet been intimate, so there was no question of
betrayal and the bad luck that comes with it. Voinovitch was
offering herself. As with Carla, he could not refuse her.

But, unlike Carla, the pleasures of lovemaking seemed
new to her as well. She would not undress fully and she
insisted that all lights be turned off. Suddenly, she was prim
and proper again. She had also been passive. She barely
moved, leaving everything to him.

Finally, came the sex. She remained limp. She stared up
at him, no expression, all the while. When it was over, she
turned on her side, curled herself up, and began sobbing.
He tried to soothe her. She shook him off. Then she leaned
over the edge of his bed and vomited on top of his shoes.

Still, he tried to comfort her. He told her that it was only
the vodka. That, and his failure to put her sufficiently at
ease. He suggested that they try again, with a little more talk
this time, even a few jokes. Sex is fun, he said. It should not
be taken too seriously. For this, she called him a dirty name.
From that day to this, they had barely spoken.

"Very well," he said to her now. "You are Lieutenant

Voinovitch. Major Rykov is telling you to come look at this screen.''

She wrinkled her nose, but she stood up. He watched her. Such a shame, he thought. A good body, proud posture, wonderful hips. She was standing at his side now, pretending to look at the screen, but there goes that nose again. He could tell that she was sniffing him. He wished he had thought to use cologne.

''What do those numbers mean?'' he asked.

She leaned over, reading them. ''You are not cleared,'' she said. She turned away.

This was too much.

Yuri grabbed her arm, snarling at her. ''Enough,'' he barked. ''I have tried my best with you. I have no more time for this. In ten seconds, *Lydia,* you are going to be across my knee.''

She trembled. A shine came into her eyes. Her chest began heaving. Yuri, seeing this, groaned inwardly. It was fast becoming apparent that he had used the wrong technique during their previous encounter. Their notions of fun, with respect to sex, were not the same.

She wet her lips. Her chest rose several times before at last she touched the screen with her finger.

''This number,'' she said thickly, ''is a numerical code. It shows the date of the restriction and who ordered it.''

Yuri studied the number. 02–4–238–4412. He touched a finger to the first two digits. ''This 02, then, is Second Chief Directorate?''

''They still seem to be calling it that, yes.''

''And the others?''

''The next two sets are a date, also in code, showing when the restriction was ordered. This one is from last September. In the last set of digits, 44 identifies the officer and 12 states the reason. 12 is always the reason. It means national security.''

''Who is the officer?''

She did not answer.

His hand still gripped her upper arm. He squeezed it. Hard.

''I . . . am not authorized.'' Her voice took a hitch. ''Even if I am beaten.''

Yuri's eyes became hooded.

"Why . . ." She swallowed hard before continuing. "Why do you smell of lemons?"

Yuri sagged. But better lemons than Carla. He thought of telling her that he scratched himself on thorns and rubbed lemon juice into his wounds to increase his suffering. The answer would probably please her, but he had no wish to arouse her appetites beyond their present state. He tapped a finger against the screen.

"Have you ever seen these names before? Barca and Corsini?"

"No."

An idea struck him. "How can I see what other files have been restricted by this same officer?"

"Turn your head," she told him.

Yuri obeyed. She reached past him and touched a series of keys. A list scrolled onto the screen. It contained about a dozen names in alphabetical order, each followed by another numerical code. All of the names, except one, meant nothing to him. But the name second from the top, after Barca, read BENEDICT, CARLA.

He pointed to the code after her name. "All the date codes are the same except for that of this woman. What date is this?"

"Eighteen, February. This year."

Nearly three months ago, thought Yuri. According to Carla, that was approximately when her relationship with Aldo became serious. Aldo must have reported his conquest and all access to her file was then ordered to be restricted. But by whom?

And what of the other names on this list, and what did they have in common? Nearly all were of different nationalities. Members of some sort of network? He memorized the names as best he could.

"Lydia . . . who is your commanding officer?"

"General Belkin."

"And I am his aide. I am asking you in his name. This 44 is obviously running illegals in the West and the SCD has no such authority. Who is number 44?"

"General Belkin must ask."

"Very well. We stay here until he calls. But I have urgent duties in Zurich and you are keeping me from them."

She grunted doubtfully. "More likely a woman in Zurich," she said. "One more to your taste."

Exasperated, Yuri made a fist with his free hand. He used it to punch his own head. "Then come with me if you like," he growled at her. "You like pain? I'll show you pain."

It was his fatigue talking. His impatience. He did not mean it. He shook his head. "I'm sorry. Never mind that."

But he felt that she had softened. He glanced up at her. An odd expression. He had thought that she was baiting him, but now what he saw looked very much like disappointment.

Yuri had an intuition. He did not much like himself for it, but the clock was running. "You would not have the stomach for it," he said. "Besides, I might end up ripping your uniform off."

She moistened her lips. "What sort of duties?"

He took the chance. "A man has been killed. Cut to bits. It is nothing for a woman to see."

She began to tremble. That shine returned to her eyes. "I am . . . not so delicate as you think."

Yuri had no doubt of that. What happened, he wondered, to the psychological testing procedures of the KGB? Had they been dispensed with in the rush toward reform? If not, how is it that this woman gets Foreign Intelligence duty instead of, for example, the job of interrogator at Lefortovo prison. All the same, he could use her. If only to have a second pair of eyes and to have a driver in case his own eyes should grow heavy.

"Who is 44? Do you know?"

She shook her head, then cocked it toward his machine. "I can ask. But why?"

Yuri took a chance. "The man who has been killed seems to work for him. Let's see what we're getting into."

She hesitated. Then, "Turn your head."

Again, Yuri obeyed. He released her arm. She rubbed it for what seemed a long time before reaching for the keys. He listened as she typed in an identifier, then another series of letters. The machine chugged.

"Hmmph," she muttered.

Yuri peeked. The screen said ACCESS DENIED, followed by another code.

She pushed his face away. "I will try something else." She worked the keys again for what seemed like a full minute. One message after another appeared on the screen and quickly blinked off as if she were picking her way through an electronic maze. She hit the return key, the screen lit up, she stood erect.

"He is one of these," she said.

Yuri looked. There were eight names, alphabetical, all with the same surname, followed by designator codes. The surname was BOROVIK. Yuri stared at it, one eye closed. It seemed to ring a distant bell.

"These two"—she touched the screen—"are television commentators in Moscow. They are father and son. No association with KGB."

Lydia squinted to read the other codes. "This one is a physicist and that one is a dancer who defected ten years ago. The other four are all KGB. One captain, one major . . . not enough rank there . . . one major general . . . and one colonel, but the colonel appears to be deceased."

She said "Hmmph" again. She played more keys.

An abbreviated biography appeared on the screen under the name BOROVIK, GENNADI YAKOVICH.

They read it together although Yuri did not know why Lydia had called it up. A dead man was hardly number 44.

Yuri glossed over the biographical details. Nothing striking in them. A man of modest credentials who nonetheless managed to be promoted fairly regularly. This deceased colonel had last been assigned to the old Fifth Directorate—ideology and dissidents—stationed in Leningrad. Dead eight years. Murdered. Body mutilated. Circumstances and details are classified. Several confessions, two executions. Confessions now regarded as illegitimate. Status of investigation: closed.

"I thought so," said Voinovitch. She returned to the alphabetical list. "Same patronymic. That one and this one were brothers. Why would they close such an investigation?"

Yuri wasn't sure that he cared. "Bring up the other one."

More keys. A second biography washed down from the top—BOROVIK, VADIM YAKOVICH.

Yuri read this one more carefully. Like his brother—born in Sverdlovsk, which is now Yekaterinburg. Father was the party boss there. No education beyond high school, no languages, no technical training. And yet he was made Deputy Minister of Mines when not even Yuri's age. Typical.

Applied KGB in 1966. Assigned Second Chief Directorate. Stationed in Prague 1968–69, promoted, Budapest after that, promoted, back to Moscow, promoted, to East Germany as deputy commander of the Karlhorst Compound, back to Moscow when Germany was reunited. Never traveled to the West. Steady promotions and yet he was never sent to the KGB Higher School or even Higher Party School.

Yuri was frowning. This was the resume of a goon.

The KGB had seen nothing in him worth developing. Take away his father's influence and he would have been pounding rocks in the gold and emerald mines of Sverdlovsk or sweeping some factory floor. A bag of stolen emeralds probably got him into the KGB in the first place.

How come the promotions? Answer is simple. More emeralds from his papa in Sverdlovsk. But also he does what he is told.

"This Borovik," he asked Lydia Voinovitch. "What is his job now?"

Lydia asked the machine. It answered with another designator code.

"Looks like . . ." She rocked her hand as if specificity was eluding her. "Investigation of black-market activities . . . smugglers . . . that sort of thing."

"It doesn't say straight out?"

She pointed to a series of numbers. "These are clearances," she said. "They refer to certain categories of files to which his orders give him access. They all involve the black market one way or the other. He seems to be on a special assignment of some kind."

"Reporting to whom?"

She shrugged. "There is no indication. But probably to his deputy chairman or to the Special Inspectorate."

Yuri frowned again. This last was the equivalent of an inspector general's office. Or it used to be. Now it had become a repository for the grayest of the gray men. Many had been members of the Party Committee—the ideological watchdogs of the KGB—until Gorbachev decreed that they no longer had jobs. Positions had to be found for them. Their incomes and privileges were to be assured but foreign travel was to be denied them. Otherwise half of them would fly to New York in search of literary agents.

On the one hand, Yuri was excited, although he took care not to show it. General Belkin had gone to Moscow hoping to beat the bushes. Flush out some men for whom he had no names or faces. This, at least, is what he claimed, and Yuri would not presume to doubt him even though such a speculative tactic was not so typical of him. Borovik, in any case, could be one of them. So much seemed to fit. An illegal network. Aldo Corsini a part of it. Carla Benedict listed as if she were part of it, but he knew that to be impossible. She is clearly seen as an asset. An entry to the Bruggs. A means of penetration.

On the other hand, he was troubled. Two things bothered him. The first was that this Borovik, if all else was true, seemed to have a great advantage over General Belkin. He would be waiting for him. On his own ground.

The second—a contradiction—was that Borovik could *not* be the man. What was being done, if General Belkin was right, required intelligence and a talent for organization. It required something of a visionary. Borovik was merely a goon.

But whose goon? The goon of how many?

How he wished that General Belkin would call.

"Major Rykov? Yuri?"

He rubbed his eyes. "Yes, Lydia."

"This dead man in Zurich. He is *svoi*?"

"Definitely not."

"An enemy?"

He nodded. "A criminal. A lowlife."

To anyone else he might have added, as encouragement, that Corsini is a man who beats women. With Voinovitch, however, it was doubtful that such a pronouncement would have the desired effect.

"Will there be danger?" she asked.

He started to shake his head. There would be the scrubbing of walls and floors. There would be the binding of a body, tying weights to it, and perhaps rowing it to the deepest part of Lake Zurich. He had not decided yet. There would be the disposition of Corsini's car. There would be fighting sleep, and afterward, there would probably be the task of relieving this woman's excitement. But there would probably be no danger.

"Very possibly," he said. An answer to the contrary would have disappointed her.

"We will need weapons."

He doubted it but he nodded. Weapons would please her. All the more if they were illegal. He could not very well go down to Embassy Security and sign out two Makarovs. General Belkin, however, kept two or three confiscated pistols in his office safe. They were not of the best quality, but they were unrecorded.

As for Lydia, he had not actually promised that he would take her with him. Not firmly. But now he could not leave her in any case. No telling what she might do, whom she might call, if left alone with her thoughts, resenting that he had gulled her.

What he really wished was that he could trust her to stay and wait for General Belkin to call. He could leave her a message, carefully worded, to be read to him verbatim. But what, he asked himself, would be the greater risk? Trusting her to do that without first calling someone else? Or leaving General Belkin in ignorance awhile longer.

The answer was neither. The greater risk would be the untimely discovery of what had become of Aldo Corsini.

Who could tell what a goon might do?

25

Red Square was brightly lit.

Cobblestones gleamed and St. Basil's glistened, its exuberant swirls of color even brighter against the darkening sky. Beyond was the Rossiya Hotel, so impersonally massive, thought Elena, when seen in daylight. Now it seemed almost inviting.

She hugged her new husband's arm. She felt good.

Soon, over a nice supper, she and Leo would explain everything to him. Everything. She would see to it that Leo filled in a few blanks. For her own part, she would explain that her intention was not so much to deceive him as it was to humor Leo Belkin and, above all, not to miss this chance to see Moscow. He would grumble for a while but he would understand. A weight had been lifted.

Not so, she feared, with poor Leo.

He was on her right arm, his lips moving soundlessly. He was probably rehearsing what he might say at dinner. Finding a way to make his theories sound more plausible than they had to her. And perhaps still puzzling over the restoration of Lesko's good humor.

KGB disease.

He kept glancing over toward the Kremlin, toward those guards at the Spassky Gate. He must have felt her eyes on him because now he raised his watch, pretending that he was only checking the time against the clock in the Savior's Tower. But she knew that he was looking for that officer.

Was the officer watching for him? Had the officer called to report that a certain General Belkin was nosing around the Kremlin with unauthorized visitors? That, after all, was surely Leo's purpose in making a scene there earlier. And if the officer did call, had anyone cared? She had seen no sign of surveillance.

Elena squeezed him. When he did not respond, she

pinched him. Relax, Leo. She scolded him with her eyes. If they want to watch us, let them watch. Let them scurry in and out of their holes. If they show themselves, so be it.

She shook her head bemusedly.

Paranoia, she thought. It must be a genetic trait here.

It begins to seem as much a part of the Russian psyche as officiousness is to a German or stoicism to a Swede. It must also be a virus, borne in the Moscow air. She feared that she was catching it herself.

Take Lesko, for example.

She had expected him to return demanding answers. She felt sure that he would rejoin them, Valentin in tow, having had a full half hour to be alone with his thoughts, and he would place his hands across the back of Leo Belkin's neck.

"Okay Leo. Time to level."

There would be no waiting for a quiet talk over dinner.

"No more games, Leo."

He would refrain, in deference to her, from saying *"No more bullshit,"* but the word would be implicit.

"I want it straight. What the hell are you getting us into?"

But he had done nothing of the sort. If anything, he seemed restored, even pleased with himself.

She knew that look. It usually bespoke some private triumph. It was there each time he came home from one of his German lessons, which she was not supposed to know he was taking. It was there when he fixed a problem with her car after it had baffled the chauffeur. Or when he had bought her some . . .

Of course.

A gift.

This was a department store. She could see a small bulge in the pocket of his topcoat. He had bought her a gift. If so, he had probably bent the law in some way and would, therefore, not give it to her in the presence of their host.

Poor Leo.

He sees a Lesko who is suddenly in high good humor and he has no idea what to make of it. This newly appreciative Lesko had rejoined them at the fountain, carrying on about the architectural glories of GUM, saying that one day it will be all Waldenbooks, Radio Shack, and Sears Roebuck.

Leo had stared in the direction from which Lesko had
come as if searching for a clue to his behavior. Next he had
shot a questioning glance at Valentin. Valentin could only
shrug.

"Ah . . . may I know what brought about this change
in you?" he asked.

Also a shrug. "The pause that refreshes, Leo."

Belkin blinked, not comprehending.

"No big deal. I got something out of my system."

A cryptic reply. The dual meaning was clear to Elena, but
she could see that Leo was struggling with it, attempting to
decode it, wondering what could possibly have transpired
during his brief absence. What he might have learned.

She sighed inwardly. KGB. CIA. Different names, same
disease.

"Come." She took Lesko's arm, then that of Leo Belkin.
"We will start our wedding trip from here."

26

This is stupid, thought the Sicilian.

All of it.

For the second time in as many hours, he had driven past
the little stone boathouse on Lake Zurich. There were no
lights inside before. There were none now. Carla Benedict's
Volkswagen was still by the stairs that led to her apartment
on the second floor. Corsini's car was nowhere in sight. He
had even telephoned the house to see if Carla, at least,
would answer. He would pretend to have misdialed. The
phone rang and rang.

So what does this mean? It means that they are someplace
else. Maybe having dinner, maybe feeding their damned
swans again. More likely, Borovik was right. They went
someplace to fuck.

Is it so strange that Corsini has failed to report when expected?

The question is a joke.

With Aldo, it is strange when he *does* report on schedule. It means that he managed to get all the way to the transmitter without spotting a big pair of tits enroute. Aldo and his tits.

But Borovik says, ''I want him now. Find him.''

He had hoped to avoid talking to Borovik. It was bad enough being told to contact Moscow Center by telephone. Or rather to have Corsini do it. The Sicilian thought he'd better call himself. Find out what's going on here.

Procedure for calling Moscow Center, emergencies only, was to ring the new Press Information Office and then ask to be transferred to a certain Major Viktor. This was Podolsk. The Sicilian did so but, to his instant dismay, they patched him through to Borovik instead.

Podolsk has a stiff neck sometimes, but at least he listens to reason. Get him to Italy and he is almost fun. Borovik, especially lately, is something else entirely. Especially since this wedding.

No. It started before that.

The Sicilian knew when it started. It started when Aldo learned that Mama's Boy would be coming and this was reported to Borovik. That he was invited should have come as no surprise but it made Borovik crazy.

Why? Who knows.

Aldo seems to know, but he is irritatingly coy about it. He says that it is a personal matter. He says that to speak of it would be to betray a confidence. He says that it has nothing to do with our business.

Fine.

Then don't involve me.

The Sicilian had refused to go anywhere near the wedding, using the excuse that someone might show up who knew him. As it happened, several did.

Now Aldo tries to make light of it. He says that all Borovik wants to know is why this wedding trip to Russia. It is *not* all. The first question Borovik asked was if Bannerman intended to accompany them. Is this a reasonable question? When he asks it you can hear the hatred in his voice. When the answer is no, what you hear is disappointment. It is like the grumbling of a cat when the mouse has safely reached its hole.

Today, once again, the Sicilian could hear that hatred. This was not a good thing. But he did not argue with Borovik. He wanted to get off the line before Borovik forgot himself and spoke a name. Borovik's end might be secure—stress *might*—but his was certainly not.

He was sorely tempted to remind Borovik that a flash-code communicator is not a toy. Nor is it a beeper that says call the office. A signal goes up, it bounces off a satellite, it comes down to Ostankino, the only satellite link in all of Russia, and then it is relayed to Moscow Center. Anyone can hear it along the way. Anyone can pick it up. They can't read the code, perhaps, but they know approximately where it originated and they know that something important must be going on. A legitimate emergency is one thing. "Aldo, call home" is something else.

"Find him," he says.

But where?

The maid at Willem Brugg's house says that they left hours ago. There is no answer at Aldo's hotel. What now? Does he get a flashlight and shine it into the back seat of every parked black Audi he sees?

Corsini and Borovik, he thought disgustedly. The two weakest links.

If they had followed the careers for which they were best suited, Corsini would star in pornographic films and Borovik would be a vivisectionist.

With Borovik, pain is everything. Some argue that it's power, but this is nonsense. Power is for the faceless men who pull his strings. To Borovik, power and wealth would mean nothing if he could no longer inflict pain.

With Aldo, it is his cock.

He likes to boast of all the different places in which he has had women. Give me five minutes, he would say, any place, any time, with any normal woman and I will have her sitting in a puddle. Give me ten minutes and I could make a veal chop come.

On one occasion, he told of making love in a church. He was there to watch an infant being baptized, but Aldo had his own idea of what constituted a christening. So he worked his fingers on the woman he was with and soon they are in the confessional and the woman is performing oral sex on him. That, at least, was what he claimed.

The Sicilian could have slapped him cross-eyed for that one. A church is a church.

Lately, however, since his seduction of Carla Benedict, Aldo's behavior has undergone a subtle change. He has never once boasted about sex with Carla. How he makes her gasp and moan. How hard she tries to please him. Instead, he only smiles. He holds his chin a little higher.

At first, the Sicilian thought that Corsini might have developed a measure of sensitivity toward an associate who does not happen to share his sexual preferences. But it wasn't that at all. His remarks about fags and queens came as frequently as before.

He might also have realized that this particular associate could be sick to death of hearing about the famous Carla Benedict. Carla and her knife. That overblown reputation. The Sicilian had a reputation of his own, and sometimes—he would admit it—it gnawed at him to always hear that she was so much better.

But it was not either of these that accounted for the change in Aldo. What was happening, the Sicilian feared, was that Aldo has discovered a new path to manhood.

To Corsini, a woman bedded is a woman reduced. If she becomes less, he becomes more. If that woman is a Carla Benedict, he becomes *much* more. If that is the direction in which his mind has turned, it will truly be time to slap his face before he gets that cock of his cut off.

Which brings us back to finding him, thought the Sicilian.

It struck him that Aldo might be in that house with Carla after all. Doubtful, but possible. His car might have been left elsewhere for any number of reasons. Or he might have parked it inside those double doors in the space where boats are stored for the winter. Hidden it so that he would not be bothered. She might have turned down the volume on her telephone. They could have spent the afternoon making love and then, drowsy from the Bruggs' champagne, have fallen asleep.

The Sicilian grunted aloud. He wiped that picture from

his mind, certain that Aldo Corsini has enough sexual fantasies of his own without more being provided for him.

Falling asleep, however, would explain no lights. Also no report to Podolsk. The Sicilian had no wish to call again and have Borovik ask him why he did not at least take a closer look inside the boathouse. Say "boathouse" over an open telephone line and you might as well say Carla's name.

He would drive by once again.

If still no lights, he would go in on foot.

27

At his uncle Pyotr's garage on Kurskaya, Ratmir's hands had at last stopped trembling.

Three glasses of good Georgian cognac had helped. So had some food. Ratmir had told his uncle that he was too upset to eat, but that was before Uncle Pyotr produced a whole half of a chicken, all for him. Also some cold beet salad and two thick slices of bread on which he could have his choice of honey, raspberry preserves, or butter.

Ratmir spread all three on the rich black *chorny*. His uncle did not object. Just the opposite. He smiled. The smile was because the first taste of this wonderful food had caused his nephew to weep. It was also because Uncle Pyotr liked to show how rich he was from time to time.

He was entitled, thought Ratmir. Uncle Pyotr had always been the smartest one in the family. The war had taught him. Twelve years in the camps had taught him. His whole life had taught him. Uncle Pyotr knew how to do more than survive.

The first thing he did when Ratmir arrived was to clean the blood from the sleeves of his jacket. Ratmir had not even realized that it was there. He knew that there was blood on his mallet, however, and he was about to throw it into his uncle's coal stove, but Uncle Pyotr said no. This wastes a good tool.

Instead, Uncle Pyotr washed the mallet and then dried it with a welding torch. In the end, the mallet was a little charred but it was otherwise good as new. As for Ratmir's clothing, his uncle had rinsed out the stains with cold water and, for the few that still showed a little, he smeared them with engine grease. No one is surprised, he said, that a taxi driver has a little grease on him. And no one will look for blood under grease.

Next, after the first cognac, Uncle Pyotr chipped a large piece of ice from his cooler and told Ratmir to hold it against his cheek. The cheek had an angry bruise from when it banged against the roof of his taxi.

"Are you sure this man is dead?" Uncle Pyotr asked.

"He is dead."

"You have seen men die? How are you so sure?"

"I have heard engines cough and die. The sound was the same."

Uncle Pyotr nodded, satisfied.

He found some clean grease and rubbed it on Ratmir's scalp, which was extremely tender where his hair had been pulled out in clumps. He rubbed a little more grease on the back and sides so that it would look like hair oil. Then he rearranged Ratmir's hair, combing it so that the gaps would be hidden.

Ratmir did not know what he would have done without his uncle Pyotr.

Count on him, he thought, to think of everything.

Uncle Pyotr was so smart.

He was also, by far, the richest of them. His garage was very small, barely more than a shed, but there were always cars waiting outside because everyone knew that he was an honest man and that his prices were fair. For most jobs he would take a down payment of perhaps a bottle of vodka, and then he would give his customer a list of things with which he could pay off the balance. For big jobs, perhaps a fur coat or a Japanese television set. He would tell you what he needed. Often he would even tell you where to get it. Almost always this would be from the apartment of a former

Communist official or that of a known informer. Meantime, Uncle Pyotr himself would steal the parts he needed.

He was not sent to the camps for stealing. He was sent because one time Stalin was giving a speech at Dynamo Stadium and Uncle Pyotr, who was trucked there from his factory to help fill the seats, was yawning throughout the speech and was the first to stop clapping when Stalin finished. This was witnessed by one of those tedious party women who speak only in slogans and who had a private grudge against Uncle Pyotr because she had once given him a stupid order and he told her that if she shaved her upper lip and clipped the hairs growing out of her moles, her face would look less like an armpit.

This woman had bided her time. Now she denounced him for insulting Stalin. Next day he was arrested. A magistrate, hearing that he had worked a double shift before going to Dynamo Stadium, let him off with a warning. But this woman got to her district party boss and word came down that an example should be made of him. The same magistrate had him brought back in and gave him two years. By the time Uncle Pyotr finished expressing his views on this subject, the sentence had grown to twelve years.

In those days, this was not so unusual. Everyone denouncing everyone else. Children reporting on their parents. Getting medals for it. Being held up as heroes.

But, before this, Uncle Pyotr had been a genuine hero. Early in the Great Patriotic War he was revealed to be such a good shot and so patient under fire that his colonel sent him back for training as a sniper. He was back in time for Stalingrad. In that one battle alone he killed more than one hundred German and Rumanian soldiers and for that he was awarded his country's highest medal by none other than Nikita Khrushchev, who was then a lieutenant general.

Afterward, Khrushchev was photographed standing with Uncle Pyotr and admiring his rifle. He sent Uncle Pyotr a signed copy of that photograph with a note saying that they must go hunting together when the war is over. But five years later this Hero of the Soviet Union is sent to the gulag over nothing.

In the camps, he met other men who had no idea why they were there. One of these learned much later that he was

there because he wiped his ass with a piece of newspaper
that had Stalin's picture on it.

What had happened was this:

One day, he is in his outhouse, shitting. Meanwhile, the
door is open because he is talking to a man he thought was
his friend. He tears off strips of newspaper to wipe himself.
His friend, who happened to owe him two goats, sees that he
is wiping himself with Stalin's face and sees a chance to
cancel the debt. Next thing you know, this man gets ten
years for anti-Soviet activity.

Uncle Pyotr only got out because Khrushchev came to
power and had already made his speech about Stalin's
crimes. Some relatives wrote to him and asked him if he
remembered the famous sniper from Stalingrad and his
promise to go hunting with him. Khrushchev did. He made
good his promise. He also got the ass-wiper released.

After this, no one should be surprised that Uncle Pyotr
hates all Communists unless they happen to be named
Khrushchev. Or that he steals from them. The woman who
denounced him was getting her apartment stripped clean
every few months and all her pension checks stolen until she
finally put a plastic bag over her head. The man who
denounced his friend for two goats moved out of Moscow as
soon as he was found out. This was too bad, thought Ratmir.
He should have been drowned in that same outhouse.

Ratmir poured another cognac and picked at the carcass
of the chicken. There was also a little beef and some other
foods in the cooler. Uncle Pyotr said he could help himself
to anything but the cheese and coffee because they were
both for trade.

The meat, he knew, was from Uncle Pyotr's monthly
food package which he gets for having been a ''repressed
person.'' Everyone who went to Stalin's labor camps is
entitled. He also gets a pension and extra ration coupons for
being a Hero of the Soviet Union and, for just being a
veteran, he gets to buy cheese and yogurt in a special store
which is open to him on Sundays. He said that he would try
to stop there on the way home. Get more cheese if the lines
were not too long.

After he stops at a kiosk and makes his phone call.

After he calls the police.

He will call the police headquarters of the Krasno-Presnensky district because GUM is in that district.

Uncle Pyotr will not give his true name, of course. But he says that it is always better to give a name and address than to give nothing, because when you give nothing they are right away suspicious and they try to trace your call. Knowing Uncle Pyotr, he will probably give the name and address of some Communist or informer.

He will say that he was just leaving GUM and he witnessed a confrontation which he thought should be reported. There was this one man, fat, very short hair, wearing a fleece-lined jacket. He seemed to be watching two other men. He seemed to be matching their faces to some photographs he was holding. Of the two other men, one was young, not so big, and the other was not so young but he was very big and he looked like a foreigner.

The big one sees the fat one watching him. Now comes the confrontation. The big one approaches the fat one. Uncle Pyotr could not hear what he said to him, but he was quite sure that he heard the fat one say that he was ''Komitet.''

Only KGB would dare say this, but the big man was not intimidated. All at once the big one and the young one seize the fat one. Maybe they stick a gun in his ribs—Uncle Pyotr doesn't know—but the fat one goes with them as they take him down 25th October to the alley where the trucks make deliveries.

Uncle Pyotr can no longer see them, but he hears the sounds of a fight. He hears blows being struck. One minute later, the young one and the big one come out alone and they go back into GUM.

Uncle Pyotr looks in the alley. He sees a dark shape on the ground. He looks closer, strikes a match. Fat man is dead. Head is all smashed up. On his chest are still the photographs. Uncle Pyotr strikes another match. One of the photographs looks like the big man from GUM. Uncle Pyotr becomes frightened. He hurries to the metro and goes home, but after a while he remembers his duty as a citizen.

Ratmir drained his fourth cognac.

His nerves were quiet now. He wished that his conscience would shut up as well.

It was, after all, not his idea to blame the big one and the

young one. This was Uncle Pyotr's idea. It came to him
after he had made Ratmir tell him again and again what had
really happened in every detail. It was only after the second
cognac that Ratmir remembered the photographs in that fat
thief's hand and the way that the pig had told him to slow
down when he saw those other two.

Don't worry about those two, said Uncle Pyotr. Even if
the police find them there will be no evidence. Main thing
is to keep the police busy chasing shadows for a while. Let
them find out if the big slob who bullied you is really KGB.
Very unlikely, but it adds to the confusion. Meantime, stay
away from the Savoy for a few weeks in case the doorman
remembers that the dead man got into your taxi.

Uncle Pyotr is very smart.

But Uncle Pyotr is also Uncle Pyotr. It would be hard for
him to remain silent if two innocent men should be arrested
and charged. Unless, of course, they were Communists.

Ratmir would try not to think about that.

28

How Leo had anguished about this trip, thought Elena. It
was on, then off, then finally on again when she insisted.

She had no doubt that the invitation, when first offered,
was entirely spontaneous, entirely free of covert intent. The
news that she was carrying Lesko's child, that they would
marry in three weeks, had taken him totally by surprise.

He had delighted in her happiness. He teased her for
blushing. Then, when she asked if he would stand up with
Lesko at the wedding, he was overcome. She remembered
how he had fumbled for his appointment booklet and, seeing
that his schedule for the weekend of the wedding was full,
happily crossed out all of it. He turned to the pages for the
following week. More appointments. He stared at them, his

tongue between his lips, a wide grin forming. Suddenly, he clapped his hands.

"Your wedding trip," he blurted. "Where will you go on your wedding trip?"

She had scarcely given it a thought. But now that the subject arose . . .

"A few days in the London flat, perhaps. Or at the house in Antibes. Lesko has never seen either of them."

"He has also never seen Russia, no?"

She blinked. "Russia for a honeymoon, Leo?"

He pretended to pout. "Russia for a honeymoon," he repeated. "Did Catherine the Great take this attitude? She was German, you know. Nearest thing to Swiss."

Not all Swiss, she thought, would agree with this last. Not many Germans for that matter. She said nothing.

"Elena the Great and Lesko the Terrible. You see? You even sound Russian."

"Um . . . all the same, Leo . . ."

"Very well. Perhaps not for a honeymoon, perhaps not right away. But a visit to my country will be my wedding present. You choose the time and I will arrange everything. I will personally be your guide."

Leo was more than a little deflated, although he tried not to show it. His eyes said, I know. You think Russia is nothing. Snow and ice. Long lines and shortages.

She took his hand. "It is a most generous wedding present, Leo. I would like very much to see your country."

She, too, meant later. Perhaps in a year. But the more that she thought of it, the more that the . . . eccentricity . . . of a Russian honeymoon appealed to her. She enjoyed travel. She especially enjoyed showing Lesko places that he never dreamed he would see.

"I will talk to Lesko," she said.

She did.

She was not sure that the conversation actually registered with him, but she did tell him of Leo's gift and she suggested that now, before the baby, might be the best time to take advantage of it. He muttered something in reply, some unclear reference to the South Bronx, but he did not object. It seemed that he was still in shock. More on his

mind was the prospect of telling his daughter that she was
about to have a brother.

Leo was thrilled. She told him, however, that her doctor
had urged her not to overdo it. A week or ten days. Just
Moscow and St. Petersburg, perhaps. Not too much flying,
no extended driving on Russian roads, stay within reach of
good medical care and use private clinics only. Leo agreed.
He would begin making arrangements at once.

But when next she saw him, over afternoon tea, everything was changed. It was a bad idea, he told her. Impulsive.
He had not thought it out. Too much confusion in Russia
today. Better to wait. She asked him what had happened to
cause such a change of heart. He gave reasons. They all rang
false. She insisted, in her disappointment, that he be frank
with her.

He told her the truth. It was Yuri, he said, who had opened
his eyes. No one, said Yuri, would believe that this was a
wedding trip. One look at these three traveling together and
what they will see is the work they did in Zurich now being
tried out in Moscow. It will make . . . them nervous. It might
frighten them. Frightened men do foolish things.

She had a sense that he'd started to say *him*—one man in
particular—not *them*. But she let it pass.

"Ah . . . who are *they,* Leo?"

He looked at his hands. "Criminals. Renegades."

"Leo, is that not the whole point of what we did here? To
frighten criminals?"

A troubled sigh. "It is surely not the point of a honeymoon, Elena. Antibes is better. Go to Antibes and lie in the
sun with your new husband."

"What is better is to keep him moving. Antibes would
have too many young blondes strolling past him with their
flat bellies and bare chests."

Belkin didn't smile.

"Leo." She gripped his sleeve. "What is it really?"

He grimaced. Again he looked away. "I will tell you
what kind of friend I am, Elena. When I realized that Yuri
was quite right, I considered saying nothing. I saw an
opportunity to find a few bad apples."

In this, she saw the reason for his pain. "From what
barrel, Leo? Your KGB?"

186 John R. Maxim

His jaw tightened. "Not *my* KGB."

Inwardly, Elena rolled her eyes. *Not my KGB.* My KGB . . . we are the good guys. Their KGB . . . they are the oppressors, the Jew hunters, the thought police. My KGB works to improve the lives of our people. Their KGB works only to keep them down.

She knew Leo. She knew that he was far too sophisticated to reduce the distinction between the First Directorate and all the other directorates to one of good versus evil. They were all chosen by the same criteria. They all took the same oath which, incidentally, had nothing to do with improving lives.

"Leo . . . to the heart of the matter." She made a vaulting gesture with her hand. "Are you saying that drug traffic in your country is controlled by the KGB?"

"I have . . . reports," he told her. "And it's not only drugs."

"These reports. Have you passed them on to your superiors?"

He nodded. "I am told, in effect, to mind my own business."

Elena eyed him skeptically. "But that was not the actual language."

He shook his head. "I am told that they are looking into it. If I should come across hard evidence, I should pass it on through channels. Otherwise, it is not my responsibility."

"In other words, it's the responsibility of the former Second Directorate. Why do you doubt that they would want to crack down on the drug traffickers before Moscow becomes another New York?"

"The police might want to. But the KGB does not operate that way. They infiltrate. They are very patient. Eventually, they are so woven into an organization at all levels that, yes, they do in fact control it."

"So?" To Elena, this seemed a sensible course of action. "And then what?"

"And then nothing. For them, control is an end in itself."

She pursed her lips. *Them* again. The bad KGB.

"Forgive me, Leo," she said. "But this begins to sound like nonsense."

He sat back, nodding slowly, wearily. His body language

said that she was not the first to make such an assessment.

"Leo." She drummed her fingers. "Look at me."

He hesitated, then met her eyes.

"Do you know how many lives I have helped to destroy?" she asked him.

He shook his head impatiently. "That was a different Elena. And you have more than atoned for her."

"The slate is far from clean, Leo. Before I am finished . . ."

He raised both hands, stopping her. "You say this to persuade me that you understand. That you do not minimize. But you will also tell me that I am allowing a pathological distrust of my own organization to color my judgment."

She lowered her eyes. "That isn't possible, Leo?"

He grunted. His expression softened. "I saw this once on the wall of a lavatory: 'Even paranoids have real enemies.'"

Elena smiled. Her tone was gentle. "And Russia has real problems, Leo. Do I minimize if I say that drugs are not so high on the list?"

"Not so high?" Belkin sniffed. "Is alcohol a drug?"

He quickly waved a hand to show that the question was rhetorical.

"Today," he said, one finger aloft, "there are at least fifteen million alcoholics in the Russian Republic alone. Nearly one person in ten. Subtract young children and it's one in seven. This rate of alcoholism is twice that of the United States and it does not tell half the story."

Elena waited. She was not, she hoped earnestly, about to hear of a KGB plot to keep Russia drunk.

"Last year"—the finger waved at her—"more than forty thousand died from drinking homemade concoctions and another twenty thousand were blinded. Last year, in Russia, there were over six million arrests for public drunkenness. Why so much drinking, Elena?"

Broken spirits. Broken hearts. And now the end of dreams. She was beginning to see what was coming.

"And now for drug abuse." The finger on his other hand came up. "Two million drug abusers in Russia. This is less than one-fifth the rate of abuse in the United States and in most of Western Europe. Not so high, eh? Not a big problem.''

Elena worked the numbers in her head. Twice as many alcoholics as in the West. It follows that there should be twice as many drug abusers as well. Not two million. Twenty million. An attractive market for the traffickers. If only these twenty million Russians had any money.

"How would they pay for the drugs, Leo?"

"Who? User or seller?"

"User. The ordinary Russian."

"Same as in the West," he answered. "By stealing."

He saw doubt in her expression. He misunderstood it.

"Even in better times," he told her, "more than half of all production was vanishing before it could be delivered. This is everything. Food, clothing, building materials, appliances . . . everything. An additional twenty percent is so-called 'ghost' production. A farm or factory produces this amount but it never appears on the books. The manager uses it for barter. This is how he gets the materials he needs and it's how he gets food and trade goods for his workers. For some commodities, vodka and caviar, ghosting and stealing account for up to ninety percent of production.''

"Yes, but if this were stopped . . ."

"It can't be stopped. This is the economy, Elena. For my lifetime at least, this is how it will function."

"You arrest them for being drunk. Why not for stealing?"

"Then who would be left to work?"

Belkin paused, reflecting on the taste that he must be leaving in her mouth. "We are not a nation of thieves, Elena. The ordinary Russian does not regard this as theft. For all his life, and for all his father's life, everything has belonged to the state, therefore to everyone and therefore to no one. If they paid him enough to buy, he would buy. If he could find what he needs in the shops, he would buy. But he cannot find it because the best still goes to those who have influence and most of what is left is reserved for export. So he helps himself. Is this theft," he asked, "or is it Marxism carried to its logical extreme?"

She tossed her head vaguely, noncommittally.

Another fine philosophical distinction, she thought. This

time between stealing communal property and stealing someone else's property. It made for an interesting conversation over tea, but it did not answer her question. How would they pay for the drugs?

That Russians stole from each other did not come as a revelation. She knew a British businessman who had lived two years in Moscow. He told the story that for a long time he could not understand why the Russians could not seem to make light bulbs that were capable of lasting more than a few weeks. Always, in his office, they were burning out. He would turn off the lights at the end of a business day and the next morning, guaranteed, several of the bulbs would be dead. Except, he told her, there was a period of about two months when they all seemed to work quite nicely.

At last, he caught two of his Russian workers in the act. They were standing on chairs, unscrewing his light bulbs, and replacing them with dead ones, which they had brought from their apartments. Why did they steal? Because there were no light bulbs in the shops. Why no stealing for that two-month period? Because the shops had light bulbs.

Very well, she thought. If a user wants drugs, he will steal or deal for them. This is normal. She still had trouble understanding what the user might steal that the dealer would want.

"Leo . . . if I wish to get high tonight, I go to my dealer. What do I give him in return for my drugs?"

"Almost anything of value."

"Which I've stolen?"

He shrugged. "Same as in the West. At first, you steal from your family. When they have nothing left or when they throw you out, you steal from others. The dealer tells you what he wants you to bring him."

"What does he do with these stolen goods?"

"He fences them. In Moscow alone, there are thousands of shops and kiosks where stolen goods can be bought."

"And paid for with what?"

"Hard currency if you have it. Jewelry, for example, if you don't."

"With which the shop pays the dealer who then buys more drugs?"

"Precisely."

"And the trafficker turns this jewelry—for example—into cash."

"One assumes so, yes."

Elena groaned within herself. Leo was no fool. But to her this made no sense. She shook her head.

"Too complicated, Leo," she said. "Drug trafficking is not a commodities exchange. It is a cash business and your country has no cash. Worse, you speak of hundreds of illegal shops, all of which must be known to the KGB by now. If they know the shops, they know the dealers who supply them."

"All true." He nodded.

"And all a house of cards. If I were still a trafficker, I would stay far away from it."

Belkin raised an eyebrow. "You would turn your back on a country that is potentially the richest in the world? More oil than Saudi Arabia, more gold and emeralds than all of South America, more coal than the United States? Or would you decide to get in on the ground floor as thousands of Western firms are doing already?"

"And as the KGB, according to you, is doing already."

"It is. Believe it, Elena."

"As a matter of policy? Or are these the renegades you mentioned?"

"First comes policy. Infiltrate and control. This is normal. In the meantime, they say, let the people have their drugs. Let them become addicts. Addicts do not riot over the price of sausage. They do not tear down statues."

Elena sipped from her cup. She did so to mask her skepticism. He saw through the attempt.

"With my own ears, Elena, I have heard SCD officers discuss the comparative merits of the various narcotics. Marijuana is bad. Too bulky, hard to ship, too easy for users to grow their own, and, worse, most people can take it or leave it alone. Hashish is more concentrated but, otherwise, shares the same disadvantages. Cocaine is good but is currently too expensive, comes from too far away, and few Russians have yet developed a taste for it. Crack cocaine is out of the question. Crack is *nekulturney*. Too low-class. Also, addicts too quickly become useless. Best drug for Russians is heroin."

"Um . . . why is that?"

"More easily imported, available from former republics, can be smoked, is already in fashion with boys who served in Afghanistan. Best of all, a heroin addict can function quite normally as long as he is not deprived of it."

Elena's expression had become distant.

In her mind she saw the Indians of Bolivia. She had grown to womanhood there. She had lived in a fine house. The Indians worked the fields. She had been taught, as a young girl, that they were nothing. They swept the streets, they picked the crops, and they had babies. It was all they were good for. And yet she was fascinated by them. These Quechuas and Aymaras, now abysmally poor, almost all of them illiterate, chewing coca leaves to give them false strength and to dull the ache of empty bellies, were all that remained of the proud Inca nation.

Her mind seemed to want to draw a parallel. But she knew that to do so was absurd. One might compare those Indians to the Russian serfs of eighty years ago but not to the next generation for whom an elementary education, at minimum, was compulsory under the Communists. Surely not to the men and women of Leo's generation who attended university and helped to conquer space and who began, gradually, to think for themselves.

The bravest, the dissidents, thought aloud.

Leo's uncle, come to think of it, had been one of them. Her uncle Urs, not Leo, had told her a little about him. Impressively accomplished. An Academician in both science and literature. Nikolai? Yes . . . Nikolai Belkin. Arrested and offered a choice between exile and a public confession of his error. Chose the latter. Kept to himself after that. Elena wasn't sure that she'd blame him, given the circumstances of the time but Leo, according to Uncle Urs, was not so generous. Spoke of him with contempt. Uncle Urs was never clear why. It was not as if Leo was on such high ground himself.

But she dismissed the question from her mind. The subject at hand was complex enough without dredging up family skeletons.

The odd dissident aside, the mass of Soviet citizens were thought to be passive, thoroughly indoctrinated, politically inert. Boris Yeltsin knew better. He had listened to them. More to the point, Leo Belkin knows better. The men and women who stood against the tanks will never again stand silent. And the KGB, most assuredly, will not turn them into zombies. The statues have not stopped coming down.

"Leo . . ." Elena was still struggling with this. "Your charge is that some within the KGB are in league with the drug traffickers . . ."

"Not just drugs. All smuggling. Whole country is for sale."

She waved this aside. "And that their motive is to anesthetize the masses?"

"Not a motive, Elena. But it's one of the justifications."

"What is another justification?"

"I've told you. Let it grow. Infiltrate and control it. Promise to destroy it when the time is right."

"But this, you think, will never happen. They will not destroy it."

He shook his head. "Too much money, Elena. Same as in the West."

"Leo . . ." She searched for a tactful way to phrase her next question. She found none. "In all the KGB, are you the only officer who believes that this is happening?"

His eyes took a chill. He shook his head. "No. I am not."

"Then why is no action taken?"

"You can ask that of any bureaucracy, Elena. Can you imagine one, anywhere, that is free of corruption? And yet genuine purges are few and far between because a bureaucracy, under attack, develops a bunker mentality. This is not so much to protect the guilty. It is because for every thief who is the target of an investigation, there are twenty more who are at least technically guilty of complicity or are open to a charge of dereliction. So what do they tell you? It is an internal matter, they say. We are looking into it. We will police ourselves."

"Fine. Why don't you let them?"

He shook his head stubbornly. His eyes had turned inward.

Elena saw the answer in them. Leo had been *letting them* for too much of his life. She could understand that, she supposed. But it was an unhealthy frame of mind. That of a vigilante.

"These renegades, Leo. What would you do if you had their names?"

"For now? Just put them in the computer. Begin to gather evidence."

"Which computer? The Zurich program?"

"Yes."

Elena frowned. The Zurich program had little to do with evidence. It had to do with retribution.

"And how would you get the names? Surely you don't expect them to reveal themselves just because the three of us turn up in Moscow."

He hesitated, choosing his words. "We . . . might have caused a stir," he said. "I am not quite alone in this, Elena. There are people who will tell me what sort of questions are asked. Perhaps even what instructions are given."

She stared at him. "What people?"

"Men who . . . believe as I do."

She sagged inwardly. Good KGB, bad KGB, and now a shadow KGB.

"Leo . . ."

"The discussion is academic. We are not going."

"But you are? By yourself?"

"I have some leave coming. Yes."

"Then all three of us will go. You will make good on your gift."

"Another time, Elena. Not now."

She reached into her purse and found a notebook. She chewed her lip. "There's the question of what to pack. What will I need, aside from plenty of Marlboros?"

Belkin started to shake his head. Resolutely. But he stopped. He started to refuse her. Firmly. But the words died on his lips.

"You'll . . . help me?" he said at last.

She shook her head. "Not on this."

Disappointment. Then relief. Relief won out. Then came vexation.

"Then why, Elena? What's the point?"

"I think to keep you out of trouble, Leo."

. . .

And because . . . why else?

Elena asked this of herself.

Is it merely curiosity?

Or is it because I think that between now and the time we get to Russia, poor Leo might decide to tell me the truth?

Cause a stir. That was the phrase he used.

But his eyes clouded over when he said it. She had a sense, then and there, that he was seeing a face in his mind. That he knew perfectly well who he hoped to stir up.

Yes, she will go to Russia with him.

But why?

Be honest, Elena.

For all that you love your new life, it does seem a bit bloodless from time to time, doesn't it. Too many board meetings. Too many lawyers.

A little excitement. A little intrigue.

Lesko could probably do with a bit of it himself.

29

The lobby of the Savoy was in an uproar.

It was the prostitutes versus the Finns.

A party of seven Japanese had returned from a trade conference at the Russian White House. There had been many vodka toasts at lunch and still more at the end of the day. They were in high spirits.

Somewhere between the White House and the Savoy, the seven Japanese men had come across two Russian hookers, both blondes, both petite, whom they were now attempting to smuggle up to their suites. They had dressed the two prostitutes in long dark topcoats and Homburg hats and formed a tight cordon around them as they made their way to the elevator. Giggles, not those of the prostitutes, gave the Japanese businessmen away.

The Finnish night manager spotted two pairs of untrou-
sered legs and stepped from behind the desk, confronting
the Japanese and insisting that the girls must leave at once.
The Japanese lowered their heads and ran for it, half for the
elevator and half for a flight of stairs that led only to a small
casino.

Two sheep ranchers from New Zealand, weathered faces,
easy grins, ambled out of the bar to watch. Beer glasses in
hand, they tried to start a bidding war for the services of the
two *putanotchkas* while hooting the stiff-necked manager.
Another Finn, wearing a red carnation, came out to enlist
the aid of the burly Russian doorman whom he was now
berating on the assumption that he had taken a bribe from
the Japanese.

In all this confusion, Viktor Podolsk saw a chance to step
behind the desk and steal a look at the message which had
come in for General Belkin some twenty minutes earlier. He
had heard the name "Yuri" repeated aloud. He presumed
the caller to be Major Yuri Rykov, Belkin's aide, and had
questioned the Finnish manager as to its nature and origin.
The Finn had refused to betray it, KGB or no KGB. It was
enough that the day manager had given one of Podolsk's
technicians prior access to the rooms assigned to the Belkin
party. This access would not extend to private mail and
messages if the night manager had any say in it.

As the Finn tried to keep the elevator doors from closing,
Podolsk found the message. There were two, actually. The
second was unsigned. It read *Confirmed. K36–8 PM. He
will be there.*

It seemed to be a confirmation of their dinner reservation.
K36, if he remembered their itinerary correctly, was the
restaurant at number 36 Kropotkinskaya. Looks as if someone else is meeting them there. Not surprising. Belkin is
bound to have friends in Moscow, but why wouldn't he
leave his name? Why not "*I* will be there?"

The Yuri message was no more enlightening. It read *Call
me. Very urgent.* The call was made from Bern. Probably
from the embassy there. Podolsk memorized the number.
He would check it later. In the meantime, Podolsk allowed
himself to hope that some crisis had developed that would
require that Belkin return to Bern immediately. That way,

perhaps this lunacy could end before any real damage was done.

Podolsk replaced the message slips and stepped from behind the desk. But too late. The recalcitrant night manager had turned, spotting him, and was making a little pink fist. The Japanese seized the moment and the elevator doors slammed shut.

The doorman was now at the foot of the casino stairs shouting, *"Valutki! Snaroo'zhi!"*—Hookers! Outside! This caused a groan of despair from the Finn, who did not feel that it elevated the tone of the dispute.

Podolsk ignored all this. He crossed the lobby, pausing to pick up some scattered newspapers as if he were staff, and returned to his post at the concierge desk where the fat German salesman, back from Detsky Mir with the toys he had bought for his children, was zipping them into one of his bags.

Suddenly, the German became agitated.

He snapped his fingers in the direction of Podolsk's face and, his voice rising, was pointing at a spot on the carpet. Podolsk spoke little German, but the salesman seemed to be indicating that one of his bags was missing.

Podolsk's reaction, less than solicitous, now infuriated the German. His voice, already loud, rose to a bellow. *"Du. Wo ist . . .* something, something *. . . meine rechenmaschine . . .* something, something *. . . gestehlen."*

Podolsk thought he understood the sense of it. An adding machine of some sort had been stolen. If so, the German was now saying, it was stolen from under the nose of the man who had been given *". . . funf Deutschemark . . ."* for keeping an eye on those bags—if not by Podolsk himself.

The Finn with the red carnation hurried over, hands raised, trying to calm him. Very difficult, thought Podolsk, to calm a German once he makes up his mind to yell. To make matters worse, General Belkin and his party chose this moment to enter the hotel lobby.

Podolsk averted his face.

The first Finn, the night manager, rushed from behind the reception desk to greet Belkin's party and to steer them past the angry scene near the door. Podolsk circled to his left, keeping the German between himself and the reception desk as Belkin's driver brought in their bags and they began the formalities of registration.

The German took Podolsk's shiftiness as inattention to his complaint. Possibly even a sign of guilt. He poked Podolsk's chest with his finger. It was all Podolsk could do not to snap it in half, especially when the German, seeing that his own language was having only a modest effect, began calling on his knowledge of Russian epithets. At this, Belkin's driver turned to look. Podolsk lowered his head. He brought a hand to his mouth as added concealment.

The ranting German was now addressing the lobby in general. He was using his hands to describe the size of his missing machine and he was pointing to the spot from which it had disappeared. Podolsk, although mortified, was at last beginning to comprehend what had happened.

He had not noticed such a machine but now he knew why. That curious exchange of jackets, that show of being hot, came back to him. The German's machine had been hidden under Kerensky's smelly coat. The sausage-maker had indeed stolen it from under his nose. Podolsk glanced toward the Hermitage Bar, where Kerensky, thankfully out of sight, was no doubt watching all this with an expression of studied innocence. Podolsk spoke to the Finn in Russian.

"This man is going to the airport?"

The Finn glanced at his watch. "His flight is in two hours."

"And this machine . . . what is it?"

"A laptop computer. A Toshiba."

"Kindly tell him who I am. Tell him quietly."

The Finn hesitated. He had no great wish to have it thought that any part of the hotel staff consisted of KGB officers pretending to be Finns. But perhaps it would quiet the German. He obeyed, first touching a finger to his lips to show that he was speaking in confidence.

The German blinked, momentarily silenced.

"Now tell him that he will have his machine by the time his flight leaves Moscow. He has my word."

The Finn translated what he said.

"Wort aus KGB?" the German spat scornfully, too loudly. This time Lesko turned to look.

"Get him out of here," Podolsk hissed to the Finn. He picked up two of the German's bags and carried them to the street. The Finn gathered the rest and followed. Next came the German, but not before a final snarl, in gutter Russian, of *"Yeb vas, KGB. Mudaki, KGB."* This was heard throughout the lobby. One of the New Zealanders sprayed a mouthful of beer. Both men cheered.

The Finn rapped on the hood of the nearest taxi, ordering the driver to open his trunk. The driver was Yakov, Kerensky's cousin. He looked questioningly at Podolsk. Podolsk hesitated, then nodded. Best, he decided, to get all of them away from this hotel before they burn it down. The bags were loaded. He watched as the German, still cursing, pulled away in Yakov's borrowed taxi.

The surveillance was now a disaster. It was his own fault. He should have refused to use these idiots. Borovik, even more, would have only himself to blame. To Podolsk, the only satisfaction would be the talk that he was about to have with Kerensky.

He looked through the door to see if the lobby was clear. It wasn't. Belkin's party was still at the desk. They were handing their passports to the night manager, who was still glaring at him over their shoulders. As Podolsk watched, the night manager made a show of holding up two magnetized cards, room keys, and pretended to study them. With a flourish, he put them aside. Now, in a slow and deliberate manner, he chose two new keys. These he handed to Belkin and to Lesko.

Podolsk groaned.

They had been given new rooms. Clean rooms. The manager had been told that General Belkin would probably make such a request but he was to say that the hotel was fully booked. Belkin would have expected that answer. He would probably not have argued.

Not that Podolsk ever thought that he would learn much of anything through eavesdropping on their private conversations. Not Belkin's, surely. On the contrary, his hope was that such conversations would help to convince Borovik that this visit is entirely innocent. Now Borovik would conclude . . . who knows what? That they have something to hide? That the Finns are in on it with them. Or worse, that everyone is mocking him again.

A disaster, thought Podolsk. A circus gone amok.

There was nothing to do but break off. Send Kerensky packing and go back to Moscow Center. With luck, he can be there when Barca or the Sicilian report in. Before Borovik can talk to them.

Before he ruins everything.

"What's a *yeb vas*?" Lesko asked Belkin in the elevator.

The Russian bellboy tried not to laugh.

"An . . . expletive," Belkin told him. "Not attractive."

"Anything like *fuck you*?"

Elena poked him. But Belkin sighed and nodded.

Lesko mouthed the phrase, tasting it. "Okay. What's a *mudaki*?"

"Lesko . . ." Elena moved to pinch him.

"Will you stop?" He covered his arm. "They appreciate it when you try to learn their language."

At this the bellboy's shoulders trembled. He showed signs of oxygen deprivation.

"Hey, kid. What's a *mudaki*?"

The young man turned. His eyes were tearing. He looked at Elena as if for permission. She turned away to hide a smile.

"*Mudak* means 'schmuck,'" Belkin answered for the bellboy. "*Mudaki* is plural."

Lesko chewed on that one as well. Then, "The guy yelling. Who was he mad at?"

Belkin hesitated. "Something about stolen luggage."

Lesko nodded as if satisfied.

Nice hotel, he thought to himself. Has everything you'd find in New York. Hookers, luggage thieves, Japs in blue suits, and pissed-off guests. Except in New York you don't hear many Germans cursing out the KGB.

Belkin hadn't mentioned that part. Maybe he hoped that it had slipped past him because the initials sound a little different in German. Maybe he hoped that he wouldn't notice who the German was yelling at, either. Tall guy, blond hair, dark suit. Could have been one of the Finns who

run the place except for his eyes. The guy had cop eyes. No
mistake.

Lots of messages in the eyes tonight.

There was the frazzled Finn behind the desk whose eyes
said *Yeb vas* to the guy who was being yelled at and, when
he got his attention, made a production out of switching our
rooms around.

There was Belkin, who never turned around but whose
eyes, Lesko felt sure, had told Valentin to see what he could
find out while we're up unpacking.

There was also the look on Belkin's face when he
checked his messages. Lesko saw Yuri's name on one of
them. No big reaction to that one. Maybe mild annoyance.
But the second one seemed to shake him up. No idea why.
All Lesko could see was the letter *K*, some numbers, and a
few words in Russian. Belkin breasted it very quickly. For
a second there, his hand was shaking.

Then there were Elena's eyes. Looking up at him. Giving
him a little squeeze. Those eyes were saying thank you.

Thank you for being patient. Thank you for trusting me.
Be patient just a while longer.

"At dinner," was all she said. "We'll have a nice
dinner."

Yeah, well . . .

Lesko had an idea that he might be using his new Russian
words before the night was over.

30

Yuri could see no other way. Next roadside phone, he
would have to call Mama's Boy. Tell him everything.

Already, a few kilometers back, he had tried once more to
get through to General Belkin. Thirty minutes later, there
was still no connection. Soviet communications system.
Worst in the world. Ridiculous to think that his country

would ever start a war. Troops in the field would be the last to hear about it.

"Next telephone you see," he said to Lydia Voinovitch, "pull over once more, please."

She made a face. "And waste so much time? Zurich from here is only thirty minutes."

"This call is not to Moscow. Takes five minutes, maybe ten."

"Who now? Mama's Boy?"

He hesitated. "Yes."

She let out a sigh. "World is changing very fast," she said. But she did not protest.

He had not intended that Lydia know so much. But as they drove out of Bern in Aldo Corsini's car, facing an unproductive ninety minutes of driving time, it bothered him that he still did not know what the Italian had said to himself on that tape recording. The receiver kit was still under the passenger seat where Corsini had concealed it.

On an impulse, he had asked Lydia if it happened that she spoke Italian. She said no, only English and Spanish. A little while later, however, she remarked that although she had no training in that language she found that she could usually communicate with Italians. Give or take an extra vowel, she said, Spanish and Italian are similar.

He thought about this for several kilometers. Then he decided. She would make what she could of Aldo Corsini's tape from the garden party. The parts in which he talked to himself.

"Reach under you," he said. "You will find a brief-case."

She played the tape, listening through earphones, making notes, and then she played it two more times. It was true that her Italian was not so good. Her translations were fragmentary. But by the third playing she felt sure that she had the sense of Aldo's remarks. Yuri asked her to drive as he studied her notes.

Very strange handwriting for a woman, he thought. No graceful loops or swirls. Only tiny little letters all cramped together. He wondered what the KGB psychologists had made of that, but he put the thought aside. This was looking gift horses in the mouth.

"I do not understand this," he said to her.

"What part?"

"If a man is talking only to himself, what is the point of talking aloud?"

"Only in the beginning is he talking to himself. Interesting part begins later but read it in sequence. This man is not right in the head."

This remark put Yuri in mind of another English proverb that warned of pots who call a kettle black. But he soon understood her meaning.

She was right about the beginning. There, Aldo is only repeating the names of people he meets so that he will not forget them. This is sensible. Next, speaking to others, he begins asking why Elena chooses Russia for a honeymoon. He learns it was not for honeymoon.

Several guests, all Bruggs, tell him that this trip was wedding present from General Belkin but trip was to be taken later, next year, after baby. They say it was Elena who decided to go now, take advantage, while she can still travel. General Belkin, they say, argued against this. Too much confusion now. Go later. But Elena, always the adventuress, has made up her mind, has already talked to Lesko. She's very curious about Russia. Wants to meet Leo's family in St. Petersburg.

Now Corsini is alone again. Talks to himself in Italian. "See, shitface? You worry for nothing."

"He calls himself *shitface*?" Yuri asked.

Voinovitch shook her head. "Reference is to name from computer file. You see down below. Shitface is this Borovik."

Yuri realized why the name had seemed familiar. He must have heard it, although it did not register as a person's name, when he first tried to listen to the tape. Too much babble around it.

He read further. He saw the name. But Lydia had not spelled it as it was on the screen. Here it is *Boriavik*.

"What is *Boriavik*?" he asked. "Why this spelling?"

"Is Corsini's pronunciation. Is contempt, I think."

"Contempt?"

She nodded. "*Boria*, in Spanish, is slang expression. Means like . . . 'puffed up.' Italians, I think, have same word, similar meaning. Is like 'arrogance.' Corsini calls him other names as well but these I cannot translate. Meaning is clear, however, from inflection. Words are insults.''

Yuri grunted. He turned the page.

Now Corsini appears to have lost interest in the purpose of the trip to Russia. He says two more names of people he sees at the party. Yuri recognized those names. They are contract agents who have worked for Bannerman in the past but who have now been retained by the Bruggs. As Corsini moves on, he speaks of them with admiration. But suddenly, Lydia writes, his tone becomes sullen.

''I could have been as good,'' she quotes him saying. ''I could have been as good as any of you.''

Now comes a long pause, says Lydia.

To himself he says, ''You think I could not?''

Now he says, ''You think there is no more to me than what you see? Two others in my life have made that mistake. My wife made that mistake.''

More silence. Indistinct mutterings. Then, ''Bare hands. Both times. Not so easy as you think.''

Yuri blinked. He turned another page but this line of thought was not developed further. Aldo's thoughts had turned to Mama's Boy.

''What does this mean?'' he asked Lydia. ''Two others. Bare hands.''

''From context,'' she told him, ''I think he has killed on two occasions.''

''Bare hands? This means he choked them?''

''He is not specific.''

''You think one was his wife?''

She nodded. ''From inflection, from choice of words, I think that both of these were women. He would like to boast that he has killed but he is afraid that these two agents would not consider killing women to be such a great achievement. Is why he says is not so easy.''

Yuri saw Carla in his mind. And Aldo with his necktie. No, he thought. It is not so easy.

He returned to Lydia's notes, holding them under the map light. Now Aldo says, ''I could still be as good. I could be as famous as Bannerman.''

Next, someone says hello. He says nice to see you again. He takes a bite of something, chews, and swallows.

"More famous," he says.

He whispers these words. He says them again and again as if he is tasting them. There is the sound of a smile in his voice. Now he says, "And you, dear Carla, will help me."

"Carla," he says. Still is whispering.

A woman approaches. Not Carla. She introduces herself. Another cousin of the Bruggs. Aldo is polite, says the note by Lydia, but he is distracted. The politeness is forced. He excuses himself. Now he is alone again. More whispers.

"Carla?

"Will you be my wife? No.

"Will you honor me by becoming . . ."

All this to himself. It has the sound of rehearsal, says Lydia.

"I offer you all that I have, all that I am, all that I may become."

This one amuses him.

"I think you will say yes, perhaps. I think now you are ready."

He is humming. Lydia says melody is Toreador song from *Carmen*. Maybe not such an irrelevancy, thought Yuri.

Now Aldo says, "Borovik.

"How much will you pay?

"Twenty thousand?

"Fifty thousand?

"No."

The voice becomes firm. "Not for twice that amount. No more crumbs from your table. What I make, from now on I keep half. That is my price."

This, says Lydia, is followed by some private musings. Very disjointed but there is the sound of glee. Westport is mentioned. Something about cutting off a head.

She is not sure about this last, she says, because the context is confused. Might be used in the sense of eliminating leadership. Might mean Mama's Boy. But then there is the word "brother" and the phrase "head for a head." Reference is very unclear. Finally, word "head" is used in the context of pride. General Borovik, says Corsini, will at last be able to hold up his head and stop pulling himself.

"Pulling himself?"

Lydia shrugged. "Reference is probably to masturbation. Corsini and Borovik . . . this is not a respectful association."

There were only a few more notes of her translations. More references to Borovik, all of them unflattering. One reference to himself. He says that one day they will be "telling stories about Aldo Corsini for a change. About Barca."

Now he approaches Carla. Speaks English. She asks how he is enjoying the party. She asks is something wrong.

"Marry me," he says to her.

She is stunned. Lydia's assessment.

Then, "I love you. In this I am helpless. You are the most beautiful woman . . ."

Here the microcassette runs out of tape. Yuri closed Lydia's notebook. He had heard this part. Carla had told him all the rest. How they would live for part of the year in Westport. How he would get to know all her friends. In his mind, he could see her dragging him from the garden party. Aldo had not found time to insert a fresh cassette.

"This cutting off of heads," he said to Lydia, "is it a figure of speech?"

She had no idea.

"He speaks of being rich. How does he accomplish this by marrying Carla Benedict?"

A shrug. "He becomes a spy in Westport? He reports on Mama's Boy?"

"Almost everyone reports on Mama's Boy," he told her. "Almost always is a waste of time."

She took a breath as if reluctant to speak. "He assassinates Mama's Boy," she suggested.

Yuri frowned. There might be that inference, he realized, in Corsini's words. Get close to him through Carla. Choose his time, then strike. But for what purpose? Just to be famous? Man who shot Billy the Kid?

There was a time when he might have tried it himself if so ordered. When he was young, fresh from training, eager to test himself. But Yuri would have handpicked a team and they would have trained together for weeks. Even then, even if successful, retribution would have been terrible. Also, that

was different world, different Bannerman. Now even hard-
line KGB agrees. Best to let sleeping dogs lie.

"You say he is not right in the head. Why?"

Yuri had his own opinion based on Carla's account, but
even she had questioned her own recollection. He wished to
hear the insights of a woman who was considerably more
detached.

"You ask why?" Her chin came up.

"Yes. Why?"

"This man who boasts of killing women?"

"Every man who kills a woman is not crazy."

Lydia sputtered.

Uh-oh, thought Yuri.

"This . . . this *wop* decides, 'I will marry Carla and
then this will happen and that will happen and I will be
rich.' Does it occur to him that she might not swoon at his
proposal? That she might say no? Does he consider that she
might see through him as if he were glass?"

"Um . . . he deludes himself, you are saying."

"He thinks with his big Italian cock, is what I am
saying."

She was glaring at him, not watching the road. Yuri
groaned inwardly. In her mind this was less an observation
about Aldo Corsini than a universal truth that embraced all
men since Adam. Yuri foremost.

He could only surrender. Next time he was tempted to
take a woman home with him, he would first get a sample
of her handwriting.

It was at this point that he decided to look for a phone and
try to catch Bannerman. He could use the reprieve. More
than that, he wanted the answer to a question. The trouble
was that it had not yet formed. But he could feel the pieces
of it, in the back of his mind, trying to come together.

He had an odd sense that Lydia had almost asked it before
she remembered that she hated men.

Hatred.

There it was again. One of the pieces.

And once again, it floated away.

31

The Krasno-Presnensky district, like all of Moscow's districts, is cut in the shape of a pie wedge. The crust is formed by a section of the Outer Ring Road. The wedge comes to a blunted point at a tiny section of the Kremlin Wall.

There is no practical reason for this configuration. It exists because every party boss of every district wanted some part of it to touch the Kremlin. He also wanted the main road through his district marked with a special lane through which he could speed in his limousine on his way to and from meetings at the seat of power. The police in the glass-enclosed traffic stations at each major intersection would stop all other traffic until he had passed.

All this was changed now. No more party bosses, not so many limousines, no more pedestrians scrambling out of the way. Even the district boundaries were scheduled for restructuring in order to reflect some measure of administrative efficiency.

For Captain Alexei Levin of the Moscow militia, this restructuring could not come soon enough. If it had been done already, or if the body had been found at the other end of GUM, it would have been in someone else's district and he could have been home having dinner by now.

But here he was and there was the dead man, just as the caller had described him. Flat on his back. Skull smashed. Three photographs on his chest. Two men and a woman. The caller had not mentioned a woman.

Captain Levin had already confirmed that the name the caller gave was false. This came as no surprise. The surprise was that he called in the first place. In Moscow, no one gets involved with the authorities if they can help it. Even now. And especially if the dead man was heard to say that he was KGB.

A lot about this was already beginning to stink. The caller, in the first place, said that he was frightened. But to Levin he sounded more like a man who was pretending to be frightened. A man who is genuinely frightened not only does not call but, if he does, does not give so much detail.

He does not walk into a dark alley, strike a match, and stand there making mental notes of a dead man's injuries and how he is dressed. In fact, if his nerves are really that steady, he likely helps himself to that expensive shearling coat and those good leather boots and that Japanese watch.

He does not report that the dead man's right ear has been nearly torn from his head. The report was accurate, of course. Both ears had been battered. But the caller would have had to turn the man's head in order to see the right ear. It could not be seen looking straight down at him.

A sergeant was taking flash pictures. He took two from a distance to record the position of the body. Now he was taking close-ups of the injuries.

"Look here," said the sergeant. "The left arm and hand."

Levin squatted at his side. The sergeant guided his eye toward two bloody imprints on the sleeve of the shearling, each circular in shape and about six centimeters in diameter. He pushed the sleeve up to the elbow, revealing matching yellow bruises on the forearm.

"Here he fended off blows," said the sergeant. "Weapon was round like a hammer. Wide head like a shoemaker's hammer. Maybe a mallet."

Levin shined his torch on the dead man's skull. "Mallet," he said, nodding. "Edges are blunt."

"And see here. See the fingers."

The hand was caked with blood, especially the palm where it had probably been pressed against the torn ear. Several long dark hairs were matted to the fingers. They could not belong to the victim. Nor, he thought, did they belong to either of the three in those photographs unless we are to believe that it was the woman who beat him to death.

"Roll him over," said Levin. "Let's see who he is."

The sergeant found the dead man's papers in the back pocket of his trousers. He carried the green, cloth-covered *pasporta* and the gray *trudovaya knizhka*, the labor book

that detailed his history of employment. He was a sausage-
maker, it said, at Abattoir #6 out on Kutuzovsky. That fact
and the name were enough for Levin.

"Sergei Kerensky," he said to the sergeant. "Better
known as Sasha. He's one of the Kerensky brothers."

The sergeant raised an eyebrow. "Chicago Brigade?"

Levin nodded.

He remembered when this gang was just the Kerensky
brothers and a few of their cousins breaking heads for the
Lubertsy Brigade. Then there was a falling out. Two of the
Kerenskys were beaten up. Then, next day, five members of
Lubertsy are lined up against a brick wall down at the
Varshavsky car-service station and machine-gunned. Like
famous Valentine's Day massacre in America. No proof
against the Kerensky brothers, but the rumor is that this one
and his cousin Yakov did it. More than rumor. They boasted
of it. Soon they are calling themselves the Chicago Brigade.

More machine-gun killings follow. Both sides have
losses. Kerensky asks for a peace conference on neutral
ground. Havana Restaurant. KGB shows up in place of
Kerensky. Suddenly there is no more Lubertsy Brigade.
Suddenly Chicago Brigade is running all prostitution, used-
car sales, porno shops, and most burglary in the whole
northwest quarter of Moscow.

"The man who called," said the sergeant. "Perhaps he
was correct about hearing KGB."

Levin shrugged. He doubted it. He doubted that the man
who called had heard or seen anything at all. Levin was now
convinced of that. He was calling to say what he had been
told to say.

But who told him to say it? The KGB? He doubted that
as well. It was no big secret that the Chicago Brigade had
enjoyed KGB protection for years. That they were certainly
informers. That their small army of ex-convicts was used to
break up demonstrations from time to time, with clubs and
brass knuckles, while Levin's men were told to busy
themselves elsewhere.

Tell the Jew policeman to look the other way if he knows
what's good for him. Tell him to go arrest some drunks.

But that KGB is now lying low. It would hardly want
attention called to itself through this tipster. More likely, the

caller was trying to deflect attention from someone else. And onto that big, hard-eyed man in the photographs.

Levin took another look at them. He had to smile.

"We are asked to believe," he said to his sergeant, "that Kerensky was following this one." He held up Lesko's photograph. "This one notices Kerensky. There is a confrontation. Kerensky claims to be KGB. This one is not impressed. He and a younger man then drag Kerensky down here and beat him to death with the mallet he carries for just such occasions. Next, so that you and I would not have to tax our brains, he leaves his photograph on Kerensky's chest."

"That one," said the sergeant, "looks like KGB himself."

Levin stared at the photograph. He tried to read the face.

No, he decided. Not KGB. The eyes were too alive. The other features were vaguely Slavic, he supposed, but there was something foreign about him.

He wondered what the photographs meant. The fact that there were three of them. And whether Sasha Kerensky ever actually had them in the first place.

He had to assume that the three were probably in Moscow at this moment. If not, he asked, what would be the point of trying to link them with this murder? Kerensky, quite possibly, had been asked to keep an eye on them. Probably by his protectors in the KGB. Which means that the KGB probably knows who and where they are.

"You know what we should do?" asked the sergeant.

"What?"

"Drag him around to the other side of GUM. One hundred meters and he's out of our district."

It was an appealing suggestion. The problem was that the police cars had already attracted a crowd outside the alley and they know there is a body in there. Someone would talk out of turn. Also, even if they did drag him to the other side, the police from that district would probably drag him right back when they see who it is.

"I have a better idea," said Levin. "You go back to the car. Patch a call to Number Two, Lubyanka."

"And tell them what? The Jew says all is forgiven?"

"Tell them to come pick up their garbage."

32

"Is Yuri again," he said when Susan's voice answered.

"He's here. Wait."

Yuri listened to the clicking sounds that meant a scrambling device was being activated. Someday, he thought, he would like to see Mama's Boy's system. Designed by Molly Farrell. All done with harmonics. Better than CIA. CIA needs same machine on both ends.

"Yuri?" Bannerman's voice. "We were just leaving for the airport. Where are you?"

"On road approaching Zurich. Not long to Carla's house. Carla is safe in my flat, asleep from pills I gave her. I estimate she will not wake for six hours."

"You'll be back before then?"

"If no difficulties, yes."

"Keep her there, even if you have to tie her up. Have you spoken to Leo?"

"I have left two messages but they have gone to dinner."

"Which means he can't reach you until you get back to Bern. I can't wait for that, Yuri. I've got to know what I'm walking into."

"I know. Is purpose of call. I have translation of Corsini tapes."

"Translated? By whom?"

"By KGB officer. A woman. She is reliable, I think. She helped me to find Corsini in restricted files. She is with me now."

A brief silence, suggestive of annoyance. Then, "Start with the files. Who is he?"

Yuri hesitated. "Please understand. Best for me if you speak first."

Bannerman understood. Accessing restricted files could mean a court-martial, Leo or no Leo. The young Russian was hoping that all he had to do was confirm.

"Corsini is an agent-in-place," said Bannerman as if it were more than a guess. "He's working for the SCD and I think that Roger Clew knows it."

"Thank you. Since when does he know?"

"Only since after the wedding."

Yuri grunted. Clew had done a background check, probably out of curiosity. Yuri wished now that he had thought to do the same.

"Clew does not know that he's dead?"

"No. Confirm or deny, please, Yuri."

"He was an agent. File gives no details but yes, he was run by SCD. He is part of a network. All totally illegal."

"Is the SCD, or a faction within it, trying to control drug distribution in your country?"

"Not just drugs. All smuggling, all organized crime."

"Why would that interest Roger?"

Yuri hesitated. "You understand that Soviet Union . . . former Soviet Union . . . has no money?"

"Yes."

"Everything is for sale. Weapons and guidance systems are for sale. Two hundred kilos of enriched uranium are missing. Many tons of nerve gas are missing."

A long silence. "Does Leo Belkin know where they've gone?"

"No."

"Does he have an opinion?"

"Is like . . . when a war is just ending. Some things are hidden for later. Some things are hidden so that others cannot use them."

"Does this include money?"

"Money, much gold, gemstones from Ural mines . . . everything."

"Including, I suppose, morphine base."

"Yes."

"Isn't that Leo's immediate interest? The drug trade?"

"Began with drugs, yes. But same distribution network would be used for most other forms of contraband. Control that network and you control all the rest."

"Which this *faction* is trying to do now?"

"We think so. Yes."

"Yuri . . . why is this necessarily sinister? I mean, might this simply be good police work?"

A part of Yuri wanted to laugh. "No one is in charge, Mr. Bannerman. At this level, all is chaos. Chaos always brings opportunists. Is important to remember that many thousands of trained KGB officers are now unemployed. Also that not all of the bad ones have been purged."

Bannerman grunted. Another thoughtful silence.

"Back to this drug network, Yuri. Leo, I take it, plans to use the Zurich program against it."

"Not just General Belkin, but yes."

"And it's all programmed and ready?"

"Is not ready. Needs names."

An exasperated sigh. "Which he hopes to get how? By thumbing his nose at Moscow Center and hoping that they'll do something stupid?"

"Not so simplistic. But yes. He means to draw them out."

"Using himself as bait. Along with Lesko and Elena."

"Elena is not being used. For most part, she agrees with what he is doing."

"She's known all along?"

"Since before the wedding, yes."

"Yuri . . ." Bannerman paused, searching for words. "Doesn't this sound just a little bit crazy to you?"

"World is crazy."

"We're talking about Leo. If there is an outlaw KGB, it's none of Leo's business. Why is he taking this on?"

"Not his business? Is his country."

"You know what I mean."

"Country is dying, Mr. Bannerman."

Yuri felt a sudden wave of sadness. As much as he respected this man, he saw no use in trying to explain General Belkin to him. Bannerman would not understand. For Bannerman there is no country. He defends only his portion of it, only his friends. For all else, his soul has turned to ice.

The question, the one that had eluded Yuri, began forming again. But once more the pieces fell away. Bannerman. It had to do with Bannerman. With cutting off a head.

214   John R. Maxim

"Yuri?"

"Still here."

"Back to Corsini. Was he a professional?"

"Some training. Not much, I think. Admiration of your people was genuine."

"They sent an amateur against Carla Benedict?"

"They sent a romantic. He knows to be attentive, to flatter, and he is probably proficient in bedroom. In this case, I think, these skills were the first requirement."

"I suppose," Bannerman said distantly. "What's on the tape?"

Yuri opened Lydia's notebook. His intention was to give only the essence of Corsini's remarks, withholding certain particulars. The identity of this Borovik was not for Bannerman to know. Or those names that he had memorized and then written down. Those were a KGB matter. Absolutely requires permission from General Belkin.

He began summarizing. Bannerman listened closely.

At the part where Corsini realized that there was no urgency to make this trip, Bannerman expressed regret that Corsini had not lived to report it. But all it probably meant was that Belkin wasn't quite ready. And perhaps all the more vulnerable.

"Yuri?"

"Yes."

"While I think of it, don't assume that Corsini worked alone, especially if he's not a trained agent. I can't believe that whoever sent him would not have assigned someone else to observe and report. That person might be wondering where he is before long."

"My thought as well," Yuri told him. "Is why I brought extra pair of eyes."

"And you'd better assume that Roger has Corsini under surveillance by now."

"While he is with Carla as well? Would he take such a risk?"

"Perhaps not. But keep it in mind."

"Thank you. I continue? Notes now get interesting."

"Please."

Bannerman listened with growing wonder to the workings of Aldo Corsini's mind. His detachment from reality.

Aldo's conviction that he could have been the best of them.
If Bannerman were to beat his doctor neighbor at one-on-
one, he would not conclude that he was ready for the Boston
Celtics.

Regarding the two women he seems to be claiming that
he killed, Bannerman had no idea what to make of that.
Corsini told Carla that his wife had died in a fire. Maybe
he'd killed her and then set it. Maybe she'd spit in his face.

As for the sudden decision to marry Carla, Bannerman
did not share Yuri's view that Carla would necessarily have
checked him out first. She might not have wanted to know.
Enjoy it while you can. Nothing lasts anyway. If a dark side
should turn up later she was more than capable of dealing
with it. No one has a side as dark as Carla's.

The most curious revelation was Aldo's intention to live
in Westport, become totally accepted, and become rich and
famous by doing so. Even assuming acceptance, which
would be polite at best, how does he get rich? He asked this
question of Yuri.

A low grunt. The equivalent of a shrug.

"Lydia suggests assassination. Most likely of Mama's
Boy."

"Why me? I'm not part of this." No alarm in his voice.
Only annoyance.

"Old grievance, perhaps. I do not know."

"Okay, then who would pay him?"

"Perhaps no one. Is possible that this is fantasy."

"Yuri . . ." Bannerman's voice had an edge. "Who
does Aldo *think* would pay him?"

The Russian hesitated. Bannerman heard the drumming
of fingers against the roadside kiosk.

"I will tell you," Yuri answered finally, "that there is a
man. He is KGB. Moscow Center. He seems to be Aldo
Corsini's control."

"But you won't tell me his name."

"Internal matter. Only with permission."

"Fair enough. Does Leo know it?"

"I learn it myself only tonight. Computer in Bern speaks
of him. Corsini speaks of him. I must emphasize, however,
that this is only one name. Not name at top. Would be far
from top. This man is strictly goon."

"Well, have you checked my file?"

"Recently, no."

"It wouldn't have been recent. Have I crossed this man in the past?"

"I would have remembered. I don't . . ."

His voice trailed off.

That question. It was trying to form again. There were pictures this time. The computer screen in Bern. Borovik's file. And there was that phrase. The cutting off of heads.

Heads.

Mutilation.

"I must ask a question." Yuri took a breath. "You have been to Leningrad?"

"Once."

"And when was this?"

"Eight or nine years ago. Why?"

"Was a man killed on that occasion? KGB?"

"Yes."

"Would you tell me . . . in what manner?"

The line fell silent for a moment. Then muffled words. Sound of Susan's voice. It was Yuri's impression that she was being asked to occupy herself elsewhere. A sliding door opened and closed. Bannerman's voice again.

"What's this about, Yuri?"

"Indulge me, please. What happened in Leningrad?"

Bannerman hesitated, then appeared to conclude that there was no harm in telling.

"There was a prisoner exchange. Your people had kidnapped one of ours. We kidnapped one of yours in return."

"KGB?"

"A colonel. I don't remember his name, but there were two of them. Brothers. Both colonels."

"You kidnapped two?"

"Just the one. We picked him up in East Germany and brought him to Helsinki for the swap. His brother negotiated for your side. Billy McHugh, John Waldo, and I made the exchange from a boat just off the Finnish coast. Our man was belted to a stretcher. He'd been beaten but he was lucid. He said there were no weapons on their boat and they hadn't wired him in any way, but he'd heard helicopters warming up on the other shore. We lifted him aboard, shoved our hostage into the water, and got out of there while the Russians were fishing him out. But I should have . . ."

Bannerman's voice trailed off. Yuri realized that he was replaying that day in his mind, clearly chastising himself for some remembered failure.

"To make a long story short," said Bannerman, "the brother had rigged a timing device inside the aluminum frame of the stretcher."

"Explosives?"

"No. Well . . . just a pop. It was . . ."

Bannerman cleared his throat.

"Alcohol and methyl difluoride," said Bannerman. "Do you know what that is?"

"Is sarin. Nerve gas."

"The charge mixed the two chemicals. The gas killed our man and the crew of an ambulance we had waiting. The rest of us were following behind. We saw the ambulance drift onto the shoulder, hit a ditch, and roll over. I had no idea what happened. I ran to pull them out but Billy knocked me down. Two girls on a motorcycle came from the other direction. They saw what they thought was an accident and rode their bike to the door before Billy could stop them. They died as well."

Yuri cleared his throat. "But this is Finland, yes? Still not Leningrad."

"Leningrad was about eight months later. We went back in for that colonel. His name was Borovik, now that I think of it. Colonel Gennadi Borovik."

"You executed him?"

"Yes. Are you ready to tell me why you're asking?"

"Possible relevance. How did he die?"

Voice became flat. "I cut his head off, Yuri."

The Russian swallowed. Lydia's translation was better than she knew. He moistened his lips. "Ah . . . Details might be useful," he said.

"What do you want to know?" Bannerman's voice showed annoyance again. "Did I take my time? Did I use a butter knife?"

Yuri thought he knew the answer to this. Profile on Mama's Boy was clear. If he goes to kill, he kills. No cruelty, no waste of time. Yuri flattered himself that he was like Bannerman in this regard. Killing was not a game.

But it was also true that Mama's Boy leaves no doubt. Always leaves signature.

"I . . . am curious what you did with this head."

A long silence, perhaps to determine that Susan could not hear. Then, "I left it on the hood of his car. I left his car parked outside number 4 Liteiny Prospekt."

Yuri closed his eyes.

Liteiny 4. KGB headquarters for Leningrad.

He remembered hearing a story, officially denied, of a terrorist attack on that building. It had happened before his time. But he recalled no mention of a head used as hood ornament. Only of firebombs.

"Firebombs," he said aloud. "That was you, by chance?"

"Yuri . . . have you read my file or haven't you?"

"File has nothing about this. Very curious."

He heard Susan's voice in the background. Anton is outside, she is saying. They must leave now or they will miss their flight. Bannerman says that he'll be right behind her.

"Not so curious," he told Yuri. "The intent was to humiliate. They dealt with that by deciding it never happened."

"Humiliation was purpose of firebombing as well?"

"No. That was a few days later. John Waldo stayed in Leningrad for a while."

The young Russian raised an eyebrow. "For what purpose?"

"Staying or bombing, Yuri?"

"Staying was to cover Mama's Boy's retreat. Bombing was to create a diversion?"

"It was more of an impulse. He thought the building was ugly."

33

The Sicilian found no car inside the boathouse. It had no room for one in any case.

He had entered from the open end, which faced the lake. He waited for several minutes, listening. He heard no sound except the stop-and-go scurrying of rats who had caught his scent. He wondered, idly, how they managed to smell him, so strong was the stink of mildew and of spilled gasoline.

In what little light there was he could make out the shape of a small motorboat. It was hanging from a davit over the launching well. To one side, he saw the wooden cradle for it. He also saw the white hull of a Sunfish leaning against one wall. Its sail had been carelessly wrapped around the mast and boom and all three left lying on the damp concrete floor.

These sights and smells annoyed the Sicilian. He had spent much of his life around boats. They deserved better care than this. He fought off an urge to hang the Sunfish mast on the wall before the rats make a nest of the sail. Pull the outboard in and lower it onto its cradle before a wind comes up and bangs it against the hoist.

Perhaps, he thought, Carla Benedict knows no better. Probably the only things she takes good care of are her knives. But Aldo should have taught her. Not that he was such great shakes at maintenance himself.

He decided to risk using his penlight.

The beam picked up a winding iron staircase which stood in the far corner. Above it was a trapdoor, very large, intended for passing nautical equipment back and forth when the apartment upstairs was still a sail loft.

Two rats began squealing. Fighting. The noise seemed deafening.

The Sicilian froze, listening for sounds from above. He heard nothing. No feet striking the floor. No evidence that

there was anyone there to hear. Carefully, silently, he
climbed the spiral steps. He had no intention of entering the
apartment, least of all being caught inside by Carla should
she return home suddenly. It simply struck him as a good
thing to know whether the trapdoor was bolted from above.
Knowing Carla Benedict's reputation, it surely was.

But it was not.

He opened it a crack and listened. Still no sound. No
snoring from the bedroom. Only the ticking of a clock and
the cloying smell that the homes of single women always
seem to have. He opened it further and froze again. He was
about to shine his light when something, it sounded like
chunks of broken glass, clattered off the tilted door. A rat
chose this moment to scream again and another caused a
bottle to tip over and roll.

He eased the door closed and stood, not moving. It
crossed his mind that the broken glass might be some sort of
booby trap, some warning device, but he knew that this was
probably nonsense. More likely, Carla Benedict was as poor
a housekeeper above as she was below. And if ever there
was proof that no one was home, all that racket provided it.
Borovik would have to be satisfied.

He switched the penlight on again, marking a path back
through the boathouse with its beam. It picked up several
pairs of glowing eyes. Two of the rats paused, briefly, and
then scurried toward the launching well where he saw them
leap the several inches into the hanging motorboat. More
squealing broke out. Rats thumping against the hull. He
wondered what had attracted them to that boat.

He swung the beam and saw it. A carpet, rolled up
loosely. At the bow end he saw what seemed to be a
defeated rat. Its face was bleeding. It was licking its paws.
Now he saw movement inside the carpet.

The Sicilian's stomach tightened. Two things were possible. Either the rats were nesting in that boat or he now
understood why Aldo Corsini had not reported, why his car
was not there.

The fool had killed another woman.

A part of him wanted to leave at once, get to his
transmitter, make his call. But he had to be certain. He
hurried down the iron staircase and picked up a centerboard

that was leaning against a wall near the Sunfish. With it, he stepped to the edge of the launching well and began beating the carpet. Four, then six rats emerged and scattered, leaping over the gunwales and plopping heavily to the concrete before vanishing into the darkness.

Satisfied that none were left, he reached into the opening at the bow end and felt the unmistakable shape of a skull. It was wet and torn. He found the end of the carpet and, with effort, began unrolling it, wiping his hand clean in the process. When only one thickness was left, he pulled it down far enough to reveal a face and he fumbled for his penlight again.

He had little doubt of what he would see. This scene was familiar to him. In his mind he saw a picture of Corsini's dead wife, wrapped tightly in a sheet, flames lapping all around her bed. He saw that other woman, the fashion model from Milan, weighted with a sack of canned goods and dropped over the side of his boat off the Corsican coast. He saw that Carla Benedict, like those two, had somehow caused Corsini to forget himself.

Cursing Aldo once more, he switched on the light.

The Sicilian gasped. In surprise, not horror.

He had been wrong.

The face, badly gnawed, both eyes gone, was not that of Carla Benedict. It was Corsini himself. He covered it again. Breathing heavily, struggling against the swaying boat, he rolled the carpet once more.

His face burning, he made his way out of the boathouse and toward the small marina where he had left his car. He needed to clear his head. To think.

What could this mean?

His first thought, as before, was that Corsini had lost control again. A wrong word was said, some imagined insult, and he had hit her. The sickness of Corsini was that once this began, he could not seem to stop it. But this time the woman he hit was not a whining wife who had grown up rich and spoiled. It was not a preening model from Milan. This was Carla Benedict, who had probably killed twenty to his two.

But he had another thought.

Carla had discovered him. Or she knew from the beginning.

This would not have surprised the Sicilian. He thought from the beginning that this would never work. This was Carla Benedict, he had argued, not some schoolgirl, not some unfulfilled housewife in search of a romantic fling. Has she stayed alive so long, he asked, by trusting a man just because he takes her sailing in the moonlight?

Perhaps, thought the Sicilian, he should go back and examine the body more closely. See how he died.

Had she questioned him first? Coring one eye socket to get him in a talking mood? That was what the Sicilian might have done. And then ended it with one quick thrust at the base of the skull.

Both of Aldo's eyes were gone, but that must have been the work of the rats. Cuts by Carla would have been clean, practiced, professional. No use going back. With a flashlight, without a pathologist, it would be impossible to tell how long she might have worked on him.

And whether she had help.

The Sicilian considered this.

In his mind, he tried to envision how Carla could have wrapped Corsini in a carpet and lifted him into that boat by herself. Would she have the strength? Perhaps. She is small, but she is wiry. He could not imagine who she might have called upon for help in any case. Possibly one of Bannerman's people who are now working for the Bruggs. But if one thing is known about Carla Benedict, it is that she is very independent. She almost always works alone.

Yes, he decided. It could have been done. Dragging him to the trapdoor would not be so difficult. Squeezing him down that winding staircase would have taken some effort, but in that case she was assisted by gravity. From there it was not far to the launching well. She would have lowered the boat to just below the edge and rolled him into it.

But the point of doing so, he assumed, was to dispose of Aldo out on the lake. Why, therefore, had she not seen it through? Where had she gone? If she had decided at last to get help, perhaps to enlist the Bruggs, tell them of Aldo's interest in the Russia visit, she could have done all that by telephone.

He could think of only one other possibility. If Corsini had named names, including the Sicilian's, she might now be out looking for him.

A second alternative flitted across his mind. She had gone after Borovik himself. He knew that this was ridiculous. Inspired, no doubt, by Carla Benedict's reputation for extravagant behavior. Getting Borovik's name from Aldo was one thing. Getting at him was another. You don't just climb on a plane and say take me to Moscow.

Yes.

An intelligent move would be to sever Aldo's one communications link with any support that might be available to him. Even now, she might be waiting for him outside the house where he had taken rooms. The Sicilian was sorely tempted to go back there. She might have gotten Aldo to describe him to her, but she would not know him on sight. He had that advantage. He could finish her first. Be able to report that he had nipped this in the bud.

A better way, he reflected, might be to stay right here. She would surely come back well before sunrise in order to dispose of Aldo. She would not expect him. The Sicilian wet his lips. To be the man who took out Carla Benedict, one against one, would raise his stock considerably.

He knew that he should ask Podolsk first. But Podolsk would say hands off. Get out of Zurich now. Go back to Genoa, lie low. We don't need problems with Mama's Boy.

So, no use asking Podolsk.

The Sicilian's excuse would be that he could not risk reporting to Podolsk on an open line and that his instructions, in any case, were to report directly to Borovik.

He took the communicator from his belt and stepped out under open sky. Extending the antenna, he tapped out a series of digits and followed them with Borovik's designator. He waited. From Ostankino, an answering code blinked across his readout. Cleared to send.

The Sicilian hesitated. There were only so many prearranged signals.

Corsini was BARCA. CAT meant dead. Carla Benedict was BLADE. BLUE meant am terminating. This last, strictly speaking, referred to operations and not to avenging Aldo. He would do his best to make his meaning clear. Mix in a few

words for which there were no codes. Doing so would
surely make Podolsk angry.

But maybe not Borovik.

All Borovik would care about was that he made her
suffer.

34

Yuri knew that he must clear his head.

Too many distracting images.

Booby traps with nerve gas. Innocent victims. Vengeance. Decapitation. Add to these the knowledge that he
had probably said too much. But there was no help for that
now. The immediate need was to get rid of a body.

He had driven, with Lydia, over the Quay Bridge where
Carla told of feeding swans with Aldo. He turned south,
down through the necklace of lights that bordered Lake
Zurich. Just a few kilometers further, where the lights began
to thin, was Carla's boathouse. Time to be alert.

Innocent victims. The phrase pushed through again.

Not only the two girls on the motorcycle. Not only the
ambulance crew. There were Russian victims as well. The
file on the late Colonel Borovik said that there had been
confessions and executions. It noted that their legitimacy
was doubtful. And yet the investigation had been closed.

It had been closed, he felt certain, because they knew
perfectly well who had done it. Mama's Boy would have
left no room for doubt. Hit me, I hit back. Twice as hard,
twice as terribly, and where you least expect it. Yuri could
only suppose that someone high in the KGB had decided to
cut his losses. Or to mollify the surviving Borovik by
sacrificing a few more Russians.

Those who were executed were certainly scapegoats,
dying to protect KGB interests. And perhaps to avoid a
diplomatic confrontation with Finland. Yuri hoped that they

were not so innocent. Criminals, at least. Rapists and murderers. But it was just as likely, he knew, that one of them had an apartment that some party official coveted.

No wonder General Belkin is ashamed.

Most distracting of all, in its way, was this business of firebombing KGB headquarters in Leningrad. It was done, according to Mama's Boy, not as additional retribution but as a statement of architectural criticism. At first, Yuri felt sure that his leg was being pulled. But no. Bannerman was quite clear. John Waldo had decided that the building was ugly.

This was completely insane.

I mean, thought Yuri, here is John Waldo, at that time surely one of the three most hunted men in all of Eastern Europe—not Russia, because no one would have imagined that he would linger in the Soviet Union—and he tosses a bomb made of petrol and rubber cement—very hot, hard to put out—through the front door of Number 4 Liteiny Prospekt.

You want to know who thinks this is not so crazy? You need to guess? The answer is Lydia. Lydia listens to this story and you know what she says?

She says, "It *is* ugly."

She does not say that he does this, perhaps, to lay a false trail, to sow confusion. She says that this building—they call it the Big House—is totally out of place among the fine czarist pastel-colored houses of Liteiny Prospekt and all of Leningrad for that matter. In this whole museum city, she says, it is the one building that the citizens of Leningrad would permit to be torn down. Not because of KGB. Not because of unpleasant associations. Plenty of buildings have bad memories. It's only because it's so ugly. Too bad, she says, about those who died from the smoke. But also too bad that the fire was extinguished.

Lydia and John Waldo. A match made in heaven.

He forced the subject from his mind. He was sorry that he mentioned it to Lydia. He was talking entirely too much this evening.

His most serious lapse has been with Mama's Boy. Where this Borovik was concerned, the cat was definitely out of the bag.

Although Bannerman had not let on that he knew, probably out of politeness, it had perhaps taken him thirty seconds to realize that the colonel he had kidnapped in East Germany, whose brother he had subsequently decapitated, was the same man who was now running Aldo Corsini's network.

Very stupid, thought Yuri. No excuse for it. Certainly none that will satisfy General Belkin. The only mitigation is that Bannerman can do little for the next seven hours except sit on an airplane. By the time he arrives in Zurich, Yuri will have spoken to General Belkin and made a very strong suggestion that he get out of Moscow immediately.

Come back to Bern. Begin building names into computer. We now have General Vadim Y. Borovik and most of his European network except for two or three names that Yuri had been unable to retain when he memorized them. No matter. Lydia will probably give him another look if he can manage to keep her moods on an even keel. After that, it is only a matter of finding dossiers to match the names. And then interrogating a few. Soon we will have all the names we need.

Better yet, forget the Zurich program. Go to the Chairman with with names and evidence. Go to CNN for that matter. *New York Times*.

But he knew that General Belkin would do neither of these. We don't hang out our laundry, he would say. Nor do we go to the Chairman, or to the KGB chief of investigations. The cockroaches would only scurry out of sight and the goon, Borovik, will have conveniently thrown himself out of his apartment window.

This would surprise anyone? Five days after the Gorbachev coup, party treasurer Nikolai Kruchina does precisely that. Jumps or is pushed. A few weeks later you look up and here comes his predecessor, Georgi Pavlov. Meanwhile, most of Soviet Union's gold is missing. Next comes Dmitri Lisovolik, chief of the party's International Department, after investigators find 600,000 American dollars in his office safe. Got so people would only walk in middle of street.

Carla's boathouse was just ahead.

He knew that it would be in darkness. It was set in a grove

of trees some thirty meters in from the road. The house was equipped with floodlights that were activated by a motion detector, but he had pulled the plug before he left. He would have motions of his own which he didn't need detected. It also helped that there was not much moon. And a haze floated over the lake. A small boat would quickly be lost in it. This was all to the good.

"House is there," he told Lydia. "Slow down but drive past."

Sliding lower in his seat, he looked as best he could for signs of visitors. He saw the shape of only one vehicle. Carla's Volkswagen. There were still no lights coming from the house. No suspicious cars parked in the vicinity.

"You see that marina?" He pointed to a sign. "Pull in there."

It was not much of a marina. Little more than a ramp for the launching of boats on trailers. But it was a place to stop and get organized.

The marina had parking for about a dozen cars but only one space was filled. A small Fiat, probably left for the night. He would check it all the same, see if it's warm to the touch. It might also be useful if he should need to borrow it. Fiats are easy to start. Yuri pulled in next to it.

Nearby, was a rack holding several canoes. They were chained and padlocked. Yuri saw one whose chain ran through the handle of a paddle. It gave him an idea. The chain would be no problem. A tire iron would suffice.

He reached into the glove box for the two automatic pistols which he had taken from General Belkin's safe. They were not the best. One was a Browning, .22 caliber, long rifle. Only useful for head shots, thought Yuri. He counted five rounds in a clip meant for ten. He chambered one of them.

The other pistol was a Turkish MKE, four-inch barrel, seven shots, caliber was .380 ACP. A ridiculous weapon, he thought. The rear sight was adjustable for windage. With a four-inch barrel, this is pretentious. He gave that one to Lydia.

She sniffed but made no other comment as she very professionally checked the mechanism and determined that the bore was not obstructed. She, too, chambered a round.

Yuri handed her the key to Carla's front door. He described the location of the lock and the direction in which it turned so that she would not be seen to fumble with it.

"I will go back by canoe," he told her. "Give me ten minutes to look things over, then you will drive to her door, enter quickly, and wait. Do not turn on the lights. I will watch a few minutes more and then come in."

"So much caution?" she asked.

"Best to be safe."

"But this is Corsini's car. If anyone is watching, they have already seen it."

Yuri had considered that. He had thought of driving directly to the boathouse as if they were Carla and Aldo returning from a day's outing. But while Lydia might pass for Carla in the dark, he was twice the size of Corsini. Better this way, he told her. Bannerman might be right about a second agent snooping about. American intelligence was another possibility. Even Swiss police, if a cleaning woman, for example, had chosen this day to enter the boathouse and had seen all the blood.

Always amazing, the things that go wrong.

35

Borovik sat slumped in his chair, a framed photo of his mother in his hands. He kissed it. Then he hugged it against his chest.

He had told her the bad news. Corsini was dead. Bannerman would have to wait a while longer.

She put up an understanding front, she comforted him as always, but he could see in her eyes, even in just a photograph, how disappointed she was.

A jangling of the olive-colored phone had intruded. The caller, a former captain, wanted an explanation of the traffic that had just been exchanged with Zurich.

He was polite enough. He said, "I am sure, Vadim Yakovich, that I must not be reading these correctly. If you would tell me precisely what these signals mean . . ."

But Borovik had looked down into his mother's eyes. Her eyes said, *"Tell him it's none of his business."*

That's just what he did. But the former captain started to give him an argument. He was not so polite now. Borovik hung up on him.

Perhaps, he told his mother afterward, that wasn't such a good idea. The former captain might go right to the man in the Scottish hat, and Borovik had had enough trouble from that one already. But his mother said, *"Vadim, my fine son, don't worry about it. They still need you more than you need them. One hand washes the other."*

Behind him, another interruption. A knocking on the door. Borovik ignored it.

He knew that it was Podolsk. He had seen him coming from two streets away, head up, arms stiff, hands made into fists. The look of a man spoiling for a fight. He was coming, no doubt, to say why he had disobeyed instructions. Why he was not at the Savoy.

That matter could wait. It seemed not so important now. More important was his poor mother. He had promised her, her photo at least, that soon he would have the man who had tortured and beheaded her youngest son. And now, before he could keep it, that promise was broken.

He had jumped the gun. He realized that.

If he had taken the time to think, he would have realized that Corsini was not the man for such a job. Not alone, certainly. Nor did he want Corsini, even if he got lucky, to put a bullet behind the ear of Mama's Boy. He wanted Mama's Boy alive.

He would have found a way to bring him back to Moscow. Not to this building perhaps. But there are other basements. Bannerman would be strapped to a table. His mother would come. He would let her see him in the beginning, let her slap his face, and he would have let her see him once more at the end. She would not have wanted to watch in between.

The door opened. He heard a clearing of the throat.

"Get out, Podolsk," he said quietly.

"Suit yourself," came the answer. "I'm going home."

The smaller man snorted, still not turning.

Except for that insolent tone, Borovik was tempted to let him go before he made an even greater mess of everything. He had completely botched a simple surveillance. He had allowed some German's computer to be stolen right in front of him. He has even failed to find that woman who met the Belkin party in the middle of Red Square. In that one wide-open area he can't find a tall woman wearing a long purple coat with green pants.

Now he is here to defend himself. He is actually defiant. He is going to complain about how they showed themselves from the beginning, how one of them stole a computer, how another one decided to take the evening off.

All this should come as a surprise? These men are gangsters. They are thieves. If you don't watch a thief, he will steal. This is why you put an officer in charge of them in the first place.

Borovik kissed his mother's picture. He returned it to his desk, then glanced up at Podolsk, who was still standing there, jaw set.

"Where is Kerensky now?" he asked.

No answer. Podolsk was staring at the desk.

"I asked you . . ."

Podolsk pointed. "Is that my communicator? My code-book?"

"It is not *your* communicator. You work for me. Therefore, it is *my* communicator. Where is Kerensky?"

"Out there," Podolsk said through his teeth. "He's going to stand outside Detsky Mir, all night if he has to, waiting for his brother to show up. He's going to get that machine back, give it to the doorman, and then he's going to forget that he ever heard the name of Leo Belkin."

A half smile from Borovik. His Stalin smile.

"And so will I," Podolsk added. "I'm finished with this Belkin nonsense."

Now Borovik blinked. He made a show of looking around his office as if searching for a clue to what had brought about this boldness.

"A lottery ticket?" he asked. "While you were out, you found some more winning tickets?"

Podolsk said nothing.

"While you were out, you moved all of your relatives to the West? The CIA has promised you a penthouse in New York and a Cadillac?"

Podolsk ignored the sarcasm. His eyes were on the communicator, his frown deepening. Next to it was a pink folder marked *Sovermenno Sekretno*—Top Secret.

"You've . . . heard from Barca," he said.

The Stalin smile faded. He nodded toward the folder. "I've heard from the Sicilian. Barca is dead."

Podolsk stood stunned. Then, "How? By whom?"

"Bannerman's slut. The Benedict woman."

His color rising, Podolsk reached for the folder. Borovik did not stop him. He opened it and read the partially encrypted message from the Sicilian. He could scarcely believe what he was seeing.

"It came in just this way? By satellite?"

A sigh. First that captain, thought Borovik, and now this one.

Podolsk could have wept. "This went out through the atmosphere? This?"

"*Yes,*" Borovik bellowed. "Now shut up about it."

Podolsk, nonetheless, read it aloud. "BARCA CAT. BY BLADE. AT BLADE HOUSE, ZU. SUGGEST BLUE BLADE NOW. CAN DO. AM IN POSITION."

Borovik sagged. No heart, this one. Cold fish. Barca is dead, and all he can think about is form.

"But this is . . ." As Podolsk stammered, in search of words, he noticed that something else was written on a sheet under the Sicilian's message. He looked. It was in Borovik's hand. It read, BLUE BLADE. WANT BLADE CAT. LEAVE HEAD, REPEAT, LEAVE BLADE HEAD, BLADE HOUSE, ZU, PLAIN SIGHT.

He thinks this is code, Podolsk screamed in his mind. Wait.

"What is HEAD?" he asked. "I don't know HEAD."

"Head is head and it's none of your business."

"This means . . . what? Kill Carla Benedict and leave her head dangling from the doorknob?"

Borovik pursed his lips. He had not thought to specify. Was it too late, he wondered, to say leave it on the hood of her car.

Viktor Podolsk felt lightheaded. A part of him wanted to laugh, a part wanted to scream, but a third part warned him to be careful. This is so incomprehensibly stupid that it cannot be genuine. Could Borovik be setting him up? Using his communicator? Signing off with his designator?

Think.

The Sicilian must surely know better than to send a message like this by satellite. But the Sicilian had clearly sent it.

And as for Borovik, for all that his mind is diseased, he is not a complete fool. Could he not know that a child could read this? To intercept such a message is a cryptanalyst's fantasy. It brightens his day. He waves it to the others in the decrypting room and says, ''You will not believe this one.'' They all have a good laugh about it. They leave it pinned to a bulletin board.

The Americans, surely the Swiss, must be keeping track of Carla Benedict. All they would need is one key—the knowledge that Barca is Corsini—and most of the the rest of it falls into place. Barca is Corsini. Corsini is with Carla Benedict. Carla must be BLADE and ZU must be Zurich. It isn't Zululand. The only confusion would involve the meaning of HEAD. No one would believe that HEAD meant *head*.

The telephone rang. The olive-colored one.

Good. It gave him time.

Think.

Do they know that Corsini is Barca?

Prudent assumption is yes. Surely, Carla must. Otherwise, why would she kill him? The question is how much more she got out of him, and what other names.

Borovik took the call. He answered, Podolsk noticed, in an irritable manner. On that phone, this was unusual. Normally he was respectful in case the call was from someone important.

But his manner changed at once. Suddenly, there was surprise, deference, perhaps even a hint of fear. Borovik had forced a smile. He was apologizing, saying that he thought it was Captain . . . something . . . calling back. The name, like the apology, was mumbled. Podolsk could not catch it.

All at once he was Borovik the toady again. Podolsk had seen it a hundred times. If he outranks you, his foot is on your neck. If you outrank him, his tongue is on your boots.

The subject at hand seemed to be Barca. And then that exchange of messages. Suddenly, Borovik winced. He turned away so that Podolsk could not see his face, but he was too late. Podolsk could hear the other voice each time it rose to an angry or sarcastic shout. Borovik said nothing for fully half a minute. His color was rising rapidly. No question, thought Podolsk, that he's being reprimanded. But by whom?

"General Belkin?" he heard Borovik ask, his voice the soul of innocence.

Another shout. He cringed. Then, defiantly, "Yes. Of course I know who you mean. Why should I play dumb?"

But his color was rising rapidly.

Next, he said, "You say don't go near him so I don't go near him. But the way he's been acting the past two years, I still think . . ."

Podolsk heard rising inflections, the sound of questions, sharply asked. When Borovik spoke again, his tone was downcast, his voice barely audible.

"I assumed . . . you meant none of our own people should go near him. I asked . . . as a favor . . . for someone else to keep an eye on Belkin."

The voice on the other end seemed to go silent for a moment. Then more questions followed.

"Chicago Brigade, yes. May I ask how you knew that?"

It was Podolsk's impression that the voice did not answer. Then came a change of subject because Borovik replied, "The signal to Zurich had nothing to do with Belkin. We have a small problem there and I am taking care of it."

Another question.

"No."

Borovik was squirming.

"My dead brother has nothing to do with this," Podolsk heard him say. "Least of all does Mama's Boy."

Podolsk rolled his eyes.

More questions.

"The man with General Belkin is named Raymond Lesko," Borovik said in response to one or more of them.

"He is an American, the husband of the Brugg woman, otherwise he is nobody important. As for a younger man, the only young man I know about is Belkin's driver."

Silence. Then, "Yes, they were at GUM this evening. In the crowds, our man lost track of them. Excuse me, but why do you ask?"

Podolsk waited.

"Man is named Sasha Kerensky, yes."

A nod.

"Yes, Kerensky brothers. They . . ." Borovik stopped himself. "Excuse me, but how is it that you know his name?"

Podolsk saw Borovik stiffen.

"Dead? But . . . how? In what manner?"

Podolsk, even through his own numbed surprise, thought that this was an odd question to ask. The image of a decapitated head flashed through his mind, unbidden. He listened closely, trying to hear all that he could, praying, above all, that Borovik would forget himself and address the caller by name.

Suddenly, Borovik became aware of him. He half turned, jabbing a finger at the door, telling Podolsk to use it. Podolsk hesitated. He took his communicator and his codebook from the desk but he made no other move. Borovik glared at him, mouthing *Get out*. Podolsk shook his head. His eyes said, *Not this time, Borovik*. They said, *I will not leave just so you can tell your handlers that whatever happened to that oaf, it happened because Major Viktor Podolsk failed to follow your instructions.*

Borovik turned away, his expression one of helpless rage—but only for a moment. The voice, and whatever it was saying, soon caused the blood to drain from his face. He listened, bent over as if in pain. Now and then he tried to interrupt, his manner servile, attempting to mollify, but each sound he uttered was cut off by the voice.

An unusual voice, thought Podolsk. Sharp but melodic. No Moscow drawl from what he could hear of it, but no recognizable accent either. The voice, when shouting, had an almost-operatic timbre. It seemed to him that he had heard it before, but he could not begin to place it. Suddenly, with a loud clatter, it was gone. Borovik now found his own voice. He began speaking, for Podolsk's benefit, over a line that was now as dead as Sasha Kerensky.

"No, you listen," he began. "No, no, Minister. You will shut up and listen."

The charade was mercifully brief. Just enough to let Podolsk know who still was boss and that he was talking to a minister of the republic who certainly did not exist. He hung up on this ghost.

Podolsk wanted desperately to leave.

He wanted to find another window to the open sky so that he could countermand that stupid order. Even now, in Borovik's office, he was working the communicator with his thumb on the chance that the signal might go through. The Sicilian's code. Then the code for *abort*. Then Borovik's sign-off. But he could not leave without knowing, at least asking, what had happened to Sasha. Borovik would smell a rat at once.

"The American killed him," said Borovik as if in answer. "The policeman named Lesko." He had turned once more to stare out into the night. "Lesko and Belkin's driver. They beat him to death outside GUM."

Podolsk was too astonished to speak.

"First he mocks me," said Borovik distantly. "He drives past my window and he gestures . . . so." He mimed Lesko's salute from Belkin's Chaika. "He knows that, meanwhile, Barca is dead or dying. Before he is one hour more in Moscow, he murders Sasha Kerensky."

"Ah . . . who says so, General Borovik, sir?"

The Stalin doll almost answered. He motioned toward the olive phone but he caught himself.

"He was seen." The voice was still small. "He left his photograph on Kerensky's chest. He left all their photographs."

Podolsk shook his head. To him, this was inconceivable.

"How many others, Podolsk?" He stood up, moving to his window.

A helpless shrug. "How many others . . . what?"

"This was coordinated," he said. "Barca in Zurich. Sasha under my nose. Both at the same hour. How many of the others, Podolsk? How many more are dead?"

"The American . . ." Podolsk struggled to grasp all this. To find some footing. "He has been arrested?"

Borovik shook his head. "I am . . . *asked* . . . to do nothing. I will wait."

"Ah . . . but you think I should signal the others. See if they respond. Tell them, meantime, to lie low."

Now he nodded. "Quickly, Podolsk. Do that now."

Podolsk turned toward the door.

"I don't see Kerensky," said Borovik.

"He's there." Or should be. "In the doorway of Detsky Mir."

"Send him home, Podolsk."

The major glanced skyward, thanking his stars. But then he frowned.

"Sir . . . this news will be hard on him. He might not be so easy to control."

For a long moment, Borovik gave no answer. He sat rocking, his fingers steepled against his lips, staring into space.

"Tell him . . ." His eyes cleared. He wet his lips. "Tell him to come here, call me from the lobby. I will go down and speak to him."

"Thank you, sir."

Podolsk, his brain reeling, stepped through the office door.

"What would Stalin do?"

His mother asked this question from her photograph.

He nodded slowly, wistfully, in reply.

"This Sasha . . . he was a nice boy?"

Borovik rocked his head. But again he nodded, not wishing to disappoint her.

"I'm surprised they didn't cut off his head as well."

He grunted. He had half expected to hear that they had.

His mother was weeping.

"They shouldn't get away with this," she told him, gathering herself. *"Arkadi Kulik or no Arkadi Kulik."*

He wanted to tell her to be patient. But he knew what she would say. For nine years now, she has been patient. Nine years is enough.

He would talk to Kerensky. Now they both had scores to settle.

36

The Siciilian stood in darkness. He was cursing himself.

He had looked out the window when the car turned in off the road. It flashed its high beams as it approached the house. The glare caught him full in the face. He could not have been seen, he felt sure, because he had looked out through curtains. But his night vision was ruined all the same.

It was Aldo's car. No doubt of it. As it passed to the side of the house, he could see that a woman was driving and that the passenger seat was empty. It was as he'd guessed. Carla had acted alone. Even now, she did not come with help. It was all the more likely, therefore, that his other guess was correct as well. She'd been out hunting him.

The Sicilian's hand brushed over the communicator that was hooked to his belt. He gave it a squeeze of appreciation. Borovik's signal had been childishly coded but at least it was not ambiguous.

Kill her.

For what she did to Aldo. And before she kills you.

The business about her head was not so unambiguous, but he had decided to take it literally. Hack it off. Leave it in plain sight. This, he assumed, is meant to instill fear in whoever walks in here and finds her. The Sicilian had misgivings about it. His primary concern was that such a thing had the look of a signature. Someone else's. Not his own. It would be hard enough, without that, to convince certain people that it was he who'd taken Carla Benedict. With a knife. On her own ground. Even if he had Carla's knife to show for it.

But he would do it. Afterward, he might do a little cutting of his own. Perhaps the thumb from her right hand. Too bad that she's not known for a tattoo. As for the head, he supposed that he could leave it on a shelf in her refrigerator.

He had seen that done in films. Filmmakers understand dramatic impact.

On the other hand, however, it might be days before someone thinks to open her refrigerator and, besides, Borovik had specified *plain sight*. Best to stick it in a flower pot and leave it facing the front door. Or perhaps on her kitchen stove, in a frying pan, with the burner turned on low. That way, they could just follow their noses to the surprise of their lives. Another way would be to . . .

The Sicilian grimaced. Stop that, he told himself. You're getting as bad as Borovik.

The car was now out of sight. He could hear only the crunch of gravel as it pulled to the side of the house and stopped by the outside staircase. The engine went silent. He heard one door open and then close very quietly. Now, on the wooden stairs, he heard two steps taken, one loud squeak, and then no more steps. He realized that she had stopped, possibly to remove her shoes.

Why the sudden caution? Had she seen him after all?

No, he decided. This might be normal for her. It's why she has lived so long.

The Sicilian, also in stocking feet, eased his way back toward her kitchen. It was where he decided he would wait for her. Behind the front door would be foolish. It would be the first place she would check before entering. She would switch on the light, watch, and wait, look for signs of disturbance. She might even have memorized the pattern of the broken glass. She would then enter. She would lock the door behind her. Then she would walk through the apartment switching on all the other lights. The kitchen would be last because her bedroom and bathroom would be first. Women always expect trouble from bedrooms and from behind shower curtains. Never from kitchens. The Sicilian had heard this from someone. He hoped it was not from Aldo.

The door opened abruptly, almost silently. No jangle of keys. The door closed again. No light came on.

The Sicilian waited, listening, his knife held across his chest. He heard a faint rustle of fabric. She was definitely inside. He realized now that the removal of her shoes was not an aberration. Somehow, she had sensed his presence. Another woman might have run. Not Carla. She is inside, probably crouched low, her own knife in her hand. She, too, is waiting, listening.

A hundred heartbeats, two hundred, and she still had not moved. At the entrance to the kitchen, the Sicilian angled his head slightly. He could now see half of her living room but not the half where she stood. He decided to risk it. His night vision was not yet at its fullest, but it had to be better than that of a woman who had just been driving. He leaned further, his knife high, ready to parry a sudden thrust.

He saw her.

She was standing, not crouching. Her back was to him. And she was looking, bent at the waist, through a window to the right of her front door. She was staring out into the night.

The Sicilian understood. Whatever she had sensed, whatever made her take off those shoes, it was out there, not here. She thinks so, at least.

She is moving now. Sideways. Again to the door. The Sicilian readied himself. His moment would come when she reaches that door, possibly to get a better look outside, more likely to bolt it. Either way, the noise of the latch would give him his chance.

She was working the lock, fumbling with it. The Sicilian hesitated. Too much fumbling, it seemed to him. Too much for someone who lives here. But that must be because she holds a weapon, this makes it awkward to grip the lock. Good time to move.

But a better time, he realized, is coming now. Door is unlocked. Being opened. Left hand still on the latch, right hand not visible so it must be extended forward. She cannot turn it in his direction. The door would be in the way.

Move, he said.

Three steps, kick the door, slam it into her. Follow it, use your body, crush her against the doorframe, and then thrust. Up through the kidneys. Avoid the ribs.

Even as he thought this, envisioned it, he was moving. The door was half open. No need to kick it. He pushed it instead, pinning her. A squeal of surprise. He had time to look down, pick his spot. He drove the knife deep. Her back arched. She went rigid.

Suddenly, a gunshot. Very close. He saw the muzzle flash and, instantly, he knew the source. Her right hand held a pistol, not a knife. His brain said that was good. Carla had a gun, cocked and ready, and he took her with a knife.

Her head was back, her mouth was open. She tried to scream, but she could only gasp. He twisted the knife to make sure. She went rigid again. Now to finish her. The Sicilian tugged the knife free. With his left hand, his body still pinning her, he reached for her hair. Grip it, pull her head back, cut her throat. Cut through to her spine.

His brain spoke to him again. It shouted at him. It said something is wrong here. What is all this hair? This bun in the back. Carla Benedict's hair is short and straight. But by the time he heard this, he had begun his cut. The body was kicking. Dancing. The pinned right hand squeezed off another shot. More noises. Something heavy, pounding on wood. And before he could focus, suddenly there was a face. Wide eyes, tortured eyes, staring into his. Enormous shoulders, wide as the doorway.

Drop the woman, his brain shouted. Free the knife. Kill this one. The Sicilian tried. But suddenly, the arm which held the knife went numb. Fingers, strong as teeth, were gripping it.

He let go of the woman. The big man caught her as she fell. The Sicilian tried to fight. With the thumb of his left hand, he tried for the big man's eyes. The man only lowered his head and punched at his chest with the hand that still held his knife arm. The punches knocked him backward, off balance. Now the arm whipped him this way and that as if he were a boy, all the while the man is still holding the woman, lowering her to the floor, calling to her, saying her name.

The name he said was Lydia.

The Sicilian's brain cried ''No.

''Not Lydia.

''Carla.''

Even the woman was shaking her head as if in denial. Violently. Side to side. One hand clutching at this man's shirt, tearing it. She was trying to speak. Pleading with him.

The words sounded Russian. "Yuri," he thought she called him.

Russians?

What are Russians doing here?

The Sicilian heard another sound. An electronic pulse. Four notes that meant *receive message.* The four notes were repeated again and again. He imagined them saying, "What's going on there? We hear all this noise." The Sicilian had no time for this. With his free hand he groped for the communicator. He could use it as a weapon. With one leg he kicked at the big man's face. The man called Yuri winced. He rocked a little. Otherwise he ignored the blow.

The Sicilian found the communicator. He held it as he would hold a brick, ready to smash it, butt end, against the big man's elbow. Make him let go of the knife arm before it lost all feeling. He hammered at the elbow once, then two times more. It had no effect.

Suddenly, the communicator was blinking at him.

ABORT, said the display in code.

Then, more urgently, ABORT—ACKNOWLEDGE—ABORT—ACKNOWLEDGE—ABORT . . . It repeated these words over and over, bathing the room in strobes of soft red light.

To a place far back in the Sicilian's mind, this was almost funny. Fine time to tell me, it said. He tried kicking again at the figure lit by the glow. But it was hard to get leverage. And again, the big man barely seemed to notice.

Ignoring him, he was talking to this one he called Lydia. Speaking Russian, but gently, as if to a lover. Comforting her. He had torn away part of his shirt and he was holding the cloth against her throat. The Sicilian twisted under the arm. He kicked, more forcefully this time.

"Hold this," the big man seemed to say to her. "Press it tight." He let it go and turned.

The Sicilian waited, his communicator in hand, timing a blow at the big man's temple. He swung. The big man blocked it easily.

Strangely, the Sicilian felt no fear. This man was strong the way an ox is strong but he seemed no more dangerous. He seemed to be saying, *This one is a distraction. Give me a few seconds. I will find a rope to tie him with.*

He felt the big one's hand at the back of his neck, pulling

him into a sitting position, bending his head forward,
embracing him. It was being done carefully. The Sicilian
understood. It was to be a choke hold. He was to be put to
sleep. Keep calm, he told himself. Wait for the pressure,
struggle a little, and then go limp. Try to fool him. It's your
only chance.

The Sicilian struggled. He went limp. But the pressure
did not ease. Now he felt a hand slipping under his jaw,
cupping it. More pressure, this time a twist. He realized, to
his horror, what was happening. This young ox meant to
break his neck.

But why so slowly? his brain screamed. Why still so
much care?

He felt a grinding of the vertebrae just under his collar.
He felt rockets shooting down his spine, down his legs,
trying to burst out through his toes. He felt hot needles in his
neck, working upward, reaching his eyes. The night exploded into flashes of light.

37

Valentin had taken the scenic route again.

"Plenty time for restaurant," he said. "I show you
Moscow at night, yes? I show you Americaland."

"What's Americaland?" Lesko asked him.

"Is like amusement park for Russians. Brief detour. Five
minutes."

Lesko glanced at Belkin, who offered no objection. This
was the same Leo Belkin, however, who had hustled them
out of their room not ten minutes after Lesko tipped the
bellboy.

"I am sorry to rush you," he said then. "Valentin is
waiting with the car, I think. Best we don't miss our
reservation."

Elena gave him a hooded look. With that one expression, thought Lesko, she said about four different things.

Oh, for heaven's sake, Leo.

Will you relax?

No, Leo, we have not been talking about you. I have barely had time to use the bathroom.

And, *Yes, Leo, I am being careful what I say in this room regardless of what seems to have happened in the lobby.*

Lesko pretended not to notice. Nor did he bother correcting Belkin as to Valentin's present whereabouts. Valentin was not cooling his heels downstairs, because Lesko had been watching him from the window.

He hadn't spotted him at first, but some other interesting things were happening down below. A man, dressed strictly blue-collar, clearly not a guest, walked out of the main entrance, head down, hands in his pockets, and crossed the street to the department store where he took a position in the lighted doorway. Lesko got a pretty fair look at him. Built like a flabby wrestler, bullet head, hair cropped short, wore a blue quilted jacket that was too small for him. He was tempted to ask Elena is this was one of the characters she saw watching the hotel before, but she was busy brushing her teeth.

Suddenly there was no need to ask. Suddenly here comes that blond guy from the lobby. The one the German was yelling at. The one who's apparently KGB. He's got a coat on now, and he crosses the street to the slob in the quilted jacket. He grabs this guy's collar and practically drags him out of the lighted doorway. He pushes him into a darker corner and, arms waving, is clearly reaming him out. Lesko couldn't tell what about, but he had a hunch or two.

Part of it, obviously, had to do with basic surveillance techniques. As in, *"Hey, mudak. You don't stand under a light bulb, you putz, making customers walk around you."* But his loudest hunch said that this bozo probably had something to do with the missing laptop which caused all that uproar and ended up blowing the blond guy's cover. Anyway, the slob is trying to get a word in edgewise. The blond looks like he wants to hit him. Instead, he points at a spot on the ground telling Bullet Head not to move from it.

The blond guy stalks off, walking fast, straight, and

obviously pissed in the direction of Lubyanka Square. The
slob flips a finger at his back, but he stays where he's told.

Now, suddenly, there was Valentin. He comes out another door at the far end. He's picked up a shopping bag
someplace; it helps him mix with the flow of shoppers. He
starts to follow the blond, but, for some reason, he decides
against it.

Lesko pressed his cheek against the window. The blond
guy, he sees, is cutting right across the square, ignoring the
pedestrian walkways. A cop wags a striped baton at him but
then hesitates and changes his mind. The cop's behavior
suggests recognition. Or else the cop sees the look on his
face, that he's making a beeline for KGB headquarters, and
decides that life's too short for the aggravation. This was
when Leo knocked on the door and said that Valentin is
downstairs waiting. Valentin showed up ten minutes later.
Apologized. Said he went to get gas.

So, okay, thought Lesko.

So we drive around for a while, listening to our stomachs
growl. Valentin conducts the tour, Belkin pretends not to be
watching for a tail, Elena gives him another of those *Be
patient, Lesko* squeezes and also a squeeze of the bulge in
his pocket that says *I know you bought something for me.
When do I see what it is?* Meanwhile, we all pretend that
Raymond Lesko is deaf, dumb, and stupid.

Valentin's route to Americaland, whatever that was, took
them past the far end of GUM. The Chaika paused for the
light. Just up from the intersection, Lesko saw that a crowd
had gathered around two police cars. People craning their
necks, peering into an alley. He hoped that the cops weren't
doing a sweep of the sidewalk entrepreneurs or, if they
were, that his friend Mikhail had been savvy enough to see
them coming.

"What do you think's happening?" he asked Belkin.

A shrug. *Nothing out of the ordinary,* it said.

"It's not a sweep, is it? Rounding up those black-market
kids?"

His interest, and the concern in his voice, brought a
flicker of surprise to Belkin's brow, but he did not question
it.

"More likely an auto accident," he answered. "See?"

He gestured toward an ambulance that was now approaching.

Lesko nodded. "Then what's with that cop over there?"

Belkin followed his line of sight. He saw, at the edge of the crowd, a policeman who was looking back at them, spreading his arms as if in welcome. It was an exaggerated gesture. It did not appear to be friendly. The cop, who obviously knew KGB plates when he saw them, was now tossing a thumb in the direction of the alley. He seemed to be saying, *Come on. It's all yours.*

"Just an accident," Belkin repeated. The light changed. The car moved forward. Lesko saw the cop's hand drop to his crotch for a parting salute.

Probably nothing, he thought. Local cops versus feds. Oil and water. Probably the same all over the world. That, however, did not explain why the local cop was inviting the KGB to settle a fender bender or, for that matter, what kind of an accident happens in an alley.

Still, Lesko could believe it. In this town, he noticed, everyone drives around with their parking lights. It's the law, Valentin explained. Probably passed, he said, so that spy satellites would have a harder time at night. More likely because some party boss's wife had complained that brights made her eyes water.

The Chaika crossed what used to be Marx Prospekt and drove north on what used to be Gorky Street.

"Very confusing," said Valentin. "In Moscow, everyplace is former this, former that. If you use old name, people think you are still Communist. If you use new name, most people never heard of it."

Lesko thought he spotted a tail.

He wasn't sure. Not that it mattered.

His first sign that they were approaching Americaland came as they passed two movie theaters in a row that were showing fairly recent American films. The titles were in Cyrillic, but he recognized the posters. One of them had Clint Eastwood on it. Made him think of Carla's boyfriend for some reason.

Belkin said that at any given time, fully half of all theaters in Moscow were showing American movies.

"Wait until you turn on your television," he said. "Can you guess the most popular program in Moscow?"

"*Leave It to Lenin*?"

"Not funny, Lesko. But not so far wrong. Most popular are *Dallas, Flintstones, Jetsons, Highway to Heaven,* and *Love Boat* in approximately that order."

"Also MTV," Valentin added. "Every Friday night is MTV."

At this, Belkin grumbled. "Soon young Russian brains will be like young American brains. All turned to oatmeal."

Lesko thought he saw that tail again. A big car. Possibly a van. The right headlight was a little cockeyed.

Maybe.

Maybe not.

38

The Sicilian was floating. All was darkness again but for one bright light in the distance. It was coming nearer. This must be death, he realized.

He had heard of people who had died but who had been revived. They told of seeing a bright light and they felt a great peace. They felt no more pain.

The bright light, they said, would welcome them, embrace them. Their whole lives would flash before them in seconds. The light would make no judgments. It would only help them to understand their lives. Why they had turned this way instead of that.

But this bright light came no closer. It stayed in one place. Now it began to soften, to diffuse. Around it he saw what looked like a ceiling. A ceiling and walls. Pictures hanging on these walls. He realized with a start that he was not dead after all. He was not even sleeping. But if this was so, why could he not move? Why did he feel nothing except a burning at the back of his neck?

The truth came upon him slowly. He understood now, although he fought to deny it, why the big one had been so careful. He was not dead. Or his brain was not dead. Only the rest of him. He wanted to scream, but his lungs would not take the breath for it.

A shadow rose.

He could see the big man clearly now. This Yuri, standing over him. There was blood on his jacket. His shirt had been ripped at the pocket and there were tears in his eyes. He bent over, reaching for something at the Sicilian's side. When he straightened, the communicator was in his hand. Coded words still flashing.

"Shoo . . ." The Sicilian tried to speak. His throat was thick. "Shoo me," he managed.

The big man seemed not to trust his voice either. He swallowed hard. "This message," he asked finally. "What is it? Who is sending it?"

"Fin . . . Finish me. Doan lee me lye this."

The big one turned away. The Sicilian felt his footsteps through the back of his head. He heard sounds of scraping. The big man returned with two house plants in heavy ceramic pots, one in each hand. He positioned these against the Sicilian's temples, immobilizing his head. He left again, returning this time with bathroom towels. He stuffed these in as padding.

Once more, the big one left him. The Sicilian's left eye followed as he knelt to pick up the woman who was not Carla Benedict. Blond hair. Body limp. He carried her into the bedroom. The Sicilian heard him talking to her. Tenderly as before. From the look of her, she could no longer answer.

Next, he heard a sound he recognized. The trapdoor opening. Broken glass tumbling from it. The squeak of metal stairs under heavy feet. The Sicilian tried to arch his neck, break it completely, end his life now. But he could not move at all.

Parts of his life did flash before him. In his mind, he saw himself when he was younger. Playing soccer. Running and leaping like a gazelle. Racing sailboats in the strongest wind.

Now he was a piece of meat. A disembodied head.

That woman.

He had no idea who she was. Or what a Russian was doing here. Perhaps they, too, had come for Carla. That must be it.

Carla was his one regret. When the white light finally comes, very soon perhaps, he will tell it without apology that he regretted only two things in his entire life: That he had never sailed the South Pacific. And that he will not be remembered as the man who finished Carla Benedict.

From below, he heard the squealing of rats. He could smell the mildew and the oil. Also sewage. But the sewer smell was there before the trapdoor opened. He realized, miserably, that he was smelling himself. His bowels had let go.

Soon, he felt the vibration of the stairs again. The big Russian came back up. The Sicilian followed him with his eye as best he could. He began cursing him, first in Italian, then in English, hoping to provoke a kick. A good kick would end it.

But the Russian ignored him. He walked into the little kitchen. The Sicilian heard him rummaging for something and he heard the rats again. He realized, to his sudden horror, that the Russian had left the trapdoor open. In his mind he saw those rats, blood on their faces, climbing the stairs. He wanted to shout, "Shut it." But he fought to stay calm. The big Russian, he knew, would not let such a thing happen. Nice-looking boy. A good face even with such scars. And he had been almost kind. Padding his head with those towels. Clearly wanting him to live.

Tears welled in the Sicilian's eyes.

He did not want to live. Strapped to a wheelchair. Needing a nurse to feed him and clean his ass. Old enemies coming to piss on him. Or their widows and sons. Spitting in his face.

Spitting.

He could still do that, the Sicilian realized. He would wait until the Russian comes back. Get him to lean close and give him a mouthful. Make him forget himself.

But when the big Russian returned, he did not lean close. His eyes, sad moments ago, were now cold and lifeless. He stood, one arm outstretched, pouring something onto the

Sicilian's chest. The Sicilian could not feel it—he could only see it falling—but it smelled, he thought, like oranges. He saw the jar that the Russian held. It looked like marmalade. He did not understand this.

The Russian put the jar aside. He reached to his belt and produced a long-barreled automatic pistol. This, he held up for the Sicilian to see. Do it, thought the Sicilian. Shoot. Or else lean close.

But the Russian did neither. Now he raised his other hand. In it, squealing and kicking, were two rats held by their necks. The Sicilian blinked.

"You are ready to die, yes?" the Russian asked him.

The Sicilian spat, but he did not have the breath for it. The spittle ran down his cheek.

Yuri waved the Browning. "Talk to me," he said, "and you die this way."

He paused, letting the idea sink in. Next, he raised the hand that held the struggling rats. He then leaned over and rubbed their faces in the marmalade.

"Don't talk," he said when he straightened, "and I leave you with the rats. You choose."

The Sicilian, eyes wide, tried to spit again. He had no moisture left.

Yuri let the two rats fall.

39

Americaland turned out to be Pushkin Square.

It would have been hard to miss. On the right, approaching it, Lesko saw a neon Coca-Cola sign at least two stories high. On the left was the famous Moscow McDonald's.

"Biggest in world," said Valentin. "Twenty-seven cash registers."

Further on, there was a Pizza Hut. And an Estée Lauder store. In the park, the centerpiece of the square, Lesko saw a group of about a dozen bikers. Black leather, shaven heads, some with facial tattoos. They were watching, with apparent distaste, a smaller group of punks with spiked hair in Day-Glo colors. There were ice-cream vendors. Street artists. Three or four guitarists. Two young kids kissing.

Americaland.

Tourists come from all the republics, said Valentin. They know all about this place from television. The TV ads for McDonald's, he said, have a slogan. The slogan is, "If you can't go to America, come to McDonald's in Moscow."

Written, Lesko assumed, by the same guy who used to write those klutzy Red Square banners.

"See the walls inside?" Valentin pointed. "See those murals? They depict life in America as all former Soviets like to think of it. Couples sunning themselves on palm-lined beaches. Picnic baskets at their sides, filled with mangoes and papayas. Everyone is rich, everyone is healthy, and winter never comes."

"Guys . . . not that this isn't interesting . . ." said Lesko.

"Yes?"

"A Big Mac is beginning to sound pretty good."

Valentin glanced at Belkin, who nodded. "Restaurant is five minutes," he said. "Kropotkinskaya. Best in Moscow."

"Say again?"

"Kropotkinskaya. K-r-o . . ."

"I got it. What time's the reservation?"

"At eight," Belkin answered.

Lesko checked his watch. Seven minutes to eight.

His brain was trying to tell him something.

He wasn't sure what.

Except that the *K* on that message slip—the one that seemed to give Leo a case of nerves—probably stood for Kropotkinskaya. Eight o'clock was on it, too. And except that being hustled out of the hotel so they wouldn't be late and then spending the next half hour poking around Americaland seemed to be aimed at getting them to that restaurant right on the dot.

Might mean nothing, he decided.

On the other hand, old Leo is starting to hyperventilate again.

Irwin Kaplan hated this.

He's now had two hours to think about it and he hates it even more.

Three times, he asked Clew and Fuller what they wanted from him. Three times, they said they didn't want a thing. For the moment.

Except maybe to see what the DEA might have picked up in the way of rumors out of Sicily. There had been talk, according to Clew, that the Sicilians were involved in a shipment of nerve gas to the Sudan. It's supposed to be coming from Russia. Maybe Kevin Aylward isn't so far wrong. Maybe there was an accident along the way.

But it can get much worse.

For openers, the talk is that the Sicilians mean to keep a couple of canisters for themselves. Maybe, with those canisters in hand, they plan to tell the Italian government to lay off them. Pardon a few bosses who were already in prison. Let them get back to business. Maybe, Clew said, they were planning a demonstration of what could happen if they didn't.

Except that now it's nerve gas instead of bombs, this kind of threat was nothing new. Kaplan tended to discount it. In his experience, Mafia underbosses are perfectly happy to see their dons knocked off or rotting in prison. It leaves room for advancement.

Nor were the Sicilians hurting for business. Heroin, their specialty, was big again in the United States; and cocaine, the Colombian specialty, was growing fast in Europe. The interesting thing was that heroin, which goes for $50,000 a kilo in Italy, fetches $200,000 a kilo in New York. Conversely a kilo of cocaine which sells for $11,000 in New York easily gets $50,000 in most of Europe.

The Sicilians decided that instead of competing with the Colombians and driving prices down, why not cooperate? The result was a deal called the Sicilian Swap. The Sicilian network sells Colombian shit and vice versa.

Might the Sicilians really be moving nerve gas?

Maybe.

They'll move almost anything if it's a condition of a drug deal. For example, the poppy growers in Turkestan might say, "Yeah, we'll sell you so many tons of base for so much a ton, but your airplane or whatever has to make a couple of deliveries for us on the way home."

Happens all the time.

But making deliveries to the Sudan struck Kaplan as a possible deal breaker. The Sudan, as of a 1989 coup, has an Islamic military government. Those guys hang drug traffickers. On the other hand, the Sudan has become a haven for Islamic terrorist groups ever since the Syrians told them to get out of Lebanon and since even Qaddafi decided to cool it for a while. If nerve gas was for sale, those groups might well be in the market for it.

Fuller, however, did not seem terribly concerned about the ultimate buyer. Maybe he's got that covered. Or maybe he knows that their Iranian sponsors would never let them play with gases that could just as easily kill everyone in Khartoum. Or everyone in Palermo for that matter. He's more interested in what the sellers are up to.

The Russians.

And what else they're peddling.

And what they plan to do with the revenues.

Roger Clew, no doubt, is looking for a hard-liner conspiracy. A grand scheme to stage another coup and make it stick this time.

Fuller would concede that such a conspiracy might exist. In fact, he'd say that there are probably dozens of them. All over Russia and in every former republic. What else do you do when you're an out-of-work Communist, no more special treatment, no one's afraid of you anymore, and there's nothing good on television?

Most of it's harmless. It gives them a reason to get out of bed.

Will anything come of it? Kaplan didn't think so.

The thing is . . . sure, a lot of these guys would like to have the power and the perks again. Have everybody jump when they give an order. But the smart ones have found a new toy. They've discovered money.

Suddenly, perks like having the use of a car and a dacha on the Black Sea don't sound so hot anymore. A villa in

Saint-Tropez sounds better. But actually owning it, this time. Also the Ferrari in the driveway.

Money.

Even Fuller thinks that this is about money. Getting rich. Not that he begrudges them. What he cares about, he says, is the damage they can do along the way, depending on what they're selling and who buys it. Anyone who'll sell nerve gas will sell nukes. We'd have to act. Fast and hard. Before some rag-head sheep fucker with an attitude has a chance to pull the pin.

Anyway . . .

Why am I part of this? Kaplan thought. Answer: Bannerman trusts me.

Just in case Lesko's honeymoon has anything to do with this . . . just in case Carla's new boyfriend is this Barca . . . and just in case any of this lays a glove on Bannerman, they're going to want him to know that they touched base with me. Because Bannerman trusts me.

Shit.

He was tempted to call Bannerman right then.

Bannerman? Just shut up and listen. Here's everything I know, everything I think. Did they level with me? Fuck, no. When *have* they? Has Clew known right along who Corsini is? Wouldn't surprise me. Why else are they so hot to set me up as an eventual peacemaker? Got all this? Good. Do me a favor? Forget I exist.

But he couldn't make that call. Not unless he wants to go to work tomorrow and find out he's been posted in Guam.

There was one other call, though, that maybe he could make.

There's this guy, Ronny Grassi, big-time smuggler, who also happens to live on a boat near Genoa. Well . . . Monaco. Close enough.

Grassi is from Brooklyn originally. Grew up two blocks away on Ocean Parkway. Classmate at James Madison High. Lesko knows him, too, but mostly from later after Lesko went on the cops.

Ronny got into smuggling while he was still in James Madison. Bought himself this old Dodge, fixed it up, and started running untaxed cigarettes to New York from North Carolina. Also handguns from Florida. By the time he got

seriously busted he had a whole fleet of trucks doing it.
Grassi jumped bail and turned up in Rome, where within a
year he was smuggling American cigarettes on an international scale. There's big money in it because the Italian
government has a monopoly on legal cigarettes.

He also branched out. Grassi deals in heavy weapons,
diamonds, even spot market oil. Not drugs, however. He
always hated drugs. And otherwise not a bad guy. A big
good-natured slob. More money than God now. Knows
everyone, including Bannerman. You can't have worked
Europe that long without knowing Bannerman.

Kaplan kept in touch. They swap favors, information,
every now and then. Maybe he also knows Aldo. If Corsini
is a smuggler, Grassi would know it, right? Or maybe he'd
know him because they both like boats.

Nah.

Grassi's in a different league. His yacht is an oceangoing
powerboat the size of a minesweeper, and he also has
several homes ashore. Aldo has a sailboat. As a rule, sailors
and powerboaters don't have much to say to each other.

Anyway, he can't call Grassi either. That would be
stupid. Corsini could be on his payroll, for all anyone knew.
And the call could blow everything that Roger is trying to
set up.

Wouldn't want that.

The thing is, given past experience, what Roger Clew is
setting up might very well include Irwin Kaplan.

Kaplan began rocking.

He rocked for fifteen minutes.

Then he reached for the phone.

40

For once, John Waldo was wrong.

"Forget about finding a decent place to eat," he told Lesko at the wedding. "The first thing you have to know about a Russian restaurant is that the waiter hates your guts for having enough money to eat there. Also for making him wait on you. So, for the first two hours, he doesn't.

"When he finally comes over, you tell him what you want but he pays no attention. This is because they're out of almost everything you see on the menu. It doesn't help to go someplace else because they all buy from the same source. This means they're all out of the same stuff at the same time.

"If the place has an orchestra, you can always kill time by dancing, except that Russian dance bands play like zombies and they only know two songs. One is 'Hello, Dolly' and the other is 'We All Live on a Yellow Submarine.'

"This brings up another problem. In Russia, women will come right up and ask you to dance, even if you're with another woman. Nothing personal, Lesko, but you won't attract the cream of the crop."

"No shit."

This last was from Katz. Putting in his two cents.

"You'll get some porker," Katz says, *"whose armpits would gag a maggot and who learned to dance by watching Wrestlemania. Probably while she was shaving."*

But private enterprise, apparently, had made some progress since Waldo's last visit.

Kropotkinskaya, the restaurant Belkin had chosen, was on an elegant old street of the same name, lined with czarist mansions and nineteenth-century apartment buildings. This could have been Vienna, thought Lesko. Valentin drove them to what looked like a townhouse with a wrought-iron awning out front. No signs, no identification as a restaurant. Just a brass plaque with the number 36 on it. Valentin started to get out. Belkin stopped him with a touch. The touch became a squeeze. It said stay with the car.

A big pleasant-looking doorman came out to meet them. He escorted them into a wood-paneled lobby that was furnished like a rich man's parlor. Two carved chairs, a few heavy antique pieces. A mirror with a gilded frame. The paintings on the paneled walls all seemed to have Dutch signatures. The doorman, speaking Russian, using sign language, helped them out of their coats. He directed them to a thickly banistered stairway which, Belkin said, led downstairs to the hard-currency dining room.

Belkin excused himself for a minute. The selection of wines was limited, he said, but there's a Berioska shop just across the street. He would send Valentin for a couple of bottles. Valentin would bring them. He will not be dining with us but he will join us for coffee and dessert.

Lesko watched him go.

"We have a few minutes," he said to Elena.

She looked up at him questioningly.

"Just so you don't think I'm totally stupid," he said, "Belkin's out there asking Valentin if he got a make on the blond guy from the lobby. I could have saved him the trouble. The guy's KGB. There's at least one more staked out across from the hotel. Looks like a leg-breaker."

Elena took his hand. She looked away. But she smiled.

Lesko hated that smile.

He hated it because it always worked. This particular smile, and this little squeeze of his hand, said, *"You are so good for me, Lesko."*

It said, *"And I am always so pleased with you. You miss nothing. You are very hard to fool. But you let me fool you all the same."*

"I'm going to hear all about this at dinner, right?"

She nodded.

"I got you a present," he said.

The smile became a grin. "I know."

"It's not that big a deal." He reached into the pocket of his suit. Elena's fingers were already working as if she were unwrapping it. "It's just this necklace."

Elena, suddenly, becomes this little kid. Suddenly it's Christmas morning.

Of all the countless things which Lesko loved about Elena, this was one that he enjoyed the most and understood the least. Here was this woman who could probably buy out Tiffany's if she wanted to, but right now her eyes are going wide over a few bucks' worth of amber beads. She's the same way if you give her a flower.

One time, after she told him about the baby, he tried writing her a poem. His first ever. Just eight lines. It sucked, probably, but she cried for two days.

She was at the mirror, taking off her pearls and carefully slipping the amber over her head. Arranging the necklace. The tip of her tongue sticking out a little the way it always does when she's trying things on.

"These are so beautiful, Lesko," she said. Her shoulders took a little hitch like she also always does when she's excited. "And so old."

She found one piece that had a flying insect trapped inside it. This caused her to gasp. Lesko's first thought was that Mikhail didn't know his amber after all. They'd dumped a piece of crap on him. But the gasp meant she was thrilled. Sixty million years, she said. Sixty million years ago this insect flew along the shores of the Baltic and landed on the flowing sap of a pine tree. Sixty million years. She kept mouthing those words. She was still rhapsodizing about pine sap when the front door opened.

Lesko turned, expecting to see Belkin. It was another party. Six men. He wouldn't have paid much attention except that the friendly doorman suddenly had an I-smell-shit look on his face. And except for the collection of hats. Two of them wore those Arab things that have the little cord around them. There was a name. He'd seen it a dozen times in crossword puzzles. Could never remember it.

One guy, younger than the others, wore a Russian fur hat but a good one. Looked like silver fox. Two others, Lesko's age, were wearing narrow brim fedoras and looked like they stepped out of those May Day newsreels.

The sixth, who seemed to be the host, was maybe in his seventies. Speaking English. Russian accent. Had a voice

like a bell. It carried. He was telling the others that their
table was downstairs.

Lesko turned away but he could see them in Elena's
mirror. They checked their coats and the two fedoras but the
Arabs kept their . . . kaffiyehs, right? The older guy kept
his hat as well. Walked to the stairs still wearing it. The
youngest one did a double take at Lesko's back, a little
squint as if he were trying to place him. The usual. He
shrugged it off and kept going.

As far as Lesko was concerned, the guy leading the way
won the hat contest.

His was a tam-o'-shanter. Red plaid. With a little pom-
pom on it.

41

"Elena has endometriosis."

Bannerman, in the aisle seat, had just closed his eyes. The
Swissair flight was over Newfoundland. Dinner trays had
been cleared. Susan had barely touched her food.

Now she turned away, looking out into the twilight. With
her right hand, she made a quick erasure motion. The
gesture said that she wished she hadn't spoken.

Bannerman sat up. "That's . . . a problem with her
uterus?" he asked, sitting up.

She hesitated, finally nodding.

"Susan, what are you telling me?"

She looked at him. "How would you know about
endometriosis?"

"Janet Herzog had it," he told her. "Maybe four years
ago. It required a radical hysterectomy."

Susan nodded. "So will Elena's. This baby is her only
shot."

Bannerman's mind, for some reason, flashed back to this
morning when they learned of Aldo Corsini's interest in the

Russian honeymoon. Susan had asked him if he thought Elena was in any danger. Elena, not her father. He had not thought much of it at the time, supposing that she felt her father could take care of himself.

"How long have you known this?" he asked.

More hesitation. "Since last November."

Before she conceived, he realized. And when Susan went over for a visit. And then those conspiratorial conversations ever since.

"Are you saying that she shouldn't be traveling?"

Susan grimaced, then shook her head. "Her doctor said she could. It's a good solid pregnancy. It's not as if she's gone bungee-jumping."

That sounded right, Bannerman supposed. Elena, if anything, would have been just as active at home. She'd been skiing as recently as Easter. And she swam laps or used a Nordic Track every day, as much so that she could enjoy eating as to stay fit.

"What's the risk to Elena," he asked, "in delaying the surgery?"

Susan tossed a hand. "It could turn into endometrial cancer. But she says the surgery would catch all that anyway. As for the pregnancy, she'll have more pain than she would otherwise, especially in the last trimester. And giving birth will be hard on her."

His frown deepened. "And then there's her age."

Susan said nothing.

"All this to give your father a child?"

"She loves him, Bannerman. And she wants one."

This last had an edge on it. He let it lie.

"Paul?"

"Yes."

"Are you going to tell me what arrangements you've made. You, Anton, and Molly?"

An edge here as well, although not as sharp.

"Susan . . ." He lowered his voice. "Anton has alerted the appropriate people. He's asked them to assist as needed. I'll never tell you who, exactly, or where, how, or for what purpose. There are two reasons for this."

"Need to know." She nodded.

"Need not to compromise them," he corrected her. "I have no right—understand this—no *right* to tell you."

She softened. She took his hand. "I understand. I really do."

"But you still feel left out."

"Paul, I'm a person. I'm human. But I'm also part of you. I want you to feel—understand this—*feel* that you can tell me anything. But that doesn't mean I need you to. Or expect you to."

He grunted inwardly.

Certainly clears that up, he thought.

He had a sense that she was holding something back about Elena. And that the leap into the subject of what he holds back from her was a try at justifying it. But Susan would freeze up if he pushed it. She already seemed sorry that she'd opened the box. He thought he'd try to lighten the mood.

"Want to hear the second reason?"

"Never mind. I was being petulant. I'm over it."

A soft smile. "You'll like the second reason better."

Her hand, on his, withdrew just a bit. A sign that she knew she was about to be managed.

"Okay. What is it?"

"I don't know much more than you do."

She patted his hand, took hers away. "Give me a break, Bannerman."

"It's true."

"Bull . . . shit." Enunciated crisply. British accent.

"Scout's honor."

She shook her head. "I know you, Bannerman. You've got this thing covered up, down, and sideways by now."

"How would I do that? I don't *know* anything, Susan."

She waited.

"Basically, all I've done is describe the situation to Anton and Molly." He looked at his watch. "By now, Anton has called anywhere from six to a dozen people in Europe and outlined it to them. Molly might or might not come over. She might or might not send Billy."

Susan closed one eye. "Who are these six to a dozen people?"

"Specifically? I don't know. But you probably saw all of them at the wedding."

"How can you . . ." She shook her head as if to clear it. "How can you not have told them what to do?"

"There was no need. They're professionals, Susan. This is how they make their living."

"Professionals," she replied blankly.

"And friends of Carla's. With that in mind, what do *you* think is the first thing they'll do?"

"Go to Bern? Protect Yuri's place?"

"Very good. What else?"

"Go to Carla's house in Zurich. Help Yuri if he needs it."

"And?"

"Go to Moscow?"

"Forget that. There's no need."

"Okay, go to Genoa. Check out Aldo's boat. Look for names, addresses, old telephone bills. Look for a transmitter."

"Now you're cooking. Let's have one more."

She had to smile. "Meet you at the airport. No. *Cover* you at the airport."

"Cover *us*."

"Show themselves when we're clear. Somewhere, probably on the highway into Zurich, a car pulls up and honks. We both pull over. He . . . or she . . . has a trunk full of weapons."

"Which won't be needed."

"But just in case."

Bannerman spread his hands. "Do you think they needed to be told to do any of these things?"

She sat back, shaking her head. She said nothing for two or three minutes. Twice, she stifled a laugh. Mostly, she shook her head.

"Nice to have friends, isn't it," she said at last.

"Paul?"

The cabin had been darkened for the movie. Bannerman was dozing again.

"Umm?"

"Sorry. You were asleep."

He shook his head. "Just resting. What is it?"

"When Yuri called . . . the last time?"

"Uh-huh?"

"Will you tell me why I had to leave the room?"

"That was . . . a personal matter."

"And you don't feel you can tell me about it."

"Well . . ." He wiped one eye. "It's something that happened years ago. And it involved John Waldo. I probably shouldn't without his okay."

"I see."

He doesn't lie.

He had never lied to her, not once, as far as she knew. But he sure leaves a lot of blanks.

She had seen his eyes when she came in to say that Anton and Molly were waiting.

You can see some scary things in a person's eyes. Hatred. Madness. The eyes of the morally bankrupt—opportunists, muggers, lawyers—who see everyone else as a fish on a line. Or eyes that imagine you tied to a bed. But the creepiest of all is to look into someone's eyes and see nothing at all. Nobody home. At least no one you knew.

Paul's eyes were dead. Cold as stone.

"Susan?"

"Umm. Yes?"

"Is there something I should know about Elena? Other than her illness?"

"No."

"No, meaning there's nothing? Or that I shouldn't ask."

"It's a personal matter."

"Oh."

She shook her head. "This isn't tit for tat. There are personal matters and there are personal matters."

"Sure. But if I—"

"Paul, honey. It's just none of your business."

___

42

Elena was thoroughly confused.

First there was Leo's behavior.

He put her in mind of a girl she'd known when she was younger. Perfectly sensible in most other respects, this girl was the sort who imagined conversations in advance. If there was a boy, for example, to whom she was attracted, she would rehearse what she would say to him and how he would respond.

Of course, the conversation never went as she imagined it. The first digression would defeat her entirely.

It seemed much the same with Leo Belkin.

They had come down the stairs to the main dining room, Valentin leading, Leo following. Valentin, it seemed, would be dining with them after all. Leo paused on the third step up, scanning the room, hands on hips, a fierce gleam in his eye. He had the look of an actor expecting applause.

Here and there a head glanced up. Then down again. No one paid any particular notice. Leo seemed . . . disappointed.

The tuxedoed maître d'hôtel had to clear his throat in order to direct Leo's attention to their reserved table, which was off to the left. After they were seated and a waiter took Valentin's wine to be chilled, Leo's eyes, no longer so triumphant, seemed drawn to the rectangular table that was directly in front of the fireplace. Six men, the group that had just arrived, sat around it.

Their host, the man who affected a Scottish cap, sat with his back to their table. And to the stairway as well. The tam had been hung over the knob of his chair. It swayed when its owner, now in animated conversation, shifted his weight. The effect on Leo Belkin was nearly hypnotic. Lesko noticed this as well.

"You know that guy?" he asked.

A stammer. A quick shake of the head. And then a nod.

"That's a yes or a no?"

"Yes," he said quietly. He began groping for his pipe.

"You want to say hello? Go ahead."

This brought a glare as if Leo had been challenged. Elena knew that Lesko meant no such thing. Belkin retreated into the menu, cursing softly. It was here that he reminded Elena of the girl she once knew.

Valentin tried to relieve some of the awkwardness by reading from the menu. Belkin leaned and whispered in his ear. Abruptly, Valentin excused himself and took the maître d' aside. More whispering. Valentin writing down what the maître d' was saying. A waiter appeared, blocking Elena's view. He set down several plates of *zakuski*—assorted hors d'oeuvres—and a bottle of chilled vodka.

At the table by the fire, they were well into their vodka already, each man in turn offering toasts. Even the two Moslems. They seemed less than devout, thought Elena.

Belkin poured the vodka into tiny glasses. His hand shook. Some spilled on the tablecloth. Elena took the bottle. She finished pouring for him.

"I think it's time, Leo," she told him.

He took a breath.

"Gomar Jost," he said, and drained his glass. Then, to Lesko, "That means 'bottoms up.' You must drink."

Lesko fingered his glass but did not raise it. "Leo . . ." he asked, frowning, "are you okay?"

Belkin sighed. He nodded. "I need a moment. To gather myself."

Valentin rejoined them. He handed a slip of paper to Belkin. Belkin read it. Elena could see, over his shoulder, that it looked like a scribbled list of names, almost certainly those of the men at the other table. Leo was mouthing them as he read. He seemed to recognize some, was memorizing others. So many emotions could be seen on his face. Anger, certainly. Disgust. Contempt.

"Leo . . . enough." Her voice was firm. "Are those your bad apples?"

His temple throbbed.

"And you expected what? To walk in here with me, with Lesko, and see them run for the exits?"

A hiss. "Don't mock me, Elena," he said, barely audibly.

"Okay." Lesko rapped the table. Sharply. "Right now, straight out," he said through his teeth, "what the hell are we doing here?"

At the table by the fire, the youngest of them had spooned caviar onto a sliver of bread and brought it to his mouth. He heard the sound made by Lesko's knuckles. He glanced over. Now he stared, blinking, disbelieving.

Her patience ended, Elena reached for Lesko's hand. Her eyes turned skyward as if to ask for strength. "We have come here to see Moscow," she told her husband. "While we are at it, we were also to save Russia. But I think there is even more to it than that."

Lesko's eyes became hooded. "Drugs, right?" He cocked his head toward the rectangular table. "Those guys are your local dealers?"

Belkin shook his head. It was more of a shiver.

"Hey!" Lesko rapped the table again. "Get hold of yourself, Leo. Talk to me."

The young one looked again. Now he was leaning across the table toward the one whose back was to them. The man with the tam on his chair stiffened. The other two Russians frowned and they also leaned forward. The Arabs glanced first at each other, then over their shoulders toward the table near the stairs. At last, the older man brought a hand to his cheek. He turned, looking past his fingers as if they were camouflage.

He searched the faces at one table, then another. He found the two who the younger one was talking about, the two whose faces had seemed familiar when he saw them in the lobby. Now the older one understood why. He knew who they were. For there, sitting with them, was Leo Belkin.

He was stunned at first. But a look of defiance, of bravado, soon crept over his face. He turned away, back to his guests. He made a small joke to put them at ease. They did not smile. He made another. They began to relax. He raised a finger and beckoned them closer. He seemed to be telling them a story.

Belkin saw none of this. His eyes were on his hands.

"This . . . encounter," he said, groping. "I have seen it so many times . . . in my mind . . . that I . . ." He grimaced, berating himself. "I don't know why this is happening."

"That is precisely why," Elena told him. "Who is that man, Leo?"

"He is . . . scum."

"More specifically, please. Start with his name."

"Kulik. Arkadi Ivanovich Kulik."

"And what is he to you?"

"He had my father arrested. He had him executed."

Elena wet her lips. "For what reason, Leo?"

"He wanted my mother."

43

It took her twenty minutes to die.

Lydia.

Yuri stayed with her. He had left the man who cut her to the rats. He had shut the bedroom door so that Lydia could not hear the sounds he made. He knelt on the floor by the bed and he took her hand. She had begged him to hold it because she was frightened. She could not see him any longer.

Yuri kissed her several times. He wet her face with his tears.

She was frightened and yet very brave.

She knew that she was dying. She said that he must not call for an ambulance. They would only move her. It doesn't hurt so much if she lies still and moving her would be of no use.

She told him that she was sorry.

He answered that it was not her fault. It was his. He should have known that there would be a second man. He should not have told her not to turn on the lights. He should have gone in first.

She reached to touch his lips. To silence him. It was not

what she meant, she said. She meant that night. After the
party for General Belkin. She was totally to blame. It is just
that she feels . . . strange emotions sometimes. She does
not want to feel them. But they come. They frighten her.
That night, she thought that the vodka might keep them
away. It made them worse. She was sorry that she was not
better for him.

It was this that made Yuri cry as he had not since he was
a boy.

Afterward, he washed her face.

He put a fresh pillow under her head and he smoothed her
hair as best he could. In a closet, he found an extra quilt. He
covered her with it.

He realized that sooner or later he must decide what to do
with her. The lake was out of the question. He would
probably bring her back to Bern in Corsini's car. The
sensible thing, he knew, was to go get it now, carry her
down to it, hide her in the trunk, but he could not bear the
thought of putting her there.

Perhaps he would keep her here until Bannerman comes.
Bannerman knows how much she has helped. She should be
more than a name to him. He should have a face to
remember.

This reminded him. He did not yet know the name of the
man on the living-room floor. Yuri heard him talking. Very
rapidly. Was someone there? He listened at the bedroom
door, the Browning in his hand.

But the man was only praying. He was speaking Italian,
but Yuri was quite sure that he was reciting the Catholic act
of contrition. Over and over. Yuri opened the door carefully
nonetheless. The man had not moved. The two rats had lost
interest in the marmalade. One was exploring the room. The
other was looking down through the open trapdoor, possibly
summoning his family. One of them seemed to have chewed
at the man's left hand, but he probably never felt it.

"Have you decided?" Yuri asked him.

The man squealed. "Gun," he shouted from his throat. It
was Yuri's sense that he was glad to see him. Also good that
he spoke English.

"Your name?"

"Zang . . . Zang . . . ow . . . iwwo."

Faster to see if he has a wallet, Yuri decided. He felt for the man's pocket. He found one. It contained two driver's licenses. One Italian, one international, but in two different names. There were also seaman papers, in still another name, showing an address in Genoa. These, thought Yuri, were probably genuine.

"You are Vincente Zangrillo?"

". . . uh."

"You work with Aldo Corsini?"

". . . uh."

"And you both work for Borovik."

". . . uh." A flicker of surprise. But no denial.

"He knows that Corsini is dead?"

". . . uh."

Yuri nodded toward the broken communicator. "And he sent you to avenge him. To kill Carla Benedict."

". . . er . . . ah . . . uh?"

This new series of sounds told him that the question was too complex to be answered with grunts and gulps of air. Also, this man seemed to be asking if he had succeeded. Yuri wished that he had thought to slice his tendons instead of breaking his neck, but there had not been time. Also, he might have bled to death. It would have meant more to clean up.

This questioning, phrased for *yes* and *no* answers, would take time. First to learn Corsini's intentions, the role of General Borovik, the extent of KGB involvement, the purpose of the network, other names, and, above all, whether General Belkin is in danger.

He thought of pulling up a chair. But no. It would make him too impatient, just sitting. Instead, he would get the bucket, some detergent, and some rags. Begin cleaning this place as he asked his questions.

Ten minutes passed.

He was on his knees, scrubbing a section of carpet by the front door. Lydia's blood. The subject at hand was heroin. It was the third subject he had tried in his effort to learn the scope of this network's activities. So far, it was involved in everything he mentioned. Missing nerve gas would come next. Already, there had been a reference to it. The man with the broken neck, the intended avenger of Aldo Corsini, had managed to pronounce "Sudanese."

Yuri heard sounds from below. A sudden scurrying of rats. He put his hand over the butt of the Browning. Probably nothing, he imagined. A dispute over one of Corsini's ears. He had left the trapdoor open for the sake of convenience and as a quick way out if needed, but possibly that was not such a good idea. This boathouse was too easy to enter.

A new squeaking sound. Very faint. Not a rat.

It sounded, perhaps, like a metal stair being tested. He drew the Browning from the small of his back and eased off the safety. Very lightly, he moved to the wall behind the front door, listening now for sounds from the wooden steps as well. If men were coming, they would come both ways.

He wished he had a Makarov. With the Browning, he would have to go for head shots. No question of shooting through walls and doors. He sighted against the lip of the open trapdoor.

"Yuri?"

A woman's voice. Down below. He held his breath.

"Friends, Yuri. Don't get anxious."

A creak outside. Now the wooden stairs were being tested. In his mind he saluted Carla. She had probably loosened the boards herself.

"Come on, Yuri. We have to be sure it's you."

He swallowed. "Name?"

"You'll know the face. May I see two hands before I show it?"

Israeli accent. It seemed familiar.

"Hands are touching ceiling," he said. He raised them, easily reaching the plaster. He rapped the Browning's barrel against it. "Now show yours."

He listened, tensed and ready, as the metal stairs took her weight. He saw the crown of a knitted cap. The eyes below it should be able to see his hands. Now he saw one black glove, then another. The second held a silenced machine pistol, upside down, dangling from one finger.

She showed her face. He did not recognize it. It had been blackened.

"It's Miriam," she said.

"What Miriam? From where?"

"From Anton Zivic." She showed more of her body. Slim, all dressed in black. "You still don't know me?"

She pulled the cap off. Dark hair tumbled to her shoulders.

"From Elena's wedding," she said patiently. "I taught your Maria how to make kreplach. She told me how to make pot-au-feu. Also we played Bach together."

Yuri remembered. So many of them at the wedding, he did not know all the names. But he remembered this one—formerly Mossad—swapping recipes for soup with Maria. Also accompanying on Elena's piano when Maria was asked to play her cello. Also teaching Billy McHugh's new wife to play "Chopsticks."

"No music tonight," she said, stepping into the room. "Tonight, it seems, I am the cleaning lady."

She whistled for the man outside.

44

None of this was his fault, thought Ronny Grassi miserably.

It's what happens when you have bodyguards.

They're all dickheads. Every one of them.

These guys . . . they spend all their time doing absolutely nothing but hanging around looking tough, watching everyone in sight, occasionally getting to put their fingers up against someone's chest who was probably only going to ask for directions.

They get bored. They keep hoping that something will happen so they can show their stuff. For your part, you try to hire guys who are reasonably levelheaded because you don't want them reaching for a piece when some poor stiff happens to be looking at you and scratching his ass at the same time.

You try to hire guys who have a little something upstairs,

bring them along, give them other jobs to do when they're ready. But bodyguards are rarely a source of executive talent, because the guys who would do that sort of work in the first place tend not to have gone to Harvard.

The only part that was maybe his fault was that he lost it a little when he heard that Corsini tried to kill Carla and she turned him into a veal chop.

Two guys show up.

They're perfectly polite. They row out to *Temptress* in a dinghy and they ask if they can come aboard. They say no to a drink and they ask, nicely, if the girls can maybe go down below. He knows at least one of them. French guy, used to do odd jobs for Bannerman. Is otherwise a tennis instructor. The other one, it turns out, lives right here in Monaco and has a shop that rents tuxedos.

These occupations cause one of the bodyguards to smirk. He winks at the other one. They've both been sizing these two up, deciding they're not so much. The French guy pays no attention but he does ask if the bodyguards, too, could give them some privacy. Sorry. House rule. They stay close.

But things are still nice. There's a little small talk about mutual acquaintances which leads to the wedding which leads to Aldo Corsini. They want to know what Corsini was up to and was he working with a partner.

Their use of the past tense is not immediately noted.

He asks them why they're interested and the French guy, tennis instructor, tells him what happened with Carla. He listens, dumbfounded. He listens through a fog because all he sees is months of his own work maybe going up in smoke and a dozen deals collapsing all because of Corsini.

He says he has to think about this. You're both in town. Give me a number and I'll get back to you.

But they don't want to leave. They want some answers. He's got too much at stake here so he says maybe tomorrow. His bodyguards take this as a cue. One of them jerks his thumb at the door and reaches for the tennis instructor's arm and the other—if you believe this—he pulls back his jacket to show his piece. The rest happens too fast to yell stop.

In half a second, one of them's on the floor with a broken thumb and the other, who was now reaching for his piece, notices that the tuxedo renter has beat him by a mile and he's looking into the squared-off muzzle of a Glock. The meatball decides to go for it anyway because when he tries this in front of a mirror he always wins. He drops to a crouch, one knee, but the knee doesn't even touch the ground before it's shot out from under him and he slams face-forward on the rug and his gun hand gets stomped.

The tuxedo guy doesn't say anything but it's clear that he considers this a breach of etiquette. He puts a round each into the icemaker and the intercom. He walks up to the wheelhouse and puts another round each into the radar, the sonar, the loran, and the computer screen. He takes out eighty grand, easy, with a dollar and a half worth of bullets. On top, he says he'll take that drink now.

He was sorry they didn't blast the cellular phone, too, when they finally left, because it rings, he picks it up, and now he hears Irwin Kaplan, who, one minute into the conversation, is threatening life-long misery if he's even *thought* about dealing in chemical weapons.

Who knew what the fuck he was talking about?

He didn't need this.

"Irwin . . ."

"Straight out, Ronny. Are you into any shit like that?"

"No."

"Don't fuck with me."

A weary sigh. He motioned for the crewman who was scrubbing up blood to leave. "Some things I don't touch. You know that."

"Are you dealing with the Russians?"

"Who isn't?"

"What are you moving?"

"Hey. Let's save time. Instead of doing this on the phone, why don't I just fly over to Atlanta in the morning and check myself into the federal prison?"

But Kaplan didn't care who might be listening.

"Okay. Let's back up. Do you know Aldo Corsini?"

He hesitated. "I did."

"Otherwise known as Barca?"

"Barca like in sailboat? I don't know. Over the years, this guy's been the Actor, the Genoan, and the Count. He likes shit like that."

"He works for you?"

"A few years back, he did. Then he went with some Russians."

"What's he doing for them?"

"As far as I know? Buying companies, mostly."

"Do you know for what purpose?"

"To make things, Irwin," he answered patiently. "To sell things. It's called investing."

A brief silence, heavy with doubt.

"Irwin, there's a ton of Communist-party money floating around. They're looking for ways to park it and make it grow. They come to Italy and they get people like me and Corsini to help set up foundations and corporations that are not tied to them or the party in case the former Soviet Union gets its act together and tries to get it back."

A pause. "So you're laundering."

"That's one way to put it."

"And they stole the money."

"They took it, yeah. Before someone else could."

"And this doesn't bother you?"

Grassi drew an exasperated breath. "Irwin . . . pay attention to this. Last winter, the Germans sent five truck-loads of donated butter to St. Petersburg. The butter *and* the trucks disappeared the same afternoon they got there. Vanished, Irwin. Never seen again. The whole country is a rathole and I didn't make it that way."

Silence. An echo of distaste. Then . . .

"Has Corsini been smuggling on the side?"

"Same answer. Who isn't?"

"Are you?"

"I'm not Mother Teresa, Irwin. That's what I do."

Another silence. This time to gather his thoughts.

"This Corsini. What might he want with Carla Bene-dict?"

"I don't know. I just heard about that. Couple of guys from Anton Zivic came asking what I know. Which is almost zilch."

"From Zivic?" A surprised pause.

"Listen, Irwin. I need you to tell Bannerman that I'd never hurt Carla. If I had any idea that Corsini would try to hurt her, I would have whacked him myself."

"Ah . . . what are you saying?"

"All I did, when I heard he was making a move on Carla—"

"Wait. Hold it. He set *out* to hook Carla? This was planned?"

"Some . . . people wanted to know what Leo Belkin was up to. This drug thing with Elena. Carla looked like a way to get close. He gave it a shot."

"What was in it for you?"

"I wouldn't mind getting close to the Bruggs myself. All I did . . . if Corsini could get Carla to maybe put in a word for me, I told him, there's some nice change in it for him. I'm leveling here, Irwin."

"Back up again. What's this about hurting Carla?"

Grassi blinked. "You don't know?"

"Know what?"

"I just heard this myself. Carla found a wire on him. He tried to kill her. She iced him but now Bannerman's going to go bullshit on anyone who had anything to do with him."

"Wait a minute. Wait."

Suddenly it's Kaplan who's going bullshit. Yelling in his ear.

Kaplan had a hundred more questions. Most of them, Grassi couldn't answer. He wanted to know when this happened, how long Bannerman knew, what he might do next, and how likely was it that someone might want to even the score. Like, for example, against Lesko and Elena who were right now in Moscow totally clueless about any of this.

He could answer about who was up in Zurich with Corsini. Sicilian wharf rat named Zangrillo. Crewed on *Temptress* a few years back. Radio operator. A fag, but good with a knife. Zangrillo just might try Carla if the guys who just shot up the boat don't get to him first.

He could answer about who was Corsini's contact in Russia. Name's Viktor Podolsk. KGB major. Been to Italy a few times. Been on Corsini's boat. But this guy's nowhere near the top yet.

This was Grassi's impression because his own Russians, the ones who'd been aboard *Temptress,* had asked him what he thought of this Podolsk. It was like they had their eye on him for bigger things.

But his own Russians were none of Kaplan's business, because that's all it is.

Business.

It's what makes the world go round.

45

This was more than Lesko could absorb.

Leo's stepfather, although he refused to call him that, was a monster, a butcher, an informer, a coward, and a criminal.

He's a sneak, a liar, and a cockatrice.

Leo said that.

He called him a cockatrice. Lesko would look it up later.

He is also a drug-smuggling, gun-running, profiteering hypocritical son of a bitch. If he's with two Arabs, it means he must be arming terrorists. It means he's probably into white slaving as well. Kidnapping young girls off Moscow streets and shipping them to the desert for when the sheeps' asses get too sore.

He was also a lousy tenor. Ask anyone.

"Tenor?"

A sneer. "Was a tenor at the Kirov. Years ago. Leningrad. Was when he met my mother."

"An opera singer? Guy covers a lot of ground, doesn't he, Leo."

"Not opera singer. Was informer for the KGB under Serov. Whole company knew it. Any drunken Irishman can sing better."

Lesko still wanted to know why they had come to Moscow, why to this confrontation in particular, and why Elena went along with this. But Belkin was flying. Lesko was reluctant to break his rhythm.

The part about Leo's mother, apparently, was news to Elena as well. And to Valentin. His chin was halfway down to the table.

The story, in a nutshell, was that Leo's father was arrested in 1956. The usual. Anti-Soviet activities. Later, same year, they heard that he died in a labor camp. Suicide.

Leo's mother had been working at the Kirov, designing costumes. They fired her because of her husband's arrest, but Kulik got them to keep her on. Brought them food. Took an interest in Leo. Was a great comfort. Before you know it, Kulik proposes. It took a while but they got married.

Kulik rises in the KGB. Encourages Leo to apply. Sponsors him. Years pass. Kulik is a general in the Special Inspectorate. Leo makes full colonel. That rank gives Leo access to old arrest records. He learns that his father had been denounced by Kulik himself, labeled a dangerous enemy of the state, accused of organizing a prison revolt—evidence from Kulik again—and summarily executed. One bullet. Back of the head.

Belkin wants to kill his stepfather but he goes to Andropov, former head of the KGB, now secretary general. Andropov didn't like Kulik anyway. Calls Kulik in, fires him on the spot, takes away all his medals. No wonder Leo is an Andropov fan. No wonder that crack about him being a family man.

But this is December 1983. Andropov dies the following February. The new guy decides to sweep this under the rug. Records disappear. Kulik's reinstated. Belkin gets a sweetheart job in Bern in the hope he'll keep his mouth shut.

"But you didn't," Lesko said, nodding.

Belkin seemed to shrink. Lesko understood. He had taken the payoff.

"Kulik's still KGB?"

He shook his head. "Out, finally, since after the Gorbachev coup. Those other three with him."

"Who are the rag-heads?"

Belkin glanced at his slip of paper. "Sudanese. A military attaché who is not in the military and a chargé d'affaires who is not diplomat. Moslem fundamentalists, now that it suits them. If you thought the Libyans were trouble," he said, "keep an eye on the Sudanese."

Elena asked Belkin what became of his mother. Another sad story. She divorced Kulik but was never the same. Blamed herself. Became a recluse.

Lesko was only half listening at this point because he was watching the other table. They were into their second bottle already. Growing more comfortable. Belkin's stepfather still telling stories. Speaking English.

Maybe he was getting louder. Or maybe it was just that his voice carried. Operatic training. But Lesko could pick up a word here and there. He heard the phrase ". . . little Leo back there . . ."

The stepfather, suddenly, put a finger to his lips. For some reason he was shushing the others. They all smiled. Looked down. Lesko wondered what this was about until he saw the waiter coming. Their waiter. Carrying a bucket of champagne. And he was bringing it straight to Leo Belkin. Someone at the other table snickered.

"Compliments of General Kulik and his party," said the waiter.

Lesko braced himself for an explosion. Lesko would have gone over and dumped it on his head.

But Belkin only nodded. He muttered a thank-you.

Come on, Leo.

That's a fucking insult.

They're laughing at you.

Lesko was embarrassed for him. Belkin had pushed the limits of their friendship but he was still a friend. Even Valentin was seething. Belkin, he was sure, wasn't going to do a thing. Fine. But Lesko damned well would.

He was rising from his chair when Belkin raised a staying hand, telling him to sit. Screw that, thought Lesko. But then he saw Belkin's eyes. There was no fear in them. No anger either.

Just real calm.

Belkin rose to his feet, taking the bottle with him. He held it by the neck. This was not so good, thought Lesko. He's going to pop him from behind. He readied himself. So did Valentin. So did the younger one who saw Leo coming.

Belkin reached the chair. His stepfather had turned, warned by the young one. He seemed less sure of himself but not quite afraid.

"Go back and sit down, Leo," he said in English. "There's a good boy."

Belkin walked on past him. Toward the fireplace. This

confused everyone, including Lesko. He began to understand when Belkin turned again to face the rectangular table.
He held up one hand, the champagne. He held up the other,
the guy's Scottish hat. Belkin dangled it.

Then he dropped it in the fire.

To Lesko, this was not the greatest *gotcha* he'd ever seen.
But sure as hell, Belkin's stepfather thought it was. He
lunged for the hat, which was already in flames. Belkin let
him try because he wasn't finished. Too late anyway.

Belkin plopped the bottle down between the two Arabs.
Into the caviar dish. Splat. When their eyes followed it, he
took both their toppers, turned again to the fire, and dropped
them in with the tam.

Agals, thought Lesko. That's what you call the little
striped cords around the head rags. These words never
came when he needed them. He did not need them now
because he was moving to intercept the two truck-driver
types who were on their feet and charging Belkin. Valentin,
meanwhile, is moving at flank speed toward the youngest
Russian, who had paused to look at the fish eggs dripping
from his shirt and was now reaching for the neck of his
vodka bottle.

46

———

Aldo Corsini had barely made a splash.

Yuri eased him over the side in at least twenty meters of
water. Perhaps much deeper. He had used that much line,
weighted with a mushroom anchor, to sound for the bottom.
He hadn't found it.

As Miriam killed the engine of the runabout, he had
wrapped Aldo's body in that same length of line, tied off
both ends of the carpet, and secured the anchor to the end
where his head was. At least one rat was still inside. It now
sensed its predicament and already was chewing to get out.

Yuri eased the bundle over the side, holding it under the surface until the carpet became waterlogged and the bubbling was reduced to an occasional burp. Then, satisfied that it would sink quickly, he released his grip on it.

Next came a bundle of bloodstained rags that smelled of household cleanser. These he had stuffed into a sail bag along with the sweepings of broken glass and a can of bottom paint for ballast. As with Aldo, he waited until it was saturated, tugging downward, and let it go.

From where they were, no lights could be seen on shore. Not even the glow of Zurich in the sky to the north. Nothing but fog. But the runabout had a small compass in the dashboard. They had steered out on a heading of 240 degrees. They would steer back by the reciprocal until they saw the lights of the marina. From there, Carla's house was only a hundred meters to the left. Avram, the man who came with Miriam, would be outside waiting for them. He was to signal with a flashlight when he heard their motor.

Yuri had not quite decided what to do about the Sicilian. Zangrillo.

Bannerman would surely have more questions for him, but Yuri doubted that the man would live until morning. Not without a respirator. He was breathing with more and more difficulty. Fluid filling his lungs.

It would be no great loss for Bannerman. Yuri now had more names. Bannerman could pick and choose and he would not have to worry about Susan being on hand for the interrogation. For Susan, seeing Lydia will be enough of a shock.

Miriam had suggested that they dispose of Lydia as well. He could not bring himself to do it. She deserved to be sent home. He had no idea where that was exactly, but he hoped it was a place where he might go and visit her one day. Bring flowers. Have a good long talk.

Because Yuri's mind was on poor Lydia, and on the urgent call that he now had to make to General Belkin—tell him to get out of Moscow fast—he did not hear the sounds that caused Miriam to place her fingers against his lips.

He listened, hearing nothing at first except the squeal of a train pulling into a station on the far shore of the lake. Some truck traffic. Nothing more. But Miriam was peering out across the stern. With one gloved hand she covered the fluorescent glow of the compass. She raised her machine pistol with the other. She pointed with it.

"There," she whispered. "And there. Two boats."

Yuri saw nothing but now he could hear. The lapping of water where there should have been none. He reached for the Browning and lowered himself. Soon he heard the soft purr of a motor. Two motors. One behind the other. He could make out their shapes. Blunt ends. Inflatables. They were roughly abeam of the runabout and perhaps forty meters away. In the bow of the first boat, Yuri saw the lumpy outline of a man with one arm raised. He seemed to be making hand signals. Now he was pointing.

Miriam saw this as well. She lifted the hand that covered the compass, then turned and nodded toward Yuri. No question. Their heading was 60 degrees. Carla's house. Yuri tensed. "Don't move." Miriam touched his shoulder. "Wait."

The two boats faded and were gone, swallowed by the night.

"Commandos," said Miriam. "Two teams. At least three in each boat. Could they be yours?"

Yuri frowned. He shook his head. Russian Spetsnaz on a lake in Switzerland? Why not on the Potomac? Why not in New York Harbor for a raid on Wall Street? Impossible.

"There would have been no time," he told her, "even if we had such units in the West."

"How long since that flash code to Zangrillo?"

"Less than one hour. No time," he repeated.

Also, he thought, even the nut cases do not send in commando teams every time an agent fails to acknowledge. And if they did, who would obey such an order these days?

"Not ours either," she said. "Could be Swiss. Enzian Unit, perhaps."

Enzian Unit. Swiss counterterrorist strike force. Zurich-based.

That these commandos were Enzian was at least plausible. But who would authorize their use? The Bruggs would have such influence, but what could be their reason? And why not just send the police?

Uh-oh.

"What about Avram?" he asked.

She did not seem concerned. "He'll hear them. When they don't signal, he will fade into nothing."

"He won't shoot?"

She shrugged. "To protect what? So they don't make a new mess?"

Yuri thought of Lydia. He hoped that they would treat her with respect while they tried to find out who she is. Her identification papers were in his pocket. He had left her handbag and its remaining contents among Carla's purses on her closet shelf.

And he hoped that Miriam was right about Avram.

Already, one too many had died for trying to help.

47

The secretary of state took Irwin Kaplan's call.

He did so reluctantly when, as his communications officer informed him, Kaplan had vehemently—not to say profanely—refused to go through Roger Clew.

Clew, still in his tennis whites, was pacing the floor of Barton Fuller's study. He was fuming, but not due to the insult. He had been cursing the DEA man for ten minutes. This began when the same communications officer advised him of a call, then in progress, between Irwin Kaplan's home and a yacht, docked in Monaco, which was registered to a man named Grassi.

If Clew was angry, Kaplan was furious.

Fuller listened to him, making notes on a pad. The notes were not strictly necessary. A full transcript of both calls would be on his desk within the hour. Highlights, written in longhand, were already at his elbow.

"Irwin . . . calm down."

Fuller raised his eyes to the heavens.

"Irwin . . . Roger did not mislead you."

He told him of the satellite communications, sent virtually in the open, between Moscow and Zurich. He explained their interpretation of them. Barca was dead. It was their first inkling of it. "Blade" had to be Carla Benedict. Carla not only had killed him, there was reason to believe that she beheaded him. The reason for thinking so was that the "Sicilian," obviously this Zangrillo, had been ordered to behead her in response.

He heard a low moan from Kaplan and hastened to reassure him. Steps had been taken. A Swiss special-forces unit is on its way as we speak. They would try to intervene. Someone in Moscow, it seems, is also trying to stop Zangrillo. They had picked up an abort signal, sent in the open.

It was not Roger, he told him, who had been disingenuous. It was Paul Bannerman. Bannerman must have known. It would be like him, in fact, if he'd seen through Corsini all along. For that matter, it would be unlike Carla Benedict to kill a man without prior approval from Bannerman.

"I got news." Kaplan was incredulous. "Carla would kill if you talked loud in a movie."

Fuller said nothing.

"What about Lesko and Elena? They could get caught in this."

"Roger called our embassy. We have armed personnel en route to their hotel."

"Have you talked to Bannerman?"

"Paul is . . . on an airplane to Zurich."

"Airplanes have radios. They even have telephones."

"I'm aware of that, Irwin. If he makes a call, we'll be listening. If Ronny Grassi's experience is any guide, he's been busy already."

"Um . . . with all respect . . ."

"That would be a nice change, Irwin."

"Don't just listen in. Talk to him. Every time you guys dick around with Bannerman . . ."

He didn't finish. "Screw it," said Kaplan. "I'm going to call him myself."

48

"We can now enjoy our meal,'' announced Leo Belkin.

He dabbed at his mouth with his napkin. There was blood where his lip had been cut. He was thoroughly pleased with himself.

It really wasn't that much of a fight, thought Lesko. The two rag-heads wanted no part of it. They backed away, babbling to each other in high-pitched Arabic, probably wondering what this little guy had against hats. Meanwhile, there was Leo, rolling around on the floor with a schoolyard headlock on his stepfather.

The two truck-driver types might have only wanted to break it up, but they both had sixty pounds on Belkin, so Lesko decided not to take the chance. He cut the legs out from under the first one and the second one went down on top of him. Lesko gave that one a quick pop in the eye when he tried to get up. It wasn't a hard punch. Just a reminder that what you see is what you get.

Valentin got in the best shot, but Lesko never actually saw it. All he knew was that the younger of the former KGB guys was suddenly on his ass and the empty vodka bottle was rolling across the rug. He sat there trying to straighten his nose.

All this took maybe five seconds. The other diners sat gaping, some with forks still poised in the air. Along came Elena, shaking her head. She took him, Lesko, by the sleeve and started leading him back to their table. With his free hand, Lesko snatched up Belkin and half carried him along. Behind him, Valentin backed away, covering their retreat. The Arabs seized this moment to lower their heads and take a bead on the exit.

The maître d' snapped his fingers at a busboy who seemed to be enjoying this. The busboy moved in and began picking up toppled chairs. The manager hissed at him. He

pointed his chin at the two truck drivers, still down and
tangled, apparently saying that the furniture can wait. The
busboy shrugged and giggled. He went to help the one with
the broken nose and got an elbow in the chest for his
trouble.

The manager ordered that one out. The younger one
answered in Russian. A stream of words that included *"Yeb
vas"* and apparently a lot worse because they even made
Valentin gasp. Valentin started after him again but Elena
said "Lesko!" and Lesko pulled him back. Two fairly big
men, however, one in an army uniform, rose from their table
where they had been dining with their wives or girlfriends
who had also gasped. More likely girlfriends, thought
Lesko, because the two men were rising to defend their
virtue. They started toward the younger one. Valentin said
something to them in Russian. Lesko picked out
". . . KGB . . ."

The younger only shouted a word. He pointed a finger
directly at Lesko—and also at Valentin but mostly Lesko—
and shouted it again, this time with a few words added. With
the pointing finger, it looked like an accusation. Belkin's
stepfather, now on his feet, barked a name—*"Oleg"*—and
told him to shut the fuck up. No need to know Russian. The
older man's meaning was clear.

The two husbands—whatever—hesitated just for a beat.
The one in civilian clothes shot a curious glance toward
Lesko, but the soldier was more interested in the man whose
language had offended the ladies. He took another step and
slapped Oleg across the face. Oleg staggered back against
the fireplace, hands to his nose. When he lowered them, the
nose was pointing at his ear again. The busboy shoved him
toward the stairs and aimed a kick at his rump. The manager
shook a scolding finger at the busboy. The gesture, thought
Lesko, reflected minimal displeasure.

Belkin's stepfather, meanwhile, seemed in shock. So did
the truck drivers. They had no idea how to react to this,
Lesko decided, because no one had treated them this way
since their first How-to-Scare-Everyone-Shitless class in
KGB school. No one messes with a KGB officer, even one
who's between jobs. It's like no one slips a whoopee
cushion under Stalin, either.

Right now all they wanted was out of there. But the maître d' stood between them and the stairs scribbling on a little pad. He tore off a page and held it out to Belkin's stepfather. Obviously a bill. One of the truck drivers started to argue, apparently saying that Belkin should pay, but the stepfather, Kulik, told that one to shut up as well. He reached into his pocket, pulled out a wad of bills, and threw most of them on the table. The four Russians clumped up the stairs.

No question who's in charge here, thought Lesko.

On his way out, Kulik's face was the color of borscht but he never glanced in their direction. The younger one sure did. Oleg. Holding his nose again, he shot a parting look at Valentin which promised that this wasn't over.

Some angry mutterings upstairs. Another "Shut up." Then Lesko heard the front door open and they were gone.

In two minutes, the room was back to normal. The furniture had been straightened and the table freshly set. The dining room had settled into a low buzz again. More than a few patrons seemed to be giving Lesko funny looks. But everyone else, the maître d' included, seemed to have forgotten that it was Leo who had fired the first shot.

"How come they're not throwing us out?" Lesko asked him.

Belkin didn't hear. He was busy getting serious heat from Elena, but he didn't really seem to mind. Guy was happy. He was glowing. All he'd say to Elena was, "It was a matter of honor. A matter of honor." In his mind, he was still burning his stepfather's hat. Valentin answered for him.

"Because we are not KGB torturers from Lefortovo who retired after looting party funds."

Lesko stared, then understood. "That's what you told those two guys who joined in?"

Valentin nodded absently. He had found blood— Oleg's—on his necktie.

"Well? Is it true?"

"Is what true, please?" He found more on his lapel.

"That they're torturers and looters."

Valentin rocked his hand. "The first is possible. The

second is probable. You notice that they offered no rebut-
tal."

"The guy Oleg did. He pointed at you and me and said
something."

"Is nothing, Mr. Lesko. It made no sense."

"Indulge me."

A shrug. "He said that we are murderers. He said that
tonight we beat a man to death."

Lesko blinked. "You and me?"

"It is what he claimed."

That would account for the funny looks, thought Lesko.
Including the one he was now getting from Elena.

"Did he happen to mention when and where exactly?"

Valentin only shrugged. His manner said that this accusation was of no importance to him.

Lesko was about to press him on it, but the waiter
appeared with a cart and began setting out more plates of
appetizers. He was describing each one in English. Pirogi
stuffed with mushrooms. More pirogi with cranberries.
Smoked sturgeon. Little crepes, called blini, filled with
cheese. He was especially proud of the carp mousse.

Waiters.

It's the same everywhere, thought Lesko. When you get
to the absolute most critical part of any conversation,
guaranteed they'll show up and start telling you about the
specials. Carp mousse, for Christ's sake.

As for that wild accusation, the more time he had to think
about it the less he liked it. It's true, he thought, that people
say weird things in the heat of the moment. But this one was
so far out in left field that he had trouble dismissing it. It
also struck him that the outburst did not seem to surprise
Belkin's stepfather. He seemed more interested in getting
Oleg to shut up about it.

"Lesko?" Elena was squinting at him.

He looked at her, assuming that she was on the same
track.

"When you left us at GUM," she asked him, "did you
have . . . difficulty with anyone?"

Nice, thought Lesko.

She's asking did someone take the last of the paper
towels so I smashed his face against the toilet. Did some-

body try to get ahead of me in line so I threw him off the balcony. "Elena . . . I went to the washroom, I bought the necklace, I came back."

Belkin came to life. He looked at Elena's throat. "You bought this necklace? The amber?"

Christ! Here we go. "Yeah, Leo. This necklace."

"Paid for how? You had rubles?"

Lesko could have told him. But that would have meant telling Elena how much he paid for it. She really liked it. Five bucks with a lot of change might have made it sound like a piece of junk. He leaned forward.

"Leo . . ." He showed his teeth, "We've been in Russia, what, five hours? So far we've been tailed by the KGB who are probably going through our suitcases while we're sitting here. We see you busting on some Kremlin guard just to make sure everyone knows you're in town. We learn that you have manipulated Elena and that both of you have suckered me. Suddenly, we just happen to run into your wicked stepfather which tells Elena that you've also suckered her. We watch you avenge your real father—so that now he can rest in peace—by burning a fucking *hat*. Are you sure you want to give me any shit about trading dollars into rubles?"

Belkin was not intimidated. "This exchange. Where was it made?"

"I sold my body, Leo. Up in the washroom."

Belkin took a breath. "But not on the street," he said, one eyebrow lifting.

For an instant, Lesko was confused. He wondered if this was Belkin's idea of snappy repartee but he saw no humor in the other man's expression.

But not on the street.

Suddenly he saw what was in Belkin's mind. It was that accident they passed. Down at the far end of GUM. A street cop flipping his crotch at a car with KGB plates. He saw it in Elena's mind as well. Only for an instant. But then she shook her head.

"The accusation includes Valentin, Leo," she reminded him. "And he was with us except for two minutes at most."

Lesko chose to say nothing. He rubbed his chin.

No.

No, he decided. It was too much of a stretch. Some guy was *maybe* beaten to death. Let's say that part's real. That was *maybe* the reason for that ambulance and the victim was *maybe* KGB. And *that's* if that cop's behavior meant anything more than that his shorts were too tight.

Let's say that someone *did* see him outside GUM with that kid, Mikhail, who just *might* pass for Valentin. Same size and build.

But then what?

They pick someone off the street and beat him to death just to set up Raymond Lesko? Worse, they pick one of their own? And, after setting up this impossibly elaborate frame, they blow it when one of them gets whacked in the nose?

It's ridiculous.

Except for two things. Why did the guy say it? And why did Leo's stepfather almost shit when he did?

Screw it, he decided. We're out of here.

"Can you get us on a plane tonight?" he asked Belkin.

The question, Lesko could see, came as no great surprise. The Russian only sighed. He looked at Elena, who was glaring at him. Her expression said *"Wait till I get you alone."*

"Not an airplane this late," Belkin replied at last. "But I can get you out of Moscow. The Red Arrow to Leningrad leaves at midnight. It's a good train. You can sleep. In the morning, first thing, I'll have you on the first flight that goes west."

Elena's lower lip came forward. A good sign, thought Lesko. A quiet pout. She's not going to fight me on this.

"Is there any reason, then," she asked, "why we should not enjoy the rest of our meal?"

This was not so good a sign. This was a *give-me-another-hour-so-I-can-wrap-you-around-my-little-finger* sign.

He wondered why they still bothered with wedding vows. The Swiss still had *honor and obey* in theirs. No big surprise. Swiss women only got the vote about twenty years ago.

Elena was happy to say it, she said. Honor and obey. Except that when she did, Lesko's ESP picked up this huge silent chorus of *"In a pig's ass"* from the packed pews behind them. Loudest of all from Katz.

But Elena saw the sense in leaving. She was talking to Belkin now, urging him to get out as well and to take Valentin with him. All six of those men, she told him, have been shamed and humiliated. Each one, as we speak, will be conjuring his personal revenge fantasy even if this Kulik should counsel patience.

Valentin nodded thoughtfully. He took a sip of wine and a mouthful of pirogi. He excused himself. Lesko knew where he was going. He would stay with the car, make sure no one tampered with it. Maybe make some calls from the lobby to see about that train and get the Savoy to have their bags ready. He did not ask Belkin's permission. Lesko appreciated that.

Carp mousse.

What the hell, thought Lesko. You only go around once.

Belkin was talking about his uncle now. The one who lived in Moscow. Leo would make a phone call, he said. His uncle Nikolai had . . . a certain influence. He would see to their safety while they were still in Moscow. From Belkin's manner, Lesko gathered that the uncle was in this with him. The whole family, probably. And that their focus, maybe, had less to do with battling organized crime than with nailing stepfather Kulik.

Elena was giving Belkin a funny look. She didn't say anything. She just sighed and shook her head sadly. It was the kind of look you get, thought Lesko, when you realize you've been had.

Belkin wanted to leave. He stood up.

"Sit," she ordered him. "We *also* came here to have dinner."

She touched Lesko's thigh, patted it.

"We are perfectly safe," she assured him. The pat said that she would explain later.

Lesko's main course, chosen for him, was a smallish entrecote awash in a cream sauce that had capers poking out of it. He hated all that shit on a steak. He looked to see what Elena was having. Her dish, Belkin explained, was a baked grouse that came encased in the original bird, feathers and all. Lesko felt better about the entrecote.

The waiter made room on the table, pushing plates and

glasses aside, moving napkins. The slip of paper with the names of those six on it ended up near Lesko's wrist. He picked it up, glanced at it. The names were printed in Cyrillic. He was about to hand it back to Belkin, but Belkin was busy showing Elena how to get at her grouse and otherwise trying to cool her down.

Lesko closed his fist over the slip of paper.

It could wait, he decided.

He folded it into his pocket.

49

"That man was your son?" seethed the chargé d'affaires who was not a diplomat. "Your son did this to you?"

They were in Kulik's new Zil. Almost new. Sostkov had learned of one that had been stored in a garage in Yekaterinburg. He'd had it stolen and then paid a bribe to have it registered in Kulik's name. It was very thoughtful of Sostkov. The memory of that gesture kept Kulik from being too hard on him. For not controlling his mouth. For as much as warning those four in the restaurant that the police were on the trail of that big ox, Lesko, and Leo's driver. Major Podolsk, one hoped, would have better command of himself.

"Stepson," Kulik answered distantly. "He is not blood."

"Islam makes no such distinction. He struck you. You cannot, with honor, let him live."

"I know."

The Zil droned on, Sostkov at the wheel, his eyes beginning to blacken.

The Sudanese touched his temples where his agal had been. It had belonged to his grandfather. New tears came to his eyes.

"He laid hands on me as well. And on my brother here. We want him first. We want him for one hour."

The military attaché who was not a soldier nodded gravely.

"We'll see."

"One hour," he demanded, "or our business is finished."

Kulik bit his tongue.

He knew why they wanted the time. Five minutes to amputate the offending hand and then bind it up lest he die too quickly from loss of blood. Five minutes for the other. The rest of it to let him stare at the stumps. He wondered if Islamic law stipulated the period of contemplation.

As for their business being finished, the threat meant nothing. These two insects were far too greedy to walk away from millions. Too tired of being poor relations of the Arabs who have the oil. Too fond of the young blond women with bare tits on Grassi's boat for whom they have developed an addiction. Bare tits and Mount Gay rum with tonic water.

Islamic law indeed.

As for settling accounts with Leo Belkin and the other two, his own humiliation ran just as deep. Ten times as deep. Little Leo had ruined him once. Tried to send him to prison. He would not get another chance.

But Kulik reminded himself that he was a patient man. A disciplined man. Never mind the skinned elbows, he told himself. Never mind the bruises that made it impossible to sit comfortably. Or the burning of his ears where Leo Belkin had slapped him. Never mind the tam-o'-shanter. It is only a hat.

At this, Kulik wanted to scream.

He had to bite his hand.

No, it was not just a hat. It was a uniform. More commanding, more intimidating than the one that had been taken from him. It said more about him than any medal.

It didn't help that he had two more exactly like it. Everyone thought that he had just the one, but he could not simply take another one out of his safe, because fifty people had seen the original burning. He couldn't kill them all.

At least there is still the golf club. But it isn't the same.

An old Russian proverb popped into his head. It goes, "In

a fight, a rich man protects his face but a poor man protects his pants.'' Here are three rich men who are more worried about their hats.

Perhaps, he thought, it is better to think of it that way. Keep things in perspective. Keep emotions out of it. Don't act in haste.

But Leo Belkin will die all the same.

Very soon.

Until then, no one touches him. Not Sostkov, not these Arab clowns . . .

No one.

Only me.

And my golf club.

50

Kerensky's cousin, Yakov, could not stop crying.

Feodor, at least, had managed to get a grip on himself.

Kerensky had called his younger brother from a kiosk in Lubyanka Square. Told him to come at once. Take the metro. Meet him outside Detsky Mir. He waited until Feodor got there before he told him, as gently as he could, that their older brother was dead and the name of the man who had murdered him. They hugged each other, tried to comfort each other, for more than an hour. That was how much time they had to wait for Yakov to get back from the airport.

There was not much comfort to be found. What made this so hard was that Sasha had done nothing to deserve it. If he had been shot during a hijacking or ambushed by another Brigade, that would have been bearable, because that is the chance you take. But all Sasha had done was to go and keep an eye on the Belkin party when they were wandering around GUM. Somehow, they had spotted him. They decided, "This one must have been sent by Borovik. Let us teach Borovik a lesson."

So the big one, Lesko, and the driver pulled a gun on him. They marched him into an alley and they beat him to death with the butt of the gun. They also searched his pockets and they found the photographs that Major Podolsk had given them. They left the photographs on his chest. It was their way of boasting about it. It was their way of saying to General Borovik, "This is what we think of you. You know we did it. Now let's see you prove it."

Even the general wiped a tear when he told Kerensky about Sasha. The worst part, he said, was that they would probably get away with it. Some Jew police captain was trying to cover it up. He was probably bribed. This Lesko's wife is very rich, said Borovik, and you know how the Jews are when they smell money.

"And do you know what they're going to do now?" Borovik had asked. "These murdering bastards? They are going out to dinner. At eight o'clock they will be sitting down at Kropotkinskaya 36, stuffing their faces, mocking us, spending enough on that one meal to feed a hundred decent Russians."

This was not the only injustice, said the general. Although it was true that he wanted these criminals watched, he would never have sent one man against all four. That was Major Podolsk's doing. As much as anything, it was Major Podolsk's stuck-up arrogance that killed Sasha. But don't you worry, said Borovik. I'll take care of that daiquiri-sipping faggot. That's if someone doesn't put a bullet through his head before I get the chance.

Kerensky understood his meaning. He understood every word including those not spoken. Kerensky would settle up with Podolsk. Borovik had as much as given permission. But Podolsk would have to wait in line.

Daiquiri-sipping faggot.

You see?

He knew right along that there was something off-center about that one.

Across the street from Kropotkinskaya 36 and a half block further up, a florist's delivery van sat parked, front end out, in the service alley between two czarist-era apartment houses.

The van had been stolen that morning. In the afternoon it was driven to Sheremetyevo, where its occupants witnessed the arrival of the Belkin party. The two men, dressed as laborers, their clothing filthy, cloth caps pulled low on their brows, watched as the party from Zurich climbed into a waiting Chaika with KGB plates. They watched to see if anyone else would follow. No one did.

Staying far behind, they saw the Chaika turn off onto the Outer Ring Road. They chose not to follow, opting instead to proceed to the Savoy by the most direct route. They parked the delivery van just off Sverdlov Square, facing the Bolshoi, with the intention of watching on foot. They were walking toward the Savoy when the Chaika suddenly reappeared, squealing around the corner, making them scurry to get out of the way.

Now they saw that the driver was slowing, pointing at the Bolshoi's facade. He picked up speed and turned left. That was the last they saw of the Chaika for almost two hours. They were not concerned. The tourists, they decided, had gone sightseeing.

They were waiting, watching, when the KGB Chaika finally arrived at the Savoy amid considerable confusion. They heard a man shouting in German and they saw two women, certainly prostitutes, being ushered out through the kitchen entrance.

They went back for their stolen van. The Belkin party, they knew, would be coming out again in forty-five minutes or so to go out for dinner. But it was more like fifteen minutes.

That the Chaika then headed toward Pushkin Square confused them somewhat. It was the wrong direction entirely. Then, in the process of following it, the driver saw the reflection of his low-beam headlights on the rear of a bus. The lights were out of alignment. It would not do for the Belkin party to see those headlights too often. The driver broke off. Better, he suggested, to wait for them on Kropotkinskaya. They are simply killing time. Doing more sightseeing. That must be why they left so early for an eight o'clock reservation. The man in the passenger seat agreed.

They had barely settled on the best place to park when the Chaika appeared. It found a place at the curb almost straight across from them. The KGB driver stayed with the car. The other three entered.

Moments later, they saw Leo Belkin reappear. Moving briskly, for some reason, he climbed back into the Chaika and just sat. Staring ahead.

Soon, in a minute or two, a big black Zil appeared. Six men in it. The Zil, too, found a place at the curb but a bit further down from the entrance. The six got out. Two seemed to be Arabs. One looked like a Scot. They entered the restaurant.

"Look," said the driver of the van.

His companion followed his eyes to the Chaika. Leo Belkin, he saw, had ducked low in his seat. He was straightening again. Clearly, he had not wanted to be seen by those in the Zil.

Both men climbed out of the Chaika. There was a conference. Now the driver went loping across to the Berioska shop. Belkin called a name, stopping him. The name was "Valentin." Belkin held up two fingers. The younger man nodded and went on.

"What do we know about Valentin?" asked the driver of the van.

A shrug. "He's KGB. Belkin trusts him. Otherwise, nothing."

This man's accent was American.

Minutes later, the young officer came out with a bag, the necks of two bottles showing, and brought it to Leo Belkin. Belkin had been pacing the sidewalk.

"It's wine, probably Georgian," said the passenger. "I piss better wine than the Russians make."

An injustice, thought the driver, but he was tired of arguing. He watched as Belkin refused the bag and cocked his head toward the restaurant. He seemed to be saying, *"No, I changed my mind. You come in and help us drink it."*

The men in the van sat back. They sipped instant coffee from a thermos. About thirty minutes passed. Suddenly, the door of the restaurant was thrown open. The six men from the Zil came out. They seemed agitated, in disarray. They headed for the Zil. The doorman came out behind them. The driver of the van assumed that it was to tell them, three of them at least, that they forgot their hats. But he didn't. He merely stood watching them, hands on his hips, looking satisfied for some reason.

"What's all that about, you think?" asked the driver. His accent was Austrian.

A shrug. "Maybe Lesko farted."

The Austrian chuckled. The American didn't smile.

"Take a picture," he said.

The Austrian groped for the autofocus camera that he'd left behind his seat. He set the zoom. Waldo reached in front of him and pressed the horn. A quick series of staccato bleats.

The use of a car horn is illegal in Moscow. Except in emergency. The sound will always cause heads to turn. As expected, the six men glanced in their direction, not sure of the source.

"Now," said the American.

The camera clicked and whirred.

"Why are we doing this?" asked the driver.

"I don't know. Get the license plate."

The camera clicked again.

"If you wanted a name and address, could you get it?"

"A name to go with the Zil?"

"For instance. Yeah."

"There aren't so many Zils. Technically, the government owns all of them. Someone would know who's using that one."

"How long would it take?"

"For enough dollars? By lunch tomorrow, probably."

"What about matching names to photographs?"

"Hard to say. Days. Weeks. But what for?"

"I don't know."

"You think something happened inside?"

"Something did. We just don't know if we care."

Yakov was crying again. It got Feodor started.

They kept it up all the way past GUM where it got worse because there were still police cars. It continued, Yakov the loudest, all the way to the storage room in the Shelepikha district where they kept a number of weapons. Kerensky tried to tell Yakov what the plan was for Sasha's killers, but it was no use. It was all Yakov could do to keep his eyes on the road.

Always, since they were children, Yakov looked up to his cousin Sasha and Sasha used to beat up anyone who picked on little Yakov. He always laughed the hardest at Sasha's jokes, even harder than Kerensky. Yakov would do anything for Sasha.

What he had to do first was stop crying.

Kerensky could not blame him but this was not good. Twice, between the Savoy and the Shelepikha house, policemen had flicked their batons at him because of the way he was driving. Kerensky made him keep going. Both policemen wrote down the plate number, probably, but it wasn't Yakov's taxi. The owner could say it was stolen. The important thing was that they get to the restaurant before the killers of Sasha finished eating. Also that a policeman in a car didn't decide to pull them over and then notice the guns on the floor of the back seat. No use trying to bribe him. He would never take their first offer. He would want to haggle and this chance would be lost. They would have to shoot him.

When they picked up the weapons—an AKM submachine gun and a Dragunov sniper rifle—Kerensky saw the Toshiba. Sasha had been here, he realized. Kerensky saw him in his mind, rubbing his fingers over it, wondering how much it would fetch. This vision caused his throat to thicken. Next, Sasha had put it down, so carefully, and then hurried off to GUM to do as Major Podolsk had ordered.

Something troubled him about the Toshiba. What? That Podolsk knew he'd stolen it? That he was now supposed to rush it out to Sheremetyevo where that fat German was waiting for it? Just so he would shut up about it? Another stupid order from Podolsk. Let the German grow old waiting.

But it wasn't that. What troubled him was how Sasha got to GUM, but he felt sure he knew the answer. You don't see many taxis in Shelepikha, so Sasha must have told his driver to wait. Probably promised to pay him extra although the driver would never have seen a kopek. Sasha was not one to throw money around.

It occurred to Kerensky that his murder must have happened very quickly by the time he got to GUM. How did his brother even have time to find them in such a big and crowded store? Could they have been waiting for him? If so, how did they recognize him? They had only that one glimpse of him as they drove on past the Savoy, and Sasha had even changed his jacket in the meantime.

Perhaps he would look for that driver. Ask him if he saw anything when he dropped Sasha off at GUM. Show him a picture of the big American.

The ride to Kropotkinskaya took only ten minutes. Kerensky explained his plan once more to Yakov, who was better now.

The first thing to do is to look for the black Chaika. KGB plates. Number MOC331. If it's still there, so are they. The KGB driver is probably inside with them because Borovik said the reservation was for a party of four.

Once they find it, they drop Feodor off one block down from the restaurant entrance. There is an apartment building with a row of thick junipers in front. Lots of deep shadow. Feodor has the Dragunov. It holds only five shots but is semiautomatic and it has a sniper scope. Also he has two extra clips. He waits under the nearest juniper, very quiet, doesn't light a cigarette. His job is to provide a crossfire when the Belkin party comes out and then covering fire after that.

Yakov drives once around the block and pulls up just above the restaurant. Kerensky stays low in the back seat with the AKM at his feet. When the Belkin party comes out, Yakov drives to the canopy and asks if they need a taxi. They will pause to say no. Kerensky will mow them down. Feodor picks off any of the men who manage to jump behind cars. If the woman is clear they will try not to shoot her, but if she isn't, too bad. Yakov then speeds off, they pick up Feodor, and then they go and get good and drunk in Sasha's memory.

Yakov acknowledged the soundness of this plan. His only complaint was that he had no weapon other than his knife and the length of pipe he kept under his seat. Perhaps, he said, he will get a chance to bash a head or two to finish them off. Perhaps, even, we can take the American alive and

bring him back to the sausage room. Watch his eyes pop out
when the grinder reaches his hips. Like the Armenian.

Kerensky regretted telling him about that.

But he let his cousin talk. It was better than crying. When
they got to Kropotkinskaya, however, he would have to be
firm with him. He had not worked out a good plan so Yakov
could improvise. Anyway, a look from Feodor said enough
was enough as far as sausage machines are concerned.
When Yakov learns how to take one apart and clean it,
maybe then we'll discuss it.

Yakov turned onto Kropotkinskaya.

"There." He gestured with his chin toward the awning in
front of number 36. It was a half-block ahead and on the
right. The entrance was brightly lit.

"And there and there," said Feodor. He pointed with his
finger at two Chaikas they were passing.

"Shit," said Kerensky. He saw Chaikas everywhere.

He counted four of them, all black. Also several other
makes. There were drivers in many of them, dozing for the
most part, waiting for their big-shot bosses to finish stuffing
their faces. Worse, down ahead, Kerensky could see a man
and woman standing at the curb outside that apartment
house. The man was now stepping into the street to try to
flag down their taxi. The plan would need to be flexible
after all.

"Keep going," he told Yakov. "Go around the block."

"I don't get off at the trees?" asked Feodor.

Kerensky's face darkened. So good with machinery, he
thought. But cement between the ears.

"*There*. That one." Yakov, excited, tossed his thumb at
a Chaika parked a few cars up from the entrance. "That was
their driver. He is staying with the car."

Kerensky put a hand on Feodor's neck to keep him from
turning to gape.

"Go around," he said again.

After four right turns they were back where they started.
None of the chauffeurs even glanced at them. Just another
taxi looking for a hard currency fare.

More good luck. The man and the woman seemed to give
up on getting a taxi. They were walking toward the
Smolenskaya metro station. No need, now, for Feodor to

explain why he's walking into their shrubbery with a sniper rifle.

"Get ready," Kerensky told his brother. "Hold the rifle against you. Don't let it show when you're getting out."

"You don't have to tell me everything," grumbled Feodor.

The taxi stopped. They waited a few seconds to make sure no one was coming through the lobby. Kerensky nudged Feodor, who quickly climbed out, banging the barrel against the taxi's roof. Kerensky cursed within himself. But Feodor managed to walk to the front door without dropping it. As instructed, he stepped briefly inside. Then, on a signal from Kerensky, he stepped out again and slipped behind the first of the junipers. He could now make his way to the last of them.

"Go," Kerensky said to Yakov.

"I have an idea," said his cousin.

"Don't have ideas. Just drive."

Yakov rounded the corner. "I can cut his throat," he said.

"Whose?"

"The driver. The one who helped to kill Sasha."

"Yakov . . . have you been listening to me?"

"Yes, but this is good. If I get the driver first, the others will stand out in front wondering where he is and you will have more time to shoot."

"Yakov . . . did you notice that he is not the only driver out there?"

"Yes, but do you know what they will see? They will see only a taxi driver who needs a light for his cigarette. He pulls up next to the Chaika, he gets out, he has the cigarette in his hand, and he goes to the window of the Chaika. The driver rolls it down. The taxi driver leans in. They see the glow of a lighter. They see the driver take a puff and walk back to his taxi."

Kerensky grunted. "And meanwhile, the driver is banging on his horn while he tries to hold his throat together."

"Okay, not his throat. I go for his eye. One thrust, one twist, and his brain is soup."

Kerensky considered this.

To polish off the driver first would certainly isolate the others. But he could not trust Yakov's knife to do the job. A

knife can kill quickly if the victim is helpless or else doesn't
see it coming. But if he gets a glimpse of it and tries to
protect himself, you can spend all night trying to finish him,
and all the time he's yelling. Besides, he had a hunch that
Yakov would want to make that one suffer.

"You just drive," he said to Yakov. "Drive and keep
your eyes open."

Yakov started to speak. But he only grumbled.

"On Kropotkinskaya, pull up just behind that Chaika. I
want to check the license plate."

"You think I don't know that car?" Yakov was offended.
"At the Savoy it emptied right in front of me."

"At the Savoy, you weren't so upset. Do what I tell you,
Yakov. Do *only* what I tell you and I'll give you a present."

"What present?" he asked glumly.

"I'll give you Major Podolsk."

Yakov brightened somewhat.

"For sausage. You can make him into sausage."

Yakov shook a fist. Triumphant.

"Just don't say nothing yet to Feodor."

51

"Now what?" said the American.

It was the second time he asked that question.

The first was when Belkin's driver came back out of the
restaurant looking like a man who suddenly expected
trouble. He was peering up and down the street, arms
folded, one hand well inside his jacket. After a while he
walked to the car and unlocked it. He reached in from the
driver's-side door and took a flashlight from the glove box.
Back out, he got down on his knees and shined it under the
chassis. He went to the rear bumper and looked there as
well, also feeling along with his fingertips. Satisfied, but
still wary, he climbed behind the wheel and sat.

The next time was when the same yellow taxi made its second pass of the block.

The first pass was already peculiar. The taxi had slowed as if its destination was the restaurant. Two passengers in back. Both men. But it didn't stop. It continued on as if to pick up two more passengers who were waiting outside a building further down. Then it drove past them as well.

It went around the block. Now it was back. It stopped in front of the apartment house where a man and woman had been waiting. They were gone. A man was climbing out of the taxi. He seemed to be hugging something against his chest. Whatever it was, it banged against the taxi before he turned and walked quickly toward the lobby.

"Probably nothing," said the Austrian. "Maybe he just didn't want to run into those people. Maybe he's behind on his rent."

"Or something," John Waldo said, nodding.

The Austrian's name was Lechmann. He yawned.

"How long are we going to do this?"

"Don't start. You're getting an all-expense-vacation here."

The Austrian hooted. "This is your idea of a vacation? An oil barge into Riga. Hard class by train to Zagorsk, sleeping with goats. To Moscow by truck with a load of rotting cabbage. What would you consider roughing it?"

"A KGB prison."

Lechmann grunted. "And I'll tell you something else. If they catch us, they don't have to ask how we got here. They can trace our route just by smelling us."

Waldo said nothing.

Ernst Lechmann pressed his shirt to his chest. This was to cut off the fumes that were rising from his body. Five days he had gone without bathing. He had chosen this truck because he thought the flowers would help. They only made it worse. The various odors seemed to be reacting chemically. The resulting scent smelled something like ammonia mixed with honey.

He appreciated the alternative—a cage in Lefortovo. But he also understood that these days you can bribe your way into this country, no problem. You could probably even tell them you're a spy if you felt like it. They would look at you

like you're crazy. Spying? Spying on what? Didn't anyone
tell you the news? Don't you get CNN at home? But they
would take your bribe and be satisfied.

Lechmann knew this because he knew the Russians. He
used to work for them. And he knows Moscow and St.
Petersburg inside out, which is why Waldo asked for him.
That, and because he can drive anything on wheels. And
steal anything on wheels. And because he could not say no
to Elena. Call it a wedding present. Call it also staying on
the good side of Mama's Boy.

Still . . .

They didn't have to come in this way. If Waldo would
admit the truth, he simply likes beating them. In his heart, he
liked the old days better.

"I meant tonight," he said. "How long tonight?"

A shrug. "If they go back to the Savoy, we'll hang
around there for a while. Then we'll knock off."

"And go get a bath?"

"You don't want a bath. You want to smell like a
Russian."

Lechmann snorted. "I have news for you," he said.
"When a passing Muscovite holds his breath, preferring
asphyxiation to gassing, it's a definite sign that this scent is
unfamiliar to them."

Waldo seemed to consider this. In his mind's eye, thought
the Austrian, he was seeing those people in the Irish Shop
on Kalinin this morning when he went in to buy his
Guinness and corned beef for lunch plus a jar of instant
coffee. Their lips were turning blue.

"Okay," he said. "We'll go to a *banya* later. Maybe pick
up some new clothes."

Lechmann felt sorry for the bather who came back and
found these in his locker. He was relieved nonetheless.

"We'll go to the Moscow Swimming Pool. It's open until
eleven."

Waldo sneered. "I hate that fucking place."

The Austrian rolled his eyes. Waldo didn't hate the pool.
It was a wonderful pool. Perhaps the biggest outdoor pool in
the world, open year round, heated. You could swim in a
blizzard. What Waldo hated was that on that site was once
a great cathedral. The Cathedral of Christ the Redeemer.

This name annoyed Stalin. He tore it down to build the new Palace of Soviets in its place. It was to be the biggest building in the world. Except then they discovered that the ground could not support its weight. The cathedral was gone. Nothing but a vast mud hole, seventy meters deep, in its place. Stalin is philosophical. At least the cathedral is gone. Stalin says, okay, so we make a swimming pool.

When it comes to architecture, don't get Waldo started.

''There's that cab again,'' said Waldo.

The two men watched as it coasted down the block, stopping, double-parked, just behind Belkin's Chaika. Belkin's driver, Valentin, was eyeing it in his side mirror. He had probably noticed the first two passes as well. More than probably. He was now reaching his right hand inside his coat, no doubt to make sure that his pistol would come out easily.

Maybe not a bad idea, thought Waldo. He reached behind his seat. His left hand found a large bouquet of mixed spring flowers wrapped in green paper. He placed it upright between his legs. With the fingers of his right hand, he probed among the ferns for the pistol grip of a German submachine gun. It was a Heckler & Koch MP5 fitted with a sound suppressor and a laser sight. The sight alone had cost him a Rolex watch in Riga. Lots of German weapons there, stashed for a guerrilla war that got cancelled when Yeltzin said screw it, let the Baltics go and good riddance.

The occupants of the taxi seemed to be arguing. The driver opened his door partway. The passenger grabbed at his jacket. The driver shook him off and stepped out. Skinny little guy. Face like a hawk. The passenger started to come after him. But he decided against it.

The driver now walked to the Chaika. He tapped on the side window with a hand that held an unlit cigarette. Waldo couldn't see the other hand. But he had a feeling. He flipped the safety off the MP5.

Hawk-face was tapping again. Waldo couldn't see Belkin's driver, but he could see part of the window and it wasn't rolling down.

Sorry. No matches. Get lost.

Back in the taxi, the passenger was watching this. He looked tight as a drum.

"Get ready to start this thing," said Waldo.

Hawk-face was getting pissed. That was part of it. The other part was that he didn't seem to know what to do next. He turned away from the Chaika. Then he turned back and kicked the door. He stepped back a bit, as if daring this Valentin kid to come out and fight him. Waldo could see Valentin's face now. No fear on it. Maybe a little anger. But he had a job to do and it wasn't swatting flies.

Hawk-face gave up. He walked back to his taxi, the unlit cigarette now in his mouth. He hesitated before getting in because the big guy in the back seat looked ready to strangle him. But he did get in. The big guy popped him one. Belkin's driver, watching all this, decided to start his engine.

He pulled away from the curb. No lights. He stopped again three car lengths down just short of the restaurant entrance. Now he climbed out, through the passenger side, leaving the motor running. He stood there, watching the taxi.

"There's Elena," said the Austrian.

Waldo looked. The doorman was first. He gave her a little bow. Next came Belkin, then Lesko. The doorman, for some reason, wanted to embrace Lesko. He was slapping his back with both hands. Lesko looked embarrassed.

Waldo glanced back at the taxi. The argument was over. The two men were sitting like statues. Now the one in the back touched the driver's shoulder. A calming gesture. Waldo felt a chill. That was no tail.

"It's a hit," he said. "Start up."

The van's engine wheezed and caught. The taxi started rolling.

Waldo opened his door partway. He tore the MP5 from the bouquet and squeezed the bulb that lit the laser sight. A red dot blinked on. He moved it to the driver's left cheek. The window was down. He waited.

An inner voice was speaking to him. Now several voices. The loudest said, *"Kill him."* Another argued for the man in back who surely had the gun. A third, a more distant voice, shouted that something was wrong here. Waldo felt that chill again. He knew what it was. That second pass. Those thick evergreens. There was another shooter there.

Waldo fired. The shot was too low. It slapped the soft

tissue just below the jaw. Waldo saw the throat explode. But
the man only stiffened as if in surprise.

Sudden movement near the Chaika. Belkin's driver had
seen the taxi start to move. He didn't like it. He raised one
hand toward the Belkin party, shouted for them to wait
while he drew his pistol with the other. Everything was slow
motion. The pistol was dropping in an arc and sighting
across the Chaika's roof.

Waldo scrambled from the van. He knew that the taxi
driver was finished. He knew that the man in the back had
a weapon. But Belkin's driver had him covered and Waldo
needed to cover that first tree. The red dot searched the
branches. It found a solid shadow. Waldo squeezed off a
burst. The shadow rocked.

But Valentin heard and saw him. Confused, he swung his
pistol toward the van. The taxi was still rolling, no one
steering. Lesko had Elena by the collar. He swung her like
a doll, pressing her against the wall, his body between her
and the guns. Belkin had the same thought. He moved
toward her, hands raised, trying to make himself bigger.

The doorman was shouting a warning, pointing. Valentin
swung his pistol again. Too late. A burst from the taxi's rear
window caught him high in the chest. His pistol flew from
his hand. It clattered to the sidewalk. Belkin turned. He saw
Valentin falling. He shouted his name and moved toward
him.

A shot came from the juniper tree. Belkin staggered. A
hand went to his hip. The taxi hit the Chaika, scraping along
its side.

"I have the tree," shouted Lechmann in Russian. His
weapon was an MP5-K, same as Waldo's but short, no laser,
no suppressor. He saw the muzzle flash. He emptied a clip
at it. But the man in the tree had loosed another burst. Stone
flew from the building's facade near Lesko's body. He
shifted his bulk to envelop Elena. He glanced over his
shoulder, toward the tree.

Lesko saw a man, now on his knees, trying to crawl. The
man pitched onto his face. Lesko saw no weapon. He
glanced to his right. He saw Belkin, still on his feet, lurching
toward Valentin. He saw Valentin's pistol. He forced Elena

to the sidewalk, shouted to her to stay there, stay low, then scrambled for that gun.

"The sniper is down," Lechmann shouted, again in Russian. "I'm covering."

Waldo had the taxi but no clean shot. He could kill the man in the back seat but Belkin was just beyond, reeling like a drunk. The same shot could kill Belkin. But the man with the Kalashnikov had no shot either, because the taxi had wedged tightly against the Chaika. The man in back was now shouting at the driver. He was shouting "Go!" in Russian. The voice suddenly went up in pitch. He yelled a name. Sounded like *jack-off*. It was just dawning on him, Waldo realized, that his driver was dead or dying. Nor did he seem aware of the other shots from the van. The grinding of metal against metal must have drowned out Lechmann's burst.

Good, thought Waldo. And he's got to come out this way.

Kerensky fought panic. He ducked low in the seat. He had no idea how Yakov had been shot. The windshield was intact. He had heard the Dragunov shoot twice but nothing else except shouted voices. This could still be done, however. Get out, shoot the rest of them, push Yakov over, and go get Feodor. He reached for the door handle, unlatched it, then kicked the door open with his foot. He backed out of the taxi and stood, using the door as protection.

Waldo, behind his own door, waited for his shot. He realized now that the laser sight was off, shooting low and left. Better not try a head shot. He aimed at the right shoulder blade and flipped to full automatic.

"Look out," cried Lechmann.

The windshield of the van shattered. Two more shots in quick succession slammed into Waldo's door. One passed through but missed him. He saw the muzzle blasts. He saw Lesko behind them, shooting from a crouch.

"Drive," he snapped. "Get out of range." He scrambled into the van, crouching behind the dashboard. Lechmann pressed the pedal and flicked the lights on full, hoping to blind Lesko. He kept his head down. He cut the wheel left and steered from memory.

"Fucking Lesko. Where'd he get a gun?"

"Hold it."

"Stop here."

They were abreast of the first juniper. Waldo wanted another shot. He looked back, knowing that Lesko would have no more time for them. He'd have to go for that other moose or get shot himself. Waldo saw his back. He had rounded the front of the cab. The moose had ducked behind the door but was rising now to aim the Kalashnikov. It hit metal. The top of the door. A half clip, by the sound of it, sprayed the air over Lesko's head. Lesko raised the pistol. Nothing. It must have jammed. He did not break stride. One foot came up. It kicked the door, hammering it against the moose.

Suddenly Lesko had the assault rifle. He'd plucked it out from the moose's hands. He held it by the barrel. The moose stumbled free of the car, backing away into the middle of the street. He was yelling a name. *"Feodor! Feodor, shoot!!"*

"I think that's Feodor," Lechmann said, pointing.

Waldo followed the finger. There was a man, the second shooter, still alive; he looked like the moose. Blood on his face and shirt, one arm broken, one leg dragging. He was hanging onto a parked car, trying to pull himself up by the hood ornament.

"Kill him," said Waldo. "I'll give you some room."

Once more, he hopped into the street. Lechmann fired. Waldo heard the slap of bullets against flesh but he did not bother to look. He squeezed his bulb and the red dot found the man who was frantically backing away. Waldo held his fire. The moose had stopped. He was weaving now. Circling Lesko. He had raised both fists. Waldo blinked. He did not believe this. From the moose's actions, he was daring Lesko to drop the gun and fight him.

"I hear whistles," said Lechmann. "They're close."

Waldo heard them. He should shoot and go. He knew that. Still, he wanted to see this guy take Lesko on. But Lesko was in no mood for sporting gestures. He turned the Kalashnikov, tried to fire it. Again, nothing. The moose had emptied the clip when he panicked. Now the moose let out a roar and charged.

"You coming?" Lechmann hissed at Waldo. "Otherwise, I'll say good night."

Lesko had caught him flush. He'd swung the butt. It
straightened him. The moose staggered. Lesko moved in.
He hit him four more times that Waldo saw. All short chops
to the elbows or the face, none meant to finish him. Waldo
could almost hear Lesko.

"You like to hurt people?"

Whack.

"You like to see pain?"

Whack.

"How's this, you fat fuck?"

Crunch . . . Crunch.

The van was rolling. The last Waldo saw, Lesko was
dragging the moose back to the taxi, smashing his face
against the trunk.

52

Irwin Kaplan sat in his kitchen waiting for the wall phone
to ring. He had the house to himself. His wife and his
youngest daughter were down at the high school watching
his oldest play field hockey.

It was twenty minutes since his call to Swissair. Plenty of
time for Clew, who had surely listened in, to go running to
Fuller.

The phone rang.

He was tempted, as he reached for the receiver, to say
"Hello, Mr. Fuller." But he didn't. Nobody likes a smart
ass. Besides, it might be Bannerman.

"It's Bart, Irwin."

He cleared his throat. "Hello, Mr. Fuller."

"Have you tried to reach Paul?"

"You told me not to."

"I know what I told you. I asked if you tried."

Okay, he thought with a sigh. The game is *Let's Pretend*.

"Yes, I did." he answered. "Swissair's going to radio the cockpit. Ask him to call."

A pause. "I could prevent that, you know."

"I know. But at least I'll have made the effort."

Silence.

"Mr. Fuller, did you know Susan's with him?"

"Yes." Another pause. "How did *you* know that?"

"I called Anton Zivic."

And another silence. But this one was gratifying. Kaplan had called Zivic from his car phone out front. It was nice to know that his car, at least, didn't have ears.

"Calling Zivic," he said, "is how I got the flight they're on. Would Bannerman be bringing Susan if he's looking to start a war? Would Zivic even have told me where he is?"

"What's your point?"

"I think he's on damage control. I think he's going to snatch Carla and get her the hell out of Switzerland."

"Irwin . . . I'm afraid Carla's dead."

Kaplan closed his eyes. He moaned inwardly.

"It just came in. That Swiss special-forces unit found her. They were too late."

"Was she . . ."

"Beheaded? No."

Kaplan took a breath. Small comfort. He waited.

"Her killer may have tried, however. The commander of the raiding party says that her throat was deeply cut. The man who seems to have done it—your Sicilian apparently— was also found dead at the scene. Someone broke his neck and then propped him up so that he wouldn't die too quickly. One assumes that this was so that he could answer questions. He was left that way to be gnawed on by rats. Roger thinks that this sounds like the sort of thing Billy McHugh might do."

Kaplan pictured the scene in his mind. He felt no pity. He offered no comment.

"Billy . . . or whomever . . . was also too late to save Carla. She was dead or dying when he arrived. He then took the time to wash her face, fix her hair, and lay her out on her bed as if she were asleep."

Kaplan was seeing that as well.

"This happened, Irwin, at about the same time that Ronny Grassi was being called upon. It would seem that—Susan or no Susan—Paul Bannerman has already mobilized his people."

If he hasn't, thought Kaplan, he sure as hell will now.

"Mr. Fuller . . . what do you want from me exactly?"

"You said it, Irwin. Damage control. What I *don't* want is Bannerman running wild until I know what happened to a shipment of nerve gas, who is selling it, where it's going, and what is its intended use."

A thoughtful pause. "Nerve gas, huh?"

Fuller heard the doubt. "Speak your mind, Irwin."

"You knew who Corsini was long before the wedding. You've had him under surveillance right along."

"Among others, yes."

"And whatever this thing is, you've got your own people inside it. You're worried Bannerman won't care about sorting them out."

This silence, and a little hissing sound, said, *"There's such a thing as being too smart for your own good, Irwin."*

Yeah, well. Fuck you.

"And this isn't about nerve gas, is it. It's not about drugs and it's not even about smuggling."

Fuller found his voice. "On the contrary," he said firmly, "both are very much a part of the equation. Get this through your head, Irwin. No one has lied to you."

Kaplan tried to believe him. No outright lies. He'd only danced around the truth a little.

"Okay, but let's talk nerve gas. There was a story a few months back. There's this town in Russia . . ."

"Vigirsk. Near Yekaterinburg."

"That's the place. Did it happen?"

"Yes."

"From more stolen nerve gas?"

"From the same shipment. One canister did that, Irwin. There were eighty canisters in all."

Another pause, longer than the last. Then, "That's pretty scary, all right."

"Yes, it is."

"Somebody ought to do something."

A patient sigh. "Irwin . . . drop the other shoe."

"It's what I asked you this morning. What makes this a State Department problem?"

"Because this nerve gas, *scary* as it is, is only one little part of an infinitely larger smuggling operation. If our information is correct, the same people who are moving that gas—and everything else that isn't nailed down—are the people who have also been moving some one hundred billion dollars in missing Communist-party funds."

Kaplan was silent for a long moment. "You said *billion*?"

"The amount, if you have trouble grasping it, is roughly equal to the gross national product of Sweden. Any part of that money, if recovered, can make the difference between anarchy and relative stability in the former Soviet Union. Helping to assure that stability, Irwin, is clearly within the purview of the State Department."

The DEA man sniffed. "As opposed to the Russians themselves? I mean, I assume they've noticed that someone cleaned out the vaults."

Fuller ignored the flippancy.

"Okay. You're saying that the people who'd know how to look for it are probably the people who took it."

"Something like that, yes."

"And your real interest in getting it back, aside from that stability business, is so this country doesn't have to make up the shortfall."

"Right on the button, Irwin. This country among others."

Kaplan considered this. He found comfort in it. He was always more comfortable when conversations got past moral principle and got down to money. Money or power. It was always one of the two.

"Well . . ." He shrugged. "You know that Grassi knows where it is. Some of it, anyway."

"Some, no doubt. But that missing hundred billion includes an estimated sixty tons of gold, one hundred fifty tons of silver, and eight tons of platinum, not to mention a rumored fortune in precious stones. I don't think *Temptress* has quite that much cargo capacity."

Fuller, having said this, let it hang in the air.

Okay, thought Kaplan, I'll bite. "What does, Mr. Fuller?"

"Sudanese ore carriers, if you want a wild guess. The Sudanese ship a lot of copper and chrome to Black Sea ports."

Wild guess, my ass.

"How does the Sudan figure in this?"

"The Sudanese government has a number of ambitions. One of them is to replace Switzerland/Luxembourg as the premier tax haven of the next century. Khartoum is licensing banks left and right. Their laws don't allow much in the way of auditing nor do they permit the freezing of accounts. The Sudan, incidentally, is where Saddam Hussein kept his traveling money."

Kaplan waited.

"In addition, we know that the Sicilian Mafia controls the second and third largest banks in Khartoum. The Islamic proscription against drug use does not extend to drug profits. Nor would they discriminate against a group that knows more about laundering cash than the Swiss and more about smuggling than the Hong Kong Chinese."

This last part, Kaplan assumed, was to convince him that he should care. But he already knew about the Sicilians.

Fuller continued.

"The primary ambition of the Sudanese is to become the center of the militant Islamic world now that all the others are either discredited or showing signs of reduced religious fervor. Already, no Arab needs a passport to travel in or out of the Sudan. The various terrorist groups find this to be a considerable convenience. The Sudanese intend to use them, not only against Israel, but against any Islamic government which embraces a more moderate view."

Kaplan was grimacing. "Which brings us back to nerve gas," he said.

Fuller nodded. "Do you begin to see the scope of the problem, Irwin?"

Kaplan muttered something. It was unintelligible.

"Irwin?"

He shook his head, clearing it. "Anyway . . ." he said, "all you want from me is to get Bannerman to cool it?"

"For the time being."

"What if something else happens?"

"Ah, yes." Fuller covered his mouthpiece. He was

asking a question, probably to Roger Clew. He came back
on. "The Lesko-Belkin party is out to dinner at the
moment. We think we know where. As soon as they're
found, they will be whisked to the embassy compound in a
bulletproof Lincoln."

Kaplan grunted softly, thoughtfully. He knew that he
should call Zivic first. Tell him about Carla and that he'd
just now heard. Maybe Zivic could help get Bannerman to
go easy. But he doubted it. Bannerman, he suspected, would
sooner hit at random than be thought not to be hitting at all.
That's what makes him such a frightening son of a bitch.

"I might have to deal," he told Fuller. "What can I give
him for Carla?"

"Corsini's control . . . that name was Viktor Podolsk?"

"He's a KGB major, yeah."

Fuller covered the phone again. More mumbling. Then,
"You can give him Major Podolsk, Irwin."

53

John Waldo was angry. Mostly at himself.

He knew that he should have seen the hit coming. At the
least, he should have assumed it and made some kind of a
move the moment that taxi showed up for a third pass.

That's when he should have known. The first pass was to
look things over, the second pass was to set up cross and
covering fire, and the third was for the hit itself.

The thing was, a hit was about the last thing he expected.

Even when he saw it building, it was too stupid to be true.
All those witnesses. The doorman out front. Six or seven
chauffeurs dozing in their cars, any one of whom could have
decided to follow the shooters home or maybe even cut off
their escape. Any one of them probably could have done it
because that wheelman driving the taxi wasn't worth a shit.

The guy was pathetic, thought Waldo.

A wheelman, for openers, never *ever* gets out of the car. This one not only got out but he decided, apparently on his own, that he would go and pop Belkin's driver himself. Belkin's driver, however, does not cooperate. He doesn't roll down his window even when little Hawk-face gets all pissed off and kicks his door.

Still . . . Waldo should have moved faster.

The Austrian—Lechmann—tried to make him feel better. Even Elena, he pointed out, never expected anything like this.

That was true, Waldo supposed.

All she wanted, she told him, was for someone to get to Moscow early, look things over, keep an eye on them once they got there. If we're followed, she said, try to find out who's interested. She told him why. That Belkin has a bug up his ass about the KGB looting the country.

That's not exactly what she said. Elena doesn't talk like Lesko yet. But she said she was asking him if he'd take the job because Bannerman says he knows his way around Moscow and St. Petersburg and might not mind dropping in again and maybe torching a few more buildings.

That wasn't exactly what Bannerman said either. And Bannerman had other reasons for making the suggestion.

A big one was that a few weeks before, in Westport, Waldo had clocked some lawyer who'd been slapping his wife around. Everyone thought Billy or Molly did it. More likely Billy. He had the history. Waldo had to tell Bannerman it was him. Bannerman wasn't happy. But he said let's keep it between us. Meantime, maybe you're getting cabin fever here in Westport. Maybe you could use a change of scenery.

When Elena made the proposition, he sort of asked Bannerman if it was okay. Sort of. He told Bannerman that he might hang around Europe for a while. Take that vacation. Bannerman just smiled and said good idea. That's when Waldo knew it was probably Bannerman's idea in the first place. Elena said bring whoever you want. Spend as much as you like. Just don't mention this to anyone else. Least of all Lesko. He was sure to make a fuss over it, she said.

He sure as hell will now, thought Waldo.

Lechmann had pulled into a darkened street just off the Arbat. He was prying what remained of the windshield from its frame and using a rag to sweep the glass from the floor and seats.

Until they pick up new wheels, Waldo told him, they'd better take the right front door off, too. Bullet holes. Without it, they still wouldn't look any different from a thousand other crates driving around this town. The place is one big spare-parts depot. It's okay not to have any doors or windows, but if your car is dirty they give you a ticket.

"Let's ditch it soon," said Lechmann. "Lesko will be giving a good description."

Waldo grumbled in agreement.

There had been no question of sticking around, identifying themselves. They'd end up doing five years just on general principles unless Bannerman could come up with something the Russians wanted in exchange.

Nor could they blame Lesko for shooting at them. To him, they were only dark shapes in deep shadow. Dark shapes with muzzle blasts. But maybe he began to get the picture when they pulled up down the street and put a few final stitches in that sniper.

Waldo tried to think what he should have done differently. He supposed that he could have told Lechmann to ram that cab. But then the van might have been disabled and he couldn't assume that spraying the tree had put the sniper out of action. As it turned out, it hadn't. He'd gotten off at least five shots before Lechmann's burst crippled him.

Then Lesko starts blasting.

Gun looked like a Makarov. It must have been the one Belkin's driver had.

"That driver," he said to Lechmann. "Valentin, right? I think he probably bought it."

"Perhaps not." Lechmann had been thinking about that as well. "The shots hit him high. Here and here." He touched his chest at the level of his collar bone.

"Belkin caught one, too. Could you see how bad?"

The Austrian touched his right kidney to show the entrance wound. "He was also in shock. Walking in circles. Finally he sat. Very hard. I think it's bad."

Don't count on a bonus for this one, thought Waldo. But

at least Elena looked okay. No thanks to them. She had the sense to stay down. And Lesko had the balls to draw their fire away from her.

They'll hold Lesko for maybe two days. Maybe longer if he killed the moose. Elena, they'll just question. They'll be very polite when they find out who she is. They'll get a statement, find out she didn't actually see much of anything, and then put her on the next plane out. Anything else, they'll get from Belkin and Valentin if those two are able to talk.

He ought to let Bannerman know, thought Waldo. But he can't risk a call. Anyway, by the time he got an overseas line Elena could be back in Zurich. She'll tell him.

If the moose is alive, they'll wring him dry. Who sent you? Why? Who were the two who escaped in a flower truck? Why did they kill your associates? Don't you see that it must have been prearranged? They were there to silence all three of you. For your own good, tell us everything.

"You know what I'm thinking, right?" he said to Lechmann.

Lechmann raised a staying hand. "I want soap and water, new clothes, some food, and a van that gives less fresh air. Any other subject, tell me tomorrow."

"I think it was that bunch in the Zil. They ordered the hit."

The Austrian snorted. "Why? Because they left the restaurant in a huff? For this you don't order a killing. For this you leave nothing for the waiter."

Waldo considered this. He thought it proved his point.

"That hit," he said. "Did it look like surgical precision to you? Or did it look like a last-minute arrangement."

Lechmann had to agree. Certainly with this last. It was also clear that the driver, Valentin, gave no sign of expecting trouble until minutes after that group in the Zil had departed.

"Tomorrow we find out whose car that is," said Waldo. "But first I want to know what happened inside."

The Austrian shook his head. "First a bath," he insisted. "We have two hours until the restaurant closes. When it closes, we can ask."

"Ask who?"

"The doorman," Lechmann answered. "Whatever happened inside, the doorman did not disapprove."

"That was Waldo," said Katz.

He said this from deep within Lesko's brain even as Lesko was pounding the big man's face against the taxi.

But Lesko said no. Moved like him, maybe. Bowlegged stance. Kind of rocks side to side. Never really saw the face because it was always behind his scope. No, he decided. No way that was Waldo. Listening to Katz could have got him shot.

It was for cover, as much as anything, that Lesko had dragged the big man behind the taxi. It was to knock the fight out of him that he kept banging this shooter's head while keeping one eye on that flower van down the street.

The van had stopped down by those trees. The man jumped out. He aimed his weapon, had a clear shot, and didn't take it, which means he couldn't have been in on this. Just then, another burst came from inside the van. It was aimed off to the side, which means they must have nailed that other shooter. Then the van starts rolling. The guy jumps back in. The van disappears around the corner.

Waldo? No way. Waldo wouldn't have cut out. All he knew about that van for sure was that it had one cockeyed headlight. It had been tailing them since they left for dinner.

The man he was holding had stopped moving. The one who shot Valentin. This one he had seen before, no question. Two hours ago. Standing in the doorway of Detsky Mir.

He realized, his anger draining, that he might have overdone it. Bloodied and broken teeth glistened on the surface of the trunk. The trunk itself was sprung from the pounding.

Lesko rolled the killer onto his back. He'd gone totally limp. One eye was open a slit. The other had been driven deep into its socket. He seemed to be breathing. Or just expelling air. Lesko had no time to worry about which. He let him slide off the trunk. He pulled the lid open, then he lifted the big man by his belt and collar and heaved him into the trunk, his thick legs dangling outside.

Elena.

Lesko slammed the trunk on this one's knees. No reaction. He stepped around the Chaika and onto the sidewalk.

Elena was the way he'd left her. She was half sitting, half leaning against the building. She looked wrung out, a sort of tired I-don't-believe-this expression on her face. She didn't look up at him. Her eyes were on Leo Belkin, who was trying to undo the buttons on Valentin's shirt.

Belkin's fingers weren't working very well. He was reeling like a drunk. Lesko heard another police whistle close by. He glanced up toward its source. A cop at the next corner. He was just standing there blowing, probably waiting for backup before risking an approach.

Lesko knelt at Belkin's side. He eased him away from Valentin. The doorman came out, wringing his hands, saying something in Russian. Lesko looked up at him, shaking his head. The doorman said "Ambulance" in English. He mimed a telephone call. "Ambulance comes," he said.

Belkin sank to the pavement, hugging his waist, curling himself into a fetal position. He had trouble speaking, but he could gesture with his head. See to Valentin, he was saying. Help Valentin.

Valentin looked bad, thought Lesko, but maybe he had a chance. He was breathing; his lungs sounded clear. The bullets may have missed them. Lesko ripped the shirt open. Two neat holes, high in the chest, and a nastier-looking wound high on his gun arm. That one had sent the pistol flying. It didn't look dangerous. He reached behind Valentin's neck and felt for the exit wounds. He found them. They also seemed clean and in line with the entry. Not too much blood, no bone fragments that he could feel, and they were well away from Valentin's spine.

Lesko shrugged off his coat and bunched it under Valentin's head lest he go into spasm and hurt himself on the cement. He stripped his necktie and used it to bind the arm. That seemed to be where most of the blood loss was coming from. It was all he could do. Now he needed to check on Belkin whose left foot was starting to twitch.

"Lesko . . ."

Katz's voice. Faint. He ignored it.

"Lesko!" The voice came again, more urgently this time.

He knew that it was only his own mind, warning him
about something that it sensed. Happens all the time. It's
probably about the Russian cops, he thought. Blue lights
were coming down the street. Belkin's needs were more
immediate. But he heard Katz speaking to him again.
Louder. Closer. He was saying something about Elena.

Good idea, he thought. Maybe Elena could keep an eye
on Valentin, keep him warm and quiet while he . . .

Elena.

It struck him that it was not like Elena to just sit. She
knew more about bullet wounds than he did. She took two,
herself, back in . . .

He looked up at her. She had not moved or changed
expression. She was looking back at him. Or maybe at
Belkin. Or maybe at neither of them. Lesko felt himself go
cold.

"Elena?" He called to her.

No reaction.

He tried to call her name again but he found he couldn't
speak. He raised himself on legs which, suddenly, could
barely hold his weight. He walked toward her, slowly,
wanting to see her eyes come up to meet his. They didn't
move.

Now he saw the blood. A fist-sized smear on some
ornamental stone two feet above her head and a few more
dabs that had marked her progress as she slid down the wall.

He heard himself calling her name. He saw his hands
reaching to touch her face and he heard himself cry out
when he felt how cold it was.

Now he felt the blood. It was behind her left ear. Her eyes
were like black opals, their pupils fully dilated. He could not
look at them. Carefully, he probed beneath the clotted hair.
The tissue, the skull itself, was spongy to his touch.

The part of his brain that was rational said that she could
not have been shot. He was covering her when the shots
were fired. He'd seen where the bullets from those trees had
hit. And there had been no impact. If there were, he would
have felt it because her head had been against his chest.

He glanced up at the ornamental stone where the trail of
blood began. It had a rounded edge, protruding. The

realization began to form that he must have crushed her against it. A low anguished howl came from deep in his stomach. He wanted to run back into the street. He wanted to find Valentin's gun and stick it in his mouth.

Elena twitched.

Quickly, too roughly, he dropped his fingers to her throat. In his agony, it had not occurred to him that she might not be dead. There was a pulse. Slow and faint but it was there.

"Elena!" He bellowed her name.

Her lips moved. They seemed to part a bit. A cheek twitched. One of the black opals drifted as if searching for him.

Desperate, hopeful, he screamed her name again. He squeezed the flesh of her arm, digging in his nails. She seemed to react. A small gasp. A stuttered intake of breath.

His left hand, balled into a fist, lashed out at someone. He didn't know who. Someone in white. The doorman was trying to say something to him. He leaned close. Lesko swiped at him as well. The doorman backed off.

The rational part of his brain knew that he . . . they . . . were trying to help. The rational part saw the ambulance. The flashing lights. Many police cars. But Elena was trying to come back. He was sure of it. Give him just a minute and he could help her break through.

The doorman was spreading his arms. A gesture of hopelessness. Lesko saw this. He misunderstood it. He wanted to scream *"No! She'll be okay."*

But the doorman was not looking at Lesko. He was looking at the two uniformed policeman who were holding back, not sure how to separate this deranged bull of a man from this woman without doing more damage.

The doorman moved out of view. Lesko could not see nor did he care where he was going. He did not see him take a baton from the hand of one officer, turn, and take careful aim for a measured backhand blow across Lesko's temple.

54

"You won't believe this," said the sergeant.

He was staring at the face of the large semiconscious man, now handcuffed, being strapped to a stretcher. The last time he saw that face it was a photograph on the chest of Sasha Kerensky.

"I'm far ahead of you," answered Captain Alexei Levin. He had in his hands a collection of identity papers. He sorted and arranged them as if they were playing cards.

He paused for a moment, absorbing the scene around him. It was lit bright as day by a truck that said CNN on the side. Behind it was a sound truck from Vremya Evening News. Two commentators, one English, one Russian, were speaking into video cameras. Half of Moscow would be watching this tomorrow. Perhaps half the world. And that doorman, he suspected, could buy a restaurant of his own with what CNN will pay him for his tip.

Well up the street, honking their horns, trying to get around the blue police Volgas, were two big cars, a Lincoln and a Mercedes. Embassy cars, no doubt of it.

Down the street was a crowd of onlookers. Some were scouring the pavement, looking under parked cars, hunting for souvenirs. Levin snapped his fingers at a uniformed militia man, telling him to go pick up shell casings before they all disappear.

He turned back to his sergeant. Levin raised an arm, pointing toward the curb near the first of the juniper trees.

"Down there, full of holes," he said, "is Feodor Kerensky."

He traced an arc to the taxi just above them.

"Behind the wheel, with no throat, is Yakov Gudin, cousin of Feodor. In the trunk, with no face and drowned in his own blood, is Kerensky himself."

The sergeant, eyes wide, started to speak. Levin raised the finger. He wasn't finished.

He pointed to the chalk marks where the three others had been. Blood still wet in all of them. He started with the nearest outline.

"KGB captain . . . based at Yasenevo . . . maybe he lives."

The finger moved to the chalk just beyond.

"KGB general . . . Foreign Intelligence . . . based in Zurich. He probably dies."

Levin's hand had come almost full circle.

"Elena Brugg . . . also from Zurich . . . very rich . . . very influential. She probably doesn't make it to the hospital."

He came to the last set of documents. Levin nodded toward the stretcher.

"Raymond Lesko . . . was once a policeman apparently . . . from New York . . . now lives at the Brugg woman's address . . . is probably her bodyguard."

He paused thoughtfully. Among the contents of the American's pockets were a slip of notepaper with six names on it. Scribbled in Russian by a hand other than this one's. Levin knew three of the names. KGB. All former generals. All three would be greatly improved by a firing squad. To be on the same list, the other three had to be just as rotten. Perhaps the Brugg woman was doing business with them.

He glanced up the street once more. The Mercedes, he felt sure, would be from the Swiss embassy. The Lincoln from the Americans. Behind them, probably, was a car from the Interior Ministry coming to tell him he is relieved. Go home, Captain. Not a word of this to anyone. Eat a matzoh or something.

He smiled ruefully.

Tell that, he thought, to the doorman who is now on camera. Tell it to the waiters inside who are wondering how much CNN will pay to know what this group had for dinner.

"Alexei?" The sergeant was staring at the chalk marks where the KGB captain had fallen. "That one matches the description of the young one who was with this big one."

Levin grunted. He had realized that as well. In the pocket of the big one—the American named Lesko—there was a receipt from a jewelry shop at GUM. So they were there, after all. But what did this tell us? That these two did in fact kill Sasha while the other two shopped? It was still too farfetched. Levin didn't believe it. What was clear, however, was that the various Kerenskys had believed it.

They believed it because someone convinced them of it. And who did that? Who else knew the details? Who else would know where these four were having dinner? Answer: their old protectors from the KGB.

Next question is why. Why the frame-up with Sasha? Why would they want these four killed? Find out why, and you're halfway to knowing who. That's if the American's list doesn't tell us who already.

There, thought Levin. Simple and straightforward. More or less.

Simple, of course, if you don't start wondering how two men in a flower delivery van knew to sit out here and ambush the Kerenskys.

He shared all these thoughts with his sergeant.

"More bodyguards?" the sergeant suggested.

Levin gave him a look. Shame on you, it said.

The sergeant wished he hadn't said it. Unless all of the witnesses had hallucinated, he realized, a man doesn't shoot at his fellow bodyguards.

In Levin's belt was the Makarov they had taken from the big American. In his pocket was the clip he had found in the street. The witnesses said that the big one suddenly stopped firing as if the gun had jammed. This allowed those other two to get away. A Makarov, however, does not jam so easily. But if you're not used to it, Captain Levin knew, you can easily press the button that releases the clip. This must have been what happened. It explains why this Lesko stopped shooting at the van, but it does not explain why the two *in* the van didn't seize that chance to kill him.

Answer: they didn't want to. They might have been friends after all.

Or . . . possibly . . . they were from a rival brigade. Survivors, perhaps, of the Lubertsy Brigade. Perhaps, thought the sergeant, they just happened to pick tonight to settle old scores. It was as good a guess as any.

Levin watched as the American, Lesko, was heaved into

the last of the ambulances. He seemed to be coming around.
Just a good bump on the head.

A morgue truck was next in line, waiting to shovel up the
remains of the Chicago Brigade. Behind it was a tow truck
for the taxi.

"So?" asked the sergeant. "Now what?"

"We take out our pads. We start taking statements."

"Waste of time. You know that this will be taken from
you. It's too big. They especially won't want the *Jew* on
CNN."

This reminded him. The doorman had been saying something about a big fight inside the restaurant. The maître d',
meanwhile, was frantically waving his hands, trying to get
the doorman to shut up about it.

Levin sighed. He riffled the sheaf of documents as he
looked up the street. The Lincoln was getting through. It
was coming down the far sidewalk. The Americans. They
won't ask his religion before they start raising hell.

"You start with the waiters," said Levin. He cocked his
head toward the Lincoln. "I think I'll start with them."

55

The commandos were definitely Enzian Unit.

Yuri saw the insignia as he drove past with Miriam. Two
soldiers dressed in combat fatigues stood in the road to keep
traffic moving.

In the gravel driveway leading to Carla's boathouse he
saw two vehicles with the markings of the Swiss military.
The assault had been made from this direction as well.
Behind them, just in from the road, he saw a Buick sedan
with diplomatic plates. The boathouse itself was illuminated
bright as day by spotlights. Two men, civilian clothing,
were climbing the wooden steps to the loft apartment. A

soldier at the top seemed to be saying that it was safe to enter.

Miriam sat close to him on the front seat of Aldo Corsini's car. Her chin rested on his shoulder. His right hand was between her thighs. Miriam's hand was inside his shirt, playing with the hairs of his chest as she tasted his cheek with her tongue.

This picture was presented to one of the sentries when Yuri slowed to ask what happened here. He expected no answer and got none. But at least it gave him the chance to look. And the sentry would be more likely to remember his amorous companion than the make and model of the car they were driving.

Yuri and Miriam had paddled—no motor—to the small marina just two hundred meters below the boathouse. Miriam's car had been left there as well, but it was gone. Avram had taken it. She knew that he would be waiting with it a few kilometers up the road. There was some risk, they realized, in taking Corsini's Audi. Those raiders might well be looking for it. On the other hand, Corsini's tapes and Lydia's notes were still inside. Also, leaving the Audi to be found at the marina might lead to the lake being dragged.

"Those were Americans, I think," said Miriam when the car picked up speed.

Yuri nodded. He was already trying to imagine who sent them and why. It wasn't Anton Zivic because Zivic had sent Miriam. It might have been Roger Clew, however. The diplomatic license plate seemed to argue in that direction. Also, Clew is fond of theatrics. A commando raid would be his cup of tea.

"When we find Avram," she said, "I have a robe and slippers in my suitcase. I can put them on and go back."

Yuri understood what she meant. She would pretend to be a curious neighbor. Very natural. No one would question it. The men in the Buick would probably ask her if she saw or heard anything before they arrived, and to do that they would have to identify themselves. Miriam was very resourceful.

But Yuri's mind was elsewhere. The first thing was to get to a telephone and get through to General Belkin. Warn him. Get instructions. Find out who in the embassy can be trusted to help. Meantime, Miriam could report to Anton Zivic. The next was to get back to Bern, get rid of this car, and see to Carla. He was reasonably sure that she would be sound asleep, probably for several more hours. And Zivic, no doubt, had sent a team there as well.

He hoped that they would be as good as Miriam. What he didn't need, the way things were going, was for the pills not to have worked so well and for Carla to slice them up the way . . .

Lydia.

He could not stop thinking of Lydia. The way he had used her. Showed her so little respect. Sent her straight into that knife. Lydia, who was so brave at the end.

"Yuri . . . stop it."

For an instant he thought this was Lydia's voice in his mind. It was only Miriam.

He could have asked, "Stop what?" but he didn't. She was reading his thoughts and he knew it.

"We all have our dead," she said quietly. "But we go on for the—"

He raised a hand, stopping her before she could say more. He knew that she meant well. But she knew nothing of Lydia Voinovitch. If Miriam were to say, "She knew what she was getting into," it would have broken his heart.

"There is Avram," she said instead.

He saw a car, hood up, a man fiddling with the engine, pretending that it had malfunctioned. He glanced into his rearview mirror and eased off on the accelerator. He saw nothing behind him, but ahead, coming from the other direction, two big sedans, Mercedes, were abruptly slowing. They stopped, one behind the other. The driver of the first was looking at Avram. He rolled his window down. Yuri snatched the Browning from his belt and stepped on the gas, prepared to ram if necessary.

"No." Miriam touched his leg. "In the second car. It's Willem Brugg."

The first Mercedes went on. Yuri recognized at least two of its occupants. They had been at the wedding. They now worked for the Bruggs.

Willem Brugg stayed with the second car. He had

gestured for Yuri to wait while he finished talking on his cellular phone. He was dressed in evening clothes. Could it have been Willem, Yuri wondered, who had arranged for the raid on Carla's house? If so, Yuri wondered how he knew that anything was happening there. More likely, he had been out to some affair when someone tipped him about the raid. Yuri could ask him soon enough.

In the meantime, he was glad for the chance to get a grip on himself. There he was, ready to ram and shoot before Miriam told him what he should have known already. Willem's car was hard to mistake. It was, perhaps, the only white Mercedes in all Zurich that had a ski pod permanently strapped to the roof along with four different antennas. Willem was equally hard to miss. Hair worn long, in waves with gray streaks. A face, good face, tanned like leather from being outdoors more than in. Willem had been known to hold board meetings while hiking and to make deals while skiing glaciers in July.

He was also a man who smiled easily. Laugh lines were etched at the corners of his eyes and mouth. He was not smiling now. He handed the phone to his driver, sat still for a long moment, then opened his door and stepped out. He seemed unsteady on his feet. Yuri started to get out, to offer assistance, but Willem Brugg motioned him to stay.

He waited as two police cars sped by, their Mars lights strobing, then crossed the road to the black Audi. His expression, Yuri saw, was grim. His eyes, normally so alive, so intelligent, seemed clouded and distant. He greeted Yuri by name and bowed his head to Miriam.

To Yuri, he said, "I am . . . so very sorry. I know that she was special to you."

Yuri thanked him but the reply was a reflex. He wanted to ask how Willem could know about Lydia.

"The man who killed her . . . it was you who saw to him, I take it?"

Yuri nodded.

Brugg gestured vaguely toward the first Mercedes, since departed. "They will see to everything else. She will be . . . treated as we all would wish. She was special to me as well."

Yuri narrowed his eyes. He was distracted but he was not

unconscious. It was finally getting through to him that Willem Brugg was talking about Carla. Yuri felt a surge of unreasoning panic. Had they gotten to Carla? Killed her in her sleep? Or was Willem, please God, talking about poor Lydia whom he'd left in Carla's bed? He had to swallow before he could ask. In that time, Willem Brugg's eyes had moistened. He gestured, stiffly, almost reluctantly toward the Mercedes with the ski pod and the four antennas.

"From Moscow," he said, "I'm afraid there is more bad news."

Irwin Kaplan was disappointed. And more than a little sad.

He stood in the driveway, leaning against his car, the car phone still in his hand. Anton Zivic, whom he always thought was the most civilized of that bunch, had taken the news of Carla's death as if he'd told him that she had the flu.

No anger. No bereavement. Just maybe a little startled. He wanted the when, where, how, and who. Then, at the end, all he said was "Hmmph!"

Kaplan told him what Fuller had asked. That Bannerman and his people shouldn't go crazy, and why. Zivic seemed more interested in that part of the conversation. But the more Kaplan told him, the madder he got, because for all the years they've been together and all the crap they've been through together, Carla Benedict ought to have been worth more than a fucking "Hmmph!"

It as much as said, "What the hell. She's been walking between the raindrops so long that it's hard to get worked up when her luck finally runs out." It said, "Don't sweat it, Irwin. No one here will make a big deal."

He didn't even bother giving him the name of that KGB major. Podolsk. If Fuller was so willing to give him up, he had to be on the bottom rung anyway. When Fuller covered the phone, it was probably to ask Clew if he knew who Podolsk worked for yet. Clew probably did. Besides, Zivic would have realized in a minute that no major could have ordered such a high-profile hit. That's if he even cared.

The phone in the kitchen was ringing. Kaplan had left the door propped open so he could hear. He walked toward it. This ought to be Bannerman, he thought, speaking of cold-blooded pricks. He reached for the wall phone and said his name.

"Irwin, I'm glad I caught you." Barton Fuller again. He sounded flustered. *Caught* me?

"Would you put Roger on, please?" he said.

Kaplan was doubly confused. "Roger?"

An annoyed hiss. "I gather he's not there yet?"

"Mr. Fuller, this is my *house*. Why would he be here?"

"He'll . . . explain everything. In the meantime, I'm going to ask you to talk to no one."

"I'm . . . ah . . . just waiting for Bannerman."

"He won't be calling. You can talk to him later."

Kaplan's expression darkened. "Does this mean you did block his call?"

"I've had to make some decisions, Irwin. I—"

"And Roger's coming here, probably with muscle, to put me out of circulation. Am I right? He's late because they stopped to pick up their ski masks."

"Irwin . . ."

"Listen, here's what I'm going to do. I'm going to lock my doors, get my gun, and if anyone shows up here whose name isn't Kaplan, I'm going to lay one across his fucking bow."

A long breath. "You're going to Moscow, Irwin. So is Roger. So are Paul and Susan. I need you to be there with them. Roger will explain."

"Yeah, well, fuck Roger," Kaplan exploded. "I wouldn't recognize Little Bo Peep if I had to listen to his version of it."

"Irwin . . . Elena Brugg has been shot."

Silence.

"It's a head wound. It's bad. It happened less than an hour ago. Leo Belkin and his KGB driver were hit as well. They're both critical."

Kaplan swallowed. "Lesko?"

"Injured. Perhaps not seriously. He . . . um . . . got his hands on one of the gunmen."

An image formed in Kaplan's mind. He forced it away. A minor satisfaction.

"Who?" he asked quietly. "I mean, who did this?"

Fuller's answer, to the extent that he could give it, came

in rambling half-sentences. Some of them confused. He was still clearly shaken by the news.

There were three gunmen. Or maybe five gunmen. Lesko may or may not have had a run-in with them earlier. Either way, Lesko seems to be blaming himself. Had to be forcibly sedated. Is homicidal. Maybe suicidal. Either or both.

The shooters were local gangsters with a grudge or they were acting for the KGB. There were rumors, theories, both ways. The KGB connection was alleged by a police informant. Or an informant who is a policeman. Not clear. They have a name. Borovik. Second time that name has . . .

Fuller let his voice trail off. He shifted, abruptly, to the details of the flight to Moscow. It was Kaplan's sense that he had not meant to say that name aloud. What was it? *Borovik*. If Kaplan was to bet, he'd say that that was the name Roger Clew turned up as that KGB major's boss.

Fuller's voice was stronger now. Bannerman, he said, knows nothing of this. When he lands, he will be placed under guard by the Swiss authorities and immediately deported. A special diplomatic flight will be waiting. It will take him to Moscow where he will remain under guard until this business is sorted out.

You and Roger will meet him there. A military aircraft will depart from Andrews as soon as you get there. You'll fly directly to Moscow's Vnukovo II airport. It's very secure. Reserved for VIPs. With luck, the two flights will arrive within an hour of each other. That's eight or nine tomorrow morning, Moscow time. From there, you'll be taken to the embassy compound where you'll get a medical briefing and you, Irwin, will be told everything we've learned in the meantime.

If you have time to pack, pack light. I'll square this with your office. No, don't stop on the way to tell your wife. Just leave her a note to call this number and I'll talk to her myself.

Irwin . . . damn it. Don't argue on this one. If I must, I'll get the *President* to call you. Otherwise, just this once, shut up and do as I ask.

Yeah, well . . . fuck him, too, thought Kaplan.

"No," he said aloud.

Screw this.

Bessie Kaplan didn't raise a schmuck.

"They're going to fucking *arrest* Bannerman, kidnap him to Moscow, and keep him there until he listens to reason. Is that what you're saying, Mr. Fuller?"

"Irwin . . ."

"Then what? You think Bannerman's going to smile and say thank you for going to so much trouble? Thank you for bringing Irwin over? Because if Irwin's here, I know that everything you're telling me must be true? Irwin makes *all* the difference. Now I'll only kill some of you."

"Very well, Irwin," came Fuller's voice wearily. "Stay on the line. You can say no to the President."

Shit.

This has to be a bluff, thought Kaplan.

It wasn't.

They got him at Camp David. Out of breath from jogging. The call lasted maybe thirty seconds. The language was very general.

The President—nice guy—made a reference to "this Moscow business" but, talking to him, Kaplan did not get the feeling that he knew much about it. He might have been distancing himself, Kaplan supposed. More likely, he really didn't know that much and the call was an act of faith in Fuller. He said maybe after this we'll all have lunch and talk about it. And one of these days, he said, he'd like to meet this Mama's Boy he's heard so much about.

You don't tell the President to be careful what he wishes for.

You also don't say no to the man.

He wanted to talk to Fuller again. Kaplan apologized for disrupting his Sunday and clicked off. For a long moment, he sat staring out at his car.

"Do it, Irwin," the President had said. "Please get on that plane."

But he never said don't use that car phone. He never said don't call Willem Brugg, for instance. To Kaplan, it seemed the decent thing to do. Kaplan slid off his stool and headed for the door.

The President never said don't call Zivic again either.

Zivic.

Maybe this, at last, will get a rise out of him.

But the main point of calling Zivic would be to explain why Bannerman's being put on ice. Don't overreact. Don't go snatching Fuller's mother, for instance. Fuller's heart's in the right place. He's just a little spooked at the moment.

Kaplan heard sirens a long way off.

A police escort, maybe.

He had maybe two minutes, he figured. Time for at least one of those calls.

56

Lesko knew that they must have drugged him.

He could remember being inside an ambulance. He could remember wanting to tear it apart. Other than that, there were just bits and pieces.

The shot they gave him had eased the throbbing of his head. But it also kept him from clearing it. His brain was in one of those four-in-the-morning states that he hated. Not quite awake. Not quite asleep either. Half in and half out of a dream. No way to know what's real and what isn't.

He knew, or was pretty sure, that this was a hospital. He was strapped to a gurney but he didn't mind that. The straps kept him from floating away.

He was in a big room that had yellow tile halfway up the walls and a ceiling that was cracked and stained. Belkin and Valentin were in the room with him. White coats all around both of them, especially Valentin. Nurses running in and out. Doctors yelling in Russian. They were cutting Valentin's clothes off.

Belkin was trying to get up, trying to get over to Valentin's table. He had managed to undo the strap across his waist and got up on one elbow. He was naked. A bloody gauze pad peeled away from his hip as he swung one leg

over the side. A male nurse ran over and eased him back
down.

They were using defibrillating pads on Valentin.
Clear . . . zap . . . clear . . . zap. Belkin tried again.
He was calling Valentin's name. Lesko knew that this was
all a dream because David Katz was standing over by
Valentin's table trying to talk to one of the lady doctors. The
doctor told him to get lost so Katz went over and stood with
John Waldo, who was watching all this with a Guinness
bottle in his hand. Katz looks at Waldo and shrugs. He
cocks his head toward Valentin and gives a thumbs-down
signal.

Waldo.

This was further proof that Lesko was dreaming, because
this was the old John Waldo. He looked the way he did
before he got his nose job and his tuck and before he dyed
his hair the color of wet sand. Earlier, in the same dream,
there was a guy in a flower truck who sort of looked like the
new John Waldo, but Waldo said it wasn't him. He said he
was over in Red Square at the time pissing on Stalin's grave.
Ask anyone.

He asked, "How is Elena, by the way?"

Lesko said she's fine but the question bothered him.
There was something about Elena. He just couldn't seem to
remember what it was.

The doctors had finished with Valentin. They unplugged
him, covered him up, and turned to Belkin. Leo started
fighting the straps again. He was waving them off, jabbing
his finger, trying to get them to go back and do more work
on Valentin.

But Valentin wasn't on the table anymore. He was
standing over with Katz, fully dressed, showing Katz where
the bullets went in and how one of them bounced off his
sternum and sent bone fragments down into his heart and
left lung. He wasn't upset about it, especially. Katz, in turn,
showed him how he got shot a few years back. Shotgun
blast. Boom. Blew off most of his face. He was using his
hands to show how it sprayed all over his windshield.

Waldo wasn't there anymore. Lesko wondered why.
Katz, who could read his mind, said that it's because Waldo
isn't dead.

Just then, the doors behind them burst open. A bunch of men. Suits. Speaking English. A surgeon in a mask waved his hands at them, yelling *"Get out."* But more men came in. They walk right through Katz and Valentin. The second bunch is quieting the surgeon, showing ID. Americans, Russians, all flashing ID at each other. One of the Americans, bald guy, short beard, is carrying a medical bag. Two others, Lesko saw, are gesturing in his direction. The gestures say we'll take that one.

Suddenly Elena waltzes in. She's holding what looks like a baby and she walks right up to Valentin, who is very excited to see her. Elena is beaming as well. It is a baby and Valentin can't wait to see it. Elena folds back the blankets. Katz peeks in over Valentin's shoulder and he screams. He turns away, sticking a vomit finger down his throat but, real fast, he tells Elena that he's only kidding. He looks over.

"Just kidding, Lesko."

He gives thumbs-up this time.

"Good-looking kid," he's saying. *"You got a son."*

Then Lesko remembered.

Hardly daring to breathe, he called Elena's name.

She didn't answer.

He kicked at the straps on his ankles as he called her again. She didn't seem to hear. In rising panic, he remembered why Waldo couldn't be there with Katz anymore but Valentin could. One foot pulled free, then the other. He whipped his legs to one side. The table danced. He whipped them again. It fell over with a crash.

Lesko tore at the remaining straps, all the while calling her name. He managed to get to one knee with the table on his back. He stood up. He tried smashing it against the tiled wall. Men were rushing toward him, grabbing the table, shouting at him. He couldn't hear them past his own roar.

The bearded one with the medical bag. He was filling a needle. Lesko tried to kick at it but the big male nurse fell on his leg. Two others turned the table, pinning him with it. The man with the syringe was on the floor with him, aiming it like a dart at his upper arm. He felt the cool sting. Lesko tried to bite at it. It was emptied and gone too quickly.

The man who injected him now reached for his head. He

took a knot of hair in one hand, Lesko's jaw in the other. He
was shouting at him. Shaking him.

"She's not dead," he was saying.

Damn it.

She's not dead.

This was what Lesko heard as the black wave came over
him.

But his last conscious thought was that it can't be true.

Four-in-the-morning dreams.

Nothing about them is ever quite true.

57

Bannerman's sleep was dreamless. For the most part, it
was sound.

The first-class cabin was fully dark but for one sliver of
light coming from the galley behind him.

At one point, he became aware that the cockpit door had
opened and closed and the flight attendant who came
through it was standing over him. Looking at him. He chose
not to stir.

She reached over his body to pick up a blanket that had
slipped from Susan's legs and covered them again. Next,
she reached again and placed a small piece of paper on the
console between the seats. Her shadow moved away. It
disappeared behind the galley curtains.

A message slip? He wondered.

Whatever it was, it could wait. He'd wake up half the
cabin if he used the phone. But he was curious all the same,
so he fished for his car key, which had a small flashlight
built in for finding the ignition in the dark. He read the
message. Call Irwin Kaplan, it said. It gave what looked like
a home number.

He could only guess why Irwin might be trying to reach
him. A reasonable guess, knowing Irwin, was that he knew

or had learned something about Aldo Corsini that Roger, being Roger, had held back. Irwin, while by no means an ally, had an aversion to being used.

The message, however, did not say *Urgent*. Bannerman put it back down and settled himself. He was asleep in seconds. An hour passed.

He was awakened again by more activity in the cabin. The cockpit door opened and closed more than once, it seemed. Shadows moving. He noticed that the message slip was gone. He stopped one of the shadows and asked about it. She whispered that she didn't know. She hadn't seen it. But he could hear the lie in her voice.

He gestured toward the air-to-ground that was built into the seat in front of him. "Is this working?" he asked quietly.

She shook her head. "There's a problem with atmospherics."

"Thank you."

Two rows up, on the aisle, Bannerman saw a shadow that had not been there before. A man. He had moved up, no doubt, from the coach section. He was, if Bannerman were to guess, a Swissair security guard such as the armed air marshals who mix with the passengers on American flights. He was positioned between Bannerman and the cockpit.

Bannerman squinted at the dial of his watch. Another two hours to Zurich. One hour, more or less, until they turn on the lights to serve breakfast and hand out customs declaration forms.

That done, and this was more than a guess, the chief steward would come and whisper in his ear. Bannerman would be asked, very politely, if he would remain in his seat until all other passengers have deplaned. The Swiss authorities, he will say, would like a word with you.

Roger, you devil, he thought. *You know Aldo's dead, don't you.*

Someone had found him. Or something had gone wrong when Yuri and that woman . . . Lydia . . . got to Carla's place.

Roger would have made a call. Got the Swiss to put him on ice until he could be reasoned with.

Fine. That meant he'd have to be leveled with as well.

His only concern was for Yuri. Wondering what he might
have walked into. But he shook it off. It was not a useful
train of thought. He settled back once more.

Another hour's sleep.

He had an idea that he might be needing it.

58

————

Viktor Podolsk, sick at heart, picked up his telephone and
dialed a number. It rang; a man's voice answered.

"Is this Brodsky?" he asked.

The voice was irritated. "There's no Brodsky here. Don't
you know it's late?"

"I'm sorry. What time is it?"

"Almost midnight. Next time, be more considerate."

The phone slammed down in his ear.

An hour later, when it *was* almost midnight, Podolsk was
pacing the lobby of the metro station between the old and
new Lenin libraries. There was no Brodsky. It was a code
designation for this meeting place. The man he called would
not have known that. He would merely set a time and then
pass the message on. Eventually, it would reach the old
gentleman in the raincoat and fur hat, small dog on a leash,
who was now entering the station.

"Viktor." The old gentleman nodded a greeting. His
expression was grim. "You heard, I take it."

"Heard? All of Moscow heard, Academician. It was on
Vremya."

The older man sighed. He had known that. It came on just
at the end of the evening's broadcast. Since then, he had
been following events by other means. There was one
report, so bizarre that he barely gave it credence, that his
mild-mannered nephew had started a small riot an hour
before the shooting happened. Took on a table of six all by
himself. *Burned their hats* and sent them packing.

Burned their *hats*? It was ridiculous. In what restaurant, least of all that one, do six men wear hats to the table? Still, he was told, the militia was investigating this report in their search for a possible motive. A waste of time, probably. But let them search. It will keep them out of the way.

"Viktor . . ." He put a hand on Podolsk's arm. "The young driver, Valentin, died during surgery. They fear that General Belkin himself might not make it through the night."

It was Podolsk's turn to sigh. "I am . . . so very sorry," he said.

The older man looked into his eyes. "It was not your fault, Viktor. He should never have come here with those two. It was both foolish and pointlessly dangerous."

It was himself, thought Podolsk, who should be offering comfort. This man is about to lose his nephew. The son of his sister.

"I should have done more," said the major. "I should have seen it coming. I should have done more to protect him."

The Academician grunted. He shook his head. "You can't protect a man from himself, Viktor. He is a good man, however. I wish you'd had a chance to know him."

He started to say more, but just then, the little fox terrier began turning in circles. The Academician tugged at its leash to keep it from squatting. "Give me a minute," he said. "She needs to go. I will take her out to the curb."

Podolsk welcomed the chance to gather himself. Should have—should have—should have. He must have sounded like an old woman. All the same, he shared the wish that he could have met General Belkin. Or, more to the point, that General Belkin would not die thinking that Viktor Podolsk is just another criminal. Another of Borovik's pimps and errand boys. But he understood, he supposed, why General Belkin could not be told.

He knew that these two had quarreled. No surprise there. Two very different personalities. One was patient, the other was not. One was orderly, the other was impulsive. One kept his objectivity while with the other you would almost think this was personal.

It was more, thought Podolsk, than the difference in

approach between the spy and the Academician. In their
most recent quarrel, General Belkin was harshly critical of
his uncle.

"You plod along while they bleed our country dry," he
said then, according to his uncle. "You want everything tied
up in a neat package with a red ribbon on it. You behave too
much like the intellectual who wants to know for the sake of
knowing. Worse, you begin to behave like *them*. Control for
the sake of control."

This was unjust.

General Belkin's problem, Podolsk had often thought,
was that he was spending too much time with this Mama's
Boy. Too much time with attack dogs. Also, it is easy to
throw stones from the safe distance of a Zurich posting.

Nikolai Belkin could have had such a sanctuary. When
they arrested him, in the first year of Gorbachev, exile had
been his for the asking. He could have said, "No, I will not
shut up, I will not retract." But they would have answered,
"Okay, pack one bag small enough to carry on a plane.
You're not a Soviet citizen anymore. Go wherever they'll
take you. Say you're a Jew and go to Israel. They'll give
you a job sweeping streets. By the way, don't pack any
papers. Not a single document, not one notebook, not a
single address or telephone number. Just get out."

But he stayed. And he retracted. He retracted because you
can't fight them from Israel.

The Academician came back into the lobby. His dog's
mood had improved. Not so his own.

"This . . . ambush." Nikolai Belkin signaled a return
to the subject at hand. "You believe, I take it, that Borovik
gave the order?"

Podolsk nodded. "There's no question."

The Academician had none either. The three gunmen had
all been identified. Chicago Brigade . . . the brother,
found earlier, dead outside GUM . . . the clumsy effort to
make it seem that the American had done it. The murder of
Borovik's man . . . that Italian. And finally Borovik himself. A twisted and diseased mind whose every action is
guided by what he thinks Stalin would have done in his
place.

"I can't go on with this," said Podolsk. "You have to get me out."

The older shook his head. "I know it's been hard on you, Viktor. But you're too close to quit now."

"But I'm not close at all," Podolsk argued. "Two years out of my life for this and I can identify no one besides Borovik who is higher than the rank of captain. Two years of being a criminal. I'm surprised my parents haven't died of shame."

Nikolai Belkin could have argued this considerable understatement. Podolsk had, after all, become the control for Borovik's entire European network. Add to that, he had learned the name of every member of the Chicago Brigade, the registry of every truck, the location of at least three warehouses, and could give evidence against scores of corrupt officials.

But all of this, for all its scope, was still only one spoke of the wheel. The trick was to get to the hub. But one cannot just go there. One must wait to be invited.

"It will change soon, Viktor," he said. "Trust me on this."

Podolsk looked away. "The problem," he replied, "is to trust myself."

The older man lifted an eyebrow.

"I waited almost one hour," Podolsk told him, "before I asked for this meeting. Do you know what I was considering?"

The older man nodded. "It's on your face, Viktor."

"I wanted to march over to Number Two. If that little son of a bitch was still in his office, I truly think I would have picked him up out of his chair and thrown him out his goddamned window."

The uncle of Leo Belkin said nothing.

"And you know something else? I could have walked straight to the elevator, straight out of the building, and every guard who heard Borovik screaming all the way down would have taken a sudden interest in the number of cracks in the ceiling. They despise him as much as I do."

Still nothing. But the older man's expression was thoughtful.

Podolsk tried several other reasons why his mission

should be given up as a bad job. Because Borovik despises him as well, advancement is impossible. Two years, and the closest he's come to those pulling the strings was an angry voice on the telephone this evening. Overheard. Berating Borovik. After today, certainly, Borovik will want to get rid of him and, very likely, try to blame him for all that has happened. One night, very soon, he's liable to open his door and be looking down a gun barrel. Behind it is Borovik. No. Worse nightmare. Behind it is Borovik's mother.

This last was not meant as a joke. Nor did Nikolai Belkin smile.

"This . . . angry voice," he said. "I assume you did not recognize it."

Podolsk started to shake his head. He changed his mind. "It was . . . very distinctive. My impression was that I've heard it before. I want to say that I've heard it giving speeches but, like all of us, I've had to listen to thousands."

"Describe it, please, Viktor."

Podolsk did his best. Singsong. From deep in the chest. He mimicked the inflection. As he did so, he thought he saw recognition in the older man's eyes.

"Who is he?" Podolsk asked quietly.

The eyes were distant. They were staring through walls.

"Do you know him?" Podolsk asked again, this time suspiciously.

Nikolai Belkin raised a hand as if asking for time. He turned away, pacing, his hand at his mouth, the dog, now confused, pacing with him. He would nod, and then he would cancel the nod with a rapid shake of his head. But the nods became more frequent. At last, he turned to give his answer.

"I should have guessed," he said. "The answer is I should have guessed."

Podolsk waited.

The old man took his arm. "Walk with me," he said.

They went outside. The two men walked, in virtual silence, down toward the Pushkin Museum, crossing toward the lights and the rising steam of the Moscow Swimming Pool. The dog barked at the sounds made by swimmers. The old man tugged the leash. They continued on, stopping only when they reached the embankment of the Moscow River.

It took this long for him to trust himself to speak. It took this long for him to stop saying to himself, Leo must have known. Somehow, Leo must have found out. It is why he came to Moscow.

But how much he knew, what he hoped to achieve, did he come in search of martyrdom . . . these questions he could not begin to answer.

The Academician knew full well the leap of logic he was taking. He had only the barest evidence that the voice on that telephone might have been Arkadi Kulik's. And yet here—he touched his chest—he had no doubt of it. That story, the burning of hats, might have credence after all.

There were two possibilities. One was that Leo, on his own, had learned all about Borovik and had followed that trail to Kulik. Nikolai Belkin did not believe it. How could he follow a trail that had, to this point, been invisible to everyone else? If Leo had even been aware of Borovik's existence, surely he would have tried to call up his file from Bern. He never had. Until a few hours ago, according to Yasenevo, no one had. A few hours ago, suddenly, a code and cipher official named Voinovitch tries to call up the Borovik file, but Leo by that time was already in Moscow, and has had no contact with Bern since he arrived.

The second possibility, while no less remote, seemed at least to sound like Leo. He had somehow tracked Kulik to Moscow. He didn't know, or care, about Borovik. All he wanted was to purge his own devils. All he wanted was to come, look Arkadi Kulik in the eye, slap his face, and apparently set a match to that hat he's so proud of.

If this were true, if this is what happened, the police would indeed go looking for Kulik. But he would be innocent of this ambush. Such an act would be impossible for him. Too impulsive, the trail would—and will, lead straight to his door. And that will infuriate him. He will want to head it off. He will have to act quickly.

"Viktor?"

Podolsk waited.

"Viktor, I'm going to ask something of you. You are free to say no. But you cannot, I'm afraid, ask many questions."

The major made a face. Still, he waited.

"First thing is to go home," said the Academician. "Get lots of sleep. Tomorrow you don't work, correct?"

Podolsk shrugged. "Monday, technically, I'm off. But Borovik takes no days off except on his mother's birthday. I always go in."

"Tomorrow, take at least the morning. Take time to think. If by lunchtime you decide to head for the woods, you'll get no argument from me."

Podolsk looked at the sky. Good old Nikolai. Always, when he most needs you to say yes, he tells you . . . feel free to say no.

"This man," Belkin began, "the man whose voice you heard?"

He paused, choosing his words carefully.

"He will not *appear* to be at the top. He is a man who hides himself in committees . . . collaboratives. He might pick out a man who he thinks can manage and then push that man into the limelight. But yes, very definitely, he will be the one who pulls the strings."

He raised a hand to keep Podolsk from speaking.

"Tomorrow . . . or the next day," he said, "I think you will hear from this man. I *think* that he will want to see you. But trust me on this. It is better that you know nothing . . . *nothing* about him in advance. If he suspects that you've been briefed, or even that Borovik has let his name slip out . . ." He stopped himself.

"This . . . mystery man," Podolsk asked. "What will he want of me?"

"He will need you now. For a while, I think he will need you."

"A while is what? A month? Six months?"

Nikolai Belkin chewed on the answer before giving it. "He will need you," he said, "until he doesn't need you. After that, he will kill you."

Podolsk took a breath and exhaled. For several moments, he said nothing. A sightseeing boat cruised by. At last, Viktor Podolsk shook his head. A rueful smile.

"With all respect, Nikolai Ilyich," he said, "you would never make a living as a salesman."

59

Ernst Lechmann had no problem getting the doorman to talk. After CNN and Vremya, you couldn't shut him up.

They had waited for him outside the restaurant, Waldo half a block up, Lechmann half a block down, on the assumption that at closing time he would head for one metro station or the other.

It was Waldo's intention to follow him home, wait for him to fall asleep, and then wake him up by tickling his nose with the muzzle of a Heckler & Koch. Typical John Waldo plan, thought Lechmann. Go directly to last resort. This man has the subtlety of a head-on collision.

Lechmann's plan, if the doorman came his way, was to fall in step with him as he walked to the Smolenskaya station and offer a pleasant greeting. The doorman would assume that he was about to be robbed by this man with the funny accent who smelled of chlorine and cheap soap and whose wardrobe must have been selected in the dark. But the doorman would be put at ease by the Austrian's friendly manner and by the fact that, as he walked, he was counting off fifty-dollar bills, American, from a wad half an inch thick.

Thankfully, the big doorman walked toward Smolen-skaya. An added blessing was that he was the last one out. No need to separate him from assorted home-bound waiters and busboys. On the dot of midnight, the doorman locked up. He was still in his uniform. Very impressive. Maroon with gold braid. Epaulets and fourragères. Worn proudly. He would have looked like something from a Viennese operetta had the effect not been ruined by a bulging plastic bag thrown over one shoulder, filled, no doubt, with booty from the restaurant's pantry.

Using one fifty-dollar bill as a calling card, Lechmann introduced himself as a journalist. The doorman seemed to

have trouble believing this, but as long as he believed in
fifty-dollar bills it was not going to be a problem.

The first fifty got his attention. The second got a detailed
account of the bloodletting that had happened two hours
earlier. Lechmann forced himself to be patient, taking notes,
as he listened to events in which he himself had participated.
He was amused to hear John Waldo described as a little
monkey who kept leaping in and out of a delivery van. More
so when he learned that the doorman had done an imitation
of him for the benefit of the CNN cameras.

The smile froze on his face, however, when he learned
that Elena had been shot. A head wound. And that the
doorman had to crack Lesko across the skull in order to let
the medics get at her. Two other men shot as well. Both
KGB. Both seriously wounded. All four taken to Hospital
#52 on Zubovsky. The three assassins, all local gangsters,
had been piled back into their taxi and towed off to the
morgue. He had overhead a militia captain telling the
tow-truck driver to . . .

The doorman stopped himself, waiting for another fifty to
appear. Lechmann peeled one off. It quickly vanished into
the doorman's pocket.

What the militia captain said, he told Lechmann, was,
"Save the trip. Dump them, taxi and all, on the sidewalk
outside Lubyanka. I should have done that with the other
one."

This reference, he explained, was to still another killing
that had happened earlier in the evening. The doorman was
foggy on the details although one of the waiters told him
that the big American was involved in that one as well. As
for the rest of the captain's statement, his meaning was
clear. The three in the taxi were in the pay of the KGB.

But you know how it is with the KGB, he said. Everyone
talks big these days but they're still afraid. That militia
captain is no exception. What he really should have done, if
he had the balls, was to drive right out to Zhukovka and
arrest that son of a bitch, Kulik, before they bust him to
sergeant and stick him in a traffic booth, which is probably
what they'll do because he wouldn't shut up and go home
when they told him to instead of sticking his Jew nose
where it doesn't belong.

Lechmann made a soccer time-out signal with his hands. He had the feeling that he had fallen one fifty-dollar bill behind. This was confirmed when the doorman stopped talking and rubbed his fingers together. The Austrian peeled off one and then another in the hope of an uninterrupted narrative. In seconds, he was scribbling furiously. He filled two pages.

There would be no need, it seemed, to track down the Zil. Lechmann now understood why that bunch had come stumbling out of the restaurant. Why three of them were suddenly hatless. Why one had a broken nose. More importantly, Lechmann now had a name and a not-so-flattering biography to go with it. But he only had a partial address.

"Zhukovka," he repeated. "For two fifties, you should be more specific."

The doorman dangled a ring of keys. "For two more on top," he said, "we go back to the restaurant and I'll look up his account."

Ernst Lechmann left Waldo to wait outside. Let him wait and wonder, he decided. The doorman was having a nice time and Waldo would only spoil it. It would do John good, he thought, to learn that you catch more flies with honey than with vinegar.

Lechmann waited at the coat-room counter, one eye on the front entrance, as the doorman went back to the office. He returned carrying what looked to be a stack of index cards, chewing on some leftover which he had apparently found en route.

"I give you five minutes with these," he said to the Austrian. "After that is renegotiation."

"Ten minutes," said Lechmann firmly. "Use it to make me some sandwiches."

The doorman gave no argument. Probably because a sandwich sounded good to him as well. He was now banging around in the kitchen, no doubt filling another plastic bag while he was at it.

Lechmann started going through the cards, all of which had to do with this Kulik.

Kulik, it seemed, made a habit of dining at Kropotkin-

skaya. Every Sunday night, with few exceptions, apparently
since the restaurant opened. The file listed his favorite
dishes, favorite wines, methods of preparation, and ingredients to be avoided. A notation said that he was severely
allergic to cheese and nuts. In the margin, someone wrote,
"He should choke on them." After a note that he likes
French onion soup with a sprinkling of coriander, another
hand wrote, "Be sure to spit in it."

Not much affection for him here, thought Lechmann.

And yet he keeps coming back. He keeps bringing three
or four guests at a time. It must be why they put up with
him.

Many of his guests had notations of their own. Same sort
of thing. Name, rank, and position, preferred dishes, eccen-
tricities. Most of the names were Russian, a few were
Moslem, perhaps from the other republics, but several
sounded European. One of the Moslems had a problem with
body odor. The card said don't put him too close to the fire
because he gives off fumes. One of the Russians, said his
card, makes sounds like a rutting pig when he eats. Try to
seat him with his back to the other diners. But the remaining
cards, by and large, were not disrespectful. Most were the
sort of records that any fine restaurant would keep, the
better to pamper important guests.

Lechmann used his ten minutes to copy as many names as
he could. You never know what's useful. Several of the
Russian names were familiar to him. Old-time bully boys,
mostly now retired. This was not a list of seminarians.

The big doorman came out with the sandwiches. Lechmann asked him for a reliable map of the greater Moscow
area. Any doorman should have one. He wanted to pinpoint
that Zhukovka address as closely as possible.

What he would do with it, however, was something else.

From what he had learned of what happened in here, and
from what he now knew of this Kulik, there was every
reason to suspect that John Waldo had been right. That
General Arkadi Kulik—KGB—Special Inspectorate—
Retired, had indeed made the phone call that set up that
ambush outside. Even the doorman was strongly of this
opinion.

"What now?" he asked. "Are you going to go after him?"

"I will . . . have to discuss it with my editor."

The doorman sniffed. "This editor of yours. Does he rock while he's standing? Does he hold his arms . . . so?" The big man did a passable imitation of an ape.

Lechmann pretended not to understand.

"I'll speak plainly," said the doorman. "I think this is twice that I've seen you tonight. I think that before you were a journalist, you were first a florist."

It crossed Lechmann's mind that he might have to kill this man. But he looked into his eyes. He saw approval in them. The doorman's eyes drifted to Lechmann's waist. They were looking for a bulge beneath the new coat he had stolen. Lechmann patted his sides to show that he had nothing. His weapon was down the street, in an old window box between the second and third juniper trees. The doorman was not convinced. "I think you and the monkey should go shoot this Kulik," he said.

Lechmann could have pointed out, he supposed, that a gunman does not often feel the need to pass out fifty-dollar bills in exchange for information. While at it, he also could have asked what it is, exactly, that this doorman could have against Arkadi Kulik.

But he knew the answer. It was always the same. It would start, "Those bastards . . . every one of them. I hate those fucking bastards."

The reply would not get much more articulate than this, and it would seldom get specific. The more vague the complaint, the more you knew that you were talking to a man who had shamed himself. He had betrayed friends. He had informed on coworkers.

"That office . . ." Lechmann pointed toward the rear. "Does it have a copying machine?"

"A good one. It's German."

"Does it have a fax machine?"

"They keep it hidden, but yes."

Lechmann took the remaining cash from his pocket. He kept a few notes for himself and left the rest, about two thousand, on the coat-room counter.

"I am going to make copies of these cards," he said.

"I'm going to try to fax them, with a note, to a number in America. If I can't get a line, will you stay here until they go through?"

The doorman stared at the money. He seemed to nod.

"Down where they found the dead sniper, there is an empty window box just past the second tree. If you get a reply, will you leave it in that window box?"

The doorman studied him. This *journalist,* he realized, had as much as made an admission. "Will this make them sweat?" he asked finally.

Lechmann nodded. "I think I can promise," he said. "At the very least, it will make them sweat."

The doorman gestured toward the money. "Don't forget that when you leave," he said.

There was a good chance, thought Lechmann, that the fax would go through. A restaurant like this, they must deal all the time with Western suppliers. Anton Zivic would know what to make of those names. He would probably recognize most of them.

The cover note would tell him of the shootings. If he doesn't know already. If someone hasn't called his house from Mario's and told him to turn on CNN.

The next question at hand is what to tell Waldo. What did I find out? Not much. But I got us some sandwiches.

No, Lechmann decided. He could not very well withhold the news about Elena. But if he tells him that she's been shot, and that the man in the Zil was probably behind it, and, by the way, I happen to have his address . . . who knows what John Waldo will do next?

Lechmann snorted. As if there could be any doubt.

"Let's just go look around," he will say. "If he's there, maybe we'll ask him why he did it."

Lechmann could picture that conversation. John Waldo on this Kulik's chest, force-feeding him on cheese and nuts, perhaps with a corkscrew half into his ear just to keep the conversation flowing.

This could be a long night, thought Lechmann with a sigh.

60

Arkadi Kulik was in a white rage.

As if the dinner, all by itself, was not enough of a disaster.

And then having to listen, all the way to the Sudanese consulate, to what Islam requires of him if his honor is to be restored. He couldn't get rid of those two fast enough.

After that, having to listen to two fat-assed former generals who probably haven't so much as made a fist in thirty years, arguing over which of them gets first crack at the American, Lesko. Man to man, the one with the black eyes was saying. Just me and him. Locked in a room. Bare hands. At this, even Sostkov was rolling his eyes.

Then at last, finally getting home, finally closing the door of his study so that he could get at the white powder he kept in his safe. Needing it to lift his mind above all this. Spilling it. All over the carpet in front of the safe. Down on his hands and knees trying to salvage pinches of it from the nap and then suddenly, in his mind's eye, imagining that Leo Belkin was standing there in the room watching all this, a smug and scornful expression on his face.

Kulik didn't even remember getting up. The next thing he knew, he was on his feet and the golf club was in his hands and it was swinging at that face. Instead it broke a floor lamp. He kept on swinging, and he must have been shouting, because Sostkov came banging on the door asking if he was all right and is someone in there with him.

He did not answer at first. He stood staring, near to tears, at the golf club, which had bent almost in half. There was a fracture at the crease. He knew that it would snap if straightened.

With effort, he composed himself.

"No . . . just an accident . . . thank you, Sostkov . . . leave me . . . please."

But his hands were trembling.

A swallow of tequila would help. Lightheaded, he knelt
once more in front of the refrigerated minibar that was a gift
to him from a shipment intended for one of the new hotels.
Tequila was better than vodka at such times. It slaps you in
the face. It put the fire back into your belly.

He would need it.

Because then, on top of everything else, the telephone
rang. He ignored it. Let Sostkov pick up. He did, but, after
two minutes, Sostkov comes to the door again and says, in
a strange voice, that perhaps the general had better take this
call.

It was one of the Sudanese. Kulik couldn't tell which one
or even what he was saying at first, because the voice was
so high and excited and he was also forgetting his English
and lapsing into Arabic. Ridiculous language. Every second
word sounds like *lollypop* or *Ali Baba*.

Even when he got the sense of it—something about a
shooting, Ali Baba . . . dead bodies all over the place, Ali
Baba lolly lolly . . . television . . . CNN, Ali Baba—he
could not imagine what this idiot was getting so hysterical
about. It was only when certain names began pushing
through the Arabic—Ali Leo Belkin Lolly—Ali Elena
Bruggallolly—that he began to realize, with wildly mixed
emotions, that it was they who had been shot. He shouted
into the phone. Slow down, he said. Start over, he said.

But the voice of the Sudanese was now belligerent. Even
abusive. More than that, it was accusatory.

"How dare you," he was saying, "to take this upon
yourself. How dare you put us in such a position. You don't
think they'll know it was you? You think this is the old days
when you could kill thousands, no questions asked?"

Kulik was too dazed to speak. Adding to the confusion
was Sostkov, waving at him from the doorway, another
phone at his ear, trying to get his attention.

Kulik shrugged helplessly. Sostkov seemed exasperated.
He put the phone down, reached for a pad, and began
scribbling furiously. He came in with the pad and held it up
for Kulik to see. For emphasis, he mouthed the message.

"It was the Kerenskys," he was saying. *"They were
waiting for the Belkin party. The Kerenskys shot them up but*

they got all the Kerenskys. All dead. Belkin's driver dead. Belkin and the Brugg woman might also die.''

When Kulik could speak, he mouthed one word.

''Borovik?''

Sostkov took a breath and sighed. *''Who else?''* was his reply.

It was a catastrophe.

First, humiliation. Then disaster, calamity, and now catastrophe. This was how Arkadi Kulik's evening had progressed.

The Sudanese was correct, lamentably, about everything except the conclusion he drew from it. He had walked past a television set, seen the doorman who had been so insolent being interviewed, got someone at the consulate to translate for him, and, disbelieving, had rushed back over to see for himself.

By then, they were towing a taxi with three dead assassins in it. Restaurant staff and patrons were outside, gossiping with anyone who would listen. The prevailing opinion was that it had all started with a fight that had broken out earlier when a party at one table insulted the party at another.

So the police know as well, Kulik realized. They know all about that disgusting brawl and the burning of three hats. They would surely have his name from the maître d' by now. They would know that his party left first and that the Belkin party was attacked when it left an hour later. They would draw precisely the same conclusion as had the hysterical Sudanese.

He needed, at all costs, to bring this under control before men he's made rich, men he'd spent years cultivating, organizing, playing them like puppets, suddenly decided that he, Arkadi Kulik, was now a liability.

He had to act quickly.

He made one phone call which, he hoped, would at least keep the Moscow police from showing up at his door. The call was to a deputy minister who had influence with the militia. It is time, he told him, to use that influence. Head off this investigation. See that the detectives now in charge are transferred, their notebooks collected, reliable people put in their place.

But this, the deputy protested, will not be so easy. It's

more complicated than you think. There was another killing, earlier, in which the American is a suspect and the victim was another of the Kerenskys.

At this, Kulik could barely speak. But more needed to be done. He sent Sostkov and the general with the black eye speeding back to Moscow. To find Borovik. Bring him back here before the detectives can get to him and start asking questions. Tell him we need his advice. Say we need to know what Stalin would do in this situation. If he doesn't go for it, stuff him in the trunk.

He told the second general, the one with the rip in his pants, to get on the other phone. Call the owners of that restaurant, wake them up, make sure they know the consequences if a single name among this evening's guests is given out, or that of any other guest from any other Sunday evening.

What else, he asked himself, should he be doing?

There was a possibility, he supposed, of retaliation by Leo's other friends. His soul mates within the KGB. Those faceless hypocrites who had turned against their own. But they would be the least of his problems. They will act only through channels, Kulik thought. They will file written demands for a thorough investigation, but they will run into stone walls. You'd think they would have learned by now.

But that still leaves the Bruggs and all their resources. It still leaves Mama's Boy and all his renegades. And, for the moment at least, it still leaves General Vadim Yakovich Borovik who had, at long last, outlived any possible usefulness he ever had.

That idiot.

That criminally stupid idiot.

As for the Brugg family, he could only guess what they might do. But they were not his most immediate concern. Any reprisals from that end will be planned out very carefully beforehand and their primary weapon will be money. They are Swiss, after all.

Bannerman, however, will want to respond at once. But even Bannerman can't pick his targets out of a hat. He will need to interview the survivors and will probably want to see the American—this Lesko—personally. That means he'll be coming to Moscow if they grant him a visa, and that alone can take many days and much debate. Once here, he'll need to confer with those he will surely have sent ahead. That done, he will need to form a plan of action and, perhaps, import even more specialists to carry it out. It could be a week or more before he's ready to act.

Plenty of time, thought Arkadi Kulik. He would even make it easy for Mama's Boy. Pick his targets for him. Lay a trail of bread crumbs to this or that address, just for the mischief of it, and hope that he is not discriminating.

But just in case he is, we will contrive to be more specific. He will have names. In the course of a deathbed confession, General Vadim Borovik will name, as his coconspirators, a select few individuals who have been annoyances lately. Perhaps even those two Sudanese since they now seem disinclined to do business.

The confession will be recorded on videotape. Sent with a note to Mama's Boy himself by certain men of conscience, certain friends of Leo Belkin who must regretfully remain anonymous.

Play the tape, the note will say. But first, so you'll know that justice has been done, open the accompanying satchel. No, it's not a bomb. It's round but it's not a cabbage either. You've seen one just like it before, Mama's Boy. Think back a few years.

This was Sostkov's idea. To send him Borovik's head.

One must give credit where due, thought Kulik.

61

Across and just down from the restaurant entrance, John Waldo sat in the darkened delivery bay of the Berioska shop. He had taken the top off his sandwich.

He was rebuilding it, discarding the smoked herring and the olive slices, munching the cucumbers separately, plac-

ing the marinated tomatoes between the roast pork and the
chicken.

He had already muttered an opinion of a man who would
place herring and chicken between the same two pieces of
bread. Dagwood, the doorman. This came during a pause in
Ernst Lechmann's account of what he had learned.

Waldo was patient. He knew from Lechmann's manner—
starting to tell him something . . . thinking better of it—
that he had probably dug up a name and address to go with
that Zil. Another indication was that Lechmann kept saying
they should wait to see if Zivic answers before they take any
action. The only action Waldo could think of, other than
maybe checking out Hospital #52, would involve paying a
visit to the guy who very probably sent the shooters. Check
out his house. Try to find out what's what.

Lechmann would hate that. He says he doesn't mind
going into a strange house as long as he can soften it up first.
Like by rolling in a grenade. In Waldo's view, this totally
misses the point of reconnaissance. The other thing . . .
Lechmann says he farts when he's nervous. A sure way to
wash out of cat-burglar school is to be someone who farts
when he's moving through a darkened house.

But it didn't matter. They had to hang around here
anyway. If Dagwood is on the level, maybe they'll get
instructions from Zivic. If he isn't and he drops a dime,
someone will be setting up a surveillance on that window
box before the doorman comes out and puts something in it.
They had to hang around because they had to know.

An hour went by.

In all that time, Waldo counted just four passing cars—
one of them a police cruiser, blue Volga sedan, nothing
special on its mind—and he saw no one at all on foot.
Typical Moscow nightlife. Muggers would starve.

So little traffic was good in one way. Any movement
stands out. But it's not so good if you're the one who's
moving. He had already decided what they would do about
that. He kept it to himself for now because Lechmann, he
felt sure, will *really* hate this new idea.

"He's coming," said the Austrian.

They watched as he came through the door, two plastic
bags this time, locked it, then lifted the bags to his shoulder.

He paused to look up and down the street as a normally prudent man would. No sign of abnormal anxiety. He was looking down at the sidewalk now, at the chalk outlines still there. With a slow shake of his head, he blessed himself backward. The Russian Orthodox way. He turned and began walking in the direction of the metro station.

Waldo felt sure he was straight. But if he isn't, he decided, it's better to louse up their timing.

"Go now," he whispered to the Austrian. "Call him."

Lechmann hesitated, but he understood. He slipped from the shadows and, as the doorman approached the row of junipers, gave a soft whistle. The doorman turned, looking for its source. He recognized Lechmann. He raised his free arm in greeting and moved toward him.

Waldo saw what he was hoping for. No anxious glances to either side. There was no hint in the doorman's demeanor that a plan had been upset. Waldo was satisfied but he did not yet relax. He kept his weapon at his cheek. He watched as the doorman drew several folded sheets from his inside pocket and handed them to Lechmann. From his outside pocket he drew two bottles. One was a Pepsi. The other was mineral water. He gave these to Lechmann as well, slapped his arm, and turned down Kropotkinskaya.

Waldo eased his finger off the trigger.

"Zivic's crazier than you are," Lechmann muttered.

Waldo nodded slowly, not sure that he disagreed.

The fax from Westport had been sent in English, open, no code, either in the belief that interception was unlikely or in the hope that the KGB would pick it up. Waldo wasn't sure which. It read . . .

Yours acknowledged. Well done.

Am aware of events on Kropotkinskaya. PB arriving Vnukovo II, ETA 08:40 Moscow time Monday, in the company of Roger Clew, Irwin Kaplan, possibly Susan L, possibly Willem Brugg and will be taken, under guard, to U.S. Embassy. Purpose of detention is to prevent independent action.

Leo Belkin, Elena, severely wounded, both doubtful. Action, therefore, must be taken regardless.

Will coordinate reprisals, this end. You will coordinate teams 1, 2, and 5. Cobra and Viper to coordinate teams 3 and 4. Primary targets, your end, are General Vadim Borovik and Major Viktor Podolsk—KGB, Moscow Center but any/all targets of opportunity are authorized.

Example: Liteiny 4.

If no abort signal by 10:00, continue to execute at your discretion. Am advising State Department, that effect, via a copy of this message.

Waldo read it a second time, and then a third. Let's take it a piece at a time, he decided.

An ETA of 08:40 Monday means that Bannerman would have to have left Westport well before he could have known what happened here. Waldo didn't understand that. Or why all those others were traveling with him. But if Zivic says they're coming, they're coming.

How Clew figures in this, he had no idea. Maybe Bannerman leaned on Clew to get him into Russia. Maybe under guard was the only way the Russians would let him in.

As for the hit, Zivic already knew more than he did. Must have heard via CNN. Or maybe he's got a source here. Waldo felt bad about Elena. Lesko, he knew, must be going batshit right now.

As for these five teams that he's supposed to divide up with Cobra and Viper . . . *what* teams? And who the hell are Cobra and Viper? None of their people use dumb names like that. Except maybe for Mama's Boy, but that's more of a nickname that got hung on him.

The answer, Waldo concluded, is that there aren't any snake names and there aren't any teams either. But Zivic wants everyone at the State Department, maybe everyone in Moscow, to think we're already here in force.

And invisible.

Speaking of invisible, he and Lechmann aren't. That

doorman could still be a problem. He's seen Lechmann's face and he knows he was driving the van. But Lechmann chose to trust him so that's that. The thing is . . . if that doorman is human, he probably made a copy of Zivic's fax for himself and will find someone who knows English to tell him what it says. He wouldn't be able to resist telling someone.

Spilt milk, Waldo decided.

As for this General Borovik—who Lechmann says is *not* the guy with the Zil—but who Zivic seems to think is behind the hit—Waldo had no idea where that had come from except that the name seemed to ring a bell. He turned to the Austrian, who was sipping the Pepsi.

"You got an address for this KGB guy?" he asked. "This Borovik?"

The Austrian searched through his folder of papers, copies of which he had faxed to Zivic, and read them in the glow of distant streetlights.

"Here it is. It's an apartment house in the Lenin Hills."

"How about the other one? Major Podolsk."

"No mention of him. Was never one of the guests."

Okay, thought Waldo. Then Borovik. He knew where he'd heard that name now. This part was getting interesting. Given the mention of Liteiny 4—that building he torched— this figured to be the same Borovik from a few years back in Leningrad. The brother. The one they snatched and traded but whose brother spiked their guy's stretcher. The brother got the bill for it a few months later. Maybe this one's been stewing about Bannerman ever since. Suddenly Bannerman's friends show up in town. The guy can't resist whacking them.

"John . . . *No!*" said Lechmann, who was glaring at him.

"No, what?"

"No, we do not drive our flower van with no windshield to an apartment house that is certainly guarded and try to shoot a KGB general."

Waldo grunted. Actually, he was thinking of something else. Borovik aside, maybe what Zivic really meant by Liteiny 4 was that he should go torch Moscow Center. But either action, he had to agree, did sound a little nuts.

Especially with the van, but he'd already made a decision about that. The one Lechmann would hate.

"What Zivic wants," he told the Austrian, "is for us to make some noise. He wants some leverage with whoever's holding Bannerman. He wants us to stick and move until he calls us off."

Lechmann looked in pain. "By means of this abort signal?"

"At ten in the morning, yeah."

"John . . . *what* abort signal?"

Waldo shrugged. He didn't know, either. "Maybe he figures we'll know it when we see it."

Lechmann groaned theatrically. But he had a point. They couldn't very well hang around the American embassy tomorrow morning waiting for a balloon to go up or some damned thing. But that, come to think of it, gave Waldo an idea about how to get in touch. First things first, however.

"We need a car," he said to Lechmann.

Lechmann nodded. He gestured toward another van, one of two that were parked in the rear of the Berioska shop. White, with a green birch tree—the Berioska logo—painted on the side.

Waldo shook his head. "They don't drive at night. We need a car that no one gives a second look at night. An ambulance, maybe."

Lechmann sniffed. He had known this was coming. Waldo was easing his way into the suggestion that they go to Hospital #52 on Zubovsky, look in on Elena, hope that none of the police or reporters notice them, and then make off with one of their ambulances. Dumbest idea he ever heard from John Waldo. Theft would be reported within ten minutes. No vehicle is easier to spot. Every ambulance in Moscow would be stopped ten times over by the police. He said all this to Waldo.

Waldo smiled within himself.

"See that?" He put an arm around Lechmann's shoulder, hugging him. "That's what makes you such a pro. It's these good ideas you have. It's why you get top dollar."

The Austrian eyed him with suspicion. "What idea, specifically?"

"You just said it," Waldo told him. "What we need is a police car."

62

It was two hours later, European time, when Bannerman's Swissair flight touched down at Zurich's airport.

As he had expected, he was asked to remain in his seat, with Susan, while the rest of the passengers deplaned. The air marshal stayed close to see that he did.

The senior flight attendant had been watching him as well, her expression a mix of curiosity and disdain. That he was some sort of criminal, she had no doubt. What sort remained to be seen.

Suddenly, she was called to the cockpit. When she emerged from it after a minute or so, the curiosity remained but the disdain had been replaced by something akin to sympathy. This new expression seemed to embrace Susan, thought Bannerman, perhaps even more so than himself.

She bent to whisper in the marshal's ear. He glanced toward their seat, one eyebrow rising. Another change of attitude. The flight attendant then approached his seat and handed him a message slip.

He didn't have to read it. She told them what it said. Mister Willem Brugg would be coming aboard in just a few minutes, accompanied by two representatives of the Swiss government. They would like to hold a private conference aboard this aircraft. Mr. Brugg apologizes for any inconvenience and has asked that we see to your comfort in the meantime.

"Someone's been hurt," Susan said to her quietly. She, too, had been reading the attendant's expression. "Will you please tell me who?"

"I'll bring you some coffee," was all she would answer.

• • •

"Willem?"

Susan, half out of her seat, called his name when he entered the cabin. Two men, wearing suits, entered behind him. Still another wore military fatigues and a submachine gun across his chest.

Willem Brugg raised his palms in a calming gesture, and asked the others to stay back. He came toward her, leaned to take her hand, kissed it, and answered the question he saw in her eyes. Her father was not hurt, he told her. Only a bump on the head. His own weary eyes went moist. He wiped them.

"Oh, God." Susan clutched his sleeve. "Oh, God, not Elena."

He nodded. "Injured," he said quickly. "But still alive."

He sat on the arm rest of the seat in front of Bannerman and told them all that he knew. The shooting outside the Moscow restaurant. The nature, as he understood it, of Elena's wound. The subsequent death of the young man who had been with them. Three assassins, all dead, one of them by Lesko's hand, two others by a second pair of gunmen who were as yet unidentified.

At this, he looked questioningly at Bannerman. Bannerman nodded, almost imperceptibly.

The men in the suits had moved closer so that they could hear. Willem Brugg turned, glowering. One man shrugged an apology. They had their orders.

"These men," Willem told Bannerman, "are here to ask you some questions and then to see that you do not remain in Switzerland. I am going to tell you why. Listen carefully, so that there's no misunderstanding. Are you listening?"

The emphasis, Bannerman assumed, had a purpose. He nodded, first tapping his finger against Susan's hand, asking her, he hoped, to show no reaction.

"You once had an agent, Carla Benedict. Blonde woman? Wears her hair in a bun?"

Bannerman nodded slowly.

"I regret to tell you she has been murdered. Here in Zurich. As she slept in her bed."

Bannerman felt an answering tap from Susan. He glanced at her. Her expression was blank. "Go on," he said.

"A man, also murdered, was found in her living room. His neck was broken. Small man. Dark skin."

Not Yuri, Bannerman realized. But not Aldo either.

"In the dead woman's apartment there are other traces of blood. They belong neither to this man or this woman. Be that as it may, the Swiss authorities are perfectly capable of getting to the bottom of it and they don't want Mama's Boy conducting his own vendetta on their soil."

One of the Swiss had moved forward as if to object. He was not a fool. He knew prompting when he saw it. But the second Swiss tugged at his jacket. This is Willem Brugg, he said with his eyes. You might want a favor someday.

"You are persona non grata in Switzerland," Elena's cousin told Bannerman. "You are free to choose any destination, but I invite you both to come with me to Moscow. My plane departs in forty minutes. It carries a full neurosurgical team and several tons of equipment. Also two of General Belkin's aides. Major Yuri Rykov, I think you know. Lieutenant Lydia Voinovitch, I think you have known even longer."

"Lydia." Bannerman nodded. "Of course."

"You'll come to Moscow?"

"I will. Not Susan."

He felt her nails. "Susan," she said through her teeth, "will speak for herself."

Willem knew that the exchange had been clumsy.

But perhaps, given the circumstances, it was all one could ask.

Before going to meet Bannerman's flight, he had tried to keep busy, not think about Elena. It was impossible, of course. But there was the medical staff to assemble, equipment to be dismantled and packed for shipping, technicians to go with it, arranging a satellite feed directly to that Moscow hospital so that his specialists could confer with the Russian doctors. There were all the special clearance and emergency visas, including one for the Israeli, Miriam, who is now a nurse, and one of Avram, who is now an interpreter.

With all this came the call from Irwin Kaplan. Next from Anton Zivic. Both expressing sorrow for the tragedy in

Moscow but only Kaplan saddened by the death of Carla.
Kaplan said a strange thing when Willem commiserated. He
said it's nice that *somebody* gives a shit.

Irwin had also told him of the plan to have Bannerman
arrested, held until he and Clew got there, then taken to
Moscow under guard to keep him from going by himself.

Willem quickly put a stop to that arrest nonsense. Kaplan
had not asked that he do so but the request was implicit.
What they do with him on Russian soil, however, could be
another matter. Moscow is not Zurich. His interference in
the matter of detaining Bannerman led to an urgent call
from the office of the American embassy secretary of state.
Willem chose not to return it. He had enough on his mind
already.

At last, with everything arranged, he goes to the airport to
meet Bannerman's flight. With him is Yuri, who has been
saying that they need to talk in private—it's about Carla—
but until now there has been no opportunity.

They are cleared through Passport Control and are
walking down the concourse toward Gate 37 when suddenly, standing by the chocolate counter, there is Carla
Benedict back from the dead.

"It's what I was trying to tell you," says Yuri, who is
almost as surprised to see her.

She woke up, she told Yuri, with a man sitting on her
chest and another one holding her legs.

It turned out that she knew them both. Anton Zivic had
sent them. They had gained access to Yuri's flat and had
been sitting with her as she slept for several hours. When
she began to stir, apparently, they thought it best to avoid a
misunderstanding. They neutralized her until her head could
clear.

She called the boathouse but no one answered. She
dressed, put on her wig, and prevailed upon the two men to
drive her to Lake Zurich. She saw the commotion, had no
idea where Yuri was, then decided that the airport was as
good a place to wait as any. There was only one flight
arriving from New York in the predawn hours. She felt sure
that Bannerman would be on it.

Willem did not like her looks. She seemed dazed and
distracted, a condition that was nevertheless preferable to

the alternative. Yuri whispered that he had given her
something to help her sleep, but it seemed more than that to
Willem. He did not dwell upon it because, just then, the
Swiss authorities appeared at the entrance to the concourse.
Yuri reached into his pocket and produced a leather folder
which he thrust into Carla's purse.

"Your name," he told her, "is Lieutenant Lydia Voinovitch, communications officer, Russian embassy, Bern."

She blinked at him, slow on the uptake. Not at all like the
Carla that Willem knew. But now, at least, he knew the true
identity of the woman who had bled to death in Carla's bed.
Situation gets more confusing by the minute.

"Take her to my plane," he said to Yuri. "Have one of
the doctors look at her. Let her rest before you . . . bring
her up to date."

Yuri nodded. Appreciatively. He turned her away from
the approaching Swiss and began marching her toward a
door that led to the tarmac. She was lagging behind him. He
turned and barked at her in Russian, urging her on with a
snap of his fingers. She did not bridle at this. Very much
unlike Carla.

Perhaps, thought Willem, the thing to do was take her
along. No telling what she might do when she hears about
Elena. They had become so close, the three of them, Elena,
Carla, and Susan. When they get to Moscow, he will try to
keep her on the plane. The Russians need not be the wiser.

Best for everyone, perhaps, that Carla Benedict stays
dead for a while longer.

63

_____

For a town that rolled up the streets at midnight, thought
Waldo, an awful lot seemed to be happening.

They had found their blue police Volga at the Varshavsky
car-service station on the southernmost arc of the Garden

Ring Road. Lechmann knew, and reluctantly admitted, that militia cars were taken there to be fixed. He'd seen as many as a dozen at a time lined up at Varshavsky.

It was more like twenty. Maintenance, Lechmann remarked, must have gone to hell since his last visit. There was only one watchman and he was asleep. It took Lechmann thirty minutes to find one that was more or less in working order. It needed a battery, which he took from another whose rear end was caved in, and it needed petrol, which he siphoned from two others. They hid the flower van among assorted wrecks that had been towed to Varshavsky for parts.

They were cruising back north in the general direction of the Kremlin—Waldo was saving their specific destination as a surprise—when he thought he heard gunfire in the distance. They pulled over and listened.

No doubt about it. They heard, no mistake, the distinctive *tat-tat-tat* of an AK-47 on full automatic and the chain-saw sound of an Uzi-type weapon. And now several guns, all shooting at once. The sound was punctuated by two dull *whoomp*s.

"Grenades," said Lechmann.

Waldo shook his head. "Incendiaries. Look at the sky."

It was glowing. First came two red swells as if from a distant fireworks display and then a softer, flickering glow. More gunfire. Waldo switched the police radio on. There was nothing at first. They waited. Then, a stream of orders in Russian. Waldo could barely make sense of them— something about sausage—but Lechmann translated.

"It's a meat-packer . . . Abattoir #6 over on Kutuzovsky . . . under attack. They don't know by whom. They are calling all cars to the scene. They are calling for fire engines."

Far up ahead, Waldo saw a set of blue lights blink on, flashing, and then turn left out of sight. A second police cruiser crossed right to left behind them. Good, he thought. Keep everybody busy.

"Let's roll," he told Lechmann. "Go straight but speed up. We better look like we're on a call."

"Are you going to tell me where we're going?"

"You promise you won't give me any shit?"

"Zivic wants noise so you're going to make noise. Just tell me where."

"KGB headquarters," Waldo answered. "Where else?"

Lechmann could have refused, he supposed, but he found the idea titillating and the conditions seemed ideal. They made one stop at a park near the embankment. Lechmann got out, took a handful of mud, and smeared it over the license plate and over the numbers on both doors. They proceeded up Novaya to Lubyanka Square, crossed it, and came to a stop outside the triple-arched front entrance of Detsky Mir. Directly across, out Waldo's side, was Moscow Center. Other than the lobby, perhaps a dozen windows were lit. No guards outside.

Waldo turned in his seat and shouldered his weapon, extending the barrel and sound suppressor through the open window. Adjusting his sights, he moved from one lit window to the next in search of movement. He saw none. But in one of these was a bronze bust of Feliks Dzerzhinski. It would do for a start. He squeezed off one shot. A loud *sput* and the head of the hollow bust exploded. In that office, a figure scrambled toward the door where he clawed at the light switch. The office went dark. Waldo moved on.

He put a round through each of the lighted windows, destroying two more busts and a chandelier in the process.

"Ammunition is not inexhaustible," Lechmann grumbled as he watched their rear. "And a sound suppressor is not a silencer."

"Just a couple more."

He put two rounds into the face of the clock that was just below the middle pediment of the roof, stopping it.

"Next time I shoot, go," said Waldo.

He dropped his sights to the main entrance. Double glass doors. Used mostly by visitors. Inside, he could see that an alarm had been given. Two men, uniformed, pistols out and held at shoulder level, were edging down the inner stair toward the glass doors, pressing themselves against one wall.

"Yeah, right," Waldo muttered. "You're backlit, shitheads. You go after a sniper, backlit, with a handgun?"

This criticism struck Lechmann as harsh. For seventy years, no one had so much as spat on the sidewalk in front of that building. The guards could be forgiven for doubting that some crazed marksman was out there, intent on decapitating every bust of their patron saint that he could draw a bead on.

Waldo fired once more. The glass in the left-hand door shattered. The two guards fell over themselves scrambling up the stairs. Lechmann put the Volga in gear and, tires squealing, sped up Pushechnaya Street passing the Savoy Hotel on his left. As he did so, his stomach rose toward his throat.

There were, at the entrance to the Savoy, at least five black Chaikas bearing KGB plates, men climbing into them, some carrying suitcases. The suitcases, he had no doubt, belonged to Lesko, Elena, and Belkin. Their rooms had been searched. Their personal effects had been taken for closer examination in the attempt to find out what had brought them to Moscow. No surprise there, of course. But if they had left one minute earlier, five cars filled with armed men would have driven right down the middle of John Waldo's little shooting gallery.

"Where now?" he asked when his heartbeat had slowed.

"There's a fountain across from the Bolshoi. Let's clean this mud off so we're normal again."

"And what after that?" he asked, his voice still a bit high. "We could always shoot our way into the Kremlin and help ourselves to the crown jewels. We could break into Lenin's tomb and turn up the thermostat."

Waldo ignored the sarcasm. He had turned the radio back up. The female dispatcher was giving more reports of gunfire. More bombings.

"Is this that same place?" he asked Lechmann. "The meat-packer on whatzizovsky?"

The Austrian listened. He shook his head, frowning. "This is a different location," he said, and then held up a hand for silence. "Two . . . no . . . three locations, all in the Krasno-Presnensky district and . . . wait . . . this one is now about us."

But from what the dispatcher was saying, their own adventure was the least of the militia's concerns. *"There's a report of a sniper,"* she was saying, *"shooting up #2 Lubyanka. Go drive past. See if there's anything to it. If you should happen to see one, tell him it's not nice, what he's doing.''*

Lechmann translated without comment, although, truth be told, he found such insolence unattractive. It had the sound of a coward's revenge. But his mind was more on this sudden rash of shooting incidents, one after another, in a city that was not New York.

''You thinking what I'm thinking?'' Waldo asked.

The Austrian nodded. ''That we are not so alone after all?''

''That maybe Zivic was straight. Maybe we *do* have five teams here, plus maybe even Molly Farrell setting off all those fireworks, and meanwhile we're driving around without a fucking clue.''

Lechmann could only shrug.

''I mean, maybe it's possible,'' said Waldo. ''Maybe they came in early, like us. Maybe Zivic thinks we know. Maybe Elena, for instance, was supposed to tell us but she got hit.''

Lechmann doubted it. Zivic, and certainly Bannerman, would not have left such a communication to chance. As for Elena, she had no reason to think that she would even lay eyes on them in Moscow. It was enough that she knew they were near.

On the other hand, farfetched as it seemed, his mind's eye was picturing Molly Farrell, an electronic device in her hand, touching off explosions all over Moscow. Why Molly, you ask? Molly was bridesmaid to Elena. She was another one, like Susan, like Carla, always whispering in private with her. Do harm to Elena while Molly is here and there would be no stopping her. She would do to this city what Hitler couldn't do.

But he knew that this was nonsense. All of it. For reasons of timing alone, it was totally impossible. Still . . .

''Let's drive out to the Lenin Hills,'' said Lechmann.

''What changed your mind?''

''Don't get ahead of me,'' said the Austrian. ''It's only to take a look.''

At what, for what, he didn't want to say. But it would not surprise him, the way things were going, to see a certain apartment building lighting up more of the sky.

64

"Hey, Lesko?"

Katz's voice.

He'd been hearing it for some minutes. Hours. Days. He didn't know. It wanted him to wake up. That was the last thing he wanted. He didn't even want to be alive.

"Come on. Snap out of it."

A hand, shaking him.

Since when does Katz have hands? he wondered without much caring.

"Mr. Lesko?"

A new voice. Not Katz this time. He opened one eye and saw them. Katz sitting on the edge of his bed. The other shape standing, one hand on the arm he couldn't move. He was rubbing it with something cold. Sticking him again.

"This will help you wake up," he said.

"David?" He had to ask. *"Is she dead?"*

Katz gestured toward the other shape. *"This guy says no."*

The shape came into focus somewhat. Yeah, he thought. Bald guy with a beard. Same guy who climbed under the table with him. Sticking him. Pulling his hair. Yelling at him that she's not dead.

"I am Colonel David Meltzer," he was saying now. "I am the resident physician attached to the United States embassy here in Moscow. Do you recall that you're in Moscow?"

". . . Elena," he whispered.

"She's alive. For the moment, she's stable. Do you see what I'm holding, Mr. Lesko?"

He tried to see. Yeah. It looked like a little white rock. It was going forward and back, forward and back, turning in this guy's fingers. Son of a bitch. Trying to hypnotize him. "Fuck you," he murmured.

The doctor took a weary breath.

"What your wife has, Mr. Lesko, is a depressed skull fracture. This fragment of a granite carving, not you, is what did the damage. A bullet from a high-powered rifle knocked it loose and sprayed the both of you with shards of granite. While you were sleeping, I took smaller fragments out of your left arm and out of the back of your neck."

Lesko hunched his shoulders. He did feel something on his neck. Pulling at his skin. A bandage. Arm felt a little sore, too. So what?

"I know that you think you hurt your wife. You think you crushed her head against that wall. You didn't. If anything, you kept her from being hurt worse than she is."

Tears welled in Lesko's eyes. "How bad?" he asked.

A sigh. "Time will tell. The wound has been cleaned, the pressure on her brain relieved, she has a drain in place. In a word, she's been stabilized. There's a neurosurgeon, they don't come any better, flying here within a few hours through the efforts of Mr. Willem Brugg. He's bringing his entire team and, from what I gather, the contents of a good-sized neurological clinic. Your wife will not want for good medical treatment."

"I want to see her." Lesko tugged at his restraints. "Get this shit off me."

"Ah . . . I'm afraid we'll have to discuss a few things first."

Lesko heaved at the nylon straps. Meltzer put a hand on his chest.

"Understand me," he said. "Do that once more and I'll call for the men I have waiting outside. They will take you, bed and all, to the embassy compound where there is a detention cell waiting for you. It's for your own good. Right or wrong, Mr. Lesko, you beat one man to death and are a suspect in the beating death of another. You also had a gun. You fired that gun. For that alone, you will otherwise rot in a KGB prison until they decide you have nothing else to tell them. If we can get you to the embassy, however, you'll be out of their reach."

Lesko let his head fall back. He had no strength anyway. It seemed useless to argue that a gun-possession charge was

bullshit. Let alone a homicide charge. That gun was
Valentin's. He picked it up off the . . .

Oh, damn. Oh, God damn.

"The kid . . . Valentin . . . he's dead?"

"I'm afraid so."

"Belkin?"

"He's in surgery now. That bullet chewed his insides
pretty good, but he's got a chance."

Lesko took a long breath. "I want to see Elena."

The army doctor stepped back from the bed. "We're told
that you're an honorable man, Mr. Lesko. If you will give me
your promise of full and absolute cooperation, give truthful
answers to a few questions I must ask, I will give you five
minutes with your wife before we go."

Lesko showed his teeth. "You're straight with me, I'm
straight with you. There's your promise."

"Okay, let's test it. Who were those men, Mr. Lesko?
The two in that van."

"I don't know. That's the truth."

Colonel Meltzer seemed unconvinced.

"Doctor . . . I was fucking shooting at them. I emptied
half a clip at them. You think they were pals of mine?"

An ambiguous shrug. "Could they have been Paul
Bannerman's people? And you just didn't realize it?"

Lesko shook his head. He meant it. "Bannerman
wouldn't have sent them. Not without telling me first."
Prick better not have.

"Let's try a name. Is one of them David Katz?" he
asked.

"Oh, for . . ." But Lesko understood. He was probably
yelling for Katz all night. Telling him to go stay with Elena.
Bring Valentin with him. Bring . . . Wait a second. Bring
John Waldo.

He was not about to mention Waldo. That was only a
dream. But he explained who Katz was. The doctor seemed
dubious. Fine. Let him check it out.

The doctor was talking about Bannerman now. Saying he
was on the way. Didn't seem happy about it. All kinds of
people coming, including Susan. Including Irwin Kaplan for
some reason. Lesko was glad about Irwin. Irwin, you could
talk to.

But Lesko didn't want to know about this now. He wanted to see Elena. All this doctor seemed interested in was containing this situation . . . saying there's a lot at stake . . . Bannerman could screw it up . . . saying they need his help to keep Bannerman under control . . . saying that if anyone has the moral authority to ask Bannerman and the Bruggs to stand down, it's the husband of Elena Brugg.

"Wait . . . wait . . . wait." Lesko squeezed his eyes shut, trying to focus on all this. "Run that by me again."

The doctor from the embassy did so. In somewhat more detail. Larger issues, he was saying. No room for personal vendettas. Not for what happened to Elena. Not for what happened to Bannerman's agent in Zurich.

"What agent?"

"A woman . . . Carla Benedict . . . dead . . . murdered."

Lesko could not believe it. People like Carla are never victims. They make victims.

All this talk of vendettas. The idea of revenge had somehow never crossed his mind. Time for that later. When Elena's out of danger. But if he had to decide now who he'd want to go after, Belkin's stepfather would have to lead off the list. It was clear to him now. Kulik. Name was Kulik. Red-faced. Humiliated. He probably got out to the sidewalk, looked for a pay phone, and an hour later the shooters are waiting.

"What do you want from me?" he asked the doctor quietly.

"I told you. Your word."

"That what? I won't go after anyone on my own?"

"And that you'll do all in your power to dissuade Paul Bannerman from doing the same."

"On his own."

"Your word on it?"

"You got it. Now where's Elena?"

They had closed her eyes.

The left side of her head was packed in gauze, a lump of it, the size of his fist. She had a tube in her nose. She was breathing. Very softly. That was good, he hoped.

Another tube led to her arm, the arm that was scarred from the other time she got shot. At the end of that arm, a finger was moving. He wanted to believe that she knew he was there, that the finger was for him. Come, Lesko. Hold my hand.

He couldn't because they had handcuffed him. The muscle from the embassy. They said it was a precaution. He had already wrecked one ambulance and half of the emergency room even when strapped to a gurney. Lesko remembered, dimly.

But he was able to lean over her bed. Kiss her. Talk to her. While he did, he kept looking at that finger. It kept moving, same way. He saw no change in response to his presence. It was just a twitch. Still, it said she was alive.

"You're going to be okay," he told her. "No question."

He said this and other things aloud because he'd heard that a coma patient knows when you're there. Sometimes just hearing your voice can bring them out of it. He had a neighbor, back in Queens, went into a diabetic coma. Was like that for weeks. Came out of it when they brought her dog to see her. And you're supposed to ask questions. One day, out of the blue, they answer you. Sometimes.

He spoke to her, quietly, tenderly, as long as he could. Until his voice began to crack and the tears spilled down his face. After that, he began talking to God. Trying to make a deal. Let her live, he said, and you can keep the baby. Let her live and you can take me. But if you let her die, you son of a bitch . . .

The embassy doctor was at his shoulder. "We have to go," he said.

You let her die and I'll fill up hell for you.

"Mr. Lesko." The doctor touched his arm. "You gave your word."

Lesko nodded slowly. He gave it and he'd keep it. Five minutes with Elena. Then go peaceably. After that, no action on his own, no action by Bannerman. Not on his own.

It won't be on his own.

65

The apartment house in Lenin Hills was still standing.

And it was guarded. But it wasn't quiet.

Out front, an old woman was yelling about something. She was running back and forth, between two guards, pulling at their uniforms. She was in a frenzy. One guard would shake her off, turn his back to her, and she would run to the other. He, too, would turn away.

Up above, a few tenants in bathrobes were watching this from darkened terraces. They were keeping to the shadows. They wanted to see. But otherwise, they wanted no part of that woman.

"Keep going," Waldo said to the Austrian. "We don't need this either."

But the old woman had spotted the blue Volga. Salvation. She threw up her hands and ran toward the street on a course that would intercept them. Lechmann had to brake quickly. He would have hit her.

The old woman put both hands on the hood, then on the left fender, then on the side mirror as if by touching it she could keep it from driving away. She reached Lechmann's window. She was yelling, wailing, spraying spittle through bad teeth.

"They took him," she was shouting. "My son. They took him and dragged him out."

Lechmann wiped his face. He looked past her at one of the guards who was gesturing to him. The guard was shaking his head at the two militia plainclothesman. He was tossing a thumb down the street. Get moving, was his message. This is none of your business.

But Lechmann felt Waldo's hand on his thigh. The touch, pressing firmly, said, *"Wait."*

"Who took your son, old mother?" asked the Austrian.

"Men," she cried. "Two men in a big car with guns. My

son is KGB. My son is a *general* in KGB and these bums did nothing.''

The guards were moving toward the Volga. They were probably on someone's payroll. Lechmann didn't want a confrontation. Too many pairs of eyes. Waldo, if he opened his mouth, could never pass for a Moscow cop. He might have to kill the guards.

But Waldo spoke anyway. "Your son. His name?" he asked.

Her expression wavered at the accent but only briefly. "Is Borovik. Vadim Borovik. Is important general."

"*You!*" One of the guards. "Nothing happened here. This one is crazy."

The thumb again. The second guard had the old woman by the collar. He was walking her, half carrying her, back toward the building's entrance.

"Her son was not taken?" asked Lechmann. "He is not a general?"

The guard made a show of noting the number of their car. "Take my advice," he said, "and don't ask for trouble."

"Good advice," said Waldo in his ear. "Go."

"What'll we bet," asked Waldo when they turned the corner, "that the black car was a Zil?"

"No takers."

"And that it's on its way, right now, to Zhukovka."

Lechmann shrugged. "Just as likely to a lime pit some-place."

"Maybe the lime pit's in Zhukovka. You got an address, right?"

The Austrian nodded glumly.

"What's the matter?"

"Zhukovka is big-shot dachas. Very well protected. To everyone but you, this means stay away. I think I am going to die tonight."

"Yeah, well, you don't think this is interesting? This says Zivic is right. Borovik sent the shooters. But he fucked up. By accident, maybe even on purpose, he made it look like it was the guy in the Zil who sent them."

A skeptical grunt.

"Where does it not make sense? You know from the

doorman that Borovik has had dinner with whatziz-name . . . Kulik . . . more than once. Borovik's in this guy's pocket, right? Like those two guards who are proba-bly sticking a pillow over that old lady's face right now. But maybe Borovik gets ambitious. Maybe he decides to set Kulik up and he . . . Make a right turn here.''

Lechmann cut the wheel, still grumbling. ''You know how many times you said *maybe* in the past few hours? By actual count, it's six million.''

''Turn right again, next corner. Flip your lights off.''

''We're going back to that apartment house? What for?''

''Zivic said make noise. I want to pop those two guards in the ass.''

66

The Brugg Industries jet had departed late.

Not by long; they could still make Moscow on schedule. The delay had been caused by Barton Fuller.

He had used his influence to have takeoff clearance denied until he could speak to Bannerman personally. He wanted a promise. Do nothing, he said, until you've met up with Irwin and Roger. Do nothing until you hear them out.

Bannerman had no trouble agreeing. He could use the time to get his people in place. As for hearing them out, he had a sense that he knew more than they did already. About who the players were, at least.

He had spoken to Zivic at length by way of Willem Brugg's communications center. He learned of the French-man's visit to Grassi's boat and of the exchange with Ernst Lechmann in Moscow. He had listened to Yuri, also at length. He now knew about the Borovik network. Yuri described its scope but declined to list the names and places.

''Yuri . . .'' Bannerman asked, not unkindly, ''who are you saving them for?''

It seemed to sadden him that Bannerman could ask. "General Belkin," he said haltingly, "is not the only honest man in KGB."

"These others, then. Have you met them?"

"Some. Yes."

"Will I?"

"If they agree. If they think that Mama's Boy can understand them."

"Yuri . . . what does that mean, exactly?"

"These are men who love their country. Good times or bad. For their country they will make any sacrifice."

"And . . . a man like me," Bannerman said quietly, "I could never understand that."

"I do not mean to insult you. Please believe, you have my highest respect. No man is more loyal to those who trust him. But you, I think, have never known the pain that even I have felt. And mine is nothing compared to that of General Belkin and these others."

Bannerman grumbled inwardly.

From Susan, he doesn't understand women.

From Anton Zivic, he doesn't understand just letting life *happen* every now and then.

And now from Yuri, he doesn't understand suffering. Or love of country.

As for suffering, he would agree that he doesn't understand making a national pastime of it. In Russia, that's what it is. Listen to their music. It's either heroic or melancholy with not much in between. Try to read their poetry without wanting to drink straight from the bottle.

Bannerman dismissed that train of thought. He was beginning to sound like John Waldo.

"No offense taken," he said to Yuri, rising. "But if that's all that's bothering you, try to put it aside until this is over."

He was not annoyed so much. It was more a measure of discomfort when people who should know better allow themselves to be distracted.

There were fourteen passengers in the main cabin. Willem Brugg was in the cockpit, flying right seat and staying close to the radio. Of the fourteen, eight were medical staff. They sat in the rows farthest back and in the main salon—a bedroom cum office—where two of the doctors were reviewing an EEG of Elena's brain that had been faxed from the Moscow hospital. They were not distracted. They knew what they had to do.

Miriam who was now a nurse sat with them, learning to act and sound like one. Avram who was now an interpreter was memorizing those medical terms which seemed likely to arise.

Next was Yuri, who was keeping to himself in spite of Carla's efforts to comfort him about Leo and especially Lydia. Carla seemed more like herself again. A stimulant from one of the doctors had helped. She was pacing the aisles now, unable to sit. Several times, she made silent eye contact with Susan. Bannerman had no idea what that meant, if anything, but he thought he could read at least a part of Carla's mind. Just three hours further east there would be someone she could punish for sending Aldo Corsini into her life.

Susan sat two rows beyond Yuri. She, too, seemed very much within herself. He had not been very attentive to her since they learned about the Moscow shooting. He'd been busy debriefing people. He sat, reached for her hand, and squeezed it. She did not acknowledge his presence.

"How are you holding up?" he asked. "Can I get you anything?"

"He's right, you know," she said, staring ahead.

"Um . . . About what, Susan?"

"That you don't feel pain. You don't even hate."

Oh boy. "No, Susan. What I don't do is indulge it. What I don't do is feel what you're feeling exactly when you want me to feel it."

"I want you to hate. This time, I want you to hate."

He had never seen her quite like this.

The look in her eyes.

It *was* hatred, and that wasn't good. Carla could hate, and so could he, for that matter. But they'd learned, over time, how to put it aside. Even to use it. The way they'd learned to use fear.

"Paul . . . that baby . . ."

Twice now she'd started to speak, using those three words, and twice she'd stopped herself from saying more.

The second time she said it, Carla was pacing up the aisle. Carla overheard it. Their eyes met and held again. There were no words in this exchange, but Carla, clearly, seemed to be telling her to shut up. Abruptly, the psychic message was completed.

''We need to talk,'' Carla said.

She reached in and took Susan's hand, pulling her out of her seat. They went back to the main salon where the doctors were closeted. Carla threw them out.

They were in there for thirty minutes. When they came out they were holding hands. Very unlike Carla. They separated. Susan stopped by Yuri's seat. She knelt, her arms folded across his knees, and made her own attempt to comfort him. Carla continued forward.

''Um . . . ahem,'' he said after she'd passed his seat.

''It's none of your business, Paul.'' She kept walking.

That does it, thought Bannerman. That was the second time he'd heard that tonight, and in what seemed to be the same context. Elena's baby. He had also, apparently, moved down the evolutionary scale from cold fish to potted plant. Enough was enough. He got up and followed her.

''Do we have weapons?'' she asked when he reached her seat.

''No, because we'll be searched at Vnukovo. Carla . . .''

''They won't search me. I'm Lieutenant Voinovitch. Who do we have in Moscow?''

''Waldo and Lechmann, but keep that to yourself. Is Susan pregnant?''

''You're asking me?''

''Carla . . .''

''We didn't talk about that.''

''Then what's going on?''

''Paul . . . it's *really* private. And it has nothing to do with you.''

''Elena's baby. Is there something wrong with it?''

A flicker of hesitation. ''Not that I know of. Aside from Elena's condition. And aside from the kid being a Lesko.''

Bannerman stared. ''You're joking about it. That means it's not serious.''

''I didn't say serious. I said private.''

''But she told you. She'll talk to you but not me.''

"Women talk to women, Paul. And I'm a woman. You can tell by the tits, such as they are."

Bannerman's color rose slightly. Carla reached for his necktie. She pulled him closer.

"Look . . . Paul. You're a little dense about some things. Like knowing when to shut up and leave something alone. But mostly, you're very smart. Very perceptive."

Bannerman waited.

"So you might even figure this out."

"Fine. Then why not—"

She tugged the tie, stopping him. "If you *do* figure it out . . . and you say one word to any human being . . . including Susan . . . I am personally going to cut your balls off."

67

Lechmann was convinced of it now. It's better to be crazy.

First Waldo shoots those two guards. Both of them. In the buttocks. He was as good as his word.

Why did he do this?

In part, he says, because one was impolite and the other is too rough with old ladies. Also because the first showed excessive interest in their car. Even Waldo, however, does not regard these as capital offenses.

"Relax," he says.

"Just a pop in the ass. Think of it as a spanking."

Also, if those two guards see this car go in one direction and a minute later they are shot from another direction, Waldo reasons that a suspicious police car will no longer be foremost in their minds.

Even so, he says, it wouldn't hurt to get out of Moscow for a while. Let's go to Zhukovka. This brings the next lunacy.

All the way to Zhukovka, twenty miles from Moscow, he

asked Waldo to please tell him the following. If we are stopped, how do we explain what a Moscow police car is doing in Zhukovka? How do we explain two Moscow detectives, one of whom speaks Russian with a Salzburg accent and the other hardly speaks it at all, are doing so far out of their jurisdiction?

"You're right," he said at last. "They stop us, we got a problem."

"So, what now? I turn around?"

"What we do . . . we stop them first."

And this is precisely what ensued. They drive into Zhukovka, all over Zhukovka, stopping every patrolling guard they see. We are Moscow Police, Sex Crimes Unit, hunting a rapist who dresses in a guard uniform. Show me your papers. No sudden moves. My partner is covering you. Ah . . . you are legitimate. Go about your duties but keep your eyes open. The bastard is somewhere in this area. My height, pockmarked, walks with a limp.

Lechmann should have known. Ask a Russian for papers, he shows you his papers. A conditioned reflex. When he drove past these same guards again they would salute to show that they were on their toes or they would spread their hands to signify that they'd seen nothing. None of them seemed to wonder why the second Moscow policeman, the one who didn't speak, was no longer in the car. What's to wonder? He is doubtless beating the bushes for that rapist. Or on a stakeout waiting to pounce on anyone who limps.

Definitely, it pays to be crazy.

Dacha means "cottage." Some cottage, thought Waldo.

The house was three stories high, made of stucco and carved wood painted white, Empire style. It was built, Waldo assumed, by some nineteenth-century nobleman who appeared to have some taste. It had a porte cochere entrance on one side and two sets of French doors facing front where there were remnants of a formal garden. A separate garage was set well back; it was once a stable. No one seemed to use it. The cars—Waldo saw three—were gathered at odd angles around the porte cochere. One was the Zil.

The property was surrounded by a seven-foot wall whose gate had been left open. An open gate meant no dogs. There were coach lamps atop the gate posts but they weren't lit. Nor were there any exterior lights around the main entrance. This struck Waldo as too good to be true until he saw the reason for it. A second Zil appeared. One man and a driver.

The driver tapped his horn as he slowed to a stop. The young one from the restaurant, broken nose, stepped out of the house and into the moonlight. He nodded, more like a bow, very respectful, to the newcomer who was climbing out of the Zil. This was a new face, not one of the suits or the Arabs from the restaurant.

Waldo memorized the plate number. The driver was holding the door for his passenger. He closed it behind him, watched him go into the house, then leaned back against the Zil and fumbled for a cigarette and matches.

Waldo waited until he struck the match, blinding himself, then moved from his place behind the open gate to the set of French doors nearest him. The room inside was unlit except for what spilled from other rooms. He was reluctant to try the doors for fear of an alarm system, but he was able, at least, to get some idea of the layout. Main entrance to his right, a big center hall, probably a grand staircase. This was a formal dining room, furnished with antiques. Next to it, on Waldo's left, a sitting room or parlor. On the far side, he got a glimpse of what looked like the library, four or five men all shaking hands, before Broken Nose stepped to the door and closed it.

Waldo moved on, proceeding in a clockwise direction around the perimeter of the house. The kitchen, he assumed, would be in the basement. He was looking for the outside entrance. He knew that it would also double as a servants' entrance and that there would be a narrow staircase leading up as well as down. He found it. It was locked. But there was an old coal chute just beyond. No longer used. The house had long been converted to oil. The delivery pipe was right next to the chute.

He forced the lid of the coal chute. Dry wood. Rusted nails. It broke apart easily. He felt no wires but the inside was caked with years of dust, spiderwebs, old hornet nests. What the hell, he thought. I'm here.

He took off his coat, turned it inside out, did the same with his trousers, and put them back on. This was so the dirt would be less obvious later. But his weapon, he decided, would have to stay up here. Too bulky to be held against his chest. Besides, he'd need both arms and all their lateral strength to slow his descent. He climbed into the chute.

"Well? Where is he?" asked the man who had just arrived.

"Down below," Kulik answered. "The kitchen. We left him handcuffed to a pipe."

"And you intend to kill him?"

"Yes. If you and the others agree."

"Agree? Of course we agree. We told you six months ago that the man has shit for brains. You needed a mess like this before you could see it."

"What I needed," Kulik answered evenly, "was a suitable replacement, patiently groomed, carefully evaluated. Now we have one. He could take over tomorrow. That is my intention unless you disapprove. I plan to have a talk with him, first thing."

"That's this Podowsk?"

"Podolsk. Not *Podowsk*."

"Put him aside for the moment. This mess, do you have it under control?"

"The police certainly. And now Borovik. As for the various other factions involved, I am confident that they can be diverted."

"For your sake, I hope so. Already, I think you can expect to be fined for that business in the restaurant. Tell me about your stepson, Arkadi."

"What about him?" And fuck you with your fine.

"How did he trace you to Moscow?"

"The . . . encounter must have been a coincidence. There is no other explanation for it."

The newcomer grunted doubtfully.

"Back to this Podowsk. What I hear from Leningrad is he's no more than a common thief."

"You don't do him justice. According to Sostkov here, he was a most inventive thief."

Still the doubt. The man looked at Sostkov, whose face was still aglow with pride at having been permitted to meet him at last. Sostkov snapped out of it. He added his own endorsement of Podolsk.

"Already," said Sostkov eagerly, "he runs Borovik's old network. In fact, he has doubled its size. He recruited the new ones himself. It's a wonder, frankly, that he has not struck out on his own, so much does he despise General Borovik."

"Not such a wonder," Kulik put in. "Borovik had the goods on him. He would have been dead or in prison before you could wink."

A grunt. "Bringing Podowsk along, Arkadi Ivanovich, that is your decision. Finishing Borovik, that is an act of charity. The sooner you put that one out of his misery, the better. But you must keep this under control. Also, if I were you, I would not be so quick to believe in coincidence."

"We . . . bow to your wisdom."

They heard a noise. A banging sound and then a ghostly wail. It seemed to come from the heating duct.

"Borovik," said Kulik. "He's been doing that since he got here."

The newcomer frowned. He glanced toward Kulik's fireplace. The famous golf club was no longer there. But now he saw it. It was on top of Kulik's desk and it was bent in half. He now felt sure that he knew the reason for the wailing.

"By the way," he asked Kulik, "why did you bring him to this house? Why couldn't he have jumped off a roof like Pavlov, Kruchina, and the others?"

"I need to ask him a few questions." Including, as those others were asked, where he has his money stashed. If there's a fine to be paid, by God, it will be Borovik who pays it. "He's going to help us control this."

"Borovik? How will he do that?"

"He's going to use his head for a change."

Waldo, frozen into a crouch, groped for his penlight to see what he had stepped on. He knew it was not a cat.

The beam fell on two white thighs. They were trembling. Higher, a pudgy waist, its belly exposed. The pants were down around the knees and the shirt was half open. No socks. One shoe on, the other off. The man had been forcibly dressed. He had a bag over his head, tied off at his neck with a drawstring. It was a thick canvas bag like the kind banks use. Waldo had no doubt who he was. The man asking "Who's there?" had to be Borovik.

He was handcuffed to the drainpipe leading from a large stone tub. Waldo had seen tubs like it. They were for keeping fish alive before there was refrigeration. Borovik, terrified, kept asking "Who is it?" That, and a low stream of pleadings in Russian. Waldo only caught some of it. He was trying to bargain. Trying to make a deal.

He scanned the room with his penlight. It was the original kitchen. Pots and pans hung from hooks. Cabinets filled with bowls and platters. A long butcher-block table stood in the center. He saw a massive iron stove that was giving off heat. Someone had fired up the oven. Maybe so Borovik wouldn't freeze.

Ignoring the Russian, he located the narrow staircase that the servants used. He started to climb. It squeaked horribly. He backed away, crossing the old kitchen to a wider set of stairs. But he heard footsteps, several pair of feet, just above him. Better look for a place to hide, he thought, in case they decided to come down. Preferably something that has a back door.

There was one large pantry, a wine cellar, and an old root cellar. They wouldn't do. Then he remembered the dumbwaiter. A house like this would have one. It would lead to an upstairs pantry just off the dining room. He found the shaft behind a Dutch door. The dumbwaiter cabinet was all the way down. He tried the rope. The cabinet moved easily. The pulleys squeaked, but they were three floors up. Servants' quarters would be at the top. Along the way, the shaft would likely pass near the master bedroom. Breakfast in bed. This was good, he thought. This gave him *three* back doors.

More footsteps. Muffled voices. And a dull shudder upstairs as if a heavy door had been opened. Someone seemed to be leaving. A moment later, he heard the start-up roar of a heavy engine. Probably the second Zil. Waldo checked his memory for the plate number. He still had it.

He had to assume that someone would be coming down. Borovik was yelling now. Trying threats. Waldo heard both fear and rage. Fear was way ahead. As quietly as he could, he climbed onto the cabinet and closed the Dutch door from inside. He tried the rope. No problem there. It could handle his weight.

"Where are you?" the Russian was calling. "Where did you go?"

Waldo grunted. He considered climbing back out and putting him to sleep. But better not. If those other guys come down, he decided, they'll know he didn't clock himself. And Borovik was not likely to ask which one of them has just been prowling around the kitchen.

And here they came. At least three, by the sound. Maybe four. They figured to be the four from the restaurant, minus the two Arabs whom he hadn't seen among those in the library. He considered hanging around to see what would happen. Hear what they said to Borovik and vice versa. Hope that they stuck to the three or four hundred words Waldo knew. He should have had Lechmann do this. Yeah, right. Lechmann would have had two heart attacks already.

So screw it. Better to use their noise to cover his. He began pulling himself up.

He bypassed the dining room in favor of the master bedroom. The dining-room pantry would be right over their heads. He might open the door into a stack of dishes. The only question about the bedroom was whether Kulik had a tootsy up there. But Kulik, given his age, probably had an even limper dick than his own. Waldo decided he could chance it.

There was no one. And no problem with the door. He tied off the pulley rope lest the cabinet go crashing back down. That done, he paused to think this over. Right about here was where Lechmann would tell him he's crazy. Like . . . um, tell me, John . . . what was the point of all this?

"What? Going in here? This is reconnaissance."

"Reconnaissance for what?"

"For when we want to hit them."

"So? Why don't you hit them now? You have five targets, authorized by Zivic, all in the same house. Go out, get your weapon, go back in, and spray the whole pack of them as they climb the basement stairs."

"I don't know. I don't think so."

"Too easy, is that it?"

"I don't know."

"You want to know the truth? You are addicted to creepy-crawly. If you lived in Paris you would know every inch of the sewers."

"Well . . . Maybe I do know. You know whose hit this should be?"

"Whose?"

"Lesko's."

Lechmann would argue with that. He'd agree with the premise . . . nice thought and everything . . . but he'd point out that Lesko is basically not a killer. I mean, he would definitely bang anyone who was involved in Elena getting shot, but he'd probably want to sort them out first and be sure he had the right guys. With us, standards are less exacting. A bird in the hand.

Lechmann might have a point. Waldo would think about it.

In the meantime . . . back to reconnaissance.

He made his way down the grand staircase. Good carpet. No creaks. In the light from the center hall he saw that he'd forgotten to turn his clothes rightside-out again. He decided to leave them. If anyone got a look at him, most of what they'd remember would be seams and shoulder pads.

He went first to the front door and made sure it wasn't bolted. Exit number one. Next, he went into the dining room. He checked the French doors for wires, found one, and traced it to its terminal. Holding his breath, he disconnected it. No alarm sounded. Shitty system. Exit number two.

Reversing himself, he passed through the pantry, which, he saw, had been made into a small office. It opened onto the center hall directly across from the library. In the library itself, the first thing he noticed was the safe. It was an antique. Beautiful old thing. Ornate brass trim with hunting scenes etched into the door and sides. It stood against the wall on one side of the desk. A hotel-type minibar sat next to it looking tackily out of place. He was moving toward the safe when he heard voices, hollow and tinny. He realized that they were coming up from the basement. He listened at the duct.

There was a struggle going on down there. Heavy

breathing. One voice, sort of melodic, was giving orders. Must be Kulik. Waldo listened. From the tone and what words he could pick up, it sounded like Kulik was telling Borovik what they're going to do to him. Now he's asking questions.

He wanted to know about some money. Waldo got that. But he was also talking about cooking something. Baking something. Feet? Sounded like feet. Waldo couldn't be sure, but if he had to guess, he was saying that either Borovik came clean about the money or they'd stick his feet in that oven.

Whatever.

From the sound of it, they'd be busy for a while. He had time to look around. He checked out the top of Kulik's desk. Nothing interesting there. He wondered about the broken golf club, but he didn't dwell on it. His mind was more on that safe. Gorgeous thing. But seriously low tech. What the hell, he decided. He'd give it a shot.

It took him six minutes. But for the shrieking down below, making the tumblers hard to hear, he could have had it in five. He opened the heavy door and sat back to look over the contents.

He saw a little bag of white powder, which he presumed to be happy dust. He ignored it. His eye was drawn to the canvas bags. More bank bags like the one over Borovik's head. Three were filled. Several more lay flat and empty. The next thing he noticed was the hats. Scottish tams. Two of them. They seemed identical to the one Kulik had worn into the restaurant. He wondered, idly, who keeps hats in a safe, but he did not dwell on that either.

On the shelf with the hats there were several folders, a number of documents, and what looked like a set of charts. He had no idea what they were, but if they were kept in a safe, they had to be important. He wondered if he should take them. Tomorrow, even tonight, they might be missed. On the other hand, if this stuff is anything good and the shit, meanwhile, hits the fan, it might be gone by the time they come back. Waldo thought of the bedroom. He was tempted to run back up for a pillowcase. The hell with it.

Waldo stripped off his coat and spread it in front of the

safe. He took all the folders, all the charts, and piled them on top of it. He went to Kulik's desk and opened a file drawer. He pulled a handful of files from the back. Waldo didn't know what these contained either, only that they were likely to be less interesting than those in the safe. He put them where the others had been. The arrangement was by no means identical but, perhaps, close enough for any casual inspection.

He opened one of the canvas bags. It was filled with German marks. Large denominations. A second bag was split between dollars and pounds. A third held Swiss francs, and, way in the back, he found a small leather pouch that felt like it was filled with gemstones. Waldo didn't bother to open it. He pocketed the pouch and then dumped the contents of all three bank bags onto his coat. He folded it and tied the sleeves across, making a bundle. Next, he took the now-empty bags and, with them, walked along the bookcases stuffing them with the thinnest volumes he could find. So filled, he returned the bags to the safe in approximately their original positions. He closed the door and spun the combination.

Like Lechmann says, a bird in the hand. Speaking of which . . .

He turned the key of the minibar, opening it. He hated these things. They all had toy ice trays that made cubes the size of teeth and they never had Guinness. This one didn't either, but it had some other good stuff, most of it foreign except for some chilled vodka and several tins of caviar. He saw a half-empty bottle of tequila. It seemed out of place because otherwise there were two bottles of single malt Scotch, eight bottles of Scottish beer, a box of Highland Shortbreads, and a slab of Scottish salmon. This guy's got a definite thing for Scotland, thought Waldo. Waldo took two cold beers from the back and shoved them into his bundle.

One minute later he was outside the house, back at the far side retrieving his weapon. He could still hear shrieks coming up through the coal chute. He almost felt pity until he thought about Elena. And Leo. And that kid, Valentin, who tried to protect them.

Two minutes after that, he was two streets away. On one of Zhukovka's main arteries. Sitting in a hedge, sipping one of the beers, waiting for Lechmann to make his next pass. Getting there was a little bit dicey because the sun was almost up and here's this bum walking through Zhukovka with his pants on inside out, a bundle of swag under one arm, and a laser-scoped Heckler & Koch in the other. But no one saw.

He used the time to decide how he would tell Lechmann about his next idea.

Lechmann, he knew, will shit when he hears it.

But not for long. Only until he finds out he's rich.

68

Kaplan almost felt sorry for Clew.

They're no sooner airborne than Clew began briefing him on the way to handle Bannerman. He trusts you, Irwin. He'll listen to you. Make him understand what's at stake here. Make sure he sees the big picture.

Wonderful.

The big picture, of course, has to do with the missing party funds. What's at stake here is nothing less than the economic viability of the former Soviet Union. It goes under and we have massive bread riots. Revolution. Anarchy. The hard-liners come back and it's the end of the democratic experiment. Except now we see ultranationalism. Ethnic hatred. Former republics nuking each other. It spreads. Before you know it we have instant global warming.

"So, Paul . . . now you understand, right? Except for this, Roger would have told you about Aldo Corsini."

"Sure, Irwin. The big picture. Now it's all clear."

This was fucking ridiculous.

"Roger . . . Bannerman's friends have been hit. He's going to hit back. It's as simple as that."

"Not if you do your job, Irwin."

"Roger . . . get some sleep."

The trouble with people in State, guys like Roger, most diplomats, is that after a while they don't know their own bullshit from substance anymore.

The substance is that they really do want to find that money. There's a presidential directive to that effect. Work with the Russians. Track it. Seize it if it's in our jurisdiction. But this is the same Washington, lest we forget, that couldn't even track the savings-and-loan money.

Still, let's say they do find some of it. They'll give it back, but they'll also find a way to make political hay out of it. Maybe, as even Fuller admits, the President will then cut American aid by a like amount and look like a hero for doing it. Or he leaves the aid in place if Russia agrees to sell off its resources to corporate America at bargain-basement rates. Who knows? In politics it's nothing for nothing. Just don't tell me, and certainly not Bannerman, that we're working for world peace here.

Anyway, most of that money is long gone and the Russians have Gorbachev to thank for it. Only a month before that coup attempt he signed a decree authorizing private investment of Communist-party funds. The top guys all knew that the old system was ending. The party was discredited, members quitting by the millions. But Gorbachev, sincerely or otherwise, still believed that the party could reform itself and was, in any case, the only bureaucracy they had. But the party, he said, might have to cool it for a while. Hide the money just in case.

Gotcha, boss.

We'll hide it so deep even you won't find it. If there's one thing we learned from the capitalists, it's how not to leave a paper trail. Meanwhile, one financial magazine estimates that there are now 15,000 millionaires in the former Soviet Union, less than 600 of whom made their fortunes legally.

Clew does try to sleep but not for long.

Five times in the first two hours, he goes to the cockpit to take a call on the scrambler. The calls are all from Fuller, usually with the Moscow embassy on the other line. For the most part, they were updates. Another bombing, another shooting. By the last call, Clew is a dishrag. To hear Fuller tell it, half of Moscow was in flames.

The first call, a half hour into their flight, was a confirmation that the three dead shooters were Moscow thugs—a gang called the Chicago Brigade—rumored to have ties to the KGB, specifically to this General Borovik again. Lesko killed one of them. Bare hands. The others were shot to death by persons unknown.

Persons unknown were having a busy night. By the second call, they had attacked, in force, a meat-packing plant that this Chicago Brigade is known to use as a base. Several dead. All known gang members. Several other hangouts, apartments, garages have been attacked in rapid succession. This might be a reprisal for the restaurant ambush, but it's more likely the work of a rival gang seizing the chance to finish them off. Clew wants to believe the latter, because if it's not a rival gang, it has to be Bannerman's people.

This, he decides, is impossible. Bannerman was stuck on a plane, denied any contact with the ground. Even with access to a phone there was no way he could get agents in Moscow that quickly. Unless they were there already. As bodyguards. Those first two persons unknown just might have been bodyguards, but if so, why did they hit and run?

The next call, someone has shot up KGB headquarters. No real damage except to KGB pride. It had the look of a message. An act of defiance. This one leaves him speechless. No way, he says, would a criminal gang pull a stunt like that. It wouldn't be worth the heat. Anyway, witnesses say the shots came from a police car. Kaplan offered no opinion.

Then comes the worst call. Fuller also reads him a fax. It's from Anton Zivic to somebody—person unknown again—who is already in Moscow. This fax says Bannerman's on his way. It also says that Bannerman has a whole fucking army in Moscow and it gives them a two-name hit list. One is the name Grassi gave. The other is this Borovik who Fuller mentioned.

Clew almost chokes on this one. He can't figure out how Zivic could have set it up. Five teams plus team leaders sounds like at least a dozen operatives. From where? Recruited locally? He especially can't figure how Zivic knows all he knows.

"I told him."

"You *what*?"

"I gave him those names. Sue me."

"Do you realize what you've done?"

"I told Willem Brugg, too."

Clew is apoplectic but he gets a grip on himself. Now he knows why Brugg sprang Bannerman. He wants to know what Zivic said and whether he seemed to know any of this already. But nothing for nothing. First Clew has to say who this Borovik is, and no bullshit.

No bullshit is against Clew's nature, but he does open up. He can't help it, because he doesn't know how much Zivic filled in already. He says Borovik is a major player in this smuggling thing. He says there's also a personal thing between Borovik and Bannerman. It goes back eight or nine years to when Clew was still running Bannerman. He tells the story.

Now . . . if Bannerman is scary *before* you get this mental picture of him hacking some guy's head off, this makes you want to pull a gun on the pilot and tell him to turn this sucker around. Clew also tells about John Waldo torching KGB headquarters in Leningrad. Partway through, his mouth goes slack. This is because it dawns on him that shooting up Moscow Center sounds a lot like torching Leningrad Center.

This leads to the realization that Waldo must be in Moscow. Zivic had to send the fax to someone, right? Wait a second . . .

"Roger . . . How did Fuller get that fax?"

"I don't know. Intercepted it, I guess."

"Then they have a number. They know where it was sent."

He shook his head. "He said they couldn't track it."

Kaplan did not pursue the subject. He had an idea, however, that if Fuller got his hands on a fax from Zivic, Zivic wanted him to have it. Besides, who ever heard of communicating with a field agent by fax?

Okay, why would Zivic do that? Part bluff, maybe. It's a warning that says don't fuck with Bannerman when he lands, because we have a dozen people there who are going to make it very costly if you do.

But why does he name the two targets? Doesn't that warn them off? Kaplan could think of two possible answers. One, it's another bluff, to make Fuller think he knows more than he does. Two, they were already dead by the time he got that fax.

Then comes the most recent call to Roger. The one he's taking now. He's shaking his head again. Big sigh. He hands the headset to the flight engineer and comes shuffling back like it's the last mile.

Borovik, he says, has been kidnapped from his home. Two guards got shot. Not critically. They could talk. They claim they tried to stop it. Two men driving a Chaika plus a backup shooter covering them. Conflicting reports from other witnesses. They say the guards are full of shit about trying to stop it and they're even lying about the kidnappers' car, which happened to be a Zil.

It gets worse, says Clew. Remember Zivic's fax? Guess what. Now CNN has a copy. No, not from Zivic. They say some Russian walked in off the street a half hour ago and sold it to them. Yes, he's reliable, and yes, they know it's genuine. He was on hand when the fax came in and he was also an eyewitness to the restaurant shooting. The witness says it was another guy, one Arkadi Kulik, who set up the hit and he claims to know why. He has further information about Kulik and Borovik, but he wants big bucks for it. CNN-Moscow is awaiting approval from Atlanta. Meanwhile, they got a description out of him of the two who picked up the fax after he copied it. Two women, late thirties, tall and slender, both brunettes, British accents.

Clew gets hung up on this last part. Doesn't sound like anyone he knows, or that Bannerman has ever used. Besides, Bannerman likes to mix nationalities. Must be disinformation. The informant is protecting his sources.

Maybe, come to think of it, the whole thing is disinformation. Including Zivic's fax.

"Roger . . ."

"Give me a second. I need to think."

"No. Don't think. If you do, you might make a decision. Guaranteed, it will be the wrong decision."

Clew held his temper. "Irwin . . . If you don't have anything constructive to offer . . ."

"You want constructive? Constructive would be instead of trying to stop Bannerman from screwing up your grand strategy, you should have gone to him in the first place."

"And said what? Go find the party treasury for us?"

"No, not for starters. For starters, you'd say, 'I know I've been an asshole but would you do me a favor for old times' sake?' You'd say, 'We've got about a thousand intelligence agents, lawyers, and accountants trying to trace all this money. So far, we're having about the same luck we had trying to find the Marcos money and the Duvalier money but now, suddenly, we think we have two solid leads to maybe a chunk of it.' "

"Corsini and Grassi? They're small-fry, Irwin."

"But if you did that, Carla Benedict might not be dead and Bannerman wouldn't be blaming us, me included, for not leveling about Corsini."

Clew looked away. "No one could have foreseen . . ."

"See that? That's my point. You didn't have to foresee. All you had to do was level. Whatever Bannerman thinks of you, his first concern would have been Carla. He'd want to know everything about Corsini, which would have taken him about two hours."

"You're overestimating him. He called me about Corsini, remember?"

"And by then it was too late. You should have called him. If you were straight with him, he would have called Grassi just like I did. Grassi leveled up to a point, but can you see him trying to bullshit Bannerman?"

"Grassi would have tried to . . ."

He didn't finish. Even Clew, Kaplan realized, did not believe what he was starting to say. True, Grassi might have tried to tap-dance. But Bannerman would have laid those dead gray eyes on him and said, "If this touches me . . . or mine . . ."

Grassi would have given up his mother.

Roger had drifted off. He awoke to see Kaplan removing the headset, emerging from the cockpit, a strange expression on his face.

"Where are we?" he asked.

"Over the Baltic, coming up on Riga. Touchdown's in about forty minutes. Fuller says the Brugg plane's about an hour behind us."

"That was Fuller? Why didn't you wake me?"

"I called him."

Clew rubbed his eyes. "Ah . . . are you going to tell me why?"

Kaplan nodded. "This is out of control, Roger. It's no good holding Bannerman. If we give him some room, maybe he can contain it."

Clew made a face. "Yeah, well . . . the Russians might have something to say about that, Irwin."

"Maybe it's in their interest. If they're straight, maybe they even come out ahead."

"Irwin . . . what did you say to Fuller?"

"That I'm with Bannerman. This once, this one time, I'm with Bannerman."

69

It was full daylight before Lesko left the hospital.

The army doctor, Meltzer, had given him five minutes to dress. That was before he had his clothing brought in and Meltzer saw its condition. Pockets were torn, one sleeve was ripped loose at the shoulder, all of it was stained with blood. Elena's, Valentin's, a little of his own. His Bally shoes had vanished during the night.

He sat with Elena until a change of clothing could be brought to him. It took three hours. Some problem finding his luggage. He didn't care. Nor did anyone come to arrest him. Nor was he surprised. Meltzer, the embassy, they weren't interested in protecting him. They wanted him out of circulation.

He spoke to Elena constantly. His voice, if she could hear it, would be all that was familiar to her here. All that could comfort and encourage her.

He told her about Meltzer, that they'd probably sent a doctor rather than an embassy official because he was less likely to throw a doctor out the window, especially one that had kept her alive until her cousin and this new surgeon could get there. Supposed to be the top guy. Fix you up in no time.

He told her all that he knew of what else was happening. Which wasn't much. That subject exhausted, he told her that he'd been learning German. That it was to be a surprise. For a while, he spoke to her in German, even counting to a hundred, until he exhausted his knowledge of that language as well.

He told her that he had other surprises for her. That he was studying to become a hairdresser. And that he was studying interpretive dance. And that while she was sleeping he had a tattoo artist come in and tattoo his face across her chest because he knew she'd really like that but was probably too shy to say so.

Nothing.

No reaction. Just that one finger.

"David?"

"She can hear you."

"How do you know?"

"I just do. She can hear you."

They brought the clothing, most of it, and most of his toiletries. He took a quick shower, shaved under it, and dressed in a dark suit and tie that Elena had picked out for him in Zurich. She said he looked like a banker in it. Or a handsome diplomat. What he looked like, he knew, was a bouncer in a better class of gin mill, but . . . eye of the beholder. He returned to her bed, asked her how he looked. She told him he should comb his hair. She said a hairdresser

should be his own best advertisement. She said this in his
mind. It wasn't her, really. But it was what she would have
said. If she could.

They drove him to the embassy in the Lincoln. Two
guards in front, himself and Doctor Meltzer in the rear. On
his lap, he held a paper bag containing Elena's personal
effects. Her purse, her rings, her other jewelry. The amber
necklace was there. He pulled it out and found the piece
with that little insect in it. He remembered how it had
pleased her. Tears started to well up again. He had to put it
away.

To the right of the Lincoln was the Moscow River. Lesko
was gazing across it, staring into the distance, mostly so that
Meltzer couldn't see his face.

"Your friends have had a busy night," the doctor said
dryly.

Lesko stirred. "What?"

"Over there." He pointed. "That smoke."

Lesko hadn't even noticed. But now he saw. Thick black
smoke way off in the distance. A fire out of control. Two
fires. Maybe three.

"I'm supposed to know who set those?"

"You'd tell me, of course, if you did."

Lesko shrugged. "What else happened?"

The doctor told him. Drive-by shootings, other fires,
someone trying to shoot a few KGB generals through their
office windows. In his mind, for some reason, he pictured
John Waldo. His mind added the flower truck. It was
careening through Moscow, back doors wide open, Waldo
in the back throwing Molotov cocktails at every building
whose design offended him.

But he didn't believe it. No one man, or two, did all that.
Besides, if Waldo was going to torch anything, it would
probably be that building up ahead.

Lesko gestured with his chin. "What's that place?"

"The big building? That's the Hotel Ukraine. The embassy is just this side of the river from it."

Lesko nodded without comment. But he remembered
what Waldo had said about it. The Ukraine. It was one of
five brown kitschy buildings just like it, same style, scattered around Moscow. Stalin wedding cakes, they call

them. Huge and ugly. The hammer and sickle on every
spire, every flat surface, every cornice. And you wouldn't
believe, Waldo told him, what they tore down to put up that
pile of shit.

Yeah, thought Lesko. That's where Waldo would have
started.

The traffic was getting busy. More people on foot,
carrying briefcases, empty shopping bags. Monday morning. Back-to-work day.

Along the riverbank, this side, some of them were setting
up sidewalk shops. Cardboard boxes, mostly, with a piece of
plywood on top. Stuff they were selling looked like junk. Used
clothing. Books, pictures, odd pieces of furniture. Even empty
bottles. Anything to pick up a few extra rubles. The pathetic
sight saddened Lesko, but he kept his mind on it because it
helped keep him from thinking about Elena. That she still
might die. And if she did, where she goes, he goes. About two
minutes behind. Unless he has some names first.

The Lincoln turned left onto Kalinin and again onto
Tchaikovsky Street. Lesko could see the embassy flag.
Main gate with Marine guards. But first an outer gate with
Russian guards. More people setting up sidewalk displays.

"Pitiful, isn't it?" said the army doctor. "It's like
America during the Depression. But worse. Much worse."

Lesko stiffened. "Flowers," he said.

The driver glanced back at him.

"Right there," Lesko pointed. "Selling flowers. I want
to buy some for my wife."

"Um . . . I can arrange that from inside, if you like.
You can have them sent over."

"No, those. They're her favorites. I want to buy them
myself."

The driver looked back again, this time at the doctor.
Meltzer shrugged and nodded. The driver pulled to the curb.
Lesko rolled down his window and called out to the two
men who were selling them.

The taller of the two seemed startled. He moved, tenta-
tively, in the direction of the car, but the second man
stopped him. He raised a finger toward Lesko, indicating
that he should wait. He then reached into the large cardboard box and selected a bouquet that was wrapped in green

paper. This he placed across the taller man's arms. He piled two more on top of it and took still another, which he carried himself.

The taller man approached Lesko. The shorter one approached the driver, who was waving him off. He came forward nonetheless. With his thumb, he pinched a carnation from its stem for the driver and another for the second guard.

"For lapel," he said in English. "Makes you look . . . what is word? Spiffy. Ladies go crazy for you."

The driver, amused, took one and passed the other.

"Look what else," said the flower seller. "Not only carnations."

The driver turned. He looked into the bouquet the smaller man was holding. He went rigid. The other guard froze as well.

Lesko didn't have to look. He could see the *what else* in the bouquet that the man on his side was holding. It was the barrel and foresight assembly of what had to be an automatic weapon. Meltzer took a breath and held it. For a long moment, no one moved or spoke.

Lesko, shaking his head, leaned forward. He reached under the jackets of the two civilian guards and relieved them of their pistols. He patted both men down, found one pair of handcuffs and a canister of Mace. These he dropped into the open paper bag and sat back. Meltzer had still not exhaled.

"You're a pisser, you know that?" he said to John Waldo.

70

Bannerman stood in the cockpit, braced, as the Brugg Industries plane made its final approach and landing. He needed to see what was waiting for them.

He spotted Clew's plane from a quarter mile out. Air Force markings. A fighter-bomber from the look of it, modified to carry passengers. Probably one of those command planes designed to stay aloft during a nuclear emergency. Such an aircraft landing at Vnukovo II was still a considerable novelty. Several figures, standing near it, were taking photographs. Others were posing with the American plane as background. Souvenir snapshots. Bannerman had expected . . . he didn't know . . . a somewhat higher level of excitement.

Closer to the terminal he saw two black Lincoln sedans, one of them a stretch. Behind them, two other sedans, probably KGB Chaikas. Knots of men talking. He could not pick Roger out, but he saw one bald head that might well have been Kaplan's.

Otherwise, not much activity. No troop trucks. No armored car at the far end of their runway, there to make sure he doesn't jump out and make a run for the trees when this thing stops.

He had no such intention. Nor did he have much of a plan. If he was going to be detained, so be it. He could threaten them, of course, but if they decided to call his bluff, he would be obliged to make good on those threats somewhere down the line. Nobody wants that.

It had crossed his mind to borrow some whites and try to slip in with the medical staff. As a group they had emergency clearance. But his face, unlike Miriam's and Avram's, was too well known. Someone would spot him and then the whole group would be held up and scrutinized, possibly at Elena's peril.

All he could really do was try to seem in control of virtually anything that happens. Actually *having* a measure of control would, of course, be better. But he had none. That's the minus, he thought. The plus is that Roger won't believe it.

Very soon now he would know how Waldo and Lechmann chose to keep themselves busy last night. Show no surprise. Sit tight until Waldo finds a way to make contact. Waldo is likely to spot Miriam, get word to him through her. Miriam and Avram can also free him if it comes to that. All he need do is nod in their direction at the hospital. Roger would not dare keep him from seeing Elena.

And failing that, Carla will be floating around as long as neither Clew nor Kaplan spot her under that wig. She'll be loose with Yuri. Yuri might or might not introduce her to whoever these friends of his are. They might or might not help. The authorities might or might not agree to deliver everyone who had a hand in that shooting or in trying to kill Carla.

If not, the real initiative will start tonight. Whether he's free or not, it won't matter. By tonight, that dozen or so ghosts will be real. Five teams, at least. Anton will have seen to that. To the five teams, add any number of free-lancers because Willem Brugg has posted 100,000 Swiss francs each on Vadim Borovik and Viktor Podolsk. On the chance that Waldo is right—that someone named Arkadi Kulik might have been responsible—Willem is ready to post another 100,000 on him plus 25,000 each on the other five who were at his table.

Bannerman returned to his seat and strapped in. He reminded Susan to fasten her belt. She did not respond.

She had become progressively more withdrawn since her talk with Carla. And, a short while ago, she had flared up at the Swiss surgeon. He had been dismissive and more than a little patronizing when she had questioned him about Elena's condition. Willem Brugg had to separate them. The surgeon did not help matters by asking that, in future, if "the girls want to chat" they should use the lavatory. He's luckier than he knows that Carla didn't hear him.

"Susan . . ." He traced his fingers over her hand. "I know that I haven't been very attentive."

She took a breath. "Would you have said that to Carla?"

Uh-oh.

"I'm not so fragile, Bannerman."

He had meant to fasten her belt for her. Now he was afraid to. But the engines changed pitch and she did it herself.

"Susan . . . John Waldo has been in Moscow for a week. That's why I told you there was no need to send anyone. I didn't lie, exactly. He was already here."

Silence.

"I'm telling you in case you should see him swinging a mop at the hospital, for example, or in a Russian army uniform. So you don't forget yourself and call out his name."

Oh boy, thought Bannerman. He would not have said that to Carla either.

"Ah . . . I could have put that in a better way."

Susan said nothing. She chewed her lip.

"Come on. I'm being a twerp again. Let me have it."

She shook her head. "I've dumped on you enough this trip. You didn't deserve it. I know you've got a lot on your mind."

"I guess we all have."

He meant nothing by that remark. But it seemed to make her stiffen. She turned her face from him. He thought of putting his arm around her. But Molly had once told him, if you have to think about it, it's too late. He reached for her hand instead. She pulled it away.

"I can deal with this, Paul," she told him.

"I know you can."

"No, you don't. I'm a little wired. I'm not myself. But I can deal with this."

"Um . . . Susan."

"One question first. Okay?"

"Anything."

"They say that when you . . . hit back . . . you hit at random. That's not strictly true, is it?"

"I . . . don't shoot up airports and schoolyards if that's what you're asking."

"But when you go after someone, he's done *some*thing.

It's just that you don't worry a whole lot about degree of guilt. The way my father would, for instance.''

"Your father won't. Not this time.''

"But . . . you, though. All you have to say is go kill this one or that one. And they'll do it.''

"Susan . . .''

"No, no. I can deal with this.''

"Susan?'' He took her hand. He lowered his voice. "You're pregnant, aren't you?''

She ignored the question. "I want to be in on this, Paul,'' she said. "I want to be part of it.''

"Your part is to control your father because you're the only one who can. Susan, *are* you going to have a child?''

A hesitation. A choosing of words. "A godchild. Elena asked me.''

"I'm sure she did. But . . .''

At this, at "I'm sure she did,'' there was a flash of Susan's eyes. As before, it meant nothing. Just something you say. But it drew a searching look. First at him and then at Carla, who was leaning across seats, looking down at the Moscow suburbs. Anger now. Carla must have felt it. She turned. Their eyes met. Carla, barely perceptibly, shook her head. Denial. Her eyes moved to his. They, too, flashed at him. A question. An accusation. Another threat.

And Bannerman knew.

Endometriosis. Elena's age. Risky pregnancy. Last chance. Godmother. Bannerman knew. He didn't want to, but he knew.''

He feigned annoyance; tried misdirection.

"Don't look at Carla. If I'm going to be a father, it's between you and me.''

Her face softened. A hint of relief. Another message, Susan to Carla. It's okay. All clear, I think.

"Susan? Am I?''

"That's one of the things I'm deciding,'' she told him.

71

Captain Levin was at home.

He had been told to go back there, stay there, speak to no one.

For three hours they had questioned him.

You were relieved, Captain, last night at eleven. What did you do after that? And after that? And then what?

I did my job. There was a gang war last night—or didn't you notice?

Never mind that now. Did you talk to the Americans who came from the embassy? We know that you did. What did you tell them? Did you talk to reporters? What did CNN pay you?

The American thug. This Lesko. Why did you not arrest him? He had a pistol and he used it. Even without it, he murdered two men that we know of and yet you let him go off to the hospital, unguarded, and you took your time making a report. Except to the Americans.

Alexei. That's not a Jewish name. Why isn't your name Yehudi or Abie? Better yet Moses because it's his law that you follow. God knows, you don't follow Russian law.

Nor, of course, did they.

He found out later that although they had no right, they had impounded the militia car that he used. They were seen vacuuming it out. They impounded his logbook, his notebook, and the files from his desk. They did tests on his hands to see if he had fired a gun. What did they think? That it was he who fired from that flower van?

It was four in the morning when he found out what they were really looking for. Some maniac had shot up #2 Lubyanka. From a blue Volga like the militia uses. What policeman would be so contemptuous? they asked. You don't have to look very far. Ask the Jew, Levin, who seems to have been everywhere tonight. He's the insolent bastard

who called from GUM and told us to come pick up our
garbage.

His telephone rang. He ignored it. They would certainly
be listening and he was too tired to watch his words. His
wife was off to work, his children off to school. All he
wanted to do was sleep until they got home. Then, after
supper, he and his wife would finally have that conversation
that he'd been avoiding. Is this what we want for our
children? Will they ever feel like citizens in their own
country? Is there any hope here for any of us?

The ringing stopped, then started again. It seemed louder
than before. It might be his wife. He knew that she was
worried about him. He picked up and said his name.

"Alexei. Are you dressed?"

His sergeant. "I'm just going to bed."

"Not yet, you're not. Be outside in five minutes. I have
a surprise."

"Boris . . ." It was not the sergeant's name, but he
would get the idea. "I've been suspended."

"I know. And fuck them. You hear me, you guys? Fuck
you."

Levin winced. "Boris, go home. Go sleep it off."

"Fuck them because you're a hero, Alexei. You were
right all the time. The canisters. They were right where you
said we would find them and don't give me any modesty.
Downstairs in five minutes."

The sergeant slammed the phone down before he could
speak.

Levin stood for a moment, blinking stupidly. Canisters? I
was right? About what? What canisters?

He hung up on his end and walked to the basin where he
splashed cold water on his face. He tried to think.

Since midnight, he knew, his sergeant had been busy.
Running from one shooting to another, one bombing to
another. Revenge attacks by what's left of the Lubertsy
Brigade on what's left of the Chicago Brigade. Other
brigades, other mafias, moving in to pick at the carcass. A
feeding frenzy. Stealing the Kerensky trucks. Looting the
Kerensky warehouses and . . .

Warehouses.

The sergeant must have found something in one of the

warehouses. Wants him to get the credit for it. But what is packed in canisters? Sausage meat would have him so excited? Tea?

Levin reached for his coat.

In five minutes, now four, he would find out how he became such a hero.

72

The Brugg Industries plane had barely touched down when two trucks came racing across the tarmac.

They were military trucks, but they were behaving strangely. As the aircraft taxied toward the terminal they followed behind, weaving, almost playfully, the way dogs run to welcome their master.

One pulled ahead and Bannerman saw the reason. Soldiers were driving, but in the rear, under the canvas, he saw only white coats. Doctors, technicians, hospital orderlies. Several were waving, grinning. They seemed greatly excited.

When the cargo bay opened a few minutes later, some scrambled aboard and others formed lines to start passing the boxes. Susan among them, pitching in.

One doctor, a woman, was beside herself. She darted from crate to crate, carton to carton, touching them, gently, as if they were living things.

Two uniformed customs officials arrived. Shouting angrily, pushing the woman aside, they told all the white coats to stay back. Get away from the cargo. Go wait in the terminal. The woman turned on them, her finger pointing, fire in her eyes. "Don't dare," she seemed to be saying. "Put your hands on this, you thieves, and I'll break your necks."

Bannerman watched this exchange from the main cabin door. It had been retracted; the ramp was in place. He saw

Yuri down below, Carla with him. Yuri beckoned to the soldiers who had come with the trucks. A brief huddle, they nodded knowingly, then each put a hand against the chest of a customs official. "You heard her," they must have been saying. "Find something else to steal."

One official tried bluster. Outraged authority or outraged innocence. He demanded the names of the soldiers. But all this time, the eyes of the other man caressed certain of the cartons. Those eyes removed all doubt. One soldier drew his sidearm and aimed it at the crotch of the senior official. He became jelly. Both men turned on their heels.

The woman doctor was a schoolgirl again. She began asking questions, one after another, her voice rising each time. Bannerman saw Avram pick up the manifest. He was nodding his head, saying *"Da"* to every question she asked. His finger was no more than halfway down the manifest before Bannerman saw that the doctor was weeping. Another was hugging her. Still another was doing a dance. Of the rest, some were crying, the others beaming.

"I brought more than they asked for," said Willem Brugg, who was watching at Bannerman's side. "I told them that if Elena lives, they can keep all of it. I will leave it in any event. That hospital has nothing."

So Bannerman had gathered.

There were cartons of painkilling drugs, antibiotics, even whole blood packed in coolers. It was treasure. Priceless. Those who were crying, he imagined, were thinking of patients, perhaps relatives, whose suffering could now be relieved. As for the army trucks, Willem had been told to expect them, he said. One of the doctors had a son who was a colonel. Without reliable guards, he told Bannerman, half of the shipment would disappear inside the terminal. What remained would be hijacked before it reached the hospital.

"I will go with the first truck," he said. "You might as well try to come with me. If they stop you, you're no worse off."

Bannerman didn't answer at first. He was watching Yuri and Carla. They were walking toward the terminal building some sixty yards away. Yuri kept himself between Carla and the small knot of Americans, to his right, who had

separated from their Russian counterparts and were now
approaching the plane.

Among them, though not in the lead, was Roger Clew.
Hands in his pockets, shoulders hunched. It struck Bannerman that he had a defeated look about him. In contrast, there
was Irwin Kaplan. Kaplan had been born with a defeated
look, which only a fool took at face value, but now he was
the one with the confident bounce to his step. It was good to
see Kaplan.

"Take Susan," he said, "but I'll stay. I've got to reach an
understanding with this bunch. Better now than later."

A third black Chaika, not seen until now, appeared
rounding the terminal off to Bannerman's left. It was
moving slowly and it seemed to be headed toward Yuri.
Yuri saw it. He nudged Carla. They kept walking.

More movement to Bannerman's right. The door of the
first Lincoln opened abruptly. A man stepped out, a radiophone in his hand. He was calling, urgently, after the
Americans. They stopped. Clew and Kaplan turned and
walked toward him.

Bannerman was more concerned about the Chaika. It
came to a stop between Yuri and the terminal doors. A rear
window was rolling down. Carla reached with her right
hand under Yuri's jacket at the small of his back. Must be
a gun there. But Yuri took her arm, restraining it.

"Mr. Brugg," the flight engineer called from the cockpit.
"I've picked up that call if you're interested."

Willem glanced at him. The engineer was holding a
headset, gesturing toward the Lincoln with the open door.
He had been playing with his dials, monitoring what he
could. Willem thanked him. He raised the headset to his ear,
but he, too, kept his eyes on the Chaika.

The rear door had swung open. A man was climbing out.
Not a young man. Yuri seemed to know him. He stepped
forward to take his arm. The man straightened his fur hat
and then, as if he had forgotten himself, tipped it politely to
Carla. He glanced over toward the Americans and, as if an
afterthought, turned so that his back was to them, and raised
the collar of his raincoat. Now he was speaking to Carla.
Carla knew no Russian—perhaps fifty words—as Yuri was

evidently explaining. A look of surprise came over the old man's face. A look of anger over Carla's.

"I think Yuri just blew her cover," said Bannerman. "I'd better get her back here."

"Binoculars," Willem said to his engineer. He kept the headset at one ear. The binoculars came. He raised them just as Yuri and the older man embraced. Carla had softened. The man separated himself from Yuri. He offered her his hand. She took it. Carla almost curtsied.

"It's Leo's uncle," said Willem Brugg, surprise in his voice. "I'm sure of it. That man is Nikolai Belkin."

"You know him?" Bannerman had never heard the name mentioned.

"From the photograph, yes. In Leo's flat. There had been an . . . estrangement of some years and yet Leo kept his photograph. It was always on Leo's piano."

The man was reaching back into the Chaika. He returned with several files and began showing them to Yuri, his manner grave but animated. Yuri's fingers rose to his temples as if what he was hearing was too much to grasp. He spread his arms, a gesture of helplessness. Now he cocked his head toward the plane while reaching a hand for the files. He wanted to bring them . . . show them. The older man was clearly hesitant but, at more urging from Yuri, he relented.

Yuri was backing away from him. Motioning for him to wait and for Carla to stay with him. Yuri turned toward the airplane and ran toward it, head down, at a trot.

Willem, with his headset, grunted. "We have another problem," he said.

"First this one, Willem. Tell me about this one."

"Nikolai Belkin . . ." said Willem, groping. "He is . . . was . . . a great man, I think. An Academician twice over . . . many honors. Became a dissident . . . but fell back into line. Leo said he should have stood up to them. Was ashamed. He said his uncle could have been as revered as Sakharov if he only had more backbone."

Yuri climbed the stairway three steps at a time.

"This man who just came," he said breathlessly, reaching Bannerman. "He is—"

"I know who he is. What's happening?"

"He said it's finished. He said we can do nothing."

"Yuri . . . *what* is finished?"

"He knows everything. He says all you have done is drive them underground. The names you have . . . all of them . . . are probably dead already. Sacrificed. He hopes you have not killed Major Podolsk. He says Major Podolsk is ours, not theirs. Two years' work, two years trying to penetrate, it's all for nothing."

"Um . . . slow down, please. What's in those files?"

He fanned them. "Borovik . . . Kulik . . . a man named Sostkov. All thrown out of KGB. Borovik goes crazy because of you. General Belkin goes crazy because Arkadi Kulik murdered his father to marry his mother and then learns he's here in Moscow after this Sostkov ordered a BMW for himself. Everything is shambles."

Bannerman grasped about a tenth of this.

"Yuri, is Academician Belkin one of those you're working with? Those I wouldn't understand?"

The Russian grimaced. "Was grief talking. Not me."

"Forget that. Will he talk to me now?"

"Too many eyes and ears." He gestured toward the two embassy Lincolns. "But it is to see you that he came. He asks that you come to his car."

"If you're going," said Willem Brugg, "go now while they're distracted."

Bannerman glanced toward the Lincolns. At the one with the open door, an argument had started. It was Irwin Kaplan, angered about something, berating Roger Clew. The other Americans had turned. They were walking back.

"What's that about? Did you hear?"

"It's our other problem. Lesko was freed at gunpoint. He's now armed, has an embassy car, and he has help."

73

"You remember Ernie Lechmann, right?"

"The wedding. Sure." Lesko reached for the Austrian's free hand and shook it, but his eyes were on the rear window. Meltzer and his muscle were a block behind them. They'd been let out in a factory area about a mile from the embassy.

The two civilians turned out to be CIA. They were out in the street, handcuffed together, frantic, looking for a car to flag down. Good luck. Even Meltzer was shaking his head at them.

"Listen." Lesko settled back. "Don't think I'm not glad to see you guys . . ."

"Here. Take a Beretta." Waldo had been checking the mechanism of both pistols. He handed one to Lesko together with the clip from the pistol he'd rejected. Lesko hesitated, but he took it.

"Ah . . . how about a few answers, John."

Waldo took a breath. "Last night? Yeah, it was us. And yeah, we could have been quicker."

"Bannerman sent you? He saw this coming?"

"Second part is no. First part is more or less. We're tourists, mostly."

A snort from Lechmann.

"Who else is here?"

"We're not sure. But we think just us."

"All that shit last night and the fires? That was just you two?"

"Some of it. We don't know who else."

Lesko rechecked the Beretta. "How illegal is this?"

Waldo jerked a thumb toward the street behind them. "It's more illegal for those two. They're not supposed to carry outside the embassy compound. It's why they had Mace, so guns could be a last resort. You want the Mace?"

Lesko waved it off. The day he needed Mace . . .

"Look," he said. "The more I think of it, if they won't let me stay with Elena, I'd just as soon stick around the embassy in case there's word on her."

He saw Lechmann's eyes in the rearview mirror. Lechmann was nodding agreement.

"How is she doing?" asked the Austrian.

"Skull fracture. Coma. But she's stable."

"Belkin?"

"Touch and go. I saw him. He doesn't look good."

"How about yourself?" Waldo asked. "You holding together?"

Lesko started to nod, but shook it off. "Not that well," he admitted.

"There's some Swiss doctors coming. Willem Brugg, Bannerman, and I think Susan. You heard that?"

"A whole mob, yeah. The Meltzer guy told me."

Waldo checked his watch. "They were due in by now. Figure another two hours before the doctors can get in and go to work. We thought you'd rather be with friends. Anyway, we might know a better way to pass the time."

"How?" Lesko closed one eye. "In a hot Lincoln with embassy plates? I don't want to tell you guys your business, but . . ."

"Relax. We got a better car stashed. You're gonna feel right at home."

Lesko saw the smirk. "I'm supposed to guess? A cop car, right?"

"Bingo."

Lesko could only sigh.

"Yeah, but . . ." Waldo's smirk faded. "That brings up something else. We gotta talk about where your head is. Like, do you still feel like a cop or do you just want the shit bag who shot your wife?"

Lesko stared. His mouth went dry. "You found him?"

"We gotta know, Lesko."

"You did find him. You found Kulik."

Waldo showed his palms. Go slow. "If we did, you gotta be clear on something. There's this house out in the suburbs. Once we go in, we don't read any rights, we don't sort them out. If they're there, they're dead."

Lesko blinked. "Who's *they*? That whole table?"

"Four of them. For starters."

"Who else?"

"Ah . . . the car is just ahead," said Lechmann, discomfort in his voice. "Also a metro station. If you want my advice, Mr. Lesko, you'll take the metro. Elena will need you."

Lesko chewed his lip. "Who else, John?"

A sigh. "I'm gonna say it again, Ray." He spoke slowly, almost gently. "If a neighbor stops in to use the phone, he's dead. If we find a Tupperware party going on, they're dead. You start trying to pick out who's who, then *I'm* dead. Who *else* can't be the issue."

Lesko's eyes dropped to the Beretta. The Lincoln slowed.

"You must decide," Lechmann told him.

Lesko nodded. "I'll take the table," he said. "Anyone else is yours."

74

"Murphy's Law, Mr. Bannerman."

The Academician sorted through the files that Yuri had returned to him. He was shuffling them, sifting through them, as if looking for a place to start. He had the glazed look of a man who was overwhelmed by events. "Murphy's Law applies nowhere else the way it applies in my country."

Leo's uncle had greeted him correctly but coolly. He showed considerably more warmth toward Carla. It was clear that Yuri had told him about her. The editing must have been substantial.

When Carla climbed into the Chaika, however, taking the right front seat, she startled the driver with a Russian endearment and an affectionate embrace. He understood the reason for it only when she backed away and he saw his pistol in her right hand, being cocked with the left. Yuri, mortified, insisted that she give it back at once. The older man patted his knee. Never mind, he told Yuri. She is everything you said she is. If Georgi's gun puts her mind at ease, perhaps it will calm Mama's Boy as well.

Yuri caught his eye. His expression seemed to say, *"You see? This is a great man."*

Bannerman grumbled inwardly. He was anxious to be done with this and do something about getting into Moscow. He watched as Leo's uncle picked through his files once again and extracted four photographs. He laid them out atop his briefcase. The four men wore KGB dress uniforms. Bannerman recognized Borovik at once. A few pounds heavier. Hair was dark. Probably dyed. Mean eyes. The Academician identified the others as Arkadi Kulik, Victor Podolsk, and Oleg Sostkov. Then he covered their faces with his hands.

"There are good men in the KGB, Mr. Bannerman. Are you able to believe that?"

"Yes, sir. I know that."

"My nephew is one. Yuri, here, is another."

"Yes sir. But could we please . . ." He gestured toward the photographs.

"Stop me if I go too fast," said Nikolai Belkin coldly. He seemed unaccustomed to being prodded.

Bannerman listened.

In a stream of nearly flawless English, Nikolai Belkin took him through the maze in which all of their lives had recently connected. The Academician was not KGB, he said. But, a few years back, he had found himself adopted as a sort of moral authority by certain elements within the KGB. These were men, he said, who had been struggling to redefine themselves. "If you know my nephew, and understand him, I hope that perhaps you get my meaning."

Bannerman sighed inwardly, feeling Yuri's eyes on him.

"They know, Mr. Bannerman, that their country is being systematically looted. They are also aware that if the KGB is not stopping it, the KGB must therefore be part of it. Need I explain KGB? That its strength has been, and continues to be, a monopoly on all information?"

"Ah . . . no sir. I know that."

"This is not like the West, Mr. Bannerman, where information is readily available. The KGB controlled everything, infiltrated everything. They do not stop a habit of seventy years just because some politician tells them they're disbanded."

He was doing it anyway.

"But let's move on."

Thank you.

"What our men have chosen to do, in effect, is to infiltrate the infiltrators. This brings us to Major Podolsk. For two years now, he's been working to win General Borovik's confidence, trying to find out who is next up the ladder. As of only last night, I think we know. At the next rung up, and possibly much higher, is Arkadi Kulik."

Bannerman listened closely. As he did, he was forming an opinion of Leo's uncle. He was a decent man, to be sure. A teacher. A philosopher. Liked to talk about the good in people. Bannerman wondered how he'd lived this long.

He caught Carla's eye. He saw the beginnings of disappointment there. And an assessment not unlike his own.

Bannerman asked about Leo. Why had he come to Moscow? Why had he brought Elena?

These questions brought a dizzying flood of new names and images. At first, the answers did not seem responsive. There was Leo Belkin's father. Leo's mother. Arkadi Kulik, again, who destroyed them both. Leo finding out. Hounding Kulik out of the KGB. But that was not enough for him. Leo wanted to kill him. Kulik, however, had vanished.

Forget him, his uncle had insisted. No personal vendettas. Don't you think I know how you feel? The man Kulik murdered was my brother-in-law. It was my sister whose bed he desecrated for all those years. But we have bigger fish to fry. We have a nation to rebuild.

Leo could not accept this. They quarreled. There was bitterness. Leo went back to Bern, but he kept pestering his uncle with reports that Kulik was seen in this or that city, that he'd gone to America, even that he was dead. But never that he was living in Moscow.

When he first made the offer of this wedding trip, therefore, he had no thought of searching for Arkadi Kulik. The Academician was now convinced of it.

"Um . . . what makes you so sure?" Carla asked, before Bannerman could.

"Murphy's Law, Ms. Benedict." He tapped a finger against the tight-lipped mouth of Captain Oleg Sostkov.

"Sostkov, it seemed, had ordered a new BMW to be shipped from Germany. One week ago—and I learned of this only this morning—my nephew received a routine request from Yasenevo. It merely asked how an unemployed KGB captain can afford such a car. Leo was to determine how it was paid for, in what currency, how the funds were transferred. A file on Sostkov accompanied the request.

"The first thing Leo saw was that Sostkov had been a junior officer on Kulik's staff. The whole staff got its walking papers when Kulik did. The address BMW had for him was a dacha in Zhukovka, which should have been even more beyond Sostkov's means than the BMW. No, it's not in Kulik's name either, but, to make a long story short, he lives there. Someone at Yasenevo told Leo. This person had been asked not to, but he did.

"This same person told him that Arkadi Kulik made a habit of dining Sunday nights at Kropotkinskaya 36. You see what happens, Mr. Bannerman, when people become impatient and lose sight of their goals. You see what happens when men let their emotions get the better of them."

Bannerman turned to Yuri. "Did you know about this?"

The young Russian shook his head miserably. "Not this. No."

"But you knew that he came here for a reason."

Yuri grimaced. "The offer of a wedding trip was sincere, Mr. Bannerman. It was only . . . he came to realize that such a visit would cause discomfort, rub some noses."

"Then why didn't he cancel it?"

"He tried. Elena said she would come regardless."

Exasperated, Bannerman took a breath. "These noses. Was one of them Borovik's?"

"He knew nothing of Borovik. Nothing of Podolsk. Nor did I until last night."

Bannerman looked at Leo's uncle. "But you did? And you said nothing?"

The old man drew himself up.

"Mr. Bannerman . . . I've read about your visit to Leningrad some years ago. Has it occurred to you that the shooting might have been an act of vengeance and that those close to you, not my nephew, might have been the real target?"

"Ah . . . what difference would that make?"

"It would clarify motive, certainly. A case of chickens coming home to roost, perhaps. And you wouldn't be looking for someone else to blame."

Yuri winced. Carla's eyes had become hooded. They met his. They were saying, *"Screw this. Let's go do something."*

Bannerman glanced back toward the plane. The first truck was loaded, its tarp secured. White coats were climbing into the second.

"Let me summarize," he said to the Academician. "Leo confronted Kulik. An hour later he was shot. Either Kulik or Borovik ordered the shooting, and I'll tell you that I don't care which. All you want of me is that no harm comes to Major Podolsk. Is that why we're talking?"

The old man's expression turned grim. "If your *death squads* haven't killed him already, yes."

Another slap. Bannerman held his temper.

"Don't you know? I would think you'd have people protecting him."

A hesitation. "He was to stay home, wait at his apartment. He is not there. Do your people have him or don't they?"

"I have no idea."

"Last night, Mr. Bannerman, General Borovik was dragged from his home. Did your people do that?"

"I'll know when I talk to them."

"If they didn't, then Kulik did. If so, it means that Borovik must have acted on his own and Kulik is trying to keep himself removed from it. He's too late, you know. Murphy's Law. Half of Moscow knows what happened inside that restaurant."

"There go the trucks." Carla flicked a finger. "And there goes Roger after them."

Bannerman turned. Roger Clew was trying to wave down

the trucks. The soldiers ignored him. One threw him a finger. They roared off. Clew ran back to Kaplan, who was making calming gestures. Bannerman could almost hear Kaplan's words. Forget it, he'd be saying. You think Bannerman's sealed up in a crate? He's back in Brugg's plane waiting for us to chase after those trucks.

Clew yelled for an embassy car all the same. It pulled out, three men in it, drove up to him. He seemed indecisive. Kaplan folded his arms. At last, Clew told the driver to follow the trucks. Kaplan began walking toward the plane. Clew threw up his hands and followed him.

"Carla . . ." Bannerman turned to look at her. "I want you to stay with Yuri. Yuri? If Mr. Belkin here approves, you might want to go to Major Podolsk's apartment and wait there. Lesko is running around loose. If he's with who I think he's with, he has Podolsk's name by now and he won't stop to wonder what side he's on. Carla?" He held her gaze again. "Do this for me, please. I'm going to see if I can get a ride with those two."

He stepped from the car and started toward the plane, counting backward from ten, waiting for the sound of a second door slamming. He heard it at *eight*. The next sound would be the angry click of Carla's heels.

"Hey, Bannerman," he heard her hiss. "What the fuck is this?"

He placed his hands on her shoulders and turned her so that she faced away from the plane. He leaned over, his lips close to her ear.

"Tell me what you thought of Leo's uncle," he said quietly.

A touch of sadness. "I know. He's a turkey."

"Is he a leader?"

"Like you, you mean?"

"Like anyone."

A tentative shrug. "He's . . . more of a chaplain. He thinks he's Jesus but at least he's honest."

"He's righteous, Carla. That's not the same as honest."

She twisted her neck to look up at him. "And maybe you're just pissed because he doesn't buy your act."

"He thinks I'm ruthless. What does that tell you?"

"That he isn't. I know."

"Would you follow that man?"

Silence.

"Well?"

She shook her head. "I can see why Yuri buys into him. It could feel good for a while. But no."

"It's Yuri that I'm worried about. He gets near that old man and his mind stops working."

"I know."

"Don't misunderstand me. Leo's uncle is a man determined that nothing should be done in the old ways. If he wants to take the high road, I think that's admirable, but he doesn't belong in this line of work. Predict his future, Carla."

She squirmed.

"Okay. Then tell me why he's still alive."

She took a breath, then nodded. "They know he's harmless. A two-year penetration just to get one name. I'd have had it in two minutes."

"He had it all the time, Carla. He just never made the connection because he was too busy proving that he could rise above private emotions. But not all his disciples feel that way."

"One of them dropped a dime. I know."

"So if this high-road business is beginning to wear thin, I don't want to see Yuri backing the wrong horse."

"I'll stick with him. He stuck with me."

Bannerman gave her a squeeze. "Thank you."

"What are you going to do?"

"Try to catch up with my death squads."

"How come Clew and Kaplan? I mean, I can see Kaplan, but . . ."

"Yuri didn't think I'd understand Leo's uncle. I'm afraid I do. But I definitely understand Roger. More to the point, Roger understands me."

75

Viktor Podolsk was blindfolded.

He himself had wrapped the red necktie twice around his head and tied the knot. The man who came for him, the man now driving the Zil, then sealed it off with adhesive tape.

"Borovik is finished," he had whispered through the door of Podolsk's apartment off Tishinsky. "Bad for him. Good for you. They want to see you, Viktor Vasilyevich."

Podolsk, a Makarov in his hand, had stood to one side of the door. With a rolled-up newspaper, he reached to block the light from his peephole to see if a bullet smashed through where his face seemed to be.

"You see?" said the voice. "Nothing in my hands, nothing under my coat. In my shirt, however, there is this."

Podolsk wouldn't look. But a second later he heard the man getting down on his knees. Fifty-dollar bills, American, began to appear under his door. Ten at a time. The voice counted them off. He stopped at five thousand.

"Next comes my *spravka*," said the voice. "It's a little out of date, but it's me."

Podolsk picked up the blue-covered KGB pass and opened it. Oleg Sostkov was the name. Captain, Special Inspectorate. The pass had expired. A little out of date was almost three years already.

He recognized the face. Very stiff. Cold and unsmiling. He had seen this man much more recently. He'd seen him wandering around Moscow Center from time to time, most often down in the basement cafeteria where the worst of the cells used to be. Drinking Pepsi. Chewing the fat. The older hands all seemed to know him. Some were cordial, most gave him the cold shoulder, but this sort of mixed reception was not uncommon when former officers stopped by to visit. Podolsk, however, had paid him no mind because this man had showed no interest in Borovik, nor had Borovik so much as looked at him. But for the past few months, to hear him tell it now, he was practically Borovik's control.

Podolsk, finally, had let him in, but he kept the Makarov in his hand. The face startled him. Still unsmiling, both eyes had been blackened and his nose was swollen and held in place by tape. The eyes, however, seemed full of good humor.

When a smile did come, he would raise a hand to cover it. His face, Podolsk realized, had an unfortunate musculature by which a simple smile looked more like a sneer. It was not an asset. Sostkov clearly knew that. Podolsk gestured questioningly toward the more recent facial damage but Sostkov waved it aside. He repeated what he'd said from the corridor. For Viktor Podolsk, this was to be a day of days. It was Podolsk's impression that great good fortune had recently visited Sostkov as well.

Even later, however, in the Zil, after agreeing to be blindfolded, he kept his pistol. It was small comfort by then, of course, but Sostkov said, "Keep it, if it makes you happy, until I say we're almost there. By that time, if you don't know I could have killed you ten times over, you're a hopeless case."

"It's the biggest day of your life," he kept saying. "All you have to do is make a good impression. Already this man wants to like you because I have personally vouched for you."

In the time that he was blindfolded—it was only thirty minutes—Sostkov coached him on how to behave, what to say. His advice was simple. "Be yourself, be truthful, don't tell him what you think he wants to hear. He knows you hated Borovik. Believe me, that will stand in your favor."

The Zil made many turns. But always, in the end, Podolsk would feel the morning sun on the back of his neck. They were headed due west. Out into the suburbs. Sostkov asked for the gun. Podolsk held it out to him.

At last, the Zil stopped. Two short beeps of the horn. Sostkov's window rolling down. Podolsk could smell lilacs. "Give me a minute with him first," said Sostkov. He climbed out of the Zil.

Podolsk listened. At first, he heard only birds and Sostkov's footsteps. Sostkov stopped, not far from the car.

New footsteps were approaching. And now a quiet voice, not Sostkov's, asking questions.

It was not the voice Podolsk was listening for. No singsong voice from deep in the chest which the Academician had seemed to recognize. This one was flat, a bit nasal, and had a minor impediment. He was pronouncing Podolsk as "Podowsk."

Sostkov was telling him how he, Podolsk, had reacted when Sostkov went to fetch him. "He was ready for anything," he said. "He thought he would be blamed for what Borovik had done. When he saw it, last night on Vremya and more this morning, he thought he would have a heart attack."

"What have you told him about Borovik?" came the voice.

"Only that he's finished. And that we have him on ice."

This last brought a chuckle from the other man. Podolsk had no idea why it was funny.

The voice cleared his throat. "There's not much else to laugh about today," he said. "This comes none too soon. Have you heard they found the canisters?"

A gasp from Sostkov. "No. I have not."

"Fucking Borovik, again. His fucking Chicago Brigade. The canisters were stored in one of their meat lockers. The Lubertsys shot their way in, took all the meat they could carry, and set fire to the building. This morning, people were coming in off the street, through the flames, to get what was left. The militia saw some of them carrying the canisters and stopped them because they look like artillery shells. By that time, it was just as well. They would have taken them home, smashed them open, and that would have been the end of Moscow."

Podolsk tried not to breathe.

"Already it's on television," continued the voice. "Yasenevo blaming the Security Ministry, the ministry blaming the army, the mayor saying I told you so, and a militia captain taking bows for finding them."

Sostkov started to speak, but it seemed that the man hushed him. His voice dropped to a whisper. Podolsk heard the word "window." He had noticed, it seemed to Podolsk, that the window of the Zil was partially open. Podolsk did his best to seem oblivious. He pretended to be occupied with a strip of tape that was stuck to his hair.

But his mind was racing. "Canisters . . . The end of Moscow." These words put him in mind of a rumor that he'd heard, officially denied, of a tragedy out in the Urals. And of another, also denied, about enriched uranium that was missing. Through all of this he tried to listen. It was no use. They were still speaking in soft murmurs although not about him. He heard Borovik's name. Lots about Borovik. Another name. Sounded like "Kulik."

Kulik.

Podolsk seemed to know that name. Yes. There was a Kulik, years ago, who came to KGB Higher School. Gave talks on party discipline. The need for vigilance. Encouraged the best young officers to apply for a Special Inspectorate posting, which nobody in his right mind would . . .

Of course. Special Inspectorate. Sostkov's *spravka*. In his mind, Podolsk could hear that lecturer now. Singsong. It had to be. It was the voice from Borovik's green telephone.

The door of the Zil opened, startling him. Then another. Men climbing in.

"Relax, Viktor Vasilyevich." Sostkov speaking. "A few questions. First, do you think you're ready for Borovik's job? You would be reporting to me."

"Reporting to you?" Podolsk was confused. "Yes," he answered. "Yes, indeed."

Sostkov saw the confusion, misunderstood it. "I don't mean in KGB. You would have to resign. You are willing?"

"I will do what is needed. But there is a condition. I will not run the Chicago Brigade. That's if there's anything left of them. Using those clowns was nothing but disaster."

Silence. Then a grunt from the front seat. It had the sound of approval.

"Major Podowsk . . ." The voice came from the same direction. "Have you ever killed a man?"

"Yes."

"Under what circumstances?"

"An . . . associate was cheating me. I had been fair with him. Even generous. He cheated me all the same."

"You sent someone? Or you did it yourself."

"I shot him. Face to face. To send someone would have been cowardly. Also, I wanted him to know why."

"So. You are the hot-blooded type, Major."

Podolsk shook his head. "It was necessary. I took no pleasure in it."

He could feel Sostkov, on his left, nodding vigorously. He seemed to like that answer. Never mind that it was all invention.

"Who was this man? Where did it happen?" asked the voice in front.

Podolsk feigned reluctance but he gave the particulars. The name was not an invention. The event was part of his cover legend. A man, shot during a robbery attempt, the case investigated but never solved. Podolsk could have told him what the man was wearing when he died, the names of his wife and children, even that of his mistress. But the voice asked him none of that.

"There is another necessity," he said. "Like you, we take no pleasure in it."

"Our hope," said the other, "is that you, with Sostkov here, will see to it for us."

Borovik, he realized. They want me to kill him. Maybe not so difficult. He nodded gravely.

"His house is not far from here. His name is Kulik. Arkadi Kulik."

Podolsk sputtered. "May I know why?" he managed.

"Sostkov will explain. You have an appointment with this man in twenty minutes."

The heavy door clicked open. The front seat creaked, one foot touched the pavement. The man hesitated.

"See to this, Major," he said. "Do this well, and the next time we meet there will be no need for a blindfold."

76

"Let's take a walk." Kaplan touched Bannerman's arm.

"I'd rather ride. Can you get me out of this airport?"

"Five minutes," Kaplan said firmly. "Just you and me."

This exchange came when Roger finally lost his grip. It was the news about the sausage machine that pushed him over the edge.

He was doing fine, Kaplan thought, up through the *We-never-lied-to-you* part and the *We-feel-as-bad-as-you-do-about-Carla* part. He was well into the *All-we're-trying-to-do-is-help-this-country-out-of-the-shithouse* part—the missing billions and all—when a flash comes in to the Lincoln that the three who were taken with Lesko have been found unharmed but Lesko is still at large.

Bannerman, to whom this should have been news, barely reacts. He checks his watch, resets it to Moscow time. To Roger, this can only mean that Bannerman knew in advance that Lesko would be sprung. The time check was to see if it was done on schedule. Bannerman doesn't bother to answer. He wants to hear the rest of it.

Clew has trouble getting back into his script because a new and more urgent flash comes in about a stash of stolen nerve gas that was found at this burning packing plant this morning.

Now Clew's sure of it. It was Bannerman's people, not some rival gang, who hit that place last night. He wants to know how long Bannerman knew about the nerve gas, and why, by the way, did he just have a meeting in a KGB Chaika?

You've been working with them right along on this, haven't you? No? Then why were they talking to you? They aren't supposed to go near you.

This last remark gets Bannerman's interest but mostly he has this dreamy look on his face like he's seen this movie

before. The phone from the embassy chirps again. The
driver calls Clew over. Clew says take a message. The
driver who is more than a driver says he'd better hear this.

It's another report on that packing plant. In a bucket next
to a sausage grinder they have found human remains. It
looked like someone had been taking the machine apart,
cleaning it out, got interrupted. Anyway, in this bucket,
someone spots a flap of skin with an ear on it. They dump
the bucket over and the ear slides across the floor. They see
that it's attached to the whole top inch or so of a man's head.
Black hair. They think it might be this kidnapped KGB
general because of such and such a tie-in he's supposed to
have had with this gang, this Chicago Brigade, who oper-
ated out of this packing plant.

Clew has no more doubts. It's clear to him now. Bannerman's people got Borovik. In fact, Bannerman's people did
everything. That includes shooting up Moscow Center just
so no one will suspect that the KGB has been in this with
them right along.

It was right about here that a private talk seemed like a
good idea.

"The guy they turned into meat loaf," Kaplan asked. "Was
that Borovik?"

"I don't know. I doubt it."

"What about Lesko? Any idea where he'd go?"

Bannerman didn't answer. He stooped to pluck a dandelion that was growing from a crack in the concrete. Rising,
he scanned the terminal area and the main gate. It was made
of double chain-link fence and topped with razor wire, but
it was wide open. Two guards at the gate. Neither seemed
especially alert. And they were facing out, not in.

He heard an automobile engine starting up, then a second.
It was those other two KGB Chaikas. They were turning and
heading for the gate. Bannerman watched them go. No one
else seemed to have more than a passing interest in four
Americans, two of them wandering around what is certainly
a restricted area, one of them a man who'd had a KGB price
on his head for the better part of fifteen years.

He glanced back at the Lincoln. Clew was leaning against

the front fender, arms crossed, one hand covering his mouth. He had that defeated look again.

"For the record," said Kaplan, "Clew was trying to be straight with you. But you see what happens. It's like his body rejects it."

A dismissive wave. "Irwin . . ."

"Why am I here, right?"

"No. But now that you bring it up . . ."

"I'm here because the President asked me, which should tell you how much shit you stirred up. I'm here because they think you trust me. Long-term, they think you're going to trust me so much that I'm the one guy in Washington you might be willing to work with. This is one reason why Roger is sulking, by the way, but they can shove that right up their asses."

"Could we . . . back up just a little bit, Irwin?"

"Just so you know I'm not a total schmuck."

Bannerman raised his hands. "Irwin . . . we're in a high-security airport that has no security. You've made some kind of deal here. What is it?"

"I didn't. Fuller did."

"Fuller then. With whom."

"With everyone. With fucking Russia. The past hour he's been on the horn with three different ministers. The bottom line is you're untouchable until half past five this evening. If you're not back here by then, in the plane that got me here, he doesn't know you."

Bannerman stared, uncomprehending.

"Here's how you spend your day. One, you're never out of my sight. Two, at ten o'clock—that's in thirty minutes—you flash the abort signal, the one from Zivic's fax. This means no more real estate gets torched and no more random sniping, but you may, and this is a quote, 'Put the Kropotkinskaya matter to rest if you can do it within that time frame.' Otherwise, you spend the rest of the day rounding up your five teams. They get safe passage same as you or they get out on the horse they rode in on. You hear what they're saying, right?"

"I . . . guess I'm slow. Spell it out, please."

"They don't need this, Bannerman. They want it over."

"Then why don't they—"

"Will you throw away that flower? You look stupid."

Bannerman closed his fist over the dandelion.

"Why don't they what? Lock everyone up? Have a trial in a couple of years? Meantime, they have to worry about every damaged personality who wants to make points with Mama's Boy plus Willem Brugg killing every deal they want to make with Europe."

"Irwin . . . whose idea was this?"

"I told you. Fuller's."

Bannerman shook his head. "Barton Fuller did not go on record plotting retributive murder with three Kremlin ministers."

A grimace. "Okay. Fuller did the broad strokes. I did the details."

Bannerman waited.

"I radioed Fuller. I told him this time around, just this once, I'm with you. He could back me or not."

Bannerman closed one eye. "I get it now. You're a KGB agent in an Irwin Kaplan mask."

"See that? Who says you're not a funny guy? Listen, Bannerman, I like Leo Belkin and he could die. I liked Carla, mostly, and she's dead. Ray Lesko is as good a friend as I've ever had and I'm a little bit in love with Elena. Not to mention that I taught Susan how to ride her first two-wheeler. She ever tell you that?"

"No."

"I want whoever did this."

"Irwin . . ."

"Fuck you, Bannerman." Kaplan gestured toward the Lincoln. "Say no and you ride in the trunk. I promised I could handle you and I will."

Bannerman groaned within himself. He tried to remember the last time he felt in control. It was probably on the Swissair flight when they asked if he wanted beef or fish.

"Weapons?" he asked.

"I got one from the driver. The Russians will give you some room but they're damned if they're going to equip you. The driver's a spook, by the way. He's supposed to be good and he's mine until sundown."

"What about Roger?"

"Roger's State. He can't be in this. He goes to the hospital in case Lesko shows up."

Bannerman was still doubtful.

"What you got here," Kaplan said wearily, "is an eight-hour window. All you have to do is agree. No matter who else lives or dies, this ends at half past five. If your people did get Borovik, maybe it's over already. As for this other guy, Kulik, my impression is they hope you make him go away."

"You didn't wonder why?"

"Who gives a shit. Yes or no, Bannerman."

He drew a breath. "You're an interesting man, Irwin." He turned back toward the Lincoln. "I have an address where Lesko might have gone. If your driver can find it, we'll start there. After that, we'll see how the morning goes."

"Uh-uh. First the abort. The deal was you call in your dogs."

"My five teams?"

"Plus whoever you snuck in with the doctors."

"We'll . . . talk about that as we drive, Irwin."

77

Waldo put his nose to the coal chute. His sense of smell had known better days, but he was pretty sure about this one. Human flesh. Burned.

Still, with the crap these people eat, he thought, it might have been lousy breakfast sausage. He turned his head and listened for other sounds that would go with cooking. He heard nothing. No shuffling of feet, no clink of utensils coming from the basement kitchen. There were lights on, though. He could have done without the lights.

He also wasn't happy that the Zil was gone. No telling who was out and who was in. He would have to take it slow.

That would not be a problem except it was coming up on ten o'clock. Zivic said knock off at ten. That, anyway, is what he and Lechmann decided it meant.

There wouldn't be any abort signal. What it was, Zivic was giving someone a deadline. Bannerman would strike a deal and then wave a hanky or some damned thing, pretending that it meant something.

Whatever. So we play Beat the Clock. The Zil shows, Lechmann will hit a couple of bleats on his siren.

He was fairly sure that the house had no servants. None living there, at least. A laundry truck had come and gone. Bundles of sheets had been left outside. An old woman pulling a wagon brought some bread and milk. A man in a bathrobe took them from her at the door. It was one of those Bobbsey Twins who were at the restaurant with Kulik. They both looked like Oscar Homolka. Shit. Half of Russia looks like Oscar Homolka. Those two must be living here, he decided.

A bad moment came when the old woman left with her wagon. She pulled it out past the gate posts, then turned and came back, walking in the direction of the open gate. Waldo held his breath. It looked as if one of the Oscars had asked her to close it behind her. That was all they'd need, because waiting behind that gate was Lesko. Waldo could guess what would go through her mind. Godzilla, here, must be the fugitive rapist everyone's talking about. With luck, her heart would stop before she could scream. But it was okay. All she wanted was to cop some free flowers. She checked out the front windows, snatched a handful of delphiniums, then scurried back to her wagon.

Waldo stripped off his coat, reversed it again, and eased himself into the chute, elbows out to support his weight. He could take his weapon now because he knew how far he'd drop. He would not need his arms to slow himself. With his free hand he reached for the wooden cover and positioned it to fall into place when released. He drew in his elbows and slid.

He saw the lump that had been Borovik. But he ignored it. He swept the kitchen with his MP5, looking for movement, listening for sounds. There was nothing, only some routine noise from upstairs. He turned toward the body.

It had been strapped to a board with antenna wire and
hoisted up across the big stone sink. Waldo recognized the
clothing and the flabby waist, but that was where it ended.
The hands, cuffed to a pipe last night, were now cuffed
behind him. Both feet were badly burned. More than
burned, they were charred. Toes curled into claws. That end
of the board was burned as well. It wasn't breakfast he
smelled through that chute.

In front of the cast-iron stove he saw cold ashes and soot
scattered all over the floor. Oven door still open, still warm.
Board or not, the guy must have bucked like a horse when
they shoved his feet in there.

Most interesting, his head was gone.

They had cut it off at shoulder level, taking the whole
neck with it. Two knives and a cleaver in the sink. One knife
was bent. Arterial spray on the wall behind it. Lots of it.
Guy was alive when they did it. From the cuts, it looked like
they worked from front to back, figuring out how as they
went along. Even dead, a neck's not that easy to cut through.

Roasting the guy's feet he could see. Last night, when he
heard them doing this, it wasn't just for fun. Between
screams they were asking him questions, so there must have
been a point. It follows, therefore, that there's a point to
cutting off his head. Right? I mean, it doesn't just run in the
family.

Blame Bannerman. Is that the idea? They say . . .
Every time he comes to Russia someone named Borovik
gets his head cut off and a KGB headquarters gets redeco-
rated?

Waldo had no time for this. Clock's ticking and Lesko
shouldn't be left out there too long. He'll start thinking
about Elena and he won't be paying attention.

Okay. Five minutes. Get upstairs, same way, see who's
here, get to the French doors, let Lesko in. We whack them
and go home.

Maybe ask where that head is first.

He could do this, Podolsk told himself as they drove.

He could shoot Arkadi Kulik. He could and he must.

It helped him to remember the Academician's words.
Arkadi Kulik will need you, he said. He will need you until
he doesn't. And then he will kill you.

To know this is true, Podolsk realized, one need only look at Sostkov. Until last night, even early this morning, Sostkov thought he was the apple of Arkadi Kulik's eye. And then he learned the truth.

There had been three of them, Sostkov said, waiting for him outside the Zhukovka gatehouse. They told him everything. Once you bring him Podolsk, they said, Kulik will not need you anymore. He wants you dead. He has been waiting for this moment.

Sostkov had not believed them at first. But they played him a tape and there it was. Kulik's voice, no mistake, telling them that Oleg Sostkov had become a liability. Could no longer be relied upon. Time for him to go.

They told him the real reason. They told him, he said, of all the others who had been at the scene of a certain accident. He had thought they were in Europe running companies, living in villas, enjoying their money. But they were dead. All of them. They died because they knew where the bodies were buried. Only Sostkov had been spared because he was needed. That need had now passed.

Podolsk was quite sure that he knew what this "accident" was. And that knowing where the bodies were buried was not a figure of speech. But Sostkov made it clear that he was not to ask.

"You can't imagine how depressed I was, Podolsk. I'll admit to you that I could have cried. And you know what they did? They embraced me. First the one you met, then both of the others in turn. Not since I was a child has another man embraced me."

"And you . . . knew then that they were your friends."

But Sostkov didn't hear the doubt behind those words. He didn't want to. They told him, he said, that they are not all like Kulik. Yes, they want to be rich, he said. They did not deny that. Yes, they want the power of wealth because without it they cannot rebuild their country. The money from a certain shipment, now lost to them, could have built hospitals, new roads, new technical schools.

This, they told Sostkov, is the kind of men we are. If we get rich it's because we make lots of our people rich. Kulik, however, cares only for Kulik. It is Kulik who has become the liability.

Why? A hundred reasons, said one of them. He is too ambitious. Too full of himself. He had boasted once too often that he put these men and others where they are and he could bring them down just as easily. Next he'll think he makes the sun come up.

There are also practical reasons, said another one. They had to do with that business last night. Trying to protect himself, Kulik made phone calls he should not have made. Trying to deflect attention from himself, he accomplished just the opposite. Never mind whether that shooting was his fault or not. Who will believe that he was innocent of it? Will General Belkin's friends at Yasenevo? Will the Bruggs? Will Mama's Boy, who was, even now, said to be on his way to Moscow?

"But the first man, the one I took you to see, Podolsk, said forget all that. The big reason for him, personally, was that he could no longer stand by and see the devotion of men like Oleg Sostkov answered with betrayal. That's what he said, Podolsk. Men like me. He meant you, too."

Podolsk forced a smile to show that he was gratified.

Sostkov slowed the Zil and prepared to turn right. Just ahead, Podolsk saw a road sign for the suburb of Zhukovka.

"Wait until you see this house," said Sostkov, brightening. "It once belonged to a count. His paintings and furniture are still in it."

Podolsk blinked. With all this, we're going to talk about a house?

"Tolstoi himself stayed there once. For an entire summer. He was hiding out from the czar's police. In the study where we will talk, he wrote 'I Cannot Be Silent.' Very famous essay. It's true. Kulik has documents and there is even a photograph of Tolstoi working in the garden. The front of the house is behind him, plain to see."

"That is . . . very exciting."

Sostkov shook a jubilant fist. "You know what's exciting? Can you guess why I'm talking like this? That house is going to be mine, Viktor. As soon as things cool down, it's my new address. And you can come visit as often as you want. That's when you're not cruising on the Mediterranean or shopping in Rome."

This kind of talk both comforted and troubled Podolsk.

Comfort, in that Sostkov's pleasure was so genuine. He, Podolsk, was not being led into a trap. At least not by Sostkov. But two things about it troubled him. Is this the way a man talks when he is on his way to kill another? Podolsk's stomach was filled with boiling stones. His bowels felt loose. It seemed to him that Sostkov should be thinking less about what those faceless men had promised him and more about the business at hand.

And now the other thing. If Kulik had become a liability, why was this not true of Sostkov? Was he not at Kropotkinskaya 36? Will the police not want to talk to him as well?

"You know, I envy you." Sostkov's mood had turned serious again. "The more I think of it, I wish they gave me Kulik to me and left the others to you."

"Others?"

"Kulik's toadies. Don't worry. Those two will be easy."

The hot stones began tumbling again. Now it's three? They are going to murder three men?

Academician Belkin would never permit this. Not three, and probably not even the one. Just get names, collect facts, he would say. There is a right way and a wrong way to do things. There are plenty of cowboys we could have used, Viktor, but I chose you because you know how to use your mind. Remember your Agatha Christie. Think how Hercule Poirot would behave and you can't go too far wrong.

Very well. What would Poirot do? Would he pass up the chance to not only get in solid with Sostkov here but also with the man who is at the top? A man who will show his face only after I prove myself?

"Kulik will want to talk to you alone," said Sostkov. "Or maybe with the other two, but me he'll ask to wait outside. Take your time. See what he has to say."

Podolsk swallowed.

"It won't be an easy interview. He wants to see what you're made of. But then, if he likes you, he will suddenly become your favorite uncle. He'll probably give you a nice present as a taste of what's to come. If it comes from his desk, that's one thing. But if he goes to his safe for it, that is when you pull out your pistol. Once he opens that safe, don't let him close it. There are things inside, documents, especially a certain videotape, which I have to bring back to our friend.''

"At what point do I . . . ah . . ."

"When you're ready, your pistol's out, give me a yell. I want to see the bastard's face.''

Sostkov gestured with his chin.

"There it is," he said, elbowing Podolsk. "My future home.''

"It's . . . quite handsome.''

"See there? Those French doors? It's where Tolstoi planted his tomatoes. He made his own shoes as well. Did you know that?''

"Shoes? No.''

"When it's mine, I think I'll plant roses.''

Lesko wasn't cut out for this.

He wasn't built for stealth.

You could be talking to Waldo and suddenly he's gone. Just as suddenly, he's standing next to you again. His feet never touch the floor. By contrast, every step Lesko took sounded like *ga-loomp*.

Waldo had waved him in from the first French door. You're clear. Come on. Clear, my ass, thought Lesko. I'm supposed to cross sixty feet of front yard and garden, some of which is crunchy gravel, passing under about twenty windows, broad daylight, gun in my hand, and hope nobody's looking out?

But he did it. He lowered his head and did it. *Ga-loomp, ga-loomp, ga-loomp*. He's halfway there when Lechmann's siren goes off. Lesko thought it was the alarm system. Visions of searchlights and Dobermans. But he realized it was Lechmann. Keep going. *Ga-loomp*. Waldo held the door for him so he wouldn't go through it closed.

"I don't want to be critical . . ." whispered Waldo.

"Will you give me a break?" Lesko covered his heart to silence it.

"I mean, I didn't expect Nijinsky, but I didn't expect you to stop and say 'Fuck' when you heard that siren either.''

Lesko showed his teeth. But he offered no rejoinder because it dawned on him that they were standing in a room that anyone could walk into at any moment. He pointed the Beretta at one door while he watched the other.

"Relax," said Waldo quietly. "It's a dining room. Nobody walks through dining rooms."

"Who says?"

"Just don't knock over a chair."

No one walks through dining rooms, he muttered to himself. There's one to file away. But again, he didn't argue. Waldo knew this house. He knew the traffic patterns.

"Who's here? You get a count?"

Waldo knew what he was asking. "No Tupperware party. Just Kulik and the two goons. They're across the hall but we wait."

Lesko felt his adrenaline pumping.

"Here's the Zil," said Waldo. "Don't move."

But Lesko did. He turned toward the French door. Waldo hissed at him. He froze. Two men in the front seat were looking right at him. It seemed, almost, that they were talking about him. The Zil passed from sight.

Waldo gestured toward the corridor door. He eased toward it, bidding Lesko to follow. "Guy driving," he said, "he's from last night. The other one's new to me."

"Not to me. He's the KGB guy from the hotel. What'll you bet he's Borovik?"

Waldo shook his head. "I'll show you Borovik. Later, though."

"Okay, that other name. Podolsk? Maybe that's Podolsk."

Waldo shrugged. He put a finger to his lips. "I gotta listen now," he said, almost mouthing his words. "But if those two come in the front, and they ask who's in the dining room, we move. They come in, they *don't* ask, we wait till everyone's settled."

Lesko nodded. He moved his spare clip to his belt where he could reach it quickly. Waldo could still hear his heart.

"You okay about this?" he asked.

"Yeah."

Yeah, he was.

The fifth guy, Podolsk or whoever, wasn't here for Tupperware either. He's in on this. He's part of Elena being hurt. And if he isn't, fuck him anyway.

• • •

Where the Minsk Road forks off to Zhukovka, there is a
sentry booth. It stands at the edge of a thick pine forest that
did not grow there naturally. It was planted so that the
dachas could not be seen.

Two cars, one of them a Zil, had gone past it, barely
pausing, but the guard in the booth waved the Lincoln to a
stop.

He was an older man, probably a pensioner. He wore the
remnants of an army uniform. He stood in pointed contrast
to the polished border guards who once kept all but the party
elite from entering. His job, all the same, was to discourage
casual visitors.

Bannerman sat back as the embassy driver—an intelligence officer named Miggs—climbed out, papers in hand,
and approached the guard. He showed him a travel authorization, then gestured urgently toward the woods behind
the booth. The guards shrugged and nodded. Miggs disappeared into the trees. The path he was taking, Bannerman
saw, followed the course of the overhead phone line that ran
from the booth.

He returned, zipping his fly, in less than a minute. He lit
a cigarette and offered one to the guard who took several.
Miggs offered him his lighter, a Zippo with the embassy
seal on it. The guard used it but did not hand it back. He
looked at Miggs, his expression hopeful.

Miggs shook his head. No free gifts. He would only trade.
The guard spread his hands, saying he had nothing. Miggs
leaned close, whispering. The guard hesitated, then nodded.
He stepped into the booth and bade Miggs to follow. Miggs
did. When he returned to the Lincoln, he smelled of cheap
brandy, but he had located, on a wall inside the booth, the
address that Bannerman had given him.

"He can't call ahead," said Miggs. "He probably won't
try."

He did not explain further, but Bannerman understood. A
swallow of the guard's forbidden brandy, traded for an
embassy lighter, had made them coconspirators. The phone
line had been cut just in case. Irwin had been right. Miggs
was a good one. And Miggs wanted Mama's Boy to know
it.

The Lincoln made a series of turns and began climbing a hill. Thick woods on either side. Fewer houses.

"Next left," said Miggs. "The guard says it's the only house, about halfway down that road. What now, Mr. Bannerman?"

"We'll see." Bannerman lowered both rear windows. "Find it, but drive past. Don't slow down."

Kaplan squirmed. He wanted to get on with this. But Bannerman was in no hurry. For the moment, all he wanted was to get close enough to Kulik's address for Ernst Lechmann to spot him. If he's out there, he will. But if Lechmann's alone, it will mean that Waldo has already gone in. Probably with Lesko. If so, they're too late.

But if Lechmann says that they're still only scouting the house, Bannerman would have him give an abort signal. Or something that passes for one, so Waldo would know to disengage until they've had a chance to talk. Tell him whose side Podolsk's on, for one thing. Rethink all this, for another. Hitting that house at the invitation of some faceless Russians, and on their timetable, did not strike him as prudent.

He had said as much to Kaplan. Kaplan saw it differently.

"You're not going to stop Lesko," he said, "so we might as well back him up."

"We'll see."

"Will you stop with *we'll see*? Fuller practically smeared lamb's blood on your forehead. You think they'd cross him just to whack you instead? I told you. They don't need this. They want it over."

"Who's this *they,* Irwin? I'd like some names."

"Are you going to tell me who you have here?"

"Not yet. No."

"Fuck you, then. Anyway, they stay in the background, it's part of the deal."

Bannerman chose not to press. Irwin talks tough when he's frightened. The names can wait until he gets that out of his system. But Leo's uncle had said much the same thing. *They* want it over. *They* don't want this to touch them. It wouldn't surprise him a bit if all these *theys* turned out to be the same people.

"Police car." Miggs tossed a thumb over his shoulder. "You see it?"

Bannerman was on the wrong side. Kaplan looked back. "It's just one cop," he said. "Parked back in the trees."

Miggs's eyes were on the rearview mirror. They narrowed.

"He's coming," said Miggs quietly. "But that's a Moscow militia car. It shouldn't be out here."

Lechmann. Bannerman didn't even have to look.

"We're okay," Waldo whispered.

His ear to the door, he heard nothing to suggest that Lesko had been spotted from outside. Just glad-handing. Good to meet you. Heard a lot about you. The youngish voice doing the honors had to be Sostkov. He was introducing Podolsk. Waldo mouthed the name.

Lesko nodded, frowning. He knew a round of introductions when he heard one. And he knew nervousness when he heard it. Podolsk was nervous. He was meeting these three for the first time and that bothered him.

The group drifted into the library. Lesko listened to their voices. He had matched each to a face and now he tried to envision where they were sitting. Kulik was easy. Distinctive voice. He was in the middle. The two bozos sounded pretty much alike. They were off to the right. Podolsk on the left. Sostkov stayed close to the door. Kulik was talking to him.

Suddenly, the double doors of the library closed and there was almost silence. Then footsteps. And humming. Sostkov, he realized, had been asked to wait outside, but he seemed pleased with himself for some reason. The footsteps approached the dining-room door. Lesko readied himself. The door creaked and bowed inward slightly but did not open. Sostkov must be leaning against it.

Waldo used hand signals. I'll pull this door, they said. He falls back, you take him. No noise. Use your hands.

Lesko hesitated. But he jammed his pistol into the small of his back and readied himself. Waldo reached for the latch.

The siren.

Both men heard it. Four bleats, not two.

"What the hell does four mean?" Lesko mouthed. *"A bus?"*

Waldo frowned. He gestured toward Lesko's watch. *"What time you got?"*

Lesko looked. He held up ten fingers.

Waldo seemed to curse. *"You're fast,"* he said.

He pressed the latch and pulled.

78

The Swiss surgeon peered into Elena's eyes.

"Your nurse thinks she spoke? What did she say?"

He asked this of the Russian doctor through Avram. Susan squeezed Willem's hand. She held her breath.

"Sounds . . . words," the doctor answered. "Not connected, I think. Dream words."

The surgeon glanced up at Willem with a look that said don't make too much of it. It could be, he supposed, an encouraging sign. But now there was nothing again. No response, even to painful stimuli.

"What words?" Susan asked Avram.

Avram huddled with the Russian. He translated.

"She said . . . Let me go. Let go. Words to that effect."

Susan moaned in relief.

"Let her die?" asked the surgeon. "It's delirium. Means nothing."

"Delirium is better than coma," Susan snapped. "And what she was saying was *Les-ko.* She was calling for her husband."

The surgeon sniffed. This was the one who had been pestering him with questions. Now she's an expert on coma.

The Russian doctor was speaking again. A question for the surgeon.

"You are aware that this woman is pregnant?"

"Five months. Yes."

"And that she has endometriosis?"

"I have her history. Yes. Tell him I know what he's going to say."

Avram translated all the same.

"Under the circumstances . . . her weakened condition . . . recovery will be difficult enough."

"No," Susan said sharply. The relief was gone, horror in its place. "Don't even think of . . ."

The surgeon looked at Willem again. "Please. It's better if you take the girl outside."

"I'm not *the girl,* you stiff-necked son of a bitch."

"Susan . . ." Willem touched her shoulder.

"You touch that baby and I'll . . ."

He guided her toward the door.

Lechmann had given his signal.

The four bleats had no prearranged meaning, but Waldo, Bannerman hoped, would understand that something unusual was happening. If he could, he might withdraw.

Bannerman stood at Lechmann's window, hearing about Waldo's first visit to the dacha. The Lincoln, behind them, had pulled onto the shoulder. Kaplan and Miggs remained in their seats. Miggs's eyes were on his sideview mirror.

"Mr. Bannerman? Behind us, sir."

Bannerman looked without turning. He saw two cars, both yellow. They had stopped at a fork in the road some one hundred yards down the hill.

"They slowed when they saw us," said Miggs. "Now they're talking it over."

Bannerman could see that. A head leaned out of the second car. The driver of the first car looked back. He was listening, now nodding.

"First one's turning off," said Miggs. "Taking that other fork."

"Could that road lead to Kulik's house?" asked Bannerman.

Lechmann answered for Miggs. "It's a longer way, but yes."

"If you go straight," he asked Lechmann, "past the road to Kulik's house, is there a back way in further up?"

"Not by car. It's forest. But I can go in on foot."

Bannerman stole a glance at the yellow car that remained. It sat, its engine idling, waiting.

The men in it were obviously trouble but he needed to know who they were. They, however, were having the same thoughts about a Moscow police car and an embassy Lincoln, and that was his advantage. The trick was to seem more a nuisance than a danger. Try to draw them in closer.

"Frisk me," he told Lechmann. "Let them see you come up empty."

Lechmann understood. He climbed out of his police car and pointed at the Lincoln's front fender. Bannerman hesitated. Lechmann shoved him. Bannerman lifted his jacket to show that he had nothing. Lechmann pushed him again, ordering him to lean against the Lincoln, arms out, legs spread. He patted him down, ankles to armpits.

"Do you have an extra weapon?" Bannerman asked.

"No. Only a useless Beretta. Lesko took the clip."

"We'll make do," he said. "Now search Kaplan. When you're finished, make a show of telling Irwin, *not me,* to turn around and get out of Zhukovka. Then let them see you drive off."

Lechmann snapped his fingers at Kaplan, ordered him out of the car. Bannerman, speaking softly, told Kaplan how to behave. Lechmann, his back to the yellow car, took Kaplan's pistol from his belt and chambered a round. "Safety's off," he told him. He replaced the pistol and pulled Kaplan's jacket over it.

Bannerman looked at Miggs. Miggs, still in the Lincoln, nodded. He chambered a round as well. Good man.

"Someone going to tell me what we're doing?" asked Kaplan.

"We're going to try to take them."

Lechmann knew that, but he didn't like it. "I should cover you," he said to Bannerman.

"You cover the house. We'll be along."

Lechmann grunted. He began his act. He gave Kaplan another shove and pointed his finger in the general direction of Moscow.

"When you see us again," said Bannerman, backing away, "watch for *us.* Not what we're driving."

• • •

"It's time we had a talk," Willem Brugg told Susan.

A nurse had brought her a glass of strong tea. Willem sat with her as she drank it.

"Where's my father?" she asked him. "Does anyone know?"

"I think Paul has gone looking for him."

She was angry with him. His place was here. He should be here to stop this.

"My father. They'd need his permission, wouldn't they?"

"I would think so. Yes."

But her mind was not eased. She knew her father. If they told him it came down to a choice, save one unborn baby or save Elena, he wouldn't hesitate for a heartbeat. Elena was his life.

"Susan . . ." Willem took her hand. "Nobody wants to take the baby. It is only that doctors must discuss every eventuality."

"Including how badly she wants it?"

"That would be a factor. Certainly."

"Excuse me, Willem, but bullshit."

She wanted to believe it, but she didn't. Once a surgeon starts working on a patient, and you're waiting outside, he can come out and tell you any damned thing at all and you have to take his word.

She thought of Miriam. Miriam would do it. She could be there in the operating room. A doctor would say, *"The patient is probably going to lose the baby anyway. The endo. Her age. Let's terminate the pregnancy now, save the strain on her system. We all agree?"* Miriam will say, *"I have a second opinion. Touch her anywhere below the neck and I'll shoot your hand off."*

"Susan?"

"I'm okay."

"No . . . you're not okay." He grimaced to show that this was difficult for him. "Susan . . . on the plane you had a talk with Carla. I think you felt the need to share a secret with her."

She stiffened but said nothing.

"I understand this need."

She closed her eyes. "Willem . . . what I discussed with Carla is none of your business. But I did *not* tell her a secret."

"Then she guessed. I saw it afterward on both your faces. Carla guessed, or she already knew."

She started to rise. "I've got to go find Miriam."

Willem Brugg took her hand, restraining her. He lowered his voice.

"You know who else guessed? My wife, Heide. Like you, she is Elena's good friend. She guessed the reason for your visits last winter. She saw the truth on Elena's face just as Carla saw it on yours. And like Carla, she would die before she would speak of it."

She glared at him. "Other than to you, you mean."

He shook his head. "Elena told us both. Over tea, just like now."

Her lips parted. She didn't speak.

"You had gone home, Susan. She was alone with her fears. Among them, what if Lesko finds out before she is ready to tell him? Would he be repulsed? Would he hate his daughter for her part in it?"

"Willem . . ." She started to shake her head. He ignored the denial.

"The reason Elena told us . . . she needed us to tell her that she'd done the right thing. We did. She had. You had. It's as simple as that."

Her throat became hot. The tears came.

"You gave her a wonderful gift, Susan. You gave her a child of her own flesh which she could not have had any other way and can never have again. But you've *given* it. You must let go of it. I've seen you with children, Susan. It's time you had some of your own."

"Willem . . ." She wanted to tell him the rest of it. That he didn't know half of what he thought he knew. The tears became sobs. Her shoulders shook. Willem had to take the glass from her. He left the napkin in her hand.

"Ah . . . have I blundered into something else here, Susan?"

She trembled. It became a shrug.

"You are . . . with child, I take it."

At last, a nod.

Movement at Elena's door distracted him. The doctors were coming out. The surgeon was looking at Susan. Not with annoyance. Not with compassion either. Fear, if anything. Avram must have told him this was Mama's Boy's woman. No longer just "the girl." Willem doubted that Susan would see this as an improvement.

"And you have . . . ambivalence? Or do you simply not want it?"

"I don't know."

"You've told Paul?"

She hesitated, then shook her head.

Willem Brugg could not think what to say. You're just upset, Susan? Those who should die will die but then it will be over? You'll go back to Westport. Paul will start reading up on the Cub Scouts or the Brownies. Little League Baseball or ballet. Molly Farrell will teach the child tennis. Billy McHugh . . . self-defense. John Waldo . . . arson.

Ah-ha.

He began, he suspected, to see the problem.

"Have you talked to anyone else? Carla perhaps?"

"No."

"Why not Elena?"

"I was going to. When she got back."

"Saying what? That you have misgivings about raising a child with Paul?"

"About even having it."

Brugg raised an eyebrow. Not that he found fault, but her views on abortion were more flexible than he'd assumed.

"You're worried about . . . what? Paul as a role model? My father, the terrorist?"

"I'm not worried about Paul. I'm worried about me. I'm becoming like Carla."

Willem had to smile. "As to loyalty, perhaps. And a very good heart. Otherwise . . . trust me, you are not at all like Carla."

She looked at him coldly. "I want some people dead, Willem. I could kill them, one by one, all by myself. And this time I wouldn't bat an eye."

He took both her hands in his.

"That's not Carla talking," he said gently. "That's your

bond with Elena talking. If you're like anyone, it's your father. And me, for that matter.''

She said nothing.

"Will you do something for me?''

"I don't want to tell Paul I'm pregnant. Not yet.''

"I'm asking you to go in and tell Elena. It could do you both some good.''

She hesitated.

"Go,'' he said. "You have a little time before they take her.''

She nodded, slowly.

"First let me find Miriam,'' she said.

79

Sostkov was embarrassed.

The door he was leaning against had given way. He was falling backward. His worst fear, before he started to die, was that they would open the library doors and find him on the seat of his pants.

But someone had grabbed him. Stopped his fall. The first message from his brain was one of relief. Then confusion.

A thick arm crossed over his face, pulling him against a body twice the size of his own. Be careful of the nose, whoever you are. But the arm was not supporting him. It was crushing him. It felt like steel against the sides of his neck, and his feet could no longer reach the floor.

His face swelled to bursting. Dried blood and fresh blood spewed from his nose. He tried to kick with his legs but two other arms seized them. Two men. They were holding him. Carrying him. Now putting him down.

Suddenly, he knew where he was. Day had turned into night and spring into winter, but he knew this place. He saw the walls of the pit. He was lying in it, among frozen pigs and sheep, looking up. He heard the approach of the bulldozer and now he saw it, pushing a car through the snow and mud. It was not the Zil. It was his silver BMW. Oh, no! He wanted to scream but he could not.

Above him, he saw many faces looking down at him from the edge of the pit. He knew some of those men. The lorry driver with his helpers. The driver of the flatbed. All eating the food he had brought them. He saw his colonel standing with them.

He tried to call out. Help me, he wanted to say. Colonel? You were always a good sort. I never felt right about any of this.

But his colonel only waved and turned away. They all turned away. There was only the bulldozer, coming to cover him.

Lesko released his choke hold.

They set Sostkov down on the dining-room carpet. Waldo went through his clothing. He took his pistol, found the keys to the Zil.

Lesko, regaining his breath, knelt to check the Russian's throat for a pulse. He felt a blip, heard a bubbling in the throat, then nothing. He reached for the edge of the Persian carpet and folded it over the gaping face.

"You ready?" Waldo asked quietly.

Lesko stood up slowly. He took the Beretta from his belt, and snapped the safety back off. He looked at Waldo and nodded.

Waldo made no sound as they entered the main hall. Lesko hesitated. He walked, lightly but not silently, to the front door where he paused to scan the driveway. No other car had appeared, but Lechmann, he assumed, had a reason for hitting that siren. He turned back toward the library.

He made an effort to be silent, but Waldo caught his eye, telling him with sign language to walk naturally. The men inside would expect to hear movement. Stepping lightly might make them wonder. As it was, he heard no sound from the library. They might have heard the struggle after all.

He put his ear to the door and listened. Now he heard a voice, speaking very softly. He heard no alarm in it. Waldo relaxed. The voice, he felt sure, was Kulik's. Its tone was

earnest, reasoning. He tried to get a sense of what was being
said. The only word he recognized was Borovik. It was
mentioned several times. The inflection had the weary
sound of exhausted patience.

Suddenly there was movement. Chairs sliding back. He
signaled Lesko to back off, wait until they sit, stay ready.

He heard a solid metallic clunk followed by the squeak of
a hinge. He knew that sound. The safe had been opened. He
listened for an outcry over the missing contents. But the safe
squeaked again, just closing over, no clunk. Kulik, he
decided, had not yet missed the haul that was now under the
Volga's spare tire.

More sounds. Plastic scratching against a lighter metal.
More mentions of Borovik. Belkin. Kropotkinskaya. And
maybe something about Mama's Boy. He wasn't sure.

Later, he would take Lesko down below, show him
what's left of Borovik. That way he'll have no regrets.
These are not the kind of people you leave standing.

He heard a new voice.

This one was a little louder, higher, very shaky, sounded
scared. Shit, he was blubbering. It seemed familiar. Waldo
tried to place it. He caught Lesko's eye and held up five
fingers. There's a fifth man in there, said the gesture. He had
not taken part in the introductions. This new voice was
talking about Borovik, too. Kropotkinskaya. Leo. Elena
Brugg. Kerensky brothers.

And Raymond Lesko.

It dawned on Waldo that the voice was saying "*Ya*" a lot.
Speaking in the first person. *Ya* did it. *Ya* sent the
Kerenskys . . . to *Kropotkinskaya* . . . to find the mur-
derer *Raymond Lesko*.

Lesko?

And those other noises before . . . plastic against
metal . . . Waldo knew what they were now. They were a
videotape machine being loaded. He was sure of it. He was
hearing Borovik's voice in a taped confession and they had
to be playing it for Podolsk.

Why? he wondered.

Hell with it.

Waldo signaled Lesko again. He wiped out five fingers,

went back to four. He signaled, *Get ready. On three, right? One . . . two . . .*

But Lesko mouthed "Wait."

He'd heard shooting, he thought. Pistol shots off in the distance. Concerned for Lechmann, he cupped a hand against his ear and listened, hoping to hear answering fire from a submachine gun.

An explosion shocked him. It came from the library. Two shots, booming, echoing off the walls. He jumped away and spun, trying to crouch, but his momentum caused him to fall backward. He crashed against the far wall, knocking a heavy gilt-framed painting to the floor, but his Beretta stayed trained on the door. Now a third shot. The concussion rattled the door.

Waldo cursed. He, too, backed away, his weapon ready.

But now there was silence. Five seconds. Ten. And then a voice from inside. Several words. They sounded . . . spent. Lesko looked at Waldo questioningly.

"You get that?" he whispered. "What'd he say?"

Waldo blinked, confused. "He said we can come in now."

Bannerman counted three heads in the yellow car that stayed. Two in the front seat. A heavyset man in back. The man in back was clearly in charge. It was he who had sent the other car on.

It was possible, Bannerman supposed, that they were private security guards. He did not think it likely. Whatever their intent, they had altered their plans at the sight of an expensive American car. It was not the police car that interested them. After Lechmann had gone they still waited and watched.

Bannerman chose to make two assumptions. One, those men were headed for the Kulik house and they were a danger to Lesko and Waldo. This near to the house, he could not afford to assume otherwise. Two, the men in the other car, whatever their intention, would take no action until the man in the back seat of this one told them that the Americans were no threat.

He had asked Kaplan to pace, to look upset, distracted. Above all, to seem in charge. He wanted their focus on

Irwin, not on himself. He had stripped off his jacket and stood, in shirtsleeves, clearly unarmed, leaning against the Lincoln's front fender within arm's length of Miggs. Miggs was to stay at the wheel, looked bored, chauffeurish. He pretended to study a road map.

"They're moving," said Miggs.

The car came slowly. It crept up, windows rolled down, all eyes on the occupants of the Lincoln. Kaplan appeared to pay them little notice. He was pretending to shout at Miggs, berating him for getting them lost, and at Bannerman for being generally useless. The men in the car stared curiously at Kaplan, who now pretended to be self-conscious, and contemptuously at Bannerman, who had meekly dropped his eyes under Kaplan's verbal assault.

The three men, two in particular, stared brazenly. It was not a policeman's gaze—trained eyes, always moving, evaluating. It was a hoodlum's gaze—eyes arrogant, intimidating, stupid. The car kept going. Bannerman was disappointed.

It seemed about to turn onto the road that led to Kulik's house. But suddenly it veered right, then swung into a U-turn left.

"They're coming back," said Miggs.

The yellow car, which Miggs said was a Zhiguli, slowed to a stop on the shoulder opposite. More stares. They said nothing. Kaplan, at the rear of the Lincoln, seemed to wilt under their scrutiny. He backed away. Bannerman merely fidgeted. Miggs turned his head toward the Zhiguli, took a weary breath, and shrugged his shoulders. The one in the back nodded slightly. Bannerman could read his mind. The chauffeur, he was thinking, had no use for these two. He would give them no trouble. Nor would the one who let little four-eyes talk to him in such a way.

"You! American!" The one in back called to Kaplan. "What are you doing here?"

He was more than heavyset. He was fat. Totally bald. No eyebrows.

Timidity from Kaplan. "We're . . . just waiting for someone."

"Go wait in Moscow. You're not allowed here."

Kaplan pursed his lips. "Who says we're not?" It came out as a whine.

"The militiaman told you," said the fat man, "and now it's me telling you. Do you need a kick in the ass before you understand?"

Indignation. "We're not bothering you."

A good line, thought Bannerman. Guaranteed, never miss, to get you stepped on. He had an even better one.

"Can't you just leave us alone?" he asked.

The one in the back turned to the man in the passenger seat. They exchanged shrugs. Both men climbed out, languidly. Bannerman had hoped for the driver as well, but he stayed in his seat, elbows out through the open window, content to enjoy the show. The other two crossed the road, slowly, deliberately, the fat one rubbing his knuckles.

Kaplan backed away further. His chin quivered. "What right do you have . . ." he sputtered. "If you're police, show me some identification."

The fat one smiled.

"Here it is," he said, and showed an open palm. Kaplan looked at it. The man slapped him across the face. Kaplan's glasses flew off. The blow knocked him sideways. He fell. The one from the front seat, ponytail, bad teeth, Euro-Disneyland T-shirt, took a stance facing Bannerman. He drew back his coat to show the pistol at his hip.

"How about you, cunt-face?" he asked Bannerman. "You want to see papers, too?"

"Ah . . . I think that will do it," said Bannerman to Miggs.

He extended a hand toward the Lincoln's window, palm up.

"It's on cock," warned Miggs. He slapped his Beretta onto Bannerman's hand. Bannerman extended his arm and fired.

The bullet struck the Russian in the neck. It missed his spinal cord. He clutched at his throat, staggered backward, but didn't fall. Bannerman wheeled on the Zhiguli's driver. Sighting with both hands, he aimed at the man's chest. Bannerman fired twice, then wheeled again. The first man had sunk to his knees. He almost seemed to be praying.

Bannerman took time for a head shot. He fired. The ponytail blew apart.

He saw Kaplan, who was no longer acting. He had pulled his Beretta and rolled to a combat stance, but he wasn't shooting. The man who had slapped him seemed in momentary shock. Mouth open. In disbelief.

"Irwin . . . now!" Bannerman barked. He lowered his pistol. The man saw this. He snapped out of it. He clawed at the holster under his arm.

"*Shit!*" came Kaplan's voice. But Kaplan fired.

The bullet struck the fat Russian in the hip. He yelped, twisted, but managed to free his weapon. Bannerman sighted on his head, but waited. Kaplan fired again. Chest shots. The Russian gasped and crumbled. He pitched forward on his face.

"Holy *shit*."

Miggs was out of the Lincoln. He had crossed to the yellow Zhiguli and reached into the driver's window.

"Still alive," he called, turning.

Bannerman had seized Ponytail by the collar, was dragging him toward the pine trees. He looked up at Miggs, shook his head. Miggs nodded. He reached back into the window. His shoulder muscles tightened briefly, then relaxed. He opened the door, dragged that one out as well.

"Holy shit." From Kaplan again.

Bannerman came back for the fat one, picked up his pistol.

"You want a shotgun?" called Miggs from the Zhiguli. "They brought shotguns and shovels."

Shovels? "Leave the shotguns in it. We're going to use that car."

Kaplan, now functioning, helped with the fat Russian. "*Taking* them?" he hissed. "This was your idea of *taking* them?"

"Irwin . . . later."

Bannerman wondered what had been unclear, but his mind was elsewhere. These men. He still knew little about them—beyond that they were killers and that it wasn't him they were here to kill and bury. They'd shown no sign that they recognized him. It was possible that they'd been called here to protect Kulik, but that, too, seemed unlikely. They would have been more vigilant, especially coming upon a car full of Americans. But all they wanted to do, it seemed to him, was to shoo away three potential witnesses.

He dropped the fat one just inside the tree line, examined his pistol, a stubby Tokarev. A shotgun would be better, but he kept it. He checked the dead Russian's pockets. No papers other than his wallet. Cards in it showed a name and address. He kept the cards and threw the wallet into a brook. He didn't bother with Ponytail. Miggs was back on the road with one of the shovels, sprinkling dirt and pine needles over the blood.

By his watch, less than two minutes had passed since the first shot. The other yellow car will have heard the gunfire. It might come looking or it might elect to wait, assuming that their friends did the shooting. Either way, better to find them first. Let them see a yellow car coming. Hope they're no brighter than this bunch.

"Irwin? How are you holding up?"

Kaplan, drained of color, sputtering now, was trying to straighten his glasses. "Bannerman . . . you . . . you're such a fucking . . ."

It was not the time, Bannerman supposed, to talk to Kaplan about his language.

"Irwin . . . I need three heads showing. If I can't count on you, I'll have to take one of these."

Kaplan gasped. A look of utter horror. Bannerman wondered what he'd said.

"Fuck you, Bannerman. Let's go."

80

Podolsk was to die this morning.

It was the videotape that had convinced him of it. Whether he passed or failed this test, it didn't matter. He would never leave this house alive.

Hear him out first, Sostkov had said. Above all, give him

every chance to open that safe. When he does, call me in. We'll shoot the dirty bastards together.

But within two minutes of sitting down with Arkadi Kulik, being offered real Italian coffee and shortbreads from Scotland, being flattered by this soft-spoken man in the Scottish hat, he knew that Kulik had a test of. his own in mind.

"A question," he had said. He leaned close, allowing his face to show that the need to ask it pained him. "Do you trust Sostkov? Or have you seen something . . . disappointing in him?"

"He is . . . ambitious," Podolsk ventured.

It seemed a good answer. The other former generals—they could have been twins—nodded gravely, knowingly.

"You're a very perceptive young man," said Kulik, sighing deeply, his sadness profound.

He did not take the subject further, but the foundation, Podolsk realized, had been laid. Before this interview was over he would hear that Oleg Sostkov is a thief, a traitor, a spy—whatever would serve—who had broken the heart of a man who had treated him like a son.

But first there was more flattery. They had heard many good things about Major Viktor Podolsk. In particular, said one of the others, they liked that stunt with the Leningrad lottery. Very clever. Shows creativity. We could use more of that kind of thinking around here.

After that came sympathy. Two years working for Borovik. That diseased mind. Was told to stay away from the Belkin party. Disobeyed orders. We know that you wanted no part of it, tried to talk him out of it, but you were in a difficult position. As for that insanity outside the restaurant, you are totally exonerated. Borovik himself has absolved you.

"I'm going to show you something," said Kulik. "It's not so pleasant but it's good that you see it."

He went to his safe, opened it, and withdrew a videotape cassette. He crossed to a TV screen and inserted the cassette. The near-twins moved their chairs so they could watch. One winked at the other.

Podolsk looked at the open safe. He was sorely tempted to end this before he lost the will for it. In some ways, he was almost beginning to like Arkadi Kulik. The old man had been charming and attentive, made him feel appreciated, important, trusted. His eyes had humor in them except when they were sad. That Scottish hat he wore indoors seemed harmlessly eccentric.

He knew, of course, that he was being manipulated, that Kulik was a master at it. The Academician had as much as said so. Still . . .

The screen lit up. Podolsk's mouth fell open. He was looking at the head and chest of General Borovik.

He was propped against a board. Perhaps tied to it. He seemed in frightful agony and yet he managed to speak. Sentences. Parts of sentences. Some of them prompted by a voice off-camera. The voice was Sostkov's. Borovik, under torture, was confessing everything.

The ambush outside Kropotkinskaya was his doing, he said. But he claimed that he did not mean harm to the ones who were shot. It was a man named Lesko he was after. He admitted to being the brains behind the Chicago Brigade. This last caused the two others to laugh.

He was a thief. He would steal anything under the sun. He confessed to stealing eighty canisters of nerve gas. Having an accident with one of them. He named the Ural village in which no living thing survived. He made it clear that his aide, Major Viktor Podolsk, had been kept totally in the dark about all this. Last of all, he named names, at least a dozen of them, who had been in these enterprises with him.

Podolsk recognized most of these names. A few did not surprise him. But he greatly doubted the guilt of some others.

Among the latter were Boris Petrov, the federal prosecutor, Andrei Kosarev, First Deputy Director of the Security Ministry, Anatoly Pimin—in charge of privatization. Podolsk had never heard so much as a whisper against these men, even when they were still Communists.

One name in particular was beyond accusation. To Podolsk's astonishment, Borovik had named the Academician Nikolai Belkin as being in his pocket.

Only one explanation was possible, thought Podolsk. Whoever had written Borovik's confession had seen a chance to discredit a few of his enemies.

It was here that Podolsk had his flash of insight. He had several.

One: All these men were Kulik's enemies. But that went without saying.

Two: He, that very morning, had spoken to one of these dozen or so men with Sostkov. But *which* one?

Three: He would *never* see that man's face. He is not to leave this house alive.

Four: It will be Sostkov who kills him. After he kills these three.

He listened in growing numbness as Kulik explained what would be done with this videotape. It would be sent to the Americans with a note. The note, signed by "The Committee for Justice" or some such thing, would tell them if they need more proof they can go to Borovik's apartment. Look in his mother's hatboxes. They'll see currency, emeralds, heroin. Not great amounts but enough to convince them. They'll also find his mother. Poor woman. In her shame, she hung herself.

"Poor woman," snorted the one who had winked. He pulled at his collar to show scratch marks on his neck.

Kulik glared at him but said nothing. Podolsk felt a scream rising from his soul. Kulik rose from his chair and walked to what seemed to be a minibar.

"With the note and the videotape we will send something else." He paused, his hand on the key to the minibar. "I should ask first if you have a strong stomach."

He managed to nod.

Kulik opened the metal door and withdrew a plastic bag. He held it up. Something wine-colored and black. Podolsk could not make out its contents at first because condensed moisture had made the bag opaque. But Kulik held it closer, turning it in his hand. Podolsk saw the face of General Borovik. He thought he would be sick.

The two other boobs were enjoying his discomfort. One was elbowing the other. Grinning eagerly, he said to Kulik, "Tell him your joke about that."

Kulik cracked a smile but declined. He returned Borovik's head to the minibar.

The same boob turned to Podolsk, chuckling. "You know what General Kulik said? He said, 'Borovik is finally making his head useful.' No. Not quite right. He said, 'It's high time that Borovik . . .' ''

He stopped himself. He cocked an ear, listening.

Podolsk heard it. The sound of pistol shots in the distance. But, just then, he was past caring. A sickening joke, told badly, had pushed Viktor Podolsk beyond his limits. The last straw can be a very small one.

He saw the Makarov before he knew he'd reached for it. All sound in the room, all motion, stopped. Only his right arm moved. It seemed to have a life of its own.

The one who could not tell a joke was first. He died before the stupid grin could fade. The other, the one with scratch marks, could only stare at the blood that splattered him from the first. The Makarov shot him through the heart.

It swung left, finding Kulik. He had backed away, his eyes darting this way and that, as if looking for a place to hide. He snatched something from his desk. A broken golf club. He hugged it, uselessly, then threw it at Podolsk. It bounced off his hip. Kulik backed away further, finally reaching the wall. Arms crossed to protect his chest, he tried to make himself smaller. He tried to talk. No sound came. Either his voice was gone or Podolsk's brain had turned off the sound. Slowly, eyes wide as saucers, he lowered himself to the floor.

The Makarov kicked, belched fire. The Scottish hat popped up, settled back. Kulik only squeaked. He quivered for a moment, and he was dead.

Podolsk stared down at him. This monster. Dead.

It seemed too quick. There should have been more to it. A man such as this should have suffered. Screamed out loud. Dragged up to a roof and thrown off the edge. Soaked with gasoline and set on fire. Something. There should have been more.

Podolsk turned toward the library's door. He backed away from it, several steps. His arms were his own now. He gripped the Makarov in both of them, ready position, poised at his right shoulder.

He cleared his throat.

"You can come in now," he said.

81

Elena could hear Susan.

She could even smell her hair.

And she could see lights and movement. Some of the time.

The trouble was . . . she didn't know how much of what she saw and heard was real. It was all mixed up with dreams. And ghosts.

Uncle Urs came by. He took her hiking, told her the names of flowers. That one was more of a memory. David Katz always seemed to be near, wearing a sport jacket with a turtleneck underneath. She knew who he was because she had seen photographs of him among Lesko's things. And he was dressed in the way Lesko had described him. Hollywood clothing. Already out of date.

He wouldn't speak to her though. He'd never quite forgiven her. But he had told Lesko, "*She can hear you.*" And that was nice of him.

There was a moment when she would have spoken to Lesko herself if he had let her get a word in edgewise. He was too busy making deals with God and proving that he could count in German. She would have told him to make whatever deal he likes but leave our child out of it.

She was fading again. Wait. Susan?

You were talking about a child just then. I'm sorry. Things take a while. You were talking about a child of your own. Are you . . . ?

I heard you. Don't you dare. Don't even think of it.

Yes, you stay close to me. Yes, and Miriam. I hear. But you especially, because the minute I'm awake I'm going to tell you what I think of talk like that.

". . . talk like that."

Yes, I know what Paul is. I know what he was and I know

why he gave it up. Need I tell you why? He was looking for *you,* Susan.

Why you in particular, I don't know. Why two people find each other, come to love each other, I can't explain. Explain Lesko and me if you can.

". . . explain."

I know only this. You are his *lifeline,* Susan, just as Lesko is mine.

"Life . . . line . . . Susan."

Oh, good grief, don't shout like that. Can't you see my head hurts?

Susan!

Why are you running off?

"Susan?"

82

Waldo was giving hand signals.

I open, draw fire, you shoot, I finish.

Lesko waved them off.

"I got a feeling," he said softly.

The voice from inside was Podolsk's. "You can come in now," he said. But there was something about the voice. A hollow sound at the end. Like in his head he was adding, "you son of a bitch."

A lot about Podolsk now bothered him. The way he sounded when he came in. Didn't really want to be here. The way he looked in the Savoy lobby. Didn't want to be there either. In front of Detsky Mir, the way he was reaming out that slug who shot Leo and Valentin. Stomping off to the KGB building like he was going to ream out someone else.

"Sostkov?" Podolsk's voice again. Concern in it.

Waldo touched a finger to his lips. Let him come look. Lesko shook his head.

"You're all alone, Viktor," he said. He took a quick step back.

Silence from the library.

"I just killed the son of a bitch."

Lesko crouched to one knee, bent low, but no bullets ripped through the wall where his head had been. Waldo's scowl said he wished one had. Lesko could hear him in his mind. You never talk to them, he was saying. You never, *ever* talk.

"You are . . . the *American*," came Podolsk's voice.

Lesko heard astonishment. He thought he heard relief. He waited.

"Please . . . you must answer. Are you the policeman? Are you Lesko?"

Heavy breathing. But definitely relief.

"Mr. Lesko, I am not your enemy."

And now desperation.

"I am *their* enemy. These three . . . Sostkov . . . that thing in the bag."

Thing in the *bag*? He looked at Waldo. Waldo rocked a hand and flipped it. *I think I know,* the gesture said. *But later.*

He reached for the doorlatch before Lesko could stop him, opened it, and pushed. But he backed away quickly. Still no shots. He signaled Lesko that he could see two men, both dead. Lesko saw the third, Kulik. He was in the far corner, crumpled, head back, mouth open, another dumb red hat down over his nose.

"Two of you," came Podolsk's voice. "And more outside? Those shots?"

Lesko hesitated.

"If they are not yours, Mr. Lesko, they have come to kill me. They must now kill you as well."

Even Waldo hesitated. But Lesko was watching his eyes. Waldo knew that room. He knew that Podolsk was standing in the middle and he knew what cover there was. Probably none. He could stick the MP5 through the door, sweep the middle with one long burst, listen for Podolsk to drop, and, that distraction gone, get ready for who else might be coming.

"Podolsk? Don't get nervous."

Gritting his teeth, Lesko showed one arm, his Beretta at the end of it, pointed toward the ceiling. From inside, he heard a deep sigh.

"Mine is same way."

A breath. Lesko showed more of himself. He saw Podolsk.

Both hands were raised, an automatic like Valentin's in one of them, finger clear of the trigger. He saw Podolsk's eyes. Expecting fear, he saw none. What he saw was exhaustion. This man was totally drained. Lesko could have shot him, he thought, and he would have died with a look of relief.

He glanced over his shoulder expecting to see Waldo backing him. Waldo wasn't there. He wasn't even in the hallway. The Russian could have shot him if he wanted.

"Your wife?" asked Podolsk hopefully. The eyes said he meant it.

"I don't know."

Lesko, the Beretta still raised, scanned the room. Three dead. Everyone on his list but the Arabs. The hell with the Arabs. His eye fell to the telephone on Kulik's desk.

"You know how to call that hospital?" he asked.

Irwin Kaplan didn't like the way he felt.

He felt guilty.

The guilt was because he was feeling good about it.

I know, he told himself. For Irwin Kaplan, angst is the normal emotional state. Self-inflicted wounds. Two thousand years of suffering.

But for anyone to tell him that he could kill a man, even a lowlife goyim thug prick who slapped his face, he would have said no chance. Wishing he had the guts, maybe. Shooting to protect his family, maybe. But not to kill, not if he could help it. Until this time.

The Russian went for his gun and he had to shoot. But now, now that it was settling, that fat fuck was everyone he ever hated.

"There's the house," said Miggs. "I don't see the other Zhiguli."

"Keep going. They'll be looking for this one."

The guys he envied, as a kid, were never the bruisers like

Lesko. He didn't want people to be afraid of him. He didn't even want to fight, especially. What he wanted was to be able to walk away from an insult without it ripping at him for weeks afterward. Sometimes years.

The guys he envied were the ones who nothing bothered. Never brooded, never cried. They would set their sights and go. As an adult, though, he began to change his thinking when he noticed that half of these guys had been through three wives and the other half turned into druggies, drunks, or dropouts.

Then he meets Bannerman. Wanting to hate him at first, mostly because he was afraid of him. He knew why and now he's seen why. That was murder back there. Those first two guys. Never mind what they *might* have done. Or what Bannerman *guessed* they were *going* to do. Even if he's right, which it looks like he is, it was murder by any standard. And you want cold-blooded? When he shot that second guy, the driver? He shot him as low as he could, avoiding his head. It was so they wouldn't have to clean brains off the windows before they could drive his car. That even shook Miggs.

"There's one of them," said Bannerman from the back. "On foot, just past the wall."

Miggs looked. "Where?"

"He's gone. He started to flag us down from those trees, but he . . ." Bannerman cursed. "Stop and get down. Fast."

Ducking low, Miggs slammed on the brakes. Bannerman snatched at Kaplan's head, throwing him against Miggs. Miggs grabbed the head and held it, bending the glasses again.

"Stay low," Bannerman told Miggs. "He'll go for the driver."

"Who will?" asked Kaplan, muffled.

Bannerman groped for a handkerchief. He shook it out, jammed one end into the barrel of his shotgun, and shoved it out the window.

"Waldo will, if you give him a shot."

He counted to three, took a breath, then stuck his head out with the handkerchief. His right eye flashed red as Waldo's laser beam washed over it. When he could focus again, he

saw the man he'd seen moments before. The man had
popped out, then was whipped back. Now he was a rag doll
tumbling toward the roadway. Waldo had taken him. He had
come within a blink of taking them as well.

Twenty minutes passed.

They were in the trees near the place where the body had
fallen. Miggs had dragged it back up the slope, covered it
with branches. Further in, they found the second Zhiguli,
empty. It had come in through the birch and pine forest as
far as it could. Kaplan and Bannerman, armed with shotguns, sat facing the house although they couldn't see it for
the trees. Miggs watched their rear.

"How long do we sit here?" asked Kaplan.

"They might still come back for that car."

"And if Waldo already got them?"

"Then we wait, Irwin. Until we're told that we're no
longer in the way."

Bannerman was embarrassed. Kaplan loved it.

Bannerman has this great idea. We use one yellow
Zhiguli as a Trojan Horse. We drive up to the second one
and whack the men in it before they know what hit them.
But he doesn't figure that Waldo might already be out there
turning them into organ donors. The guy who waved from
the woods fell for the Trojan Horse but so did Waldo, who
probably would have shot us. Give Bannerman credit for
realizing it in time but the prick doesn't get straight A's.

"So our part's over."

"The day is young." Bannerman gestured toward his
pistol. "You can carve a notch if you're bored, Irwin."

Embarrassed. And now snippy. Kaplan loved this.

They heard the first short bleat of Lechmann's siren.
Bannerman relaxed. He asked Miggs to take their Zhiguli,
go get the Lincoln, and bring it back to Kulik's house. A
second bleat sounded, then a third, each closer than the last.
Bannerman stood up, began walking toward the road.
Kaplan followed.

"This means Waldo got them all?"

Bannerman nodded.

"How could he know how many?"

"He would have asked the first or second."

Asked. Nice. "Now what? We hit the house?"

"There's no need. The house is secure."

"How do you know?"

"Because Lechmann left his post."

So now its Twenty Questions. "Okay. How could Lechmann know? Wait . . . Waldo went and told him. But how
would Waldo know where you sent Lechmann?"

"Irwin . . . he just knew."

"Hey. Excuse *me*. We're taking a walk in the fucking
woods here while you're assuming that no one from that
second car is still functional. It's not like you're never
wrong, Bannerman."

A sigh. "Waldo knows me. He knows I'd have sent
someone to cover the rear and that could only be Lechmann.
He also knows Lechmann. He knows what position he'd
choose."

"Thank you."

"My pleasure."

"Just don't screw up again."

Boomalacka-boomalacka.

Kaplan couldn't help it. He knew that he was on an
adrenaline high. And that he'd crash. What the knowledge
that he'd killed a man would do to him, he'd have to wait
and see. But for right now, fuck him. For the first time in his
life, he felt that he could handle anything. He'd been on a
mission with Mama's Boy, been in a gunfight with him,
more than held up his end. He wished people could know.

Certain people.

"Hoooh-ly shit!"

Kaplan paused at the entrance to Kulik's library. He felt
the adrenaline draining.

Two men, big bellies, blue suits, sat in matching chairs.
Except for the blood, they could have dozed off watching
TV. The TV was on. It was a program about private
vegetable gardens.

A third man, skinny, older, was slumped in one corner, a
red tam down over his face. His knees were drawn up, his
hands clutched at his chest. No visible blood. He could have
been a wino sleeping it off.

Lesko is standing behind the desk. He's on the phone,

talking away, as if there's nothing wrong with this picture.
He looks up, gives the high sign. It's like, Hey, Irwin, good
to see you, be with you in a minute. At his side, chair pulled
up, is a guy wearing KGB collar tabs. He's holding a
videocassette under his chin, looks shell-shocked. He's
sticking close to Lesko while he's staring out at Bannerman.

Bannerman had looked in, but he's still in the hallway.
He's huddled with Waldo, who had let them in through the
dining room. Why is Waldo's coat on inside-out? A fourth
body on the dinning-room floor. A rug has been folded over
it.

What does this make? Ten dead? Three from the first car,
figure three from the second, four in these two rooms.
They're like ninety minutes into their eight-hour window
and already it's like Stalingrad.

Why is nobody else bothered by this? But as the thought
floated through his mind, it struck him that he isn't either.
Not that much. It's like the times he's had to visit a morgue.
You'd see five or six people laid out on tables. Heart
attacks, overdoses, stabbings. After a while, they're just
stiffs unless they happen to be someone you know. Or
unless they're children.

The guy with the cassette, Waldo is telling Bannerman, is
Podolsk. Maybe he's okay . . . he popped those
three . . . Lesko clocked this one. Waldo lowers his voice,
says something about the basement, something else about a
minibar.

Miggs comes in, says his own holy shit, spots the open
safe, and makes a beeline for it. Lesko wonders who he is
but he doesn't really care. He looks like his horse just came
in. Must be the hospital. Good news about Elena? Kaplan
spreads his hands to ask. What?

Lesko gives thumbs-up. Yeah, it's Elena, he says. She's
awake . . . or she was . . . and the EEG something-
something is looking good . . . she's going into
surgery . . . this is Susan . . . less damage than they
feared, but some . . . will know better when they go in,
but she was talking, making sense, recognized faces, was
even bawling out Susan for something . . . I don't
know . . . Hey, Bannerman . . . she wants to talk to
you . . . Susan.

The KGB guy understands English. He's listening to all

this. Tells Lesko how glad he is to hear it, but he still looks suicidally depressed.

Miggs says he's also glad to hear it. He introduces himself, shakes Lesko's hand. But Miggs doesn't look so happy, because whatever he's looking for, he doesn't seem to be finding it. He's been shuffling through file folders, discarding them, now he's pulling books out of those heavy canvas bags like banks use, leafing through them, tossing them aside.

Bannerman crosses to the desk. Waldo walks over to Miggs. He says, "Nothing good, huh?"

Miggs introduces himself . . . You must be John Waldo . . . heard about you . . . never believed half of it until today . . . and no, this is all junk . . . can't understand why it's even in a safe.

Bannerman's on the phone with Susan, speaking softly. Kaplan knows he must still be wired because he can hear almost every word. All his senses seem heightened.

Yes, Bannerman is saying . . . it's wonderful news . . . Yes, me too . . . Here? . . . Well, we've just . . .

Lesko's waving at him, shaking his head. From his gestures, what he's saying is let's not go into a lot of detail here.

Bannerman says he'll let her father explain . . . no real trouble, no . . . Irwin's been with us right along, he says, as in *If Irwin the Harmless is here, you know there can't have been any violence.* No, sweetheart. He drops his voice. You have nothing to apologize for . . . If anything, I'm the one who . . .

Bannerman stops himself. Takes a breath like he's changed his mind about something. Looking directly at Lesko, he says, "Susan . . . I will tell you *everything* when I see you . . . No, I want to . . . you have every right . . . you're a part of my life. Susan . . . you *are* my life.

"No, I said *life*.

"Lifeline? . . ."

Bannerman's eyes seem to melt. Even go moist. Kaplan can't believe it. Bannerman's getting emotional. "Lifeline . . . yes . . . yes, that's the word . . . that's the *only* word," he says.

Kaplan looked away. He had no business listening. But maybe he liked Bannerman just a little better now.

Waldo steps over Miggs and goes to this metal cabinet . . . opens it . . . it's the minibar he was talking about . . . little bottles in the door. He reached in, way back, comes out with two bottles of beer, asks who else wants one. Three stiffs in the room and he's raiding the icebox.

Podolsk points at the lower shelf, stammers something. Waldo says what? He pulls out this big plastic bag, examines it, makes a face, puts it on the pile with Miggs's discards. Kaplan can't see what's in it. Waldo reaches back in, finds some vodka and tequila, passes both bottles to Podolsk, who is just sitting there rocking now, eyes vacant. He puts his cassette down and takes the two bottles. Come to think of it, Kaplan thought, I could use a beer myself.

Lesko's drumming his fingers, scowling, waiting for Bannerman to get off the phone. It's easy to read his mind. Listen, Bannerman . . . my daughter doesn't have to know shit . . . at least not about me . . . tell her Podolsk blew all four of them away.

Kaplan felt the same way, sort of. Well . . . no, he didn't. Bannerman could tell her about him if he wanted. The way he sucked in that putz who thought he could push the little four-eyed Jew around. The way he handled himself. He wouldn't tell Roger, though. It's more satisfying if Roger hears it from someone else. Bannerman, he has a hunch, will enjoy telling him. If he doesn't, Miggs will.

Bannerman's saying maybe an hour, two at the most, they'll be back. Sounds like Susan wants to tell him something . . . he's asking why she can't tell him now. Whatever. She doesn't want to. Maybe she's worried about a tap.

Waldo finds four more beers. He pops their caps and lines them up on one side of the desk. He sips from one, says everyone help yourselves. He reaches back in, finds some smoked salmon, caviar, and an open box of shortbreads. He puts these on the desk and begins slicing the salmon with a knife he pulls out of his sleeve.

Podolsk, watching all this, has a look of utter disbelief. Kaplan doesn't blame him. I mean, this is the scene of a

massacre here, and all anybody seems to care about is how
the women in their lives are doing and fixing a snack. But
it occurs to Kaplan that yesterday, even an hour ago, it
would have been him who had that look on his face. What
the hell, he'll let himself feel a little smug about it. He raised
his beer bottle to Podolsk.

"To better days," he said.

Podolsk blinks. But slowly, he raises his little vodka
bottle, salutes with it, and drains it.

Bannerman's off the phone. For a long moment, he stares
into space, eyes soft, almost dreamy. Suddenly, a grimace.
He shakes it off. Bannerman's all business again.

He huddles for a minute with Lesko, and then with Lesko
and Podolsk together. "Go ahead," Lesko says to Podolsk.
"Tell him what you told me."

Kaplan could only catch parts of it—Podolsk was nervous, struggling with his English—but the part he heard
clearly was where Podolsk didn't think any of them would
get back to Moscow alive. Something about the safe.

Miggs looks up. He's been listening. Not *this* safe, he
says. There's nothing here. But the man has a point, he says,
about us making it back to Moscow. Zhukovka's real easy
to seal off, and whoever sent that bunch outside will be
wondering why they haven't heard from them.

Bannerman nods. "Irwin?"

"Yeah."

"I want you to go out to the Lincoln, call Roger on the
radiophone, tell him we need an armed escort of at least four
embassy cars and we need it now."

"I can call the Russians. They said if—"

"Call *Roger,* Irwin. Tell him to assume that the moment
he hangs up, he'll be in a race with someone else. Save the
address and directions until last. Give no names, no other
details."

"Bannerman, we have a pass here. Why shouldn't I—"

"Irwin." Lesko's voice was weary. "Make the call."

"Do it, Irwin." Bannerman was polite. "Please."

"*Okay,* for Christ's sake."

"When you've done that, stay out there with Lechmann.
Help him watch the road until you're relieved."

"Take him a beer," said Waldo.

"Hey, screw you guys," he flared. "This is to get rid of me, right? Get lost, Irwin, so us big boys can talk?"

"And take my gun," said Waldo. "You could need it."

Kaplan hesitated. He stared at Waldo's weapon, this Star Wars thing with two different scopes and a silencer. "Uh . . . how does that work?" he heard himself asking.

Lesko rolled his eyes. They could have sent a letter by now. Waldo showed him the MP5. Here's the safety, he says, and this switch is for rate of fire but leave it at three-round bursts. You don't shoulder this thing, he says. You just shine the beam and shoot. He demonstrates by beaming a red dot to the forehead of the only Russian who still had one.

As Kaplan studied the German gun, Waldo recapped the beer and stuck the bottle in his pocket. Oh yeah, he said. And take him this. He picked up the cloudy plastic bag and placed it under Kaplan's free arm.

Kaplan had turned and started walking before the glint in Waldo's eye registered. As had the fact that the room was dead silent except for someone being shushed and that the fingers of his left hand had a secure grip on what felt very much like a nose and mouth. Kaplan's ears began to ring.

Whose head it was, he had no idea. Borovik's, if he had to guess. Who says Waldo doesn't have a sense of humor. He wanted to drop it, get away from it, fling it back at Waldo.

He'd be damned if he'd do either.

He stopped, framed in the doorway to the hall. He turned the bag, twisting it in his hand so he could grip it by the gathered neck. He held it out at arm's length, appearing to study it. He counted three, brought it to his face, and kissed it.

Boomalacka-boom.

He dropped his arm. Just get me outside, he told his legs.

83

The motorcade, six cars in length, left Zhukovka well before noon.

Leading it, lights flashing, was a blue Volga of the Moscow militia. Four heavy sedans, two men in each, had come from the embassy. The men were armed with Ingram submachine guns, diplomatic status, and full authority to protect the person of the American ambassador, whose armor-plated Lincoln, flags streaming from the fenders, had been borrowed by Roger Clew.

Clew's car was in fourth position. The two behind it were assigned as chase cars, instructed to block pursuit. The two in front were authorized to ram if a roadblock should be encountered. Of these, Miggs drove the first.

The motorcade met its first challenge just beyond the gatehouse leading to the Minsk Highway. Two black Chaikas appeared, KGB plates. Men in raincoats, cigarettes in their mouths, leaped out, tried to flag it down. They were ignored. One man was knocked aside. A second drew his weapon but another restrained him. They scrambled back into their cars. One sped off toward Kulik's house. The other turned and gave chase.

On the Minsk Highway, several Russian-made cars appeared. Some had been waiting on the road and pulled out as the motorcade approached. Others roared up from behind, then slowed, keeping pace. One car, a Mercedes, moved up one Lincoln at a time, peering into each of them, a man in the front seat taking photographs. The windows of the ambassador's car were smoked, frustrating his effort.

These men seemed unsure of what action to take. The Mercedes pulled up to the blue Volga. The man in the back shouted over the road noise to the plainclothes militiaman driving, demanding to know why he was escorting these Americans.

"You think they tell me why?" Lechmann answered in Russian. "They tell me go do it and shut up."

He took a folded piece of paper from his shirt pocket, and displayed it. "Five signatures," he shouted. "With big shots like this, you don't argue."

The man seemed to want to reach for the paper. It was impossible, of course. The man snarled in disgust. Lechmann smiled within himself. In Russia, paper was still everything. Even if it was only the repair authorization that he found in the glove box.

Roger Clew was too angry to be nervous.

Lesko really couldn't blame him. Nobody would tell him much. Clew sat at his side facing Irwin Kaplan, who had taken the jump seat, the better to watch their rear. But Kaplan wasn't watching the pursuit cars. He was staring into space.

Kaplan was coming down fast. His swagger was pretty much gone and Lesko knew that stare. The makings of future nightmares were beginning to form. Kaplan was cradling a shotgun. Waldo had given it to him when he reclaimed his MP5, but now Kaplan was holding it too distractedly for Lesko's comfort. Lesko told him it would be just as handy lying on the floor. Kaplan refused to put it down.

Back at the house, before Clew showed up, Waldo and Bannerman had gone off into the trees. When they came back a minute later, Bannerman was struggling under the weight of a body and Waldo had picked up that shotgun. Together, they eased the dead man into the back seat of the Zil. Bannerman reached in, took the man's wallet, replaced it with another, and backed away. Waldo aimed the shotgun at the dead man's face and pulled the trigger. Kaplan let out a yip. This was when Waldo traded guns with him.

Taking the MP5, Waldo fired a burst into the fuel tank of the Zil. It didn't ignite. Muttering something about Russian gas, he waited until most of it had drained and then tossed a match. The back half of the Zil was quickly engulfed.

Suddenly, Waldo had a worried look. He hurried to the driver's-side door, opened it, released the hand brake, and pushed the Zil several yards forward. By the time he stepped clear, his coat was smoking. He asked Lesko to check his back for sparks.

"John . . . why'd you do that?" Lesko had asked him.

"Nice house. It might have caught."

Lesko closed his eyes. "I meant the stiff, John. Why'd you shoot off his face?"

"Looks more like Podolsk that way."

"You gave him Podolsk's wallet?"

"Yeah."

He found Borovik's head where Kaplan had put it down. In a planter right outside the door. The way Kaplan left the house with it, Lesko would have bet that he'd had thoughts of dropping it on Roger Clew's lap. Not now, though.

Waldo took the head out of the bag and tried to balance it on the hood without success. He pulled out his sleeve knife and was about to do some trimming when Bannerman saw Irwin turn green and said lying the head on its side would do just as well. Lesko didn't even ask about this one.

"So where's Bannerman now?" Clew asked Lesko, bringing him back to the present.

Lesko gestured vaguely. "He went ahead."

"And Waldo's with him?"

A shrug. "You know Waldo. You turn around and he's gone."

Both statements were more or less true. Bannerman was up on the floorboards behind Lechmann, covered by the drapes from Kulik's French doors. Poor Podolsk drew the trunk, but at least he was cushioned by the rest of the drapes.

Bannerman says he needs an hour or two. The plan, such as it is, is to get to the embassy. Lechmann will pull ahead to block traffic while the Lincolns lined up to show ID at the Russian security checkpoint. If they're waved through, fine. If they're stopped for a search or if undue attention is paid to Lechmann and his cop car, Miggs will blow through the checkpoint and ram the gate trying not to crush any Marines. Lechmann will drive off in the confusion. Miggs will say his accelerator stuck.

As for Waldo, he was walking toward the woods again the last time Lesko saw him. He asked Bannerman where he was going. "John likes to go out the back way," was all Bannerman would tell him.

"Irwin . . ." Clew tried appealing to Kaplan. "You asked me to come and I came. I brought eight men who are risking their lives to get you back to the compound safely. And this is all you're going to tell me?"

"Roger, I don't even know what I know."

Kaplan held up a hand to show that he was not being evasive. "You looked in the house. I told you who did what to who." He gestured toward the Mercedes that was keeping pace with them. "If you want to know why these guys wanted us before they even saw what happened out there, pull over and we'll ask them."

"How did Bannerman know they'd be coming?"

"He just seemed to know it."

Clew turned to Lesko. "There was an empty safe back there. What was in it?"

"I don't know. That's the truth."

He could have told him to ask Miggs, who had gone through it. Or that the contents of the safe were nothing Bannerman seemed to care about, which was true. Come to think of it, it was odd that Bannerman showed no interest at all. So Lesko had asked Waldo, on a hunch, if he'd already cleaned the safe out. Waldo gave a little twitch that said yes.

"So? What did you find?" he had asked him.

A shrug. "It's all in Russian. Except the money."

"Where is it?"

"Later."

Podolsk was not much more informative.

Whatever was in there, he said, Sostkov was to bring it back to that man whose face Podolsk never saw. Podolsk was convinced that Sostkov would have left him among the dead. But Bannerman was fairly sure that neither man would have left that house alive. Someone wanted a clean sweep, and to get it he needed all of them in the house at the same time. The men in those two yellow cars were a cleanup crew. They even brought shovels with them, possibly to drag six bodies deep into the woods and bury them. Too bad, he said, that we couldn't have kept one of them alive for a while. But having Podolsk might be second best. For the time being, let's keep it among ourselves that he survived.

Miggs had a problem with this because he was career

Intelligence and that career would be over if he made a false
report. Bannerman made him a promise. Make a *late* report,
he said, and I'll give you enough intelligence for *ten* careers.

"Listen," Lesko told Clew, who was starting to fume.
"You came right out and we appreciate it. But you want us
to tell you what's in Bannerman's head and we can't."

"You didn't ask him?"

"Yeah, I did." Lesko nodded. "He wants to get out of
this town in one piece. He wants to take Susan back to
Westport and look for a bigger house. That's pretty much all
he said."

"Bigger house?"

"Don't ask."

The domestic image brought a rueful grunt. Clew blinked
it away. "What's stopping him?"

"Roger . . . look out the window."

Clew glanced at the cars. He seemed unimpressed. In
fact, Lesko realized, those cars were showing progressively
less enthusiasm for the broadside they'd get if they made an
aggressive move.

"Speaking of windows," said Clew, "I thought Bannerman had this wonderful eight-hour pass that Irwin here
worked out for him."

Lesko heard the sarcasm. "He thinks that's bullshit. He
wasn't going to touch it."

The answer seemed to gratify Clew, but it brought Kaplan
to life. He jabbed the shotgun back toward Zhukovka.
"Eleven dead. You call that not touching it?"

Lesko cursed his own big mouth.

"That deal was straight," Kaplan insisted. "The Russians had no use for those assholes either. They said help
yourself and he did."

"Okay, Irwin. I guess that's right." Lesko's eyes said,
"Irwin . . . later."

"They wanted it over. They just didn't want Bannerman
hitting at random while they had their own man . . ."

A glare. *"Irwin . . . Shut the fuck up."*

You're getting upset, Irwin. You don't want to believe
you were being used, especially by Fuller. Jesus Christ,
Irwin. You're DEA, not State. Of *course* you were being

used. You were also, I think, about to make reference to
Podolsk and we don't want to do that yet.

Kaplan seemed to get the message. He settled down. The
motorcade, Lesko saw, had reached the Garden Ring Road.
Less then ten minutes to the embassy. Those other cars were
starting to drop back and now the Mercedes was turning off.
To get new instructions, maybe. Christ, how big *is* this
thing?

"They said help yourself and he did," says Kaplan.

The thing is, he didn't.

Bannerman didn't go to Zhukovka to whack anyone. He
went there because it was the one address he had—from
some faxes Zivic sent him—where a berserk Raymond
Lesko might have gone and Irwin, here, was even offering
him a ride.

If anything, he wanted to prevent a killing. Podolsk's.
Leo's uncle turns up out of nowhere and tells him that
Podolsk is a plant for the good guys, that he's very close to
penetrating Kulik, and Bannerman's going to blow two
years of undercover work if he doesn't back off.

Normally, Bannerman could care less and, besides, he
thinks this guy has his head in the clouds. But he doesn't
want his future father-in-law . . . which is how he's starting to talk suddenly . . . which might *still* get his legs
broken . . . killing the wrong man.

Considerate guy, Bannerman.

Next he hears Irwin's deal. He can see how Fuller might
have bought into it. The Russians want to stop the destruc-
tion, which they still think is all Bannerman's doing. So
does Fuller. But Fuller thinks Bannerman's people have
Borovik already so maybe it's pretty much over. He says,
let's give Bannerman some room, see if he'll gather his
people and get out. Not prolong this thing.

"Would Fuller shaft you?" Lesko had asked when he
heard about this window.

"He would . . . try not to."

Nice relationship, thought Lesko. But that, as it happened, was his own take on Fuller. Guy's basically straight
but he's a diplomat. A job like that, sometimes you have to
make choices. The thing is, so do the Russians.

Bannerman thinks it's possible that these three Russian ministers felt that Borovik, Kulik, and that bunch brought it on themselves. Let Mama's Boy take his best shot. But he says don't bet on it, even if they're basically straight themselves. In their shoes, says Bannerman, he'd look for a way to use this.

"They'd go back on their deal with Fuller?"

He rocks his hand. "It won't look like their doing."

"What won't? How will they use it?"

"The temptation might be strong to do a little house-cleaning of their own. And let Mama's Boy get the credit."

"So what if they do? You'd lose sleep over it?"

"I don't have to be alive to get the credit, Lesko."

"Mr. Clew, sir?"

The voice came from the Lincoln's squawk box. Up front, the guard in the passenger seat was scribbling on a notepad, the radiophone hunched to his ear. He tore off the sheet, lowered the glass divider a crack, and passed it through.

Clew studied it, shielding it. He was frowning deeply. As he read further, however, he broke into a grin. He tried to mask it with his hand. Finally, he folded it to hide a part of the message and showed the rest of it to Lesko.

"Do you know any of these names?" he asked.

There were five. Lesko said he thought he knew two of them. He'd only seen them in Cyrillic before, but they looked like they might be those two Arabs from the restaurant. The other three, he'd never heard of.

"What about them?" he asked.

Clew unfolded the sheet. "An hour ago, your two were shot to death as they left the Sudanese consulate. A witness says the shooters were two men, early forties, short and tall, the short one wore glasses. Sound like anyone you know?"

Bannerman and Irwin here. Lesko curled his lip.

"Of the other three," said Clew, "two jumped from their apartment windows and the third was crushed under a train. This is all in the past hour. A witness claims this last one was *thrown* onto the tracks by a very large, rough-looking man who shouted in English . . ."

That choked laugh again. Clew's eyes were watering. He raised a hand. "I'm sorry. It's funny and it isn't."

Lesko glowered. "Shouted what, Roger?"

"This is in recompense for Elena."

84

Carla was beginning to like Viktor Podolsk.

She was coming to know him through the sort of books he read and through the single photograph of a slender young man posing with his parents. The face, though perhaps five years younger, matched the one in Nikolai Belkin's file folder.

In the photograph, taken at an outing of some kind, all three were laughing. Podolsk was almost doubled over. She had no idea what the joke was, only that they had shared it and enjoyed it. The mother, trim and stylish, had a wonderful grin. The father had an equally open face. A lot like Yuri's. These people liked and loved each other. She envied Podolsk.

The apartment, on the fourth floor of an older high-rise near the Moscow Zoo, was tiny. It was only one room, really, with a thin partition down the middle giving him a bedroom. But the living-room half had floor-to-ceiling windows from which she could see polar bears swimming. Both windows had cushioned seats. One had a wicker back rest. Judging by the stack of books near that one, Viktor Podolsk sat there when he read.

There were quite a few Agatha Christie mysteries, all Russian translations. And some Father Brown mysteries by G. K. Chesterton. But there were just as much Balzac and Flaubert, Dickens and Mark Twain, some in French and English, but much of it translated into Russian. About half of the books seemed to be in manuscript form—fourth or fifth carbon copies.

Yuri explained that many of these books, while no longer forbidden, are extremely hard to get. A rare book, once found or borrowed, would be copied on a typewriter and passed among friends. Or friends would meet and form a circle, passing each page as it was read. Someone had actually sat down and copied the *Oxford Book of English Verse*. Possibly Podolsk himself. It must have taken years. There was a length of ribbon marking a love sonnet by Elizabeth Barrett Browning. It seemed strange. Browning was her favorite as well.

Carla had read quite a few of these books, especially the Balzac and a good deal of the poetry. But she could not imagine herself leaving them around like this for other people to see. She never kept books. Or even talked about them. People know you too well when they know what you read.

"Yuri?"

He didn't answer. He was sulking a little, pretending to be watching the street for John Waldo or Lesko. At the same time listening for sounds from outside the door, which he broke to get in here. She'd told him that there was no use watching. Waldo would never approach from the front, and he doesn't make noise. The best thing to do is talk. If he does come for Podolsk, let him hear their voices. Yuri snorted. That's all well and good if it's Waldo, he said, but suicidal if it's someone else.

Well . . . as long as we're on the subject of dying . . .

"Yuri, I don't think I'm going back. I think I'll just stay dead."

He wrinkled his nose. "Staying dead? What use is that?"

"I don't choose to discuss it."

Besides, you big prick, you haven't even touched me since Bern.

"Well, you must discuss it. The notion is absurd."

"Will you talk to me about Leo's uncle?"

"You will be respectful for a change?"

"Yes."

"First you, then. Did you suppose you can go on being Lydia?"

She shook her head. "You'll want to claim her body, send it home. If the Swiss haven't made her already, they will. Which means they'll be looking for me. If they dredge up Aldo, they'll charge me with murder.''

''I don't think so.''

''That was my damned rug you wrapped him in.''

''It wasn't murder, and an arrest can be dealt with.''

''I'm not going back. I hate Zurich now.''

''Then return to Westport with Paul. You'll be safe among friends who care about you.''

''Screw that.''

''And why this attitude?''

''They'll feel sorry for me, Yuri. They'll take me to fucking lunch.''

Finally, Yuri understood. Carla, who feared nothing, could not bear to be pitied. In the week since the wedding, the sight of Carla Benedict in love must have been the talk of her whole world. All the same, the secret could never be kept. Too many people had seen her alive. The Academician among them, Willem Brugg and Susan among them. He pointed this out to her.

Her response was that her side could be trusted to keep silent. If she asked them. Susan especially. Carla hinted that Susan had a secret of her own, which they shared, and Carla would never betray her. Yuri ignored the digression. Betrayal was not the issue.

''In any case, where would you go?'' he asked her.

''I might stay here. Here I can be Lydia for a while longer.''

''Carla Benedict, who speaks no Russian, stays in Moscow with false papers? It's too ridiculous. You would be picked up as soon as they see you are not with a tour group.''

''Get real, Yuri. This country's a sieve now and the language is money. I can get all I need.''

Total nonsense, he thought. Not at all like Carla. ''I have leave coming. Why don't I stay for a while, show you my Russia. After that, I will take you home.''

''What about Maria?''

''I will . . . ask her permission.''

Carla laughed. ''Talk about dream worlds,'' she said. ''But as long as we are, let's talk about Leo's uncle.''

''You said you'd be respectful.''

She tried to think of a way. Yuri, meanwhile, dropped his eyes.

"What was Mr. Bannerman's impression?" he asked her.

She told him, adding her own.

Yuri did and did not want to hear it. But he listened, sometimes nodding in reluctant agreement. At last, he reached for one of the manuscripts that were stacked by the window. It was one of the Chesterton stories.

"In Bern," he said, "in General Belkin's office, he had a quotation from this man pinned to a corkboard. It reads, 'When people stop believing in something, the danger is not that they will believe in nothing, but rather that they will believe in *anything*.'"

Carla started to speak. Yuri raised a hand.

"You can't imagine the pain in this country," he told her. "All the old ways are totally rejected, even those that worked, even those that were humane. Add to that, there is hardly a man or woman in this country who is not deeply ashamed of *something*. For forgiveness, some go to a church and you know what they find out? That the priest was a KGB informant. That for years, he reported any confessions that might be of interest to them."

"You knew about that?"

He shook his head. "To find out was just as sad for most KGB. So we look for our own priests. We find men like Academician Belkin or we find an Arkadi Kulik. This is what we have come to, Carla."

"You'd pick Nikolai over Leo?" She stood watching the polar bears.

Another shake. Almost a blush. "That . . . attraction was very recent. Only since I learned how much General Belkin had misled me . . . misled Elena. It was, I think . . . bounce-back?"

"Rebound," she smiled, partly in relief.

"I said very bad things to Mr. Bannerman."

"It's Paul and forget it. I do that all the time."

She was watching a police car now. The same one had passed minutes earlier, moving slowly.

"At Elena's wedding, shall I tell you what I was going to ask him?"

"If you could come to Westport. He knows."

"Would it . . . I mean, if you were to go back there, and I were to come . . . for only a visit at first . . . and I brought Maria . . . would that be unpleasant for you?"

"Why would it?"

That driver, plainclothes, had a machine gun on his lap.

"It is only . . . considering that you and I . . . that we have been . . ."

"Yuri, don't be a jerk."

She heard a dull crunching sound coming from the cheaply carpeted hall. The sound was from Podolsk's light-bulb stash, which she had crushed and scattered along the hallway. She reached for her borrowed Makarov. Yuri was already in a crouch, his pistol trained on one side of the doorframe. Carla's came up on the other. Yuri was speaking softly, tenderly in Russian. She realized he was faking sex. She answered with a moan of pleasure. Yuri's breath came faster. More words, grunts. Carla almost shouted *"Da . . . Oh, Da. Da. Da."* But she didn't know if Russians did that.

From outside, the clearing of a throat.

"Um . . . If this is a bad time . . ." came Bannerman's voice from the hallway.

85

Before this morning, the recovery room at Hospital #52 had been the office of the Communist-party administrator. His qualifications for managing the affairs of a major hospital consisted of similar positions at a cement plant in Rybinsk and a factory making busts of Lenin in Lvov. His job was to see that treatment was given according to party rank and to see that treatment standards met party norms. He was to assure, for example, that patient mortality figures below 1.85% were published no matter how many actually died.

Until Willem Brugg's equipment came, Hospital #52 had no other recovery room, no intensive-care unit worth the name. Now it had both.

Elena's surgery had taken two hours. Barring complications, the Swiss surgeon told Willem and Susan, she would recover but the news was not all good. A degree of facial paralysis could be expected, possibly permanent. Some hearing loss, same side, was possible. She might have limited use of her left arm. Paralysis was indicated there as well, suggesting damage to the motor area of the brain.

More serious, one sliver of bone had been driven deep into the limbic system. It is embedded, the surgeon explained, in an area of the hypothalamus that is associated with memory, the capacity to feel pleasure or pain, and the brain's ability to balance extremes of emotion. To remove it would have done further damage. The effect would remain to be seen. The patient will face many months of close observation and therapy. There is an excellent facility near Munich. The surgeon could recommend it without reservation.

"Your father," said Willem to Susan when the surgeon excused himself, "has an expression that is not so polite but is often appropriate."

"In a pig's ass?"

"Wonderful expression. It speaks volumes."

A more detailed report came from Miriam and Avram, who had witnessed the procedure. When they spoke of Elena, they used her name where the Swiss surgeon had not. Yes, he was quite good, Miriam agreed. But so was the mechanic who had once restored a sports car she owned after it had been accidentally immersed in salt water.

Elena was conscious or semiconscious throughout some of it. Parts of her brain had been stimulated with electrodes in order to determine loss of function. It was one of the Russian neurosurgeons who wanted to know, in detail, what sort of person Elena was. He asked, Miriam realized, because he considered her outlook, her strength of character, to be relevant to which invasive procedures they would undertake and which they would forgo. This doctor, she said, she would trust with more than her sports car.

The Russian, on the other hand, had resisted one procedure on the grounds that the risk of infection was too great. Miriam had been about to side with him until she realized that his reservation had to do with the unavailability of the proper antibiotics. There were none to be had in all of Moscow. He relented, happily, when he realized that Willem Brugg had brought enough for fifty such patients.

"Tell that man," said Willem Brugg, "that he will have all that he needs. For the rest of his life, if necessary."

Lesko, with Clew, Kaplan, and two bodyguards in his wake, arrived forty minutes later. He had come from the embassy. All five men carried flowers. Hundreds of them. A corsage, clearly meant for a woman, was pinned to Lesko's lapel. His left eye was swollen and discolored. His trousers were split up the seam. What had happened was this.

Upon reaching the embassy compound, Lechmann had gone past to block traffic from one direction while the last two cars blocked traffic from the other. There was no sign of the pursuers, but the guard at the Russian checkpoint had been increased and a Chaika blocked the entrance. Blowing through was no longer an option.

It became apparent that the guards had instructions to search each of the embassy cars, trunks and undercarriages included. The officer in charge was polite, even apologetic. He said that he had been ordered to detain any Russian national, any foreigner, who could not show the proper papers, and to seize any materials that appeared to be Russian in origin. His orders, he said helplessly, were no more specific than that.

Lesko had little doubt that the object of the search was Podolsk, probably Bannerman, and perhaps the contents of Kulik's safe. That aside, he had no intention of sitting there when he could be with Elena. He climbed out of the ambassador's Lincoln, ignoring a guard who told him to wait inside, and walked up to the checkpoint where Miggs was in discussion with the officer in charge. His intention was to say, "Here's my name, the hotel has my passport and visa, I'm grabbing a taxi."

But he saw alarm in Miggs's eyes and followed them. Two men, black raincoats, had been standing among the

vendors, watching. They seemed anxious. One had been
eyeing the police car where Lechmann was standing at the
door, arms folded across the roof, trying to look bored. The
black raincoat nudged his companion and cocked his head
toward Lechmann. The body language said *"Let's just go
take a look."*

Lesko called to Lechmann, asked if he spoke English.
The two men hesitated. Lechmann shrugged. Lesko reached
into his pocket, flashed some money, said he'd pay twenty
dollars for a ride to Hospital #52. Lechmann answered by
giving him the finger. Lesko blinked but he quickly understood. Lechmann wanted to stage a brawl.

Showing his teeth, he advanced on Lechmann. Miggs
tried to grab his arm, Lesko pushed him away. Lechmann
had rounded the police car where he stood, an insolent smirk
on his face, daring Lesko to come closer. Lesko did, fully
expecting that Miggs would seize him from behind and
make a show of dragging him away. Miggs didn't. Lesko
hesitated. Lechmann feinted with his left and threw a
chopping right that hit high on his cheek.

Lesko didn't know what to do. Grab Lechmann by the
neck? Chase him around the car? But now he felt two sets
of arms on him, one of them in uniform. Miggs and the
Russian officer. Lechmann moved in, aimed a kick at his
groin; Lesko took it on his hip. Screw this, he decided. You
want realism? He wrenched himself free and stormed after
Lechmann, who was dancing away, taunting him. Lesko
went for the police car instead.

He threw his back against the passenger-side door and
dropped into a weightlifter's squat, gripping the car by the
rocker panels. He heaved. Two tires rose slowly off the
ground. With a roar, he heaved again. He heard the vendors
cheering as he managed to straighten his legs. He heard his
trousers split. He heard Miggs shouting, *"Don't."* Yeah,
well, then pitch in here, for Christ's sake.

Miggs and the officer grabbed him again. They pulled
him away from the car, which came down with a crash that
popped two of its hubcaps. He heard Lechmann yelling
something-something *"Amerikanski"* with a *"Yeb vas"* in
there someplace. He could only imagine what Bannerman,
on the floorboards, was calling him. Now Lechmann, who

had suddenly turned pale and wasn't faking it, was arguing with the officer . . . I want to arrest this man. The officer was shaking his head, pointing up Tchaikovsky Street telling Lechmann to get lost. Lechmann threw another finger, this one for all of them. He drove off without the hubcaps.

The only good thing about this, other than that Bannerman and Podolsk were now clear, was that the Russian officer decided to do the ambassador's car first just to get this tanklike American out of there. Lesko found another flower vendor, dropped the same twenty, and needed Kaplan to help him with all the flowers he'd just bought. The grinning vendor threw in a small corsage, which he insisted on pinning to Lesko's lapel.

"For good show," he said in English. "For very good show."

"Don't ask," he said to Elena, softly.

One eye had flickered when he entered the room. It was when Willem turned and said his name. He would have sworn that she started to smile. Not just because he'd come. Because of the way he looked. In his mind, he saw her grinning at him, hands at her cheeks, saying, *"I don't believe this."*

Yeah, well . . .

She was sleeping now, breathing quietly without the help of oxygen. Her color was better than when he'd seen her this morning. The finger had stopped twitching. He touched a hand to her throat, checking her pulse against his own. Elena's seemed so slow. It alarmed him until Susan gestured toward the monitor and whispered that Elena's was the normal one.

Willem had given up his chair to Lesko. He had signaled Susan that perhaps they should wait outside, but Lesko said no, stay, both of you. This is a family. They sat down again, taking seats at a small conference table that had a wet bar behind it.

Lesko, for the first time, noticed his surroundings. Recovery room? The bar was flanked by life-size portraits of Marx and Engels. On the far wall, over a leather couch, was a larger one of Lenin. On an antique sideboard were a dozen

or so framed photographs of another of those trucker types
shaking hands with twenty years' worth of Kremlin leaders.
An orderly was clearing them away to make room for the
flowers.

"Don't ask," he heard Elena say in his mind.

86

The MosKopy store on Kalinin Prospekt is a joint venture
between Russian entrepreneurs and an American franchise
chain. Podolsk had told Lechmann about it. For hard cash,
they ask no questions.

The store offers a mailing and messenger service, four
high-speed copying machines, and several fax machines.
During daylight hours, the fax machines are virtually
useless in terms of any communication beyond greater
Moscow. A city of eight million, Moscow has fewer than
two hundred long-distance telephone lines. Only that many
calls can be made at one time. You could make more,
Lechmann knew, from Main Street in Westport. Ask why a
market economy is slow to catch on, and that's all you have
to know.

If it had not been late on a Sunday night when he thought
to try faxing Anton Zivic, all these circuits would surely
have been busy. As it was, he was lucky. He had expected
an operator to come on the line and, if she was in the mood
to be helpful, suggest that he try again at sunrise.

He was not there, however, for the fax machines. He was
there for the Japanese color copier that was kept in a small
walk-in closet that had a heavy curtain across the door. The
machine was strictly for self-service use. The fee, per
copied page, was several times the normal rate with a hard
currency surcharge for each quarter hour of use. This was on
the assumption that any papers that were not to be seen by

staff had probably been stolen. The machine was seldom idle.

Lechmann busied himself with the contents of Arkadi Kulik's safe. When finished, he was to messenger the duplicate set to the hospital, into Miriam's hands only, with a note from Bannerman that says "Get this back to Zurich." The original was to be wrapped and left for Yuri to pick up. Yuri, leaving nothing to chance, was now watching from outside while Bannerman keeps an eye on the blue Volga and while Carla discusses literature with Podolsk.

Hours earlier, Lechmann had also photographed the documents. This left three possible ways of getting them out of Russia. Not such bad odds. He had photographed them when he and Waldo hid the militia car before going to try to free Lesko. Getting the papers on film was Waldo's idea. Someone might steal their police car, he said. Waldo, Lechmann felt certain, was innocent of the irony in that observation.

Waldo kept the four rolls of film plus the fifth partial roll, which Lechmann had shot outside Kropotkinskaya 36. It was no longer needed to identify the occupants of Kulik's Zil, but Waldo kept it all the same. That done, Waldo dropped the camera down a sewer. This saddened Lechmann—it was a very expensive Pentax SLR—but he understood. Never keep a camera when you no longer need it. When they see a camera, they look for film.

The copying was almost finished. It's anyone's guess, thought Lechmann, where Waldo is now. Probably well out of Moscow on the back of another truck. The five rolls of insurance film are inside a hollowed-out cucumber or some such thing. Waldo will get out when he gets out. He will turn up when he turns up.

Click-hum, click-hum.

It must be wonderful, thought Lechmann, to see the world as Waldo sees it. Everything so simple. That Waldo is seriously crazy no one would argue. But try to go the one step further and classify his derangement.

Are not all lunatics delusional? Try to find anyone more logical. Are they not dysfunctional? Try to find anyone more resourceful. Bannerman, perhaps. But no one else. Waldo is lethal in the extreme, but is he therefore dangerous? Answer: He is if you are. If you are not, he is merely grumpy.

Click-hum.

Someday a psychologist will stumble on Bannerman's Westport and think he's gone to heaven. They'll set up world headquarters. They will have a whole wing just to study Carla Benedict. All the way here she is in deep conversation with poor Podolsk, who, it's clear on his face, had thought she had come to kill him. All she wants, however, is to persuade him that Gertrude Stein was a quack.

Click-hum. Rose is a rose is a rose.

Just two more charts.

On their way to the MosKopy store, Lechmann had gone through the papers with Bannerman, translating for him as best he could. They were quite a hodgepodge. Hundreds of names, addresses, titles, all sorts of nationalities. The papers sketched an enormous network certainly, but, beyond that, Lechmann had no idea what to make of them.

It is not as if these charts say *"Mafia"* across the top and then show in little boxes who are the capos and who are the soldiers. Nor do they say, *"Here is how we will regain power"* or even *"Here is how we will steal Russia blind."* All they seem to show is a network of connections that are not even necessarily criminal.

There is one chart, for example, on which Aldo Corsini's name had caught his eye. Follow the dotted lines in one direction and they lead to twelve other names, with Ronnie Grassi's off to the side. Follow them in another direction and one line, color-coded, leads to Elena Brugg—who the hospital says is out of surgery, looking not so bad, thank God—and from there to Leo Belkin—who is conscious but not so good. From there it splits off and changes color. One line to Nikolai Belkin, one line to Bannerman himself. Should one assume that this incriminates Elena? Bannerman? Leo's uncle?

This was only one chart. Another showed connections between the Bruggs and a number of European industrialists, financiers, even several big-shot politicians. Here, lines connected them to names that were plainly criminal. Known traffickers in drugs and munitions. Smugglers. Money launderers. A lot of lawyers.

There were notes in abundance, but they were usually cryptic. Some were obviously in code. Bannerman knew many of the names, and Podolsk knew many others, but between them they could make little sense of the whole.

"Could so many be corrupt?" Podolsk had asked Bannerman.

"Sure."

No hesitation. Just "Sure."

Hear him say this, hear the way he says it, you understand fortress Westport.

"But here is Elena Brugg," said Podolsk. "Here is you."

This was when Bannerman begins to stare hard at the pile of papers. He begins to rock a little, saying nothing. His eyes go soft and his fingers start to drum. You know that he is listening to inner voices.

And then suddenly the drumming stops. There is almost a smile. You know that he knows. Bannerman, who speaks little Russian and reads even less, now seems to understand everything.

"Ernst . . . You said Irwin's at the hospital?"

"Also Clew. Yes."

Bannerman turns to Carla, asking if she has a pen and paper. She produced a notebook from her purse, first putting her Makarov and hairbrush on Podolsk's lap. He begins writing down a list of names, some from one chart, several from the others. Lechmann helped him with the Cyrillic. Some of these he checked against names on the sheets of fax paper he took from his pocket. Lechmann recognized these pages. They listed those who had dined with Kulik. Bannerman numbered the names, stopping at sixteen.

"Copy this as well, please," he said. "Wrap the copy inside Yuri's package. Take the original to Irwin, personally, with this note."

He begins writing. "Carla, are you still dead?"

"For a while."

"Then you stay with Major Podolsk. Major? Where can you lay low for a few hours but still be reached?"

"Ah . . . Hotel Savoy? I have room sixteen, reserved for four more days."

Bannerman hesitated. "Can you get in without being seen?"

"Through Hermitage Bar, yes. Is why I chose that room."

Bannerman looked at Carla, who nodded. She would check it out first, the nod promised.

"Major . . ." Bannerman was still writing. "I'm going to try to get you out of the country. After that, but only then, I'll tell you everything you're entitled to know."

"Out of Russia?" Podolsk blinked. "This means defect?"

"It means visit until it's safe to come back."

It also, thought Lechmann, means let's get rid of you before you remember that you're a KGB officer and, like Yuri this morning, get confused about your loyalties.

At a glance from Bannerman, Carla opened her door and took Podolsk by the hand. He is reluctant, but he does not resist. Bannerman watches as they cross Kalinin together. Carla is talking to him, calming him. She puts his hand around her waist, shaking it to make it relax. Pretend we're lovers, she seems to be saying. We're just out for a stroll. This, for some reason, causes Yuri to pout a little.

"Yuri . . . do you have any friends at the Swiss embassy?"

"Contacts. Not friends so much."

"I need two things. A secure phone so that I can call Anton, and I need these originals sent to Zurich, Willem Brugg's attention, in the Swiss diplomatic pouch. Will they do that for you?"

"Better if Willem asks. Then would be no question."

"We'll go to the embassy, call him from there." Bannerman felt at his shirt pocket, found a slip of paper, glanced at it. "There was a second Zil at Kulik's house last night. Waldo saw one passenger and a driver. If I give you the plate number, is there a fast and discreet way to learn who had the use of it?"

"Not discreet if fast, not fast if discreet."

"The man will know who's asking?"

"Within minutes, I think."

There is, thought Lechmann, a certain sullenness about Yuri. Twice now he sneaks a look in the direction Carla had taken. This is what? Jealousy? Yuri doesn't like that they go to a hotel room?

If Bannerman noticed, he ignores it.

"Never mind," he says. "We'll ask Roger to do it."

He adds a postscript to the note he's written to Kaplan, tears it off, writes his short note to Miriam. He begins another note addressed to Susan, but this one he tears off and crumples.

"I want Roger to see that list of names, but make sure Irwin gets it first. Use the MosKopy messenger for Miriam because I don't want you seen with a package, but find her and let her know it's coming. After that, take Susan aside and tell her what's happening."

"Ah . . . I'm not so sure I know myself."

"I'm going to tell Anton to start hitting them. You tell Irwin that I want a response within one hour. I'll be somewhere near the Swiss embassy. You bring it, I'll be watching for you."

Lechmann glanced at his watch. "They will ask if you intend returning to Vnukovo. The deadline is now in four hours."

Bannerman grunted. "Irwin might ask. Roger will know better."

87

Viktor Podolsk had given up.

There was no sense to be made of this day. The famous Mama's Boy flies into Moscow and he does in one hour what the Academician would not have done in two lifetimes. Podolsk could see that now. It saddened him terribly. Two years of his own life wasted.

So much death. It left him numb. Numb even to the body of Carla Benedict, who had removed her clothing right in front of him while she waited for the bathtub to fill. He could not believe it. First came her blonde wig. Next she kicked off her shoes, hung up her jacket, pulled her blouse over her head— she wears nothing underneath—and down came her skirt. She stood at the entry closet, checking her Makarov, wearing only panties. On the bathroom door was a Savoy Hotel bathrobe. It was provided to make such exposure unnecessary, but she ignored it totally. Podolsk shielded his eyes with his hand.

Carla Benedict.

His first surprise was that she was alive. The second was that she bore him no grudge. Walking here, he tried to talk to her all the same. He wanted her to know that the Aldo Corsini business was none of his doing and how frantically he had tried to stop the Sicilian.

She would not discuss it. He persevered. "Leave it alone, Viktor," she said. They walked a few more blocks, he tried again, she said, "Viktor . . . leave it the fuck alone."

Her attitude was now clear. Also clear was that there was great pain. Great loss. Very lonely woman. This saddened Podolsk all the more. He was glad to change the subject to the one that still baffled him.

"How did Bannerman know?" he asked.

"Hmm?" She turned off the tap. Now went the panties. Oh, God.

"Ah . . . Bannerman," he repeated. "How could he, so soon, have put so many pieces together?"

"He's a pretty smart guy. Can I use your razor?"

"Razor?"

"I want to do my legs."

He gestured, still not looking. "My kit is on the sink."

In the bathroom doorway she started to turn, then stopped. He felt that she was staring at him. He parted two fingers. She was. Slowly, she reached behind the door and took the robe. She held it bunched against her chest, the hand with the Makarov over her privates. Ridiculous, but at least it is modesty. She is still staring.

"Viktor?"

A weary sigh. He sensed what was coming. "Yes?"

"Nothing. Never mind."

"Viktor?"

Podolsk groaned softly. And a little angrily. Ten minutes,

she's been in there soaking. Hardly a splash. Door open in case someone comes. She has been sitting there wondering about him and now she will ask. He took a breath.

"The answer," he told her, "is no. It so happens."

"Um . . . the answer to what?"

"You read Gertrude Stein. Does that make you a lesbian?"

Silence.

"I know what you thought. All those books in his flat, you say. No wife, no pictures of lady friends. A KGB officer who sniffs flowers. You say, why hide such a beautiful body from this one? It will mean nothing to him."

Podolsk grimaced. He had not meant to say all that. Better she thinks that he is homosexual than be certain he's an idiot.

"Viktor . . ."

"Forgive me. It has been a difficult day."

"You think I'm beautiful?"

He chewed his lip. "You know it perfectly well."

A longer silence. Then, "Viktor, how long has it been?"

An exasperated sigh. "Can't you tell me about Bannerman? I want to talk about Bannerman."

"How long? Months? Years?"

Even to himself, he did not know how to answer. How long since what? Since he's been with a woman or since he's been any *use* to a woman. All he knew was that the pains in his stomach came first. He would need to coat it with milk each morning, so much did it rebel against starting another day with Borovik.

"Two years," he answered. "Almost two years."

"And before that?"

"There was someone. She died."

And that was all he was going to tell her. He could have said how kind she was. How she taught him to love poetry. How one day a mole on her back got bigger and in one month she was gone.

"Viktor?"

"Yes. Sorry." He was biting on his knuckle.

"Is that when you took this job?"

"Soon after. Yes."

"They told you it was dangerous. And you hoped it was. Viktor, I know that feeling."

His throat grew hot.

"Come talk to me, Viktor."

88

Bannerman heard the bleat before he saw the blue Volga.

He watched from behind a sheltered tram stop as Lech-mann, Susan in the front seat with him, made one slow pass, doubled back, and began a second. He had not expected Susan but he was glad she came. If Lechmann allowed it, it was safe. Still, he waited one more pass before he showed himself. Lechmann pulled to a stop at the far curb.

Only Susan got out. She put a hand on Lechmann as if bidding him to stay. She came to him. As she drew near, Bannerman started to speak. She walked through the words, reached her arms around his neck, and held him tightly.

He wanted to tell her that Russians don't do this, not out in the open. But he knew what she would say. *"Just shut up, Bannerman. Shut up for a minute."* He held her, smelling her, feeling the warmth and the life of her. No one would have taken them for Russians anyway.

She bit his ear. "Let's take a walk," she whispered.

It was a broad, tree-lined street of mansions and town-houses. Several were now embassies or consulates. The Swiss embassy was just ahead and across the street. Bannerman could see Yuri at an open second-floor window, watching their backs. He caught Bannerman's eye and shrugged.

Susan had not spoken again. She had punched him, however. He began to move out of range when he saw the fist rising again, but she grabbed his sleeve and pulled him back. Lechmann, he gathered, had not left much out.

"Elena's talking a little," she said at last.

"I know. Yuri spoke to Willem. I can't imagine better news."

This last caused Susan to look up at him, but she said nothing. They walked a little further in silence. Only a toss of her hair, a couple of private sighs.

"You do know how to shake people up, don't you, Bannerman."

He grumbled softly. He wanted to hear Irwin's response to his note, but it could have waited. In another half block or so he might have thought of something personal and affectionate to say that did not sound foolish. Given the circumstances. Given that she was more inclined to hit him.

"Paul?" She stopped, folding her arms. "Have you ordered the deaths of sixteen men?"

He hesitated. There went the moment. He shook his head.

"Irwin sure thinks you have."

He shook it again. "Nothing will happen if we get home safely."

"Are they the men behind all this?"

A noncommittal grunt.

"Bannerman . . . talk to me."

"They are . . . the names of prominent people, mostly from Europe, who would have to be involved in what I think is happening. A couple were named on Borovik's videotape. The others I picked pretty much at random from Kulik's papers."

"Roger doesn't think they were so random."

"Then Roger knows more than I do."

Bannerman steered her toward an ice-cream vendor. He felt a need to do something normal. He ordered two cones, paying with a dollar bill, and handed one to Susan.

"You said you had something to tell me. You said it was personal."

"It's . . . a candlelight kind of subject. Later, okay?"

"Later is fine."

"Paul, those sixteen men . . ."

He stopped her. "My note said *hit*, by the way. Not *kill*."

"There's a difference?"

"Hitting can be a car that blows up with nobody in it. If

you mean people harm, you don't warn them first. That list
was a warning.''

"A bluff?''

"Not a bluff. No.''

"What happens now? If you don't get what you want, I
mean.''

"Anton has the list. By now, he's on the phone. He'll put
out word that all sixteen are my enemies and he'll arrange
a few near misses. He will escalate at his discretion until I'm
physically back in Westport. It's just insurance, Susan.''

She was silent for a long moment. Chewing, he supposed,
on the morality of random terror. He supposed wrong.

"Well, I have news,'' she said finally. "Whoever you're
up against doesn't do near misses.''

She produced a slip of paper from her purse. It was
another list of names, shorter, only five.

"These men have been murdered,'' she told him, "here
in Moscow, during the past few hours. Ernst Lechmann says
none of you did it. But my father says you knew it would
happen.''

Bannerman studied the list. It had been copied in Lesko's
hand. The last two names were Arabic. Probably those two
Sudanese, he imagined. The other names were Russian, and
they seemed familiar. He'd probably seen them on Kulik's
charts. He had half expected to see Nikolai Belkin on it.
Perhaps they don't think he's worth bothering with.

Susan touched her finger to the second name.

"This one was pushed in front of a train—by my father,
according to witnesses—at a time when he was twenty
miles away with you and Irwin. You and Irwin were seen
killing two Arab diplomats.''

She told him what her father was said to have shouted.
Bannerman had to smile, but, on reflection, it wasn't so
funny. Whoever had given that order was all the more
dangerous for being stupid. If not stupid, then vain. It
bespoke a party-boss mentality shaped by too many years of
no one daring to question a witless order.

"Did Roger trace a license number for me?'' he asked.

She nodded. "He says it's a pool car, a Security Ministry
limo used by no one in particular. But the Russians say it

never left its garage last night. Roger thinks John must have misread the plate.''

"I suppose he might have."

But Bannerman didn't think so. Waldo had a burglar's night vision. He could probably have read a newspaper at that distance. More likely, either the Russians were covering or it was someone whom Roger had chosen to protect.

Either way, Bannerman wasn't sure that he cared. Except that he'd like to have given Podolsk a name.

"Paul, I need to ask you something," she said. "Am I putting you at a disadvantage here?"

"Um . . . how do you mean?"

"Is it *hitting* instead of *killing* because you said you'd tell me everything? I mean, are you starting to do things differently for my sake?"

He thought for a moment, then shook his head. "It could come to that, I guess. But no."

"We'll talk about that later, too." She looked at her watch. "That plane you're supposed to be on by five-thirty. Is there a bomb on it? Irwin told me to ask you."

"He thinks I'd know?"

"Irwin thinks you know everything."

A soft smile. "I have no idea. I'm just not about to go near a plane that so many people think I'll be boarding."

"Roger told him you'd say that." She gestured toward the Swiss embassy. "He guessed that you'd be coming here, by the way. He really wants those papers. He'll try to get them from the Swiss."

"There's more than one set. But then he knows that, too."

She nodded. "Which brings us to Mr. Fuller. On the chance that Elena can be moved, he's sending an Air Force MedEvac plane from Wiesbaden. The deal is that you and *anyone you care to designate*—that's his emphasis—are guaranteed safe conduct into our embassy, from the embassy to Vnukovo-II, and from there to Wiesbaden. You will be searched but not detained, you go out with the clothes on your back. He asks if you realize how generous that offer is."

"He's saying I can take Russians out. What does he want in return?"

''You're to take no further action from this moment. You
will leave none of your people behind. You'll either
surrender all documents to Roger or deliver them to Fuller
personally within twenty-four hours of departing Russian
soil. Agree and you leave Vnukovo noon tomorrow.''

''Wiesbaden's a two-hour flight. Why not today?''

''Because I'm going with you when you leave but I want
some more time with Elena.''

She touched his lips when he started to object. ''And
especially some time with you. My father's going to stay at
the hospital. He gave us his hotel room.''

''Um . . . the embassy compound would be safer,
Susan.''

She shook her head. ''The embassy has Roger, Irwin, and
about nine other people waiting to talk to you privately. It
has Barton Fuller waiting for you to call him. It also, I
assume, has a microphone in any room they'd put us in. Not
that I'm bashful, but at some point I might want to screw
your brains out and have no wish to be the entertainment at
the next embassy smoker.''

''Ah . . . yes, but . . .''

She spoke to the sky. ''He blows two men away without
blinking, but he stammers if I talk dirty.''

''Susan . . . your father's room . . .''

''Is wired too?''

''Almost certainly, yes.''

''We'll take a very long shower.''

''Listen . . . Paul . . . I'm not an airhead. I know this
isn't over.''

He said nothing.

''Are you going to take Fuller's deal?''

They had turned back toward Lechmann's police car.
''I'll take the plane ride. We'll talk about the rest of it when
everyone's out. That includes Elena whenever she can
travel.''

''He's not going to like that.''

''Susan, he expects it.''

She licked ice cream from her fingers. ''That's what
Irwin said. He told Fuller to go fuck himself.''

''Susan . . .''

"Irwin said it, not me. He thinks you're amazing, by the way."

An indifferent grunt.

"You *are* amazing. You're in Moscow eight hours and you've got two governments jumping through hoops."

"Susan, not to burst your bubble . . ."

"You didn't do a thing, right? You're just passing through."

"I did almost nothing. I have those papers because John Waldo can't walk past a safe without trying it. That includes mine at home."

"But John didn't know what he had. Lechmann said it's this massive conspiracy but it took you to understand it."

"It's not a conspiracy. Not the way you mean."

"Then what's in those papers that's so important?"

"If I'm right, it's more in the nature of a business plan."

Use the words "business plan," thought Bannerman, and people start to nod off. But that, he was fairly sure, was what he had.

Most of the documents had to do with cash transfers into some thirty Western banks and the purchase of large blocks of stock in what looked like hundreds of European corporations.

Some of the banks and a few of the corporations were listed by name. Most were in code. The cash amounts were also coded, but the dates were not. About half the dates fell during the third quarter of 1991. Given the timing, from just before to just after the Gorbachev coup, that money seemed likely to have come from the party treasury.

Everyone seems to see the looting of that treasury as part of some grand design. He didn't. To him, it had the look of a free-for-all. Everyone grab what you can.

This money, in any case, is what Fuller is trying to recover for the former Soviets. That's according to Kaplan. But even Kaplan, given his outburst at Fuller, has apparently developed some doubts.

Bannerman could hardly blame him. First Fuller tells him they're after some stolen nerve gas to keep terrorists from getting their hands on it. Next it's a drug network, the Sicilian Mafia, and then global smuggling in general. Finally it's the missing party funds and something about the

Sudan, of all places, becoming money launderer to the world.

There would be no cash in the Sudan. Certainly not ore ships full of gold and diamonds. Irwin realized, on reflection, that no one would be so stupid as to trust infidel treasure to an Islamic military government. Any laundering through Khartoum banks, cash transfers, would be done strictly electronically. The only actual money there would be the bribes that were paid. The gold reserves, at least, are probably still in Russia.

Either way, Fuller claims it's all of a piece and it probably is. But what he was doing, Irwin finally realized, was laying a trail of crumbs, telling Irwin just enough to get him to help keep Mama's Boy under control while giving him as little of the big picture as possible.

Okay, then . . . what's the big picture?

Looking at Kulik's papers, it was the odd mix of criminal and apparently legitimate enterprises that started him thinking. What Kulik *seemed* to have charted out was a good portion of his country's economy, criminal and otherwise—he makes no distinction—and a fair-sized portion of the European market as well. In particular, that part in which Russians—not Russia—have a substantial financial interest via the dispersal of the party funds. It was, Bannerman suspected, a blueprint for trying to control all of it.

He told Susan what he thought. She had not nodded off.

"You don't call that a conspiracy?"

"Well . . . he's basically charting out where the money is now, who controls it, and where the power and influence is generally. That's why the Bruggs are on several of the charts. I'd call that doing one's homework."

"Homework," she said blankly.

"It's what CIA analysts do, Susan. It's also what corporate raiders do."

"Except these people are gangsters."

"Yes, but you can't think that way. The trick, I guess, is to understand that the market economy here *is* essentially criminal. Most ways of making money still break the law and require wholesale bribery. All the things you think of as criminal—smuggling, black market, drug dealing, theft of resources—try to think of them as industries, because that's what they are. They provide jobs, Susan. They put food on the table and keep money in circulation."

She scowled. "That's pretty cynical, Bannerman."

"Susan, I'm quoting Yuri. The criminal economy, for now at least, is the only one that works."

She chewed her lip. "The stolen party treasury. Do these papers lead to it?"

"Some of it. Maybe most of it, eventually."

"If Fuller had them, would he help the Russians get it back?"

"Probably not."

"Irwin doesn't think so either anymore. Why don't you?"

"Because Fuller works for his own country, not this one. I'm sure he wants to keep it from total collapse, but he'd also like the fire sale to go on for another twenty years. Is that pretty much what Irwin said?"

"Just about."

"That's not a conspiracy either, Susan. That money, remember, isn't stashed in a vault somewhere. It's been invested in the West. Whatever portion is returned to the former republics, therefore, would have to be pried out of some other economy—say Italy or France—that has benefited from the infusion. If Fuller asked those governments to give it up, they'd tell him to get lost."

"Then why do he and Roger want the papers so badly?"

"There are other ways to milk them. All those names, for one. Everyone who's now in power was a major party figure when the party grabbed that money. A lot of them seem to have a piece of this. Most of the Western names are business and political leaders who have knowingly helped them launder the money. Kulik would have put the squeeze on them one way or the other. So will Roger if he gets those documents."

"You're talking blackmail."

"It's called diplomacy at that level."

Susan made a face. "And you won't give them to the Russians either, because you think they're all a pack of thieves."

Bannerman shook his head. If he felt that way, he told

her, the solution would be simple. Get out, print up a hundred copies, and mail them to the world press.

But what made this such a rats' nest is that some of those names, now high in government of the various former republics, are, at least in Yuri's opinion, essentially honest men. Some, he says, are convinced Communists who wanted that money stashed away for the eventual return to Marxist values. They feel entirely justified: Let the workers get a taste of dog-eat-dog and unemployment and they'll come to their senses soon enough.

Others, who are more pragmatic, knew that if they didn't take it, someone else would. They, at least, intend to put it to good use once the political situation stabilizes. But on the whole, Yuri agrees with Susan. The majority were probably thieves. Some rationalized it. Some just took it.

Going public with Kulik's papers might easily do more harm than good. It might bring down a few governments, cause financial chaos, years of lawsuits. And to no good purpose. What the lawyers don't grab for themselves will probably vanish all over again.

Giving them to the Russians was no solution either. Give them to the wrong man and he'll just take over where Kulik left off. Give them to an honest man and having them could get him killed.

"Well, what's left? Do you have a plan or don't you?"

"My plan is to get us home. Maybe dig a moat around Westport."

"I'm serious. I meant what to do with these papers."

"Susan . . . look at us. We're walking down the street in a city where we don't want to be, trying to dope out a situation that was never any of our business. This isn't my problem to solve."

She said nothing.

"I'm just one man."

"Paul . . ."

"What?"

"Like it or not . . ."

He took a breath, expelled it wearily.

"I know. They think I'm still Mama's Boy."

He knew what Susan meant.

"Like it or not," she said to him, "you scare a lot of

people. They know you have those papers. Make a plan or
they will.''

She was right. But it was all so damned dumb.

On the question of what made him so important, why
Fuller wanted him out of it, he knew that answer.

It wasn't just him. Fuller saw Carla involved with one
Aldo Corsini, who was clearly part of a Moscow-based
network. He saw Lesko and Elena heading for Moscow with
Leo Belkin. He could not imagine that the two were
unrelated. He reasoned—correctly, as it happened—that
Leo meant to use the Zurich program against the people
who were looting his country. He assumed—not correctly—
that Lesko and Elena had thrown in with Leo and maybe
Carla was part of it as well. If that was true, it would only
be a matter of time before Mama's Boy got into the picture.
If he wasn't in it already.

What's Fuller's real interest? Basically, he probably
agrees with Yuri. The criminal economy is the only part that
works. The new robber barons *will* be running this country,
and that has no end of implications where U.S. policy is
concerned. Fuller's thinking probably ran something like,
Let's not have Bannerman opening up this box while we're
still learning where the real power is, and who we need to
talk to when we want to get something done. And let's not
have him hitting, by chance or design, the ones who are
already in our pocket.

Bannerman looked at his watch.

If Corsini hadn't worn that wire, if Arkadi Kulik had
decided to stay home and watch TV last night, he and Susan
would be back out on their terrace, right now, having their
morning coffee.

On the other hand, he'd still be wondering whether he and
Susan have a future together. That's no longer a question.
She's carrying their future in her belly. Not that being
pregnant made the difference. Anton was right. He would
never have let her go anyway.

"You want a plan?" he asked her. "Here it is. I'm going
to dump all this on Willem Brugg."

"What does that do?"

"It lets me walk away from it."

"Fine, but why would the Bruggs want it?"

"These documents, if I'm right, are a mother lode for insider trading. The Bruggs could end up owning half of Russia."

She made a face. "How does that help the Russians?"

"Food on the table. The Bruggs would build, not loot."

It wouldn't take them a week, he told her, to have these documents decoded, analyzed, interpreted. The Bruggs would know how to exploit them. Kulik's banks would cooperate. If one didn't, the Bruggs would probably buy it. The Bruggs work with money, not guns.

Well . . . they start with money.

They would probably call Ronny Grassi in, scare him half to death, and then take him on as a consultant. And Leo, if he lives. And Yuri, of course. It's only right that Yuri should have a voice in this.

Yuri is finished in the KGB. There's nothing left for him there. But with Brugg money behind him, he can start one of his own. Maybe he'll make Viktor Podolsk a general.

They reached Lechmann's car. Susan touched his arm.

"But not my father, Paul. And not Elena. Let's leave them out of this, too."

"They'll have . . . other things to think about."

"Elena's got a lot of healing ahead of her. She's going to stay in bed, even if I have to tie her down."

"I agree. Absolutely."

He opened the door for her.

And he did agree. But fat chance, thought Bannerman.

89

Carla was beginning to wonder if she'd been had.

Not that she was complaining.

She was probably about twenty when she learned one of the great and enduring truths of human nature. The best way to get a guy you've just met to make love to you . . . not just fuck you, but really make love and do it slowly, patiently, lots of touching and soft whispers, lots of tongue . . . is to tell him you think you're frigid.

He'll spend hours at it. And he won't be a shit the next morning because he'll feel so good about himself. He'll think he's the one and only. He was the cure. Years could go by and you'll always be special to him.

It had never occurred to her, somehow, that this might work both ways. It sure as hell worked for Viktor. The first time took her almost three hours. She would have thought that she could make a corpse come in less time than that.

One problem was the phone. It rang once for quite a long time. He didn't answer, of course, but they had to disengage and listen at the door for fifteen minutes, Makarovs in hand, in case someone decided to check out the room in person. No one did. When they came back to the bed, the message light was blinking. She told him to ignore it.

The call was not from Bannerman, because Bannerman, the second problem, came to the door, knocking softly, saying his name. She wrapped herself in the bedspread, let him in, and steered him into the bathroom.

With the hairdryer, shower, and exhaust fan going— fairly safe unless they thought to bug the hairdryer— Bannerman briefed her on what was happening. He also dried his hair, which was wet for some reason. All this took another ten minutes, a considerable loss of momentum.

He told her who else Anton had sent, that they would check in with Miriam as they arrived and that Miriam would send some over here. They might not be needed, this was just in case, don't make any contact with them. They'll stay until Elena, and maybe Leo, can travel.

He told her about the plane from Wiesbaden. It would take Yuri and Viktor out, himself and Susan with them. Lechmann's already gone out to Vnukovo to watch for any unusual activity. If she doesn't want to be seen, she can wait and go out with Willem. In the meantime, however, try to keep in mind that someone still wants Podolsk dead. That charred corpse in Kulik's Zil might not fool them very long.

The "try to keep in mind . . ." was as close as he came to a lecture on maybe trying to be a touch more combat-ready in here. Carla wondered why she was being spared until he told her he'd been upstairs, room 404, with Susan. When he sort of mumbled the "with Susan" part, she knew in a flash why he wasn't throwing stones and why his hair was wet.

When Bannerman finally left, she was afraid she'd have to start from scratch with Viktor. But that pump had been primed. He went off like a rocket about twenty minutes later. Too fast. Explosive decompression. But a half hour after that, he was ready again.

The second time wasn't bad at all. Except Viktor, she was pretty sure, was wishing, pretending, that she was someone else. There's a look they get. But she didn't mind. Probably that girl who died.

Afterward, however, he couldn't do enough for her. He washed her with hot towels and sprinkled her with some talcum he found among the bathroom amenities. He went to the minibar and broke out the caviar and crackers. There were four little bottles of Stolichnaya that had been kept on ice and two thimble-sized shot glasses for offering toasts. Between toasts, he fed her the caviar with a little wooden spoon.

The toasts were sweet. To her, to her rare beauty, to her parents for giving the world such a gift. But they also took forever because he felt the need to summon and recite an appropriate verse with each one. Worse, some of these were Russian, which meant he had to struggle with a translation and then apologize for how much of it had been lost in the attempt.

He toasted his own parents, the two in the photograph she'd seen. He wanted her to meet them. Some day, perhaps very soon, he wanted her to come to St. Petersburg with him. She said it's a date. What the hell.

Leo was forever telling her she had to see the place anyway. It would be nice to drop in on his family, tell them he was a good guy, see what she could do to help them. Depending on her mood, she thought, she might even do a flyby of KGB headquarters. Funny idea. It wasn't exactly in the post–cold war spirit but if she could do a better job on it than Waldo did, maybe they'll put up a plaque.

But St. Petersburg might have to wait awhile.

"Viktor?" He was tickling her back now. "Have you ever seen Paris?"

"Never. Only wonderful pictures."

"Want to go?"

"Someday. Of course."

"I mean tomorrow night. I'll show you where Balzac lived. I know whole streets, and one cafe in particular, that are still just the way he described them."

Podolsk only smiled. He did not believe that she was serious.

Carla realized that she was getting a little swacked—seven vodka toasts and counting—but the more she thought about it, why not?

After two years he's due for some R&R. So is she. Preferably someplace where she'd never been with Aldo. Where she won't have to keep trying to wash him off.

Viktor's just as good looking as Yuri. Not as tough, maybe, but that's okay. He's about ten times as well-read, however, and now his plumbing's back in working order. He has to keep using it, though. Gotta blow out those pipes at least twice a day.

But it's not just the sex. Or that they can talk about books. He likes her. He really does.

And they have one other thing in common. They're both ghosts. They're both supposed to be dead.

Abruptly, Carla kissed him and rolled out of bed. She gathered her clothing, her wig, shoved the Makarov in her purse.

"You are going out?" asked Podolsk, startled.

"Just up to tell Bannerman. We're going to Paris."

The Finn with the carnation was fuming.

KGB or no KGB, five days or no five days, he wanted Major Podolsk out.

He had called Podolsk's room personally to tell him to pack up. He wouldn't pick up the phone, but he was in there, no question. He had snuck in like a thief. Brought some chippy with him. A chambermaid had heard them as she pushed her cart past his door. The chambermaid came running. From what she'd heard about last night, she didn't know why that one was still walking around loose.

The whole staff had seen it on television. Three Hotel Savoy guests, the ones Podolsk was "keeping an eye on," were shot on Kropotkinskaya not three hours after they checked in. One dead, two others wounded. Two of them KGB themselves.

Who shot them? Those Kerensky gangsters. Their faces were on the morning news. Why did two of those faces look so familiar? Because they had both been with Podolsk last evening, right here in this lobby. Who could doubt that Podolsk must have given the order.

One of them, no question, had also stolen the computer of that ghastly German. Which Podolsk swore that he would recover. And which he never did. Also, it would not surprise the Finn if that dreadful business with the prostitutes was actually a diversion set up by Podolsk. And finally, this morning by fax, there is a bill from the German. Pay it, he says, or I tell all the world what kind of a place you run. KGB snoops pretending to be Finns.

The manager thought of going back there, pounding on his door. But this is the Savoy, not the Kosmos. Already, there has been one disgusting scene too many. Let his bosses come and get him.

He looked at his watch. Where are they? When he called them, even that was strange. Are you sure, they kept asking? Could there be a mistake?

Just get him out, and quietly, he told them, or I call the militia.

No, don't do that. We'll see to it.

Well? What's keeping you, then?

Susan had been drying her hair when Carla knocked. Their eyes met when Bannerman let her in. A little smile from Carla and then a questioning look. Susan answered with a shy grin.

Yes, the grin said. I told him I'm pregnant. And it's okay. It's even okay with me now. And I can see you've just been laid. It's all over your face. I'm sure it's all over mine.

Now a frown from Carla and, with it, another unspoken question. Susan understood. No, she said with a different kind of smile, a slight shake of her head. Not about Elena. I'll never tell him about Elena.

Bannerman watched this exchange with something less than patience. He interrupted, asking Carla with lip movements and gestures whether she left Podolsk alone downstairs. Carla held up two fingers, then both hands. Relax, Bannerman. Two minutes.

Bannerman steered her toward the bathroom. More sign language. Susan, will you excuse us? Leave the hairdryer going. If you will, go turn on the TV and radio. Make some noise. Carla? Talk fast, please.

I want to take him to Paris . . . Paris? . . . Yes, right from here . . . You came up here to tell me you want to go to Paris? . . .

That was all Susan heard as she squeezed past them. Poor Paul. If after all those years together, he's still surprised by anything Carla does . . .

She turned on the radio, turned it up, then crossed to the TV and did the same. The program, she was startled to see, was *The Rifleman*. Lucas McCain telling the bad guys to *dosky-vosky-narodya*. Must be Russian for "Get out of town."

She still had her brush. She went to one of the tall arched windows and opened both panels inward. A breeze came in. It would help to dry her hair.

As she brushed it, flipped it, she took in the scenery outside. There wasn't much to see. A department store blocked the view. If it were not there, Paul had told her, she would be looking directly at Lubyanka Square and KGB headquarters. She had still never seen it. She wondered if it's all boarded up, snipers on the rooftop, waiting to see if John Waldo comes back.

Below, the far side of the narrow street was lined with sidewalk vendors, some looking bored, others hopeful. Much of what they were selling looked used. One old woman had only a single pair of gloves to offer, holding them up to each passing pedestrian. No one even glanced at her.

A movement to the right caught her eye. A black car had turned onto the street and abruptly slowed. A man in a raincoat hopped out before it had fully stopped. The car moved on, pulled over once more, and a second man, dressed like the first, got out. Both of them, fifty yards apart, took an immediate interest in window displays of camping equipment and toys. Both had newspapers folded over their hands. The vendors nearest them seemed to stiffen. They moved aside to give them room.

"Paul?"

He didn't hear. The hairdryer.

Now a second black car came up. Not as slowly. It pulled up to the center entrance. The driver got out, helped an old man from his seat. He had a little dog with him. The old man was looking around him. He seemed confused.

He turned his head sharply as if someone had called his name. Susan looked in that direction. Still another man, well dressed, not as old, had stepped out from inside the department store. He beckoned to the man with the dog, then gestured, impatiently, toward the car. "Leave the damned dog," was what Susan sensed he was saying. The driver came around and took it. He put it back inside. Remained standing by his door.

More huddled conversation. The older man seemed more confused than ever. He kept looking toward the hotel entrance. At one point he looked to his driver as if for help. The driver turned away. He caught the eye of one of the window shoppers. They exchanged nods.

"Paul," she said sharply. "Come look at this."

He came to the window, Carla with him. He followed her line of sight, and grunted.

"Leo's uncle," he said to Carla. "Do we know the other one?"

She shook her head. She saw the driver whose gun she had taken. She scanned the street. "I see two raincoats."

"Three," Susan heard herself saying. "The driver's with them, not him."

"Carla?"

"On my way."

"Susan, call the embassy. Roger or Miggs."

Carla was out the door. Susan had the phone. The hotel operator clicked on, she asked her to ring the embassy, then waited. She waved a hand at the walls. "Won't they hear?"

Bannerman made a dismissive gesture. It no longer mattered. He had reached for the Tokarev, which he'd left under a fold of the bedspread, and was back at the window. Susan listened, then spoke into the phone.

"They're getting Roger. What do I tell him?"

"Does he know we're here?"

"Yes."

"Say I said the agreement's been broken and now they're all going to die."

"Um . . . that's it?"

"Only that. Sound hysterical. Then hang up."

"Shit!" Clew slammed the phone down. *"Miggs!"*

He was already at the door, Kaplan with him.

"Bannerman?" Kaplan asked.

Clew nodded. He pointed at Miggs. "Every man you have, to the Savoy *now*! I want a plane *now,* not tomorrow. I want everyone at the hospital out *now*."

"Hold it." Kaplan raised a hand. "Elena can't—"

"Now, Miggs. Make it happen."

Miggs reached for the intercom.

"Paul, I have a gun, too."

He didn't turn. He kept his eyes on the street, but she felt his displeasure. "Where did you get it, Susan?"

"None of your business. What can I do?"

He was silent for a long moment. "Come here with it. I'll show you."

Carla, her hand in her purse, watched as Podolsk moved through the bar, walking toward the street exit. His back was to the several patrons sitting there. But they paid no attention. That established, Podolsk turned and retraced his steps, now heading toward the lobby. Carla followed, staying back, listening for movement in the bar behind her. There was nothing. The bar, at least, seemed clear.

Two Japanese men sat in the lobby writing postcards. They did not look up, but a uniformed porter did. He blinked at the sight of Podolsk, then shot a glance toward the desk. Carla followed it to a man in a dark suit, red carnation. The man's jaw tightened visibly. Keeping both eyes on Podolsk, he reached for a telephone.

Carla stepped to the door that led behind the desk. She

opened it and, smiling pleasantly, stepped close to the man with the carnation. He went rigid.

"That's a gun against your nuts." She jabbed him with it. "Who did you call about the man in room sixteen?"

He couldn't speak. She jabbed him again.

"I . . . I only want him out," the Finn managed.

"Who did you call? Give me a name."

"Name? I called KGB. Only the switchboard. I didn't ask for names."

"How many are inside already?"

"None. No one came. Just now, I was about to call and ask why."

She tugged at his sleeve. "Lie down now."

He started to kneel. "Wait," she said. "Give me that carnation."

Nikolai Belkin's brain was reeling. And his heart was breaking.

"Don't argue with me," this man had said to him. "Just get him out here. For you, he'll come out."

But first he said Podolsk was a traitor . . . that he went over to those others for money . . . those who would destroy this nation . . . try to make beggars of us. The Academician told him no, it was impossible. At that, this man grabbed him by the shirt.

Belkin looked into the deputy director's eyes, trying to comprehend this. He saw panic. More than that, he saw a man he no longer knew. He turned to his driver, Georgi, to say come here, help me persuade Kosarev that Podolsk would never . . .

But in Georgi's eyes also, he saw a stranger. He saw contempt. Georgi? You have been with me from the beginning. Why do you—

"Useless old fool," the man snarled at him, shoving him. "Get back in the car. Sit there with your fucking dog. You can do that much, can't you?" And he called to Georgi, "Go. Get him out here. Tell him the Academician needs him."

Georgi nodded. He turned and seemed to signal among the vendors. And now the men in the raincoats. The Academician knew those two as well. They had come to

him months ago, begging for the chance to work with him.
We want to help you save our country, they said. And now
they ignore him? They listen only to Georgi?

Susan fought to calm herself.

All he told her was they've come to kill Podolsk. How he
knew that at a glance, he didn't say. To Carla, he just says
her name and she's gone. She knows what to do. Do they
rehearse these things? Like . . . here's what we do if
we're ever in Moscow and . . .

Don't think, he told her. Your part is to disrupt. You'll
know when to shoot. When you wonder if you should, that's
the time. Aim to shatter those display windows. Toss
furniture out of this one. Anything. Disrupt.

Then Bannerman was out the door.

"Uncle David? What the fuck do I do?"

"Do like he says, Susan."

Big help. *"There are fifty people down there selling stuff.
What if I hit them?"*

No answer.

And some of them were moving now. The woman with
the pair of gloves and a man selling pots. They made eye
contact—she was almost sure—with that old man's driver.
The old man was back in his car, sitting with his face in his
hands. The other one had backed into the store. The
raincoats with the newspapers weren't looking at toys
anymore, and two of the vendors were crossing toward the
hotel entrance.

*"They're part of this, right? Or are they taking a pee
break? Carla, what would you do?"*

Dumb question. She'd let God sort them out.

Disrupt disrupt disrupt. Buy time until the cavalry comes.
But that could mean more shooting, more bystanders hit.
She had one idea, maybe dumb, maybe not. She groped for
the phone.

Podolsk did not want to think the worst. Perhaps all the
Academician wanted was to ensure his safety. Not Carla,
not even Mama's Boy, can read minds from a fourth-floor
window.

"He's not calling this," Carla told him. "That other guy is."

Podolsk had caught only a glimpse of him through the lobby entrance. He could not be sure, but it looked like Andrei Kosarev. Kosarev, he told Carla, is first deputy director of the Ministry of Security, new KGB. Also one of the names on the Borovik tape, but one that Podolsk greatly doubted. Kosarev is a reformer, he told her, not old school, not corrupt. Academician Belkin might well have gone to him for help.

"You want to bet your life on that?" she asked him. "Get in the gift shop, stay out of sight."

She says this as she stands behind the front desk, very Finnish in her blonde wig and her blue blazer with the red carnation. One foot is on the poor manager's back. Her eyes are shining. He had not seen this look before, but this, he thinks, is at last the Carla Benedict they tell stories about. For a moment, however, as she is sending him away, a new look comes over her. It is like fear. Her eyes open, her lips part.

"Viktor . . ." Her voice is also strange. "Don't you get killed on me," she says to him.

Bannerman had come and gone.

It would have been nice, thought Carla, if he'd stopped to touch base. A little coordination here. Instead he edged into the lobby, did a double take on her in her manager suit, and laid an I-don't-believe-you look on her. He gave this little whirl of his hand and he was gone. She took it to mean that he was covering the back.

Bad plan, Bannerman. Out front is where the heat is.

She saw the two vendors—a thin, balding man with no chin and a frumpy thin-lipped woman with a butch haircut—crossing the street. The doorman moved to stop them. The woman leaned toward his ear. The doorman backed right off. Now they were coming in, she with a big purse, him with a shopping bag. The woman flashed a mystery ID at Carla, touched an if-you-know-what's-good-for-you finger to her lips, and took a seat behind a potted palm. The man wandered over to the gift shop. Carla held her breath. But he stayed outside, perusing a tall revolving rack of foreign newspapers, largely concealed by it. Back across, that driver whose gun she lifted had been watching, waiting for them to get inside and settled.

Think Carla. You're a little shit-faced but you still have the edge.

These two are obviously backup. The driver—Georgi, right?—would come in, knock on Room sixteen, say who he is, and a relieved Viktor Podolsk, he hopes, will open the door. He might not kill him on the spot. They'd want to take him out quietly, strap him down, find out what's in those papers. If he's not there, kick the door in on the chance of finding a set.

And here he comes.

Carla lowered her head, pretending to be sorting mail. He'd know her if he looked too closely, but she was betting he'd want to keep his own face averted. And he was doing that. Let him go back, she told herself. He'll come up empty, go back outside, and waste more time getting told what to do next. Maybe they'll give up. Just leave. Maybe they'll pick a better time like when that plane we're taking is over Poland.

Come to think of it, fuck that.

"Hey, Georgi. Looking for someone?"

He froze. He turned toward her, startled. The woman blinked. The man, partly hidden by the rack, kept turning it.

"You have to get by me, Georgi. Me and your Makarov here."

She held it up for him to see. She held it carelessly, in her left hand, letting it dangle from one finger. The Finn under her foot tensed. She glanced at him. "Viktor, you stay down," she said.

She could see the driver trying to stare through the desk. She knew that he was weighing his chances. This woman, the famous Carla, could she be so reckless as to hold a gun in that way? He could beat her easily, he was thinking. Get the drop on her, see if Podolsk's really there. He fought to keep from looking at the other two. But the dyke in the chair had made her own decision.

Her hand, and the butt plate of a machine pistol, cleared her purse. Carla raised her right hand from behind the desk, a second Makarov in it.

She fired.

• • •

"You can walk or you can die," Bannerman told the man. "You choose."

He had come in behind him, first leaving through the Savoy kitchen, walking briskly up to Lubyanka Square, through the front entrance of Detsky Mir, through the crowds of shoppers, to the rear entrance facing the hotel.

There was another man with him, a bodyguard, but he, too, had been watching the street. Bannerman chopped him down. Without breaking stride, he seized the older man's collar, jammed the Tokarev under his jaw. The man stiffened. He managed to turn his head slightly.

"You are Mama's Boy?" he asked, wincing in pain.

"Walk."

"You don't know what you're doing. I've helped you. Now we only want to contain this."

"Then you won't mind walking. Go."

Carla's bullet chanced to hit the rising weapon, slamming it against the woman's rib cage. Her head hit the wall, the chair collapsed under her. The two Japanese sat frozen, the porter dropped to the floor, and the Finn yelped and bucked, knocking Carla's leg from under her. She fell to one knee and her chin struck the desk. It stunned her, but she regained her feet. The driver saw her eyes, started to reach inside his coat, but he threw up his hands instead. It would not have saved him. What did was the sound of breaking glass from the far end of the lobby. The tall rack was falling over, spilling newspapers. She swung both Makarovs on the man who had been standing there.

Bannerman heard the muffled shot as he and his hostage reached the sidewalk. He could not tell the source at first. On both sides of him, vendors saw his gun and scrambled for safety. Boxes tumbled, goods were scattered.

More shots. Much louder. He looked up. Now it was Susan who was firing. A display window to his left rained glass. One of the raincoats, a gun in his hand, danced away from it. He ran into the street, into the path of a CNN sound truck that had come screeching around the corner. It struck him a grazing blow, knocking him into the path of fleeing vendors.

CNN? So quickly?

The other raincoat was running toward Bannerman, his attention divided between Bannerman, the CNN truck, and Susan's fourth-floor window. Bannerman swung the Russian to face the running man. The Russian barked an order. The raincoat backed away.

He heard two more muted shots like the first. And then he heard a muffled scream. A woman's voice. The door of the Savoy burst open. He saw Nikolai's driver backing out, hands raised, crouching. He broke and dove for cover. As the door was swinging shut, Bannerman heard that scream again, more clearly now. It was Carla's voice. She was screaming *"Viktor!"*

Podolsk had seen the man come in, saw him take his position. He had seen them all. And he saw on Georgi's face, when Carla challenged him, that Carla had been right.

Why Carla shot, he could only guess. It echoed off the marble like a clap of thunder and he saw her stagger as if she herself had been hit. He had no weapon—Carla wanted both Makarovs—but he could not stay and hide. And this man by the newspapers was also pulling out a gun. He could take that one at least.

Podolsk snatched a brandy bottle from the shelf and charged out of the gift shop. The man heard him coming, turned, but Podolsk caught him full across the temple. The bottle shattered. The man fell backward, taking the newspaper rack with him. Podolsk snatched his weapon as he fell. He looked up to where Carla had been. He saw belches of flame where her hands should have been. He heard the thunder again and he felt the lightning strike his chest.

He felt himself rising, lifted off the floor. There was very little pain. This was all that he remembered.

90

Rozhdestvenka Street, the short and narrow block separating the Savoy and Detsky Mir, was jammed with vehicles and people.

Five embassy Lincolns, their way blocked by sound trucks from CNN and now Vremya, had mounted the sidewalk on the Savoy side. On the Detsky Mir side, two ambulances, several police cars, and a half-dozen black Chaikas had done the same. Even the mayor of Moscow showed up, his office having been alerted by Vremya that those responsible for last night's carnage, today's rash of killings, were said to be at the Savoy trying to finish the job.

It was Susan who had called CNN, who in turn had called Vremya. It seemed as good as anything to tell them. It might even have been true, for all she knew. Disrupt, Bannerman had told her. Nothing disrupts like a swarm of reporters.

She had rushed down to the lobby as soon as Bannerman and the man he was holding made it safely through the door. She knew that there had been shooting in the building. The three dull booms and their vibrations had come right up through the floor. When she emerged from the lobby stairwell, there seemed to be bodies everywhere, but most of them were moving. The woman who was not a vendor was on her knees, clutching her chest, trying to crawl toward the exit. The man, his head bleeding, was also trying to rise, and a Japanese was trying to hold him still. Another Japanese was kneeling with Carla over a man who, Susan feared, was probably Major Podolsk. Carla was talking to him, desperation in her voice. The Japanese was packing newspaper against wounds high on his chest.

She saw Bannerman, his pistol under that man's chin, his attention still on the street, trying to get Carla to answer him. What happened here? Who shot him? From the look in his eyes, he was within a blink of blowing the man's head off if the answer was Nikolai Belkin's driver.

The next five minutes were a blur of faces and running feet. The first of the Lincolns pulled up outside, Roger, Irwin, and Miggs. More embassy suits followed, Yuri with them. The suits sealed off the lobby, searching and guarding the two who had pretended to be vendors. They let no one in or out until the first EMS crew arrived and, with it, a Doctor Meltzer from the embassy.

Yuri picked Carla off the lobby floor so that Meltzer had room to work. He took her aside, got her to speak a few words. A suit scooped up two Makarovs that had been on the floor beside her. Yuri steered Carla toward Bannerman but seemed to think better of it. Bannerman was busy with Roger and the man he was holding. Carla shook Yuri off and was down with the injured man again. Holding his head. Stroking it.

Susan called Yuri's name. "Is that Podolsk?" she asked him.

He sighed and nodded.

"I think I know who shot him. He's right outside."

Yuri started to shake his head, his eyes terribly sad, but he followed her finger. The driver was still out there, blocked in. He stood talking to one of the raincoats, seemed exceedingly nervous, kept glancing at the figure that was slumped in the back seat of the black Chaika. She told Yuri what they'd seen, and what she'd seen, from the fourth-floor window. That man, the driver? Whoever he works for, it's not Leo's uncle. Leo's uncle tried to stop him.

Yuri's sad eyes slowly widened. His nostrils flared. Without a word, he was out the front door. The driver saw him coming, saw his face, turned, and tried to run. Yuri reached him, gripped his jacket, was asking him questions and getting denials. Yuri pulled him toward the left rear door of the Chaika, opened it, and seemed to freeze. As if in slow motion, Susan saw him reach in and place the fingers of his free hand on the throat of Nikolai Belkin. Just as slowly, he straightened. He touched the little dog as if to comfort it. Slowly, almost tenderly, he closed the door again. Susan knew that the old man was dead.

Yuri seemed to explode. The hand gripping the driver lifted him onto his toes and the other stripped him of his pistol. Yuri was dragging him back toward the Savoy. The raincoat came after him, reached to grab his shoulder. Yuri whirled on him, brought the pistol down across his ear. The raincoat pitched forward. CNN got all of this. Film at eleven.

Susan had never seen Yuri angry. She was now almost afraid of him. He burst through the front entrance with this man, glanced once around the lobby, then dragged him through a door marked Office. Several hotel staff scurried out. They scattered to find other places of safety. Yuri slammed the door behind them. More bangs and thumps came from inside.

Susan's impulse, rather than to hear a man being beaten, was to go and sit with Carla, at least try to be of comfort whether Carla welcomed it or not. She had started in that direction when a new uproar started outside. Her father had arrived.

His appearance caused a near stampede when the CNN and Vremya crews recognized him as the berserk American from last night's Kropotkinskaya massacre. He pushed through the gang of reporters, all of them shouting questions at once. The CNN correspondent asked him to confirm rumors of a retaliatory massacre at a certain dacha outside Moscow. The embassy suits kept them back. Susan noticed, meanwhile, that a similar line of KGB suits was forming opposite them. They had the look of men who thought they should be doing something, but no one seemed to be telling them what that was.

Of all those in the lobby, the most relaxed seemed to be the man whom Paul had dragged across the street at gunpoint. Paul had lowered his weapon and turned to ask about Podolsk's condition. The man—someone named Kosarev—strolled over to the glass of the lobby doors and gestured with open palms to those outside, telling them to calm themselves.

But behind them, there was still another commotion. A man in a blue police uniform was wading through microphones, making his way to the lobby. Kosarev sagged visibly at his appearance. His manner was not so much concern as *I-don't-need-this.*

"*Dobrij vechir, Kaptain Levin,*" said the Russian wearily.

Must mean good evening, thought Susan.

"*Yeb vas, Kosarev,*" the policeman answered.

Irwin Kaplan, who had been standing in that group with Bannerman, was no longer listening to whatever was being said. He was staring, mouth open, at the blonde woman with the red carnation, blood on her hands, and a man's head in her lap. He approached her, disbelieving, touched her shoulder, and lowered himself to her side. She looked up at him. Neither spoke. Irwin touched her wet face. He kissed her.

Susan's father, remembering how to parent, yelled at her for being safe. That done, he asked if she had swiped his Beretta and yelled at her for that. If she got shot, he said, it would have served her right. He would not have even come over here, he said, if Elena hadn't made him.

"Pay attention to your daughter for a change," Elena had told him.

"Meanwhile," she said, "I could use the peace and quiet."

"And if all is well at the Savoy," she told him, "take time to shower as a favor to me."

No, he said in answer to the brightening of Susan's face. Elena is *not* okay and no way in hell is she going to be moved. She is not going to fly, drive, walk, or even sit up until he tells her she can. He had thrown those embassy clowns out of her room, he said, when they even suggested it.

Susan agreed, of course, that she shouldn't be moved yet. Still, in her mind's eye, she saw Elena tossing back the covers the minute her father left the room. Telling someone to unplug her, give her a hand. Telling Willem to call Vnukovo and get that sucker revved up. Reminding him that it's a flying hospital. And that although she had vowed to obey, that was only for Zurich. This is Moscow.

Susan saw Podolsk move.

He was suddenly conscious and trying to touch Carla's

face. She was keeping him from doing it, backing away for
some reason, her teeth clenched, tears streaming; she was
shaking her head at him. Irwin turned to her. He seemed to
be scolding her.

Carla struggled to her feet. Irwin rose with her. She ran,
half doubled over, toward the corridor leading to the guest
rooms. Irwin followed.

"Carla shot him, right?" said her father at her ear.

"No . . . No, I think it was . . ."

But Lesko knew the look. "She shot him," he said.

The door marked Office opened.

Yuri came out dragging the driver with him. The driver
was holding his ribs. He was bleeding from the mouth.

"Who has comb?" he asked Susan and her father. "Also
handkerchief."

Startled, she produced both from her purse, then tried to
snap it shut on her father's fingers, which were relieving her
of the Beretta. Her father pulled it free.

Yuri combed the driver's hair, roughly, approximately,
and returned the comb to Susan. Next he spat into the
handkerchief and used it to wipe the blood from the driver's
face.

"This you don't want back, I think."

"Um . . . it's okay."

He looked around him. "Carla is where?"

"With Irwin. He took her—"

"You go too, please. Needs woman."

But by this time he was looking past her. His eyes, still
hot with rage, found those of the man named Kosarev.
"Watch TV tonight," he said. *"You son of a bitch."*

This last phrase was mouthed. No doubt, Susan felt sure,
so as not to offend her ears. It did not greatly offend
Kosarev, who only grumbled softly as if at a minor
frustration. By the time that thought registered, Yuri was out
the front entrance, climbing onto the hood of a Lincoln,
pulling Georgi up with him, inviting the cameras to come
forward.

The police captain, Levin, followed him out. He wanted
to hear this himself. Yuri looked down at him, hesitated,

then reached into his pocket. He pulled out what looked like a video cassette and handed it to Levin. He gestured toward the Vremya unit. Go play it, he seemed to be saying. Play it for everyone.

"Any idea what that's about?" Susan asked.

Lesko shook his head. Bad enough he'd probably have nightmares about it himself. But Bannerman was now telling the Russian, and Clew, what was on Borovik's confession tape. Just the highlights. Like a place called Vigirsk, wiped out by stolen nerve gas. Naming names. Kosarev's name among them.

The Russian wilted, just for a second, but quickly recovered. From where Lesko stood, the existence of that tape did not seem to be news to him. Now, in fact, he was trying to brush it off. Coerced by torture from a piece of garbage like Borovik . . . zero credibility . . . all Kulik's doing . . . trying to blame the innocent for his own criminal acts . . .

But he was looking outside, watching the faces of the reporters as they listened to the driver and to Yuri.

The army doctor, Meltzer, glanced up at Lesko.

"You've been busy," he said, scowling.

Lesko grunted. "For the record," he answered, "you asked me not to do anything on my own. I didn't. How bad's he hit?"

"I've seen men die from leg wounds. This is a chest."

"He's not bubbling," Lesko said hopefully.

"He's not doing cartwheels, either." Meltzer cocked his head toward Clew. "I hear you're flying him out."

Lesko frowned. "Can he make it that long?"

The army doctor blew air. "He's stabilized, I think. The question, I gather, is will he make it if he stays."

Podolsk's hand came up. He was trying to speak. Lesko knelt, took the hand. "You heard, right? You just have to hang in. You'll make it."

"That man . . ." Podolsk squeezed. "Kosarev."

"Easy, okay? What about him?"

"Ask him to say my name."

"Say your name? What for?"

"Please. I want to hear him say my name."

What the hell, thought Lesko. If only to keep him quiet. He crooked a finger at the man named Kosarev, calling him forward. The Russian held back. Lesko showed his teeth.

"Lighten up, Lesko." Clew stepped between them. "This man's your ticket out."

Lesko had assumed as much. He was clearly not everybody's favorite human being at the moment, but he did seem to have a lot of clout. Lesko's guess was that he'd be going along for the ride to Zurich or Wiesbaden, wherever, so no one should develop engine trouble.

The thing was, though, he wasn't acting much like a hostage. He was acting, now, more like a guy who's had a very bad day and would just like it to be over. It wasn't helping that the cameramen outside were all suddenly trying to get shots of him through the glass. Nor was it helping anyone's nerves, come to that, that those two Japs—born with cameras around their necks—were snapping everything in sight. One was now posing with those two shooters . . . guy with the bandaged head and the ugly woman wheezing through broken ribs. What a fucking circus. This whole thing. Beginning to end.

Lesko rose to his feet.

He approached the Russian, patting Bannerman and Clew on their shoulders to show his good intentions. He put an arm around Kosarev. The Russian tensed but did not struggle.

"What's your name? Andrei, right?"

Kosarev nodded warily.

"Tell me," he said to Clew, "that our friend here had nothing to do with last night."

"He didn't. That was the last thing he wanted."

"But he was in this thing with Kulik."

Clew shook his head. "That . . . hasn't been proven."

Lesko looked at Bannerman, whose mind was elsewhere. "Roger's not a guy you can just shoot the shit with, is he?"

A flicker of a smile.

"That was Andrei's boys who showed up with the shovels this morning? And who chased us all the way back from Kulik's?"

Bannerman raised an eyebrow toward Kosarev. He had

apparently not bothered to ask. Kosarev shrugged. It was not a denial.

"Lesko . . . let's save time," said Clew. "What he wants is no more trouble. What he *did* want was Kulik's papers. He now understands that they're gone."

With his free hand, Lesko rubbed his eyes.

Nice, he thought. Guy says I gave it a shot, it didn't work out, water under the bridge. Never mind all the dead. And maybe the dying.

Miggs whistled from the front door. He was waving a Motorola, pointing at his watch. Any time you're ready, he was saying.

Bannerman reached for Kosarev, but Lesko tightened his grip and walked him to Podolsk's side. "He wants you to say his name. It can't hurt, right?"

Podolsk looked up, waiting. Kosarev mumbled it. Gutturally. It was Lesko's sense that he was trying to alter his voice. Lesko began to understand.

"Out loud," he said, squeezing. "Into the mike."

"*Podowsk,*" the Russian said through clenched teeth. "He is Major Viktor *Podowsk.*"

Podolsk's breath came in gaps. "That is him," he said. "That is the man who . . ." He tried to claw at Lesko's gun.

91

The MedEvac plane from Wiesbaden arrived as the setting sun touched the horizon. Viktor Podolsk, Meltzer attending him, was carried aboard first and connected to a respirator.

The convoy from Hospital #52 brought Leo Belkin in one ambulance, Elena in another, Valentin's body in a third. It was Belkin who begged them not to leave Valentin behind. It was bad enough he got him killed, he said. He couldn't leave him in a Moscow morgue for some clerk to contact his family.

Three Lincolns and the two army trucks escorted them. Riding in the truck, as additional escort, were a dozen or more hospital staff and several Russian soldiers—relatives of staff—who were determined to witness the safe departure of the Brugg Industries plane and the MedEvac aircraft. Several of the Swiss medical team had elected to stay in Moscow. They would teach the use of the equipment they had brought. They would come home when the Russians were proficient. Miriam and Avram stayed in case anyone else breaks the truce. And to direct traffic when the teams from Zivic start arriving.

The Swiss surgeon, to the surprise of many, was among those who chose to remain. He made it clear that this was not a humanitarian gesture. He expected to be paid the full salary per diem of a Russian staff surgeon. That the amount in question is less than one Swiss franc, he said, has no relevance to the principle at hand. Also tell that Lesko *girl* that she can kiss my ass.

Elena, though pale and weak, wanted a few minutes with Leo before he was lifted aboard the MedEvac. There was time, because the MedEvac had brought with it a maintenance team that had been ordered to inspect the Air Force plane on which Kaplan and Clew had arrived. Almost at once, they found evidence of tampering.

They met, stretcher to stretcher, on the tarmac between the two planes. Belkin, himself even weaker, groaned at the sight of her. Her head was thickly padded, her left eye wandered slightly, her speech was slurred. He was totally to blame, he said. He had been no friend. He was deceitful and stupid. And when trouble came, as he should have known it would, he was worse than useless. Poor Valentin. It was unforgivable. It was shameful. It was . . .

". . . a matter of honor, Leo," she reminded him.

She would hear no more of his breast-beating, she said. She will expect him in Zurich as soon as he is well enough. They will discuss, among other things, when she is to get the rest of her wedding gift. At the very least, she told him, she expects him to make good on St. Petersburg.

Lesko had come over. He heard the part about St.

Petersburg. Over my dead body, he thought to himself. But he was glad to see that Leo's color was a little better. Get well, Leo. Get nice and strong so I can pound the living shit out of you. After that, no hard feelings.

Lesko was just leaving the Savoy when he learned that Elena was already on her way to Vnukovo. He had wanted to hit someone then as well, starting with that Russian prick, Kosarev, but Bannerman stopped him. We want him walking, he said. We want him clearing the way outside. Lesko still had no idea why this little shit was helping them.

Outside, that Russian cop, Levin, tried to arrest him, but Bannerman got him to back off. Promised he'd be in touch. Then Yuri tried to go for him. This was after they had to drag Yuri down off the Lincoln. He fought them off and then waved the reporters over to Nikolai Belkin's car, haranguing them in Russian. Meltzer ducked in to take a look. He confirmed that the old guy was dead, but he didn't think he'd been murdered. Looked like a stroke, he said.

Yuri wanted to go to Wiesbaden with the MedEvac, look after Podolsk and Leo, make arrangements for Valentin. Valentin and then someone named Lydia. Just as much, he didn't want to fly back with Andrei Kosarev, because he couldn't trust himself not to kill him. After Wiesbaden, he didn't know. He said he didn't think he'd go back to Bern except to clean out his flat.

Bannerman shook his head. Come back with us, he said. We have some things to talk about with Willem. And tomorrow we'll go to Bern one more time to collect your mail. If you go to Wiesbaden, he said, you'll face about a week of interrogation. You might end up killing Roger Clew instead.

Fucking Bannerman.

Just once, Lesko would like to see him shut down the computer and, like, *feel* things. But Susan says that's not fair. You should know him, she says, when there's no shit like this going on. He's gentle, and sweet, and he can be endearingly inept around the house.

Some standard, right? Endearingly inept.

The other extreme, he supposed, would be someone like Carla Benedict, who doesn't do anything *but* feel. That was

one more thing that slowed them down at the hotel. Carla
tried to get away from Irwin. She tried to climb out the
window of Podolsk's room. God knows where she thought
she was going. Irwin thinks she would have hurt herself. He
had to tackle her and hold on, trying to protect his eyes and
his balls until the rest of them got back there. But when they
did, yeah, you'd have to say Bannerman was gentle. And
sweet. He carried her out like a little girl he was putting to
bed. Her face buried in his neck. Her whole body trembling.
In fact, seeing that was what finally calmed Yuri down.

Carla's already on the Brugg plane, still a basket case.
Irwin's staying with her. He refused to go back with Roger.
Susan's with them both. From what Lesko understood,
Carla had gotten a little snockered, which is something she
never does. The booze affected her judgment when those
three shooters came in. There was no urgent need, otherwise, to force a fight. But once it started, she was on
autopilot.

Except for the vodka, he couldn't see how it was all her
fault. Podolsk made a dumb move. Ballsy, maybe, but
dumb. He popped up like a target on a combat range. Carla
couldn't see his face, she said, with all the flying newspapers, but she saw a gun, which she knew Podolsk didn't
have. She never saw him grab it from the other guy.

Now she's convinced she's the kiss of death. If she feels
anything for you, you die. Cause of death—Carla. She
thinks they put that on your toe tag. There was her sister last
year, she says, couple of guys before that, her mother years
back . . . everyone. Then Aldo yesterday and Podolsk
today. Not that Podolsk is dead, but she thinks he will be if
she ever goes within one country of him again.

Right now she's getting lots of female empathy from
Susan and a lot of TLC from Irwin, who turned into a
puddle for some reason when he found out she wasn't dead.
Irwin will have his own problems in a day or two. Wait and
see.

Anyway, let them have their counseling session with
Carla. Before they get to Zurich, maybe he'll give it a shot
himself. It's called Lesko therapy. You pick her up, shove
her into the lavatory, shut the door behind you, and scream
at her.

You say, "Get *over* it."

You say, "This is self-indulgent, self-pitying bullshit and I'm tired of hearing it."

You say, "Podolsk's hurting worse than you, he's all alone, and you promised the guy a trip to Paris. You got two minutes to tell me what you're going to do about that or your pants come down and I spank your ass raw."

Of course, you pat her down for weapons first.

And you protect your eyes and your crotch.

Epilogue

From the Brugg Industries jet, Bannerman could see the lights of Dresden below. Russian airspace was some forty minutes behind, Moscow more than ninety. Well to the north, he could still see the MedEvac plane reflecting the afterglow of sunset.

The airborne office, aft, converted to a bedroom suite at night. Elena had been made comfortable there. Susan was with her. She had chased out all other visitors including Lechmann, who had turned up with a huge bouquet of drooping carnations he had somehow managed to find.

The main cabin had been darkened. Yuri and most of the medical staff were asleep, exhausted or emotionally spent. Lechmann sat huddled with Willem, briefing him, probably telling him about the documents that were on their way. The Russian, Kosarev, sat off by himself, staring out into the night. Carla's tiny body lay across two seats, her legs drawn up, her head on Irwin Kaplan's lap. One hand clutched a spray of violets, also from Lechmann. Bannerman had covered her with blankets. Kaplan tucked them in. He whispered that she looked about twelve years old.

The stillness was broken only by Lesko. He was in the galley, rummaging for a fresh piece of ice to hold against his lip where Carla had kicked him. She understood, she told him, that he meant well. She even agreed. Yes, damn it, she would go to see Podolsk in Wiesbaden. Maybe . . . maybe even Paris someday. But that split lip should teach you. Don't ever put your hands on a lady.

Lesko found the ice and grabbed two cold Löwenbräus. He walked back up the aisle, and took the seat next to Bannerman.

"Ready for a few questions?" he asked.

Bannerman took the offered beer. "I've got one myself. You first."

"Kosarev's the guy behind all this?"

"He's chairman of the board, apparently. Elected by a council. It's structured very much like a corporation."

"But he's the one who wanted you running loose so he could thin out the competition."

"Not the only one, but yes."

"And he would have killed you to get those papers."

"At the Savoy? He didn't know I was there. He just wanted Podolsk."

"Let's shorten this. You made a deal with him, right? He calls off his dogs, he comes along so no one blows us out of the air. In return, he gets what was in Kulik's safe."

"He gets a ride to Zurich. Nothing more."

A pained expression. "Am I missing something here? Why, then, did he get us out of Russia?"

"We got *him* out, Lesko. He's running."

Lesko rubbed his eyes in a show of utter weariness. "Bannerman . . ." He groped for words. "With you, is anything ever what it looks like?"

"You were there, Lesko. What isn't clear?"

"I tuned in late. Indulge me."

Bannerman sipped his Löwenbräu. "The bottom line, I guess, is that Kosarev thinks those papers will put him in front of a firing squad."

"So why wouldn't he tear the Savoy apart looking for them?"

"He was on Candid Camera, Lesko. We have Susan, by the way, to thank for that."

"Yeah, well . . . I still liked it better when she was dating lifeguards. How did you know to go after Kosarev?"

"He was over in that doorway. He was obviously calling the shots. It was Susan, again, who spotted him."

"But you knew him, right? You knew who he was."

Bannerman hesitated, then shook his head. "Never heard of him before today."

Lesko thought he understood the hesitation . . . and why getting answers from Bannerman can be like pulling teeth. The thing is, Bannerman knows he has this reputation for always being two steps ahead of you. Sometimes, maybe, he actually is. But what he really does is make it *seem* that way because it forces mistakes by the other guy. Keeps him off balance.

So Bannerman's telling the truth. He had no idea who Kosarev was when he went over to Detsky Mir and stuck a gun up his nose. Kosarev gets dragged out in the street, which is suddenly filling up with the television news media and his goons are being shot at from windows. He hears the people he just sent inside being blasted. He says, shit. Mama's Boy knows *everything*. Somehow he set me up.

"Okay . . . so you pull him out of Detsky Mir."

"Have you been in there?"

"Where? The store?"

"There's a Ford showroom in there."

"There's a what?"

"European Fords. About a dozen new models, all encased in glass."

"Bannerman . . ."

"Sorry. It just struck me."

"Yeah, well, I'll strike you if you don't stay with the program here. You're saying Kosarev threw in the towel."

He nodded. "Especially when Roger showed up with the cavalry. Next there was Yuri's performance with Georgi. Georgi, by the way, babbled something about a witness to that nerve-gas disaster still being alive and kept on ice by Kosarev. To use, I assume, against Kulik. That's when Levin tried to arrest him. Podolsk wanting to shoot him didn't do much for his peace of mind either."

"But you said he's not alone in this? Why didn't someone else at least stop us from taking off?"

"I don't know. Maybe they thought Kosarev had it under

control. And because we beat the evening news. By now,
however, they know that he's defecting to save his skin.''

''Who are *they,* by the way? Do you know?''

Another hesitation. Bannerman shook his head.

''Okay. Kosarev. He was willing to leave with just the
clothes on his back?''

''He didn't mind. We had a plane going to Zurich and I'm
sure he has plenty of money there.''

There was something wrong here, thought Lesko. Maybe
it's just the way Bannerman says things. I mean, everything
everyone does, to hear him tell it, is perfectly logical. You'd
like to get a sense of good guy–bad guy here. Maybe a little
anger. Like Yuri had. Like Podolsk had.

It's the computer again. And it's pissing him off. Lesko
thought he'd better go for another beer, look in on Elena.

''Uncle David?''

Susan had called him twice in her mind. He wasn't
answering.

She wished he would. He was her father's ghost, but he
was still her uncle David. Or at least that was what she'd
called him since grade school.

She was kneeling at Elena's bedside, being careful not to
disturb the tubes that dripped fluid into both her arms.
Elena, exhausted by the move, was dead to the world.

Susan stared at the growing swell of her belly. She could
not resist reaching to touch it.

''Uncle David . . . is it mine?''

''I don't know. I bet it isn't.''

She closed her eyes. Held her breath.

''Why don't you think so?''

*''Like her cousin told you . . . Elena had second
thoughts, I think. Using yours hit a little too close to home.''*

But they had talked about that from the beginning. It
didn't bother the doctor. He said that genetically, clinically,
Susan's egg would be the best possible match. Forget horror
stories, he said, about inbreeding. The risk of the child being
defective is no greater, in fact much less, than if Elena tried
to have the child on her own. He recognized, however, that
dealing with this on an emotional level was another matter
entirely.

Elena seemed okay about it. In some ways, she loved the idea. The genes were right, the coloring was right. Even the personality. She said that a new Susan was exactly what anyone would expect . . . hope . . . to come out of such a union. The *crapshoot* that Lesko talks about would be at a minimum.

Susan also got Janet Herzog's vote. Janet couldn't donate an egg because she didn't have a uterus anymore. She came over, mostly, for moral support and to show Elena that losing her plumbing had an up side. That was when Elena asked them all to be bridesmaids if she ever got up the nerve to ask Lesko and if he said yes.

Janet agreed, on the other hand, that there was much to be said for using Molly Farrell's egg. Coloring is similar. Molly is very athletic—was NCAA champion at tennis. Very strong character and a nice personality there as well.

The option that tickled Elena the most, however, was that of using Carla's contribution. Can you imagine such a combination? she asked. Lesko and Carla? The world would tremble. Red hair, however, might raise some eyebrows.

"David? It's a son, right?"

"Who knows?"

"My father said he had a dream. You were in it. The baby came and you said it was a boy."

"That was a dream, Susan."

"Like this one?"

"Like this one. Look, why don't you just ask Elena who she used."

"Because we agreed that we'd never, ever, speak of it. None of us. And because I'm not sure I want to know."

"So? Wait and see, right?"

She felt herself smiling.

"I guess. Wait and see."

Lesko sat again.

"How's Elena doing?" Bannerman asked him.

"I just looked in. Susan's praying by the bed. I left them alone."

Bannerman arched an eyebrow. Another facet to Susan he'd never seen.

"I've got more questions," Lesko told him, "but let's have yours."

A long pause. Then, "I'm going to ask Susan if she'll be my wife. I guess I want to ask for your blessing."

Lesko stared. "Are you shitting me?"

"I . . . um, thought it was traditional to ask."

"Fuck tradition. Would *you* give *you* your blessing?"

"Lesko, maybe if you talked this over with Elena . . ."

"Let's get back to a subject I can handle, okay? What's the story with Leo's uncle?"

Bannerman, thought Lesko, came close to sulking. He had clearly rehearsed his dumb proposal. This must be some of that endearing ineptitude shit. This, and weaving through Detsky Mir, gun in hand, knowing there's every chance you won't get through this alive and yet a part of your head is saying, *"Oh, wow. New Fords where they used to have Infants & Toddlers."*

Bannerman answered anyway.

Nikolai Belkin was basically a schmuck, he said, although Bannerman's actual language was a little more charitable. Kosarev had recruited him just after the Gorbachev coup. He told him that us reformers who were never really Communists need a man of your moral stature to help clean up the KGB. Raise your banner and see who flocks to it. Even provided him with a car and driver.

For Kosarev, this was a good way to find out who was reliable and who, like Leo and Yuri for example, had a conscience. Then, through old Nikolai, he'd have these guys infiltrate anyone who was a threat to him. He'd build his own power base while pretending to be the great white knight of the new Russia.

It was so, so sad.

When Leo's uncle finally caught on, it broke his heart.

"I'll ask you again. What did you promise Kosarev?"

"I promised Roger. I said I'd do him no harm."

"Yeah, well, I didn't promise."

"No . . . you didn't."

No way, thought Lesko. No fucking way is Kosarev going to waltz into a Zurich bank tomorrow and then head for the nearest Mercedes dealer. Then start doing deals with Roger

Clew. On the other hand, let him. Let Carla or Yuri see him driving it. He'll be his own hood ornament before the week is out. Which Bannerman must know damned well.

Lesko still felt bad about something.

In his mind, he saw that lady in Red Square. Elena gave her that book and that nail polish. He saw her big happy grin, he felt her warmth. He saw that kid, Mikhail, who had bought the amber necklace for him. And he saw all the Russian doctors and nurses who had been so terrific . . . and who had cried when they saw all the stuff that Willem brought.

"Bannerman?"

"Hmmm?"

"What will happen to Russia?"

"The hard times will blow over. Everything blows over."

"Will there be anything left?"

Bannerman had to think how he would answer. The Kuliks and the Kosarevs will always be around. On the whole, however, he tended to agree with Yuri. The buccaneers, the opportunists, and the borderline criminals are the ones who make things happen. Like them or not, they make an economy grow. People like Fuller and Clew don't. They try and they might even mean well. But they spend all their time hatching grand strategies that never work because the people they don't bother to consult always have ideas of their own. The trick is to get out of their way, but no government in the world can bring itself to do that.

But that's not what Lesko wanted to hear.

"It could be the richest country in the world. In my lifetime."

Lesko nodded slowly. "That's what Mikhail said. He's this kid I met."

"And the poorest. But the poor won't have to stay that way. I guess that's the difference."

Lesko chewed on that as well. "I like those people, Bannerman."

"I know you do."

"Maybe I can . . . ." He stopped himself.

Yes, thought Bannerman. With those files, with a little Brugg money, maybe you can.

• • •

"Lesko?"

"Yeah."

"I want my life. I want a home."

Lesko said nothing.

"If there's a wedding, will you come to it?"

"You know I will."

"Will you give Susan away?"

"Yeah. Sure. And thanks."

"When the baby comes, maybe you and Elena . . ."

Lesko seemed to swell. Godzilla rising. Bannerman knew that he'd made a mistake. "What baby?" Lesko hissed.

"Um . . . yours? Yours and Elena's."

He receded slightly. "What about it?"

"Ah . . . have you thought about who you'll ask to be godfather?"

Lesko put a hand on his shoulder.

"Bannerman . . . don't push your luck," he said.

ABOUT THE AUTHOR

JOHN R. MAXIM lives in Westport, Connecticut, except when he's in places like Moscow and Zurich. He won't tell us what he does there.

The author has written seven previous books, including *Abel Baker Charlie* and *Time Out of Mind,* both coming soon from Bantam, and is currently at work on a new novel.